> "EVIL IS A COMPLETELY
> DIFFERENT CREATURE, MAC.
> EVIL IS BAD THAT BELIEVES IT'S *GOOD*."

MacKayla Lane was just a child when she and her sister, Alina, were given up for adoption and banished from Ireland forever.

Twenty years later, Alina is dead and Mac has returned to the country that expelled them to hunt her sister's murderer. But after discovering that she descends from a bloodline both gifted and cursed, Mac is plunged into a secret history: an ancient conflict between humans and immortals who have lived concealed among us for thousands of years.

What follows is a shocking chain of events with devastating consequences, and now Mac struggles to cope with grief while continuing her mission to acquire and control the *Sinsar Dubh*—a book of dark, forbidden magic scribed by the mythical Unseelie King, containing the power to create and destroy worlds.

In an epic battle between humans and Fae, the hunter becomes the hunted when the *Sinsar Dubh* turns on Mac and begins mowing a deadly path through those she loves.

Who can she turn to? Who can she trust? Who is the woman haunting her dreams? More important, who is Mac herself and what is the destiny she glimpses in the black and crimson designs of an ancient tarot card?

From the luxury of the Lord Master's penthouse to the sordid depths of an Unseelie nightclub, from the erotic bed of her lover to the terrifying bed of the Unseelie King, Mac's journey will force her to face the truth of her exile, and to make a choice that will either save the world . . . or destroy it.

P9-DCD-520

Praise for the Novels of
Karen Marie Moning

SHADOWFEVER
The #1 *New York Times*, *Wall Street Journal*, and *Publishers Weekly* bestseller

"Moning has taken her heroine—and her readers—on a turbulent, emotionally devastating and truly unforgettable ride! Enormous kudos!"
—RT BOOK REVIEWS, TOP PICK AND GOLD MEDAL

"Epic is the word that first came to my mind after I read the words 'The End' and closed the book on what was an amazing journey. I don't think I've ever read a more satisfying final book in a series. I can't even count how many times I was taken by surprise, shocked, blindsided and thrilled. I was left emotionally spent and completely happy with the many unexpected paths this story took." —FICTION VIXEN BOOK REVIEWS

"A simple review can never adequately describe *Shadowfever*, words on a page being spectacularly poor substitutes for the strength of feeling and broad emotional spectrum captured between its covers. Ms. Moning is more than a storyteller, her characters far more tangible than fictional beings could ever be thought to be, and she has created a world of infinite complexity that openly challenges us, dares us to experience it and remain only a passive observer, and then yanks us in with a shocking brute strength as it subjects us to the sharpest of pains sparsely interspersed with the warmest of joys. Enter into this final piece of the puzzle with a first-aid kit at the ready, as Ms. Moning is a master at inflicting wounds designed to injure but not kill, and she subjects both her characters and us to numerous events that leave indelible marks on the soft flesh of our hearts. Despite the pain, we revel in the emotional injuries, honored to be privy to a book capable of having such a remarkable effect."

—SUPERNATURAL SNARK

"*Shadowfever* delivers an outstanding conclusion to a fabulous series." —NIGHT OWL PARANORMAL, TOP PICK

"*Shadowfever* did not end the Fever series world with a whimper. It definitely was a bang. A big, wet and fulfilling bang. Take that however you feel is necessary."

—PARAJUNKEE'S VIEW

"Ms. Moning, much like Mac, takes her story and runs with it, balls to the wall, 550 pages to its uncompromising and satisfying conclusion." —FRESH FICTION

"*Shadowfever* is an explosion of mystery, action, passion, lust, love and magic. As I read this last book in the series I experienced surprise and wonder, shock and horror, sorrow and grief, hope and joy, and, in the end, satisfaction; I couldn't have hoped for more."

—BEYOND HER BOOK

"I cried, I laughed, I screamed, I cursed, I dropped my Kindle due to astonishment, and I'm sure that I repeated that cycle several times throughout the book. I had this perfect way of how things would come together, and none of it happened the way I had it planned in my head. What KMM did was so beyond anything I could have divined, it made the book that much more awesome in my eyes. So, I'm sure as you may have guessed, I give this five stars. I would give it five hundred if I could. It was just that perfect for me."

—THE ROMANCE REVIEWS

"This series is exactly what an epic fantasy should be. An adventure. In every way."

—PENELOPE'S ROMANCE REVIEWS

"*Shadowfever* surpassed every expectation I had. For as many theories as I have discussed, I was completely shocked at most of the outcomes. There was not a single aspect I was disappointed in. My favorite part is that Barrons and Mac stay so true to their characters. Barrons doesn't change, or yield to Mac. And I think KMM does an excellent job with keeping him so consistent. He stays broody, and possessive, and mysterious. An excellent end to my favorite series. This book gets an A++++++ from me. Thank you Karen Marie Moning for this extraordinary series."   —SMEXY BOOKS

"I was in shock at how perfectly Karen was able to write this. She is an absolute genius."
—YUMMY MEN AND KICKASS CHICKS

"This book was everything I expected, wanted, needed, craved . . . and so much more."
—CANDACE'S BOOK BLOG

"I can't remember the last time I'd had so much fun watching a story unwind."   —MY VAMP FICTION

DARKFEVER

"A wonderful dark fantasy . . . give yourself a treat and read outside the box."   —CHARLAINE HARRIS

"Moning's newest foray contains suspense and plenty of setup. It's a compelling world filled with mystery and vivid characters, and this, combined with the hint of sparks between Jericho and Mac, will stoke reader's fervor for *Bloodfever*, the next installment."
—PUBLISHERS WEEKLY

"*Darkfever* is masterfully rendered, a dark and sexy fantasy featuring a Buffy of the Fae, with a sly sense of humor and maturity of handling that's a delight to read."
—BOOKPAGE

"Moning launches a remarkable new series that's exotic and treacherous. . . . Clear off space on your keeper shelf—this sharp series looks to be amazing!"
—RT Book Reviews

"A seductive mix of Celtic mythology and dark, sexy danger."
—Chicago Tribune

BLOODFEVER

"I loved this book from the first page. . . . More. I want more."
—Linda Howard

"Moning's delectable Mac is breathlessly appealing, and the wild perils she must endure are peppered with endless conundrums. The results are addictively dark, erotic, and even shocking."
—Publishers Weekly

"Spiced with a subtle yet delightfully sharp sense of humor, Bloodfever is a delectably dark and scary addition to Karen Marie Moning's Fever series."
—Chicago Tribune

"Moning brilliantly works the dark sides of man and Fae for all they are worth."
—Booklist

FAEFEVER

"Erotic shocks await Mac in Dublin's vast Dark Zone, setting up Feverish . . . expectations for the next installment."
—Publishers Weekly

"Ending in what can only be described as a monumental cliffhanger, the newest installment of this supernatural saga will have you panting for the next. Breathtaking!"
—RT Book Reviews

"A gift of epic proportions to paranormal romance fans."
—Penelope's Romance Reviews

"An exciting read, with wonderfully described fight scenes and sizzling scenes with the Fae princes."
—Night Owl Romance

DREAMFEVER

"Freaking fabulous! So utterly wonderful that you really must read this series, if you're not already."
—LITERARY ESCAPISM

"This book is absolutely riveting. By far, the most fascinating book I have read this year."
—PENELOPE'S ROMANCE REVIEWS

"Mac's evolution from typical twenty-something to unrelenting warrior has been shocking, graphic and painful. Moning pulls no punches as she sets Mac on this ghastly path!"
—*RT BOOK REVIEWS*

"This series should come with a warning on it. Because it's about as addictive as any illegal drug and will take over your life until the next book is finished!"
—BOOK CHICK CITY

"Brutal, deep and leaving us with heaps and heaps of questions, *Dreamfever* is an undeniably great urban fantasy."
—VAMPIRE BOOK CLUB

SHADOWFEVER

Books by Karen Marie Moning

THE FEVER SERIES

Darkfever

Bloodfever

Faefever

Dreamfever

Shadowfever

THE HIGHLANDER SERIES

Beyond the Highland Mist • To Tame a Highland
Warrior

The Highlander's Touch • Kiss of the Highlander

The Dark Highlander • The Immortal Highlander

Spell of the Highlander

SHADOWFEVER

A MacKayla Lane Novel
BOOK 5

Karen Marie Moning

DELL
NEW YORK

Shadowfever is a work of fiction. Names, characters, places, and incidents are the products of the author's imagination or are used fictitiously. Any resemblance to actual events, locales, or persons, living or dead, is entirely coincidental.

2011 Dell Mass Market Edition

Copyright © 2011 by Karen Marie Moning, LLC

All rights reserved.

Published in the United States by Dell, an imprint of The Random House Publishing Group, a division of Random House, Inc., New York.

Dell is a registered trademark of Random House, Inc., and the colophon is a trademark of Random House, Inc.

Originally published in hardcover in the United States by Dell, an imprint of The Random House Publishing Group, a division of Random House, Inc., in 2011.

Owing to limitations of space, the permission acknowledgments are located on page 682.

ISBN 978-0-440-24441-7
Ebook ISBN 978-0-440-33974-8

Cover design: Eileen Carey
Cover image: © Ben Heys/Shutterstock (woman)
Step Back cover images: © Yolande De Kort/Trevillion (tree branches), © David Muir/Getty Images (lock), © Fancy/Jupiterimages (woman), © Susan Fox/Trevillion Images (part of scarf), © Ronya Galka/ Trevillion Images (part of scarf)

Printed in the United States of America

www.bantamdell.com

9 8 7 6 5 4 3 2 1

Dell mass market edition: September 2011

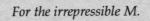

For the irrepressible M.

PART

1

Between the idea
And the reality
Between the motion
And the act
Falls the Shadow
          —T. S. ELIOT

I feel it deep within
It's just beneath the skin
I must confess that I feel like
    a monster.
    —SKILLET, "MONSTER"

YOU WISH TO KNOW ME?

POSIT YOURSELF AS THE PINPOINT CENTER OF ONE OF YOUR KALEIDOSCOPES, AND GRASP TIME AS THE COLORFUL FRAGMENTS ERUPTING FROM YOU IN A MULTITUDE OF DIMENSIONS THAT CONSTANTLY EXPAND OUTWARD IN AN EVER-WIDENING, EVER-SHIFTING, INFINITE ARRAY. SEE THAT YOU CAN CHOOSE AND EXPAND FROM ANY OF THOSE UNCOUNTABLE DIMENSIONS AND THAT, WITH EACH CHOICE, THOSE DIMENSIONS WIDEN AND SHIFT AGAIN. INFINITY COMPOUNDED EXPONENTIALLY. UNDERSTAND THAT THERE IS NO SUCH THING AS REALITY: THE FALSE GOD YOUR RACE WORSHIPS WITH SUCH BLIND DEVOTION. REALITY IMPLIES A SINGLE POSSIBLE.

YOU ACCUSE ME OF ILLUSION. YOU—WITH YOUR ABSURD CONSTRUCT OF LINEAR TIME. YOU FASHION FOR YOURSELF A PRISON OF WATCHES, CLOCKS, AND CALENDARS. YOU RATTLE BARS FORGED OF HOURS AND DAYS, BUT YOU'VE PADLOCKED THE DOOR WITH PAST, PRESENT, AND FUTURE.

PUNY MINDS NEED PUNY CAVES.

YOU CANNOT GAZE UPON TIME'S TRUE FACE ANY MORE THAN YOU CAN BEHOLD MINE.

TO APPREHEND YOURSELF AS THE CENTER, TO SIMULTANEOUSLY PERCEIVE ALL COMBINATIONS OF ALL POSSIBLES, SHOULD YOU CHOOSE TO MOVE IN ANY DIRECTION—"DIRECTION" BEING A VERY LIMITED METHOD OF ATTEMPTING TO CONVEY A CONCEPT FOR WHICH YOUR RACE HAS NO WORD—*THAT* IS WHAT IT IS TO BE ME.

—CONVERSATIONS WITH THE *SINSAR DUBH*

1

Hope strengthens. Fear kills.

Someone really smart told me that once.

Every time I think I'm getting wiser, more in control of my actions, I go slamming into a situation that makes me excruciatingly aware that all I've succeeded in doing is swapping one set of delusions for a more elaborate, attractive set of delusions—that's me, the Queen of Self-Deception.

I hate myself right now. More than I'd ever have thought possible.

I squat on the cliff's edge, screaming, cursing the day I was born, wishing my biological mother had drowned me at birth. Life is too hard, too much to handle. Nobody told me there'd be days like these. How could nobody tell me there'd be days like these? How could they let me grow up like that—happy and pink and stupid?

The pain I feel is worse than anything the *Sinsar Dubh* has ever done to me. At least when the Book is crushing me, I know it's not my own fault.

This moment?

Mea culpa. Beginning to end, all the way, I own this one, and there will never be any hiding from that fact.

I thought I'd lost everything.

How ignorant I was. He warned me. I had so much more to lose!

I want to die.

It's the only way to stop the pain.

Months ago, on a hellishly long night, in a grotto beneath the Burren, I wanted to die, too, but it wasn't the same. Mallucé was going to torture me to death, and dying was the only chance I had of denying him that twisted pleasure. My death had been inevitable. I saw little point in drawing it out.

I'd been wrong. I'd given up hope and nearly died because of it.

I *would* have died—if not for Jericho Barrons.

He's the one who taught me those words.

That simple adage is master of every situation, every choice. Each morning we wake up, we get to choose between hope and fear and apply one of those emotions to everything we do. Do we greet the things that come our way with joy? Or suspicion?

Hope strengthens . . .

Not once did I permit myself to feel any hope about the person lying facedown in a pool of blood. Not once did I use it to strengthen our bond. I let the onus of our relationship rest on broader shoulders. Fear. Suspicion. Mistrust drove my every action.

And now it's too late to take any of it back.

I stop screaming and begin to laugh. I hear the madness in it.

I don't care.

My spear sticks up, a cruel javelin, mocking me. I remember stealing it.

For a moment, I'm back in the dark, rain-slicked Dublin streets, descending into the sewer systems with Barrons, breaking into Rocky O'Bannion's private cache of religious artifacts. Barrons is wearing jeans and a black T-shirt. Muscles ripple in his body as he casts aside the sewer lid with the ease of a man tossing a Frisbee in the park.

He's disturbingly sexual, to men and women alike, in a way that sets your teeth on edge. With Barrons, you aren't sure if you're going to get fucked or turned inside out and left a new, unrecognizable person, adrift with no moorings, on a sea with no bottom and no rules.

I was never immune to him. There were merely degrees of denial.

My respite is too brief. The memory vanishes and I am again confronted with the reality that threatens to shatter my hold on sanity.

Fear kills . . .

Literally.

I can't say it. I can't think it. I can't begin to absorb it.

I hug my knees and rock.

Jericho Barrons is dead.

He lies on his stomach, motionless. He hasn't moved or breathed in the small eternity that I've been screaming. I can't sense him in his skin. On all other occasions, I've been able to feel him in my vicinity: electric, larger than life, vastness crammed into a tiny container. Genie in a bottle. That's Barrons: deadly power, stopper corking it. Barely.

I rock back and forth.

The million-dollar question: What are you, Barrons? His answer, on those rare occasions he gave one, was always the same.

The one that will never let you die.

I believed him. Damn him.

"Well, you screwed up, Barrons. I'm alone and I'm in serious trouble, so *get up*!"

He doesn't move. There's too much blood. I reach out with my *sidhe*-seer senses. I sense nothing on the cliff's edge but me.

I scream.

No wonder he told me never to call the number on my cell that he had programmed as IYD—*If You're Dying*—unless I really was. After a time I begin to laugh again. He's not the one who screwed up. I am. Was I played or did I orchestrate this fiasco all by myself?

I thought Barrons was invincible.

I keep waiting for him to move. Roll over. Sit up. Magically heal. Cut me one of those hard looks and say, *Get a grip, Ms. Lane. I'm the Unseelie King. I can't die.*

That was one of my biggest fears, whenever I was indulging in any of a thousand about him: that he was the one who'd created the *Sinsar Dubh* to begin with, dumping all his evil into it, and he wanted it back for some reason but couldn't trap it himself. At one point or another, I'd considered everything: Fae, half Fae, were-wolf, vampire, ancient cursed being from the dawn of time, perhaps the very thing he and Christian had tried to summon on Halloween at Castle Keltar—key part there being immortal, as in *unkillable*.

"Get up, Barrons!" I scream. "Move, damn you!"

I'm afraid to touch him. Afraid if I do, his body will be cooling noticeably. I'll feel the fragility of his flesh, the mortality of Barrons. "Fragility," "mortality," and "Barrons" all packed together in the same thought feels about as blasphemous as stalking through the Vatican hammering upside-down crosses on the walls.

I squat ten paces from his body.

I stay back, because if I get close I'll have to roll him over and look in his eyes, and what if they're empty like Alina's were?

Then I'll know he's gone, like I knew she was gone, too far beyond my reach to ever hear my voice again, to hear me say, I'm sorry, Alina, I wish I'd called more often; I wish I'd heard the truth beneath our vapid sister talk; I wish I'd come to Dublin and fought beside you, or raged at you, because you were acting from fear, too, Alina, not hope at all, or you would have trusted me to help you. Or maybe just apologize, Barrons, for being too young to have my priorities refined, like you, because I haven't suffered whatever the hell it is you suffered, and then shove you up against a wall and kiss you until you can't breathe, do what I wanted to do the first day I saw you there in your bloody damned bookstore. Disturb *you* like you disturbed *me,* make you see me, make you want me—*pink* me!—shatter your self-control, bring you crashing to your knees in front of me, even though I told myself I'd never want a man like you, that you were too old, too carnal, more animal than man, with one foot in the swamp and no desire to come all the way out, when the truth was that I was terrified by what you made me feel. It wasn't what guys make girls feel, dreams of a future with babies and picket fences, but frantic, hard, raw loss of self, like you can't live without that man inside you, around you, with you all the time, and it only matters what *he* thinks of you, the rest of the world can go to hell, and even then I knew you could change me! Who wants to be around someone that can *change* them? Too much power to let another person have! It was easier to fight you than admit that I had undiscovered places inside me that hungered for things that weren't accepted in any kind of world I knew, and the worst of it is that you woke me up from my Barbie-girl world and now I'm here and I'm wide awake, you bastard, I couldn't be more awake, and you *left* me—

I think I'll scream until he gets up.

He was the one who told me not to believe anything was dead until I'd burned it, poked around in its ashes, then waited a day or two to see if anything rose from them.

Surely I'm not supposed to burn him.

I don't think there are any circumstances under which I could do that.

I'll squat.

I'll scream.

He'll get up. He hates it when I'm melodramatic.

While I wait for him to revive, I listen for sounds of scrabbling at the cliff's edge. I half-expect Ryodan to drag his broken, bloody body up over the edge. Maybe he's not really dead, either. After all, we're in Faery, maybe, or at least within the Silvers—who knows what realm this is? Might the water here have rejuvenating powers? Should I try to get Barrons to it? Maybe we're in the Dreaming and this terrible thing that has happened is a nightmare, and I'll wake up on a couch in Barrons Books and Baubles and the illustrious, infuriating owner will raise a brow and give me that look; I'll say something pithy, and life will be lovely, chock-full of monsters and rain again, just the way I like it.

I squat.

No scrabbling in the stones and shale.

The man with the spear in his back doesn't move.

My heart is full of holes.

He gave his life for me. Barrons gave his life for me. My self-serving, arrogant, constant jackass was the constant rock beneath my feet, willing to die so I could live.

Why the hell would he do that?

How do I *live* with that?

A terrible thought occurs to me, so awful that for a few moments it eclipses my grief: I would never have killed him if Ryodan hadn't appeared. Did Ryodan set me up? Did he come here to kill Barrons, who was never invincible, merely difficult to kill? Maybe Barrons could be killed only in his animal form, and Ryodan knew he'd have to be in it to protect me. Was this an elaborate ruse that had nothing to do with me? Was Ryodan working with the LM, and they wanted Barrons out of the way so I'd be easier to deal with, and the abduction of my parents was mere sleight of hand? *Look over there while we kill the man who threatens us all.* Or maybe Barrons had been cursed to live out some hellish sentence and could be slain only by someone he trusted, and he'd trusted me. Beneath all the cold arrogance, the mockery, the constant pushing, had he given over that most private part of himself to me—a confidence I'd never earned, as I couldn't have proven any more surely than if I'd stabbed him in the back?

Oh, gee, wait, I did. On Ryodan's word alone, I'd turned on him.

The accusation of betrayal in the beast's gaze hadn't been an illusion. It had been Jericho Barrons in there, staring at me from behind that prehistoric brow, baring his fangs, reproach and hatred blazing in his feral yellow eyes. I'd broken our unspoken pact. He'd been my guardian demon and I'd killed him.

Had he despised me for not seeing through the hide of the beast he'd worn to the man within?

See me. How many times had he said that to me? *See me when you look at me!*

When it mattered most, I'd been blind. He'd been dogging my every step, treating me with that characteristic Barrons' combination of aggression and animal possessiveness, and I'd never once recognized him.

I'd failed him.

He'd come to me in a barbaric, inhuman form, to keep me alive. He'd set himself up as IYD regardless of what it might cost him, knowing he would be turned into a mindless, raging beast capable only of slaughtering everything in his immediate vicinity but for one thing.

Me.

God, that look!

I cover my face with my hands, but the image won't

go away: beast and Barrons, his dark skin and exotic face, its slate hide and primal features. Those ancient eyes that saw so much and asked only to be seen in return burn with scorn: *Couldn't you have trusted me just once? Couldn't you have hoped for the best, just once? Why did you choose Ryodan over me? I was keeping you alive. I had a plan. Did I ever let you down?*

"I didn't know it was you!" I gouge my palms with my nails. They bleed for a brief moment, then heal.

But the beast/Barrons in my mind isn't done torturing me. *You should have. I took your sweater. I smelled you and granted you passage. I killed fresh, tender meat for you. I pissed around you. I showed you in this form, as in any other, that you are mine—and I take care of what is mine.*

Tears blind me. I double over. It hurts so bad I can't breathe, can't move. I hunch over, curl in on myself, and rock.

Beyond the pain, if there is such a place, I know things.

Things like: According to Ryodan (if he's not a traitor, and if he is and somehow still alive, I'll kill him as dead as we killed Barrons), I have a brand on the back of my skull placed there by the Lord Master, who probably still has my parents, because Barrons is here, so obviously he never got through to Ashford.

Unless . . . time passes differently in the Silvers and he *did* have time to get to Ashford before I punched IYD, summoning him here to the seventh dimension I've been in since entering the Lord Master's slippery pink corridor back in Dublin.

I have no idea how long I was in the Hall of All Days or how much time passed in the real world while I sunned with Christian by the lake.

Once, courtesy of V'lane, I spent a single afternoon

on a beach in Faery, with an illusion of my sister, and it cost me an entire month in the human world. When I returned, Barrons was furious. He'd chained me to a beam in his garage. I'd been wearing a hot-pink string bikini.

We fought.

I close my eyes and embrace the memory.

He stands there, furious, surrounded by needles and dyes, about to tattoo me—or, more accurately, *pretend* to tattoo me where he's already tattooed me but I haven't discovered it yet—so he can track me if I ever decide to do something as stupid as agree to stay in Faery for any period of time again.

I tell him if he tattoos me, we're through. I accuse him of never feeling anything more than greed and mockery, being incapable of love. I call him a mercenary, blame him for losing his temper when he couldn't find me and trashing the store, and, while I scathingly concede that he might get an occasional hard-on, it's undoubtedly for something like money, an artifact, or a book—never a woman.

I remember every word of his reply: *Yes, I have loved, Ms. Lane, and although it's none of your business, I have lost. Many things. And, no, I am not like any other player in this game and I will never be like V'lane, and I get a hard-on a great deal more often than occasionally. Sometimes it's over a spoiled little girl, not a woman at all. And, yes, I trashed the bookstore when I couldn't find you. You'll have to choose a new bedroom, too. And I'm sorry your pretty little world got all screwed up, but everybody's does, and you go on. It's how you go on that defines you.*

In retrospect, I see through myself with pathetic ease.

There I am, chained to a beam, nearly naked, alone with Jericho Barrons, a man who is so far beyond my comprehension, but, God, he excites me! He plans to work slowly and carefully on my naked skin for hours. His hard, tattooed body is an unspoken promise of initiation into a secret world where I could feel things I can't begin to imagine, and I *want* him to work on me for hours. Desperately. But not to tattoo me. I goad him to the best of my naïve, sheltered abilities. I want him to take from me what I lack the courage to offer.

What a complicated, ridiculous, self-destructive feeling! Afraid to ask for what I want. Afraid to own up to my own desires. Driven by circumscription of nurture, not nature. I'd come to Dublin wearing shackles on my bonds. I'd been all nurture.

He was all nature—trying to teach me to change.

Like I said: degrees of denial.

He'd leaned into me, in that garage, sex and barely leashed violence, and when I'd felt his hard-on, it made me feel so alive and wild inside that later I'd had to peel off my bikini and take care of myself in the shower again and again, fantasizing a very different outcome in his garage. One that had taken all night.

I'd told myself it was because I'd spent the day in close proximity to a death-by-sex Fae. Another lie.

He'd unchained me and let me go.

If I were chained to that beam now, I'd have no problem telling him exactly what I wanted. And it wouldn't involve unchaining me. At least not at first.

I focus through my tears.

Grass. Trees. Him.

He lies facedown. I need to go to him.

The earth is wet, muddy from last night's rain, from his blood.

I need to clean him. He shouldn't be messy. Barrons doesn't like to be messy. He's meticulous; a sophisticated, exquisite dresser. Although I've straightened his lapel a few times, it was only for the excuse of touching him. Stepping into his personal space. Exercising familiarity to underscore that I had the right. Unpredictable as a hungry lion, he might be feared by everyone else, but he never ripped out *my* throat, only licked me, and, if his tongue was a little rough sometimes, it was worth it to walk beside the king of the jungle.

My heart is going to explode.

I can't do this. I just went through this with my sister. Regret upon regret. Missed opportunities. Bad decisions. Grief.

How many more people will have to die before I learn how to live? He was right. I'm a walking catastrophe.

I fumble in my pocket for my phone. First thing I do is dial Barrons' cell. The call doesn't go through. I press IYCGM. Call doesn't go through. I hit IYD and hold my breath, watching Barrons intently. The call doesn't go through.

Like the man himself, all lines are down.

I begin to shake. I don't know why, but the fact that the cell phones don't work convinces me more than anything else that he's beyond my reach.

I flip my head down, scrape my hair forward, and, although it takes me a few tries to get the angle right, I take a shot of my nape. Sure enough, two tattoos. Barrons' brand is a dragon with a *Z* in the center that shimmers with faint iridescence.

To the left of his tattoo is a black circle crammed with strange symbols I don't recognize. It seems Ryodan was telling the truth. If the tattoo was put there by the LM, it explains a lot: Why Barrons so heavily warded the basement where he dragged me back from being *Pri-ya*, how the LM found me at the abbey once the wards had been painted over, how he found me again at the house Dani and I squatted in, and how he'd tracked me to my parents' in Ashford.

I pull out the small dirk I lifted from BB&B.

My hand trembles.

I could end my pain. I could curl up and bleed out next to him. It'd be over so quickly. Maybe I'd get another chance some other time, some other place. Maybe he and I would be reincarnated like in that movie, *What Dreams May Come,* that Alina and I hated so much because the kids and husband died, then the wife committed suicide.

I love that movie now. I get it, the whole idea of willingly going to hell for someone. Living there, insane if you have to, because you'd rather be insane with them than endure life without them.

I stare at the blade.

He died so I would live.

"Damn you! I don't *want* to live without you!"

It's how you go on that defines you.

"Oh, shut up, would you? You're dead, shut up, shut up!"

But a terrible truth is shredding my heart.

I'm the girl that cried "wolf."

I'm the one that pressed IYD. I'm the one that didn't think I could survive the boar on my own. And guess what?

I *did.*

I'd driven it away and already been safe by the time Barrons appeared and blasted into it.

I hadn't really been dying after all.

He died for me and it hadn't been necessary.

I overreacted.

And now he's dead.

I stare at the dirk. Killing myself would be a reward. I deserve only punishment.

I stare at the snapshot of the back of my head. If the Lord Master found me right now, I'm not sure I would fight for my life.

I consider attempting surgery on my own skull, then

realize I am not in the best frame of mind for that. I might not stop cutting. It's close to my spinal column. Easy way out.

I slam the blade into the dirt before I can turn it on myself.

What would that make of me? That I got him killed, then killed myself? A coward. But it's not what it would make of me that bothers me. It's what it would make of him—a wasted death.

The death of a man like him deserves more than that.

I bite back another scream. It's trapped inside me now, stuffed down into my belly, burning the back of my throat, making it painful to swallow. I hear it in my ears even though my mouth makes no sound. It's a silent scream. The worst kind. I lived with this once before, to keep Mom and Dad from knowing that Alina's death was killing me, too. I know what comes next, and I know it's going to be worse than last time. That *I'm* going to be worse.

Much, much worse.

I remember the scenes of slaughter Barrons showed me in his mind. I understand them now. Understand what might drive a person to it.

I kneel beside his naked, bloody body. The transformation from man to beast must have shredded his clothing, exploded the silver cuff from his wrist. Nearly two thirds of his body is inked with black and crimson protection runes.

"Jericho," I say. "Jericho, Jericho, Jericho." Why did I ever begrudge him his name? "Barrons" was a stone wall I erected between us, and if a hairline fracture appeared, I hastily mortared it with fear.

I close my eyes and steel myself. When I open them, I wrap both hands around the spear and try to pull it from his back. It doesn't come out. It's lodged in bone. I have to fight for it.

I stop. I start again. I weep.

He doesn't move.

I can do this. I can.

I work the spear free.

After a long moment, I roll him over.

If there was any doubt in my mind that he was dead, it vanishes. His eyes are open. They are empty.

Jericho Barrons is no longer there.

I open my senses to the world around me. I can't feel him at all.

I am on this cliff, alone.

I've never been so alone.

I try everything I can think of to bring him back to life.

I remember the Unseelie flesh we crammed into my backpack what seems a lifetime ago, back in the bookstore when I was getting ready to face the Lord Master. Most of it is still there.

If only I'd known then what I know now! That the next time I saw Jericho Barrons, he'd be dead. That the last words I would ever hear him say were "And the Lamborghini," with that wolf smile and promise that he would always be at my back, breathing down it, keeping it covered.

The wriggling, chopped-up Rhino-boy flesh is still neatly trapped in baby-food jars. I force it between his swollen, bloodied lips and hold his mouth shut. When it crawls out the jagged gash in his neck, my trapped scream nearly deafens me.

I'm not thinking clearly. Panic and grief ride me. Barrons would say: *Useless emotions, Ms. Lane. Rise above them. Stop reacting and* act. There he is, talking to me again.

What wouldn't I do for him? Nothing is too disgusting, too barbaric. This is Barrons. I want him whole again.

Ryodan had flayed him from gut to chest, before he slit his throat. I carefully peel back the meat of his tattooed abdomen and stuff Unseelie into his exposed, sliced stomach. It crawls out. I consider trying to sew the stomach up, so his body would be forced to digest the flesh of the dark Fae, and wonder if it would work, but I lack needle, thread, or any other means of repairing his torn flesh.

I attempt to put his entrails back into his body, arrange them in some semblance of order, dimly aware that this is perhaps not a normal, sane thing to do.

Once he said: *Get inside me, see how deep you can go.* With my hands on his spleen, I think, *Here I am. Too little, too late.*

I use my newfound proficiency in Voice and command him to rise. He told me once that student and teacher develop immunity to each other. I'm almost relieved. I was afraid Voice might raise a zombie, reanimated but not truly revived.

I prop his mouth open with a stick, slit my wrist, and drip blood into it. I have to slice deep to get a few drops and keep slicing because I keep healing. It only makes him bloodier.

I search my *sidhe*-seer place for magic to heal him. I have nothing of such consequence inside me.

I am suddenly furious.

How could he be mortal? How *dare* he be mortal? He never told me he was mortal! If I'd known, I might have treated him differently!

"Get up, get up, get up!" I shout.

His eyes are still open. I hate that they're open and so empty and blank, but closing them would be an admission, an acceptance I don't have in me.

I will never close Jericho Barrons' eyes.

They were wide open in life. He would want them open in death. Rituals would be wasted on him. Wherever Barrons is, he would laugh if I tried something as mundane as a funeral. Too small for such a large man.

Put him in a box? Never.

Bury him? No way.

Burn him?

That, too, would be acceptance. Admission that he was dead. Never going to happen.

Even in death he looks indomitable, his big black-and-crimson-tattooed body an epic giant, felled in battle.

I settle on the ground, gently lift his head, maneuver my legs beneath it, and cradle his face in my arms. With my shirt and hot tears that won't stop falling, I bathe away dirt and blood and clean him tenderly.

Harsh, forbidding, beautiful face.

I touch it. Trace it with my fingers, over and over, until I know the subtlest nuances of every plane and angle, until I could carve it out of stone even if I were blind.

I kiss him.

I lie down and stretch out next to him. I press my body to his and hold on.

I hold him like I never permitted myself to hold him when he was alive. I tell him all the things I never said.

For a time, I have no idea where he ends and I begin.

The Dani Daily

91 Days AWC

GET YOUR SHADE-BUSTERS!!!

READ ALL ABOUT IT!!!

Yep, you heard me right! The feckers CAN be killed! Brought to you by *The Dani Daily* your ONLY source for all the news AWC (After the Wall Crash, morons. I ain't gonna keep spelling things out for you).

The Dani "Mega" O'Malley SHADE-BUSTER

- 1 chunk Unseelie flesh.
- Fuse.
- Flash powder. Use only pyrotechnic industry-standard mix. Do NOT use chlorate or sulfur. HIGHLY unstable. Take it from me, I know what I'm talkin' about!

Make cherry bomb. Pack in center of flesh. Run fuse. Mold Unseelie flesh into round shape for easier rolling. Corner Shade, roll in SHADE-BUSTER, and cover your ears! The feckers are cannibals!!! Watch Shade devour snack and disintegrate when the bomb explodes inside it. If it eats LIGHT, it dies!

CAVEATS!

*Kids under 14: Do NOT do this without help. Ain't gonna do nobody no good if you blow your hands off. We need you in this fight. Be cool. Smart is the new cool.

*You gotta be fast! If you find a 'specially bad nest, write down the address of it on *The Dani Daily*, stick it on the wall inside the G.P.O., O'Connell Street, Dublin 1, and I'll take care of it for you. (They don't call me MEGA for nothing!)

*Do NOT use SULFUR! It makes the mix WAY unstable. I'm still growing back my eyebrows and nose hair.

*'Times the cherry bomb blows before the Shade eats it. Some of 'em are stupid enough to eat the next one you throw in.

LEGAL DISCLAIMER!

The Dani Daily (TDD, LLC) and affiliates are NOT responsible for collateral blast damage or injury!

2

I t's funny the things people say when someone dies.

He's in a better place.

How do you know that?

Life goes on.

That's supposed to comfort me? I'm excruciatingly aware that life goes on. It hurts every damned second. How lovely to know it's going to continue like this. Thank you for reminding me.

Time heals.

No, it doesn't. At best, time is the great leveler, sweeping us all into coffins. We find ways to distract ourselves from the pain. Time is neither scalpel nor bandage. It is indifferent. Scar tissue isn't a good thing. It's merely the wound's other face.

I live with the specter of Alina every day. Now I will live with Barrons' ghost, too. Walk between them: one on my right, one on my left. They will talk to me incessantly. I'll never escape, bridged between my greatest failures.

The day is cooling by the time I'm able to force myself to move. I know what that means. It means night is about to come slamming down on me with the finality of steel shutters on the glass façade of an upscale shop in a rundown neighborhood. I try to disentangle myself from him. I don't want to. It takes half a dozen attempts to make myself sit up. My head aches from crying; my throat burns from screaming. When I sit up, only the shell of my body moves. My heart is still lying on the ground next to Jericho Barrons. It beats one more time, then stops.

Peace at last.

I cross my legs beneath me and stiffly push myself up. I stand like I'm a hundred years old, creaking in every bone.

If the Lord Master is hunting me, I've sat on this cliff's edge for a dangerously long time.

The Lord Master, Darroc, leader of the dark Fae, bastard that tore down the walls on Halloween and turned the Unseelie hordes loose on my world.

The son of a bitch that started it all: seduced and either killed Alina or got her killed; had me raped by the Unseelie Princes, lobotomized, and turned into a helpless slave; abducted my parents and forced me into the Silvers; and drove me to this cliff's edge, where I murdered Barrons.

If not for one ex-Fae hell-bent on regaining his lost grace and exacting retribution, *none* of this would have happened.

Revenge will never be enough. Revenge would be over too quickly. It wouldn't satisfy the complexity of the needs of the creature I became while I was lying here, holding him.

I want it all back.

Everything that was taken from me.

A geyser of rage explodes in me, seeping into all the nooks and crannies my grief occupies. I welcome it, encourage it, genuflect to my new god. I baptize myself in its steaming, hissing fury. I give myself over. *Claim me, take me, own me, I am yours.*

Sidhe-seer is only a few letters away from *Ban-sidhe*: my birth country's harbinger of death, that shrieking mythic creature driven by fury.

I seek that dark glassy lake in my mind. I stand on the black-pebbled beach. Runes float on the shiny ebon surface, glistening with power.

I bend, trail my fingers through the black water, scoop up two fistfuls, and offer the bottomless loch a deep bow of gratitude.

It's my friend. I know that now. It has always been.

My fury is too vast for nooks and crannies.

I don't try to contain it. I let it build into a dark, dangerous melody. I throw my head back, making room for it as it rises. It swells, blasts up my throat, puffs out my cheeks. When it erupts from my lips, it's an inhuman cry that soars above the trees, rips into the air, and shatters the tranquillity of the forest.

Wolves startle awake in their dens, howling in mournful chorus; boars squeal; and creatures I cannot name scream. Our concert is deafening.

The temperature drops and the forest around me is abruptly encased in a thick silvery coating of ice, from smallest blade of grass to highest bough.

Birds flash-freeze and die, beaks parted, feeding their babies.

Squirrels ice, mid-leap, and drop like stones to the ground, where they shatter.

I glance at my hands. They are stained black, my palms cup silvery runes.

I know now where Barrons ends and I begin.

When Barrons ended, *I* began.

Me.

Mac O'Connor.

Sidhe-seer that a certain Seelie Prince said the world *should* fear.

I kneel and kiss Barrons a final time.

I do not cover him or perform any ritual. It would be for me, not him. There is only one thing left that I will do for me.

Soon, none of this will matter anyway.

I had to be ripped in half to stop feeling so torn in two. Divided, never knowing who to trust.

I'm now a woman with a single ambition.

I know exactly what I'm going to do.

And I know how I'm going to do it.

3

After leaving Barrons' body, I travel in the direction my guardian demon had been herding me. I believe he must have wanted me to go this way for a reason.

I trust him in death like I never did in life.

What a piece of work I am.

I follow the river for miles. As he disappears behind me, so, too, do I. With each step I take, I strip off another piece of myself. The weak parts. The parts that won't help me accomplish my goals. And if they are the so-called human parts, oh, well. I can't feel and still survive what I've got to get through.

When I am certain I am ready, I stop and wait for my enemy.

He does not disappoint.

"I thought you'd never get here," I say, my voice husky from screaming. It hurts to talk. I savor the pain. It's what I deserve.

The LM is still some distance away, concealed in the forest, but I see the shadows that move too sinuously to be cast by any tree.

"Come out." I lean back against a tree, one hand in a

pocket at my cocked hip, the other at my waist. "I *am* what you want, aren't I? What you came here for. What all this is about. Why hesitate now?"

My spear is in the holster beneath my arm, my dirk in my waistband. The black-leather rune-covered pouch holding the three stones the LM wants—three-quarters of what we all hope will form some kind of cage for the *Sinsar Dubh*—are tucked securely in my backpack, which hangs over my shoulder.

Shapes glide from the darkness: the LM and the last two Unseelie Princes.

Jack and Rainey Lane are not with them.

That would disturb me, except the Mac who loves her parents was in those pieces I left behind with Barrons' body. Barrons is dead. It's my fault. I have no parents. No love. No weaknesses. There's not a single shaft of sunshine in my soul.

I feel immeasurably lighter, stronger.

Darroc—I will no longer call him the LM; even the abbreviation of his smug-ass title implies superiority—has been eating a great deal of Unseelie flesh. Power is thick in the air between us. I'm not sure what comes from him and what is rolling off me. I wonder how his minions feel about him cannibalizing their own. Perhaps what is an abomination to the Light Court is a common vice at the Dark Court, an acceptable hazard of being Unseelie.

As he approaches the circle of silvery light in which I stand, his eyes widen infinitesimally.

I laugh, a throaty purr. I know what I look like. I washed after leaving Barrons and prepared myself with care. My bra is in my backpack. My hair is softly curled and wild around my face. It took time to get the black stain off my palms. There is nothing about me that is not a weapon, an asset, something to use to get what I want, including my body. I've learned a thing or two from Barrons: Power is sexy. It shapes my spine, infuses my beckoning hand.

I have not been devastated by Barrons' death. The alchemy of grief has forged a new metal.

I have been *transformed*.

There's only one way I can make his death okay. Undo it.

And, while I'm at it, undo Alina's, too.

Every person I've met who's known something about the *Sinsar Dubh* was cryptic about it. No one has been willing to tell me exactly what's in it. The only thing everyone kept telling me was that it was imperative I find it, and quickly, because it could be used to keep the walls from crashing.

Well, the walls are down now. It's too late.

Considering that I've been hunting this Book with single-minded dedication for months, it's startling how little thought I've given to its contents. I swallowed what I was told and obediently chased it.

I suspect now that everyone was keeping me tightly focused on the goal of finding it in order to keep the walls up, so I'd never get around to thinking too hard about *other* possible uses for the *Sinsar Dubh*.

There I was, hunting an object of unspeakable power, surrounded by people that wanted it for reasons of their own, and never once did I think: Wait a minute—what might it do for *me*?

Darroc told me that with the *Sinsar Dubh* he could bring Alina back. He said he wanted it to reclaim his Fae essence and exact revenge.

V'lane told me that the Dark Book holds all the Unseelie King's knowledge, every last damnable bit of it. He said he wants it for the Seelie Queen, so she might use it to restore their race to their former glory and to re-imprison the Unseelie. He believes it contains fragments of the Song of Making, lost to their race so long ago, and that the queen will be able to use them to re-create the ancient melody. I don't know exactly what the Song of Making is or does, but it seems to be the ulti-mate in Fae power.

It was Barrons that told me the most. He said the *Sinsar Dubh* contained spells to make and unmake worlds. Something to do with those fragments of the Song. He never would tell me why he wanted it. Said he was a book collector. Right. And I'm the Unseelie King.

Lying there, holding Barrons' body, I'd contemplated the *Sinsar Dubh*'s potential uses, for the first time, in a very personal way.

Especially the part about making and unmaking worlds.

It had all become perfectly clear to me.

With the *Sinsar Dubh,* a person could create a world with a different past—and a different future.

Essentially, a person could turn back time.

Erase anything they didn't like.

Replace those things they couldn't bear to have lost, including people they couldn't stand to live without.

I'd torn myself away from Barrons' body with one purpose.

To get the *Sinsar Dubh,* and when I did, I wasn't turning it over to anyone. It was going to be *mine*. I would study it. Grief had focused me like a laser. I could learn anything. Nothing would stand in my way. I would rebuild the world the way I wanted it.

"Come." I smile. "Join me." My face radiates only warmth, invitation, pleasure at his presence. I am the last thing he expected. He believed he would find a ter-rorized, hysterical girl.

I'm not and never will be again.

He motions the princes back and takes a casual step forward, but I see the studied grace in the movement. He is wary of me. He should be.

Coppery Fae eyes meet mine. How did Alina fail to see that those eyes were not human, no matter how human his body appeared?

The answer is simple: She did. She knew. That was why she lied to him, told him that she didn't have any family, that she was an orphan. Protected us from the very first. She knew there was something dangerous about him, and she wanted him anyway, wanted to taste that kind of life.

I don't blame her. We are flawed. We *should* have been banned from Ireland for everyone's good.

He assesses me. I know he passed Barrons' body. He's trying to figure out what happened but is unwilling to ask. I suspect nothing could have convinced him more surely than seeing Barrons dead that the MacKayla he thought he was dealing with wasn't home anymore. His gaze drops to the thin, jagged-edged silvery runes on the ground encircling me, bathing me in cool, eerie light. His eyes widen again as he scans them, and, for the briefest of instants, he looks rattled.

"Nice work." His gaze flicks between the runes and my face. "What are they?"

"You don't recognize them?" I counter. I sense deception. He knows what they are. I don't. I'd like to.

The next thing I know, his copper eyes lock with mine and a vibrant blue-black light blazes from his fist. I hadn't even seen him reach inside his shirt for the Hallow.

"Step out of the circle now," he commands.

He's not using Voice. He's holding the amulet, one of the four Unseelie Hallows, an ornate necklace that houses a fist-sized stone of inexplicable composition. The king created it for his concubine to enable her to bend reality to her whim. The amulet reinforces an epic person's will. Months ago, I sat at a very exclusive auction in an underground bomb shelter and watched an old Welshman pay in excess of eight figures for it. He'd had stiff competition. Mallucé had murdered the old man and taken it before Barrons and I had been able to steal it. But the wannabe vamp couldn't use it.

Darroc can. I believe I could, too—if I can get it from him.

I held it once, and it responded to me. But, like many things Fae, time imbued it with a degree of sentience and it had sought something from me—a binding, or pledge. I'd not understood—or, if I had, hadn't been willing to make it, afraid of what it would cost me. I'd lost the Hallow to Darroc when he'd Voiced me into turning it over, before I learned to use Voice myself. I'd have no compunction about exploring the amulet's desires now. No price is too high.

I feel the blue-black power it radiates, lacing his command with compulsion. The pressure is immense. I want to leave the circle. I could breathe, eat, sleep, live without pain forever, if only I would leave the circle.

I laugh. *"Throw me the amulet now."* Voice explodes from me.

The heads of the Unseelie Princes swivel and they regard me. It's hard to tell with them, but I think they suddenly find me very interesting.

A chill runs up my spine. There is no fear, no terror left inside me, yet those . . . things . . . those icy, unnatural aberrations . . . they still manage to affect me. I have not looked directly at them yet.

Darroc's hand tightens on the blazing amulet. *"Step out of the circle!"*

The pressure is crushing. It can be eased only by obeying.

"Throw me the amulet!"

He flinches, raises his hand, snarls, and jerks it back down.

For the next few minutes, he and I each try to bend the other to our will, until we are finally forced to concede that we are at an impasse. My Voice does not work on him. Neither amulet nor Voice works on me.

We are matched. Fascinating. I am his equal. My, what a creature I've become.

He circles me, and I turn with him, a faint smile curving my lips, my eyes alight. I am charged. I am exhilarated. I'm pumped on the power of my runes and myself. We study each other as if confronting a new species.

I offer my hand, an invitation to step to my side.

He looks down at the runes. "I am not that great a fool." His voice is deep, musical. He is beautiful. I understand why my sister wanted him. Tall, golden-skinned, there is an otherworldly eroticism to him that being made mortal by his queen did not eradicate. The scar on his face draws the eye, begs the finger to trace it, to learn the story behind it.

I cannot ask how great a fool, because it would betray that I don't know what my runes are.

"What happened to Barrons?" he says after a time.

"I killed him."

He searches my face, and I know he is trying to come up with any scenario that might explain the way Barrons was mutilated and killed. If he examined the body, he saw the spear wound, and he knows I carry it. He knows I stabbed him at least once.

"Why?"

"I wearied of his incessant boorishness." I wink. Let him think me mad. I *am*. In every sense of the word.

"I didn't think he could be killed. The Fae have long feared him."

"Turns out the spear was his weakness. It's why he never wanted to touch it."

He absorbs my words, and I know he's trying to decide why a Fae weapon could kill Jericho Barrons. I'd like to know, too. *Was* it the spear that dealt the killing blow? Would he have died of that wound eventually regardless of whether Ryodan had slit his throat?

"Yet he armed you with it? You expect me to believe that?"

"Like you, he thought I was all fluff and no teeth. Too stupid to be worth suspicion. 'Lamb to the slaughter' was how he liked to phrase it. Little lamb killed the lion. Guess I showed him, huh?" I wink again.

"I burned his body. There is nothing left but ash." He watches my face carefully.

"Good."

"If there was any way he might rise, he never will now. The princes scattered his ashes to a hundred dimensions." His gaze is piercing now.

"I should have thought of that myself. Thank you for finishing it so well." My mind is on the new world I plan to create. I've said good-bye to this one.

Copper eyes narrow, glittering with scorn. "You didn't kill Barrons. What happened? What are you playing at?"

"He betrayed me," I lie.

"How?"

"It's none of your business. I had my reasons." I watch him watch me. He wonders if the rape of the Unseelie Princes and my time in the Hall of All Days has unhinged me. He wonders if I'm unbalanced enough to have gone crazy and actually killed Barrons for pissing me off. When he glances down at the runes again, I know he thinks I have enough juice to have pulled it off.

"Step out of the circle. I have your parents and will kill them if you don't obey me."

"I don't care." I scoff.

He stares. He heard the truth in my words.

I *don't* care. An essential part of me is dead. I don't mourn it. This is no longer my world. What happens here doesn't matter. In this reality, I'm already on borrowed time. I will rebuild a new one or die trying.

"I'm free, Darroc. I'm really, truly free." I shrug my shoulders, toss my head, and laugh.

He sucks in a sharp breath when I say his name and laugh, and I know that I've reminded him of my sister. Did she say those words to him once? Does he hear joy in my laughter, as he once heard in hers?

He stalks a tight circle around me, eyes narrowed. "What changed? In the days since I abducted your parents and today, what happened to you?"

"What happened to me started happening a long time ago. You should have kept Alina alive. I hated you for that."

"And now?"

I look him up and down. "Now is different. Things are different. *We* are different."

His eyes search mine, left to right and back again, rapidly. "What are you saying?"

"I see no reason we cannot be . . . friends."

He tries the word. "Friends?"

I nod.

He contemplates the possibility that I am sincere. A human would never entertain the notion. Fae are different. No matter how much time they spend among us, they just can't nail the subtleties of human emotion. It's that difference I'm counting on. When I left Barrons, all I wanted was to lay in wait for Darroc, use my runes and my newfound dark glassy friend to kill him the moment he appeared.

I exorcised it swiftly.

This ex-Fae turned human knows more about both the Seelie and Unseelie courts, and the Book that I am determined to possess, than anyone. When he has told me everything he knows, I'll relish killing him. I'd considered allying myself with V'lane—and when I'm done taking everything I need from Darroc, I still may. After all, I'll need the fourth stone. But V'lane doesn't seem to have any real knowledge about the Book, aside from a few old legends.

It's a better bet that the Unseelie know more about the Dark Book than the Seelie Queen's right hand. Maybe even where to find the prophecy. Like Barrons, Darroc has actually seen pages of the arcane tome. I was forced to concede that hunting the *Sinsar Dubh* was an exercise in futility until I discovered how to control it. But Darroc has never stopped his search. Why? What does he know that I don't?

The sooner I pry his secrets from him, the sooner I learn to contain and use the *Sinsar Dubh,* the sooner I can stop living in this agonizing reality that I will have no hesitation about destroying to replace with *my* world. The right one. Where everything ends happily ever after.

"Friends work toward common goals," he says.

"Like hunting books," I agree.

"Friends trust each other. They don't barricade each other out." He looks at my feet.

The runes came from within me. I *am* my circle. He doesn't know this. I kick them aside. I wonder if he has forgotten my spear. As heavily laced with Unseelie as he is, a single prick would sentence him to the same slow, gruesome death that Mallucé suffered.

When I step out, he slowly looks me up and down.

I see the thoughts that flash through his eyes as they travel over my body: *kill her/fuck her/assault and bind her/explore her uses?* It takes a lot to make a man kill a beautiful woman he has not yet slept with. Especially if he enjoyed her sister.

"Friends don't try to coerce each other," I say with a pointed look at the amulet.

He inclines his head and slips it back inside his shirt.

I offer my hand with a smile. Barrons taught me well. *Keep your friends close . . .*

Darroc takes it, leans down to place a light kiss upon my lips. The tension between us is a palpable thing. One sudden move from either of us and we'll be all over each other, trying to kill each other, and we know it. He keeps his body pliant. I infuse my limbs with languor. We are two scorpions with coiled tails, trying to mate. It is no more than I deserve, the punishment of letting him touch me like this. I sentenced Barrons to death.

I part my lips beneath his, but demurely, teeth standing guard. I exhale a soft whisper of a breath into his mouth. He likes it.

. . . and your enemies closer.

Behind us, the Unseelie Princes begin to chime softly like dark crystal. I remember that sound. I know what it precedes. I tighten my hand on his. "Never them. Never again."

Darroc turns to them and barks a harsh command in a language that hurts my ears.

They vanish.

The moment I no longer know where they are, whether they might be closing in on me, I reach for my spear. It is gone, too.

The Unseelie Princes cannot sift within the Silvers with any predictability. Darroc tells me it's a crapshoot every time they try. Cruce's curse again, screwing things up.

I tell him the stones are no better, that whatever dimension I'm in tries to expel them once uncovered, in an effort to return the rune-covered blue-black stones to the cliffs of the icy Unseelie prison from whence they were chiseled.

I'm surprised he doesn't know this and tell him so.

"You do not understand what life is like at the Seelie

court, MacKayla. Those with true knowledge, true memories of our past, guard it zealously. There are as many versions of the Old Days and conflicting tales of our origins as there are dimensions to choose from within the hall. The only Unseelie we ever saw were those we battled the day the king and queen fought and the king slew our queen. Since then, we have drunk from the cauldron countless times."

He moves along the cliff's edge with unnatural fluidity and grace. Fae move like sleek, kingly predators, born of the sure knowledge that they can never die—or at least very rarely and only under special circumstances. He hasn't lost that arrogance, or perhaps he's reclaimed it, from all the Unseelie he's been eating. He's not wearing the crimson robes that once terrified me. Tall, gracefully muscled, he's dressed like an outdoorsman in a Versace ad, with a long fall of moon-silvered hair secured at his nape. He's undeniably sexy. In his power and confidence, he reminds me of Barrons.

I don't ask why they drink. I understand. If I found the cauldron and drank from it, it would erase all pain and allow me to start life over, a blank slate. I couldn't grieve for what I didn't remember ever having. That they drink implies that on some level the Fae feel. If not pain, at least significant discomfort.

"So how *are* we going to get out of here?" I ask.

His reply gives me a sudden chill, a sense of something more vast and incomprehensible than déjà vu—an inevitability finally manifesting.

"The White Mansion."

4

The night the walls came crashing down, I cowered in a belfry, my only goal to survive until dawn.

I had no idea if the world would survive with me.

I thought it was the longest night of my life. I was wrong.

This is the longest night of my life, walking side by side with my enemy, mourning Jericho Barrons, drowning in my own complicity.

It stretches on and on. I live a thousand hours in a handful. I count from one to sixty beneath my breath, over and over, ticking away the minutes I make it through, thinking if I put enough of them between me and his death, the immediacy of the pain might dull and I will be able to catch a breath without a knife stabbing through my heart.

We do not pause to eat or sleep. He keeps Unseelie flesh in a pouch and periodically chews it while we travel, which means he can keep going far longer than I. At some point, I'll be forced to rest. The thought of relinquishing consciousness in his presence is not a pleasant one.

I have weapons in my arsenal that I've not yet tried

on him. I have no doubt he is concealing armaments, too. Our truce is a floor of eggshells and we're both wearing combat boots.

"Where is the Unseelie King?" I ask, hoping distraction might make the minutes move faster. "It's his book on the loose out there. I heard he wants it destroyed. Why isn't he doing something about it?" I may as well embark on an Unseelie fishing expedition, casting my nets for anything I can use. Until I know how powerful Darroc is and better understand what I have in my dark glassy lake, subtlety is the name of my game. I will make no rash moves that jeopardize my mission. Barrons' resurrection depends on it.

He shrugs. "He vanished long ago. Some say he's too insane to care. Others believe he cannot leave the Unseelie prison and lies encased in a tomb of black ice, slumbering eternally. Still others claim the prison never contained him to begin with and that remorse for the death of his concubine was the only bond he ever permitted."

"That implies love. Fae don't."

"Debatable. I recognize myself in you and find it . . . compelling. It makes me less alone."

Translation: I serve as a mirror and the Fae enjoy their own reflection. "Is that desirable to a Fae—to be less alone?"

"Few Fae can endure solitude. Some posit that energy cast into an ethos that fails to reflect or rebound it permits that energy to dissipate until nothing remains. Perhaps it is a flaw."

"Like clapping for Tinker Bell," I mock. "A mirror, validation."

He gives me a look.

"Is that what the Fae are made of? Energy?"

He gives me another look that reminds me of V'lane, and I know that he will never discuss what the Fae are comprised of with me or *any* human. His superiority complex has in no way been diminished by time as a mortal. Rather, I suspect it has grown. He knows both sides now. This gives him a tactical advantage over other Fae. He understands what makes us tick and is more dangerous because of it. I file the energy idea away for further contemplation. Iron affects the Fae. Why? Are they some kind of energy that could be "shorted out"?

"You admit to flaws?" I press.

"We are not perfect. What god is? Examine yours. According to your mythos, he was so disappointed with his initial efforts creating your race that he tried again. At least we imprisoned our mistakes. Your god permits his to roam free. At a mere few thousand years old, your creation myths are far more absurd than ours. Yet you wonder why we can't recall our origins, from a million or more years in the past."

We have drawn closer to each other while speaking and both realize it at the same time. We glide back in instant retreat, regaining enough distance between us that we would see an attack from the other coming. Part of me finds this amusing.

The princes have not yet reappeared. I am grateful. Although they no longer impact me sexually, they have a profoundly terrible presence. They leave me feeling oddly two-dimensional, minus something essential, guilty, betrayed in a way I can't understand and don't want to. I don't know if I feel this because I was once beneath them, with my entire sense of self being stripped from my skin and bones, or if they are fundamentally anathema to all humans. I wonder if the "stuff" of which they were made by the Unseelie King is so alien and horrific to us that they are the equivalent of a psychic black hole. That they are unspeakably beautiful only makes it worse. Their exquisiteness is the event horizon from which there is no escape. I shiver.

I remember.

I will never forget. Three of them and an invisible fourth, moving over me, in me.

Because Darroc commanded it. That, too, I will never forget.

I thought being raped by them was terrible, that it had carved me in deep places, changed my innate makeup. I'd known nothing of pain, of transforming change. I do now.

We clear the forest, and the terrain begins to slope downward. With the moon lighting our way, we hike through dark meadows.

I give up my fishing expedition for now. My throat is raw from screaming, and putting one foot in front of the other while keeping an impassive expression on my face takes all my concentration. I slog through a lifetime of hell in the interminable darkness before dawn.

I replay the scene on the cliff through my head a thousand times, pretending it ended some other way.

Thick grass and slender flat rushes rustle at my waist and brush the undersides of my breasts. If there are animals in the dense thicket, they keep their distance. If I were an animal, I would keep my distance from us, too. The climate grows more temperate; the air warms with the perfume of exotic night-blooming jasmine and honeysuckle.

As abruptly as night falls here, dawn breaks. The sky is black one moment, pink, then blue. Three seconds, night to day.

I made it through the night. I draw a shallow, careful breath.

When my sister was killed, I discovered that the light of day has an irrational leavening effect on grief. I have no idea why. Maybe it's just to shore us up so we can survive the lonely, bleak night again.

I didn't know we were on a high plain until we were

suddenly at the edge of the plateau, and I am startled by the valley dropping sharply away before me.

Across that valley, on an oceanic swell of hill, it looms. It soars. It sprawls for miles in every direction.

The White Mansion.

Again I get that uncanny feeling of inevitability that, one way or another, life would have deposited me here, that in any reality I would have made the same choices that drove me to its door.

Home to the Unseelie King's beloved concubine for whom he killed the Seelie Queen, it is so enormous it boggles the mind. I turn my head from side to side, up and down, trying to take it all in. One could hope to behold its entirety only from miles away, as we are now. Was this where Barrons had been trying to lead me? If so, why? Had Ryodan been lying when he found me on the cliff's edge and told me that the way back to Dublin was through an IFP, an Interdimensional Fairy Pothole, as I'd dubbed the slivers of Fae reality that splintered our world now that the walls were down?

The walls are alabaster, reflecting the sun, and blaze with such brilliance that I narrow my eyes to slits. The sky beyond the House—I cannot think of it without a capital; it is far more than a mere residence—deepens to a dazzling blue that exists only in Faery, a shade that will never be seen in the human world. There are certain Faery colors that have dimension, are comprised of myriad seductive subtleties upon which the eye could linger for time uncounted. The sky is nearly as addictive as the golden floor in the Hall of All Days.

I force my gaze back to the White Mansion. I explore its lines, foundation to rooftop, terrace to tower, garden to fountain to turret. A Möbius strip of tiered structures on an Escher-esque landscape, it turns back on itself here and there, continuous and unbroken, ever-changing and unfolding. It strains the eye, tests the mind. But I've seen Fae in their true form. I find it . . . soothing. In my dead black heart, I feel something. I don't understand how anything could stir in there, but it does. Not a full-blown feeling, but an echo of an emotion. Faint yet undeniable.

Darroc watches me. I pretend not to notice.

"Your race has never built a thing of such beauty, complexity, and perfection," he says.

"Nor has my race ever created a *Sinsar Dubh*," I parry.

"Small creatures create small things."

"Large creatures' egos are so big they don't see the small things coming," I murmur. *Like traps,* I don't say.

He intuits it. He laughs and says, "I will remember the warning, MacKayla."

After he found the first two Silvers at an auction house in London, Darroc tells me, he had to learn to use them. It took him dozens of tries to establish a static link into the Fae realms, then, once he was inside the Silvers, it took him months to find a way to the Unseelie prison.

There's pride in his voice as he speaks of his trials and triumphs. Stripped of his Fae essence, he not only survived when his race didn't believe he would, but he accomplished the goal he'd been pursuing as a Fae, the very thing for which he'd been banished. He feels superior to others of his kind.

I listen, analyzing everything he tells me, looking for chinks in his armor. I know Fae have "feelings" such as arrogance, superiority, mockery, and condescension. Listening to him, I add pride, vengeance, impatience, gloating, and amusement to the list.

We've been making small talk for some time, watching each other intently. I've told him about growing up in Ashford, my first impressions of Dublin, my love of fast cars. He has told me more about his fall from grace, what he did, why he did it. We compete to disarm each other with trivial confidences that betray nothing of importance.

As we cross the valley, I say, "Why go to the Unseelie prison? Why not the Seelie court?"

"And give Aoibheal the opportunity to finish me off for good? The next time I see the bitch, she dies."

Was that why he'd taken my spear—to kill the queen? He'd lifted it without my awareness, just like V'lane had. How? He wasn't Fae anymore. Had he eaten so much Unseelie that he was now a mutant with unpredictable abilities? I recall being in the church, sandwiched between Unseelie Princes, turning the spear on myself, throwing it, striking the pedestal of a basin, holy water splashing, steam hissing. How had he made me throw it away then? How had he taken it from me now?

"Is the queen at the Seelie court right now?" I cast my net again.

"How would I know? I have been banished. Assuming I found a way in, the first Seelie that saw me would kill me."

"Don't you have allies at the Seelie court? Isn't V'lane your friend?"

He snorts disdainfully. "We sat on her High Council together. Though he gives lip service to Fae supremacy and speaks of walking the earth freely again without the odious Compact governing us—*us*, as if humans could govern their gods!—when it comes to action, V'lane is Aoibheal's lapdog and always has been. I am now human, according to my fairer brethren, and they despise me."

"I thought you said they worshipped you as a hero for tearing the walls down and freeing them."

His eyes narrow. "I said they *will*. Soon, I will be heralded as the savior of our race."

"So you went to the Unseelie prison. That was risky."
I prod to keep him talking. As long as he's talking, I can
focus on his words, on my goals. Silence isn't golden, it's
deadly. It's a vacuum that fills up with ghosts.

"I needed the Hunters. As a Fae, I could summon
them. As a mortal, I had to physically seek them."

"I'm surprised they didn't kill you on sight." Hunters
hate humans. The black-skinned, winged demons have
no love for anything but themselves.

"Death is not a Hunter's delight. Too final."

A memory flickers through his eyes, and I know that
when he found them, they did things to him that made
him scream for a long time.

"They agreed to help me in exchange for permanent
freedom. They taught me to eat Unseelie. After tracking
weaknesses in the prison walls, where Unseelie had escaped before, I patched them."

"To make yourself the only game in town."

He nods. "If my dark brethren were going to be freed,
they would be thanking me for it. I discovered how to
link Silvers and created a passage to Dublin through the
White Mansion."

"Why here?"

"Of all the dimensions I explored, this one remains
the most stable, aside from a few . . . inconveniences. It
seems Cruce's curse had little effect on this realm, other
than to splinter dimensions that are easily avoided."

I call them IFPs but I do not tell him this. It made Barrons smile. Little made Barrons smile.

I think I'm under control, that I've stripped away all
weaknesses. That committing to my mission has made
me impervious. I'm wrong. The thought of Barrons
smiling brings other thoughts.

Barrons naked.

Dancing.

Dark head thrown back.
Laughing.

The image doesn't "gently swim up in my mind" in a dreamy sort of way, like I've seen in movies. No, this one slams into my head like a nuclear missile, exploding in my brain in graphic detail. I suffocate in a mushroom cloud of pain.

I can't breathe. I squeeze my eyes shut.

White teeth flashing in his dark face: *I get knocked down but I get up again. You're never gonna keep me down.*

I stagger.

But he didn't get up, the bastard. He stayed down.

With my spear in his back. How am I supposed to find my way each day without him here to help me? I don't know what to do, how to make decisions.

I can't survive this grief! I stumble and go down on one knee. I clutch my head.

Darroc is at my side, helping me stand. His arms are around me.

I open my eyes.

He is so close that I see gold speckles in his coppery eyes. Wrinkles crease the corners. Faint lines bracket his mouth. Has he laughed so often in his time as a mortal? My hands curl into fists.

His hands are gentle on my face when he pushes my hair back. "What happened?"

Neither image nor pain is gone from my brain. I cannot function in this state. In moments, I will be on my knees, screaming with grief and fury, and my mission will go straight to hell. Darroc will see my weakness and kill me, or worse. Somehow I have to survive. I have no idea how long it will take me to find the Book and learn how to use it. I wet my lips. "Kiss me," I say. "Hard."

His mouth tightens. "I am not a fool, MacKayla."

"Just do it," I snarl.

I watch him weigh the idea. Two scorpions. He is skeptical. He is fascinated.

When he kisses me, Barrons vanishes from my head. The pain recedes.

On the lips of my enemy, my sister's lover, my lover's killer, I taste the punishment I deserve. I taste oblivion.

It makes me cold and strong again.

I have dreamed of houses all my life. I have an entire neighborhood in my subconscious that I can get to only while sleeping. But I can't control my nocturnal visits any more than I've ever been able to avoid my Cold Place dreams. Sometimes I'm granted passage and sometimes I'm not. Certain nights the doors open easily, while others I stand outside, denied entrance, longing for the wonders that lie within.

I don't understand people who say they can't recall their dreams. With the exception of the Cold Place dream, which I began blocking long ago, I recall all the others. When I wake in the morning, they're floating through my mind in fragments, and I can either spring out of bed and forget them or gather up the pieces and examine them.

I read somewhere that dreams about houses are dreams of our souls. In those dwellings of our psyche, we store our innermost secrets and desires. Perhaps that's why some people don't remember them—they don't want to. A girl I knew in high school once told me she dreamed of houses, too, but they were always pitch black and she could never find the light switch. She hated those dreams. She wasn't the brightest bulb in the box.

My houses are endless, filled with sunshine and music, gardens and fountains. And for some reason there are always a lot of beds. Big beds. Way more than any house needs. I don't know what the deal is with that, but I think it might mean I think about sex a lot.

Sometimes I worry that there's not enough room in my brain for both my dreams and reality, that I'm a hard drive with limited gigabytes and one day I won't be able to maintain the firewall between them. I wonder if that's what senility is.

Over the years, I've begun to suspect that all the houses of which I've been dreaming are just different wings of the same great house.

Today I realize it's true.

Why have I been dreaming of the White Mansion all these years?

How could I possibly have known it existed?

Now that I'm a little over the edge anyway, I can admit something: My whole life, I've secretly been afraid that beneath my fiercely focused grooming and accessorizing, I'm, well . . . psychotic.

Never underestimate a well-dressed bimbo.

The real thinkers of the world aren't the best dressed. Staying on top of the latest fashions, accessorizing, and presenting oneself is time consuming. It takes a lot of effort, energy, and concentration to be incessantly happy and perfectly groomed. You meet somebody like that— ask yourself what they're running from.

Back in high school, I began to suspect I was bipolar. There were times when, for no good reason at all, I felt downright, well . . . homicidal was the only word for it. I learned that the busier I stayed, the less time I had to feel it.

I sometimes wonder if before I was born someone showed me the script or filled me in on the highlights. It's déjà vu to the worst extreme. I refuse to believe I would have auditioned for this role.

As I stare at the White Mansion and I know what parts of it look like inside—and I know there's no way I could know those things—I wonder if I'm a serious nutcase. If none of this is happening, because I'm really locked up in a padded cell somewhere, hallucinating. If so, I hope they change my drugs soon. Whatever I'm on isn't working.

I don't want to go in there.

I want to go in there and never leave.

Duality is me.

The House has countless entrances, through elaborately manicured gardens.

Darroc and I enter one of the gardens. It's so lovely it's almost painful to look at. Paths of glistening gold pavers unfurl through exotic, perfumed bushes and circle clusters of willowy silver-leafed trees. Dazzling pearl benches offer respite from the sun beneath lacy leaves, and silk chaises dot outdoor rooms of billowing chiffon. Flowers bend and sway in a light, perfect breeze, the precise degree of sultry—not too hot or moist but warm and wet, like sex is warm and wet.

I have dreamed of a garden like this. Small differences but not many.

We pass a fountain that sprays rainbows of shimmery water into the air. Thousands of flowers in every dazzling shade of yellow circle it: velvety buttercups and waxy tulips, creamy lilies and blossoms that do not exist in our world. For a moment I think of Alina, because she loves yellow, but that thought reeks of death and brings other thoughts with it, so I turn away from the beauty of the fountain and focus on the hated face and voice of my companion.

He begins to give me instructions. He tells me we're looking for a room with an ornate gilt-framed mirror that is approximately ten feet tall by five feet wide. The last time he saw the room, it was empty of all furnishings, save the mirror. The corridor off which the room opened was light, airy, and had a floor of unbroken white marble. The walls of the corridor were also white and adorned with brilliant murals between tall windows.

Keep an eye out for white marble floors, he instructs me, because only two of the wings—as of the last time he was here—have them. The floors in other wings are gold, bronze, silver, iridescent, pink, mint, yellow, lavender, and other pastels. The rare wing is crimson. If I see a black floor, I am to turn back immediately.

We enter a circular foyer with a high glass ceiling that collects the sunny day. The walls and floor are translucent silver and reflect the sky above in such vivid detail that, when a cream-puff cloud scoots overhead, I feel as if I'm walking through it. What a clever design! A room in the sky. Did the concubine create it? Did the Unseelie King design it for her? Could a being capable of creating such horrors as the Unseelie also create such delights? Sunlight bathes me from above, bounces back at me from the wall and floors.

Mac 1.0 would have hooked up an iPod and stretched out here for hours.

Mac 5.0 shivers. Not even this much sun can warm the part of her that has gone cold.

I realize I've forgotten my enemy. I tune him back in.

Assuming, of course, Darroc is saying, that the room we seek still opens off one of those white-marbled halls.

That gets my attention. "Assuming?"

"The mansion rearranges itself. One of those inconveniences I mentioned."

"What is *with* you fairies, anyway?" I explode. "Why does everything have to change? Why can't things just be what they are? Why can't a house be a normal house and a book a normal book? Why does it all have to be so complicated?" I want to get back to Dublin *now*, find the Book, figure out what needs to be done, and escape this damned reality!

He doesn't answer, but I don't need him to. If a Fae were to ask me why an apple eventually rots or humans eventually die, I would shrug and say it was the nature of human things.

Change is the nature of Fae things. They are always becoming something else. That's a critical thing to remember when dealing with anything Fae, as I learned from the Shades. I wonder how much further they've evolved since I last saw them.

"Sometimes it rearranges itself on a grand scale," Darroc continues, "while other times it merely swaps a few things around. Only once did it take me several days to find the room I seek. I usually find it more quickly."

Days? My head swivels and I stare. I could be stuck in here with him for days?

The sooner we get started, the better.

A dozen halls open off the foyer, some well lit, others soothingly dim. Nothing is frightening. The House exudes a sense of well-being and peace. Still, it is a grand labyrinth, and I wait for him to choose our path. Although I have long been dreaming of this place, I do not know this foyer. I suspect the House is so large that an entire human life of dreams would not be enough to explore it all.

"There are several rooms in the mansion that house Silvers. The one we seek holds a single mirror." He gives me a sharp look. "Avoid the other mirrors if you stumble upon them. Do not gaze into them. I am not forbidding you knowledge, merely trying to protect you."

Right. And the White Mansion is really black. "You make it sound as if we're splitting up." I'm surprised. He worked so hard to get me at his side. Now he's letting me go? Have I been so convincing? Or does he have an ace up his sleeve I don't know about?

"We cannot afford to waste time here. The longer I'm

here, the more chance there is for someone else to find my book."

"*My* book," I correct.

He laughs. "*Our* book."

I say nothing. My book—and he's dead the moment I've got it and know how to use it. Sooner, if he's no longer useful.

He leans back against the wall and crosses his arms over his chest. In this room of sky, he is a golden angel, shoulders propped against a cloud. "We can both have everything we want, MacKayla. With you and I allied, there are no limits. Nothing and no one can stop us. Do you realize that?"

"I get to use it first." He won't exist to use it by the time I'm done with it. No, wait, unmaking him would be too easy a death.

I want to *murder* him.

"We have plenty of time to decide who does what with it first. But, for now, are we friends or not?"

It is on the tip of my tongue to mock him, to tell him words mean nothing. Why does he ask me absurd questions? I can so easily lie. He should judge my actions, but I don't share advice with the enemy. "We are friends," I say easily.

He gestures for me to take the nearest corridor on my right, one with a dusky-rose floor, and turns for the first one on his left, which gleams deep bronze.

"What do I do if I find it?" I ask. It's not like we have cell phones programmed with nifty little acronyms.

"I branded you at the base of your skull. Press your fingers to the mark and call for me."

He has already turned away and begun walking down his hall. I hiss at his back. The day will come, and soon, when I remove his brand, if I have to scrape my skull down to bare bone. I'd do it now, except I don't want to run the risk of damaging Barrons'. It's all I have left of him. His hands were on me there, gentle, possessive.

There is a smile in Darroc's voice when he warns, "If you find the Silver and return to Dublin without me, I will hunt you."

"Right back at you, Darroc," I say in the same light, warning tone. "Don't even think of leaving without me. I may not have a mark on you, but I'll find you. I'll *always* find you." I mean it. The hunter is now the hunted. I have him in my sights and will keep him there. Until I decide to pull the trigger. No more running. From anything.

He stops and glances over his shoulder at me. The tiny gold flecks in his eyes flare brighter, and he inhales sharply.

If I know Fae as well as I think I do, I just turned him on.

The Dani Daily

97 Days AWC

Dani "Mega" O'Malley SLAYS a HUNTER!!!

READ ALL ABOUT IT IN *TDD*, YOUR ONLY SOURCE FOR THE LATEST NEWS IN AND AROUND DUBLIN!

Sidhe-seers celebrate! We did it, we took one down!!! Took us all feckin' night, but Jayne and the Guardians finally bagged one of the flapping fecks! Pumped it full of so much iron it crashed to the street. I stabbed the blimey feck straight through the heart with the Sword of Light! It was something to see, you shoulda been there! Thing bled dark up into the sword, all the way to the hilt, & for a sec I worried it mighta broke it or something, but it's working again fine, so tell Ro not to get her panties in a twist!

Call to arms, dudes! Get outta that abbey and fight, fight, fight!!! Enough reconnoitering already! Rhymes with loitering, dudes—*USELESS!* DO something. We CAN make a difference. Haul ass to Dublin Castle. 'S' new headquarters for the new Garda, and they're way cool. Said all *sidhe*-seers welcome. 'SPECIALLY **SINGLE** ONES!!!!

Need to repopulate Dublin, ya know. Ain't gonna happen by itself. Lots of heroes on the streets, risking their lives, kicking Fae ass. Hook up NOW!

MEET TONIGHT!!!

DUBLIN CASTLE!!!

EIGHT O'CLOCK!!!

JOIN THE HUNT!!!

PS: Mac's sorry she can't be there, still busy with other stuff, but she'll be back REAL soon.

I slap the latest edition of my rag to the streetlamp and pound in a nail. I tell 'em what'll work for me and don't tell 'em what won't. 'Times you gotta lie.

I cram a candy bar in my mouth and freeze-frame to the next streetlamp on my route. I know my rags are getting to the peeps. I been seeing results. Couple *sidhe*-seers ditched the abbey already. I'm taking over where Mac left off—shit-stirrer extraordinaire, bucking Ro's rules and regs, all the while telling her whatever she wants to hear.

Two candy bars and a protein pack later, I'm done with my route and burning up the pavement for my fave place. I got hours for myself now and gonna spend 'em all circling Chester's, slicing and dicing everything that comes within a ten-block radius of it.

I swagger down the street.

Ry-O and his men are in there—least I think they are. Ain't seen none in a while but keep hoping. See, 'cause they piss me off. They threatened me.

Nobody threatens the Mega.

I snicker. Pub ain't no good if patrons can't get in. I can't keep 'em out all night, 'cause I hunt with the Guardians and kill what they trap, but I do 'nuff damage during the day. Jayne caught me one afternoon, said they'll kill me for it. He's heard tales of 'em, steers clear. Says they're no more human than the Fae.

Told 'em the pricks can just try to mess with me. See, 'nother thing I didn't tell nobody is, when I stabbed the Hunter, something weird happened: The dark came all the way up my sword and got into my arm a little. Infected me like a splinter. For a couple days, my hand had black veins and was icy like it was dead. Had to wear a glove to hide it. Thought I might lose it, hafta learn to fight right-handed.

Looks okay now.

Ain't in no hurry to kill a Hunter again.

But I think I'm faster. And Ro's orders don't seem to make me feel near as conflicted as they used to.

Think Ry-O and his dudes maybe got nothing on me, and I'd like to test it. Like to show Mac, but it's been more than three whole weeks since I saw her last. Since we broke into the libraries.

Barrons ain't 'round neither.

I don't worry. Ain't my nature. I live. Leave the worrying for the warts.

But I sure wish she'd show up. Any time now'd be real good.

Sinsar Dubh's been all over this city past few days. Took out a dozen of Jayne's men in one night, like it was playing with us. Kept dividing us, picking us off.

Kinda starting to wonder if it's looking for me.

5

In the House, away from my enemy, I find solace for a time.

Grief, loss, pain melt away. I wonder if they cannot exist inside these walls.

The weight of my spear in the holster beneath my arm is back, heavy against my side. Like V'lane, Darroc has some way of taking it from me, but when we are apart he returns it. Perhaps so I can defend myself. I can't imagine needing to in a place such as this.

There has never been and will never be another place in any realm, in any dimension, that holds me in such thrall as the White Mansion. Not even the bookstore competes for dominance in my soul.

The House is mesmerizing. If, deep down inside where I feel psychotic, I am angered by this, I'm too lulled by whatever drug it feeds me to focus on it for long.

I wander the rose-floored corridor, absorbing it in a dreamy daze. Windows line the right side of the hall, and, beyond the crystal-edged panes, dawn blushes over gardens filled with pink roses, wreathed heads nodding sleepily in the gentle morning breeze.

The rooms that open off this corridor are decorated in hues of morning sky. The colors of the hall, the day beyond, and the rooms complement one another perfectly, as if, from every angle, this wing was designed as an outfit, flawlessly accessorized, to be donned depending on the mood.

When the rose floor ends and a sudden turn in the corridor sets me on a lavender path, violet dusk clings to the windows. Nocturnal creatures frolic in a forest glade beneath a moon rimmed with brilliant cerulean. The rooms in this corridor are furnished in shades of twilight.

Yellow and reflective floors open onto sunny days and sunnier rooms.

Bronze corridors have no windows, only tall arched doors that lead into enormous, high-ceilinged, kingly rooms—some for dining, some filled with books and comfortable chairs, others for dancing, and still more for what I think are forms of entertainment I don't understand. I imagine I hear echoes of laughter. Lit by candles, the rooms off bronze corridors are masculine and smell of spice. I find the scent intoxicating, disturbing.

I walk and walk, looking into this room and that, delighted by the things I find, the things I recognize. In this place, every hour of day and night is always available.

I have been here many times before.

There's the piano I played.

Here is the sunroom where I sat and read.

There's the kitchen where I ate truffles smothered in cream and filled with delicate fruits that don't exist in our world.

Here, a flute lies on a table, beside an open book, next to a teapot decorated with a pattern as familiar to me as the back of my own hand.

There's the rooftop garden, high atop a turret where I've gazed through a telescope at an azure sea.

Here, a library of endless rows of books, where I've passed time uncounted.

Each room is a study in beauty, each item in it adorned with intricate detail, as if its creator had infinity in which to work.

I wonder how long the concubine was here. I wonder how much of this house is her creation.

I taste forever in this place, but, unlike in the Hall of All Days, forever here is exquisite, gentle. The House promises a blissful eternity. It does not terrify or cow. The House is time as it was meant to be: endless, serene.

Here—a room of thousands of gowns! I dash through row after row, my arms spread wide, my hands fanning the fabulous fabrics. I love these gowns!

I pluck one from its hanger and spin around, dancing with it. Faint strains of music drift upon the air and I lose track of time.

Here's a curio cabinet housing items I cannot name but nonetheless recognize. I pocket a few of the smaller trinkets. I open a music box and listen to a song that makes me feel I am drifting in space, enormous and free, more *right* in my skin than I've ever been, poised on the brink of all possibles. I forget everything for a time, lost in joy that is larger than the mansion itself.

In room after room, I find something familiar, something that makes me happy.

I see the first of many beds. As in my dreams, there are so many that I lose count after a time.

I wander sumptuous room after room, see bed after bed. Some of the rooms have nothing but beds.

I begin to feel . . . uneasy. I don't like looking at these beds.

The beds disturb me.

I turn my head away, because they make me feel things I don't want to feel.

Need. Desire. Alone.

Empty beds.

Don't want to be alone anymore. So tired of being alone. Tired of waiting.

After a time, I stop looking in the rooms.

I was wrong when I thought it might not be possible to feel negative things inside the White Mansion.

Grief wells up inside me.

I've lived so long. Lost so many things.

I force myself to focus. I remind myself that I'm supposed to be looking for something. A mirror.

I love that mirror.

I shake my head. No, I don't. I just need it. I don't have any emotions about it!

It brings me such pleasure! It brings us together.

White marble, Darroc said. I need to find white-marble floors. Not crimson, not bronze, not pink, and especially not black.

I envision the mirror as he described it: ten feet tall, five feet wide.

Gilt-framed, like the ones at 1247 LaRuhe.

The mirror is a part of the vast Unseelie Hallow that is the network of Silvers. I can sense Hallows. I can sense all Fae OOPs—Objects of Power. It is perhaps my greatest advantage.

I reach out with my *sidhe*-seer senses, expand and search.

I sense nothing. It didn't work in the Hall of All Days, either. Impossible, I suppose, to sense a Silver while inside the Silvers.

My feet turn me, and I begin walking in a new direction with complete confidence. I'm suddenly certain I have seen the mirror I need many times and I know exactly where it is.

I'll find the way out long before Darroc does. And although I will not leave without him—I have much use for him—it will please me to best him.

I hurry down a mint corridor, turn without hesitation onto an iridescent path, and rush down a pale-blue hall. A corridor of silver turns to blush wine.

The mirror is ahead. It draws me. I can't wait to get to it.

I'm focused, so focused that the crimson hallway barely makes a dent in my awareness.

I'm focused—so focused on my goal that, by the time I realize what I've done, it's too late.

I don't know what makes me look down, but something does.

I freeze.

I'm at a crossroads, the intersection of two halls.

I can go east, west, north, or south—if such directions exist in the House—but whichever way I choose, the floor is the same color.

Black.

I stand uncertainly, berating myself for screwing up *again,* when suddenly a hand slips into mine.

It is warm, familiar. And much too real.

I close my eyes. I've been played with in Faery before. Who am I to be tortured with now? What is my punishment to be? Which ghost will nip at me now with needles for teeth?

Alina?

Barrons?

Both?

I fist my other hand so nothing can hold it.

I know better than to think if I keep my eyes closed my ghost will go away. It doesn't work that way. When your private demons decide to mess with you, they demand their pound of flesh. It's best to pay it and get it over with.

Then I can focus on finding my way off the black floor. I brace myself for how bad it's going to be. I speculate that if golden floors in the Hall of All Days were bad, black floors in the White Mansion will be . . . forgive the pun . . . beyond the pale.

Fingers twine with mine. I know the hand as well as my own.

Sighing, I open my eyes.

I jerk away and scramble back frantically, boots slipping on the shiny black surface. I sprawl flat on my back with such a jolt that I bite my tongue.

I begin to hyperventilate. Does she see me? Does she know me? Is she there? Am I?

She laughs, a silvery sound, and it makes my heart hurt. I remember laughing like that once. Happy, so happy.

I don't even try to get up. I just lay there and watch her. I'm bewildered. I'm hypnotized. I'm carved in two by a sense of duality I cannot reconcile.

Not Alina. Not Barrons.

At the juncture of east, west, north, and south, she stands.

Her.

The sad, beautiful woman who haunts my dreams.

She is so dazzling it makes me want to weep.

But she's not sad.

She's so happy that I could hate her.

She glows radiantly, she smiles, and it curves lips of such soft, divine perfection that mine part instinctively to receive her kiss.

Is this her—the Unseelie King's concubine? No wonder he was obsessed!

When she begins to glide away down one of the

corridors—the blackest of the four, the one that *absorbs* the light cast by candles in sconces—I push myself up.

Moth to a flame, I follow.

According to V'lane, the concubine was mortal. In fact, her mortality was the first domino in a long, convoluted line that toppled out of control and led to this moment.

Nearly a million years ago, the Seelie King asked the original Seelie Queen—since her death, many queens have risen, only to be ousted by another who achieved greater power and support—to turn his concubine Fae, to make her immortal so he could keep her forever. When the queen refused, the king built his concubine the White Mansion inside the Silvers. He secreted his beloved away from the vindictive queen, where she could live without aging until he was able to perfect the Song of Making and turn her Fae himself.

If only the queen had granted his one simple request! But the leader of the True Race was controlling, jealous, and small.

Unfortunately, the king's efforts to duplicate the Song of Making—the mystical stuff of creation, a power and right that the queen of their matriarchal race selfishly hoarded—created the Unseelie, imperfect half-lives that he couldn't bear to kill. They lived. They were his sons and daughters.

He created a new realm, the Court of Shadows, where his children could play while he continued his work, his labor of love.

But the day came when he was betrayed by one of his own children and found out by the Seelie Queen.

They clashed in a battle to end all battles. Seelie struck down their darker brethren, who sought only the right to exist.

The dominoes fell, one after another: The death of

the Seelie Queen at the hands of the king; the suicide of the concubine; the act of "atonement" in which the Seelie King created the deadly *Sinsar Dubh*.

He rechristened himself the *Un*seelie King—never again would he be associated with the petty viciousness of the Seelie; henceforth he would be Unseelie, literally meaning *not* of the Seelie. He no longer called his home the Court of Shadows, in which he hid to perform his labor of love. It became simply Unseelie court.

By then, however, the court was a prison for his children, a macabre place of shadows and ice. The cruel Seelie Queen's last act had been to use the Song of Making—not for creation, not to make his beloved immortal!—but to destroy, trap, and torture for all eternity any who had dared disobey her.

And the dominoes fell . . .

The Book containing the Unseelie King's knowledge, all his darkness and evil, somehow ended up in my world, being protected by humans. It was set loose in a manner that I have yet to determine, but of this I am certain: Alina's murder, my screwed-up life, and Barrons' death—all are the result of a chain of Fae events that began a million years ago over a single mortal.

My world, we humans, we're just pawns on an immortal chessboard.

We got in the way.

Jack Lane, attorney extraordinaire, would put the Unseelie King, not Darroc, on trial and make a persuasive case against the concubine for guilt by association.

Because the unthinkable occurred and the original queen died before she had the chance to pass on the Song of Making to one of the princesses as her successor, the Fae race began to decline. Many princesses rose to the Seelie throne, but few lasted long before another wrested away her power. Queens were killed, others merely deposed and banished. Infighting grew and coups became more frequent. The Fae race became limited. All that was already was all that could *ever* be.

No new things could be made. Old powers were lost, and, over the eons, ancient magic was forgotten, until one day the current queen was no longer capable of reinforcing the weakening walls between realms and retaining control of the deadly Unseelie.

Darroc exploited this weakness and brought the walls between our worlds crashing down. Now Fae and human vie for control of a planet that is too small, too fragile, for both races.

All because of a single mortal—the domino that started all the others falling.

I follow the woman who I suspect *is* that mortal—in a not-quite-really-there kind of way—down the inky corridor.

If she is the concubine, I can summon no anger toward her, try though I might.

On their immortal chessboard, she was a pawn, too.

She is lit from within. Her skin shimmers with a translucent glow that illuminates the walls of the tunnel. The hall grows darker, blacker, stranger with each step we take. In contrast, she is holy, divine: an angel gliding into hell.

She is warmth, shelter, and forgiveness. She is mother, lover, daughter, truth. She is all.

Her pace quickens and she races down the tunnel, passing soundlessly over obsidian floors, laughing with joy.

I know that sound. I love that sound. It means her lover is near.

He is coming. She feels his approach.

He is so powerful!

It is what first drew her to him. She'd never encountered anyone like him.

She was awed that he chose her.

She is awed every day that he continues choosing her.

The stuff of him explodes through from the Court of Shadows, telling her he comes, filling her home (prison) where she lives a fabulous life (a sentence not of her choosing) surrounded by everything she wants (illusions, she misses her world, so far away and all of them long dead) and waits for him with hope (ever-growing despair).

He will carry her to his bed and do things to her until his black wings open wide, so wide, eclipsing the world, and when he is inside her, nothing else will matter but the moment, their dark, intense lust, the endless passion they share.

No matter what else he is—he is *hers*.

What is between them is without blame.

Love knows no right or wrong.

Love *is*. Only is.

She (I) rushes down the dark, warm, inviting hall, hurrying to his (my) bed. We need our lover. It has been too long.

In her chamber, I behold the duality of which I am carved.

Half the concubine's boudoir is dazzlingly white, brilliantly illuminated. The other half is a dense, seductive, welcoming blackness. It is split evenly down the middle.

Light and the absence of light.

I savor both. Neither disturbs me. I suffer no conflict over things upon which a simpler mind would be forced to bestow labels such as Good and Evil or embrace madness.

Against one frosted crystalline wall of the white half of the room is a huge round bed on a pedestal, draped in silks and snowy ermine throws. Alabaster petals are scattered everywhere, perfuming the air. The floor is carpeted with plush white furs. White logs, from which silvery-white flames pop and crackle, blaze in an enormous alabaster hearth. Tiny diamonds float lazily on the air, sparkling.

The woman hurries for the bed. Her clothing melts away and she (I) is naked.

But no! This is not his pleasure, not this time! His needs are different, deeper, more demanding tonight.

She spins and we gaze, lips parted, at the black half of the room.

Draped in black velvet and furs, covered with soft ebony petals that smell of him, that crush so softly beneath our skin, it is *all* bed.

From wall to wall.

He needs it all. (Wings unfolding, no mortal can see past them!)

He is coming. He is near.

I am naked, wild, ready. I need. I need. This is why I live.

She and I stand, staring at the bed.

Then *he* is there and he gathers her up—but I can't see him. I feel enormous wings closing around us.

I know he's there, she's enveloped in energy, in darkness, wet and warm like sex is wet and warm, and I'm breathing lust. I am lust and I strain to see him, strain to feel him, when suddenly—

I am a simple beast, on crimson sheets with Barrons inside me. I cry out, because even here in this boudoir of duality and illusion, I know it is not real. I know I have lost him. He is gone, forever gone.

I'm not back there in that basement with him, still *Pri-ya* but beginning to surface enough to know that he just asked me what I wore to my prom, and shutting it all down, racing from reality back into my madness, so I don't have to face what happened to me or deal with what I'm beginning to suspect I might have to do.

I'm not standing there a few days later, looking back at his bed with those fur-lined handcuffs, contemplating climbing back in and pretending I hadn't recovered so I could keep doing it—every raw, animal thing we'd done in my sexually insatiable state—fully aware of what I was doing and who I was doing it with.

Dead. Dead. I've lost so much.

If only I'd known then what I know now . . .

The king lifts the concubine. I see her sliding down a body I cannot discern in the darkness, and (I straddle Barrons and slam him home inside me; God, it feels so good!) the concubine strains, arches her neck, and makes a sound that doesn't come from our world (I laugh as I come, I'm alive, so alive), and when his vast wings spread wide, when they fill the blackness of his boudoir and pass beyond, he knows more joy in this moment than he has ever known in his entire existence, and the bitch queen would deny him this? (And I know more joy in this moment than I've ever known, because there is no right, no wrong, only now.)

But, wait—Barrons is vanishing!

Moving away from me, melting into the darkness. I will not lose him again!

I lunge to my feet, get tangled in sheets for a moment, then I am hurrying to catch him.

It grows colder, my breath ices the air.

Ahead I see only black, blue, and a white that is bled of all light.

I run toward the black as fast as my feet will carry me.

But hands are on my shoulders, turning me, forcing me away, fighting me!

They are too strong! They drag me down a black corridor, and I beat at the body that dares interrupt us!

No others are allowed here!

This is our place! The intruder will die! If only for *gazing* upon us!

Cruel hands push me, slam me into a wall. My ears ring from the impact. I am dragged, shoved again, and again. I bounce off wall after wall, until finally it stops.

I shudder and begin to weep.

Arms band me, hold me tightly. I press my face to the warmth of a hard, muscled chest.

I am too small a vessel to survive on a sea of such emotion! I grip his collar and cling. I try to breathe. I am raw, aching with need, and I am empty, so empty.

I lost it all, and for what?

I can't stop trembling.

"What part of 'if you see a black floor, turn back immediately' didn't you understand?" Darroc growls. "For fuck's sake, you went straight to the blackest of them all! What's with you?"

I lift my head from his chest, but barely. For a moment, all I can do is stare down. The floor is pale pink. He has dragged me all the way back to one of the dawn-themed wings. I fumble for my spear. It is gone again.

Awareness returns in slow degrees.

I shove him away.

"I warned you," he says coolly, offended by my anger.

Well, bully for him; I'm offended by him, too. "You didn't tell me enough, just to stay away! You should have told me more!"

"I do not explain Fae matters to humans. But since you clearly will not obey otherwise—black floors are *his* wings. Never enter them. You are not strong enough to survive there. The residue of all that once transpired there still walks those wings. It can trap you. You forced me to come in after you, putting us both at risk!"

We glare at each other, breathing hard. Although he is pumped on Unseelie flesh and far stronger because of it than I am, I gave him a hell of a fight. It hadn't been easy getting me out of there.

"What were you doing, MacKayla?" he says finally, softly.

"How did you find me there?" I counter.

"My brand. You were in extreme distress." The tiny gold flecks in his eyes glitter. "You were also extremely aroused."

"You can sense my feelings from your brand?" I am incensed. He subjects me to violation after violation.

"Only intense ones. The princes pinpointed your precise location. Be glad they did. I found you just in time. You were rushing for the black half of the boudoir."

"So?"

"The line that divides the two halves of that chamber is no line. It is a Silver. The largest ever made by the king. It is also the first and most ancient of them, unlike any of the others. When needed, it was used for punishment, to execute. You were running for the Silver that leads straight into the Unseelie King's bedchamber, in the fortress of black ice, deep in the Unseelie prison. In a few more of your human seconds, you would have been dead."

"Dead?" I choke out. "Why?"

"Only two in all existence could ever travel through that Silver: the Unseelie King and his concubine. Any other that touches it is instantly killed. Even Fae."

6

The Dani Daily—102 Days AWC . . .

I glare down at the sheet of paper, but 'cept for the title of my rag and the date, nothing's coming. Nothing's been coming for a feckin' hour.

Here I sit in the abbey's dining hall, in the middle of this brainless feckin' herd of *sidhe*-sheep that are so easily led they should wear feckin' halters and waggle fluffy sheep asses, and the words just ain't coming. And they got to. I gotta take up the slack 'til Mac gets back. Stupid sheep are back to obeying Ro and she's yanked 'em back in line again, got 'em all busy trying to clear the feckin' Shades from the abbey.

News flash, dudes, I keep telling you, *they're reproducing.* They eat, they grow, they split. Like feckin' amoebas. I been tracking 'em. I been watching 'em so hard I can tell 'em apart now. 'Times I play with 'em, mess with the lights, see how close they can *really* get to me. That's how I know so much about 'em, but nobody listens to me. Only time I'm heard is when they read my paper. They don't talk 'bout it, but everybody's using the Shade-Busters now. Anybody say thanks?

Nope. Not a single "good job, Mega," not even the teeniest little acknowledgment that I invented 'em.

I need Mac. Been nearly a month and I'm starting to worry that she's . . . Nah, ain't going there.

But where the feck is she? Ain't seen her since we broke into the Forbidden Libraries together. She in Faery again? She don't know it, but I read her journal when she was locked up in that cell, *Pri-ya,* and nobody was paying attention to her stuff 'cept Ro. She read it, too. But I took it back. Had to know what Ro knew. It's one of my hang-ups: I gotta know everything Ro knows and figure out where she's going 'fore she goes there. If I can do that, *dude,* I can run this place!

I know time spent in Faery don't move the same way as time in the real world, so I ain't as worried about Mac as I might be. See, V'lane's gone, too, so I figure she's with him.

Weird thing is, I keep stopping by BB&B and it looks like Barrons is gone, too!

Tried to get in to Chester's last night to ask about him, but the stupid feckin' feckers bounced me at the door.

Me. The Mega!

I grin and swagger a little in my seat.

It took six of 'em! Six of Barrons' freaky fecks had to work their *arses* off to keep me out, and we went at it for over an hour.

I wouldn'ta given up at all but that kinda freeze-framing starves me, and I didn't have enough candy bars crammed in my pockets. Got hungry. Had to eat. Said screw it and left. One of 'em followed me to Dublin's edge, like he thought he was throwing *me* outta the city—as if! I'll try again soon.

Still, I'm getting a little worried. . . .

Where the feck did everybody go? Why ain't nobody

talking about the LM anymore? Where's the *Sinsar Dubh*?

'S been quiet, way too quiet, and that creeps the feck outta me. Only other time things got *this* quiet . . . yeah, well—*dude*—the past ain't me.

What's already happened is for has-beens.

I'm all about the future. Tomorrow's my day.

Today sure as feck ain't. I ain't never had it before, but s'pect I got writer's block. S'pect it's 'cause I been sitting here watching a couple hundred *sidhe*-sheep do the equivalent of knit. Got an assembly line set up in the dining hall, making iron bullets. But get this—not for *us*!

For Jayne and his Guardians.

Don't know how Ro managed to make 'em all scared of their shadows again, but she did. Little things she says make 'em doubt themselves. Only took her two weeks after Mac disappeared to convince 'em all Mac was dead and to give up on her.

Sheep, I tell ya! Takes everything I got not to stand up, waggle my ass, and yell: *Baaaaa!*

But I guess the sheep shit's too deep in here for me to move, 'cause I sit and chew on my pen and wait for in-spiration.

While I'm biding time, I watch Jo. Used to be friends with her. Thought she had a mind of her own. She's smart, real smart. Puts things together the other sheep don't.

But she got weird a few months back. Started hanging all the time with Barb and Liz and never had time for me anymore. Used to be she was the only one didn't treat me like a baby. Used to be they all treated me like a kid. Now they hardly treat me at all. Nobody sits at my table.

Good feckin' thing, too! Ain't no room for sheep at my table.

Jo's sittin' real quiet, watching Liz. Watching her hard.

I wonder if she turned lezbo or somethin' and that explains why she changed. Came out of her closet and moved on, maybe got herself a ménage twat with Liz and Barb. I snicker at my joke. Dude, if ya can't crack yourself up, ain't never gonna crack anybody else up.

At first, the gunshots are so faint that even my superhearing don't register what they are. Then, when I do, I sorta figure Barrons' dudes musta come back for some reason and, like last time, they're firing warning shots. Even though we got a shitload of Uzis and other guns, we got no use for 'em here. Only in Dublin. They don't work on Shades. We don't bring our guns into the abbey. We leave 'em on the bus.

Dawning on me quick now how stupid that is.

Later, I find out it started at the west end of the abbey. Started where Mac slept when she stayed here, where I been sleeping lately, in the Dragon Lady's Library.

When the screaming begins, I freeze-frame into motion but with caution: Automatic gunfire is something I gotta factor in to my superspeed equation.

I'm fast, but, *dude*, the *rat-a-tat-tat* of that kinda spray is feckin' fast, too. Tough to dodge. And what I'm hearing is constant.

I'm in one of the corridors, heading for the screams, but suddenly everything is as dark as it must be where Rowena's head is—straight up her ass. I snicker again. I'm cracking myself up tonight.

I stop, plaster against the wall, and start moving like a Joe. Watching, straining to see down the dark corridor. I ain't got my 'Halo, but I got a couple flashlights in my pockets. I pull one out, click it on.

We ain't never got all the Shades outta the abbey. Nobody puts on their boots without shining flashlights in 'em and shaking 'em out real good first. And then only in broad daylight.

Nobody—but *nobody*—walks down dark halls here.

So why's it dark and who the feck is doing all that shooting?

Lots of moaning. Lots of wounded. Ain't warning shots. This is the real deal.

I take a Joe step forward, quiet as I can. Glass crunches beneath my high-tops, and I know why it's dark. Shooter took out the lights.

I hear a soft, awful laugh that makes my blood run cold. I shine my flashlight down the dark hall, and the darkness kinda *absorbs* it.

I hear somebody breathing fast.

I hear more glass crunching and it ain't me.

Pretty sure the shooter's headed straight for me!

I flex my fingers, curl 'em tight around my sword. Ro tried to take it away. Told her I'd be her own personal guard if she let me keep it. I stand watch while she sleeps. I'm learning about trade-offs.

What the feck is moving down the hall at me?

Later, when I tell the story, I don't tell the whole truth.

Truth is, the unthinkable happened. I got scared in that dark hall. I felt something coming and it freaked me.

I say I never got to the corridor.

Never admit I backed out with my tail tucked between my legs, retreated to the light, and then freeze-framed back to the dining hall.

The shooting starts again and so does the screaming and we all run, but there's only one way out and that's the way *in,* so we're knocking over tables and scrambling behind 'em.

Jo and me, we end up behind the same table. Long as she doesn't try any funky lezbo stuff on me, I don't mind sharing my spot. I tap the table. It's thick, made of solid wood. Might hold up, depending on bullets and distance.

More screams. I wanna hold my ears.

I'm cowering. I disgust myself.

I gotta look. I gotta know what the feck is doing this to us!

Jo and I move for opposite ends of the table at the same time and crack heads. She glares at me.

"Like it's *my* fault," I hiss defensively. "You moved, too."

"Where's Liz?" she hisses back.

I shrug. On my hands and knees, I waggle my ass. Whole abbey's falling apart and she's worried about her little girlfriend. *"Baaaaa,"* I say.

She looks at me like I'm nuts. Then we're both poking our heads around the table.

Bullets are ripping across the room, ricocheting off walls and wood. Blood's spraying everywhere, gory as feck, and the screams keep coming. The shooter is framed in the door of the dining hall.

Jo gasps and I just about fall over choking.

It's Barb!

What the feck's this all about?

She's draped in rounds, toting the biggest Uzi I ever seen. White-faced, she's screaming curses at us, taking us down like sitting ducks. I gape. "Barb?" I mutter. Don't make no sense.

Weird thing is, Jo looks stunned and bursts out, "I thought it was Liz!"

I stare down the table at her. All I can see is her head, but she kinda shrugs it. "Long story."

I assess the room, the scene. We're at the back of the hall. We'll be last to die. What the feck do I do? Why is Barb shooting us?

I look at Jo. She's no help. Looks blank as the page I was writing *The Dani Daily* on.

Dude, I wish Mac was here! What would she do? Should I freeze-frame in while Barb's shooting everybody and try to take her gun? Am I fast enough? I don't wanna die today. Tomorrow's gonna be my day. And I just know it's gonna be a good one, too! 'Sides, I got too much to do. Somebody's gotta keep an eye on Ro.

But we're dropping like flies! Holy feckin' crikey, Barb's wiping us out!

I cram a candy bar in my mouth whole, chew it just enough to get it in my gut. I'm gonna need every ounce of energy I got to pull this off. I gotta do *something.* Barb ain't gonna run outta bullets for a long time. The Mega can't cower behind a table and do nothing.

I poke my head out from behind the table, take a snapshot of the scene, and lock it down hard in my head. I map where every person, table, chair, and obstacle is.

Problem is Barb. She's the unknown. She's moving and spraying fire so erratically, I can't slam a grid of possibles down over my mental map.

Feck!

I stare, trying to pick up some kinda pattern.

I duck back behind the table as a shot zings by. Poke my head out again. Ain't no pattern.

I pump breaths superfast, puffing my cheeks in and out, kicking my adrenaline up. I ease my head out, lock the grid down best I can, and am about to give my feet wings, when Barb goes kinda fuzzy around the edges and the room gets so fecking cold my breath comes out white.

Jo makes a strangled sound.

We both see it at the same time.

What's shooting at us ain't Barb at all.

Well . . . it is, and she's screaming, but not like the psycho-rage-bitch-from-hell I thought she was.

She's screaming in horror.

She's fighting for control of the gun and failing. She forces it down and sprays the floor, but it comes up again. She tries to swing it left, toward the wall. It yanks back to the right. Her finger's tight on the trigger the whole time.

She blurs again.

She's just Barb.

No, she ain't! She's—*dude*—what the feck is that? She's got too many heads, too many teeth! She's some kinda monster! And it ain't no Shade!

It's Barb again.

Being forced to kill us.

Behind her, a shadow climbs the wall. It's huge! It towers, it expands, and when it laughs, my blood clots up in my veins and can't get to my brain, 'cause it's got so many ice chunks in it.

"Where is the Grand Bitch?" it roars. "I want her fucking *heeeeeead*!"

Jo and I look at each other.

We get it.

We both know what's got her, what's *really* firing those rounds, and it gets driven home like a spike through my skull that I ain't nearly The Shit Mac thinks I am.

Me and Jo *ooze* real slow back behind the table.

Just two brave little sheep.

Hiding from a book.

The Book.

The one we been hoping to find. Talking real big

about locking it down again. Yeah, right, just what the feck did we think we were gonna do with it?

The nerve of it. It came *here*. Here, where it was trapped for so long. It must feel pretty feckin' invincible. Pisses me off so bad I'm shaking. It came *here*. *Gah*—that's so feckin' wrong!

I read Mac's journal. I know how it works. Makes folks pick it up. Me and Barb and Jo and about fifteen others went into Dublin this morning for supplies. We didn't stick together the whole time. Split up and went off after different things.

It musta got Barb alone and made her pick it up.

I get a creepy chill that goes all the way up my spine so fast I get brain freeze when it hits my head.

Feckin' A! The *Sinsar Dubh* rode back to the abbey with us this morning! Right there on our bus!

I was sitting on the same bus with the Unseelie King's Book and didn't even know it!

I sort through my options. I ain't impervious to bullets. Dying today ain't gonna do nobody no good, 'specially not me. Don't know how to stop it. Ain't beating myself up for that. Nobody knows how to stop it.

Don't dare get close enough to let it take me.

Riding me, it could wipe out the entire abbey in record time.

I swallow. I'd been starting to wonder if it was looking for me. Guess it was looking to get any *sidhe*-seer alone, so it could take us down from the inside and gain revenge for its captivity.

They're dying. They're all dying out there, beyond my table. It's killing me that they're dying.

And I can't come up with one feckin' thing to do about it.

Got one chance, and it ain't to stop it. I grab Jo and freeze-frame outta there.

* * *

Ro's face is pale, bloodless. I ain't never seen her like this. She looks like she's aged twenty years in a single day. One hundred eighteen *sidhe*-seers were killed before Barb shot her way out of the abbey, took our bus with all our weapons, and disappeared.

A hundred more were wounded.

The *Sinsar Dubh* paid us a visit, gave us a little look-see, thumbed its Beast nose at us, flipped us the mother-feckin' bird of all birds.

Jo and me, we sit across the desk from Ro.

"You didn't even try to stop it," she finally says. She's been letting us stew. She likes to do that. Potatoes and carrots, they turn to mush if they stew long enough. Time was, I did, too. But I don't cook down so fast anymore.

I didn't need to hear Ro say it. I been staring at the accusation blazing in her fierce blue eyes for the past five minutes. I don't answer. I'm done answering her. She shoulda told us. She shoulda warned us. I never ever imagined the *Sinsar Dubh* could pull a stunt like that. She ain't training us. She's keeping us small. Afraid. Just like Mac said. What—I shoulda died so she could say, *Dani tried*? Feck that noise. Ain't dying just so she can feel better 'bout things.

Jo says, "Grand Mistress, it looked like Barb was fighting it. From the information Jayne and his men gathered about the Book, we were pretty sure what that meant."

"Och, and now you're trusting Jayne? *I* teach you! *I* train you!"

Jo turns her face away a moment, and I remember that Barb was one of her best friends. But Jo, she surprises me with a little steel. When she turns back and starts talking again, her voice is steady. "She was going to kill herself soon, Rowena. Our first goal was to keep the Book from getting a new body. If Dani had gone near it, it could have taken a virtually unstoppable body."

Ro cuts me a scathing glance. "Ever the liability, are you not, Danielle?"

I make a face, can't help it. She's always blaming me for something. Done trying to blow smoke up her ass. Sick of pretending to be things I'm not. "D'pends on how you look at it, Ro," I say coolly. "And you're always looking at it wrong."

Jo sucks in a sharp breath.

I've gone too far, and I'm about to go farther. I don't care. Ever since Mac disappeared, Ro's made it plain she'd take me back into her good graces if I'd cooperate the tiniest bit. I been skirting around the subject, flirting with appeasing her just enough to keep her guessing, thinking I'll come to heel.

But that ain't never gonna happen.

I just watched a hundred of my sisters—so what if they're sheep? They're still my sisters—get butchered. And this old woman stands and glares at me? At least I own up to my sins. I go to sleep with 'em every night. Wake up with 'em every morning. See 'em in the mirror, staring right back at me. And I say, dude, get over yourself already.

"How'd the Book get loose, Ro?" I'm on my feet, sword in my hand. "Why'n'tcha ever tell us that? 'Cause maybe you fell asleep on the job? 'S that it?"

Her voice is tight and she's even paler when she looks at Jo and snaps, "You will escort that child to her room *now*! And lock her in!"

As if *that's* gonna happen. Nobody here can control me. Ever since I killed that Hunter, I been feeling like the dude that shot a giant with his slingshot. Ro can't feck with my head like she used to.

"All I did is say what everybody's been thinking but been too afraid to say. I ain't afraid of you no more, Ro. I saw the *Sinsar Dubh* tonight. I know what I'm afraid of." I back-kick my chair so hard it slams into the wall behind me. "I'm leaving. I'm done here." I mean it. I really am. Used to think I was at least a little safe in the abbey, but we got Shades in the shadows, and now the Book snuck in, and fact o' the matter is, I can make myself a safer place than this in a feckin' Dark Zone!

'Sides, nobody here'll even notice if I'm gone. Maybe I'll check out Jayne, hang with the Guardians for a while.

"You will go to your room this very instant, Danielle Megan!"

Gah, I hate that name! Sissy name. Sissy girl.

"What would your mother think of you?" she snaps.

"What would my mother think of what you *made* me?" I snap back.

"I made you a proud and true weapon for the right."

"Guess that's why I feel like my sword most of the time. Cold. Hard. Bloody."

"Ever the melodrama with you, isn't it? Grow up, Danielle O'Malley! And sit down."

"Feck you, Ro."

I freeze-frame out.

The chilly Irish air blasts me, and if a couple places on my cheeks are especially cold, I ignore 'em. I ain't crying. I never cry.

I miss my mom sometimes, though.

The world's big.

So am I.

Dude—I'm homeless!

I swagger into the night.

Free at last.

7

"Why did you hang a Silver to Dublin in one of the white wings, when you know the House rearranges itself? Why didn't you put it somewhere more stable and easily accessible?" I resume my questions as we walk.

That bipolar feeling from my high school days is back with a vengeance. He's everything I despise. I want to kill him so badly that I have to keep my hands in my pockets, balled into fists.

He's also the person who was intimate with my sister during the final months of her life, the only one who can answer all those questions no one else can—and who can seriously shorten the amount of time I have to spend in this wasteland of a reality.

Did you take her journal? Did she know Rowena or any of the sidhe-*seers? Did she tell you about the prophecy? Why did you kill her? Was she happy? Please tell me she was happy before she died.*

"No rooms in the White Mansion ever get completely dark, not even where night falls. I erred the first time I opened a Silver. I hung it in a place that did. A creature

I believed securely imprisoned—one I did not ever intend to free from the Unseelie prison—escaped."

"What creature?" I demand. This man who looks like a Versace ad, who walks and talks like a human, isn't. He's worse than someone possessed by a Gripper—one of those dainty, beautiful Unseelie that can slip inside a person's skin and take over. He is one hundred percent Fae in a body that should never have been his. He's a cold-blooded killer, responsible for butchering *billions* of humans, hundreds of thousands of them in Dublin on a single night, without a second thought. If there was a creature in the icy Unseelie hell that he never intended to set loose, I want to know why, exactly what it is, and how to kill it. If it worries him, it terrifies me.

"Watch the floors, MacKayla."

I look at him. He's not going to answer me. Pressing would only make me appear weak.

We've resumed the search together. He's unwilling to leave me on my own. I'm in no hurry to be on my own again. I'm still raw from what happened to me in the black wing. I'd gotten cemented in memories, and if Darroc hadn't busted me out, I might never have escaped.

Chasing Barrons, I might not have *wanted* to escape. I remember the bones in the Hall of All Days. I think of the beach in Faery with Alina. If I'd chosen to stay with her then, would I have eventually died from eating food with no substance, drinking water that was no more real than my sister?

Damn Faery with its killing illusions!

I push memories of sex with the king, with Barrons, away. I distract myself with hatred for the man who killed my sister.

Was Alina happy? It's on the tip of my tongue again.

"Very," he fires back at me, and I realize I've not only

said it aloud but it seems he's just been *waiting* for me to ask.

I'm appalled that I've been so weak. Offering my enemy the opportunity to lie to me! "Bullshit!"

"You are impossible." Disdain etches his handsome face. "She was nothing like you. She was open. Her heart was not sealed away behind walls."

"Look what *that* got her. Dead."

I stalk off ahead, down a brilliant yellow corridor. The windows open on exactly the kind of summer day Alina and I always loved. I can't get away from her ghost! I quicken my pace.

We hurry down a hall of mint, then one of indigo with French doors that open onto a turbulent stormy night, before turning onto a path of pale pink, and finally there it is—a towering arched entrance into a white marble hall. Beyond the elegant entrance, windows open onto a dazzling winter day, ice-encased trees sparkling like diamonds in the sun.

Peace settles over me. I've been here in my dreams. I loved this wing.

Once, long ago on her world, a sunny day in spring was her favorite, but now a sunny day in winter delights her more. It is the perfect metaphor for their love.

Sunshine on ice.

She warms his frost. He cools her fever.

"You said Alina called you," Darroc says behind me. "You said she was crying on the phone, that she was hiding from me. Did she make that phone call the day she died?"

He startles me from my reverie and, without thinking, I nod.

"What exactly did she say?"

I toss him a look over my shoulder that says, *You really think I'm going to tell you that?* If anyone is going to be answering questions about her, it's going to be *him* answering to me. I step into the white marble corridor.

He follows me. "All you accomplish by persisting in your inane and erroneous belief that I killed Alina is guaranteeing that you will never find her true murderer. Humans have an animal of which you remind me. The ostrich."

"My head is *not* buried in the sand."

"No, it's up your ass," he snaps.

I whirl on him.

We glare at each other, but his words give me pause. Am I being an ostrich? Do I deny myself the opportunity to avenge my sister, because I'm stuck in a rut I refuse to get out of? Will I let my sister's *real* murderer get away, because I can't open my mind to see beyond my preconceptions? Barrons warned me from the beginning to not so blithely assume Darroc was definitely her killer.

A muscle works in my jaw. Each time I remember something about Barrons, I hate Darroc more for taking him from me. But I remind myself why I'm here and why I haven't already killed him.

To accomplish my goal, there are certain answers I need.

I eye him speculatively. There are others I just *want*.

And once I get the Book in my hands and change things, I'll never have another chance to ask. He'll be gone. I'll have killed him. Here and now is my one shot.

"She said she was going to try to come home but she was afraid you wouldn't let her leave the country," I say stiffly. "She said I had to find the *Sinsar Dubh*. Then she sounded terrified and said you were coming."

"Me? By name? She told you 'Darroc' was coming?"

"She didn't have to. What she said earlier made it clear."

"And what was that? What so thoroughly incriminated me?"

I still have her message memorized. I dream it sometimes, word for word. "She said, *I thought he was helping me, but—God, I can't believe I was so stupid! I thought I was in love with him and he's one of them, Mac! He's one of* them! Who else could that have been? You keep telling me she loved you. Was there someone else she was involved with that she thought she—"

"No! There was only me. She would never have sought another. I gave her everything."

"Then you understand why I believe you killed her."

"I do not, and did not. There are holes larger than Hunters in your puny human logic!"

"Who else could it have been? Who else did she fear?"

He turns and paces to one of the windows, where he stands gazing out at the dazzling winter day. Ice-crusted trees sparkle like they've been diamond-dipped. Drifts of powdery snow shimmer in the sunlight. The scene seems lit from within, like the concubine herself.

But there is only darkness inside me. I feel it growing.

"You are certain that the day you had this conversation with her was the day she died?"

It wasn't a conversation, but I don't tell him that. "Although the Garda didn't find her body for two days, they estimated her time of death at about four hours after she called me. The coroner in Ashford said it was possible she died as much as eight to ten hours after she made the call. She said it was difficult to estimate exact time of death due to the way her body had been savaged." I refuse to say "chewed on."

Still staring out the window, his back to me, he says, "One morning after I left, she followed me to the house on LaRuhe."

I catch my breath. These are words I've been waiting to hear since the day I identified my sister's body. To learn what she did the last day she was alive. Where she went. How it came to such a bitter end.

"Did you know?" I demand.

"I eat Unseelie."

He knew. Of course he knew. It amps up all the senses, hearing, sight, taste, touch. It's what makes it so addictive—and the supersized strength is icing on the cake. You feel alive, incredibly alive. Everything is more vivid.

"We'd been in bed all night, fucking—"

"T-the-fuck-M-I," I snarl.

"You think I don't know what that means. Alina used to say it. Too much information. It disturbs you to hear of the passion your sister and I shared."

"It sickens me."

When he turns, his gaze is cool. "I made her happy."

"You didn't keep her safe. Even if you didn't kill her, she died on *your* watch."

He flinches almost imperceptibly.

I think, *Nice, real nice, got that fake emotion down real well.*

"I thought she was ready. I believed what she felt for me would win in one of your idiotic human battles of morality. I was wrong."

"So she followed you. Did she confront you?"

He shakes his head. "She saw me through the windows at LaRuhe—"

"They're painted black."

"They weren't yet. I did that later. She watched me meet with my Unseelie guard and overheard our conversation about freeing more of the Dark Court. She heard them call me Lord Master. After my guard left and I was alone, I waited to see what she would do, if she would come in, if she would give us a chance. She didn't. She fled, and I followed, at a distance. She spent hours walking around Temple Bar, crying in the rain. I waited, gave her space, time to clarify her thoughts. Humans do not think as quickly as Fae. They struggle with simple concepts. It is astounding your species ever managed to—"

"Spare me your condescending judgments and I'll spare you mine," I cut him off, in no mood to listen to him condemn my race. His race already did that. Billions dead. All because of their petty power struggles.

He inclines his head imperiously. "I went to her apartment later that day. I found her in the bedroom, climbing out the window, onto the fire escape."

"See? She *was* afraid of you."

"She was terrified. It made me angry. I had given her no reason to fear me. I dragged her back in. We fought. I told her she was human, stupid and small. She called me a monster. She said I tricked her. That it was all a lie. It was not. Or, rather, it was at first but then it wasn't. I would have made her my queen. I told her that. And that I still would. But she wouldn't listen. She wouldn't even look at me. Finally I left. But I did not kill her, MacKayla. Like you, I do not know who did."

"Who trashed her apartment?"

"I told you we fought. Our anger was as intense as our lust."

"Did you take her journal?"

"I went back for it after I learned she was dead. It was not there. I took photo albums. It was then, when I found her calendar book, that I discovered her 'friend' Mac was really her sister. She lied to me. I was not the only one who was duplicitous. I have lived among your kind long enough to know this means she knew from the beginning something about me was not what it seemed. And wanted me anyway. I believe that if she had not been murdered, in time she would have come to me, chosen me of her own free will."

Yes, I think, *she would have come to you. With a weapon in her hand, just like I will.*

"I needed to know if you shared her unique talents.

Had you not arrived in Dublin when you did, I would have had you brought to me."

I absorb that and am furious. It's very important to me to pinpoint the exact moment my life started going wrong. Especially now.

It goes back farther than I'd realized.

The moment Alina left for Dublin and began heading toward the day she would encounter him, there'd been no hope of my life turning out any other way. Events had been set in motion that trapped me. I would have embarked upon exactly the same path, through a different door. If I'd not disobeyed my parents and flown to Ireland to investigate Alina's murder, would he have sent the Hunters after me? The princes? Maybe dispatched the Shades to devour my town and drive me out?

One way or another, I would have ended up here, with him, in the middle of this mess.

"Because of your sister, I resisted harming you."

More than anything he has ever said, those words stun me. I stand half dazed as they echo through my brain, knocking loose conflicting thoughts, nudging them to where they no longer oppose. Without warning, my convictions shift and settle into a new position. I'm startled by where they end up, but they moved with such logic and simplicity that I can't deny the veracity.

Darroc *did* care about Alina.

I believe him.

There was something I'd never been able to explain to my own satisfaction: I'd wondered why Darroc hadn't been more aggressive, more brutal with me from the very first. It had made no sense to me. He'd seemed almost lackadaisical in his efforts to abduct me and had kept offering me the chance to come willingly. What kind of world-destroying villain did that? It was certainly not what I'd expected from my sister's murderer. Mallucé had been far deadlier, far more ruthless. Of the two, I'd been much more terrified of the wannabe vamp when I'd first arrived.

Occam's razor: The simplest explanation that accommodates all variables is most likely the truth. Darroc had resisted harming me because of Alina. He'd restrained himself because he'd cared about my sister.

Just how much—and how much I could use it against him—remained to be seen.

"My deference undermined my efforts, and the Hunters began to question my conviction."

"So you had me raped and turned *Pri-ya*," I say bitterly. How quickly he'd gone from deference to murder, because that's what turning me *Pri-ya* had been tantamount to. Until Barrons had pulled me back, no one had ever recovered from being made a mindless Fae sex slave. They died from it.

"I needed to solidify my position. Then I lost you before I even had the chance to begin using you."

"Who was the fourth, Darroc? Why don't you just tell me?" He'd stood there watching as the Unseelie Princes destroyed me. He'd seen me naked on the ground, helpless, weeping. I calm myself by imagining the many ways I might kill him when the time comes.

"I have told you before, MacKayla, there was no fourth. The last prince of the Court of Shadows that the king created was the first dark prince to die. Cruce was killed in the ancient battle between the king and queen. Some claim it was the queen herself who killed him."

"*Cruce* was the fourth Unseelie Prince?" I exclaim.

He nods. Then he frowns and adds, "If a fourth being was at the church, neither I nor my princes were capable of seeing it."

He seems as disturbed by that thought as I am.

"I repeatedly offered you an alliance. I need the Book. You can track it. Some believe you can corner it. Some believe you *are* the fourth stone."

I bristle. There's little I'm certain of lately, but this much I'd bet the bank on. "I am *not* a stone." I was pretty sure V'lane had the fourth and final one.

"Fae things change. They become other things."

"Not people," I scoff. "Look at me. I wasn't carved from the cliffs of the Unseelie hell! I was born to a human woman!"

"You know that for a certainty? My sources say you and Alina were adopted."

I say nothing, wondering who his sources are.

He laughs. "No one knows what the king truly did after he went mad. Perhaps he made one of the stones different, the better to hide it."

"Stones don't become people!"

"It's what the *Sinsar Dubh* is trying to do."

I narrow my eyes. Was Ryodan right? Was that what this was all about—the Book taking on a corporeal, sentient form? Interesting that both he and Darroc believed this, as if perhaps they had discussed it while forming other plans—plans such as killing Barrons and getting him out of the way! After all, it was Barrons that brought me back from the *Pri-ya* state where I could have so easily been used. Damned inconvenient for them.

"But the people it takes over keep killing themselves," I say.

"Because the Book has not found the one strong enough to endure the merging."

"What do you mean, 'endure the merging'? Are you saying the right person could pick up the *Sinsar Dubh* without killing themselves?"

"And control it," he says smugly.

I inhale sharply. This is the first I've heard of anything like this. And he sounds so confident, so certain. "Use *it* rather than being used?"

He nods.

I'm incredulous. "Just pick it up and open it? No harm, no foul?"

"Absorb it. All the power."

"How? Who is this 'right person'?" I demand. Was it me? Was that why I could track it? Was that why everyone was *really* after me?

He gives me a mocking smile. "Oh, trifling human, such delusions of grandeur you suffer. No, MacKayla. It has never been you."

"Then who?"

"I'm the one."

I stare at him. He is? I look him up and down. Why? How? What does he know that I don't know? That Barrons didn't know? "What's so special about you?"

He laughs and gives me a look that says, *You really think I'm going to tell you that?* I hate it when people throw my own looks back in my face.

"But I *did* tell you. I answered your questions."

"Trivial questions."

My eyes narrow. "If you know how to merge with it, why did you insist I bring the stones into the tunnel with me when you took my parents captive? Why are you so interested in them?"

"It is said the stones can immobilize it. I have had little success getting near it. If I cannot get close enough on my own, I may need to use them. I have you to track it, the stones to corner it, and I can do the rest."

"Is it because you eat Unseelie? Is that why you'd be able to do it?" I can slice, dice, and devour with the best of them. See Mac gorge.

"Hardly."

"Is it something you are? Something you did? Something you know how to do?" I hear the franticness in my voice and it appalls me, but if he has some way of bypassing the whole absurdity of getting the fourth stone from V'lane, gathering the five Druids—Barrons seemed pretty sure one of them was Christian, and he's still lost in the Silvers—figuring out the prophecy, and performing some complicated ceremony, I want to know what it is! If there's a shortcut, any chance I can reach my goal in a matter of hours or days rather than trying to live through agonizing weeks or even months, I want it! The less time I have to spend in this hellish reality, the better.

"Look at you, MacKayla, all flushed and glowing, salivating over the idea of merging with the Book." The gold flecks in his eyes begin to glitter again.

I'd know that look on any man's face.

"So like Alina," he murmurs, "yet so unlike her."

It's a difference he seems to appreciate. "What is it about you? Why will *you* be able to merge with it?" I demand. "Tell me!"

"Find the Book, MacKayla, and I will show you."

When we finally locate the room with the Silver in it, it's just as Darroc described: empty of furnishings, save a single mirror, five feet by ten.

The mirror appears to have been inserted seamlessly into whatever the walls are made of in the House.

But my mind's not on the Silver at all. I'm still reeling from what Darroc told me.

Another piece of the puzzle that had been giving me fits clicks into place. I'd been perplexed by his determination to get the Book, when none of us knew how to touch it, move it, corner it, do a single damned thing with it, without getting taken over, turned evil, then killed, after being forced to kill everyone around us.

Along with wondering why Darroc hadn't been more brutal, I'd wondered why he was hunting it when he'd never be able to use it, when even Barrons and I had been forced to admit that chasing the thing was pointless.

Yet Darroc had never relented. He'd kept his Unseelie scouring Dublin for it incessantly. The whole time I'd been stumbling in the dark, trying to figure out the four, and the five, and the prophecy, Darroc had been following a much easier path.

He knew a way to merge with the *Sinsar Dubh*—and control it!

There's no question in my mind that Darroc's telling the truth. I have no idea how or where he got this information, but he definitely knows how to use the *Sinsar Dubh* without being corrupted.

I need that knowledge!

I watch him through narrowed eyes. I'm no longer in a hurry to kill him. Fact is, I'd kill to *protect* the bastard at this point.

I mentally refine my mission. I don't need the prophecy, stones, or Druids. I'll never need to ally myself with V'lane in the future.

I need one thing: to uncover Darroc's secret.

Once I have it, I can corner the Book myself. I don't have any problems getting near it. It likes to play with me.

My hands tremble with excitement that's difficult to contain. Trying to fulfill the absurd conditions of the prophecy would have taken forever. My new plan could be achieved in a matter of *days,* bringing my grief to a swift end.

"Why did you bring Unseelie through the dolmen in the warehouse at LaRuhe when you had a Silver you could have used instead?" I employ small questions to lull him. Get him off guard. Then I'll sneak a big one in. Like most men-who-would-be-king, he likes to hear himself talk.

"Low-caste Unseelie are distracted by anything upon which they might feed. I needed a short passage, void of life, through which to herd them. I would never have gotten them out of this world and into yours. Besides, many of them would not have fit through such a small opening."

I remember the horde of Unseelie—some wispy and diminutive, others fleshy and enormous—that had poured through the giant dolmen the night I'd caught my first glimpse of the crimson-robed Lord Master and realized, much to my horror, that he was my sister's boyfriend. The night that Mallucé had nearly killed me and would have, if Barrons hadn't miraculously appeared and saved me. I try to evict the memory, but it's too late.

I'm in the warehouse, trapped between Darroc and Mallucé . . .

Barrons drops down next to me, long black coat fluttering.

Now that was just stupid, Ms. Lane, he says, with that mocking smile of his. *They would have figured out who you were soon enough.*

We battle Darroc and his minions. Mallucé injures me badly. Barrons carries me back to his bookstore, where he heals me. It's the first time he ever kisses me. Like nothing I've ever felt before.

Once more he saved me—and what did I do when he needed me?

Killed him.

The silent scream is back, welling up inside me. Biting it down takes all the strength I possess.

I stumble.

Darroc catches my arm and steadies me.

I shake him off. "I'm fine. Just hungry." I'm not. My body has shut down. "Let's get out of here." I step into the Silver. I expect to meet resistance, because I always have in the past when entering a Silver, so I duck my head and push forward a little. The silvery surface is thick, gluey.

I explode out the other side into a headlong sprawl. I

scramble to my feet and whirl on him, as he glides from the mirror with smooth grace. "What did you do? Push me?"

"I did no such thing. Perhaps it is the Silver's way of saying 'good riddance' to the stones," he mocks.

I'd not considered the effect they might have. Tucked away in the rune-covered leather pouch in my backpack, I'd forgotten them. My *sidhe*-senses don't seem to work in the Silvers. I don't feel their cold, dark fire in the pit of my brain.

He smirks. "Or perhaps it's saying good riddance to *you*, MacKayla. Give them to me. I will carry them through the next Silver and we will see what happens to you then."

The next Silver? Only then do I realize we're not back in Dublin but in another white room which has *ten* mirrors hanging on the wall. He's made it difficult for anyone to follow him. I wonder where the other nine go.

"As if that's going to happen," I mutter. I adjust my backpack and dust myself off.

"You do not wish to know. Are you human or are you stone?" he goads. "If I carry them, and the mirror expels you with such force again, we'll have our answer."

I'm *not* a stone. "Just tell me which mirror goes to Dublin."

"Fourth from the left."

I push in, but warily this time, in no mood for another fall. This Silver is strange. It takes me into a long tunnel where I move through one brick wall after the next, as if he has stacked *Tabh'rs,* like the one in Christian's desert that was inside a cactus, only these are concealed in brick walls.

But where?

I catch a blurred glimpse of a street at night through the next Silver and am buffeted by a chilly breeze. Then

I'm blasted so hard across a cobbled alley into a brick wall that it stuns me. This one is solid and impenetrable.

I'd know my city blindfolded. We're back in Dublin. I hug the wall, determined to stay standing. I've been on my ass enough today.

I might be shaky on my feet—but at least I'm on them when my *sidhe*-seer senses kick in with a vengeance, as if awakening after a long, resented sleep enforced by being in the Silvers. Alien energy slams into my brain: The city is teeming with Fae.

Objects of Power and Fae used to make me feel sick to my stomach, but continued exposure has changed me. Their presence no longer incapacitates me. Now I get a dark, intense adrenaline rush from them. I'm shaky enough already from lack of food and sleep. I don't care where the Unseelie are, and I'm not about to start looking for the Book. I close my eyes and concentrate on turning down my "volume" until it goes silent.

Then Darroc's arms are around me, pulling me to him, holding me up. For a moment, I forget who I am, what I feel, what I've lost, and know only that strong arms support me.

I smell Dublin.

I'm in a man's arms.

He turns me around, drops his head to mine, holds me like he's sheltering me, and for a moment I pretend he's Barrons.

He presses his lips to my ear. "You said we were friends, MacKayla," he murmurs, "yet I see none of that in your eyes. If you give yourself to me, completely give yourself, I will not ever—how did you say it?—let you die on my watch. I know you are angry about your sister, but together we could change that . . . or not, if you wish. You have attachments to your world, but could you not see a place for yourself in mine? You are even less like other humans than Alina. You do not belong here. You never did. You were meant for more." His melodious voice deepens seductively. "Do you not feel it? Have you not always felt it? You are . . . larger than others of your kind. Open your eyes. Take a good look around. Are these petty, breeding, warring humans worth fighting for? Dying for? Or would you dare to taste forever? Eternity. Absolute freedom. Walk among others that are also larger than a single mortal life."

His hands cup my head, cradle my face. His lips move against my ear. His breath is harsh, shallow, and fast, and I feel the hard press of him against my thigh. My own breath quickens.

I pretend again that he is Barrons and suddenly he *feels* like Barrons, and I'm fighting to keep my head clear. Images flash through my mind, those long, incredible hours spent in a sex-drenched bed.

I smell Barrons on my skin, taste him on my lips. I remember. I will never forget. The memories are so vivid. I swear I could reach out and touch those crimson silk sheets.

He sprawls on the bed, a dark tattooed mountain of man, arms folded behind his head, watching me as I dance naked.

Manfred Mann plays an old Bruce Springsteen cover on my iPod: I came for you, for you, I came for you . . .

He did. And I killed him.

I would give my right arm to be back there, for just one day. Live it again. Touch him again. Hear those sounds he makes. Smile at him. Be tender. Not be afraid to be tender. Life is so fragile, exquisite, and short. Why do I keep realizing that too late?

The brand on the back of my skull burns, but I can't tell if it's Darroc's mark that scalds my scalp or Barrons' brand that burns me because Darroc is touching it.

"Abandon your vows to drag me down and destroy me, MacKayla," he whispers against my ear. "Ah, yes, I see it in your eyes every time you look at me. I would have to be blind not to see it. I have lived for hundreds of thousands of years in the Court of Grand Illusion. You cannot deceive me. Decry your pointless quest for vengeance, which will only end up destroying you, not me. Let me raise you up, teach you to fly. I will give you everything. And *you* I will not lose. That is a mistake I will not make again. If you come to me knowing what I am, there need be no fear, no mistrust between us. Take my kiss, MacKayla. Accept my offer. Live with me. Forever."

His lips move from my ear; he brushes kisses across my cheek. But he stops and waits for me to turn my head that last inch. To choose.

I turn to vomit hatred all over him. He claims feelings for my sister and tries to seduce me, too! Can what he felt for Alina be so easily betrayed? I hate him for seducing her. I hate him for not being faithful to her memory.

Neither of those emotions is anything Barrons would have called "useful." I have a memory to live up to. Two ghosts to bring back to life.

I focus on the here and now. What can be used. What can't.

Beyond his shoulder, I see where we are. If I felt anything anymore, I'd double over, fist in my stomach.

Clever, clever ex-Fae. The bastard.

We're in the alley, catty-corner to Barrons Books and Baubles. He hid a Silver in the brick wall of the first building in the Dark Zone across from my bookstore.

It was right out back, all this time. In my backyard. He was always watching me. Us.

When I was last here, even though I knew I was leaving to walk straight into a trap, there was buoyancy in my step. Barrons had just told me that when I came out, with Darroc dead and my parents alive, he was going to *give* me BB&B, deed and all.

I'd had no doubt that I was going to get that deed. I was so cocky, so sure of myself.

Darroc watches me carefully.

The games here are treacherously deep. Always were. I just never saw things as clearly as I do now.

He has called me on my hatred of him and done something probably only a being that had been Fae for a small eternity could do—he has accepted it and offered a full pardon. He has proposed far more than a mere business arrangement and waits for my response. I understand his game. He has studied my race with his coldly analytical Fae mind and knows us well.

By agreeing to be intimate with him, I expose myself on two levels: physically I get close enough to him that he could harm me, and emotionally I run the risk that every woman runs when she's intimate with a man—where the body goes, a tiny piece of the heart tries to follow.

Fortunately for me, I have no heart left. I'm safe on that score. And I've grown damned tough to injure.

My ghosts whisper to each other across me, but I can't hear them. There's only one way I'll ever be able to hear them again.

I turn my head for Darroc's kiss.

As his lips close over mine, the duality inside me threatens to tear me in half, and if it succeeds, I will lose my best chance at accomplishing my mission.

I hurt.

I need punishment for my sins.

I bury my hands in his hair and channel all those feelings into passion, pour them into my touch, kiss him hard, violently, with explosive feeling. I turn us both around and slam him up against the wall, kissing him like he's all that ever existed, kissing him with a full measure of humanity. It's a thing a Fae can never feel, no matter the form they wear—humanity. It's why they crave us in bed.

He staggers for a moment, draws back, and stares down at me.

My eyes are wild. I feel something inside me that terrifies me, and I just hope I can hang on to the edge of this cliff I'm on. I make a sound of impatience, wet my lips, and shove at him. "More," I demand.

When he kisses me again, the last part of me that could stand myself dies.

8

It took me a bloody fucking month to get back.

I died three times.

It was worse than the 1800s when I had to book passage on a steamer to cross the bloody ocean.

Fragments of Fae reality everywhere, took down every plane I took up.

I consider the possibility that, by the time I return, he will have caught her, cut my brand off her skull, and made her impossible to track.

Then I begin to feel her.

She is alive. She still wears my mark.

But what I sense is incongruent with her situation. I expect grief. The woman killed me and, in humans, familiarity breeds a certain emotional bond.

But lust? On the heels of murdering me, who does she lust for?

I entertain myself with thoughts of searing my brand from her skull.

When I finally arrive at the bookstore, what do I see in the alley behind it?

The woman that summoned me to save her, then

stabbed me in the back at the first opportunity, isn't lost in the Silvers, in need of saving.

She's standing in my alley, kissing the bastard that had her raped and turned her *Pri-ya*.

No, let us be perfectly precise: She's grinding herself against him and shoving her tongue halfway down his throat.

My monster rattles its cage.

Violently.

9

"Mac! Hey, Mac! Din't'cha hear me? I said, 'What
the blimey feck you doing?'"

I stiffen. I'm drifting in a dark place where I feel nothing, because if I did, I'd kill myself. No right, no wrong.
Just distraction.

"Ignore her," Darroc growls against my mouth.

"Mac, it's me! Dani. Hey, who the feck you kissing?"

I feel her zinging from side to side behind me, stirring
my hair with the breeze she creates, trying to see who
I've got up against the wall.

She's seen him twice before and would recognize him.
The last thing I need is her carrying news back to the
abbey: *Mac's teamed up with the Lord Master, just like
her sister! Just like Ro said! Feckin' traitor—must run in
the feckin' blood!*

Rowena would exploit it ruthlessly, send every *sidhe-
seer* she has to get in my way and try to take me down.
The narrow-minded bitch would put more effort into
hunting me than she'd ever spent hunting Fae.

A sudden gust ruffles my shirt, and my hair flies
straight up in the air.

"That ain't Barrons!" Dani snaps indignantly.

The name goes through me like a knife. No, it *ain't* Barrons and, unless I'm convincing, it never will be again.

"It ain't V'lane, neither!" Anger mixes with bafflement in her voice. "Mac, what'cha doing? Where the feck you been? I been looking all over for you. Been a month. Ma*aac*!" she wails the last part plaintively. "I got scoop! Pay attention to me!"

"Shall I get rid of her?" Darroc murmurs.

"She's a little tough to shake," I murmur back. "Give me a minute."

I step back, smiling up at him. No one can accuse the Fae of lacking in the lust department. It blazes in his not-quite-human eyes. Banked in that heat, I see surprise he tries but fails to mask. I suspect my sister was a little more . . . refined than I am.

"I'll be right back," I promise, and turn slowly, buying time to brace myself for dealing with Dani. I'm going to have to hurt her to get rid of her.

Her face is bright, eager. Her unruly mass of auburn curls is tamed beneath a black bike helmet, lights ablaze. She has on a long black leather coat and high-top black sneakers. Somewhere under that coat is the Sword of Light, unless Darroc sensed it and took it, too. If it's still there, I wonder if I could draw it swiftly enough to impale myself before she managed to stop me.

I have goals. I focus on them. No time to indulge my guilty conscience and even less point. When I'm done with what I plan to do, everything that happens in this alley tonight will never have taken place, so it doesn't matter that I hurt *this* Dani, because she won't have to live through it in the future I create.

The enormity of freedom that grants me makes me suddenly breathless. Nothing I do from this moment forth will ever come back to bite me in the ass. I'm in a penalty-free zone. I have been since the moment I decided to remake it all.

I study Dani with strange detachment, wondering how much I should change for her. I could keep her mother from being killed. Give her a life that would never harden her, that would let her be open, soft. Let her have fun like Alina and me, play on a beach, not be out in the streets hunting and killing monsters by the tender age of . . . however old she was when Rowena turned her into a weapon. Eight? Ten?

Now that she has my attention, she beams, and when Dani beams her whole face lights up. She bounces from foot to foot, burning off excited energy. "Where you been, Mac? I missed you! *Dude*—I mean, *man*," she corrects hastily, with a gamine grin, before I can make good on a threat I made in what feels like another lifetime that I would call her by her full name if she ever "duded" me again. "You ain't never gonna believe what's been going on! I invented Shade-Busters, and the whole abbey's been using 'em—even though they ain't saying nothing about how brilliant I am, like I musta accidentally stumbled onto it or something, when those stupid *sidhe*-sheep never woulda in a gazillion years," she mutters sourly. But then she brightens again. "And you're never gonna believe it—even I can't hardly—but I kicked a Hunter's ass and killed the fecker!" She frowns and looks a little irritated. "Well, maybe Jayne helped some, but *I'm* the one that killed it. And, feckin' A, you ain't never gonna guess this one—*dude!*" She begins bouncing from foot to foot so quickly and agitatedly that she becomes a black leather smudge in the night. "The feckin' *Sinsar Dubh* came to the abbey and it—"

Abruptly, she's no longer bouncing but standing still, looking at me, mouth hanging open, but nothing's coming out.

She stares past me, *at* me, then past me again. Her lips tighten and her eyes narrow. Her hand flashes inside her coat.

I can tell by the look on her face that it encounters emptiness where her sword should be. But she doesn't back up, not Dani. She stands her ground. If I had anything left inside me, I'd smile. Thirteen and she's got the heart of a lion.

"Something going on here I ain't getting, Mac?" she says tightly. "I'm standing here, see, trying to think of a reason, any ol' reason at all, you might be kissing that fecker, but I ain't finding none." She glares at me. "Thinking this is a little worse than me watching porn. Dude."

Oh, yes, she's upset. She just unapologetically "duded" me. I steel myself. "Lot going on here you ain't getting," I say coolly.

She searches my face, wondering if I'm playing double agent or something, undercover with the enemy. I need to convince her, beyond a shadow of a doubt, that I'm not. I need her to go away and stay away. I can't afford a superspeedy supersleuth interfering with my plans.

I also don't want her around long enough for Darroc to realize she could cause serious problems for us if she felt like it. Penalty-free zone or not, there's no reality in which I could kill Dani or watch her be killed by anyone else. Family isn't always born; sometimes it's found.

She said the Book was at the abbey. I need to know when. Until I discover how Darroc plans to merge with the *Sinsar Dubh* and am certain I can do it myself, I'm not getting him anywhere near it. I'm going to play the same game with Darroc that I played with V'lane and Barrons—only now for a very different reason—called "Dodge the Dark Book."

"Like what, Mac?" She props her fists at her waist. She's so upset she's vibrating, shivering so fast that her edges are getting blurry. "Prick tore down the walls, killed billions, wiped out Dublin, had you gang-raped—

I'm the one that saved you, 'member? And now you're sucking on"—she grimaces and shudders—"the feckin' tongue of an Unseelie-eater! What the feck?"

I ignore all of it. "When was the Book at the abbey?" I don't ask if people were hurt. The woman who is willing to ally herself with Darroc doesn't care. Besides, I won't let it happen in my new and improved version of the future.

"Gonna try this again, Mac. What the feck?" she fires.

I fire back, "Gonna try this again, Dani. When?"

She stares a long moment, then her jaw pokes out stubbornly and she crosses her skinny arms over her chest. She glares at Darroc, then back at me. "You *Pri-ya* or something again, Mac? Only without the being-naked-and-horny-all-the-time part? What'd he do to you?"

"Answer the question, Dani."

She bristles. "Barrons know what's going on? Think he needs to. Where's Barrons?"

"Dead," I say flatly.

Her slender body jerks and she stops vibrating. She had a major crush on Barrons. "No, he ain't," she protests. "Whatever he is ain't killable. Least not easy."

"Wasn't easy," I say. It took two of the people he trusted most in the world, a spear in the back, a gutting, and a slit throat. I wouldn't call that easy.

She stares at me hard, searching my gaze.

I focus on dripping scorn.

She gets it and stiffens. "What happened?"

Darroc moves in behind me and slips his arms around my waist. I lean back into him.

"MacKayla killed him," he says bluntly. "Now answer her question. When was the Book at the abbey? Is it still there?"

Dani sucks in a breath. She's vibrating again. She won't look at Darroc, only me. "This ain't funny, Mac."

I agree. It's not. It's hell. But it's necessary. "He had it coming," I lie coldly. "He betrayed me."

She puffs up, fists at her waist. "Barrons ain't the betraying kind. He never betrayed you! He wouldn't do that!"

"Oh, grow up and pull your head out! You didn't know shit about Barrons! You're not old enough to know shit about *anything*!"

She goes still, brilliant green eyes narrowing. "I left the abbey, Mac," she says finally. She gives a hollow laugh. "Think I kinda burned my bridges, ya know?" She searches my face. And I feel another blade in my heart. She burned them because of me. Because she believed that I was out there somewhere and we had each other.

I console myself with the thought that at least she won't be rushing back to Rowena to tell her I'm sleeping with the enemy and I won't have a pack of rabid *sidhe-seers* on my tail.

"Thought we were friends, Mac."

I see in her eyes that all I have to do is say, *We are,* and she'll find some way to deal with what she's looking at right now. How dare she put so much faith in me? I never asked for it, never deserved it.

"You thought wrong. Now answer the question." I'm the only one who never treated her like a child. She hates being called "kid" more than anything. "*Kid,*" I say. "Then get the hell out of here. Take your toys and go play somewhere else."

Her brows climb her forehead and her mouth pulls down. "*What* did you just say?"

"I said, *kid,* answer my question and go away! We're a little busy here, can't you see?"

She's bouncing from foot to foot again, a smudge of

darkness in the dark. "Feckin' grown-ups," she bites out through clenched teeth. "All the feckin' same. Feckin' glad I feckin' left the feckin' abbey. *You can just go to hell!*" She shouts the last words, but they catch a little as they come out, like they get tangled up on a sob she's forcing back down.

I don't even see the blur of black move away. There's a burst of light from her MacHalo as she flashes into motion like the *Enterprise* entering warp speed, then an empty alley.

I'm startled to realize that I think she's just the tiniest bit faster. Is she eating Unseelie? I'm going to kick her ass all over Dublin if she's eating Unseelie.

"Why didn't you stop her, MacKayla? You could have exploited her trust in you to get information about the Book."

I shrug. "Kid always got on my nerves. Let's go hunt ourselves a *sidhe*-seer. If we can't find one, Jayne's men are bound to know what's going on."

I turn away from Barrons Books and Baubles toward what used to be the biggest Dark Zone in Dublin. It's a wasteland now, not a single Shade left. When Darroc brought the walls crashing down on Halloween and Dublin went dark, the amorphous vampires escaped their prison of light and slithered on to greener pastures.

Hurting Dani took all my energy. I'm in no mood to walk past BB&B. I'd have to confront the obvious—that, like the man, the store is big, silent, and dead.

If I walk past it, I'll have to force myself not to stare hungrily at it. Have to ignore that, in this reality, I'll never enter those doors again.

He's gone. He's really, truly gone.

My bookstore has been lost to me as completely and irrevocably as if the Dark Zone had finally swallowed it up.

I'll never own it. I'll never open those diamond-paned cherry doors for business again.

I'll never hear my cash register's tiny bell ring or curl up with a cup of cocoa and a book, warmed by a cozy gas fire and the promise of Jericho Barrons' eventual return. I'll never banter with him, practice Voice, or be tested against pages of the *Sinsar Dubh*. I'll never steal hungry glances when I think he's not looking at me, or hear him laugh, or climb the back stairs to my bedroom that's sometimes on the fourth floor and other times on the fifth, where I might lie awake and practice things to say to him, only to end up discarding them all because Barrons doesn't care about words.

Only actions.

I'll never drive his cars. I'll never know his secrets.

Darroc takes my arm. "This way." He turns me around. "Temple Bar."

I feel his eyes on me as he guides me back toward the bookstore.

I stop and look up at him. "I thought there might be things you needed from the house on LaRuhe," I say casually. I *really* don't want to walk past BB&B. "I thought we should rally your troops. We've been gone a long time."

"There are many places I keep supplies, and my army is always near." He makes a slicing gesture in the air and murmurs a few words in a language I don't understand.

The night is suddenly twenty degrees cooler. I don't have to look behind me to know the Unseelie Princes are there, in addition to countless other Unseelie. The night is suddenly thick with dark Fae. Even with my "volume" muted, there are so many, so close to me, that I feel them in the pit of my stomach. Does he keep a contingent of them a mere sift away at all times? Have the princes been hovering all this time, listening for his call, a half dimension beyond my awareness?

I'll need to remember that.

"I am *not* walking around Dublin with the princes at my back."

"I said I will not let them harm you, MacKayla, and I meant it."

"I want my spear back. Give it to me now."

"I cannot permit that. I saw what you did to Mallucé with it."

"I said I won't harm you, Darroc, and I meant it," I mock. "See how that feels? Little hard to swallow, isn't it? You insist that I trust you, but you won't trust me."

"I cannot take the risk."

"Wrong answer." Should I force the issue and try to take the spear? If I succeed, will he trust me less? Or respect me more?

When I seek the bottomless lake in my head, I don't bother closing my eyes to do it. I just let them go a little out of focus. I need power, strength, and I know where to find both. With almost no effort at all, I'm standing on a black-pebbled beach. It has always been there for me. It always will be.

Distantly, I hear Darroc speaking to the princes. I shiver. I can't bear the thought of them behind me.

Deep in its cavernous depths, the black water churns and begins to bubble.

Silvery runes like the ones I encircled myself with on the cliff's edge break the surface, but the water keeps boiling, and I know it's not yet done. There's something more . . . if I want it. I do. After a few moments, it pushes up a handful of crimson runes that pulse on the inky water like slender deformed hearts. The bubbling stops. The surface is once again as smooth as black glass.

I bend and scoop them up. Dripping blood, they flutter in my fists.

Distantly, I hear the Unseelie Princes begin to chime, but not softly. It's the sound of broken, jagged crystal scraping against metal.

I don't turn to look at them. I know all I need to know: Whatever gift I've been given, they don't like it.

My gaze refocuses.

Darroc looks at me, then down at my hands, and goes still. "What are you doing with those? What were you doing in the Silvers before I found you? Did you enter the White Mansion without me, MacKayla?"

Behind me, the princes chime louder. It's a cacophony that slices into the soul like a razor, severs tendon, and chips bone. I wonder if that's what comes of being fashioned from an imperfect Song of Making, a melody that can unmake, unsing, uncreate at a molecular level.

They hate my crimson runes, and I hate their dark music.

I won't be the one to yield.

"Why?" I ask Darroc. Is that where the runes I've scooped up came from? What does he know about them? I can't ask him without betraying that, while I have power, I have no idea what it is or how to use it. I raise my fists and open them, palms up. My hands drip thick red liquid. Slender tubular runes twist on my palms.

Behind me, the princes' jagged chiming becomes a hellish shriek that even Darroc looks rattled by.

I have no idea what to do with the runes. I was thinking of the Unseelie Princes, that I needed a weapon against them, and they appeared in my mind. I have no idea how I translated them from that dark glassy lake into existence. I understand no more about these crimson symbols than I did about the silvery ones.

"Where did you learn to do that, MacKayla?" Darroc demands.

I can barely hear him over the princes. "How do you

plan to merge with the Book?" I counter. I have to raise my voice to a near yell to make myself heard.

"Do you have any idea what those things are capable of?" he demands. I read his lips. I can't hear him.

The shrieking behind me rises to an inhuman pitch that pierces my eardrums like ice picks. "Give me my spear and I'll put them away," I shout.

Darroc moves closer, trying to hear me. "Impossible!" he explodes. "My princes will not remain and protect us if you have the spear." His gaze slides with distaste over the runes in my hands. "Nor with *those* present."

"I think we can take care of ourselves!"

"What?" he shouts.

"We don't need them!" The ice picks in my ears have begun drilling into my brain. I'm on the verge of a massive migraine.

"I do! I am not yet Fae again. My army follows me only because Fae princes lead at my back!"

"Who needs an army?" We're inches apart, shouting at each other, and still the words are nearly lost in the din.

He rubs his temples. His nose has started to bleed. "*We* do! The Seelie are amassing, MacKayla. They, too, have begun hunting the *Sinsar Dubh*. Much has changed since you were last here!"

"How do you know?" I hadn't seen any handy newsstands in the Silvers while *I* was in there.

He grabs my head, pulls it to his. "I stay informed!" he snarls against my ear.

The chiming has become an unbearable orchestra of sounds that the human ear was never meant to hear. My neck is wet. I realize my ears are bleeding. I'm mildly surprised. I don't bleed easily anymore. Haven't ever since I ate Unseelie.

"You must obey me in this, MacKayla!" he shouts. "If you wish to remain at my side, dispose of them. Or is it war you wish between us? I thought it was an alliance you sought!" He wipes blood from his lips and cuts a sharp look at the princes.

Blissfully, blessedly, the chiming stops. The ice picks through my eardrums vanish.

I inhale deeply, gulping clean, fresh air greedily, as if it might wash my cells clean of the stain from the princes' horrific symphony.

My relief is short-lived, however. As abruptly as the hellish music stopped, my shoulders and arms are freezing, and I think sheets of ice might crack and drop away if I move.

I don't need to turn my head to know that the princes have sifted into position, one on my left, one on my right. I feel them there. I know their inhumanly beautiful faces are inches from mine. If I turn my head, they will look *into* me with those piercing, mesmerizing, ancient eyes that can see beyond where the human soul is, that can see into the very matter that comprises it—and can take it apart piece by piece. Regardless of how much they despise my runes, they're still ready to take me on.

I look at Darroc. I'd wondered what his reaction would be if I tried to take the spear. I see a look in his eyes now that was not there a short time ago. I am both a greater liability than he knew and a greater asset—and he likes it. He likes power: both having it and having a woman who has it.

I despise walking with Unseelie Princes at my back. But his comment about the Seelie amassing armies, my ignorance about the runes I hold in my hands, and the icy dark Fae sandwiching me make compelling arguments.

I tilt my head, toss my dark curls from my eyes, and

look up at him. He likes it when I use his name. I think it makes him feel like he's with Alina again. Alina was soft and Southern to the core. We Southern women know a thing or two about men. We know to use their name often, to make them feel strong, needed, as if they have the final say even when they don't, and to always, *always* keep them believing they won the best prize in the only competition that will ever matter on the day we said, "I do."

"If we get into a battle, Darroc, will you promise to return my spear so I can use it to help defend us? Will you permit that?"

He likes those words: "help defend *us*" and "permit." I see it in his eyes. A smile breaks across his face. He touches my cheek and nods. "Of course, Mac-Kayla."

He looks at the princes and they are no longer beside me.

I'm uncertain how to return the runes. I'm not sure they *can* be returned.

When I toss them over my shoulders at the princes, they make sounds like exploding crystal goblets, as they sift hastily to avoid them. I hear the runes steam and hiss as they hit pavement.

I laugh.

Darroc gives me a look.

"I *am* behaving," I reply sweetly. "You can't tell me they didn't have that coming."

I'm getting better at reading him. He finds me amusing. I wipe my palms on my leather pants, trying to get rid of the bloody residue from the runes. I try my shirt. But it's no use; the red discoloration has set.

When Darroc takes my hand and leads me down the alley between Barrons Books and Baubles and Barrons' garage, which houses the car collection I used to covet, I don't look to either side. I keep my gaze trained straight ahead.

I've lost Alina, failed to save Christian, killed Barrons, am becoming intimate with my sister's lover. I hurt Dani to drive her away, and now I've teamed up with the Unseelie army.

Eyes on the prize, there's no turning back.

10

Snow begins to fall, carpeting the night in a soft white hush. We march across it, a stain of Unseelie, stomping, crawling, slithering toward Temple Bar.

There are castes behind me that I've seen only once before—the night Darroc brought them through the dolmen. I have no desire to inspect them any more closely than I did that night. Some of the Unseelie aren't so bad to look at. The Rhino-boys are disgusting, but they don't make you feel . . . dirty. Others . . . well, even the way they move makes your skin crawl, makes you feel slimy where their eyes linger.

As we pass a streetlamp, I glance at a flyer, drooping limply on it: *The Dani Daily, 97 days AWC.*

The headline brags that she killed a Hunter. I put myself in Dani's head, to figure out the date. It takes me a minute, but I get it—after the walls crashed. I perform a rapid calculation. The last day I was in Dublin was January 12.

Ninety-seven days from Halloween—the night the walls crashed—is February 5.

Which means I've been gone at least twenty-four

days, probably longer. The flyer was faded, worn by the elements. Much more snow and I'd never have seen it.

However long I've been gone, Dublin hasn't changed much.

Although many of the streetlamps that were ripped from the concrete and destroyed have been replaced and the broken lights repaired, the power grids are still down. Here and there, generators hum, dead giveaways of life barricaded in buildings or holed up underground.

We pass the red façade of *the* Temple Bar, of the bar district. I glance in. I can't help myself. I loved the place BWC—before the walls crashed.

Now it's a dark shell, with shattered windows, overturned tables and chairs, and papery husks of human remains. From the way they're piled, I know the patrons were crammed inside, huddled together when the end came.

I remember the way the Temple Bar looked the first time I saw it, brightly lit, with people and music spilling from open doors into the cobbled streets of the corner beyond. Guys had whistled at me. I'd forgotten my grief over Alina for a blessed second or two. Then, of course, hated myself for forgetting.

I can almost hear the laughter, the lilt of Irish voices. They're all dead now, like Alina and Barrons.

I remember spending the long week before Halloween walking the streets of Dublin for hours on end, from dawn 'til dusk, feeling helpless, worthless, for all my supposed *sidhe*-seer skills. I wasn't sure any of us would survive Halloween, so I'd tried to cram as much living into those last days as possible.

I'd chatted up street vendors and played backgammon with toothless old men who spoke a version of English so heavily distorted by dialect and gums that I'd understood only every fifth word, but it hadn't mattered. They'd been delighted by a pretty girl's attention, and I'd hungered for paternal comfort.

I'd visited the famous tourist hot spots. I'd eaten in dives and slammed back shots of whiskey with anyone who'd do them with me.

I'd fallen in love with the city I couldn't protect.

After the Unseelie had escaped their prison and savaged her—dark, burned, and broken—I'd been determined to see her rebuilt.

Now I longed only to replace her.

"Do you sense it, MacKayla?" Darroc asks.

I've been keeping my *sidhe*-seer senses as closed as possible. I'm tired and have no desire to find the *Sinsar Dubh*. Not until I know everything he knows.

I open my senses warily and turn the "volume" up to a two on a scale of one to ten. My *sidhe*-seer senses are picking up the essence of countless things Fae, but none of them is the *Sinsar Dubh*. "No."

"Are there many Fae?"

"The city is crawling with them."

"Light or Dark Court?"

"It doesn't work like that. I can only pick up Fae, not their allegiance or caste."

"How many?"

I adjust the volume to three and a half. A tenth this much Fae in close proximity used to have me holding my stomach and trying not to puke. Now I feel charged by it. More alive than I want to be. "They're on all sides of us, in twos and threes. They're above us, on the rooftops and in the skies. I don't get the feeling that they're watching us, more that they're watching *everything*." Are they, too, hunting my Book? I'll kill them all. It's mine.

"Hundreds?" he presses.

"Thousands," I correct.

"Organized?"

"There is one group to the east that is considerably larger than the others, if that's what you're asking."

"Then east we go," he says. He turns to the princes and barks a command. They vanish.

I voice a growing suspicion. "They're not really gone, are they? They never are when you send them away."

"They remain close, watching but unseen. A sift away, with more of my army."

"And when we find this group of Fae?" I press.

"If they are Unseelie, they are mine."

"And if they're Seelie?"

"Then we will drive them from Dublin."

Good. The less Fae in my way, the better.

Few have ever seen the Seelie, save the rare mortal stolen away and kept at the Fae court and, of course, Barrons, who once spent a great deal of time there, sleeping with a princess, before killing her and pissing off V'lane for all eternity.

I've seen thousands of Unseelie, but until now even I—*sidhe*-seer extraordinaire—have seen only a single Seelie.

I'd begun to wonder why.

In the dark hours of the night, I'd wondered if maybe he was the only one left, if he was hiding something, if perhaps he wasn't Seelie at all, despite evidence supporting his claim.

Seeing him as he is now, all my doubts evaporate.

Here are the Seelie.

They've finally gotten off their asses and started paying attention to the mess they've made of my world. I guess they couldn't be bothered before now.

Even filled as I am with hatred for all Fae, I can't deny that V'lane looks like an avenging angel, charging down from heaven to set my world back on its axis and clean this whole mess up. Radiant, golden, and mesmerizing, he leads an army of angels.

Tall, gracefully muscled, they stand shoulder to shoulder with him, filling the street. Stunning, velvety-skinned, dusted with gold, they are so chillingly exquisite that I have a hard time looking at them—and I'm immune from having been *Pri-ya,* a Fae sex addict. They are otherworldly, divine.

There are dozens of V'lane's caste, male and female. They possess a terrifying eroticism that makes them deadly to humans. If a scientist managed to get his hands on one to study, I wouldn't be surprised to learn their skin exudes a pheromone we crave.

The perpetual promise of a smile hovers on irresistible lips, below ancient, iridescent, alien eyes. Despite all I've suffered at their hands, I want to rush forward and fall to my knees before them. I want to slide my palms over their flawless skin, discover if they taste as amazing as they smell. I want to be gathered into a Fae embrace, yield my memories, my mind, my will, and be carried off to a Faery court where I could stay forever young, cocooned by illusion.

Flanking V'lane's caste—which I assume is the highest ranking by how the other castes seem to protect it—are the stuff of fairy tales. There are rainbow-colored, delicate Fae that dart like hummingbirds on gossamer wings; silvery nymphs that dance on dainty feet; and others that I can't even see, except for blinding trailers of light they leave behind as they move. They're so brilliant and fiery, they could only be earthbound stars.

I scoff at the delicacy of his army. It's ethereal, born to wisp about, seduce, and be served.

Mine is earthy, solid. Born to gorge, kill, and rule.

We stalk toward one another, down a snow-filled street.

Where Seelie feet touch the earth, the snow melts

with a hiss. Steam rises and flowers push up through cracks, blooming brilliantly, anointing the air with the scents of jasmine and sandalwood. The Seelie end of the street is bathed in golden light.

Where my army's hooves and scaled bellies pass over the stones, a crust of black ice forms. The night embraces us; stealthy shadows, we ooze forward from the blackness.

Only once before have Seelie and Unseelie met like this—and on that day the Seelie Queen died. This is the stuff of legends, never seen by humans, except perhaps in our dreams.

Deformed monsters and hideous demons stare with baleful, hate-filled eyes at their perfect golden counterparts.

Angels glare with disdain at abominations that should never have been born, who blemish the perfection of the Fae race, tarnish their existence simply by being.

I wonder what Darroc is thinking, bringing them together like this.

We stop a dozen paces apart.

Ice and heat slam together in the street.

My breath frosts the air, then turns to steam as it passes an invisible demarcation. Eddies swirl on the pavement between us, gathering the indigestible rinds of people the Shades left behind, and tiny tornadoes begin to form.

I realize that whoever began the fairy tale that Fae don't feel was selling pure bullshit. They feel the entire range of human emotion. They just handle it differently: with patience born of eternity. Schooled in courtly manners, they don masks of impassivity because they have forever to play out their games.

As we study each other through the rapidly growing tornadoes, I remember V'lane telling me that they destroyed their own world by fighting. It cracked from end to end. Was this why? Will the weather disturbance that's being generated by the clash of these two mighty courts continue to grow if they fight and tear this world apart, too? Not that I'd particularly mind, since I intend to re-create it with the Book, but I need the Book *before* this world is destroyed.

Which means this stormy posturing really needs to stop.

"Enough with the melodrama, V'lane," I say coolly.

His eyes are those of a stranger. He regards me with the same expression he turns on the monsters at my back. I'm a little irritated to realize he doesn't look at Darroc. His gaze slides over him as if he's not even there. *He's* the fallen Fae, traitor to their race, the one responsible for tearing the walls down. I'm just a *sidhe*-seer trying to survive.

The gold-dusted Greek god standing on V'lane's right sneers, "That . . . *thing* . . . is the human you said we need to protect? She consorts with abominations!"

The gilt-skinned goddess to his left growls, "Destroy her now!"

Hundreds of Seelie, walking, dancing, and flying, begin to clamor for my death.

Without taking my eyes off them, I snap at Darroc, "I could really use my spear right now." I assume he still has it, that V'lane hasn't somehow plucked it from him the same way he takes it from me.

As the tiny, dainty Fae begin proposing methods for my execution, each one slower and more painful than the last, the god and goddess bracketing V'lane hammer him.

"She is human and has chosen the dark ones! Look at her! She wears their colors!"

"You said she worshipped *us*!"

"And she would obey us in all things!"

"They have *touched* her! I smell it on her skin!" The god looks revolted—and aroused. Iridescent eyes glitter with gold sparks.

"They have used her!" the goddess snarls. "She is soiled. I will not suffer her at court!"

"Silence!" V'lane thunders. "I lead the True Race for our queen. *I* speak for Aoibheal!"

"This is unacceptable!"

"Outrageous!"

"Beyond bearing, V'lane!"

"You will do as I say, Dree'lia! I decide her fate. And only I will carry it out."

I mutter at Darroc, "You need to make a decision, and fast."

"They always overreact," Darroc murmurs. "It is one of the many things I despised at court. A session in High Council could go on like this for several human years. Give them time. V'lane will bring them to heel."

One of the tiny, winged Seelie breaks formation and darts straight for my head. I duck, but it whizzes around me.

I'm startled to hear myself burst out laughing.

Two more of them break rank and begin to zip tight circles around my head.

As they buzz past me, my laughter takes on a hysterical edge. There's nothing funny about what's happening—still, I hoot and snort. I can't help it. I've never been so amused in my entire life. I hold my sides and double over, chortling, guffawing, choking on sobs of forced gaiety, as they weave closer and closer around me. I'm appalled by the sounds coming out of my mouth. I'm horrified at the uncontrollable nature of it. I hate the Fae and their way of stripping away my will.

"Stop laughing," Darroc growls.

Hilarity has me on the edge of hysterics and it *hurts*. I manage to raise my head from my knees just enough to shoot him a dirty look. I'd love to stop laughing. But I can't.

I want to tell him to make the damned things go away, except I can't breathe, I can't even close my lips long enough to grit consonants. Whatever these lovely little Seelie monsters are, their specialty is death-by-laughter. What a hellish way to go. After only a few minutes, my sides ache from heaving, my gut burns, and I'm so breathless I'm light-headed. I wonder how long it takes to die of forced mirth. Hours? Days?

A fourth tiny Fae takes up the game, and I brace myself to dive inward, to find a weapon in my dark, lake-filled cave, when suddenly a long tongue, dripping venom, whizzes past my ear and plucks the dainty Seelie straight from the air.

I hear crunching noises behind me.

I snicker helplessly.

"V'lane!" the golden goddess shrieks. "That thing, that awful *thing*, it ate *M'ree*!"

I hear another snap, followed by more crunching noises, and a second one is gone. I cackle madly.

The remaining two retreat, shaking tiny fists and screaming in a language I don't understand. Even angry, the sound they make is more beautiful than an aria.

My laughter loses its forced edge.

After a long moment, I'm able to relax and I stop making crazed sounds of amusement. Peals fade to moans to silence. I release my sides and gulp cool, soothing air.

I stand, suddenly furious, and this emotion is all mine. I'm sick of being vulnerable. If I'd had my spear, those nasty little death-by-laughter fairies would never have dared approach me. I'd have skewered them midair and made Fae kebabs out of them.

"Friends," I hiss at Darroc, "trust each other."

But he doesn't. I see it in his face.

"You said you would give it to me so I could defend us."

He smiles faintly, and I know he's remembering how Mallucé died: slowly, gruesomely, rotting from the inside out. The spear kills all things Fae, and because Darroc has been eating so much Unseelie, he's laced with veins of Fae. One tiny little prick of the tip of my spear would be a death sentence. "As yet, *we* are not under attack."

"Who are you talking to, human?" the goddess demands.

I look at Darroc, who shrugs. "I told you the first Seelie that saw me would try to kill me. Hence they do not see me. My princes keep me concealed from their vision."

Now I understand why V'lane's gaze slid over him like he wasn't there. He's not. "So it looks like I'm the only one standing here? They think *I'm* running your army!"

"Never fear, *sidhe*-seer," V'lane says coldly. "I smell the foulness of what was once Fae and now cannibalizes our race. I know who leads this army. As for his being your friend, the one you so unwisely walk with has no friends. He has always served only his own purposes."

I tilt my head. "Are you my friend, V'lane?"

"I would be. I have offered you my protection repeatedly."

The goddess gasps. "You offered our protection and she refused? She chose those . . . *things* over us?"

"Silence, Dree'lia!"

"The Tuatha Dé Danann do not offer twice!" she fumes.

"I said, 'Silence!'" V'lane snaps.

"Clearly you do not under—"

I gape.

Dree'lia has no mouth. There is only smooth skin

where her lips used to be. Delicate nostrils flare beneath ancient, hate-filled eyes.

The golden god moves to embrace her. She rests her head in the hollow of his neck and clutches him. "That was unnecessary," he tells V'lane stiffly.

I'm struck by the absurdity of the moment. Here I stand, between opposing halves of the most powerful race imaginable. They are at war with each other. They despise each other and are vying for the same prize.

And the Seelie—who have enjoyed absolute freedom and power their entire existences—are squabbling among themselves over trivialities, while the Unseelie—who've been imprisoned, starved, and tortured for hundreds of thousands of years—patiently hold formation and wait for Darroc's orders.

And I can't help but see myself in them. The Seelie are who I was before my sister died. Pink, pretty, frivolous Mac. The Unseelie are who I've become, carved by loss and despair. Black, grungy, driven Mac.

The Unseelie are stronger, less breakable. I'm glad I'm like them.

"I will speak with the *sidhe*-seer alone," V'lane says.

"He will not," Darroc growls at my side.

V'lane extends his hand when I don't move. "Come, we must speak privately."

"Why?"

"What subtle nuance of the word 'private' do you not understand?"

"Probably the same subtle nuance of the word 'no' you never understand. I'm not sifting anywhere with you."

The god at his right gasps at my disrespect of his prince, but I see a small smile shape the corners of V'lane's mouth.

"Consorting with Barrons has changed you. I think he will approve."

The name is poison in my veins, from which I will die a slow death every minute I have to spend in this world without him. I'll never be on the receiving end of one of those looks again. Never see that infamous mocking smile. Never have one of those wordless conversations in which we said so much more with our eyes than either of us ever was willing to say with our mouths. Jericho, Jericho, Jericho. How many times did I actually ever speak his name? Three? "Barrons is dead," I say coolly.

The Seelie rustle, murmur disbelievingly.

V'lane's eyes narrow. "He is not."

"He is," I say flatly. And I'm the queen bitch from hell that's going to make them all pay. The thought makes me smile.

He searches my eyes a long moment, lingers on the curve of my lips. "I do not believe you," he says finally.

"Darroc burned his body and scattered the ash. He's dead."

"How was he killed?" he demands.

"The spear."

The soft murmurs swell and V'lane snarls, "I must have confirmation of this. Darroc, show yourself!"

My sides are suddenly icy. I am flanked by Unseelie Princes.

V'lane stiffens. The entire Seelie army goes still. And I think, *Darroc may have just started a war.*

How many hundreds of thousands of years ago did Seelie and Unseelie royalty last look each other in the face?

I hate looking at the Unseelie Princes. They mesmerize, they seduce, they obliterate. But there is something happening here that no human has ever seen. My curiosity is morbid and deep.

I position myself for a better view to see them both at once.

The Unseelie Prince stands beside me, stunningly naked. Of the four—who have been so aptly compared to the Four Horsemen of the Apocalypse—I wonder which two remain. Pestilence, Famine, War? I hope I stand next to Death.

I want to walk with Death, bring it crashing down on this immortal, arrogant race.

The dark powerful body, capable of such soul-rending pleasure, is exquisite. I examine every inch with macabre fascination. Even hating the princes as I do, it . . . excites. It thrills. Which makes me hate it even more. It turned me inside out. I remember the kaleidoscopic tattoos rushing beneath its skin. I remember the black torque slithering around its neck. Its face has a savage beauty that obsesses even as it terrifies. Its lips are drawn back, baring sharp white teeth. And its eyes . . . oh, God, those eyes!

I force my gaze to V'lane. Then I widen my view to absorb them both, being careful to avoid the Unseelie Prince's eyes.

Thesis and antithesis. Matter and antimatter.

They stand like statues, neither moving nor seeming to breathe. They study each other, assess, measure.

Prince of Consuming Night. Prince of Glorious Dawn.

The air between them is so charged that I could power all of Dublin if only I could figure out how to plug into it.

Black ice rushes forward from the Unseelie Prince's feet, encompassing the cobblestones.

It is met halfway by a bed of brilliantly colored blossoms.

The ground shudders beneath my feet. There is a thunderous *crack,* and suddenly the cobbled pavement splits jaggedly between them, revealing a narrow, dark fissure.

"What are you doing, Darroc?" I demand.

"Tell him," Darroc orders, and the prince opens his mouth to speak.

I clamp my hands to my ears to shut out the hellish sound.

V'lane uses language to communicate with me. All the Seelie have been using my language in my presence. I realize it has been a great concession.

The Unseelie Princes grant no concessions. Their language is a dark melody that the human ear was not made to hear. Once, I was forced to listen helplessly as they crooned to me, and it drove me mad.

By the time the Unseelie Prince stops speaking, V'lane is regarding me with an expression of faint astonishment.

Warily, I remove my hands from my ears but keep them close in case the UP decides to start "talking" again.

"He claims *you* killed Barrons, *sidhe*-seer. Why?"

It hasn't escaped me that V'lane won't use my name. I suspect that, if he did, those of his race would think him weak.

"Who cares? He's dead. Gone. Out of both of our ways. It's not like you didn't want him dead, too." I wonder if they really burned his body. I will never ask.

"And it was the spear that killed him?"

I nod. I have no idea, but it's simplest to agree. The less time I spend thinking about Barrons, the better.

He looks from me to the prince at my side. "And after you killed Barrons, you decided your enemy was your friend?"

"A girl needs friends." I'm bored. Tired of this posturing. I need to sleep. I need to be alone. "Look, V'lane, the Seelie are immortal, and the Unseelie are immortal. What are you going to do? Waste everyone's time beating each other up all night? As far as I know, there's only one weapon here tonight that kills Fae, and I've got it."

"You do not."

"You do," Darroc corrects.

Just like that, my spear is heavy in my holster. I jerk a hard look his way. "About damned time." I guess he finally feels the threat level has risen sufficiently. Or maybe he's bored, too.

I slip my hand inside my jacket and close my fingers around the hilt. I love my spear. I'm going to keep it in the new world I create, even though it will be a world without Fae.

"You do not," V'lane says.

"I thought you couldn't see or hear him."

"I smell the stench of him."

My spear is gone.

My spear is there.

Gone again.

I look from V'lane to Darroc. V'lane is staring in Darroc's general direction. Darroc is staring hard at the Unseelie Princes. They're having a silent battle over me and my weapon, and it infuriates me that I have no control. One instant, V'lane takes my spear; the next, Darroc gives it back. It flickers in my fingers, solid then gone, solid then gone.

I shake my head. This could go on all night. They can play their silly games. I have more important things to do—like get enough sleep that I'm sharp enough to be on the hunt. I'm dangerously exhausted. I no longer feel numb. I'm brittle, and brittle can crack.

I'm preparing to turn and walk away from it all, when the sound of automatic gunfire shatters the night.

The Seelie hiss, and all those capable of sifting vanish—including V'lane—leaving roughly a third of them still standing in the street. They turn on their attacker, snarling. As the bullets hit them, some of the lesser castes flicker and stumble. Others turn toward us and launch themselves into the Unseelie to escape.

I hear the voices of Jayne and his men, shouting to each other, closing in behind them. I catch the glint of a rifle up on the rooftop a block down and know snipers are moving in.

Good. I hope they take down hundreds of Fae tonight, cart them off and imprison them with iron. I hope Dani makes rounds and kills the ones they catch.

But I'm not about to die from friendly fire in this screwed-up reality. I have a whole new world waiting for me in the future.

I turn to the Unseelie Prince to command it to sift me out of here. My enemy, my salvation.

Darroc barks a harsh order.

The prince's hands are on me and it's sifting before I even manage to get the words out.

TIME IS THE ONLY TRUE GOD, AND I AM FOREVER. THEREFORE, I AM GOD.

Your logic is flawed. Time is not forever. It is *ALWAYS*. Past, Present, and Future. There was a time in the past when you did not exist. Therefore, you are not God.

I CREATE. I DESTROY.

With the whimsy of a spoiled child.

YOU FAIL TO DIVINE THE MASTER DESIGN. EVEN THAT WHICH YOU CALL CHAOS HAS PATTERN AND PURPOSE.

—CONVERSATIONS WITH THE *SINSAR DUBH*

11

I stand on a balcony, staring out at the darkness. Snow swirls around my face, lands in my hair. I catch a few flakes in my hand and study them. Growing up in the Deep South, I didn't get to see a lot of snow, but what I did see didn't look like this.

These flakes have complex crystalline structures, and some are tinged with faint color at the outer edges. Green, gold, dirty like ash. They don't lose cohesion on the warmth of my skin. They're tougher than the average snowflakes, or I'm colder than the average human. When I close my hand to melt them, one of the flakes cuts into my palm with sharp edges.

Lovely. Razor snow. More Fae changes in my world. Time for a new one.

Time.

I ponder the concept. Ever since I arrived in Dublin at the beginning of August, time has been a strange thing. I have only to look at a calendar to confirm what my brain knows—six months have passed.

But of those six months, I lost the entire month of September to a single afternoon in Faery. The months of November, December, and part of January were calendar pages torn from my life while I was in a mindless, sex-crazed oblivion. And now part of January and February had flashed by in a few days, while I was in the Silvers.

All told, in the last six months, four of them whizzed past, with me virtually unaware of the passage of time, for one reason or another.

My brain knows it's been six months since Alina died.

My body doesn't believe a word of it.

It *feels* like I found out my sister was murdered two months ago. It feels like I was raped on Halloween ten days ago. It feels like my parents were kidnapped four days ago, and I stabbed Barrons and watched him die thirty-six hours ago.

My body can't catch up with my brain. My heart has jet lag. All my emotions are raw because everything feels as if it took place over a short period of time.

I push my damp hair back from my face and breathe deeply of the cold night air. I'm in a bedroom suite at one of Darroc's many strongholds in Dublin. It's a penthouse apartment, high above the city, furnished in the same opulent Louis XIV Sun King style of the house at 1247 LaRuhe. Darroc certainly likes his luxuries. Like someone else I know.

Knew.

Will know again, I correct.

Darroc told me he keeps dozens of such safe houses and never stays more than one night in any of them. How am I ever going to find them all to search for clues? I dread the thought of remaining with him long enough for him to take me to each for a night.

I fist my hands. I can handle this. I know I can. My world depends on it.

I unclench my hands and rub my sides. Even hours after the Unseelie Prince touched me, my skin is still chilled in the shape of its handprints. I turn away from the cold, snowy night, close the French doors, and scatter my remaining runes at the threshold, where they pulse like wet crimson hearts on the floor. My dark lake promised I would sleep safely if I pressed one into each wall and warded the thresholds and sills with them.

I turn and stare at the bed, in the same daze I've been functioning in for the past several hours. I shuffle past it to the bathroom, where I splash cold water on my face. My eyes feel swollen and gritty. I look in the mirror. The woman that looks back frightens me.

Darroc wanted to "talk" when we arrived. But I know what it was really about. He was testing me. He showed me pictures of Alina. Made me sit and look at them with him and listen to his stories, until I thought I might go insane.

I close my eyes, but my sister's face is burned into the backs of my eyelids. And there, standing next to her, are my mom and dad. I said I didn't care what happened to them in this reality, because I'm going to make a new one, but the truth is I'd care in any reality. I've just been blocking it.

I will not ask Darroc what happened to my parents after I was swept off to the Hall of All Days, and he doesn't offer the information.

If he told me they were dead, too, I don't know what I'd do.

I suspect this is another of his tests. I will pass it.

That's my girl, Daddy encourages in my mind. *Chin up; you can do it. I believe in you, baby. Sis-boom-bah!* he says, and smiles. Even though he hadn't wanted me to pursue cheerleading, he'd still driven me to tryouts, and when I'd made the first cut, he'd had one of his clients at Petit Patisserie bake me a special cake shaped like a pair of pink and purple pom-poms.

I double over like I've been kicked in the stomach,

and my mouth wrenches wide on a sob that makes no sound because I inhale it at the last second.

Darroc is out there with the princes. I don't dare betray grief. I don't dare make a sound that they might hear.

Daddy was my greatest cheerleader, always telling me wise things I rarely listened to and never understood. I should have taken the time to understand. I should have spent more time focused on who I was inside and less on who I was outside. Hindsight, 20/20.

Tears run down my face. As I turn away from the mirror, my knees go out from under me and I collapse to the bathroom floor in a heap. I curl into a ball, silently heaving.

I've held it at bay as long as I can. Grief crashes over me, drowning me. Alina. Barrons. Mom and Dad, too? I can't bear it. I can't keep it all in.

I cram a fist in my mouth to stop my screams.

I can't let anyone hear. He would know I'm not what I pretend to be. What I *must* be to fix my world.

There I sat on the couch with him, looking at my sister in all those pictures. And each one reminded me how, when we were little, in every single picture taken of us together, her arm was around me, protecting me, watching out for me.

She was happy in the pictures Darroc showed me. Dancing. Talking with friends. Sightseeing. He'd taken so many of her photo albums from her apartment. Left us with hardly any. As if the paltry few months he'd spent with her gave him more right to her possessions than *me*—who'd spent my whole life loving her!

I hadn't been able to trace my fingers over her face in front of him because it would have betrayed emotion, weakness. I'd had to lavish all my attention on *him*. He'd watched me the entire time with those glittering copper eyes, absorbing every detail of my reaction.

I knew it would be a deadly mistake—and the last I ever made—to underestimate the ancient, brilliant mind behind those cold metallic eyes.

After what seemed like years of torture, he finally began to look tired, yawning, even rubbing his eyes.

I forget his body is human, subject to limits.

Eating Unseelie doesn't keep you from needing sleep. Like caffeine or speed, it wires you hard but, when you crash, you crash just as hard. I suspect that's a large part of the reason he never sleeps more than one night in the same place. It's when he's most vulnerable. I imagine it must chafe, to have a human body that needs sleep after having been Fae and not needing anything for eternity.

I decide that's when I'll kill him. When he's sleeping. After I've gotten what I want. I'll wake him and, while he's still feeling humanly muddled, I'll smile and drive my spear through his heart. And I'll say, "This is for Alina and for Jericho."

My fist isn't keeping my sobs down.

They're beginning to leak around it in soft moans. I'm lost in pain, fragments of memories crashing over me: Alina waving good-bye at the gate the day she left for Dublin; Mom and Dad tied to chairs, gagged and bound, waiting for a rescue that never came; Jericho Barrons, dead on the ground.

Every muscle in my body spasms and I can't breathe. My chest feels hot, tight, crushed beneath a massive weight.

I fight to keep the sobs in. If I open my mouth to breathe, they'll come out, but I'm waging a hopeless battle: Sob and breathe? Or don't sob and suffocate?

My vision starts to dim. If I lose consciousness from holding my breath, at least one great cry will explode from me.

Is he at my door, listening?

I dredge my mind for a memory to banish the pain.

When I recovered from being *Pri-ya,* I was horrified to realize that, although my time with the princes and afterward at the abbey was blurred, I retained every single memory of what Barrons and I had done together in bed in graphic detail.

Now I'm grateful for them.

I can use them to keep myself from screaming.

You're leaving me, Rainbow Girl.

No—that's the wrong one!

I rewind, fast.

There. The first time he came to me, touched me, was inside me. I give myself over to it, replaying every detail in loving memory.

In time, I'm able to remove my fist. The tension in my body eases.

Warm in memories, my body shivers on the cold marble bathroom floor.

Alina's cold. Barrons is cold.

I should be cold, too.

When I finally sleep, the cold invades my dreams. I pick my way through jagged-edged ravines gouged into cliffs of black ice. I know this place. The paths I walk are familiar, as if I've walked them a hundred times before. Creatures watch me from caverns chiseled into the frozen walls.

I catch glimpses of the beautiful, sad woman slipping barefoot across the snow, just ahead. She's calling to me. But each time she opens her mouth, an icy wind steals her words. *You must*—I catch, before a gust carries the rest of her sentence away.

I cannot—she cries.

Make haste! she warns over her shoulder.

I run after her in my dreams, trying to hear what she's saying. Stretching out my hand to catch her.

But she stumbles at the edge of an abyss, loses her footing, and is gone.

I stare, stunned and horrified.

The loss is unbearable, as if I myself have died.

I awaken violently, snapping up from the floor, gasping.

I'm still trying to process the dream when my body jerks and begins to move like a pre-programmed automaton.

I watch in terror as my legs make me rise, force me to leave the bathroom. My feet carry me across the room, my hands open the balcony doors. My body is propelled by an unseen power into the darkness, beyond the protection of my crimson ward line.

I'm not functioning of my own volition. I know it, and I can't stop myself. I'm completely unprotected where I stand. I don't even have my spear. Darroc took it away before the prince sifted me out.

I stare out at a shadowy outline of rooftops, awaiting, dreading whatever command might come next. Knowing I won't be able to refuse subsequent orders any more than I could this one.

I'm a puppet. Someone is yanking my strings.

As if to underscore that point, or perhaps merely to make a mockery of me, my arms suddenly shoot straight up into the air, flail wildly above my head before dropping limply back to my sides.

I watch my feet as they shuffle a cheery two-step. I wish I could believe I'm dreaming, but I'm not.

I dance on the balcony, soft-shoeing it faster and faster.

Just as I begin to wonder if I'm going to be the fairy-tale girl that danced herself to death, my feet go still. Panting, I curl my fingers tightly around the wrought-iron railing. If my unknown puppet master decides I'm to fling myself off the balcony next, it's in for a hell of a fight.

Is it Darroc? Why would he do this? *Can* he do this? Does he have so much power?

The temperature drops so sharply that my hands ice to the railing. When I jerk them away, ice shatters and falls into the night below, tinkling against pavement. Small patches of skin from my fingertips remain on the railing. I back up, determined not to commit forced suicide.

Never hurt you, Mac, the *Sinsar Dubh* croons in my mind.

I inhale sharply. The air is so bitterly cold it burns my throat and lungs.

"You just did," I grit.

I feel its curiosity. It doesn't understand how it hurt me. Skin heals.

That was not pain.

I stiffen. I don't like its tone. It is too silky, too full of promise. I try desperately to get to my dark lake in time to arm myself against it, to defend myself, but a wall erupts between me and my watery abyss, and I can find no way around or through it.

The *Sinsar Dubh* forces me to my knees. I strain against it every inch of the way, teeth clenched. It whips me around and I collapse onto my back. My arms and legs fly out as if I'm making snow angels. I'm pinned to cold metal girders.

This, *Mac,* the *Sinsar Dubh* purrs, *is pain.*

I drift in agony. I have no idea how long it tortures me, but the entire time I'm excruciatingly aware of one thing: Barrons isn't going to save me.

He isn't going to roar me back to reality like he did

the last time the Book crushed me in the street, the last time it "tasted me."

He isn't going to carry me back to the bookstore when it's over, make me cocoa and wrap me in blankets. He isn't going to make me laugh by demanding to know what *I* am or later cause me to weep when I steal a memory from his head and see him shattered by grief, holding a dying child.

While the Book keeps me spread-eagled against the cold steel of the balcony floor, while every cell in my body is charred, and every bone is systematically crushed one by one, I cling to memories.

I can't get to my lake, but I can get to the outer layers of my mind. The *Sinsar Dubh* is there, too, examining my thoughts, probing. "Learning me," as it said once before. What is it looking for?

I tell myself I just have to survive it. That it isn't really harming my body. It's only playing with me. It came for me tonight. I hunt it. And for some reason beyond my fathoming, it hunts me. The Book's idea of a macabre joke?

It's not going to kill me. At least not today. I guess I amuse.

It will only make me wish I was dead, and, hey—I know that feeling. Been walking around with it for a while.

After an indefinite, endless length of time, the pain finally eases and I'm yanked to my feet.

My hands grab the railing, and my upper body is contorted over it.

I curl my fingers tightly. I lock my legs down. I summon every ounce of energy I have to make my bones whole and strong again. I stare out at the rooftops, fortifying my will.

I will not die.

If I die tonight, the world will stay the way it is right

now, and that's unacceptable. Too many people have been killed. Too many people will continue to die if I'm not here to do something about it. Fueled by the need to defend something greater than myself, I gather my will and launch myself like a missile for the lake inside my head.

I slam into the wall the *Sinsar Dubh* has erected between me and my arsenal.

A hairline fracture appears.

I don't know who's more startled, me or the *Sinsar Dubh*.

Then suddenly it's angry.

I feel its fury, but it's not angry because I cracked the wall it erected. It's angry for some other reason.

It's as if I, personally, have pissed it off somehow.

It's . . . disappointed in me?

I find that inexpressibly disturbing.

My head is ratcheted around on my spine and I'm forced to stare down.

A person stands below me, a dark splash against the brilliant snow, a book tucked beneath its arm.

The person tilts its head back and looks up.

I chomp back a scream.

I recognize the hooded cloak that swirls softly back, teased by a light breeze. I recognize the hair.

But I don't recognize anything else because—if it really *is* Fiona, Barrons' ex-storekeeper and Derek O'Bannion's mistress—she's been skinned alive. The horror of it is that, because O'Bannion taught her to eat Unseelie, she hasn't died from it.

Instinct makes me reach for my spear. Of course it's not there.

"Mercy!" Fiona screams. Her skinned lips bare bloodied teeth.

And I wonder: Do I have any mercy left in me? Did I reach for my spear because I pity her?

Or because I hate her for having had Jericho Barrons before me, and for longer?

The Book's anger with me grows.

I feel it spilling out, filling the streets. It's immense, barely contained.

I'm baffled.

Why does it hold itself in check? Why not destroy everything? I would, if it would just hold still long enough to let me use it. Then I'd re-create it all the way I wanted it.

Suddenly it morphs into the Beast, a shadow blacker than blackness. It expands, soars, towers up and up, until it is eye level with me.

It hangs there in the air, flashing back and forth between its own terrible visage and the meat of Fiona's flayed face.

I squeeze my eyes shut.

When I open them again, I'm alone.

12

Stupid feckin' stupid feckers!" I kick a can down the alley. It whizzes into the air, hits a brick wall, and flattens into it.

And—*dude*—I mean "into" it. Couple inches deep. I snicker, knowing somebody'll walk by one day and be like: *Dude, how the feck did that can get embedded in the wall?*

Just one more Mega O'Malley Mystery! City's full of 'em.

I leave traces of me all over Dublin. My way of saying "*I* was here!" I been marking it up for years, ever since Ro started sending me out on my own to do stuff for her. Used to stick with little things, like bending sculptures in front of the museum just enough that *I* knew they were different but nobody else would prolly notice. But since the walls came down, it don't matter no more. I embed things in brick and stone, rearrange chunks o' rubble to spell out *MEGA,* hammer lampposts into twisty *D*s for "Dani" and "Dangerous" and "Dude."

I put a little swagger in my step.

Superstrength is me.

I scowl. "Stupid feckin' feckers," I mutter.

Hormonal is me. Up one minute, down the next. My moods change quick as my feet fly. One minute I can't wait to grow up and have sex; the next I hate people, and men are people; and, *dude*—isn't semen about the most disgusting thing you ever seen? Like, *eew,* who wants some dude to squirt snot in their mouth?

Been on my own for a couple days now, and it's swee-*eeeet!* Nobody telling me what to do. Ain't gotta go to bed. Nobody telling me what to think. Just me and my shadow—and we are two cool fecks. Who wouldn't wanna be me?

Still . . . I worry about those stupid sheep at the abbey.

Feck, no, I don't! If they don't wanna pull their heads outta their asses, ain't my trubs!

Too bad some peeps don't know to take me seriously. Gonna have to mess up their world to get 'em to see me.

Been at Chester's again.

Took seven of the slithery fecks to keep me out this time. Kept telling 'em I needed to talk to Ry-O, 'cause I think he's their leader when Barrons ain't around.

And Barrons *ain't* around.

Hunted high and low for him last night after my eye-balls got grossed out by Mac swapping nasties with the Lord Monster.

Dude—what's with that? She could have V'lane or Barrons! Who'd wanna swap spit with an Unseelie-eater? 'Specially the one that caused this whole fecking mess! Where'd she go for so long? What *happened* to her?

They wouldn't let me into Chester's. A-fecking-gain! Getting old, real old, it is. Ain't like I wanna drink or nothing. Stuff's poison. Just wanted to clue 'em in.

Finally told 'em to tell Ry-O I think Mac's in trouble. Hanging out with Darroc. Two princes protecting him.

Think he's brainwashed her or something. Gotta get her back again. Wanted backup to cover me while I take 'em all out. Ain't got my *sidhe*-sheep behind me. Since leaving the abbey, I'm Persona Non Grovel, and groveling's the only way you get anything from Ro and her herd. Even Jo wouldn't leave the abbey. Said it's too late for Mac.

That's where Ry-O was s'posed to come in. Told his freaks I was taking the Lord Monster out tonight and they could help if they wanted.

Or not.

Don't need nobody. Not me.

Mega on the move! Faster than the wind! Leaps tall buildings in a single bound!

Dude!

Zzzoooom!

I study myself in the mirror with cold detachment. A smile curves the lips of the woman looking back.

The *Sinsar Dubh* paid me a visit last night. It reminded me of its crushing power, treated me to a taste of its sadism. But, far from being cowed by it, I'm more resolved than ever.

It must be stopped, and the person who knows how to accomplish that most quickly is sitting in the adjoining room, laughing at something one of his guards just said.

So many people are dead because of him. And he's out there laughing. I realize now that Darroc was always more dangerous than Mallucé.

Mallucé looked horrific and behaved like a monster, but he rarely killed those in his enclave of worshippers.

Darroc is attractive, charming, affectionate, and he can orchestrate the annihilation of three billion humans without batting an eye, without losing an ounce of that charm. On the heels of mass homicide, he can smile at me and tell me how much he cared about my sister, show me pictures of them "having fun" together. Then kill three billion more if he gets his hands on the Book?

Merged with it, what would he be capable of? Would he stop at anything? Is he using me as detachedly as I'm trying to use him and the moment he gets what he wants I'm a dead woman?

We're locked in mortal combat. It's a war I will do anything to win.

I smooth my dress, turn to the side, point a toe, and admire the line of my leg in heels. I have new clothes. After wearing functional clothing, being pretty feels strange, frivolous.

But necessary for the monster of frivolous appetites out there.

Last night after the Book vanished, I'd tried to sleep but had succeeded only in getting tangled up in half-awake nightmares. I was at Darroc's mercy, being raped by the princes again; then the unseen fourth was there, turning me inside out; then I felt the sting of needles at my nape as he tattooed my skull; then the princes were on me again; and then I was at the abbey, shivering with unquenchable lust on the floor of the cell, my bones melting, fusing to each other, my need for sex was pain beyond imagining; then Rowena was looming over me, and I clung to her, but she crushed a funny-smelling cloth to my face. I fought, I kicked, I clawed, but I was no match for the old woman and, in my nightmare, I'd died.

I'd not tried to sleep again.

I'd stripped, stood in the shower, and let the scalding spray punish my skin. Sun worshipper to the core, I've never been cold so often in my life as I have these past few months in Ireland.

After scrubbing myself pink and as clean as I was

going to ever be again, I'd toed my pile of black leather with distaste.

I'd been wearing the same underwear for too long. My leather pants had been soaked, dried, shrunk, stained. It was the outfit I'd killed Barrons in. I wanted to burn it.

I'd wrapped myself in a sheet and stepped into the living room of the penthouse, where dozens of Darroc's crimson-clad Unseelie were standing guard. I'd given them detailed instructions on where to go and what to get for me.

When they'd moved toward another bedroom suite to wake Darroc to obtain permission, I'd snapped, *He doesn't let you make your own decisions? He freed you only to dictate your every move and breath? One or two of you can't go run a few simple little errands for me? Are you Unseelie or lapdogs?*

The Unseelie are chock-full of emotion. Unlike the Seelie, they've not learned to conceal it. I got what I wanted—bags and boxes of clothing, shoes, jewelry, and makeup.

All weapons, good.

Now, as I admire myself in the mirror, I'm grateful I was born pretty. I need to know what he responds to. What his weaknesses are. How much weakness I can get him to feel for me. He used to be Seelie. It is what he is at the core, and I got an intimate look at what the Seelie are like last night.

Imperious. Beautiful. Arrogant.

I can be that.

I have little patience. I want answers and I want them quickly.

I finish my makeup with care, dusting extra bronzer across my cheeks and the upper curves of my breasts, mimicking the gold-dusted skin of the Fae.

My yellow dress clings to a body toned to perfection

by marathon sex with Barrons. My shoes and accessories are gold.

I will look every inch his princess.

When I kill him.

He stops talking when he sees me and looks at me for a long moment. "Your hair was once blond like hers," he says finally.

I nod.

"I liked her hair."

I turn to the nearest guard and tell him what I need to change my hair. He looks at Darroc, who nods.

I toss my head. "I ask for simple things, yet they question me. It's infuriating! Can you not give me two of your guards for my own?" I demand. "Am I to have nothing for myself?"

He's looking at my legs, long and sleekly muscled, and my feet, pretty in high heels. "Of course," he murmurs. "Which two do you wish?"

I wave a hand dismissively. "You choose. They're all the same."

He assigns a pair to carry out my wishes. "You will obey her as you would obey me," he tells them. "Instantly and without question. Unless her orders conflict with mine."

They will become accustomed to obeying me. His other guards will become accustomed to seeing them obey me. Tiny gains, tiny erosions.

I join him for breakfast and smile as I choke down food that tastes of blood and ashes.

The *Sinsar Dubh* is rarely active during the day.

Like the rest of the Unseelie, it prefers the night. Those who were so long imprisoned in ice and darkness seem to find the sunlight jarring, painful. The longer I walk around with this grief inside me, the more I understand that. It's as if sunshine is a slap in the face that says, *Look, the world's all bright and shiny! Too bad* you're *not.*

I wonder if that's why Barrons was rarely around during the day. Because he, too, was damaged like us and found comfort in the secrecy of shadows. Shadows are wonderful things. They hide pain and conceal motives.

Darroc leaves for the day with a small contingent of his army and refuses to take me with him. I want to push, I feel like a caged animal, but he has lines that I know better than to cross if I want him to trust me.

I pass the afternoon in his penthouse, fluttering around like a bright butterfly, picking up things, flipping through books and looking in cabinets and drawers, exclaiming over this or that, searching the place under guise of curiosity, beneath the watchful eyes of his guards.

I find nothing.

They refuse to let me in his bedroom.

Two can play that game. I refuse to let anyone in mine. I beef up my protection runes to keep my backpack and stones safe. I'll get into his bedroom one way or another.

Late in the afternoon, I color my hair, blow it dry, and style it into a tousle of big, loose curls.

I'm blond again. How strange. I remember Barrons calling me a perky rainbow. It makes me long for a white miniskirt and pink camisole.

Instead, I slip into a blood-red dress, high-heeled black boots that hug my legs all the way up to mid-thigh, and a black leather coat with fur at the collar and cuffs, which I belt snugly at my waist to show off my curves. Black gloves, a brilliant scarf, and diamonds at my ears and throat complete my ensemble. With most of Dublin dead, shopping is a dream. Too bad I don't care anymore.

When Darroc returns, I know by the look in his eyes that I've chosen well. He thinks I picked black and red for *him*, the colors of his guard, the colors he has told me he selected for his future court.

I chose black and red for the tattoos on Barrons' body. Tonight I wear my promise to him that I will make things right.

"Isn't your army coming with us?" I ask as we step from the penthouse. The night is cool and clear, the sky glittering with stars. The snow melted during the day, and the cobblestone streets are dry for a novel change.

"Hunters abhor the lesser castes."

"Hunters?" I echo.

"How did you expect to search for the *Sinsar Dubh*?"

I've ridden one before, with Barrons, the night we tried to corner the Book with three of the four stones. I wonder if Darroc knows this. With his clever mirror hidden in the back alley of Barrons Books and Baubles, there's no telling how much he knows about me. "And if we find it tonight?"

He smiles. "If you find it for me tonight, MacKayla, I will make you my queen."

I give him a once-over. He's dressed richly, in Armani tweed, cashmere, and leather. He carries nothing. Is the key to merging with the Book knowledge? A ritual? Runes? An object? "Do you have what you need to merge with it?" I ask point-blank.

He laughs. "Ah, it's to be the full frontal attack tonight. With that dress," he says silkily, "I had hoped for seduction."

I lift a shoulder and let it fall in a carefree shrug that matches my smile. "You know I want to know. I don't see any point in pretending otherwise. We are what we are, you and I."

He likes that I classify us in the same category. I see it in his eyes.

"And what is that, MacKayla? What are *we*?" He turns slightly to the side and bites out a sharp command in an alien tongue. One of the Unseelie Princes appears, listens, nods, and vanishes.

"Survivors. Two people who won't be ruled, because we were born to rule."

He searches my face. "Do you really believe that?"

The street cools and my coat is abruptly dusted with tiny shimmering crystals of black ice. I know what that means. A Royal Hunter has materialized above us, black leathery wings churning the night air. My hair stirs in an icy breeze. I glance up at the scaled underbelly of the caste specially designated to hunt and kill *sidhe-seers*.

A great Satanic dragon, it tucks its massive wings close to its body and drops heavily to the street, narrowly missing the buildings on either side.

It's enormous.

Unlike the smaller Hunter that Barrons managed to bend to his will and "dampen" the night we flew across Dublin, this one is one hundred percent undiluted Royal Hunter. I get a sense of immense ancientness. It feels older than anything I've seen or sensed flying the night sky. The hellish cold it exudes, the sense of despair and emptiness it radiates, is intact. But it doesn't depress me or make me feel futile. This one makes me feel . . . free.

It takes a delicate mental jab at me. I sense restraint. It doesn't have power, it *is* power.

I jab back with my glassy lake's help.

It *chuffs* a soft noise of surprise.

I return my attention to Darroc.

Sidhe-*seer?* the Hunter says.

I ignore it.

SIDHE-*SEER?* The Hunter blasts into my mind so hard it gives me an instant headache.

I whip my head around. "What?" I snarl.

A great black shape, it crouches in the shadows. Head low, the underside of its chin brushes the pavement. It shifts its weight from taloned foot to foot, as its massive tail sweeps the street clean of long-unused trash cans and husks of human remains. Fiery eyes blaze into mine.

I feel it pressing at me mentally, carefully. Fae legend says that the Hunters either aren't Fae or aren't entirely Fae. I have no idea what they are, but I don't like them inside my head.

After a moment it says, *Ahhhh,* and settles onto its haunches. *There you are.*

I don't know what that means. I shrug. It's out of my head, and that's all I care about. I turn back to Darroc, who resumes our conversation where it left off. "Do you really believe what you said about being born to rule?"

"Have I ever asked you where my parents are?" I counter with a question that it hurts my heart to ask, hurts my soul to even think, but I'm in an all-or-nothing mood. If I can get what I want tonight, I'm out of here. My pain and suffering will end. I can stop hating myself. By morning, I could be talking to Alina again, touching Barrons.

His gaze sharpens. "When you first saw that I was holding them captive, I thought you weak, ruled by maudlin attachment. Why have you not asked?"

I understand now why Barrons was always insisting I stop asking him questions and judge him by his actions alone. It's so easy to lie. What's even worse is how we cling to those lies. We beg for the illusion so we don't have to face the truth, don't have to feel alone.

I remember being seventeen, thinking I was head over heels in love, asking my date at the senior prom—tight-end hot-Rod McQueen—*Katie didn't* really *see you kissing Brandi in the hall outside the bathroom, did she, Rod?* And when he said, *No,* I believed him—despite the smudge of lipstick on his chin that was too red to be mine and the way Brandi kept looking at us over her date's shoulder. Two weeks into summer, no one was surprised when he was her boyfriend, not mine.

I stare into Darroc's face and I see something in his eyes that elates me. He's not kidding about making me his queen. He *does* want me. I don't know why, perhaps because he imprinted on Alina and I'm the closest thing that remains. Perhaps because he and my sister discovered who they were together, and what they were capable of, and conjoined self-discovery is a powerful bond. Perhaps because of my strange dark glassy lake or whatever it is that makes the *Sinsar Dubh* like to play with me.

Perhaps it's because part of him is human, and he hungers for the same illusions the rest of us do.

Barrons was a purist. I get him now. Words are *so* dangerous.

I say, "Things change. I adapt. I cut away what is unnecessary as my circumstances change." I reach up and caress his face, brush my index finger to his perfect lips, trace his scar. "And often I find my circumstances have not worsened, as I initially thought, but improved. I don't know why I refused you so many times. I understand why my sister wanted you." I say it all so simply that it rings of truth. Even I am startled by how sincere I sound. "I think you *should* be king, Darroc, and if you want me, I would be honored to be your queen."

He sucks in a sharp breath, his copper eyes glittering. He cups my head and buries his hands in my hair, playing the silky curls through his fingers. "Prove that you mean those words, MacKayla, and I will deny you nothing. Ever."

He angles my head and lowers his mouth to mine.

I close my eyes. I open my lips.

That's when it kills him.

13

I've had a few paradigm shifts since the day my plane landed in Ireland and I began hunting Alina's killer—big ones, or so I thought—but this one takes the cake.

There I stand, eyes closed, lips parted, waiting for the kiss of my sister's lover, when suddenly something wet and warm slaps my face, drips from my chin, drenches my neck, and runs into my bra. More splatters my coat.

When I open my eyes, I scream.

Darroc is no longer about to kiss me, because his head is gone—just gone—and you're never ready for that, no matter how cold and hard and dead you think you are inside. Being sprayed by the blood of a headless corpse—especially someone you know, whether you like him or not—gets you on a visceral level. Doubly so when you were about to kiss that person.

But even more upsetting is that I don't know how to merge with the Book.

All I can think is: *His head is gone and I don't know how to merge with the Book.* He eats Unseelie. Can I put his head back on? If I do, can he talk? Maybe I can patch him up and torture it out of him.

I fist my hands, furious at this turn of events.

I was a kiss away—okay, maybe a few nights of sleeping with the enemy and despising myself more than I ever thought possible—from getting what I wanted. But it was going to happen. I was gaining his trust. I'd seen it in his eyes. He was going to confide in me. He was going to tell me all his secrets and I was going to kill him and fix the world.

And now his head is no longer on his body, and I don't know what I needed to know, and I can't *live* in this hellish reality for the months it could take me to get the four, the five, and the prophecy.

My entire mission was distilled to one goal—and now that goal is tottering, decapitated, in front of me!

It's a total bust.

I let him touch me for nothing.

I stare at the bloody stump of his neck as his body staggers in a small circle without a head. I'm astounded he's still moving. It must be the Unseelie in his veins.

He stumbles and collapses to the ground. Somewhere nearby, I hear garbled sounds. Oh, God, his head is still talking.

Good! Can he form sentences? I'm in a strong bargaining position. *Tell me what I want, and I'll put your head back on.*

I frown. Where are the princes? Why didn't they protect him? Wait a minute! *Who* did this to him?

Am I next?

I glance wildly around.

"Whuh," I manage. I can't process it.

Sidhe-*seer,* the Hunter purrs in my mind.

I stare blankly. The Hunter that Darroc summoned for us to ride is crouched a dozen paces away, dangling Darroc's head by the hair, swinging it from a taloned claw.

If Hunters smile, this one is. Leathery lips crack on saber teeth, and it *oozes* amusement.

Its . . . hand, for lack of a better word, is the size of a small car. How did it so tidily rip off Darroc's head?

Did it pinch it off with its talons? It happened absurdly fast.

Why would it kill him?

Darroc was allied with the Hunters. It was the Hunters that taught him to eat Unseelie. Did they—as I once warned him they would—tire of him and turn on him?

I reach for my spear. It's back. Great, the princes are definitely gone. But before I can pull it out, the Hunter laughs, dry and dusty, in my mind, and I am assaulted by a sense of age that defies time, of sanity that was forged down a long path of madness. It *was* muting itself before. This one is very different from the other Hunters.

I wouldn't be surprised to discover it was the granddaddy of them all.

It calls itself K'Vruck. Humans have no word for it. It means a state beyond death. Death is small compared to K'Vruck.

"Huh?" I stammer. The voice was in my mind.

K'Vruck is so much more complete than death. It is the reduction of matter to a state of utter inertness, from which nothing can ever rise again. It is less than nothing. Nothing is something. K'Vruck is absolute. Your species would postulate the loss of soul to try to wrap their puny brains around it.

I stiffen. I know this voice. This mockery. My spear will be no use against it. If I kill the Hunter, it would probably just hop a ride on me.

I will tell you a secret, it says silkily. *You do go on. Humans. Unless you are*—it laughs softly—*K'Vrucked.*

I suck in a ragged breath.

MacKayla, I permit none to control me. Darroc will never use his shortcut, and you will never learn it.

The Hunter pops Darroc's head like a grape. Hair

and bone slap to the pavement. And now that I'm no longer transfixed by the gory sight, I see what the Hunter holds in its *other* hand. Had been holding all along.

I back away faster.

There was never any chance that Darroc and I would soar up into the night, and hunt the *Sinsar Dubh*.

It beat us to the punch.

It hitched a ride on our Hunter and came to us.

And here I am, helpless. I have no stones, my spear is useless—

The amulet! When the Hunter ripped Darroc's head off, it stayed on his body! I feint a wild glance around, trying hard to look at nothing in particular and everything, to keep from telegraphing my intentions.

Where the hell are the princes? They could sift me out of here! What did they do—vanish the moment Darroc was killed? Cowards!

It's there! When Darroc's body collapsed to the ground, the amulet slid off the stump of his neck. Silver and gold, it's lying in a pool of blood, a dozen feet from me! I have power in my glassy lake. With the amulet to reinforce me, is it enough to hold my own?

I turn inward to step onto my black-pebbled beach, but that damned wall springs up before I can get there. The *Sinsar Dubh* laughs. I fractured this wall last night. I'll do it tonight or die trying.

Power is earned, and you have not.

I don't need to look to know it's rising, separating from the Hunter, soaring up, becoming the towering Beast form of the Book, getting ready to crush me with pain.

Or, who knows this time? Maybe it's worse. Maybe it's going to K'Vruck me.

I lunge forward and grab. My fingers brush the chain. I've got it! I'm pulling it toward me!

Then suddenly something slams into my side, and the

amulet is knocked from my grasp and gone. My arm is caught at a bad angle, extended mid-reach, and I hear it snap as I'm pushed into a long, helpless slide on my side, scraping pavement. My head hits the ground and my forehead drags. I feel skin ripping away.

Then I'm being picked up and tossed into the air. I glance wildly around but don't see the amulet anywhere. As I come down, someone flings me over their shoulder. My hair is in my face, my arm dangles limply, and my forehead is bleeding into my eyes. I nearly scalped myself on the pavement.

Everything is moving so fast it's a blur.

Superstrength. Superspeed. I feel motion sickness coming on.

"Dani?" I gasp. Did she come to save me, even though I was such a bitch and drove her away?

"Dani, no! I need the amulet!"

I hang upside down, watching pavement whiz by.

"Dani, stop!"

But she doesn't. I hear snarling receding rapidly behind us.

The Hunter roars.

Bloodcurdling howls shatter the night.

I jerk. I know those sounds. I've heard them before.

"Take me back, take me back!" I scream, but for an entirely different reason now. Who are they—these beasts that sound like Barrons? I need to know!

"Dani, you have to take me *back*!"

But she doesn't. She keeps running. Doesn't listen to a word I say. She runs me straight to the one place I never want to see again.

Barrons Books and Baubles.

14

My first suspicion that it wasn't Dani carrying me reared its head when we blasted through the front door of the bookstore.

Or, rather, that suspicion *turned* its head and licked blood from the back of my thigh.

Unless Dani had some serious issues I didn't know about, this wasn't her shoulder I was over.

It licked me again, dragging its tongue across my leg, just beneath the curve of my ass. My dress was hitched up, trapped between my stomach and its shoulder. It bit me. Hard.

"Ow!"

With fangs. Not deep enough to draw blood but enough to sting. I wiped my sleeve across my face, scrubbing blood from my eyes with the fur cuff.

I was dazed by Darroc's abrupt murder and my shock over K'Vruck being the Book. If I'd been thinking clearly, I'd have known from the first that I was much too high from the ground for it to have been Dani. Several feet too high.

The shoulder I was over was massive, as was the rest of it, but it was too dark to see clearly. Rooftop spotlights no longer illuminated the exterior of the book-store, nor did the customary amber glow bathe the interior. There was only the light of a three-quarter moon, spilling in through tall windows.

What had me? An Unseelie? Why had it brought me here? I never wanted to see this place again! I hated BB&B. It was dark and empty and ghosts were every-where. They perched with sad eyes on my cash register, drooped along my book aisles, and draped, paper-thin and defeated, on my sofas, shivering before fireplaces that would never be lit again.

I wasn't prepared to be flung from its shoulder. I went flying backward through the air, slammed into the ches-terfield in the rear seating cozy, bounced off it, crashed into a chair, got tangled in one of Barrons' expensive rugs, and skidded across the polished floor. My head smacked into the enameled fireplace.

For a moment, all I could do was lie there. Every bone in my body was bruised. Blood was crusted on my face and in the corners of my eyes.

With a moan of pain, I rolled over and propped my-self up on an elbow to assess the damage. At least my arm wasn't broken, as I'd thought it was.

I pushed my hair from my face.

And froze. Standing in the dim light of the bookstore was a shape that was devastatingly familiar. "Come out of the shadows," I said.

A low growl was the only reply.

"Please, can you understand me? Come out."

It hulked near a bookcase, panting. It was enormous, at least nine feet tall. Silhouetted against the moonlight filtering through a window behind it, it had three sets of sharp, curved horns spaced at even intervals along two bony ridges that spanned the sides of its head.

I'd seen horns like that before. My pouch of stones had been tied to similar ones. Horns I'd watched melt away when the beast wearing them resumed its human form.

In the Silvers, Barrons had been slate gray with yellow eyes during the day and black-skinned with crimson eyes at night. This one was in full night mode, velvety black in the darkness but for the glint of feral eyes. I'd heard more of these beasts back in the street, before this one had carried me off. Where had they come from?

My hands began to tremble. I pushed gingerly into a sitting position, acutely aware of every stretched tendon and strained muscle. I leaned back against the fireplace, drew my knees up and hugged them. I didn't trust myself to stand. This creature was the same kind of beast Barrons had been and was a connection to the man I'd lost.

What was it doing here? Was he still somehow protecting me, even in death? Had he assigned others of his kind to guard me if the worst happened and he was killed?

The thing in the shadows suddenly turned and smashed a taloned fist into the bookcase. Tall shelves rocked on floor bolts. With a metallic *screeeech*, the ornate case ripped from the floor and began to fall. It crashed into the one next to it, and the one next to that, taking them down like dominoes, making a complete wreck of my bookstore.

"Stop it!" I cried.

But if it could understand, or even hear me over the noise, it didn't care. It turned on the magazine rack and shattered it next. Dailies and monthlies flew in a storm of pages and splinters of shelving. Chairs slammed into the walls. My TV was stomped. My fridge crushed. My cash register exploded in a tinkle of bells.

It raged through the store, trashing the entire first floor, decimating everything I loved, reducing my cherished sanctuary to ruins.

All I could do was huddle and stare.

When there was nothing left to smash or break, it whirled on me.

Moonlight silvered its ebony skin and glinted off crimson eyes. Veins and tendons stood out on its arms and neck, and its chest pumped like a bellows. Bits of debris were stuck to its horns. It shook its head violently, and bits of plaster and wood sprayed the air.

It stared at me from a prehistoric face, through long hanks of matted black hair, with hate-filled eyes.

I stared back, afraid to breathe. Had it saved me to kill me? It was no more than I deserved, really.

It was a walking reminder of what I'd had—and lost. What I'd never seen clearly—and killed. It was so much like my creature in the Silvers, yet so different. Barrons had been uncontrollably homicidal, unable—or unwilling—to prevent himself from slaughtering everything in sight, no matter how small or helpless. Back on that cliff's edge, in Barrons' eyes, I'd glimpsed madness.

This beast was a killing machine, too, but not a mindless one. There was no insanity in its eyes, only fury and bloodlust.

It was Barrons .·. . but it wasn't.

I closed my eyes. Looking at it hurt my soul.

It growled deep in its chest, much closer than it had been a moment ago.

My eyes snapped open.

It stood a half dozen feet away, towering over me, brimming with unspent rage. Feral eyes were fixed on my neck, taloned hands opened and closed as if it wanted nothing more than to wrap them around it and squeeze.

I rubbed the base of my skull, grateful for Barrons' mark. Apparently it was still protecting me, because the creature hadn't harmed me, although it wanted to. I wondered if his mark protected me from the entire "pack" of Barrons-like creatures. He'd said he'd never let me die. It seemed he'd taken measures to continue his protection if something happened to him. Like Ryodan and me and a spear.

"Thank you," I whispered.

My words seemed to enrage it. It lunged for me, grabbed me by the collar of my coat, raised me in the air, and shook me like a rag doll. My teeth clacked together and my bones rattled.

Perhaps the mark wasn't protecting me after all.

I wasn't dying here tonight. The itinerary of my mission might have changed, but my goal had not. As I dangled, toes skimming the floor, I let my gaze go unfocused, sought my lake, and summoned my crimson runes. They'd kept the Unseelie Princes at a standoff, and the Fae princes were far more deadly and powerful than this beast.

Other things floated on the surface of my lake, but I ignored them. There would be plenty of time—more time than I wanted, I was sure—in my future to explore all that was concealed beneath those dark, still waters. I cupped my hands, scooped up what I'd come for, and snapped out of it, fast.

The beast was still shaking me. Staring into its narrowed eyes, I realized I might need to revise my earlier assessment that it wasn't as insane as Barrons had been.

I raised my fists, dripping blood. The ebon-skinned beast shook its horned head and roared.

"Put me down," I commanded.

It moved so fast that it had my entire hand in its mouth before I could even gasp. The word "down" hadn't even left my lips when my hand was gone and sharp black fangs were locked around my wrist.

But it didn't rip my hand off, as I expected. It *sucked*. Its tongue was wet and warm on my fingers, working delicately between them.

As suddenly as it had swallowed my hand, it dropped it. My fist was empty.

I stared blankly at it. Runes that the most deadly of the Fae feared, this thing *ate*? Like a succulent appetizer? It licked its lips. Was I the main course? In a blur of motion, my other fist disappeared.

Wet pressure on my skin, the silky precision of a tongue, a scrape of fangs against my wrist and that fist, too, was empty.

It dropped me. I landed unevenly on my feet, bumped into the wreck of the chesterfield, and steadied myself.

Still licking its lips, it began to back away.

When it stopped in a milky pool of moonlight, my eyes narrowed. Something was . . . wrong. It didn't look right. In fact, it looked . . . pained.

I had a terrible thought. What if it was a simpleminded beast and I'd just fed it something deadly and it hadn't known better than to eat anything it saw that was bloody—like a dog that couldn't walk away from poisoned hamburger?

I didn't want to kill another of these creatures! Like Barrons, it had saved me!

I stared at it in horror, hoping it would survive whatever I'd done to it. I'd just wanted to get away from it, to find someplace to regroup and summon my strength to forge on. I had a finite number of weapons at my disposal. I had to make good use of them.

It staggered.

Damn it! When would I learn?

It stumbled and dropped heavily to its haunches with a deep, shuddering groan. Muscles began to twitch beneath its skin. It flung its head back and bayed.

I clamped my hands to my ears but, even muffled, it was deafening. I heard answering cries in the distance, joining in mournful concert.

I hoped they weren't loping straight for the bookstore

to join their dying brother and tear me to pieces. I doubted I could trick them all into eating poison runes.

The beast was on all fours now, tossing its massive head from side to side, clearly in its death throes—jaws wide, lips peeled back, fangs bared.

It bayed and bayed, a cry of such desolation and despair that it drove a spike through my heart.

"I didn't mean to kill you!" I cried.

Crouching on the floor, it began to change.

Oh, yes, I'd killed it. This was exactly what had happened when I'd killed Barrons.

Apparently dying forced them to transform.

I was transfixed, unable to look away. I would own this sin like I owned all my others. I would wait until he changed and would commit his face to memory so, in the new world I created with the *Sinsar Dubh*, I could do something special for him.

Perhaps I could save him from becoming what he was. What man breathed inside this beast's skin? One of the other eight Barrons had brought to the abbey the day he'd broken me out? Would I recognize him from Chester's?

Its horns melted and began to run down the sides of its face. Its head became grossly misshapen, expanded and contracted, pulsed and shrank before expanding again—as if too much mass was being compacted into too small a form and the beast was resisting. Massive shoulders collapsed inward, straightened, then collapsed again. It gouged deep splinters of wood from the floor as it bowed upon itself, shuddering.

Talons splayed on the floor, became fingers. Haunches lifted, slammed down, and became legs. But they weren't right. The limbs were contorted, the bones didn't bend where they were supposed to—rubbery in some places, knobbed in others.

Still it bayed, but the sound was changing. I removed

my hands from my ears. The humanity in its howl chilled my blood.

Its misshapen head whipped from side to side. I caught a glimpse through matted hair of wild eyes glittering with moonlight, of black fangs and spittle as it snarled. Then the tangled locks abruptly melted, the sleek black fur began to lighten. It dropped to the floor, spasming.

Suddenly it shot up on all fours, head down. Bones crunched and cracked, settling into a new shape. Shoulders formed—strong, smooth, bunched with muscle. Hands braced wide. One leg stretched back, the other bent as it tensed in a low lunge.

A naked man crouched in the moonlight.

I held my breath, waiting for him to lift his head. Who had I killed with my careless idiocy?

For a moment there was only the sound of his harsh breathing, and mine.

Then he cleared his throat. At least I think he did. It sounded more like a rattlesnake shaking its tail somewhere deep in the back of his mouth. After another moment, he laughed, but it wasn't really a laugh. It was the sound the devil might make the day he came to call your contract due.

When he raised his head, raked the hair from his face, and sneered at me with absolute contempt, I melted silently, bonelessly, to the floor.

"Ah, but my dear, dear Ms. Lane, that's precisely the point. You *did*," Jericho Barrons said.

PART
11

Between the conception
And the creation
Between the emotion
And the response
Falls the Shadow
—T. S. Eliot

There's truth in your lies
Doubt in your faith
What you build you lay to waste.
—Linkin Park, "In Pieces"

Why do you hurt me?

I LOVE YOU.

You're incapable of love.

NOTHING EXCEEDS MY ABILITIES. I AM ALL.

You're a *book*. Pages with binding. You weren't born. You don't live. You're no more than the dumping ground for everything that was wrong with a selfish king.

I AM EVERYTHING THAT WAS RIGHT WITH A WEAK KING. HE FEARED POWER. I KNOW NO FEAR.

What do you want from me?

OPEN YOUR EYES. SEE ME. SEE YOURSELF.

My eyes *are* open. I'm good. You're evil.

—CONVERSATIONS WITH THE *SINSAR DUBH*

15

I never told anyone, but when I first arrived in Dublin, I had a secret fantasy that kept me from buckling during the worst times.

I'd pretend that we'd all been fooled, that the body sent home to Ashford wasn't really Alina's but some other blond coed that looked amazingly like her. I staunchly refused to acknowledge the dental records Daddy had insisted on comparing, a perfect match.

As I'd walked the streets of Temple Bar, hunting her killer, I'd pretended that any minute I was going to turn a corner and there she'd be.

She'd look at me, startled and thrilled, and say, *Junior, what's up? Are Mom and Dad okay? What are you doing here?* And we'd hug each other and laugh, and I'd know that it had all been a nightmare but it was over. We'd have a beer, go shopping, find a beach somewhere on Ireland's rocky coast.

I wasn't prepared for death. Nobody is. You lose someone you love more than you love yourself, and you get a crash course in mortality. You lie awake night after night, wondering if you really believe in heaven and hell and finding all kinds of reasons to cling to faith, because you can't bear to believe they aren't out there somewhere, a few whispered words of a prayer away.

Deep down, I knew it was just a fantasy. But I needed it. It helped for a while.

I didn't permit myself a fantasy with Barrons. I let rage take me because, as Ryodan astutely observed, it's gasoline and makes great fuel. My fury was plutonium. In time, I would have mutated from radiation poisoning.

The worst part about losing someone you love—besides the agony of never getting to see them again—are the things you never said. The unsaid stalks you, mocks you for thinking you had all the time in the world. None of us do.

Here and now, face-to-face with Barrons, my tongue wouldn't move. I couldn't form a single word. The unsaid was ash in my mouth, too dry to swallow, choking me.

But worse than that was the realization that I was being played, *again*. No matter how real this moment seemed, I knew it was nothing but more illusion.

The *Sinsar Dubh* still had me.

I'd never really left the street where it had killed Darroc.

I was still standing, or probably lying in a heap, in front of K'Vruck, being distracted with fantasy while the Book was doing whatever it liked to do to me.

This was no different than the night Barrons and I tried to corner it with the stones and it had made me believe I was crouched on the pavement reading it, when all the while it had been crouching at my shoulder, reading *me*.

I should fight it. I should dive deep into my lake and do what I did best—blunder ahead in a generally forward direction, no matter how bad things got. But as I stared at the perfect replica of him, I couldn't dredge up enough energy to drive the mirage away. Not yet.

There were worse ways to be tortured than with a vision of Jericho Barrons naked.

I would seek my *sidhe*-seer center and shatter it in a minute. Or ten. I leaned back against the fireplace with a faint smile, thinking: *Bring it on*.

The Barrons illusion rose from his half lunge and stood in a ripple of muscle.

God, he was beautiful. I looked up and down. The Book had done an amazingly accurate job, right down to his more generous attributes.

But it had gotten his tattoos wrong. I knew every inch of that body. The last time I saw Jericho Barrons naked, he'd been covered with red and black protection tattoos, and later his arms had been sheathed in them from biceps to wrist. Now the only tattoos he had were on his abdomen.

"You screwed up," I told the Book. "But nice try."

The fake Barrons tensed, knees bending slightly, weight shifting forward, and for a moment I thought he was going to launch himself at me and attack.

"*I* screwed up?" the Barrons figment snarled. He began to stalk toward me. It was difficult to look at his face when there was so much bouncing around at eye level.

"Which word didn't you understand?" I said sweetly.

"Stop staring at my dick," he growled.

Oh, yes, it was definitely an illusion. "Barrons *loved* me staring at his dick," I informed it. "He would have been happy if I'd stared at his dick all day long, composing odes to its perfection."

In one fluid motion, he had me by my collar and was yanking me to my feet. "That was *before* you killed me, you fucking imbecile!"

I was unfazed. Standing toe-to-toe with him was a drug. I needed it. I craved it. I couldn't end this charade for anything. "See, you *admit* you're dead," I parried smoothly. "And I'm not an imbecile. An imbecile would be fooled by you."

"I am *not* dead." He slammed me back against the wall, pinning me with his body.

I was so delighted at being touched by Barrons-esque hands, so thrilled to be staring into the illusion of his dark eyes, that I hardly even felt my head smack into the wall. This was far more realistic than my brief moments with the memory of him in the black wing of the White Mansion. "Are, too."

"Am not."

His mouth was so close. Who cared if it wasn't really him? It had his lips. His parts. Was one fake kiss too much to ask? I wet my lips. "Prove it."

"You expect me to prove I'm not dead?" he said disbelievingly.

"I don't think it's so much to ask. After all, I *did* stab you."

He braced his palms against the wall on either side of my head. "A wiser woman would stop reminding me of that."

I inhaled his scent, spicy, exotic, a cherished memory that made me feel alive. The electric current that always charged the air between us sizzled on my skin. He was naked and I was up against a wall, and even though I knew I was being played by the Book, I could barely focus on his words. It felt so real. Except for those missing tattoos. The Book knew how big his dick was but couldn't get the tattoos right. A small oversight.

"I'm impressed," I murmured. "I really am."

"I don't give a bloody fucking hell if you're impressed, Ms. Lane. I care about one thing and one thing only. Do you know where the *Sinsar Dubh* is? Did you find it for that bloody fucking half-breed bastard?"

"Oh, that's just rich." I snorted with laughter. The *Sinsar Dubh* had created an illusion of a person, and that extension of the *Sinsar Dubh* was asking me where the *Sinsar Dubh* was. "Infinite-regress much?"

"Answer me or I'm going to rip your head off."

Barrons would never do that. The *Sinsar Dubh* had just made another mistake. Barrons had vowed to keep me alive, and he'd stayed true to that vow until the very end. He'd died to save me. He would never hurt me and certainly wouldn't kill me. "You don't know a thing about him," I sneered.

"I know everything about him." He cursed. "About *me*."

"Do not."

"Do, too."

"Bull!"

"Not!"

"Too," I spat.

"Not!" he fired back, then exhaled explosively. "Bloody hell. Ms. Lane, you drive me bloody fucking crazy."

"Right back at you, Barrons. And you can lose all the 'bloodys' and 'fuckings' anytime now. You're overdoing it. The real Barrons never cursed that much."

"I bloody fucking know exactly how many bloody fuckings Barrons would use. You don't know him as well as you think you do."

"Stop pretending to be him!" I shoved at his chest. "You're not and you never will be!"

"Besides, that was *before* you killed me and decided to replace me with Darroc in less than a month! Grieve much, Ms. Lane?"

Oh, how dare he? Grief was all I was. Grief and revenge, walking. "For the record, you've been dead for three days. And I am *so* not doing this. Get out of here. Go. Away." I knocked his hands away from my head and stormed past him. "I'm not defending my reasons for doing what I did to you, when you aren't even really here. That's too psychotic, even for me."

He grabbed me and swung me back around. "You'd better believe I'm here, Ms. Lane, and you'd better believe I'll kill you. You could not have proved your loyalties—or lack thereof—any more completely. You jumped on me the second Ryodan said I was a threat and took me out without an instant's hesitation—"

"I hesitated! I hated killing my guardian beast! Ryodan told me I had to! I didn't know it was you!" Great. Now I was arguing with the *Sinsar Dubh*'s fake Barrons about killing him. Why would it want to do this to me? What could the Book possibly gain from making me live this fight?

"You *should* have known!" he exploded.

I knew I should end it, stop the illusion now, but I couldn't.

Being around Barrons has always made me fire on all pistons, and it didn't seem to matter a bit that I knew this Barrons was a mirage. Some people bring out the worst in you, others bring out the best, and then there are those remarkably rare, addictive ones who just bring out the *most*. Of everything.

They make you feel so alive that you'd follow them straight into hell, just to keep getting your fix.

"How should I have known? Because you've always been so honest with me? Because sharing information is what Jericho Barrons does best, where he *really* shines? No, because you'd bothered to warn me what might happen if I pressed IYD. Wait, I have it: I should have known because you'd confided in me—in the same trusting and open way we've shared so many confidences—that sometimes you turn into a nine-foot-tall, horned, insane monster!"

"I am *not* insane. I was sane enough to piss circles around you. I killed food for you. I picked up your things. Who else do you know that would have done that? V'lane doesn't have dick enough to piss with. Your little MacKeltar doesn't have the balls to own his actions. He certainly isn't capable of doing what it takes to own a woman!"

"Own? You think women can be *owned*?"

He gave me a look that said, *Oh, honey, of course they can. Have you forgotten so quickly?*

"I was *Pri-ya*!"

"And I liked you much better then!" His eyes narrowed as if he'd only finally processed something I'd said earlier. "I've been dead for you for only three bloody *days*? And you already had Darroc up against my wall out back two nights ago? You waited one fucking *day* to line up my replacement? I spent weeks worrying about whether he would scrape my brand off your skull and I wouldn't be able to track you in the Silvers. The entire time I was trying to get back to save your ass from him, you were giving him a piece of it!"

"I didn't give Darroc a piece of anything!" Get back from what, where? Being dead?

"A woman doesn't rub herself up against a man like that unless she's fucking him."

"You don't know the first thing about what I was and wasn't doing. Ever heard of going undercover? Sleeping with the enemy?"

" 'I think you *should* be king, Darroc,' " he mocked in falsetto, " 'and if you want me, I would be *honored* to be your queen.' "

I gaped.

"Isn't that what you said?"

"What were you doing—spying on me? And if you're Barrons, you know better than to believe words."

"Because your actions speak so well of you, do they? Where did you sleep last night, Ms. Lane? It wasn't here.

My bookstore was wide open. Your bedroom was upstairs waiting. So was your fucking honor."

I opened my mouth, then closed it again. Honor? Barrons was flinging the word "honor" at me? Er . . . actually, the *Sinsar Dubh* was. I couldn't decide which was more anachronistic. I frowned. There was something wrong here. Something was very, very off. Although "Barrons" and "honor" weren't two words I'd think to use together in a sentence, I couldn't come up with a single reason for the *Sinsar Dubh* to pull this kind of stunt. It had never inflicted such a prolonged and detailed illusion on me before. I could see nothing it might gain by doing it.

"Do you know why I was in the street with you and Darroc tonight?" When I didn't reply, he snarled, "Answer me!"

I shook my head.

"I wasn't there to spy on you and your little boyfriend. Speaking of which, what's it like to slurp down your sister's sloppy seconds?"

"Oh, fuck you," I said instantly. "That's low even for you."

"You haven't seen anything yet. I came to kill him tonight. I should have done it a long time ago. But I didn't get that pleasure. The *Sinsar Dubh* beat me to it," he said bitterly.

"Enough already. You *are* the *Sinsar Dubh*!"

"Hardly. But I'm every bit as deadly. We can both destroy you. Nothing can save you from me if I turn on you."

It was past time for this illusion to end. The only reason I'd let it go on this long was because it had begun enjoyably and I'd kept hoping it might turn around. But whatever bizarre game the Book was playing, it wasn't going to play nice, and this icy, sneering Barrons wasn't the man I wanted to remember.

"Time for you to go now," I muttered.

"I'm not going anywhere. Ever. If you think for one minute I'll let you flip sides mid-game, you're wrong. I'm invested. You're in too deep. You owe me. I will chain you up, tie you down, leash you with magic, whatever I have to do, but you *will* help me get that Book. And when I've got it, I might let you live."

"You're the *Sinsar Dubh*," I said again, but my protest was weak. While he'd been talking, I'd sought my *sidhe*-seer center—that all-seeing eye that can rip away illusion and reveal the truth beneath it—and I'd focused it like a laser on the mirage.

Nothing had happened. No bubble had burst, no mirage had fractured. My hands were shaking. I couldn't get enough air into my lungs.

It wasn't possible.

I'd *killed* him.

And when I'd realized what I'd done, I'd channeled my grief into a weapon of mass destruction. I'd made a plan, with a set-in-cement past and a concrete future.

This . . . this . . . inexplicability didn't fit anywhere in my understanding of reality. Not with any of my goals, not with what I'd become.

"But then again, I might not," he said. "Unlike some people, *I* don't do sloppy seconds."

I inhaled sharply. I was growing dangerously lightheaded. It couldn't be. He was not actually standing there.

Was he?

It looked like Barrons, felt like Barrons, smelled and sounded like Barrons, and certainly had his attitude.

Screw my *sidhe*-seer center. I needed juice. And I knew where to find it. I let my gaze drift out of focus and frantically sucked raw power from my glassy lake.

Refocusing again, I turned everything I had on the figment.

"Show me the truth," I commanded, and blasted it to bits.

"You wouldn't know the truth if it bit you in the ass, Ms. Lane. Case in point: It just did." He gave me that wolf smile, but it didn't hold an ounce of charm. It was all teeth, reminding me of fangs against my skin.

My knees gave out.

Jericho Barrons was still standing there.

Towering, naked, and pissed off as hell, hands fisted as if he was about to beat the crap out of me.

Puddled on the floor, I stared up at him. "You're n-not d-dead." My teeth were chattering so hard I could barely force the words past my lips.

"Sorry to disappoint." If looks could kill, the one he shot me would have sunk me six feet deep in scorpions. "Oh, wait a minute. No, I'm not."

It was too much. My head was spinning and my vision began to go dark.

I fainted.

16

Consciousness returned in slow degrees. I came to on the floor of the bookstore in the dark.

I always thought fainting showed an inherent weakness of character, but I understood it now. It was an act of self-preservation. Confronted by emotion too extreme to handle, the body shuts down to keep from running around like a chicken with its head cut off, potentially injuring itself.

The realization that Barrons was alive had been more than I could deal with. Too many thoughts and feelings had tried to coalesce at once. My brain had tried to process that the impossible was possible, make words for all I was feeling, and I'd silently imploded.

"Barrons?" I rolled over onto my back. There was no reply. I was gripped by the sudden fear that it had all been a dream. That he wasn't really alive, and I was going to have to come to terms with that unbearable fact—again.

I shot up to a sitting position, and my heart sank.

I was alone. Had it all been a cruel illusion, a dream? I glanced wildly around, seeking proof of his existence.

The bookstore was a wreck. *That* much hadn't been

a dream. I began to stand and stopped, realizing there was a sheet of paper taped to my coat. Dazedly, I pulled it off.

If you leave this bookstore and make me track you, I will make you regret it to the end of your days. ~Z

I began to laugh and cry at the same time. I sat, clutching the paper to my chest, elated.

He was alive!

I had no idea how it was possible. I didn't care. Jericho Barrons lived. He walked this world. That was enough for me.

I closed my eyes, shuddering as a crushing weight slipped from my soul. I breathed, really breathed for the first time in three days, filling my lungs greedily.

I hadn't killed him.

I wasn't to blame. I'd somehow been granted with Barrons what I'd never gotten with my sister—and I hadn't even had to demolish the world for it: *a second chance!*

I opened my eyes, read the note again, and laughed.

He was *alive*.

He'd ruined my bookstore. He'd written me a letter. A lovely, lovely letter! Oh, happy day!

I stroked the sheet upon which he'd scrawled his threat. I loved this sheet of paper. I loved his threat. I even loved my wrecked shop. It would take time, but I would restore it. Barrons was back. I would rebuild the shelves, replace the furniture, and one day in the future I would sit on my sofa and stare into a fire and Barrons would walk in, and he wouldn't even have to say anything. We could just sit in companionable or—who cared?—grumpy silence. Whatever bizarre scheme he came up with, I'd go along with it. We'd squabble over what car to take and who got to drive. We'd kill monsters and hunt artifacts and try to figure out how to capture the Book. It would be perfect.

He was alive!

As I moved to stand again, something slipped from my lap and I dropped back down to the floor to retrieve it.

It was the picture of Alina that I'd left in my parents' mailbox the night V'lane had taken me to Ashford to show me that he'd restored my hometown and was keeping my family safe. The night Darroc had tracked me by the brand on my skull and later abducted my mom and dad.

This was the calling card Darroc had tacked to the front door of BB&B, demanding I come to him through the Silvers if I valued their lives.

That Barrons had left it for me now told me one thing: He *had* rescued my mom and dad before I'd IYD'd him into the Silvers.

But he hadn't given me the picture as a present or to make me feel better. He'd left it for the same reason Darroc had. To make the same point.

I have your parents. Don't fuck with me.

Okay, so he was a little pissed off at me. I could deal with that. If *he'd* killed *me,* I'd be a little pissed off, too, no matter how irrational it was. But he would get over it.

I couldn't have asked for more. Well, I could have, like Alina back and all the Fae dead, but this was good. This was a world I wanted to live in.

My parents were safe.

I clutched the letter and photo. I hugged them to my chest. I hated that he'd stormed off and left me lying on the floor, but I had proof of his existence and I knew he'd be back.

I was the OOP detector and he was the OOP director. We were a team.

He was alive!

* * *

I wanted to stay awake all night, basking in the glow that Jericho Barrons wasn't dead, but my body had other ideas.

The moment I stepped into my bedroom, I nearly collapsed. If there's one thing I've learned since Alina's death, it's that grief is more physically draining than running a marathon every day. It wipes you out and leaves you bruised, body and soul.

I managed to wash my face and brush my teeth, smiling like an idiot at myself in the mirror, but flossing and moisturizing was beyond me. Too much effort. I wanted to puddle in a brainless heap, curl up in the comforting arms of the knowledge that I hadn't killed him. I wasn't guilty. He wasn't dead.

I was sorry he hadn't waited around. I wished I knew where he was. I wished I had a cell phone.

I would have told him all the things I'd never said. I would have confessed my feelings. I wouldn't have been afraid to be tender. Losing him had clarified my emotions, and I wanted to shout them from the rooftop.

But not only didn't I have any idea where he went at night, I could barely move. Pain had been the glue keeping my will strong and my bones together. Without it, I was limp.

Tomorrow was another day.

And he was going to be alive in it!

I stripped and crawled into bed.

I passed out while I was still pulling the covers up and slept like a woman who'd hiked through hell without food or rest for months.

My dreams were so vivid, I felt like I was living them.

I dreamed I was watching Darroc die again, enraged that his death was being stolen from me so anticlimactically, my revenge snatched away, in the pinch of a Hunter's talons. I dreamed I was back in the Silvers, searching for Christian but never finding him. I dreamed I was at the abbey, on the floor of the cell, and Rowena came in and slit my throat. I felt the lifeblood gurgle out of me, turning the dirt floor to mud. I dreamed I was in the Cold Place, chasing the beautiful woman that I couldn't catch up with, and then I dreamed I'd actually done it—destroyed the world and replaced it with one I wanted. Afterward, I flew over my new world, astride the mighty, ancient K'Vruck. His great black wings whipped my hair into a tangle, and I laughed like a demon while the dissonant, haunting notes of Pink Martini's remix of "Qué Sera Sera" tinkled like a harpsichord from hell.

I slept for sixteen hours.

I needed every minute of it. The past three days were a surreal nightmare and had exhausted me.

The first thing I did when I woke up was pull Barrons' note out from under my pillow and read it again to reassure myself he was alive.

Then I dashed down the stairs so fast I slid down the last five steps on my pajama-clad ass, desperate for confirmation that the bookstore was indeed still trashed.

It was. I did a celebratory dance in the debris.

Because it was afternoon and Barrons rarely came around until early evening, I went back upstairs and took a long, hot shower. I conditioned, exfoliated, and shaved.

I leaned back against the wall, stretched out my legs, and watched water splash over the spear strapped to my thigh, letting my mind go blank while I relaxed.

Unfortunately, my mind wouldn't stay blank and my body wouldn't relax. The muscles in my legs kept tensing, my neck and shoulders were tight, and my fingers tapped a fast staccato on the shower floor.

Something was bothering me. A lot. Beneath my happy surface, a dark storm was brewing.

How could anything be bothering me? My world was blue skies all the way, despite Dublin's constant rain.

How could I not be blissfully happy at this moment? It was a good day. Barrons was alive. Darroc was dead. I was no longer stuck in the Silvers, fighting myriad monsters and dodging illusions.

I frowned, realizing that was exactly the problem.

At this moment, there was *nothing* wrong, besides the usual fate of the world stuff I'd become mostly inured to.

I couldn't deal with that. I'd been compressed, gripped in a painful vise. I'd gotten used to it.

It was things being wrong that had given me shape and purpose and kept me going.

But in the past twenty-four hours, I'd gone from being one hundred percent consumed by grief and rage to having every single reason for feeling those emotions stripped away.

Barrons was alive. Grief—*poof!*

The man I'd believed had murdered my sister, the one I'd been so committed to killing, was dead. The infamous Lord Master was gone.

That chapter of my life was over. He would never again lead the Unseelie, wreak havoc in my world, or hunt and hurt me. I didn't have to constantly watch over my shoulder for him anymore. The bastard who'd turned me *Pri-ya* was beyond my vengeful grasp. He'd gotten his just deserts. Well . . . he was dead, anyway. His just deserts would have been a whole lot worse if I'd been in charge of doling them out.

Regardless, he'd been my raison d'être for the longest time. And he was gone.

What did that leave me? Revenge—*poof!*

I'd always envisioned a final showdown between the two of us, and I would kill him.

Who was my villain now? Who would I hate and blame for Alina's death? It wasn't Darroc. He'd had a genuine weakness for her. He hadn't killed her and, if he'd been somehow responsible for her death, he hadn't known it. Six months in Dublin, and I was no closer to uncovering my sister's murderer.

With Barrons alive and Darroc dead, there went my all-consuming focus on revenge.

My parents were safe and in Barrons' care. There was no one I needed to save.

I had no urgent purpose, no express deadline. I felt lost. Directionless.

Sure, I had most of the same primary goals I'd had before I'd gone into the Silvers and everything had gone so terribly wrong, but grief had poured me into a tight box and those walls had shaped me. Now that the box was gone, I could feel myself collapsing into a shapeless blob.

What was next? Where to from here? I needed time to absorb the sudden changes in my reality and recalibrate my emotions. Confusing me even more, beneath the joy I felt that Barrons was alive, I was . . . well, angry. Furious, actually. There was something seething inside me. And I didn't even know what. But deep down, underneath it all, I was working up a major temper and feeling . . . stupid. Like I'd leapt to conclusions that didn't hold water.

I got out of the shower, thoroughly disgruntled, and picked through my clothes, dissatisfied with them all.

Yesterday I would have known exactly what to wear. Today I had no idea. Pink or black? Maybe it was time for a new favorite color. Or maybe no favorite color at all.

Rain pattered against the window while I dithered. Dublin was once again gray.

I pulled on a pair of gray capri sweats with *JUICY* stamped across my ass, a zip-up sweatshirt, and flip-flops. If Barrons still wasn't around, I would start cleaning up downstairs a little.

After all, I'd done what he'd asked.

My parents were free, I was alive, Darroc was dead, and I had the stones tucked securely away in the heavily runed bedroom of a penthouse.

According to my understanding of the law, that made it *my* bookstore now.

That meant it was also my Lamborghini. My Viper, too.

"It wasn't *my* fucking idea, either," I heard Barrons growl as I descended the rear stairs.

The door to his study was open a few inches, and I could hear him moving around in there, picking things up and putting them back down.

I stopped on the last step and smiled, reveling in the simple pleasure of hearing his voice again. Until he'd been gone, I hadn't understood how empty the world was without him.

My smile faded. I shifted from foot to foot on the stairs.

My mood might be sunshine glinting off water, but there was a dark undertow beneath the placid surface.

I'd gone further off the deep end than I liked to think about, with the whole decimate-the-universe kick I'd been on. I'd been one hundred percent committed to wresting whatever dark knowledge I'd needed from the Book, no matter the cost to myself or anyone else. I'd been willing to do anything it could teach me in order to replace this world with a new one. All because I'd believed Jericho Barrons was dead.

I hadn't even had a concrete plan, except to get the Book and wing it, believing I could master whatever spells of making and unmaking it had to offer. Looking back on my behavior, I was stymied by it. Rabid ambition, insane focus.

Alina's death hadn't done that to me.

I pushed my hands into my hair and tugged as if the gentle pain might clarify my thoughts. Shed light on my recent temporary insanity.

It must have been the betrayal aspect of it all that had made me so crazy. If only it hadn't been *me* who'd stabbed him, I never would have cracked like I had. Sure, my grief at losing Barrons had been intense, but it was the guilt that had crushed me. I'd turned on my protector, and my protector had turned out to be Barrons.

Shame, not grief, had fueled my need for revenge. That was it. Guilt had turned me into a woman obsessed, willing to consider erasing one world to create a new one. If I'd been the one who'd stabbed Alina, if I'd participated in killing her, I would have felt exactly the same way and considered doing the same thing. It wouldn't have even been love motivating me as much as a desperate need to erase my own complicity.

Now that grief wasn't a fist around my heart, I knew I would never have gone through with it.

Re-create the world just for Jericho Barrons? The thought was ridiculous.

I'd lost Alina and hadn't turned into a world-destroying banshee, and I'd loved *her* all my life.

I'd known Barrons only a few months. If I was going to re-create the world for anyone, it would have been my sister.

Okay, that was resolved. I hadn't betrayed Alina by not going all Mad Max over her.

So why did I still feel something dark, twisting and turning inside me, trying to get to the surface? What was eating at me?

"Bloody hell, Ryodan, we've been over this a thousand times!" Barrons exploded. "The whole bloody way back we talked about it. We had a plan, you deviated. You were supposed to get her to safety. She was never supposed to know it was me. It's *your* fault she knows we can't die."

I froze. Ryodan was alive, too? I watched him get ripped to shreds and be flung down a hundred-foot ravine. I frowned. He'd said "can't die." What did that mean? As in never? No matter what?

He was quiet for a moment and I realized he was on the phone.

"You knew I'd fight. You knew I'd win. I always win. That's why you were supposed to separate us and shoot me, so she wouldn't know I was dead. Bring more ammo next time. Try a rocket launcher. Think maybe you could manage to hit me with that?" he said sarcastically.

A rocket launcher? Barrons would survive that?

"You're the one that fucked up. She watched us die."

Indeed, I did. So why weren't they dead? There was another pause. I held my breath, listening.

"I don't give a shit what they think. And don't give me this vote crap. Nobody voted. Lor doesn't even know what century it is, and Kasteo hasn't said a word in a thousand years. You're not killing her and neither are they. If anyone is going to kill her, it's me. And that's not happening right now. I need the Book."

I stiffened. He'd said "right now," strongly implying that there might be another time it *was* happening. And the only reason he wasn't killing me was because he needed the Book.

This was the jackass I'd been grieving? Whose return I'd been celebrating? I didn't ponder the "thousand years" comment. I'd work on that later.

"If you think I've hunted it this long to kill the best chance I've got, you don't know shit about me."

There it was again, the phrase Fiona had used the night he'd stabbed her to shut her up. I was his "best chance." At what?

"Bring it on. You. Lor. Kasteo, Fade. Whoever wants to get in my way. But if I were you, I'd back the fuck off. Don't give me a reason to make you live to regret it. Is that what you want? A pointless, eternal war? You want us at each other's throats?"

Silence.

"I never forget my loyalties. You've forgotten your faith. Keep her parents alive. Follow my orders. It'll be over soon."

I fisted my hands. What exactly was going to be over?

"That's where you're wrong. One world isn't just as good as any other. Some worlds are better. We've known she's a wild card since the beginning. After what I learned about her the other night, I have to let this hand play out. Have you located Tellie yet? I need to question the woman. Assuming she's still alive. No? Get more people on it."

What did he mean by after what he'd learned about me? That I'd teamed up with Darroc? That according to him I'd been willing to betray him? Or was there something else? Who was Tellie and what did he need to question her about?

"Darroc is dead. She'll tell V'lane she made it up. No one will believe the kid." Another long pause. "Of course she'll do what I say. I'll take V'lane out myself if I have to." He paused. "The fuck you could."

The silence stretched so long that I realized he must have terminated the call.

Hand on the door frame, I stood, eyeing the stairs.

"Get your ass in here, Ms. Lane. *Now.*"

"I heard—" I began.

"I *let* you hear," he cut me off.

I shut my mouth, closed the door, and leaned back against it. The corners of his lips turned up as if at some private amusement, and for a moment I thought we were having one of those silent conversations.

You think it's safe to close yourself in with the Beast?

If you think I'm afraid of you, you're wrong.

You should *be afraid.*

Maybe you *should be afraid of* me. *Go ahead, piss me off, Barrons. See what happens.*

Little girl thinks she's all grown up now.

His mouth moved into a smile that I've grown familiar with over the past few months, shaped of competing tensions: part mockery, part pissed off, and part turned on. Men are so complicated.

"Now you know what they think of you. I'm all that stands between you and my men," he said.

That and a very deep glassy lake. I'd dive to the bottom if I had to. Even though he was alive again, even though I now understood I never would have destroyed this world to resurrect him, I was no longer the woman I'd been before I'd helped kill him and never would be again.

The transformation I'd undergone had done permanent damage. The emotions I'd felt, believing he was dead, had cut deep, leaving my heart battle-scarred, my soul changed. The grief might be over, but the memory of those days, the choices I'd made, the things I'd almost done, would be a part of me forever. I suspected some part of me was still slightly numb and might be for a long time.

My gaze strayed to his neck. It was as if his throat had never been cut. There was no wound, no scar. He was completely healed. I'd seen him naked last night and knew there were no scars on his torso, either. His body bore no evidence of the violent death he'd endured.

I glanced back at his face. He was staring at my newly dyed hair. I pushed it back, tucked it behind my ears. From the hostility in his gaze, I knew if I opened my mouth again, he'd just cut me off, so I waited, enjoying the view.

One of the things I realized when I'd been grieving him was how attractive I find him. Barrons is ... addictive. He grows on you until you can't begin to imagine anyone you'd like to look at more. He wears his dark hair slicked back from his face, sometimes cut, sometimes long, as if he can't be bothered to regularly get it trimmed. I now know why, at well over six feet of long, hard muscle, he moves with such animal grace.

He's an animal.

His forehead, nose, mouth, and jaw bear the stamp of a gene pool that died out long ago, blended with whatever it is that makes him the beast. Though symmetrical, with strong planes and angles, his face is too primitive to be handsome. Barrons might have evolved enough to walk upright, but he never relinquished the purity and unapologetic drives of a born predator. The aggressive ruthlessness and bloodlust of my demon guardian is his inherent nature.

When I first arrived in Dublin, he terrified me.

I inhale deeply, inflating my lungs with a long, slow breath. Though ten feet and a wide desk separate us, I can smell him. The scent of his skin is one I will never forget, no matter how long I live. I know the taste of him in my mouth. I know the smell we make together. Sex is a perfumery that creates its own fragrance, takes two people and makes them smell like a third. It's a scent neither person can make alone. I wonder if that third smell can become a drug of blended pheromones that can be generated only by the mixture of those two people's sweat, saliva, and semen. I'd like to shove him back on the desk. Straddle him. Dump a storm of emotion across his body with mine.

I realize he's staring at me, hard, and that my thoughts might have been a bit transparent. Desire's a hard thing not to telegraph. It changes the way we breathe and subtly rearranges our limbs. If you're attuned to someone, it's impossible not to notice.

"Is there something you want from me, Ms. Lane?" he says very softly. Lust stirs in his ancient eyes. I remember the first time I glimpsed it there. I'd wanted to run, screaming. Savage Mac had wanted to play.

The answer to his question was a resounding yes. I wanted to launch myself across his desk and expel something violent from my system. I wanted to beat him, punish him for the pain I'd suffered. I wanted to kiss him, slam myself down on him, reassure myself that he was alive in the most elemental way I could.

If anyone is going to kill her, he'd said moments ago, *it's me.*

God, how I'd grieved him!

He speaks of killing me so casually. Still not trusting me. Never trusting me. Those dark currents gurgle, begin to gush. I am furious. With him. He deserves a dose of grief himself. I wet my lips. "As a matter of fact there is."

He inclines his head imperiously, waiting.

"And only you can give it to me," I purr, arching my back.

His gaze drops to my breasts. "I'm listening."

"It's long overdue. I haven't been able to think about anything else. It nearly drove me crazy today, waiting for you to get here so I could ask for it."

He stands up and rakes me with a scathing look.

Sloppy seconds, his eyes say.

You had it first, I counter silently. *I think that means he got the leftovers.*

I push away from the door, circle the desk, trailing my fingertips lightly over his Silver as I pass it. He watches my hand and I know he's remembering how I once touched him.

I stop a few inches from him. I'm humming with energy. He is, too. I can feel it.

"I've become obsessed with getting it, and if you say no, I'll just have to take it."

He inhales sharply. "You think you can?" Challenge stirs in his dark gaze.

I have a sudden vision of the two of us having an all-out fight from end to end of the bookstore, culminating in fierce, no-holds-barred sex, and my mouth goes so dry I can't swallow for a moment.

"It might take me a while to . . . get my hands on exactly what I want, but I have no doubt I could."

His eyes say: *Bring it on. But you've got a lot to pay for.*

He hates me for teaming up with Darroc. He believes we were lovers.

And he'd have sex with me in a heartbeat. Against his better judgment, with no tenderness at all, but he'd do it. I don't get men. If I thought he'd betrayed me with . . . say, Fiona, a day after he'd helped kill me, I'd make him suffer for a good long time before I slept with him again.

He believes that I had sex with my sister's lover the day after I stabbed him, that I forgot all about him and moved on. Men are wired different. I think for them, it's about stamping out all trace, all memory, of their competitor as quickly and completely as possible. And they feel that the only way they can do it is with their body, their sweat, their semen. As if they can re-mark us. I think sex is so intense for them, they can be so easily ruled by it, that they think we can, too.

I look up at him, into those dark, bottomless eyes. "Can you die—ever?"

For a long moment he doesn't speak. Then he moves his head once, in silent negation.

"As in: *never?* No matter what happens to you?"

I get that silent slice to the left and back to the middle again.

The bastard. Now I understand the anger I've been feeling beneath the elation. Some part of my brain had already put this together:

He'd *let* me grieve.

He never told me he was a beast that couldn't be killed. He could have spared me all the pain I'd endured with one tiny little truth, one small confession, and I'd never have felt so violent and dark and broken. If he'd only just said: *Ms. Lane, I can't be killed. So if you ever see me die, don't sweat it. I'll be back.*

I'd lost myself. Because of him. Because of his idiotic need to keep everything about himself secret. There was no excuse for it.

But even worse was this: I'd thought he'd given his life to save me, when all he'd really done was the equivalent of take a little nap. What did "dying" for someone mean when you knew you couldn't die? Not a damn thing. An inconvenience. IYD hadn't been a big deal after all.

I'd wept, I'd mourned. I'd built a massive and utterly undeserved Monument to Barrons, The Man Who'd Died So I Could Live, in my head. I'd thought he'd made the ultimate sacrifice for me, and it had milked my emotions brutally. I'd let it consume me, take me over, turn me into someone I couldn't believe I'd been capable of becoming.

And he'd *never* been willing to die so I could live. It had been business as usual—Barrons keeping his OOP detector alive and functioning, coolly impersonal, focused on his goals. So what if he was the one who would never let me die? It didn't cost him anything. He wanted the Book. I was the way to get it. He had nothing to lose. I finally understood why he was always so fearless.

I'd thought he'd cared about me so much he'd been willing to give up his life. I'd romanticized it and gotten swept away in a misguided fantasy. And if he'd stayed here last night, I'd have made a complete fool of myself. I'd have confessed feelings to him that I'd felt only because I'd thought he'd given his life for mine.

Nothing had changed.

There was no deeper level of understanding or emotion between us.

He was Jericho Barrons, OOP director, pissed off at me because he thought I'd taken up with the enemy, irked that he'd had to endure an inconvenient death, but still not telling me a thing, using me to achieve his mysterious ends.

He bristles with impatience. I feel the lust rolling off him, the violence beneath it.

"You said you wanted something. What is it, Ms. Lane?"

I smile coolly. "The deed to my bookstore, Barrons. What else?"

The Dani Daily

106 Days AWC

DING-DONG THE DICK IS DEAD!

Read all about it!

THE LORD MASTER WAS MURDERED!!!

Dude, like it was my 14th birthday or something already, 'stead of next week on the 20th, I got the über-coolest present: Darroc, the fecker that brought the walls down between our worlds, is DEAD! These eyeballs saw it happen up close and personal last night! And get this—one o' his own Hunters killed him! Took off his head!

Time to fight is NOW, while we got 'em on the run with nobody in charge! Jayne and his men got a method; join the madness at Dublin Castle!

Annie, I got the nest of Creepers in the back of your place last night.

Anonymous847, I cleared the warehouse, but—dude—you didn't need me. There was only two. 'Member, you can build your own Shade-Busters. I told you all about it coupla rags ago. If you need supplies, check out Dex's on Main. I tacked the recipe to the wall by the bar.

Keeping it short, got a lot of Fae ass to kick while I'm still thirteen! Which ain't much longer, only SIX more days!!!!!!!!!!!!!!!

MEGA OUT!

PS: Happy V'day, which I'm officially changing to V'lane's Day. Speaking of—anybody seen the prince recently? If so, gotta tell him the Mega's looking for him. Got some stuff he needs to know about.

17

"Turn right, here," I said.

Barrons shot me a look that pretty much said, *Fuck off and die.*

I returned it. "I left the stones at Darroc's penthouse."

He yanked the wheel of the Viper to the right so hard, I nearly ended up in his lap. I knew what a mistake that would be. Since our sexually charged incident back at the bookstore, he hadn't spoken a single word.

I'd never seen him so angry. And I've seen Barrons angry a lot.

When I'd delivered my frosty coup de grâce, he regarded me with such contempt that, if I'd been a lesser woman, I'd have withered up and died. I'm not lesser. He deserved it.

Then he'd stalked away from me and stood staring into the Silver for long moments. When he'd finally turned back, he raked a glance from my tousled blond hair to my wedge flip-flops, then shot a look at the ceiling, telling me as clearly as if he'd spoken aloud to go change into something a grown woman would wear, because we were leaving.

When I'd come back down, he herded me into the

garage without touching me. I'd felt tension ebbing and flowing like a violent surf beneath his skin, the same way the colors had crashed ceaselessly beneath the skin of the Unseelie Princes.

He'd chosen the Viper from his collection and slid into the driver's seat. I knew he'd done it to provoke me. To remind me that nothing was mine. Everything was his.

"This is bullshit, and you know it," I snapped. I couldn't fight about what was really pissing me off, so I'd work with the material at hand. "Mom and Dad are out, I'm alive, and Darroc is dead. You never specified who had to do what or how it had to happen. You only demanded an end result. Your terms were met."

The Viper rumbled down the street, and I felt a flash of envy. I knew the thrill of the exhaust pipe's heat in the driver's compartment, the sleek pleasure of the gear stick in my hand, the rush of massive muscle idling hungrily, waiting for my next command. I sighed and looked out the window, watching the darkness slide by.

I didn't have to give Barrons directions. He knew exactly where I'd stayed two nights ago. He turned right, then left, twelve blocks to the east, and seven to the south.

The city was as silent as he was. Although I sensed a great number of Fae, they weren't out in the streets. I wondered if they were having a Fae summit somewhere, planning their next move. I wondered if the Unseelie nation had been unsettled by the loss of their liberator and leader and if they were meeting to choose a new one. I wondered who would step up to take over. One of the Unseelie Princes?

In a way, Darroc hadn't been a bad choice to have leading the Dark Court. He'd wanted our world intact, because he'd wanted to rule it alongside the Fae realm. He'd liked his human pleasures and had intended to continue them. His years among us had increased his appetite for mortal women and mortal luxuries; ergo, he'd have preserved them.

But there was no guarantee that whoever stepped up to the plate next would feel the same. In fact, there was little likelihood that the new Unseelie leader would feel anything even remotely human.

If one of the dark princes took over—say, Death or Pestilence—they'd have no long-term goals, no restraint. They'd indulge until there was nothing left to devour. We'd actually been lucky to have an ex-Seelie leading the Unseelie. I knew what the princes were made of: emptiness darker and vaster than the night sky. Their appetites were boundless, insatiable.

I'd seen what had happened in the street between the Seelie and Unseelie when they'd faced off. The ground had begun to split. If the two courts clashed on a grand scale, if they went at each other en masse, they would destroy our world.

While they could move on to a new planet, we couldn't.

The human race would die out.

I'd thought I had no pressing obligations, no express deadlines. But I did. The longer the Book was loose and the Fae battled each other, the greater the danger of total human annihilation.

I wondered if Barrons realized any of this. I wondered if he even cared. Whatever he was could probably survive any fallout, nuclear or Fae. Would he simply hook up with the other immortals on our planet and move on with them? I needed to know where he stood. "We've got serious problems, Barrons."

He slammed the brakes so hard I got whiplash. If I hadn't had my seat belt on, I'd have gone through the windshield. I'd been so lost in thought that I hadn't realized we'd arrived.

"Mortal over here!" I said irritably, rubbing my neck. "You might try remembering tha—ack, what the—*Barrons!*" I was yanked out of the car by my arm so hard, it nearly popped out of socket.

I hadn't even seen him get out and come around to my side. Then I was over the curb, up on the sidewalk, and flattened against the brick wall of a building.

He leaned into me, trapping my legs with his, completing the cage with his arms.

I braced my palms against his chest to hold him at bay. His rib cage rose and fell beneath my hands, pumping like bellows. He was rock hard against my thigh, much bigger than I'd ever felt him. Too big. I heard the sound of ripping fabric.

I looked up at his face and did a double take. His skin was the color of mahogany, darkening by the second. He was taller than he should be, and sparks of crimson glittered in his eyes. When he snarled, I caught the flash of long black fangs in the moonlight.

He was changing. His hair was getting longer, thicker, matting around his face. He dropped his head close and sharp fangs grazed my ear.

"Never. Use sex. As a weapon. Against me. Again." The words were guttural, misshapen by teeth too large for a human mouth, but I understood them perfectly.

I shrugged.

"Don't give me a fucking shrug!" he snarled. His cheek was against mine and I could feel the planes of it sharpening, broadening. Again, I heard cloth ripping.

"I was angry." I'd had every right to be.

"So am I. You don't see me playing head games."

"You manipulate me all the time."

"Am I ruthless? Yes. Do I keep my own counsel? Sure. Do I push you sometimes to get you to say something you want to say anyway? Certainly. But I never mind-fuck you."

"Look, Barrons, what do you want from me? It was . . . " I searched for the right word and didn't like what I found. "Immature. Okay? But you aren't blameless. You were talking about killing me."

The rattlesnake moved in his throat.

"You owe me an apology, too," I snapped.

"For what?" Something grazed my ear, tore the tender skin, and I felt a warm rush of blood, then his tongue touched my skin.

"For not telling me you couldn't die. Do you have any idea what watching you die *did* to me?"

"Ah. Let's see. Yes. Made you fuck Darroc within hours."

"Jealous, Barrons? Sounds like it." There was no way I was explaining myself. He hadn't given me any explanations. Because he hadn't, I'd assumed all kinds of things and very nearly made a grand ass of myself in front of him last night.

Air hissed between his fangs as he shoved away from the wall. I hadn't realized how cold the night was until the heat of his body was gone. He stood in the middle of the street with his back to me, hands fisted at his sides, long talons sliding through monstrous fingers, shuddering, snarling.

I leaned against the wall, watching him. He was fighting for control over which form was going to achieve dominance and, although I was pissed off at both of them at the moment, I preferred the man. The beast was more . . . emotional, if that word could be applied to Barrons in any form. It made me feel confused, conflicted. I would never get the image of stabbing it out of my head.

When I'd been provoking him, it hadn't occurred to me that this might be the outcome. Barrons was always so controlled, disciplined. I'd thought his transformation into the beast had been a conscious one. That, like everything else in his world, it happened if he willed it to, or it didn't happen at all.

I remembered the first time I'd ever heard the strange rattle in his chest, the night he and I had gone after the Book with the three stones and failed. He'd carried me back to the bookstore and I'd wakened on the sofa to find him staring at the fire. I remembered thinking that Barrons' skin might be a slipcover for a chair I never wanted to see. I'd been right. Beneath his human form was an utterly inhuman one. But why? How? What was he?

Not once had he lost control like this around me. Was his ability to contain his animal nature getting weaker?

Or was I more deeply rooted beneath that changeable skin?

I smiled, but it held no mirth. I liked that thought. I wasn't sure who that made more screwed up: him or me.

I stayed against the wall, and he stayed in the street with his back to me, for a good three or four minutes.

Slowly, with what looked like a great deal of pain, he changed back, shuddering, snarling all the while. I understood why I'd thought I killed him with my runes last night. The transformation from beast to man appeared to be intensely painful.

When he finally turned around, there was no trace of crimson in his dark gaze. No stump of horns erupting from his skull. He grimaced as he stepped up on the curb, as if his limbs hurt, teeth flashing white and even in the moonlight.

He was once again a powerfully built man of thirty or so, wearing a long coat that was ripped at the shoulders and split down the back.

"You mind-fuck me again, I'll fuck you back. But it won't be with my mind."

"Don't threaten me." I was tempted to do it right

then and there and see if he'd really follow through. I was furious at him. I wanted him. I was a mess where Barrons was concerned.

"I didn't. I warned you."

A sharp retort was on the tip of my tongue.

He shamed it into silence with "I expect better from you, Ms. Lane." Then he turned for the door and entered the building.

I half-expected there to be Unseelie guards on the top floor, but either Darroc had been too arrogant to bother leaving any or, since he'd been killed, his army saw no point in protecting his hideouts anymore.

Once inside, Barrons went straight for the bedroom suite Darroc had occupied. I followed him, because it was the one place I'd not gotten the chance to search. I stood in the doorway, watching him ransack the opulently furnished room, pushing chairs and ottomans out of his way, overturning the dresser and kicking through the contents, before he turned to the bed. He ripped the blankets and sheets from it, flung the mattress from the frame, pulled out a knife, and gutted it, searching for anything hidden inside, then stopped and breathed deeply. After a moment, he cocked his head and inhaled again.

I got it instantly. Barrons has extremely heightened senses. Being in touch with your inner animal has its advantages. He knows my scent, and he couldn't smell me on Darroc's bed.

I knew the second he decided we'd probably done it on the kitchen table, or in the shower, or bent over the couch, or on the balcony, or maybe just had an orgy with all the Rhino-boys and guards watching.

I rolled my eyes and left him to finish searching Darroc's bedroom by himself. He could believe whatever he wanted to believe. I hoped he drowned in images of me having sex with Darroc. He might not feel emotions about me, but he certainly had the territorial instincts of an animal. I hoped the idea of somebody else playing on his turf drove him nuts.

I hurried to the suite I'd slept in. My runes were still throbbing crimson at the threshold and in the walls. They were larger, pulsating more brightly. I didn't linger. I'd searched the place thoroughly the other night. I grabbed my pack, hurried out into the living room, and began stuffing the photo albums of Alina into my pack. They were mine now, and when this was all over, I was going to sit down and lose myself in them for days, maybe weeks, and tell myself the happy part of her story.

I heard Barrons in the den, knocking over lamps and chairs and tossing things around. I walked in and watched books fly, papers explode into the air. He had his beast under control, but he wasn't bothering to try to control the man. He'd swapped his torn coat for one of Darroc's. It was too small for him, but at least it covered the rest of his shredded clothes.

"What are you looking for?"

"Allegedly, he knew a shortcut, or I'd have killed him long ago."

"Who told *you* about the shortcut?" Was there anything Barrons didn't know?

He shot me a look. "I didn't need anyone to. Prima facie, Ms. Lane. Facts speak. Didn't you wonder why he kept tracking it, even though he had none of the stones and would have been corrupted the moment he picked it up?"

I shook my head, disgusted with myself. It had taken me months to get around to wondering that. What a great sleuth I was.

"You think he left notes?"

"I know he did. The limits of his mortal brain posed problems for him. He was accustomed to the memory capabilities of a Fae."

So, Barrons knew there was a shortcut, too, and had been seeking it for some time.

"Why didn't you ever tell me?"

"They're called shortcuts for a reason. The shorter they are, the more they usually cut. Nothing is without price, Ms. Lane."

Didn't I know it. I knelt and began scanning sheets of paper on the floor. Darroc hadn't written in notebooks; he'd used thick, expensive vellum sheets and written on them in fancy calligraphy, as if he'd expected his work to one day be memorialized: documents from Darroc, liberator of the Fae, displayed like we showcase the Constitution, in a museum somewhere. I looked back up at Barrons. He was no longer throwing things; he was sorting through papers and notebooks. There was no trace of temperamental beast or angry man. He was icy, impervious Barrons again.

"Didn't anybody ever tell him about laptops?" I muttered.

"Fae can't use them. They fry them."

Maybe there *was* something to my energy theory. As more sheets rained down, I gathered them up and examined them. Under the watchful eyes of Darroc's guards, I hadn't been able to snoop through his personal documents. It was fascinating stuff. This particular cache of notes was about the different Unseelie castes—their strengths, weaknesses, and unique tastes. It was jarring to realize he'd had to learn about the Unseelie, just like we had. I folded the pages and began stuffing them in my backpack. This was useful information. *Sidhe*-seers need to be passing it down, one generation to the next. We could put together a set of Fae encyclopedias from his notes.

When I ran out of room in my pack, I began stacking the pages up to return for them later.

Then I saw a page that was different from the rest, filled with scribbled bits of thoughts, bulleted lists, circled comments, and arrows pointing from one note to another.

Alina's name was on it, along with Rowena's and dozens of others. Scribbled next to their names were their special "talents." There were lists of countries, addresses, and names of companies I assumed were the foreign branches of Poste Haste, Inc., the courier service that was our front. One bulleted list contained the six Irish bloodlines of our sect, plus another I'd never heard of: O'Callaghan. Was it possible there were more bloodlines than we knew about? What if another Fae got their hands on this information? They could wipe us all out!

I continued scanning and gasped. Rowena had a touch of mental coercion? Kat had the gift of emotional telepathy? How the hell had Darroc figured these things out? According to him, Jo was in the now-secret Haven! Dani's name was also on the page, heavily underlined and punctuated with a question mark. I wasn't on the list, which meant he'd written it before he'd become aware of me, last fall.

At the bottom of the page was a short bulleted list:

- *Sidhe*-seers—sense Fae.
- Alina—senses *Sinsar Dubh,* Fae Hallows, and relics.
- Abbey—*Sinsar Dubh*
- Unseelie King—*sidhe*-seers?

I blinked at it, trying to make sense of it. Was Darroc saying that it hadn't been the Seelie Queen, as Nana O'Reilly had claimed, who'd delivered the Dark Book to the abbey so long ago? Had the Unseelie King himself brought it to us, because we could sense Fae, and Fae Hallows, and that made us the perfect guardians for it?

Suddenly Barrons was behind me, looking over my shoulder. "Makes you think about yourself a little differently, doesn't it?"

"Not really. I mean, who cares who brought it to the abbey? Point is, we're the guardians."

"Is that what you get from his notes, Ms. Lane?" he purred.

I glanced up at him. "What do you get from them?" I said defensively. I didn't like his tone any more than I liked the amused glitter in his dark gaze.

"It's said the king was horrified when he realized that his act of atonement had resulted in the birth of his most powerful abomination yet. He chased it from one world to the next, for eons, determined to destroy it. When he finally caught up with it, their battle lasted centuries and reduced dozens of worlds to ruins. But it was too late. The *Sinsar Dubh* had become fully sentient, a dark force of its own. When the king first created the *Sinsar Dubh,* he was greater, and the Book was lesser. It was a repository for the king's evil, but without drive and intent. Yet while it roamed, it evolved, until it became all the king was, and more. The creation—abandoned by its creator—learned to hate. The *Sinsar Dubh* began to pursue the king." He paused and gave me one of his wolf smiles. "So what else might the dark king have created? Perhaps an entire caste that could track his greatest enemy, contain it, and keep it from destroying *him*? Are you going to tell me you never once considered that?"

I stared. We were the good guys. Human to the core.

"*Sidhe*-seers: watchdogs for the U.K.," he mocked.

I was chilled by his words. It had been bad enough to discover I was adopted and the parents who'd raised me weren't my biological parents. Now what was he implying? That I'd *had* no parents?

"That's the biggest pile of BS I've ever heard." First Darroc had suggested I was a stone. Now Barrons was proposing that the *sidhe*-seers were a secret caste of Unseelie.

"If it walks like a duck and quacks like a duck."

"I am *not* a duck."

"Why does it offend you so much? Power is power."

"The Unseelie King didn't make me!"

"The idea frightens you. Fear is more than a wasted emotion. It's the penultimate set of blinders. If you can't face the truth of your reality, you can't be a part of it, can't control it. You may as well throw in the towel and yield to the whims of anyone with a stronger will. Do you like being helpless? Is that what you get off on? Is that why the moment I was gone you turned to the bastard that had you raped?"

"So, what are you and your men?" I countered coldly. "Another of the Unseelie King's secret castes? Is that what you are, Barrons? Is that why you know so much about them?"

"None of your fucking business."

He turned away and resumed his search.

I was trembling, and there was a sour taste in my mouth. I pushed the papers away, got up, and walked to the balcony, where I stood staring out at the night.

Barrons had shaken me deeply with his suggestion that the *sidhe*-seers were a caste of Unseelie. I had to admit that Darroc's notes could certainly be construed that way.

And just the other night, I'd stood between two Fae armies, thinking how glad I was to be like the Unseelie, strengthened by pain, less frivolous and breakable.

Then there was that dark glassy lake in my head, that

had so many inexplicable "gifts" to offer, like runes that an ex-Fae had recognized, that had given him pause, runes that the Unseelie Princes had disliked intensely.

I shivered. I had a new question to be obsessed with besides what was Jericho Barrons?

What was *I*?

18

When we left, I snatched a *Dani Daily* from the lamppost outside the building, slid into the passenger's seat of the Viper, and began to read it. Her birthday was coming up. I smiled faintly. Figured she'd tell the whole world. She'd make it a national holiday if she could.

I wasn't surprised to learn she'd been in the street last night and had seen the Hunter kill Darroc. Dani didn't take orders from anyone, not even me. Had she been there to try to kill Darroc herself? I wouldn't put it past her.

As I fastened my seat belt, I wondered whether she hadn't stuck around long enough to see that the Hunter had been possessed by the *Sinsar Dubh,* or if she'd decided to omit that bit of news. If she had stuck around, what did she make of the beast that blasted into me and carried me off? Probably figured it was some other kind of Unseelie she hadn't seen before.

Although I was shocked to realize so much time had passed while I was in the Silvers and it was the middle of February, I should have known today was Valentine's Day.

I glanced sourly over at Barrons.

I'd never had a happy one. They'd been various shades of sucky since kindergarten, when Chip Johnson ate too many iced cookies and threw up all over my new dress. I'd been drinking fruit punch, and when his puke hit me, I had an involuntary sympathetic response and spewed punch everywhere. It had set off a chain reaction of five-year-olds vomiting that I still couldn't think about without getting queasy.

Even back in second and third grade, Valentine's Day had been a stressful experience for me. I'd wake up dreading school. Mom always got Alina and me cards for everyone in our class, but a lot of moms weren't as sensitive. I'd sit at my desk and hold my breath, praying someone besides Tubby Thompson or Blinky Brewer would remember me.

Then, in middle school, we had the Sadie Hawkins dance, where the girls had to ask the guys to go, putting on even more pressure. Adding insult to injury on what was supposed to be the most romantic day of the year, I was forced to risk rejection by asking out the guy of my dreams and praying that, by the time I got my nerve up, there'd be someone left besides Tubby and Blinky. In eighth grade, I waited too long and nobody popular was left, so I'd blow-dried my forehead on the high-heat setting, spritzed my sheets with water, and faked the flu that morning. Mom made me go anyway. The scorch mark on my forehead gave me away. I'd hastily cut bangs to try to cover it and had ended up at the dance dateless, miserable, with a painful burn and a bad haircut.

High school brought along a whole new set of problems. I shook my head, in no mood to relive teenage horrors. Bright side was, this Valentine's Day could have been a whole lot worse. At least I'd get to sleep tonight with the comforting knowledge that Barrons was alive.

"Where to now?" I asked.

He stared straight ahead. The rattlesnake moved in his chest.

We pulled up at 939 Rêvemal Street, in front of the demolished entrance to Chester's, the club that had once been Dublin's number-one hot spot for the jaded rich and beautiful bored, until it was destroyed on Halloween. I stared at him disbelievingly.

He parked and turned off the engine.

"I'm not going in Chester's. They want me dead in there."

"And if they smell fear on you, they'll try to kill you." He opened the door and got out.

"Your point?"

"If I were you, I'd try to smell like something else."

"Why do I have to go in?" I groused. "Can't you visit your buddies by yourself?"

"Do you want to see your parents or not?"

I leapt out, slammed the door, and ran after him, skirting rubble. I had no idea why he was offering—certainly not because he was trying to be nice—but I wasn't about to miss the opportunity. As unpredictable as my life was, I wasn't going to miss a single chance to spend time with the people I loved.

As if he'd read my thoughts, he tossed over his shoulder, "I said *see* them. Not visit with them."

I hated the thought of my parents being held in the belly of the seedy Unseelie hangout, but I had to concede that underground, in the middle of Barrons' men, was probably the safest place for them. They couldn't go back to Ashford. The Unseelie Princes knew where we lived.

The only other possibilities were the abbey, the bookstore, or with V'lane. Not only were there Shades in the abbey still, the *Sinsar Dubh* had paid a deadly visit, and I didn't trust Rowena with a butter knife. I certainly didn't want them hanging around me, seeing what a mess I'd become. And V'lane—with his dim understanding of humans—might decide to tuck them away on a beach with an illusion of Alina, which my dad could handle, but it would definitely push my mom over the edge. We might never get her out of there.

Chester's it was.

The club had once been the most popular place in the city, accessible by invitation only, with marble pillars that framed an ornate entrance into the three-story club, but lavish French-style gas lamps had been ripped from the concrete and used as battering rams against the façade. Fallen roof supports had crushed a world-renowned hand-carved bar and shattered elegant stained-glass windows. The club sign dangled in pieces above the entrance, chunks of concrete blocked the door, and the building was heavily covered with graffiti.

The new entrance to the club was around back, secreted beneath an inconspicuous, battered metal door in the ground, close to the crumbling foundation. If you didn't know about the club, you wouldn't give a second thought to what appeared to be a forgotten cellar door. The dance floors were so far underground and so well soundproofed that, unless you had Dani's superhearing, you'd never know there was a party going on.

"I can't be part of an Unseelie caste," I told him as he opened the door. "I can touch the Seelie spear."

"Some say the Unseelie King created the *sidhe*-seers with his imperfect Song. Others say he had sex with human women to found the bloodlines. Perhaps your blood is diluted enough that it poses no such problem."

Typical Barrons. He had an answer for all the things I didn't want to know but none for the things I did.

After descending a ladder, pushing open another

door, and going down a second ladder, we arrived at the real entrance to the club, an industrial foyer with tall double doors.

Since I'd last been here, someone had hired a decorator and replaced the tall wood doors with new ones that were black and glossy, the height of urban chic, so highly polished that I could see the couple who'd followed us down reflected in them. She was dressed like me in a long slim skirt, high-heeled boots, and a fur-trimmed coat. He stood near, his body angled in on her, like a walking shield.

I jerked. No couple had followed us down. I hadn't recognized myself. It wasn't that my hair was blond again—the black doors reflected only shape and movement, not color—it was that I looked like someone else. I stood differently. Gone was the last vestige of baby softness I'd brought with me to Dublin last August. I wondered what Mom and Dad would think of me. I hoped they could see past the changes to the Mac I still was somewhere beneath it all. I was excited and nervous to see them.

He pushed the doors open. "Stay close."

The club hit me like a blast of overblown sensuality, cool in chrome and glass, black and white, the height of industrial muscle dressed in Manhattan posh. The décor promised uninhibited eroticism, pleasure for pleasure's sake, sex worth dying for. The enormous interior was terraced with dance floors, each served by their own bars on a dozen different sublevels. The mini-clubs within the club had their own themes, some elegant on polished floors, others heavy on tattoos and urban decay. The bartenders and servers reflected the theme of their sub-club, some in topless tuxes, others in leather and chains. On one terrace, the extremely young servers were dressed like uniformed schoolchildren. On another—I turned sharply away. Not looking, not thinking about that one. I hoped Barrons was keeping my parents somewhere far from all this debauchery.

Although I'd mentally prepared myself to see humans and Unseelie mingling, flirting, and pairing off, I'm never ready for it. Chester's is anathema to everything I am.

Fae and human were not meant to mix. The Fae are immortal predators, with no regard for human life, and those humans foolish enough to think for one moment that their tiny inconsequential lives matter to the Fae . . . well, Ryodan says those humans deserve to die, and when I see them in a place like Chester's, I have to agree. You can't save people from themselves. You can only try to wake them up.

The static of so many Unseelie crowded into one place was deafening. Grimacing, I turned off my *sidhe-seer* volume.

Music spilled from one level to the next, overlapping. Sinatra dueled with Manson; Zombie flipped off Pavarotti. The message was clear: If you want it, we've got it, and if we don't, we'll create it for you.

Still, there was one theme the whole place shared: Chester's had been decorated for Valentine's Day.

"This is just wrong," I muttered.

Thousands of pink and red balloons dangling silken cords drifted through the club, emblazoned with messages that ranged from sweet to cheeky to horrifying.

At the entrance to every mini-club was a huge golden statue of Cupid holding a bow that sported dozens of long golden arrows.

The human contingent of Chester's clientele was chasing the balloons from one level to the next, climbing stairs, perching on stools, yanking them lower, and popping them with their arrows, which I didn't get at all until I watched a folded bit of paper explode from one, and then a dozen women piled up in a heap of fighting, clawing wildcats, determined to get whatever the prize was.

When one woman finally broke free from the mess, clutching her treasure, three others ganged up on her, stabbed her with their arrows, and took it away. Then they turned on one another with shocking brutality. A man rushed in, snatched the wad of paper, and ran.

I looked around for Barrons, but we'd gotten separated in the crowd. I shoved dangling silk cords from my face.

"Don't you want one?" a redhead chirped, as she snatched the cord of one I'd just pushed away.

"What's in them?" I said warily.

"Invitations, silly! If you're lucky! But there aren't many! If you get one, they'll let you in to the private rooms to dine upon the sanctified flesh of the immortal Fae for the *whole night*!" she twittered rapturously. "Others have gifts!"

"Like what?"

She stabbed at the balloon with a delicate golden arrow, and the balloon popped, raining green goo mixed with tiny bits of writhing flesh.

"Jackpot!" people screamed.

I scrambled out of the way just in time to avoid being trampled.

The redhead shrieked, "See you in Faery!" Then she was on her hands and knees, licking the floor and fighting for pieces of Unseelie.

I looked around for Barrons again. At least I didn't smell like fear. I was too disgusted and angry. I pushed through the press of sweaty, jostling bodies. This was my world? This was what we'd come to? What if we never got the walls back up? Was this what I was going to have to live with?

I began to shove people out of the way.

"Watch where you're going!" a woman snapped.

"Chill, bitch!" some guy snarled.

"Are you *asking* for an ass-kicking?" a man threatened.

"Hey, beautiful girl."

My head whipped around. It was the dreamy-eyed guy that had worked with Christian at the Ancient Languages Department at Trinity College, then had taken a bartending job at Chester's when the walls fell.

The last time I'd seen him, I had a creepy experience, looking at his reflection in a mirror. But here he stood, behind a black-and-white bar walled with mirrors, tossing glasses and pouring shots with smooth, showy flair, and both he and his reflection looked every inch the perfectly normal young, gorgeous guy with dreamy eyes that melted me.

Though I was eager to see my parents, this guy kept showing up and I no longer believed in coincidences. My parents were going to have to wait.

I pulled up a stool next to a tall, gaunt man in a pinstriped suit and top hat, who was shuffling a deck of cards with skeletal hands. When he turned to look at me, I jerked and looked away. I did not look back again. Beneath the brim of his hat, there was no face. Shadows swirled like a dark tornado.

"Divine your future?" it said.

I shook my head, wondering how it spoke without a mouth.

"Ignore him, beautiful girl."

"Show you who you are?"

I shook my head again, silently willing it to go away.

"Dream me a song."

I rolled my eyes.

"Sing me a line."

I angled my body away from it.

"You show me your face, I'll show you mine." Cards snapped together as it shuffled.

"Look, buddy, I have no desire to see—"

I broke off, physically unable to say another word. I opened my mouth and closed it, like a fish gasping for water, but I was gasping for words. It was as if all the sentences that I had been born with, enough to last a lifetime, had been sucked from me, leaving me utterly blank, silenced. The shape of my thoughts, the way I would phrase them, had been taken. Everything I'd ever said, everything I ever would say, *it* held now. I felt a terrible pressure inside my head, as if my brain was being vacuumed clean of who I was. I had the crazy thought that, in moments, I would be as blank behind my face as it was beneath its hat, leaving only a dark tornado, ceaselessly whirling, inside my skull. And maybe, just maybe, once it had everything it wanted from me, a fragment of a face would appear beneath its brim.

Terror gripped me.

I shot a frantic look at the dreamy-eyed guy. He turned away and poured a shot. I mouthed a silent plea at his reflection in the mirror behind the bar.

"I keep telling you not to talk to things," the reflection of the dreamy-eyed guy said.

He poured and served, moving from one customer to the next, while my identity was erased.

Help me, my eyes screamed in the mirror.

The dreamy-eyed guy finally turned back to me. "She is not yours," he told the tall, gaunt man.

"She spoke to me."

"Look deeper."

After a moment, "My mistake," the card-shuffling thing said.

"Don't repeat it."

As abruptly as they'd vanished, I had words again. My brain was full of thoughts and sentences. I was a person, complete with ideas and dreams. The vacuum was gone.

I fell off my stool and stumbled away from the face-less man. On shaky legs, I tottered three stools down, hoisted myself back up, and clutched the counter.

"He will not bother you again," the dreamy-eyed guy said.

"Whiskey," I croaked.

He slid a shot of top-shelf whiskey down the counter. I slammed it back and demanded another. I gasped as fire exploded inside me. Though I wanted nothing more than to put a mile between myself and the card-shuffling monster, I had questions. I wanted to know how the dreamy-eyed guy could command something like that. For that matter, what was the faceless thing?

"The *fear dorcha,* beautiful girl."

"Reading my mind?"

"Don't have to. Question's all over your face."

"How does it kill?" I'm obsessed with the many ways the Fae dole out death. I make meticulous notes in my journal on the various castes and their methods of exe-cution.

"Death is not its goal."

"What is?"

"It seeks the Faces of Humanity, beautiful girl. Got one to spare?"

I said nothing. I had no desire to know more. Ches-ter's was a Fae safety zone. On my last visit to the club, it was made abundantly clear to me that if I killed any-thing on the premises, I would be killed. Since Ryodan and his men already wanted me dead, tonight probably wasn't the best night to test my luck. If I learned more about it, or the killing weight of my spear in my shoul-der holster grew any heavier, I might do something rash.

"Some things can't be killed that easy."

I glanced, startled, at the dreamy-eyed guy. He was

looking at my hand inside my coat. I hadn't even realized I'd reached for it.

"It's Fae, right?" I said.

"Mostly."

"So, how *can* it be killed?"

"Does it need to be killed?"

"You'd stick up for it?"

"You'd stick a spear in it?"

I raised a brow. Apparently, a prerequisite for working at Chester's was that you had to like the Fae and be willing to put up with their unique appetites.

"Haven't seen you in a while." He changed the subject smoothly.

"Haven't been around to be seen," I said coolly.

"Almost weren't just now."

"Funny guy, aren't you?"

"Some think so. How you been?"

"Good. You?"

"All in a day's work."

I smiled faintly. Barrons had nothing on the dreamy-eyed guy's evasive answers.

"Gone light again, beautiful girl."

"In the mood for a change."

"More than the hair."

"Suppose."

"Looks good on you."

"Feels good."

"May not be useful. Times like these. Where you been?" He tossed a glass into the air and I watched it tumble lazily, end over end.

"In the Silvers, walking around the White Mansion, watching the concubine and the Unseelie King have sex. But I spend most of my days trying to figure out how to corner and control the *Sinsar Dubh*."

The name of the Unseelie King's Book seemed to hiss

sibilantly through the air, and I felt a breeze as every Unseelie head in the club turned toward me in unison.

For a split second the entire club was silent, frozen.

Then sound and motion resumed with the tinkle of crystal as the wineglass the dreamy-eyed guy had been tossing hit the floor and shattered.

Three stools down, the tall, gaunt thing made a choking sound and his deck of cards sprayed the air, raining down on the counter, my lap, the floor.

Ha, I thought, *got you, dreamy-eyes.* He was a player in all this. But who was he and which team was he playing for?

"So, who are you really, dreamy-eyed guy? And why do you keep popping up?"

"Is that how you see me? In another life, would you take me to the prom? Home to meet the parents? Kiss me good night on the stoop?"

"I said, 'Stay close,' " Barrons growled behind me. "And don't talk about the bloody Book in this bloody place. Move your ass, Ms. Lane, *now.*" He took my arm and pulled me from the stool.

Cards spilled from my lap as I stood up. One had slipped inside the fur collar of my coat. I removed it and began to toss it away but at the last moment stopped and looked at it.

The *fear dorcha* had been shuffling a tarot deck. The card I held was framed in crimson and black. In the center, a Hunter flew over a city at night. The coast was a dark border for the silver sheen of the ocean in the distance. On the Hunter's back, between great, dark flapping wings, was a woman with a soft tousle of curls blowing around her face. Between strands of hair, I could see her mouth. She was laughing.

It was the scene from my dream the other night. How could I be holding a tarot card with one of my dreams on it?

What was on the rest of the cards?

I glanced down at the floor. Near my feet was the Five of Pentacles. A shadowy woman stood on a sidewalk, peering through the window of a pub, watching a blond woman inside who was sitting at a booth, laughing with her friends. Me watching Alina.

On Strength, a woman sat cross-legged in a church, naked, staring at the altar as if praying for absolution. Me after the rape.

The Five of Cups showed a woman who looked startlingly like Fiona, standing in BB&B, crying. In the background I could see—I bent and peered closer—a pair of my high heels? And my iPod!

On the Sun were two young women sprawled in bikinis—one lime green, the other hot pink—soaking up the rays.

There was the Death card, a hooded grim reaper, scythe in hand, standing over a bloody body, female again. Me and Mallucé.

There was one with an empty baby carriage abandoned near a pile of clothing and jewelry. One of those parchment-like husks the Shades left behind protruded from the carriage.

I ran my hands through my hair, pushing it back as I stared down.

"Prophecies, beautiful girl. Come in all shapes and sizes."

I glanced up at the dreamy-eyed guy, but he was no longer there. I looked to my right. Mr. Tall, Pin-striped, and Gaunt was also gone.

On the bar, beside a freshly filled shot and a Guinness, another tarot card had been placed with care, facedown, black-and-silver side up.

"Now or never, Ms. Lane. I don't have all night."

I tossed back the shot and chased it, then picked up the card and slipped it into my pocket for later.

* * *

Barrons steered me to a chrome staircase that was guarded at the bottom by the same two men that had escorted me to the top floor to see Ryodan the last time I was here. They were enormous, dressed in black pants and T-shirts, with heavily muscled bodies and dozens of scars on their hands and arms. Both carried snub-nosed automatics. Both had faces that drew the eye but, the moment you saw them, made you want to look away.

As we approached, they swung their weapons toward me.

"What the fuck is *she* doing here?"

"Get over it, Lor," Barrons said. "When I say jump, you say how high."

The one that wasn't Lor laughed, and Lor slammed him in the gut with the butt of his gun. It was like hitting steel. The guy didn't even flinch.

"The fuck I jump. In your dreams. Laugh again, Fade, and you'll be eating your balls for breakfast. Bitch," Lor spat in my general direction. But he didn't look at me, he looked at Barrons, and I think that's what pushed me over the edge.

I glanced between the two guards. Fade stared straight ahead. Lor glared at Barrons. I stepped away from Barrons and walked directly in front of them. Their gazes never wavered. It was as if I didn't exist. I had no doubt I could stand there and do a dance, naked, and they'd still stare at anything but me.

I grew up in the Deep South, in the heart of the Bible Belt, where there are still a few men who refuse to look at a woman that isn't a relative. If a woman is with a man they need to speak with—whether it's her daddy, boyfriend, or husband—they'll look at the man the entire time. If the woman asks a question and they bother answering at all, they direct their reply to the man. They even turn to the side a little, as if catching a glimpse of her in their periphery might condemn them to eternal damnation. The first time it happened to me, I was fifteen, and dumbfounded. I kept asking question after question, trying to get old man Hatfield to look my way. I'd begun to feel invisible. Finally I'd moved to stand right in front of him. He'd stomped off in the middle of a sentence.

Daddy had tried to explain to me that the old man considered it a kind of respect he was paying. That it was a courtesy given to the man the woman belonged to. I hadn't been able to get past the words "the man the woman belonged to." It was a property thing, pure and simple, and apparently Lor—who, according to Barrons, didn't even know what century it was—was still living in a time when women had been owned. I hadn't forgotten his comment about Kasteo, who hadn't spoken in more than a thousand years. How old were these men? When, how, where had they lived?

Barrons took my arm and turned me toward the staircase, but I shook him off and turned back to Lor. I was getting way too much bad press. I wasn't a stone. I hadn't been created by the Unseelie King. And I wasn't a traitor.

One of those things I could have a satisfying fight about.

"Why am I a bitch?" I demanded. "Because you think I slept with Darroc?"

"Shut her up before I kill her," Lor told Barrons.

"Don't talk to him about me. Talk to me about me. Or do you think I'm not worthy of your regard because, when I believed Barrons was dead, I hooked up with the enemy to accomplish my goals? How terrible of me," I mocked. "I guess I should have just laid down and died with a whimper. Would that have impressed you, Lor?"

"Get the bitch out of my face."

"I guess taking up with Darroc makes me pretty . . . well"—I knew what word Barrons hated, and I was in the mood to try it out on Lor—"mercenary, doesn't it? You can blame me for that if you want to. Or you can pull your head out of your ass and respect me for it."

Lor turned his head and looked at me then, as if I'd begun to speak his language. Unlike Barrons, the word didn't seem to bother him. In fact, it seemed he understood, even appreciated it. Something flickered in his cold eyes. I'd interested him.

"Some people wouldn't see a traitor when they looked at me. Some people would see a survivor. Call me anything you like—I sleep fine at night. But you *will* look at me when you say it. Or I'll get so far in your face you'll be seeing me with your eyes closed. You'll be seeing me in your nightmares. I'll scorch myself on the backs of your eyelids. Get off my back and stay off it. I'm not the woman I used to be. If you want a war with me, you'll get one. Just try me. Give me an excuse to go play in that dark place inside my head."

"Dark place?" Barrons murmured.

"As if *you* don't have one," I snapped. "Your cave makes mine look like a white beach on a sunny day." Shouldering past them, I pushed up the stairs. I thought I heard a rumble of laughter behind me and glanced over my shoulder. Three men stared at me with the dead, emotionless gazes of executioners.

But, hey—they were all looking.

Behind a chrome balustrade, the upper floor stretched: acres of smooth dark-glass walls without doors or handles.

I had no idea how many rooms were up here. From the size of the downstairs, there could be fifty or more.

We walked along the glass walls until some tiny detail

I couldn't discern signified an entrance. Barrons pressed his palm to a dark-glass panel, which slid to the side, then he pushed me into the room. He didn't step in with me but continued moving down the hall to some other destination.

The panel slid closed behind me, leaving me alone with Ryodan in the room that was the guts of Chester's. It was made entirely of glass—walls, floor, and ceiling. I could see out, but no one could see in.

The perimeter of the ceiling was lined with dozens of small LED screens fed by cameras that panned every room in the club, as if you couldn't see enough of what was going on merely by looking down past your feet. I stayed where I was. Every step you take on a glass floor feels like a leap of faith when the only solid floor you can see is forty feet below.

"Mac," said Ryodan.

He stood behind a desk, couched in shadow, a big man, dark in a white shirt. The only light in the room came from the monitors above our heads. I wanted to launch myself across the room and attack him, claw his eyes out, bite him, punch him, stab him with my spear. I was astonished by the depth of hostility I felt.

He'd made me kill Barrons.

High on that cliff, the two of us had beaten, cut, and stabbed the man who'd been keeping me alive almost since the day I arrived in Dublin. And I'd wondered for days that had felt like years if Ryodan had wanted Barrons dead.

"I thought you tricked me into killing him. I thought you'd betrayed him."

"I kept telling you to leave. You didn't. You were never supposed to see what he was."

"You mean what you *all* are," I corrected. "All nine of you."

"Careful, Mac. Some things don't get talked about. Ever."

I reached for my spear. He could have told me the truth on the cliff, but, like Barrons, he'd let me suffer. The more I thought about how both of them had withheld a truth from me that would have spared me so much agony, the angrier I got. "I was just making sure that when I stab and kill you, you'll come back so I can do it again."

The spear was in my hand, but suddenly my hand was in a huge fist, and the tip was pointed at my own throat.

Ryodan could move like Dani, Barrons, and the others. So fast I couldn't defend myself. He stood behind me, arm snaked around my waist.

"Never make that threat. Put it away, Mac. Or I'll take it for good." He jabbed me with the tip of the spear in warning.

"Barrons wouldn't let you do that."

"You might be surprised what Barrons would let me do."

"Because he thinks I'm a traitor."

"I saw you with Darroc myself. I heard you in the alley last night. When deeds and words align, the truth is plain."

"I believed both of you were dead. What did you expect? The same survival instinct you admire in each other offends you in me. I think it worries you. Makes me more unpredictable than you'd like."

He guided my hand to the holster and tucked the spear back in. " 'Unpredictable' is the key word there. Did you flip, Mac?"

"Do I look like I flipped?"

He brushed hair from my face, tucked it gently behind an ear. I shivered. He bristled with the same kind of energy Barrons did—heat, muscle, and danger. When

Barrons touches me, it turns me on. But when Ryodan stands behind me, locking me in place with an arm of steel, touching me tenderly—it scares the hell out of me.

"Let me tell you something about flipping, Mac," he said softly against my ear. "Most people are good and occasionally do something they know is bad. Some people are bad and struggle every day to keep it under control. Others are corrupt to the core and don't give a damn, as long as they don't get caught. But evil is a completely different creature, Mac. Evil is bad that believes it's *good*."

"What are you saying, Ryodan? That I flipped and I'm too stupid to know it?"

"If the shoe fits."

"It doesn't. Point of curiosity: Which camp are you and Barrons in? Corrupt to the core and don't give a damn?"

"Why do you think the Book killed Darroc?"

I knew where this was going. Ryodan's theory was that I wasn't tracking the *Sinsar Dubh*; it kept finding *me*. He was about to tell me that it had killed Darroc to further its goal of getting closer to me. He was wrong. "It killed Darroc to stop him. It told me no one was going to control it. It must have learned from me that Darroc knew a shortcut to containing and using it, and it killed him to prevent me or anyone else from discovering it."

"How did it learn that from you? A cozy chat over tea?"

"It found me the night I stayed at Darroc's penthouse. It . . . skims my mind. Tasting me, knowing me, it says."

His arm tightened painfully around my waist.

"You're hurting me!"

His arm relaxed minutely. "Did you tell Barrons this?"

"Barrons hasn't exactly been in a talkative mood."

Ryodan was no longer standing behind me. He was at his desk again. I rubbed my stomach, relieved he was no longer touching me. He was so much like Barrons that his body against mine was disturbing on multiple levels. I couldn't make out much of his face in the shadows, but I didn't need to. He was so furious that he didn't trust himself not to harm me if he remained close.

"The *Sinsar Dubh* can pick thoughts out of your mind? Have you considered the potential ramifications of that?"

I shrugged. It wasn't as if I had much time to consider anything. I'd been so busy jumping from the frying pan into the fire and back into the frying pan again that reflection upon the various possibles wasn't top on my list of priorities. Who could worry about potential ramifications when the real ones kept kicking you in the teeth?

"It means that it knows about *us*," he said tightly.

"First of all, why would it care? Second, I hardly know anything about you at all, so it couldn't have gotten much."

"I've killed for less."

Of that I had no doubt. Ryodan was stone-cold and suffered no conflicts about it. "If it even bothered skimming for information about you, the only thing it knows is that I thought the two of you were dead and you're not."

"Not true. You know a great deal more than that, and that the Book might know about us at *all* should have been the first thing you told Barrons the moment he changed back and you knew he was alive."

"Well, forgive the fuck out of me for being shocked senseless when I realized he wasn't dead. Why didn't you tell me he was the beast, Ryodan? Why did we have to kill him? I know it's not because he can't control himself when he's the beast. He controlled himself last night when he rescued me from the Book. He can change at will, can't he? What happened in the Silvers? Does the place have some kind of effect on you, make you uncontrollable?"

I almost slapped myself in the forehead. Barrons had told me that the reason he tattooed himself with black and red protection runes was because using dark magic called a price due, unless you took measures to protect yourself against the backlash. Did using IYD require the blackest kind of magic to make it work? Would it grant his demand to magically transport him to me no matter where I was but devolve him into the darkest, most savage version of himself as the price?

"It was because of how he got there, wasn't it?" I said. "The spell you two worked sent him to me like it was supposed to, but the cost was that it turned him into the lowest common denominator of himself. An insane killing machine. Which he figured was all right, because if I was dying, I'd probably need a killing machine around. A champion to show up and decimate all my enemies. That was it, wasn't it?"

Ryodan had gone completely still. Not a muscle twitched. I wasn't sure he was breathing.

"He knew what would happen if I pressed IYD, and he made plans with you to handle it." That was Barrons, always thinking, always managing risks where I was concerned. "He tattooed me so he would sense his mark on me and not kill me. And you were supposed to track him—that's why you both wear those cuffs, so you can find each other—and kill him so he'd come back as the man form of himself, and I'd never be any wiser. I'd get rescued and have no clue it was Barrons who'd done it or that he sometimes turns into a beast. But you screwed up. And that's what he was mad at you about this morning on the phone. It was *your* failure to kill him that let the cat out of the bag."

A tiny muscle twitched in his jaw. He was pissed. I was definitely right.

"He can *always* circumvent the price of black magic," I marveled. "When you kill him, he comes back exactly the same as he was before, doesn't he? He could tattoo his whole body with protection runes and, when he ran out of skin, kill himself so he could come back with a clean slate, to start all over." That was why his tattoos weren't always the same. "Talk about your ultimate get-out-of-jail-free card! And if you hadn't botched the plan, I would never have known. It's *your* fault I know, Ryodan. I think that means it's not me you should kill, it's yourself. Oh, gee, wait," I said sarcastically, "that wouldn't work, would it?"

"Did you know that when you were in the Silvers, the Book paid a visit to the abbey?"

I winced. "Dani told me. How many of the *sidhe-seers* were killed?"

"Irrelevant. Why do you think it went to the abbey?"

Irrelevant, my ass. Being unable to die—I was still having a hard time wrapping my brain around that and was certain I could come up with some creative ways to test it—had given him a Fae share of arrogance and disdain for mortals. "Let me guess," I said tartly. "This is somehow my fault, too?"

Ryodan pressed a button on his desk and spoke into an intercom. "Tell Barrons to leave them where they are. They're safer there. I'll bring her to them. We've got a problem. A big one." He released the button. "Yes," he said to me, "it is. I think that when it couldn't find you, it went to the abbey, hunting for you, trying to get a lead on you."

"Do the others believe this, too, or is it your personal delusion? Perspective, Ryodan. Get some."

"I'm not the one that needs it."

"Why do you hate me?"

"I have no emotion about you at all, Mac. I take care of my own. You are not my own." He moved past me, pressed his palm to the door, and stood waiting for me to exit. "Barrons wants you to see your parents so as you go about your business you will remember they are here. With me."

"Lovely," I muttered.

"I suffer them to live, against my better judgment, as a favor to Barrons. He's running out of favors. Remember that, too."

19

Y ou put them in a *glass* room? Can't you give them a little privacy?" I stared at my parents through the wall. Although comfortably furnished with rugs, a bed, a sofa, a small table, and two chairs, the room was made of the same kind of glass as Ryodan's office, only in reverse. Mom and Dad couldn't see out, but everyone else could see in.

I glanced to the left. The shower had an enclosure of sorts; the toilet didn't. "Do they know people can see in?"

"I spare their lives and you ask for privacy. This isn't for you. Or them. It's insurance for me," Ryodan said.

Barrons joined us. "I told Fade to bring up sheets and duct tape."

"For what?" I was horrified. Were they going to roll my parents up in sheets and duct-tape them?

"They can tape sheets to the walls."

"Oh," I said. "Thanks," I muttered. I was silent a moment, watching them through the glass. Dad was sitting on the sofa, facing my mom, holding her hands, talking softly. He was robust and handsome as ever, and the extra silver in his hair only made him look more distinguished. Mom had that glazed look she got whenever she couldn't deal, and I knew he was probably talking about normal, everyday things to ground her in a reality she could face. I had no doubt he was assuring her everything was going to be okay, because that was what Jack Lane did: exuded safety and security, made you believe he could deliver on anything he promised. It was what made him such a great lawyer, such a wonderful father. No obstacle had ever seemed too large, no threat too scary with Daddy around. "I need to talk to them."

"No," Ryodan said.

"Why?" Barrons demanded.

I hesitated. I'd never told Barrons that I'd gone to Ashford with V'lane, or admitted that I'd overheard a conversation between my parents in which they'd been discussing the circumstances of our adoption, or that Daddy had mentioned a prophecy about me—one in which I supposedly ended up dooming the whole world.

Nana O'Reilly—the ninety-seven-year-old woman whom Kat and I visited in her house by the sea—had mentioned *two* prophecies: one that promised hope, the other warning of a blight upon the earth. If I genuinely was part of either one, I was determined to fulfill the former. I wanted to know more about the latter so I could avoid it.

I wanted the names of the people Daddy had spoken to all those years ago when he'd gone to Ireland to dig into Alina's medical history when she was sick. I wanted to know *exactly* what they'd told him.

But there was no way I could ask him about any of it in front of Barrons and Ryodan. If they got the smallest whiff of some prophecy in which I supposedly doomed the world, they might just lock me up and throw away the key.

"I miss them. They need to know I'm alive."

"They know. I videoed you walking in, and Barrons showed them the clip." Ryodan paused, then added, "Jack insisted on it."

I glanced sharply at Ryodan. Was that a faint smile on his face? He *liked* my father. I'd heard it in his voice when he called him Jack. He respected him. I glowed inside. I'm always proud of my daddy, but when somebody like Ryodan likes him . . . Even though I couldn't stand the owner of Chester's, I took it as a compliment.

"Too bad you're not really his daughter. He comes from strong blood."

I gave him a look I learned from Barrons.

"But nobody's sure exactly *where* you came from, are they, Mac?"

"My biological mother was Isla O'Connor, leader of the Haven for the *sidhe*-seers," I informed him coolly.

"Really? Because I did some digging when Barrons told me what the O'Reilly woman said, and it turns out Isla had only one child, not two. Her name was Alina. And she's dead."

"Obviously you didn't dig deep enough," I retorted. But I suddenly felt uneasy. So that was why Nana had called me Alina. "She must have had me later. Nana just didn't know about it."

"Isla was the only member of the Haven who survived the night the *Sinsar Dubh* was set free from its prison."

"Where are you getting your information?" I demanded.

"And there was no 'later' for her."

"How do you know that? What do you know about my mother, Ryodan?"

Ryodan glanced at Barrons. The look they exchanged spoke volumes, but unfortunately I had no idea what language they were speaking.

I glared at Barrons. "And you wonder why I don't confide in you? You don't tell me anything."

"Leave it alone. I'm handling this," Barrons told Ryodan.

"I suggest you do a better job."

"And I suggest you go fuck yourself."

"She didn't tell you that the Book visited her the other night at Darroc's. It skims her mind, picks up her thoughts."

"I think it only picks up the surface ones," I said hastily. "Not everything."

"It killed Darroc because it learned from her that he knew a shortcut. Wonder what else it learned."

Barrons' head whipped around and he stared at me. *You said nothing of this to me?*

You said nothing to me about my mother? What do you know about her? About me?

His dark gaze promised retribution for my oversight. So did mine.

I hated this. Barrons and I were enemies. It confused my head and hurt my heart. I'd grieved him as if I'd lost the only person who mattered to me, and now here we were, adversaries again. Were we destined to be eternal enemies?

One of us is going to have to trust the other, I told him.

You first, Ms. Lane.

That was the whole problem. Neither of us would take the risk. I had a lengthy list of reasons why I shouldn't, and they were sound. My daddy could take the case all the way to the Supreme Court, arguing my side. Barrons didn't inspire trust. He didn't even bother trying.

When hell freezes over, Barrons.

Same bloody page, Ms. Lane. Same bloody—

I turned my gaze away in the middle of his sentence, the ocular equivalent of flipping him the bird.

Ryodan was watching us, hard.

"Butt out," I warned. "This is between him and me. All you need to do is keep my parents safe and—"

"Little hard to do when you're such a fucking loose cannon."

The door burst open, and Lor and two others stalked in. Tension rolled off them, so thick it seemed to suck the oxygen right out of the room.

Fade followed behind them, carrying a pile of sheets and a roll of duct tape.

"You're never going to believe what just walked into the club," Lor told Ryodan. "Tell me to change. Say the word."

My eyes narrowed. Did Lor need Ryodan's permission? Or was it a courtesy in his club?

"The *Sinsar Dubh,* right?" Ryodan gave Barrons a pointed look. "Because it skimmed Mac's mind and now it knows where to find us."

"You are so frigging paranoid, Ryodan. Why would it even *want* to find you?" I said.

"Maybe," one of the other men said, "we'd make a damned good ride for it, and we don't like being used."

"Have you taught her nothing of strategy?" Ryodan fired at Barrons.

"I haven't had all that much time," Barrons said.

"A Seelie. A fucking prince," Lor said. "He's got a couple hundred more Seelie from a dozen different castes waiting outside. Threatening war. Demanding you shut the place down, stop feeding the Unseelie."

I gasped. "V'lane?"

"You told him to come!" Ryodan accused.

"She knows him?" Lor exploded.

"It's her *other* boyfriend," Ryodan said.

"Besides Darroc?" one of the other men demanded.

Lor glared at Barrons. "When are you going to wise up and shut this bitch down for good?"

The testosterone level was rising to a dangerous high. I suddenly worried they might all transform into beasts. I'd be stuck in the middle of a pack of snarling monsters with talons and fangs and horns, and I didn't think for one minute Barrons' brand would protect me from the other five. I wasn't even sure it would work on him.

"You think it's the Seelie you need to be worrying about?" said Fade.

"What the fuck do *you* think we should be worrying about?" Barrons said impatiently.

Fade swung his gun up and pumped a half dozen rounds into Barrons before anyone even managed to move. "Me."

20

The only reason it worked was because Fade caught him off guard. Barrons can move so fast that shooting him isn't the easiest way to kill him.

But he didn't expect Fade to shoot him, and Fade is as fast as Barrons.

I don't know what Barrons and the others are, but until someone tells me otherwise, I'm going to assume they're all the same. They have heightened senses: smell, vision, and hearing. Barrons has the strength of ten men, and his bones are extremely resilient. I imagine they have to be, so he can transform the way he does. I've watched Barrons drop thirty feet and land on his feet, as light as a cat.

Fade surprised them all. He managed to gun down Ryodan, too, before the others attacked him and took his gun away.

Fade stumbled back against the wall, and I thought how strange it was that he'd lost his weapon but was still hanging on to the sheets.

"What the fuck, Fade?" Lor snarled. "Forget your meds again?"

Fade looked at me. "Your parents are next," he purred. "I will destroy everything you love, MacKayla."

I sucked in a horrified breath. Ryodan wasn't paranoid. He'd been right. The *Sinsar Dubh had* skimmed me, lifted information about them from my mind, and acted on it swiftly.

It was right here—in the room with me!

It had learned about Chester's and had come to take a look around, see what it might see.

I'd been out of the Silvers for three days—and this was the third day in a row it had found me!

Was it really my fault that it had gone to the abbey because it hadn't been able to find me in Dublin? Was I indirectly responsible for all the *sidhe*-seers who'd died that night? How long had it been here, moving from person to person, working its way closer to me all the while?

Long enough to have discovered my parents—

"It's in the sheets," I cried. "Get the sheets!" I regretted the words the instant I said them. Whoever touched it would also be possessed, and the other men still had guns. "No, don't touch the sheets!" I screamed.

Fade flashed into motion and was gone.

The others followed, leaving me alone.

I dashed for the door, but it slid shut before I could get there, and I had no clue how to open it. I pressed my palm frantically to half a dozen places, with no success.

I whirled, staring into the other room. If the *Sinsar Dubh* got to my parents . . . if Fade carried it in there . . . if it killed them . . .

I couldn't bear to think about it.

My parents were standing up, looking at me, but I knew they couldn't see me. They were merely staring in the direction from which the gunfire had come.

The door hissed open and closed behind me.

"I have to get you out of here," Lor growled.

I spun around, spear in my fist. "How do I know you're not the Book?"

"Look at me. Where could I hide it?"

His pants and shirt clung to his muscular body like a second skin. I checked his shoes. Boots. "Take them off."

He kicked them off. "Now you. Lose the coat."

I slipped out of it.

"Skirt, too."

"We don't have time for this," I snapped. "My parents—"

"Fade left the club. They're safe for now."

"That's not good enough!"

"We'll take precautions. We're on guard now. Someone has to carry it in. No one will enter the upper levels of the club or your parents' cell with clothes on."

My brows shot up. *That* was going to be a real shocker for my mom.

"I said lose the skirt."

"How could Fade have passed it to me?"

"Minuscule possibility. I take no chances."

Sighing, I unzipped and dropped it. My sweater was snug. I had on a black thong. My boots clung to the shape of my legs. No place to hide a book. "Happy?"

"Hardly."

As I zipped my skirt back up, I took a last longing glance at my parents and turned away. My gaze hitched as it passed over Barrons' crumpled body, and I flinched violently.

Here I was with Barrons dead. Again.

I knew he wasn't really dead, or at least he wouldn't be for long, but my grief was too fresh and my emotions too complicated.

"How long until he—" I broke off, horrified to hear the catch of a sob in my voice.

"Why do you give a fuck?"

"I don't, I mean, I just—*shit!*" I turned and beat at the wall with my fists. I didn't care that my parents could hear the dull thud or that the wall shuddered beneath my blows. I didn't care what Lor thought of me. I hated Barrons being dead. Hated it. Beyond reason. Beyond my understanding.

I punched until Lor caught my bloody fists and pulled me away.

"How long?" I demanded. "I want to know! Answer me or else!"

He grinned faintly. "What, you gonna feed me bloody runes?"

I scowled. "Do you guys tell each other *everything*?"

"Not everything. *Pri-ya* sounded pretty fucking fascinating to me. Never did get all the details."

"How long? *Answer me.*" I used Voice to force him.

"Not sure this time. But it won't be as long as last time. And if you ever try to Voice me again, woman, I'll kill your parents myself."

21

"What must a prince do to get a Valentine's Day kiss, MacKayla?"

The words floated out of the darkness, Eros skittering across my skin, pricking me with a hundred tiny little Cupid bows. Even with *Pri-ya*-induced immunity, I still thrill to the musical, sensual sound of V'lane's voice. I no longer begin stripping when he appears, but deep down inside me there's a summer girl who never stops wanting to, especially when he's being playful, seductive.

How many Valentine's Days in my life had ended with a kiss?

I could count them on two fingers.

And those had been decent kisses, not great ones. Certainly nothing to rock a woman's world.

I paused with my hand on the doorknob of Barrons Books and Baubles. Barrons had changed the locks on the garage and the back door, so I'd had to park the Viper in the alley and walk around to the front. It had been a difficult night. I was ready for it to end. I wanted covers over my head and deep, dreamless sleep.

Mere hours ago I'd been consoling myself that, even

though Barrons was furious with me, at least I would be going to sleep tonight with the comforting knowledge that he was alive.

Right. Happy Valentine's Day to me.

"I believe human males present flowers."

I was abruptly wreathed in the delicate scent of roses. A bouquet appeared, tucked into my arm. Petals tickled my nose. The ground at my feet was strewn with them. Dewy, lush, they gave off an otherworldly, spicy scent.

I leaned my forehead against the diamond-paned cherry door. I could see my demolished shop through it. "Did you come here to accuse me of being a traitor, too?" It would be just like a Fae to shower me with gifts while threatening me. I was through justifying myself. Seeing Barrons' lifeless eyes again had nearly put me back on the cliff's edge. I had no idea why I hated seeing him dead so much, when I knew he wasn't really. Lor had assured me he would be back, although he couldn't say when. *Why* couldn't he say when? Did Barrons' body have to heal, and certain injuries took longer than others?

I couldn't get the image out of my mind. Now I had two visions of Barrons to torture myself with: gutted and shot. On top of that, I was terrified for my parents. Terrified by how easily the Book had infiltrated those closest to me. First the abbey, then Darroc, Barrons, and now a threat to my parents. I could no longer dispute Ryodan's conviction that the Book was finding me. Playing with me. But why not just kill me and get it over with? Did it really think I would—as Ryodan said— "flip"? Nothing about the *Sinsar Dubh* made sense. Sometimes it gave me a splitting, crushing headache and I could sense it coming a mile away. Other times, like tonight, I didn't have a clue it was in the same room with me.

It killed everyone else it came into contact with. But not me. It hurt me, but it always left me alive. Why?

I'd demanded Lor remove Mom and Dad from Dublin. He'd refused to even consider it. Said nobody would lift a finger unless Barrons told them to. So much for their demands for my head—apparently Barrons had the final say about everything.

I could always persuade V'lane to sift in, get them, and whisk them somewhere safe, except . . . well, maybe it was the *sidhe*-seer in my blood, but I just couldn't trust my parents to a Fae.

"I am not a fool, MacKayla. You were playing Darroc. My only question is why."

A weight slid from my shoulders. It was about time somebody believed in me. Figured it would be V'lane. "Thank you," I said simply.

I turned around and my eyes widened appreciatively. V'lane is always a vision. He'd muted himself, donned his "human" form, but it did little to diminish his otherworldly allure. In black pants, boots, and a black cashmere sweater, with his long hair spilling down his back and his velvety skin dusted with gold, he looked like a fallen archangel.

Tonight, he was even more majestic than ever. I wondered if leading a Seelie army had given him purpose he'd lacked, if he was no longer an immortal riddled with ennui and petty desires but was becoming a true leader of his people. He would have his hands full trying to lead the Seelie court. Perhaps if Jayne and the Guardians shot and caged enough of them, they'd pull their heads out. A little hardship and suffering would do the Seelie a world of good.

"You never doubted me? Even when I was standing there in the street with the Unseelie army?"

"I know the woman you are, MacKayla. Were you Fae, you would belong to my court." He studied me with ancient, iridescent eyes. "My army is not as discerning as I. They believe you are his ally. We will persuade them otherwise." A smile touched the corners of his lips. "If nothing else, your claim that Barrons was dead gave you away. I saw him tonight with you at Chester's." He paused. "I am uncertain how you managed to deceive the Unseelie Princes. They were convinced he was dead."

He delivered the statement so blandly that I almost missed the question, and the threat. Lacing his silken words was steel. Beneath his playfulness, V'lane was in a dangerous mood. But why? I knew he'd been at Chester's. Had something happened after Lor had whisked me out and dumped me at the Viper? Did he know the *Sinsar Dubh* had also been there?

"Just a little trick I learned," I evaded.

"Barrons was never dead? Was he . . . incapacitated for a time?"

V'lane and Barrons hate each other, something to do with Barrons killing V'lane's princess a long time ago. Instinct deeper than I could fathom made me lie. "You're kidding, right? Barrons is unkillable."

"I would know how you deceived the Unseelie Princes, MacKayla." There was the steel again, lacing the silk. It was not a question. It was a command.

He moved into the alcove with me, and the intoxicating fragrance of the Fae court, of jasmine and sandalwood, perfumed the delicate spice of the purple petals crushing beneath his boots. Danger stepped in with him.

I cocked my head, studying him. I suddenly knew where his anger was coming from. He was on a dangerous edge not because he thought I had managed to deceive the dark princes but because he was worried they'd known all along that Barrons wasn't dead and had somehow managed to deceive *him*.

V'lane sat on the queen's High Council. He'd been

handpicked by the leader of their race to see through court intrigue to the truth of matters. And he'd failed. His inability to discern truth from lie—from an Unseelie, no less—had shaken him. I understood that. It's debilitating to realize you can't trust your own judgment.

However, in this case he hadn't been wrong. Barrons really *had* been dead, and the Unseelie Princes hadn't deceived V'lane. But I wasn't about to tell him that. Not only had Barrons insisted I lie to V'lane, it seemed I was programmed with an unshakable imperative to keep Barrons' secret.

Knowing him, he'd probably tattooed it on me somewhere.

Still, I could give V'lane some of the truth. "Remember when you said that I had only begun to discover what I was?"

His gaze sharpened and he nodded. He touched my hair. "I am pleased you restored it, MacKayla. It is lovely."

Yeah, well, Barrons hadn't seemed to think so. "You were right. I've recently become aware of a place inside me where I know things that I can't explain knowing. I find things I don't understand."

He inclined his head, waiting.

"I found runes that the princes didn't like. I used them with a combination of others to create an illusion that Barrons was dead," I lied.

He processed my words: The Unseelie hadn't duped him. *I'd* duped the Unseelie. Faint lines of tension eased in his face.

"You convinced Darroc and the princes that Barrons was dead so Darroc would believe you genuinely sought an alliance with him?"

"Exactly."

"Why?"

I hesitated.

"MacKayla, can we not finally trust each other?" he said softly. "What must I do to convince you? Command me, I am yours."

I was so tired of lying and being lied to, of not trusting and not being trusted. "He knew a shortcut to controlling the *Sinsar Dubh*. It's why the Book killed him."

"It is true, then, what we heard," he murmured. "It was not a Hunter after all."

I nodded.

"And what is this shortcut?"

"I wasn't able to get it out of him before he died."

He studied me. "Deceiving the princes so thoroughly would have required immense power." He began to say something, then seemed to change his mind and stopped. After a moment he said carefully, "These runes you used, what color were they?"

"Crimson."

He went still, regarding me as if he wasn't entirely sure what he was looking at. It made me extremely uncomfortable. Then he said, "Did they beat like small human hearts?"

"Yes."

"Impossible!"

"Would you like me to summon them now?"

"You could, with such ease?"

I nodded.

"That will not be necessary. I accept your word, Mac-Kayla."

"What are they? Darroc wouldn't tell me."

"I imagine he was even more interested in you after he saw them. Tremendous power, MacKayla. Parasites—they graft onto anything they touch, grow, and spread like a human disease."

Great. I remembered how they'd seemed larger in the bedroom at Darroc's penthouse. Had I inadvertently loosed another Unseelie evil on the world?

"Used with the Song of Making, they can form an impenetrable cage," he said. "I have never seen them myself, but our histories tell us they were employed on occasion by the first Seelie Queen for punishment and were one of the ingredients used in the walls of the Unseelie prison."

I jerked. "How could I possibly know anything about runes used to build the Unseelie prison walls?"

"That is precisely what I would like to know."

I sighed and rubbed my eyes. More questions. They were beginning to gnaw at my sanity.

"You are weary," he said softly. "On this night for lovers, where would you sleep, MacKayla? In a silken hammock tied between palm trees, swaying over tropical surf, with a devoted Fae lover to attend your every desire? Would you share a Fae prince's bower? Or would you climb the stairs in a ruined bookstore to sleep alone in the building of a man who has never trusted you and never will?"

Ouch.

He touched my jaw, slid a finger beneath my chin, and tipped my face back. "What a lovely woman you've become. You are no longer the child that arrived here months ago. You have been tempered. You display strength and determination, conviction and purpose. But are you wise? Or are you ruled by a heart that foolishly imprinted on the wrong man? Like most humans, are you incapable of change? Change requires an admission of error. Your race devotes itself to justifying its errors, not correcting them."

"My heart hasn't imprinted on anyone."

"Good. Then it may yet be mine." He lowered his head and kissed me.

I closed my eyes and melted into his body. It was a novel change to have someone believe in me, answer my questions when I asked them, just plain be *nice* to me, and there was no denying his erotic allure. When his Fae name eased gently into my mouth, teasing, offering, waiting for me to invite it to settle, I breathed into his kiss and he breathed back. Consonants I would never be able to pronounce, with vowels comprised of delicate arias, began to pierce the meat of my tongue, causing my entire body to flush with sensual pleasure.

I inhaled the scent of Fae prince and the intoxicating aroma of spiced roses into my lungs. Not a bad Valentine's Day kiss, not bad at all.

He took his time giving me his name, letting the impossible syllables work tenderly, slowly, into me, until at last they settled and I exploded, shuddering against him. I stood in the alcove of BB&B, kissing him long after his name was mine again.

I was still glowing when I climbed the stairs and fell across my bed.

"Dude, what *happened* in here?"

I leaned my broom against a fallen bookcase and turned to see Dani framed in the open door of BB&B, cramming a protein bar in her mouth. Her eyes narrowed as she absorbed the destruction. Morning sunlight shafted into the alcove, framing her auburn curls with a halo of fire. Though the day was bright, nearly windless—a whopping sixty degrees after the recent snow—I couldn't get warm, even with both gas fireplaces on.

"Close the door, will you?" I said. I'd dreamed of the Cold Place all night. Repeatedly, I'd been jarred to near-waking by some fright—a slip into a treacherous drift, a nameless terror stalking me—but each time the nightmare had sucked me back down.

I'd scaled icy cliffs, searching for the beautiful, sad

woman, calling out, certain I would find her just over the next ridge. But at the crest of each summit, the only thing I'd found were dozens of hourglasses, with fine black sand rapidly trickling to the lower half. I'd raced from one to the next, frantically turning them over, but they'd kept emptying again in seconds.

Moments before I'd awakened for the final time, I realized the reason I couldn't find her was because I'd waited too long. Time had been of the essence and I was too late. She was gone. Hope, like the fine grains of trickling black sand, had vanished, too.

I'd blown it.

I'd showered and dressed, failure weighing heavy on my bones. Desperate to make progress, to see accomplishment of any kind, I'd attacked the debris in the demolished bookstore with a broom and a vengeance. I'd been at it for hours, beating sawdust and splinters from Barrons' rugs, sweeping broken glass into neat piles.

Dani swaggered in and closed the door. "V'lane said you wanted to see me. Don't know what for, but seeing I ain't too busy this morning, figured I'd give you a listen. But it better be different kinda stuff, 'cause last time I saw you, you weren't talking like no friend of mine." She preened. "He brought me chocolate. *Dude*—like I'm his Valentine or something. Me and him, we had a talk. Told him I'm almost fourteen and I'm gonna give him my virginity one day."

I groaned. She'd actually *told* him that? Before I'd sent him for her, I'd made him swear to turn off the lethal eroticism. "We're going to have a long discussion about your virginity and V'lane, as soon as things calm down."

"News flash, Mac, they ain't never calming. World is. What it is. This is life now." Despite her casual swagger, her flippant tone, her eyes were cold. Wary.

Tough words. Tougher truth to swallow. I never

would. "It's not staying this way, Dani. We're not going to let it."

"What can we do 'bout it? World's too big. 'Sides, ain't so bad. 'Til you go and get all pissy. Thought you and me were, like, peas in the Mega pod and there ain't no other veggies on the plate. Then you go playacting you're humping the Lord Monster. Pissing me off." She shot me a glare crammed full of the words she would never say: *You abandoned me. Left me alone. I'm here, but this better be good.* She pulled an apple out of her pocket and began munching it.

Last night, before V'lane left, I'd asked him to find her this morning and tell her Barrons had never been dead, that I'd been undercover, and I was sorry for the deception. But no apology-by-proxy could replace the real thing. She needed to hear it from me. And I needed to say it.

"I'm sorry, Dani. I hated hurting you."

"Dude, get over yourself. Didn't hurt me. It'd take *way* more than that. Figured you were PMS'ing. No big. Just wanted to hear you say you were a dick."

"I was a dick. And it may not have bothered you, but it drove me crazy. Forgive me?"

She jerked and gave me an uncomfortable look. The precocious, gifted teen had been treated one of two ways at the abbey: ordered around or ignored. I doubted anyone had ever bothered to apologize to her for anything.

"Saying you're a dick was 'nuff, already, jeez. Getting all touchy-feely like a grown-up. Gah!" She stepped around the wreck of the cashier's counter and tried to flash me a grin, but it came out lopsided. "So, what gives? Mini-tornado blow through?"

"Lose the coat," I evaded. I could hardly say, *After I killed Barrons, he was so pissed off at me that he trashed the bookstore.*

"Right. Forgot."

She shrugged out of it, left it in a puddle of black leather on the floor. Beneath it, she had on skintight black low-ride jeans, a tight sweater, and black high-tops. Her green eyes sparkled.

"With the Book hitching rides, hiding on people, guess we're all going to be dressing like skanks for a while, huh? Skintight or skin. Dude, everybody's *everything's* gonna be hanging out, and some o' those fat chicks at the abbey are gonna gross my eyeballs right outta my head. Muffin tops and camel toes, gah!"

I bit my lip, trying not to laugh. That was Dani. Not an ounce of tact. Like the world around her, she was what she was, no holds barred. "Not everybody has superspeed metabolism," I said drily. And what I wouldn't give for it. I'd eat chocolate for breakfast, pastries for lunch, and pie for supper.

She polished off the apple and tossed it into a pile. "Looking forward to seeing Barrons, though," she said enthusiastically. "You? Nah, guess you don't care. You seen him naked for, what, like—months, din't'cha?"

There were times I seriously wished she'd bar some of those holds. I was suddenly in a basement again, watching Barrons walk naked across the room, telling him he was the most beautiful man I'd ever seen.

I changed the subject hastily. "What's going on at the abbey? I know you left, but what were things like before you did?"

Her face darkened. "Bad, Mac. Real bad. Why? You thinking of going back? Gotta tell you, don't think it's a good idea."

Good idea or not, I had no choice. According to Nana, when the *Sinsar Dubh* had escaped the abbey twenty-some years ago, my mother was Haven Mistress. According to Ryodan, the entire Haven had been wiped out that night, with the exception of my mom.

Nana had called me Alina.

According to Ryodan, Alina was the only child Isla ever had. Not only would trying to interrogate Ryodan be an exercise in futility, given how tight-lipped he was, but he was currently dead and I had no idea for how long.

That left Nana or the abbey.

The abbey was closer, and the occupants weren't nearly a century old and prone to nodding off in the middle of a sentence.

The original members of the Haven might all be dead, but some of my mom's peers had to be alive still, even after the Book's recent massacre. Others, besides Rowena, had known my mother. Others knew something—if only rumors—about what happened that night.

And there were those libraries I needed to get into. The ward I'd not been able to pass, the one that had given even V'lane fits. Speaking of which, I'd forgotten to ask him about what had happened to him that day when I'd summoned him to the abbey. I made a mental note to follow up.

I was also toying with the idea of confronting Rowena and trying to force truth from her. I wondered if the power of mental coercion Darroc believed the old woman possessed was a match for the power I'd recently discovered in myself. One of the things holding me back from testing it was that I knew if I did, I'd not only be burning a bridge, I'd be torching the ground I stood on with all *sidhe*-seers. Whether or not they agreed with Rowena's decisions, the majority of the *sidhe*-seers were intensely loyal to her. Another thing holding me back was that I wasn't sure where that power came from and was reluctant to betray anything the Grand Mistress might use against me. Besides, what if all the runes I had were parasites of some kind that could inflict further damage on our world?

Still, there was another weapon at my disposal I

could try. I'd become proficient at Voice and could easily explain it away as a Druid art Barrons had taught me.

"I need answers, Dani. You with me?"

"Ro'll blow a gasket if she catches us," she warned. Her eyes sparkled, and she was beginning to blur with excitement.

I smiled. I loved this kid. We were okay with each other again. One more pain in my heart was gone. "Oh, she's definitely going to catch us. I intend to have a few words with that old woman." If things went south, I'd keep my power in check and let Dani whiz us out, or I'd summon V'lane. "Want to come along?"

"You're kidding, right? Wouldn't miss this gig for the world!"

22

Even with Dani whizzing us in at superspeed, they found us in the south wing in less than three minutes.

Ro must have laid new wards, to sense us and tip her off if we entered the abbey. I wondered how she did it, if it was like witchcraft and required a pinch of hair, blood, or nail. I could too easily see the old woman standing over a bubbling cauldron, dropping items in, stirring away, cackling with delight.

However she'd accomplished it, a group of *sidhe-seers* led by Kat confronted us at the intersection of two corridors before we were even halfway to the Forbidden Library I'd broken into the last time I was here. I'd left a group searching it while I tried to get past a holographic guardian down yet another seemingly "dead-end" hall in the abbey.

Like us, they wore snug clothes no Book could hide under. I imagined that, between the Shades and the *Sinsar Dubh*'s visit, things were pretty tense at the abbey.

"What's in the bag?" Kat demanded.

I opened the translucent plastic grocery bag I'd brought and showed her there was no Book inside it.

Once they were assured I wasn't carrying concealed, they got right to the point.

"The Grand Mistress said you were dead, she did," Jo said.

"Then she said you weren't, but we were to be thinking of you as dead because you'd taken the Lord Master's side, just like Alina," accused Clare.

"But you aren't Alina's sister at all, are you, now?" Mary demanded.

"After we visited Nana O'Reilly," Kat said, "I spoke with Rowena, and she confirmed what Nana told us about the Haven Mistress being an O'Connor. But she said Isla died a few nights after the Book escaped, and it was believed Alina died as well, although the girl's body was never found. Regardless, Alina was her only child. So, Mac, who are you?"

Dozens of *sidhe*-seers stared at me, waiting for my answer.

"She don't hafta answer to you," Dani said belligerently. "Buncha sheep can't even see what's in fronta your own eyes."

"Sure we can. We see a *sidhe*-seer that supposedly doesn't exist. Worries us some, as it should," Kat said. "Then there's you, so determined to defend her. Why would you be doing that?"

Dani compressed her lips into a thin line and folded her skinny arms over her chest. She tapped a foot and stared up at the ceiling. "Just saying, things ain't always bad just 'cause you don't understand 'em or ain't like 'em. That's like thinking anybody who's smarter or faster is dangerous just 'cause they got more brains or quicker feet. Ain't fair. Peeps can't help how they're born."

"We're standing here, waiting to understand." Kat turned her level gray gaze on me. "Help us, Mac."

"Is it true?" I said, point-blank. "Is emotional telepathy your *sidhe*-seer gift?"

Suddenly self-conscious, Kat tucked her shirt in and smoothed her hair. "Where did you hear that?"

I withdrew Darroc's notes from the grocery bag, stepped forward, and offered them to her, but she was going to have to meet me halfway to take them.

I hadn't brought all of what I'd crammed into my pack, just enough for a gesture of good faith. I didn't give a rat's ass what Rowena thought of me, but I wanted in with the *sidhe*-seers. Part of me hated this abbey, where Rowena tightly controlled the *sidhe*-seers' power yet had failed to control the greatest responsibility she'd had. Part of me still wanted to belong. My bipolarity was showing again.

"I found these when I was *undercover*," I stressed the word, "with Darroc. I searched his penthouse. He had notes on everything, including Unseelie I've never heard of or seen. I thought you might want to add them to your libraries. They'll be useful when you encounter new castes. I don't know how he got the scoop on what happens inside these walls, but he must have had someone on the inside. Perhaps he still has." Dani had told me someone had sabotaged the wards outside my cell when I was *Pri-ya*. "You might find it interesting that he says Rowena's gift is mental coercion," I said pointedly.

"How do we know these papers aren't some load of malarkey you've been making up yourself?" Mary demanded.

"You decide. I'm through defending myself."

"You haven't answered my question," Kat said. "Who are you, Mac?"

I met her serene gray gaze. Kat was the only one that I trusted to think things through and make a wise decision. The slender brunette was tougher than she looked, levelheaded, calm in times of stress, and I hoped one day she would replace Rowena as Grand Mistress of the abbey. The position didn't require the most powerful *sidhe*-seer, like the Haven did, but the wisest, a woman with long-term goals and vision. Kat exuded quiet capability, an almost complete lack of ego, a quick mind, and a solid heart. She had my vote all the way.

If she was indeed emotionally telepathic, she would sense my sincerity when I told her as much of the truth as I knew myself.

"I don't know who I am, Kat. I really did believe I was Alina's sister. I'm still not convinced I'm not. Nana said I looked like Isla. Apparently enough that I looked the way she expected Alina to appear grown up. However, like you, I've heard that Isla didn't have a second child. If you think that upsets you, imagine what it does to *me*." I gave her a bitter smile. "First I find out I'm adopted, then I find out I don't exist. But here's a shocker for you, Kat: According to Darroc's notes, he knew the origin of the *sidhe*-seers. Supposedly—"

Three shrill blasts of a whistle split the air, and *sidhe*-seers snapped to attention.

"Enough!" Rowena commanded, as she sailed up behind them, dressed in a smart, fitted suit of royal blue, her long white hair braided in a regal crown around her head. There were pearls at her ears and throat and tiny seed pearls on the chain that draped from her glasses. "That will be all! Restrain the traitor and bring her with me. And Danielle Megan O'Malley, if you think for one bloody moment to whisk her away, think twice. Be very, *very* careful, Danielle." Turning to Kat, she said, "I gave an order. Obey it now!"

Kat looked at Rowena. "Does she speak the truth? *Is* your gift mental coercion?"

Rowena's brows drew together over her fine, pointed nose. Blue eyes blazed. "You would believe her lies about the claims of an ex-Fae over what I have told you?

Och, and I thought you wise, Kat. Perhaps the wisest of all my daughters. You have never failed me. Do not disappoint me now."

"My gift *is* emotional telepathy," Kat said. "He was right about that."

"The best liar knows to salt his deception with an occasional truth, to lend the flavor of credibility. I have not coerced my daughters. I never will."

"I say it's time for truth all around, Grand Mistress," Jo said. "There are only three hundred fifty-eight of us left. We weary of losing our sisters."

"We've lost more than our sisters," Mary said. "We're losing hope."

"I agree," said Clare. "Yes," murmured Josie and the rest.

Kat nodded. "Tell us what Darroc believed about the origin of our order, Mac."

Rowena glared down her nose at me. "Don't you dare!"

I felt it then—a subtle pressure on my mind—and I wondered if she'd been using it on me whenever I'd been around her since the night we'd met. Regardless, it was no threat to me now. I'd learned to resist Voice, and the pressure coming from her was nothing compared to that. I'd been on my knees, cutting myself, with Barrons. I'd had a hell of a teacher.

I ignored Rowena and addressed the *sidhe*-seers. "Darroc believed it was not the Seelie Queen who brought the *Sinsar Dubh* to the abbey to be interred so long ago—"

Rowena shook her head. "Don't do this. They need faith. They've precious little else. It is not your place to take it from them. You've no confirmation of his claims."

I felt the subtle pressure grow stronger as she tried to cow me. "You knew. You've always known. And, like so many other things, you never told them."

"If you believe a seed of evil exists within you, it may consume you." She searched my face. "Och, surely *you* understand that."

"One might also argue that if you believe a seed of evil exists within you, you have the opportunity to learn to control it," I countered.

"One might also argue ignorance is safety."

"Safety is a fence, and fences are for sheep. I would rather die at twenty-two, knowing the truth, than live in a cage of lies for a hundred years."

"You sound so certain of that. Were it put to the test, I wonder where you would truly stand."

"Illusion is no substitute for life," I said.

"Allow them their sacred history," Rowena said.

"What if it's not so sacred?" I said.

"Tell us," Clare demanded. "We have the right to know."

Rowena turned her head away and looked at me from the side, down her nose, as if I were too distasteful to regard directly. "I knew from the moment I saw you that you would try to destroy us, MacKayla—or *who-ever* you are. I should have put you down then."

Kat inhaled sharply. "She's a person, not an animal, Rowena. We don't put people down."

"Right, Ro," Dani said tightly, "we don't put peeps down."

I glanced at Dani. She was staring at Rowena, eyes narrowed and filled with hatred. Oh, yes, it was long past time for truth in these walls, whether we liked those truths or not. Maybe Darroc was wrong. Maybe what he'd written was mere conjecture. But we couldn't question something we refused to face. And unquestioned suspicions had a nasty tendency to grow. Didn't I know; one was expanding exponentially in my head, in my heart, even now.

"Rowena has a point," I conceded. "I don't know

whether or not Darroc was right. But you should know that Barrons suspects it, too."

"Tell us," Kat demanded.

I drew a deep breath. I knew how this had affected me, and I hadn't spent my entire life indoctrinated into the *sidhe*-seer credo. I'd skimmed Darroc's notes again before I'd brought them. Farther into the pages, he'd written it not as a bulleted supposition but as a fact: *The Unseelie King created the* sidhe-*seers.* "Darroc believed it was the Unseelie King himself who trapped the *Sinsar Dubh* and created a prison for it, here, on our world. He believed the king also created prison guards." I hesitated, then added grimly, "*Sidhe*-seers. According to Darroc, it was the last caste of Unseelie the dark king created."

You could have heard a pin drop. Nobody said anything. Nobody moved.

Now that *that* was out, I turned my attention to Rowena. I had no doubt she knew what I needed to know. "Tell me what the prophecy says, Rowena."

She sniffed and turned away.

"We can do this the easy way or the hard way."

"Bollocks, child. We won't be doing this at all."

"Tell me what the prophecy says, Rowena," I said again, and this time I used Voice to command her. It resonated, echoing back at me off the abbey's stone walls. *Sidhe*-seers rustled and murmured.

Eyes bulging, hands fisted, Rowena began to spit out words in a language I didn't understand.

I was about to order her to speak in English, when Kat cleared her throat and moved forward. Her face was pale, but her voice was calm and determined when she said, "Don't do this, Mac. You needn't coerce her. We found the book containing the prophecies in the Forbidden Library you opened. We can tell you all you need to know." She held out her hand for the papers I'd brought. "May I?"

I gave them to her.

She searched my gaze. "Do you believe Darroc was right?"

"I don't know. I could Voice Rowena and see what she knows. I could interrogate her thoroughly."

Kat looked back at Rowena, who was still speaking. "It's Old Irish Gaelic," she told me. "Took a bit of time, but we've translated it. Come with us. But hush her, will you?" She shivered. "It's not right, Mac. It's like what you did to Nana. Our wills must be our own."

"You can say that, knowing she's probably been using coercion on all of you for years?"

"Her power doesn't begin to compare to yours. There is seduction and there is rape. Some of us suspected she had . . . compelling leadership abilities. Still, she made wise and fair decisions."

"She lies to you," I said. Kat was far more forgiving than I was.

"Withholds. A small but important difference, Mac. She was right about faith. Had we been told as children we might be Unseelie, we may have walked a very different path. Release her. I'm asking you."

I looked at Kat a long moment. I wondered if she had something besides emotional telepathy, a kind of emotional balm she could apply if she chose. As I looked into her eyes, my anger at Rowena seemed to diminish. And I could see a grain of truth in what Kat had said. Alina and Christian had called them "necessary lies." I wondered if someone had told me when I was, say, nine or ten that I was Unseelie, if I would have thought I was destined to be bad and never even tried to be good. Would I have thought: *What's the point?*

I sighed. Life was so complicated. *"Forget the prophecy, Rowena,"* I commanded.

Instantly, she stopped speaking.

Kat raised a brow and looked amused. "Is that truly what you wished her to do?"

I winced. *"Don't forget it! Just stop talking about it!"*

But it was too late. I'd Voiced her to forget it, and I could tell by the look of disdain on the old woman's face that every word of it had been wiped from her mind.

"You are a danger to us all," she said haughtily.

I raked my hands through my hair. Voice was tricky.

"My daughters will tell you of the prophecy I no longer recall thanks to your ineptitude at Druid arts. They will tell you freely, without coercion. But you will consent to my terms: You work with our order and no one else. If I recall the shape of it, we know what we need. You will track it. We will do the rest, with . . . " She trailed off, rubbing her forehead.

"The five Druids and the stones," Kat supplied.

"You found the prophecy and it actually tells us what to do?" I said.

Kat nodded.

"I want to see it."

We gathered in the Forbidden Library, a small, windowless room that had failed to impress me when I'd first found it, spoiled as I was by Barrons Books and Baubles. Dozens of lamps were positioned around the low-ceilinged stone room, bathing it in a soft amber glow, bright enough to keep Shades at bay but diffuse enough to minimize damage to ancient fading pages.

Now, as I glanced around, it affected me differently than it had the first time. In my absence, *sidhe*-seers had organized the dusty chaos, dug old tomes out of trunks, carried in bookcases, and arranged things for easy access and cataloging.

I love books, they're in my blood. I wandered the dry

stone room, stopping here and there to pass my hands over fragile covers I longed to touch but wasn't willing to risk harming.

"We're copying and updating everything," Kat said. "For millennia, only the Haven was permitted access to these histories and records. In a few more centuries many of them would have been dust." She gave Rowena a look of gentle rebuke. "Some of them already are."

"Och, and if you one day carry the scepter of my position, Katrina," Rowena said sternly, "you'll come to appreciate the limits of a single lifetime and the difficult choices that must be made."

"The prophecy," I said impatiently.

Kat motioned us all to a large oval table. We pulled out chairs and tucked in around it.

"We translated as best we can."

"Some of the words aren't Old Irish Gaelic," Jo said, "but appear to have been invented by a person self-schooled."

"Jo's our translator," Dani said, with equal measures of pride and disdain. "She thinks research is fun. As fecking *if*."

"Language!" Rowena snapped.

I blinked at her. She was still on that kick? I'd gotten so inured to "fecking" that it hardly even seemed like a cussword to me anymore.

"Ain't your problem no more. You ain't the boss of me." Dani gave Rowena a hard stare.

"Och, and you're so happy on your own, are you, Danielle O'Malley? Your mam would rise from her grave were she to ken her daughter left the abbey, consorts with a Fae prince and others of dubious blood, and takes orders from none at the tender age of ten and three."

"Don't give me no tender-age bunk," Dani growled. " 'Sides, I'm gonna be ten and *four* soon." She beamed around the table. "February twentieth, don't forget. I like chocolate cake. Not yellow. Hate fruit in my cakes. Chocolate on chocolate, the more the better."

"If you two can't be quiet, leave," I said.

The book Kat opened was surprisingly small, thin, clad in dull brown leather, and tied with a worn leather cord. "Moreena Bean lived in these walls a bit over a thousand years ago."

"A *sidhe*-seer whose gift was vision?" I guessed.

Kat shook her head. "No, a washerwoman for the abbess. They called her Mad Morry for her ramblings, ridiculed her insistence that dreams were as real as those events we lived. Mad Morry believed life was not a thing shaped of past or present but possibles. She believed that every moment was a new stone tossed into a loch, causing ripples that those 'revered among women' for whom she toiled were too dull of mind to see. She claimed to behold the entire loch, each and every stone. She said she was not mad, merely overwhelmed." Kat smiled faintly. "Much of what she's written makes no sense whatsoever. If it has come to pass, we can't tie it to current times or understand her signs. If all she penned in these pages is supposed to pass in order, we are only at the beginning of her predictions. A mere twenty pages in, she tells of the escape of the *Sinsar Dubh*."

"She actually calls it that?"

"Nothing in here is ever that clear. She writes of a great evil that slumbers beneath our abbey, that will escape, aided by 'one in the highest circle.'"

"A washerwoman knew of the Haven?" I exclaimed.

"Like as not, she eavesdropped on her betters," Rowena pronounced.

I rolled my eyes. "Elitist to the core, aren't you?"

Kat removed a sheet of yellow legal pad upon which Jo had scribbled a translation and handed it to me.

"There's a great deal of rambling before she gets to

the point," Jo told me. "This was a washerwoman circa 1000 A.D., who'd never seen a car, a plane, a cell phone, an earthquake, and had no words to describe things. She goes on and on about 'in the day of,' in an effort to define when this event would take place. I focused on translating only what pertained to the *Sinsar Dubh* itself. I'm still working on the rest of her predictions, but it's slow going."

I scanned it, eager to find proof of my heroic role, or at least no proof of a villainous one.

The Beast will break free and scourge the earth. It cannot be destroyed. It cannot be damaged. An unholy tree, it will grow new leaves. It must be woven. (Walled? Caged?) From the mightiest bloodlines come two: If the one dies young, the other who longs for death will hunt it. Jewels from icy cliffs laid to the east, west, north, and south will make the three faces one. Five of the hidden barrier will chant as the jewels are laid, and one who burns pure (burned on a pyre?) will return it to the place from which it escaped. If the inhabited . . . possessed (not sure of this word . . . transformed?) seals it in the heart of darkness, it will slumber, with one eye open.

"Dude—sucky! Who writes that kinda drivel?" Dani exclaimed over my shoulder.

Jo sniffed. "I did the best I could what with the woman not spelling a single word the same way twice."

"Would it've killed her to be a little more specific?" Dani groused.

"She probably thought she *was* being specific," I said. The nuances of language changed constantly, especially dialect and lingo. "Really, Dani, who'd be able to translate 'dude—sucky' a thousand years from now?"

But it wasn't only language that compounded things.

Communicating a dream was difficult. I'd been so troubled by my Cold Place dreams in middle school that I'd finally told Daddy I was having a recurring nightmare. He'd encouraged me to write it down, and together we'd tried to decide what it meant.

Logical, pragmatic Jack Lane believed the brain was like a vast computer, and dreams were the conscious mind's way of backing up and storing the day's events in the subconscious, filing away memories and organizing lessons. But he'd also believed that if a dream kept recurring, it suggested the mind or heart was having a problem dealing with something.

He'd proposed that my dream reflected a child's natural fear of losing her mother, but even at ten, that hadn't quite rung true for me. Now I wondered if Daddy had secretly worried that the recurring dream had something to do with the biological mother I'd lost, that perhaps I'd been trapped somewhere cold, forced to watch her die.

That was what I'd been thinking, too, until my recent experience in the White Mansion with the concubine and king, when I'd realized she *was* the woman from my dreams, coupled with my latest dream, where watching her die felt like *I* had perished. Now I was troubled by an entirely different possibility.

Regardless, when I'd attempted to write down my Cold Place dream, it had come out looking a lot like this prophecy: vague, dreamy, and confusing as hell.

"Besides, we think we have it sorted out," Jo said. "The word 'Keltar' means magic mantle. The clan of the Keltar, or MacKeltar, served as Druids to the Tuatha Dé Danann thousands of years ago, when the Fae still lived among us. When the Compact was negotiated and the Fae retired from our world, they left the Keltar in charge of honoring the Compact and protecting the old lore."

"And we've learned there are five male Druids living," said Mary.

"Dageus, Drustan, Cian, Christian, and Christopher," Jo said. "We've already dispatched a message to them, asking them to join us here."

Unfortunately, Christian was going to be a problem.

"You said you knew where the four stones are," Kat said.

I nodded.

"So all we need is you to tell us where the Book is, one of the Keltar to pick it up and bring it here, the four stones laid around it, and the five of them to re-inter it with whatever binding song or chant they know. It sounds like one of them will know whatever needs to be done at the end. I spoke to one of their wives, and she seemed to understand what was meant by 'the inhabited or possessed.'"

"Re-inter it where?" I demanded, watching Rowena closely. It looked as if my only role in the entire matter was to track it. This entire time I'd been feeling as if I had to do it all, but my part in the prophecy was really very small. There was nothing in the prophecy about me that was bad. Just that Alina might die and I would long for death—been there, done that. I felt a huge weight slip from my shoulders. There were five other people responsible for the bulk of it. It was all I could do not to punch the air with a fist and shout, *Yes!*

"Where it was before," she said coolly.

"And where's that?"

"Down the corridor Dani said you couldn't pass," Jo said.

The Grand Mistress shot her a quelling look.

"Can you get past the woman who guards it?" I asked Rowena.

"Don't fash yourself with my business, girl. I'll do my part. You do yours."

"V'lane couldn't get past it, either," I fished, wondering why.

"No Fae can." Smugness dripped from her words, and I knew she'd had something to do with that.

"Who is the woman that guards the hall?"

Jo answered, "The last known leader of the Haven."

Rowena's current Haven was cloaked in secrecy. "You mean my mother?"

"Isla was not your mother! She had only one child," Rowena snapped.

"Then who am I?"

"Precisely." She managed to try, convict, and execute me with the single word.

"The prophecy said there were two of us. One dies young, the other longs for death." Had she and I been alone, I wasn't sure how far I would have gone to force answers from her, but I knew this much: I wouldn't have liked myself when it was over.

"Like as not, a washerwoman ate a bad bit of fish, had dreams on an uneasy stomach, and declared herself a prophet. The word is bloodlines. Plural."

"Her spelling was appalling. There are extra letters in many words," Jo said.

"You'll need to neutralize those particular wards," I said coolly.

"There will be no Fae present when we seal the abomination away!"

"V'lane won't give me the stone," I told her. "There's no way he'll just hand it over."

"Spread your legs for another Fae and whore it out of him," she said flatly. "Then you will turn them all over to us. There is no need for you to be present when the ritual is performed."

My cheeks pinked, and it infuriated me. This old woman got under my skin like nobody else could. I wondered if my mother—*Isla*, I corrected hastily—had felt the same. I'd been so elated to discover the identity of my biological mother, and now, with everyone telling me she'd had only one child, I felt as if not only my mother had been stolen away from me but maybe even my sister as well. I'd never felt so alone in all my life.

"Feck you, old woman," I said.

"Don't waste it on me," she retorted. "I'm not the one with the stone."

"What was it you said to me once? Wait—I remember." I used Voice at the full extent of my power when I said, *"Haud yer whist, Rowena."*

"Mac," Kat warned.

"She's allowed to call me names but I can't tell her to shut up?"

"Sure, and you can, on equal ground, without compulsion. You rely on such powers in times of no need, you run the risk of losing what makes you human. You've a hot temper and a hotter heart. You need to cool them both."

"You may speak, Rowena." Voice had never sounded so pissy when Barrons used it.

"Your loyalty must be first to us, the *sidhe*-seers," she said instantly.

"Do you want the walls back up, Rowena?" I demanded.

"Och, and of course I do!"

"Then the Seelie will have to be involved. Once the Book is re-interred, the queen will need to come search it for the Song of Making—"

"The Song of Making is in the *Sinsar Dubh*?" she exclaimed.

"The queen believes fragments of it are, and from them she can re-create the entire Song."

"And so certain you are you wish that to happen?"

"You don't want the Unseelie locked away again?"

"Ayc, I do. But they've been without the Song of

Making since long before we encountered them. If the Fae regain that ancient melody, their power will once again be limitless. Have you any idea what those times might have been like? Are you so certain the human race would survive it?"

I blinked at her in startled silence. I'd been so focused on getting the Unseelie reimprisoned and sending the Seelie back to their court that I'd not deeply examined the possible repercussions of restoring the Song of Making to the Fae. It must have shown on my face, because Rowena's tone softened when she said, "Och, so you're not a complete fool."

I gave her a look. "I've had a lot on my plate. And I sure learned Voice fast, didn't I? But we have other, more-immediate problems: I know Christian MacKeltar, and he's missing. He's been trapped inside the Silvers since Halloween. We can't do a thing until we find him."

"In the Silvers?" Kat exclaimed. "We can't go in the Silvers! None can!"

"I was there myself recently. It can be done."

Rowena appraised me. "You've been in the Silvers?"

"I stood in the Hall of All Days," I said, and was surprised to hear a touch of pride in my voice. I finally allowed myself to ask the question that had been gnawing at me ever since I'd heard there were two prophecies and, in one of them, I supposedly doomed the world. Was it really about me? Or was it as vague as this one? "I heard there were two prophecies. Where's the other one?"

Kat and Jo exchanged uneasy glances.

"The washerwoman rambled 'til the end of the page about how many stones there were to throw into a loch at any given moment and that some were more possible than others," Jo said. "She claimed she dreamed of dozens such stones, but only two seemed likely. The first could save us. The second was far more likely to doom us."

I nodded impatiently. "I know. So what's the second prophecy?"

Kat handed me the slim volume. "Turn the page."

"I can't read Old Irish Gaelic."

"Just turn it."

I did. Because the ink she'd used had stained through the sheets of vellum bound into the thin journal, Mad Morry had written on only one side of the page. The next page was missing. Small pieces of parchment and torn threads protruded from the binding. "Someone tore it out?" I said disbelievingly.

"A good while ago. This is one of the first volumes we cataloged once you removed the wards protecting the library. We found it open, on a table, with this page and several others missing. We suspect it was whoever destroyed the wards outside your cell when you were *Pri-ya*," Kat said.

"There's a traitor in the abbey," Jo said. "And whoever it is either translates as well as me or took random pages."

"To have bypassed my wards and gained access to this library," Rowena added grimly, "it could only have been one of my trusted Haven."

23

I parked the Viper behind the bookstore and sat staring down into what was once the city's biggest Dark Zone—crammed full of Shades, with one giant amorphous life-sucker in particular that had seemed to enjoy threatening me as much as I'd enjoyed threatening it.

I wondered where it was now. I hoped I would get the chance to hunt it and try out some of my newfound runes, destroy it once and for all, because as large as it had been before it escaped on the night the lights went out in Dublin, I imagined it could devour small towns in a single swallow now.

I glanced at the garage. I looked at the bookstore. I sighed.

I missed him. Ironically, now that I'd become obsessed with wondering who and what I was, I was less worried about who and what he was. I was beginning to understand why he'd always insisted I judge him by his actions. What if the *sidhe*-seers really *were* Unseelie? Did that make us innately bad? Or did that just mean we—like the rest of the human race—had to choose whether to be good or evil?

I got out of the car, locked it, and turned for the bookstore.

"Barrons say you can drive his Viper?" Lor said behind me.

Hand on the doorknob, I turned, dangling the key ring from my finger. "Possession. Nine-tenths of the law."

The corners of his mouth twitched. "You been around him too much."

"Where's Fade? Did you catch him?"

"Book left him dead."

"And just when do you expect *him* back?" I said sweetly.

"Report. What did you learn at the abbey?"

"You think I'm reporting to you now?"

"Until Barrons gets back and takes control of you again."

"Is that what you think? He takes control of me?" My temper flared.

"You'd better hope so, because if he doesn't, we kill you." The threat was delivered tonelessly, with utter disinterest. It was chilling. "We don't exist. That's the way it always has been. That's the way it always will be. If people find out about us, we kill them. It's not personal."

"Well, excuse the hell out of me if you try to kill me and I decide to take it pretty damned personally."

"We're not trying to. At the moment. Report."

I snorted and turned to enter the store.

He was behind me, his hand on my hand on the doorknob, his face in my hair, lips close to my ear. He inhaled. "You don't smell like other people, Mac. I wonder why. I'm not like Barrons. Ryodan is downright civilized. I don't suffer Kasteo's problems, and Fade is still having fun. Death is my morning coffee. I like blood and the sound of bones breaking. It turns me on. Tell me what you learned about the prophecy and, next time, bring me the seer's book. If you want your parents to remain . . . intact, you will cooperate only with us. You will lie to everyone else. We own you. Don't make me give you a lesson. There are things that can break you. You wouldn't believe the madness certain kinds of pain can induce."

I turned to face him. For a moment he didn't let me, made me push against his body and struggle to move. His body was every bit as electric as Barron's and Ryodan's. And I knew he was enjoying it, quite possibly on a level of primitive carnality I didn't understand.

There are things that can break you, he'd said. I almost laughed. He had no idea the thing that had broken me most completely was my belief that Barrons was dead.

One look at Lor's eyes and I decided I would wait until Barrons was back before pressing any issues with him. "You think Barrons has a weakness for me," I said. "That's what worries you."

"It is forbidden."

"He despises me. He thinks I slept with Darroc, remember?"

"He cares that you slept with Darroc."

"He cared that I burned his rug, too. He gets a little pissy about those things he likes to think of as his property."

"You two drive me bug-fuck. Prophecy. Talk."

He interrogated me for nearly half an hour before he was satisfied. I let myself into my fourth-floor bedroom, weary to the bone. My room was a mess—protein-bar wrappers, empty water bottles, and clothes everywhere. I washed my face, brushed my teeth, slipped into pajamas, and was about to crawl into bed, when I remembered the tarot card from last night that the dreamy-eyed guy had given me.

I dug in the pocket of my coat and pulled it out. The back of it was black, covered with silver symbols and runes that looked a lot like the silver etchings I'd glimpsed on one of the three forms of the *Sinsar Dubh*—the one of an ancient black tome with heavy locks.

I turned it over. THE WORLD was inscribed at the top.

It was a beautiful card, framed in crimson and black. A woman stood in profile on a white landscape tinged with blue that looked icy, forbidding. Against the back-drop of a starry sky, a planet revolved in front of her face, but she was looking away—not at the world at all but staring off into the distance. Or was she looking at someone who wasn't on the card? I had no idea what THE WORLD card was supposed to mean in a tarot reading. I'd never had my cards read. Mac 1.0 had con-sidered having your future divined through tarot cards as ridiculous as trying to dial up a dead relative on a Ouija board. Mac 5.0 would happily take any help she could get from any source. I studied it. Why had the dreamy-eyed guy left it for me? What was I supposed to learn from it? That I needed to look at the world? That I was distracted by other things and people and not see-ing clearly? That I really was the person holding the fate of the world in my hands?

No matter how I looked at it, the card implied way too much responsibility. The prophecy had made it clear that my involvement wasn't much at all. I tucked it be-tween the pages of the book on my bed stand, got into bed, and pulled the covers over my head.

Once again, I dreamed of the sad, beautiful woman and, once again, I had the oddest sense of duality, seeing from her eyes and mine, feeling her sorrow and my con-fusion. *Come, you must hurry, you must know.*

Urgency gripped me.

Only you can. No other way in . . . Her words echoed off the cliffs, growing fainter with each rebound. *Trying to . . . for so long . . . so hard . . .*

Then an Unseelie Prince was there beside her (us).

But he was not one of the three I knew, one of the three that had raped me. It was the fourth. The one I'd never seen.

In that strange way of knowing things in dreams, I knew it was War.

Run, hide! she screamed.

I couldn't. My feet were rooted to the ground, my eyes locked on him. He was far more beautiful than the other Unseelie Princes and far more terrifying. Like the others, he looked *into* me, not at me, and his gaze felt like razors slicing through my most private hopes and fears. I knew that War's specialty was not merely to turn opposing factions, races, or populations upon one another but to find sides within a person and turn them upon themselves.

Here was the ultimate trickster, the destroyer.

And I understood that Death wasn't the one to be feared. War was the one that laid waste to lives. Death was just the cleanup guy, the janitor, the final act.

Though the same black torque writhed around War's neck, it was threaded with silver. Though kaleidoscopic colors rushed beneath his skin, a nimbus of gold surrounded him, and, at his back, I glimpsed the flash of black feathers. War was winged.

You are too late, he said.

24

I was jarred awake the next morning by an unaccustomed noise and sat up, looking around. Twice more I heard the sound before I figured out what it was. Someone was throwing a rock against my window.

I rubbed my eyes and stretched. "Coming," I groused, and tossed back the covers. I figured it was Dani. Since cell phone service still wasn't back up and the store had no doorbell, it was the only way she could get my attention, short of breaking in.

I pushed aside the drape and glanced out into the alley.

V'lane reclined on the hood of Barrons' Viper, leaning back against the windshield. Though supposedly the car wasn't mine (we'd see about that), I instantly assessed V'lane for rivets or any other abrasive elements that might mar the paint job. I love sports cars. All that muscle just does it for me. I decided it was a safe bet the soft white towel knotted loosely at his waist wasn't going to scratch anything. His perfect body was dusted gold, and his eyes were sunshine sparkling on diamonds.

I pushed the window up. Chilly air wafted in. The

temperature had dropped, low-hanging clouds had moved in. It was once again cold and gloomy in Dublin.

He lifted a cup of Starbucks. "Good morning, Mac-Kayla. I brought you coffee."

I eyed it with equal parts suspicion and longing. "You found an open Starbucks?"

"I sifted to a store in New York. I ground the beans and made it myself. I even . . . how do you say? Frothed the milk." He held up some packets. "Splenda or raw sugar?"

My mouth watered. Raw sugar and caffeine in the morning. Only sex could make it better.

"Is Barrons around?" he said.

I shook my head.

"Where is he?"

"Busy for the day," I lied.

"Anything pressing on your agenda?"

I narrowed my eyes. V'lane wasn't talking like he normally did. Usually he spoke with great formality. Today he sounded almost . . . human. I eyed the towel, trying to decide if there might be a Book beneath it. It was possible. "Could you swap that towel for something like, well, skintight shorts?"

He was suddenly nude.

Definitely no Book. "Put your towel back on," I said hastily. "Why are you talking funny?"

"Am I? I endeavor to learn from humanity, Mac-Kayla. I thought you would find me more appealing. How am I doing? No, wait. I am appropriating human contractions. How'm I doing?"

He was still nude. "Towel. Now. And you contracted the wrong words. 'I am' becomes 'I'm.' 'How am' does not become 'how'm.' But, really, it's okay. Contractions don't sound right coming out of your mouth anyway."

He flashed me a dazzling smile. "You like me as the

prince I am. That is promising. I came to take you for a day at the beach. Tropical surf and sandbars. Coconuts and palm trees. Sand and sun. Come." He offered a hand. It wasn't the only part of him extended in my direction.

I'm surrounded by intensely sexual men at every turn. "*Towel*," I demanded. I bit my lower lip. I shouldn't. I had no right. I had the weight of the world on my shoulders. I even had the tarot card to prove it.

"I do not know why you do not enjoy seeing me nude. I enjoy seeing you nude."

"Do you want me to go to the beach with you or not?"

His iridescent eyes were brilliant. "You have accepted my invitation. I see it in your eyes. They have taken on a languorous sheen. I find it arousing."

"But not to a beach in Faery," I said. "No illusion. Can you sift us to somewhere like Rio, in the human world, where only human hours will pass?"

"Command me, I am yours, MacKayla. We shall spend a finite number of human hours, to be specified by you."

I was fatally flawed. I couldn't say no. "I'll take that coffee now." I reached out the window for it, expecting him to float it up or something.

"I am unable to oblige. The paranoid one's wards are still active. They keep me several feet from the building."

"But not off his car," I said, a smile tugging at my lips. Barrons would go nuts if he knew V'lane had touched his Viper. And stretched out on it nude? He'd have an aneurysm.

"It is all I can do not to sear my name into the paint. I am afraid you will have to come down for your coffee. It is hot; make haste."

I ran a brush through my hair, splashed water on my face, slipped into shorts, a tank, and flip-flops and, ten minutes later, I was in Rio.

I can't be on a beach without thinking of Alina. I keep telling myself that, when all this is over, I'll ask V'lane to give me an illusion of her again and we'll spend a day playing volleyball together, listening to tunes, and drinking Corona and lime. I'll say good-bye, once and for all. I'll let go of the pain and the anger, tuck the wonderful parts of the life we shared into a sacred corner of my soul, and accept living without her.

If Barrons had truly been dead, and enough time had passed, would I have eventually accepted living without him? I was afraid I never would have.

I turned my attention to the Seelie Prince walking beside me. I was glad he'd come to find me this morning. If he hadn't, I would have summoned him with the sensual sting of his name through my tongue. My dreams last night had unsettled me deeply. I had questions, and he was the only one who might have the answers.

We walked a short distance down the powdery beach to a pair of silken chaises sunk in white sand, close to the salty spray of the sea. My clothes melted away and were replaced by a hot-pink string bikini and a gold belly chain adorned with fiery stones. The beach was deserted. I had no idea if there were no people left or if V'lane had sent them away for privacy.

"What's with the belly chain?" He seemed to have a fondness for them.

"When I have sex with you from behind, I will use it to pull you closer, push in deeper."

I opened my mouth and closed it again. I was the idiot that had asked.

"And now whenever you see the gold of it glinting in the sun, you will think about fucking me."

I sank into the chair and tipped my head back, watching birds fly overhead. The soft rush of waves soothed my soul. "Baseball cap and sunglasses, please."

He reached over and tucked a cap on my head, propped sunglasses on my nose. I looked at him. He was nude again, towel mounded between his legs.

"I have found it burns. It is most unpleasant."

"Is your skin real?"

He removed the cloth. "Touch it." When I made no move to do so, he said, "I regret that you are immune to me. Human seduction of one such as you may take an eon. Yes, MacKayla, in this form my skin is every bit as real as yours."

A drink appeared in my hand, a creamy blend of pineapple, coconut, and spiced rum.

"Tell me about Cruce," I said.

"Why?" V'lane said.

"He interests me."

"Why?"

"It seems he was somehow different from the other Unseelie Princes. The others didn't have names. Why did Cruce? When I first met you, you offered me the cuff of Cruce. Why was it called that? How did Cruce learn to curse the Silvers? There seems to be so much more history about him than any of the other princes."

V'lane sighed, in perfect human mimicry. "One day you will wish to talk of *me*. You will have as many questions of *my* existence and my place in Fae history. It is majestic, far more so than Cruce's. He was a fledgling prince. I have more to offer."

I tapped my fingers, waiting.

He ran his hand along my arm, wove his fingers with mine. His hand was warm and strong and felt just like a real man's. He was seriously putting on the human today.

"I have already told you more about ancient Fae history than any human has ever known."

"And I still know only the barest sketch of events. You say you want me to see you as a man, to trust you, but trust comes from sharing knowledge and finding common ground."

"If others of my race were to discover how much I tell you . . ."

"I'll take that chance. Will you?"

He stared out at the sea, as if seeking wisdom in the turquoise waves. Finally he said, "As you wish, Mac-Kayla, but you must never reveal your knowledge to another Fae."

"I understand."

"Once the Unseelie King was satisfied that he had sufficiently improved upon the initial, imperfect efforts of his experiments that resulted in the lesser castes of Unseelie, he began to replicate the Seelie hierarchy. He created four royal houses, dark counterparts to the Seelie royal lines. The house of Cruce was the final one he made. Cruce himself was the last Unseelie ever brought into existence. By the time the king began to work on the fourth royal house, he was a virtuoso at bringing into being his half-life children, even without the Song of Making. Though with their raven hair, black torques, and haunting melodies, they would never pass for Seelie, they were still a match in beauty, eroticism, and majesty for the highest-ranking light Fae. Some say the king stopped with Cruce because he knew if he made even one more of his 'children'—much like in your own mythologies—the child would kill the father and usurp his kingdom."

I nodded, remembering my Oedipus from college.

"In the beginning, the king rejoiced in Cruce and

shared his knowledge freely. He had found a worthy companion, one to work with in his efforts to make his beloved concubine Fae. Cruce was clever, learned quickly, and invented many things. The cuff was one of his first creations. He made it as a gift for the king to give his concubine, so that when she desired his presence, she had only to touch the cuff and think of him to make it so. It also protected her from certain threats. The king was delighted with the token. Together they forged several amulets to grant her the gift of weaving illusion. The king alone created the final one he bestowed upon his beloved. Some say she could deceive anyone with illusions woven from it, even him. He gave Cruce greater access to his studies, his libraries and laboratories."

"But how did *you* get Cruce's cuff?"

"My queen gave it to me."

"How did she get it?"

"I assume it was taken from Cruce when he was killed, then passed from queen to queen to be protected."

"So, while the king was trusting Cruce with everything he knew, the prince decided to overthrow him and steal his concubine?" I said. I couldn't keep the note of condemnation out of my voice.

"From whom did you hear that?"

I hesitated.

"Trust must be reciprocal, MacKayla," he chided.

"I saw Christian in the Silvers. He said he'd learned that Cruce hated the king, wanted his concubine, and cursed the Silvers to keep the king away from her. He told me Cruce planned to take the king's woman and all the worlds inside the Silvers for himself."

V'lane shook his head, tawny hair shimmering in the sun. "It was not so simple. Things rarely are. To use a human word, Cruce loved the king, first and above all.

The creator of the Unseelie is a being of unbearable perfection. If he is indeed Fae, he is from the most ancient, most pure line that ever existed. Some say he is the Father of All. Some say he had outlived hundreds of queens before the time of the queen he slew. Many of the forms he can take are beyond even Fae ability to absorb. He has been described as having enormous black wings that can enfold the entire Unseelie court. Were he to attempt to take human form, he would have to occupy multiple bodies and divide facets of himself. He is too vast to be contained in a single mortal vessel."

I shivered again. I'd seen the hint of those wings in the White Mansion. I'd felt the concubine's awareness of them, had empathically shared her fascination with their feathery touch on her naked skin. "I thought the queen was the most powerful of your race."

"The queen is heir to the magic of our people. It is a different thing. That magic has never accepted a male of the True Race, although . . . "

"Although what?"

He gave me a sideways look from beneath his lids. "I tell you too many things." He sighed. "And enjoy it too much. It has been a long time since I knew another worthy of confidences. There is an ancient myth that, should all the contenders for the matriarchal throne be no more, the magic would likely gravitate toward the most dominant male of our race. Some say our rulers are your Janus head, your yin and yang: The king is the strength of our people; the queen is wisdom. Strength draws from brute force, wisdom draws from true power. In harmony, the king and queen lead a united court. Opposed, we war. We have been opposed since the day the king killed the queen."

"But other queens came along. Couldn't the king make peace?"

"He did not try. Again, he abandoned his children.

Upon finding his concubine dead, through his act of atonement he did what he had sworn never to do. By pouring all his dark knowledge into the pages of an ensorcelled tome, he inadvertently created his most powerful 'child' yet. Then he vanished. It is rumored among Seelie and Unseelie alike that he has been trying to—as you humans would say about a lame horse—put it down ever since. The Hunter that killed Darroc was allegedly the king's own for hundreds of thousands of years. It carried him from world to world, hunting his nemesis. The king, like any Fae, loves nothing so much as his own existence. As long as the Book is free, he knows no peace. I suspect the *Sinsar Dubh* was amused to take the king's steed. I also suspect that if the king is no longer using that Hunter, and that Hunter is here in your city, then the king is, too."

I gasped. "You mean in Dublin?"

V'lane nodded.

"In human form?"

"Who could say? There is no predicting one such as he."

He would have to occupy multiple bodies. I thought of Barrons and his eight. I shook my head, rejecting the thought. "Back to Cruce," I said hastily.

"Why this fascination with Cruce?"

"I'm trying to understand the chronology. So the king trusted Cruce, worked with him, taught him, and Cruce betrayed him. Why?"

V'lane's eyes narrowed and his nostrils flared with cool disdain. "The king's devotion to his concubine was unnatural. It is an aberration in our race. Humans prize monogamy because they have a mere blink of an eye to suffer each other. You are born beneath the shadow of death. It makes you crave unnatural bondage. We do not spend more than a century, perhaps two, with a partner. We drink from the cauldron. We change. We go on. The king did not."

"Speaking of which, how do you know any of this?"

"We have scribes and written histories. As one of the queen's High Council, it is my duty to recount our past, on those occasions she passes an edict. She insists I be able to recite any part at any time."

"So the king was faithful, and fairies don't like that."

He gave me a look. "Spend a thousand years with another and tell me it is not unnatural. At the very least, tedious."

"Apparently the king didn't think so." I liked the king for that. I liked the idea of true love. Maybe, just maybe, some people were lucky enough to find their other half, the one that completed them, like a Janus head.

"The king had become a danger to his children. His court began to talk. They decided to test him. Cruce would seduce the king, turn his obsession from the concubine, make him abandon his singleminded focus on the mortal."

"Is the king bisexual?"

V'lane gave me a blank look.

"I thought the Fae were gender-specific."

"Ah, you refer to who fucks whom and are we—how do you say it—monosexual?"

"Heterosexual," I said. Hearing V'lane say the word "fuck," in his musical, sensual voice, was foreplay in and of itself. I took a sip of my drink, hung my leg over my chair, and cooled a toe into the surf.

"When I speak of Fae seduction, it is different from human lust. It is the captivation of another's . . . " He seemed to be struggling for words. "Humans do not have an appropriate word. Very psyche? That which is all one is? Cruce was to become the king's favored, re-placing the mortal with whom he'd so long been obsessed, who was not even of our kind. Cruce was to make the king once again enamored of our race. When the king returned his attention to the Court of Shadows, he would raise them to their rightful place in the light with the others of their race. His halflings were weary of hiding. They wanted to meet their brethren. They wanted to taste the life their counterparts enjoyed. They wanted the king to fight for them, make the queen accept them, to unify the courts into one. They felt all was as it should be. The queen was the wise and true leader of the Seelie, the king was the strong and proud leader of the Unseelie. They were a Janus head, complete, if only the king and queen would let them live together as one."

"Did the Seelie feel the same?" I couldn't imagine they did.

"The Seelie were completely unaware the Unseelie existed."

"Until someone betrayed the king to the queen."

"Betrayal is in the eye of the beholder," V'lane said sharply. He closed his eyes a moment. When he opened them again, the angry gold glints were gone. "I shall rephrase that properly for you: Someone should have told the queen the truth long before she learned it. The queen is to be obeyed in all things. The king disobeyed her repeatedly. When the king refused Cruce, the Unseelie knew he would never stand up for them. They spoke of mutiny, civil war. To avoid it, Cruce went to the queen to speak on his dark brothers' behalf. While he was away, the other princes designed a curse to be cast into the Silvers. If the king would not give up his mortal, they would forbid him access to her, by blocking him from entering the Silvers and ever seeing her again."

"So it wasn't Cruce who corrupted the network of the Silvers?"

"Of course not. Among my race, the name Cruce has

become synonymous with one of your humans . . . I believe his name was Murphy and a certain edict was passed? If something goes wrong, it is blamed on Murphy. It is the same with Cruce. If Cruce had indeed cast the curse into the Silvers, it would not have corrupted their primary function. It simply would have prevented the king from entering. Cruce studied with the king himself; he was far more adept than his brethren."

"What did the queen say when he went to her?" I asked. It almost seemed that Cruce was a renegade hero. Really, although the Unseelie were vile, so were most of the Seelie I'd met. As far as I was concerned, they deserved each other. They *should* have reunited in one court, policed their own, and stayed the hell out of our world.

"We will never know. Upon hearing what he had to say, she confined him to her bower. She then summoned the king and they met in the sky that very day. Although I possess no memory of it, according to our histories it was me she sent for Cruce, and when I brought him to her, she lashed him to a tree, took up the Sword of Light, and killed him before the king's eyes."

I gasped. It was so strange to realize V'lane had been alive during that time. That he'd had firsthand experience of it all yet recalled none of it. He'd had to read about it in written histories to recall what he'd willingly forgotten. I wondered: What if whoever wrote Fae histories, like our humans, distorted things a bit? Knowing their penchant for illusion, I couldn't see any Fae telling the whole truth. Would we ever really know what had happened back then? Still, I imagined V'lane's version was the closest I might ever get to it. "And war broke out."

He nodded. "After the king killed the queen and returned to his court, he found his concubine dead. According to the princes, when she learned of the battle and discovered that the king had begun to slaughter his own race in her name, she stepped from the Silvers, lay down in his bed, and killed herself. They say she left him a note. They say he carries it still."

What ill-fated lovers! It was such a sad story. I'd felt their love on those obsidian floors in the White Mansion, even though both of them had been deeply unhappy: the king because his beloved was not Fae like him, and the concubine because she was trapped, waiting alone, for him to make her "good enough" for him—that was how she'd felt, inferior. She would have loved him as she was, one small mortal life, and been happy. Still, there'd been no question of their love. They were all each other wanted.

"The next we heard of the *Sinsar Dubh*, it was loose in your world. There are those among the Seelie that have long coveted the knowledge in its pages. Darroc was one of them."

"How does the queen plan to use it?" I asked.

"She believes that the matriarchal magic of our race will enable her." He hesitated. "I find that you and I trusting each other appeals to me. It has been long since I had an ally with power, vitality, and an intriguing mind." He seemed to be assessing me, weighing a decision, then he said, "It is also said that any who knows the First Language—the ancient language of . . . I believe the only human word that suffices is 'Change,' in which the king scribed his dark knowledge—would be able to sit down and read the *Sinsar Dubh*, once it was contained, page after page, absorbing all his forbidden magic, all the king knew."

"Did Darroc know this language?"

"No. I know that for a certainty. I was there when he last drank from the cauldron. Had any of our race known the *Sinsar Dubh* had been rendered inert beneath your abbey before they'd drunk from the cauldron so many times that the ancient language was lost in the mists of their abandoned memories, they would have razed your planet to get to it."

"Why would they want the knowledge the king had so regretted acquiring that he'd banished it?"

"The only thing my race loves as much as itself is power. We are drawn to it without reason, much as the mind of a human man can be so numbed by a stunningly sexual woman that he will follow her to his own destruction. There is that moment you call 'before,' in which a man—or Fae—can consider the consequences. It is brief, even for us. Besides, while the king chose to do foolish things with his power, another of us might not. Power is not good or evil. It is what it is in the hands of the wielder."

He was so charming when he was open, speaking freely about the shortcomings of his race, even comparing his people to ours. Maybe there was hope that one day Fae and human could learn to—I shook my head, terminating that thought. We were too different, the balance of power between us too exaggerated.

"Repay my trust, MacKayla. I know you went to the abbey. Have you learned how the Book was originally contained?"

"I believe so. We found the prophecy that tells us the basics of what to do to re-inter it."

He sat up and removed his sunglasses. Iridescent eyes searched my face. "And this is the first you think to mention it?" he said incredulously. "What must we do?"

"There are five Druids that have to perform some kind of binding ceremony. Supposedly they were taught it long ago by your race. They live in Scotland."

"The Keltar," he said. "The queen's ancient Druids. So that is why she has long protected them. She must have foreseen that such events might transpire."

"You know them?"

"She has . . . meddled with their bloodline. Their land is protected. No Seelie or Hunter can sift within a certain distance of it."

"You sound upset about that."

"It is difficult to see to my queen's safety when I cannot search all places for the tools I need to do so. I have wondered if they guard the stones."

I appraised him. "Since we're trusting each other, you *do* have one, right?"

"Yes. Have you had any success locating any of the others?"

"Yes."

"How many?"

"All three."

"You have the other *three*? We are closer than I had dared hope! Where are they? Do the Keltar have them, as I suspected?"

"No." Technically, I had them at the moment, safely warded away, but I felt more comfortable letting him believe Barrons did. "Barrons does."

He hissed, a Fae sound of distaste. "Tell me where they are! I will take them from him, and we will be done with Barrons for good!"

"Why do you despise him?"

"He once slaughtered a broad path through my people."

"Including your princess?"

"He seduced her, to learn more about the *Sinsar Dubh*. She became temporarily enamored of him and told him many things about us that should never have been revealed. Barrons has been hunting it a long time. Do you know why?"

I shook my head.

"Nor do I. He is not human, he can kill our kind, and he seeks the Book. I will kill him at the earliest opportunity."

Good luck with that, I thought. "He will never give up the stones."

"Take them from him."

I laughed. "Not possible. You don't steal from Barrons. It doesn't work."

"If you find out where they are, I will help you obtain them. We will do this, just the two of us. Of course, the Keltar are also necessary to restrain it, but no others, MacKayla. When you and I have secured it for the queen, she will reward you richly. Anything you wish can be yours." He paused a moment, then said delicately, "She could even restore to you things you have lost and grieve."

I stared out at the sea, trying not to be tempted by the carrot at the end of that stick: Alina. Rowena was insisting I work only with the *sidhe*-seers. Lor was demanding I work only with Barrons and his men. Now V'lane wanted me to ally myself with him and shut everyone else out.

I trusted all of them about as far as I could throw them.

"Since the day I arrived in Dublin, everyone has been trying to force me to choose sides. I won't. I'm not going to choose any of you over the others. We'll do this together or not at all, and when we do, I want the *sidhe*-seers to watch, so if anything ever goes wrong again in the future, we know how to stop it."

"Too many humans involved," he said sharply.

I shrugged. "Then bring some of your Seelie if it makes you feel better."

The balmy day suddenly cooled. He was deeply displeased. But I didn't care. I felt that we finally had a solid plan, one that would work. We had the stones and the prophecy; we just needed Christian. I refused to worry about what we would do once the Book was secured, if the queen should be permitted to read it. I could tackle only one seemingly insurmountable obstacle at a time, and I had no idea how we were going to locate Christian in the Silvers. Too bad Barrons hadn't branded him, too.

I had one more question. It had been gnawing at me the entire time we'd been talking. I couldn't help but feel there was something about myself I needed to know, a truth that would make clear the dreams I'd been having all my life. "V'lane, what did Cruce look like?"

He lifted a shoulder and let it drop, then folded his arms behind his head and tipped his face to the sun. "The other Unseelie Princes."

"You said they kept getting better as the king made them. Was Cruce different in any way?"

"Why do you ask?"

"Just something one of the *sidhe*-seers said," I lied.

"When do you plan to attempt to fulfill the terms of the prophecy?"

"The moment we can get all the Keltar together and I locate it."

He looked at me. "Soon, then," he murmured. "It will be very soon."

I nodded.

"It must be as soon as possible. I fear for the queen."

"I asked you about Cruce," I reminded.

"So many questions about an insignificant prince who ceased to exist hundreds of thousands of years ago."

"And?" Was that petulance in his voice?

"Were he not dead, I might feel . . . what is it you humans are so often driven by? Ah, I have it, jealousy."

"Humor me."

After a long moment, he gave another of those perfectly imitated human sighs. "According to our histories, Cruce was the most beautiful of all, although the world will never know it—a waste of perfection to never have laid eyes upon one such as he. The torque of his royal line was threaded with silver, and his visage was said to radiate pure gold. But I suspect the reason the king felt such kinship to him—before he permitted his love for a mortal to destroy all they could have been—was because Cruce was the only one of the king's children to bear a paternal resemblance. Like the king himself, Cruce had majestic black wings."

25

Shortly after midnight, I was pacing the alley behind Barrons Books and Baubles, arguing with myself and getting nowhere.

Barrons still wasn't back, which was driving me crazy. I planned to have it out with him the moment he showed up. Knock-down, drag-out, air all the dirty laundry between us. I wanted to know exactly how long I could anticipate him being gone if he got killed again. I was on constant edge, waiting, half afraid he might never come back. I wouldn't be satisfied that he was really alive until I saw him with my own eyes.

Every time I'd closed my eyes tonight, I slipped into my Cold Place dream. It had been waiting to ambush me the moment I'd relaxed. I'd flipped endless hourglasses of black sand; I'd scoured miles and miles of ice, with increasing urgency, for the beautiful woman; I'd repeatedly fled the winged prince we both feared.

Why did I keep dreaming the damned dream?

Ten minutes ago, when I'd woken from it for the fifth time, I'd been forced to accept that I simply wasn't going to get any sleep without having it—and that was no sleep at all. The fear and anguish I felt in the dream were so draining that I kept waking up feeling even more exhausted than when I'd closed my eyes.

I stopped pacing and stared at the brick wall.

Now that I knew it was there, I could feel it—the hidden *Tabh'r* in the brick, the Silver Darroc had carefully camouflaged within the wall catty-corner to the bookstore.

All I had to do was press into it, follow the brick tunnel to the room with the ten mirrors, and pass through the fourth one from the left to get back into the White Mansion. I'd have to hurry, because time passed differently inside the Silvers. I would just take a quick look around. See if there was anything I'd missed the first time.

"Like maybe a portrait of myself hanging on the wall, arm in arm with the Unseelie King," I muttered.

I closed my eyes. There it was, out in the open. I'd voiced my fear. Now I had to deal with it. It seemed to be the only thing that explained all the loose ends that wouldn't connect.

Nana had called me Alina.

Ryodan said Isla had only one child (which Rowena confirmed, unless she was lying) and she was dead, and there'd been no "later" for the woman I wanted to believe was my mother.

Nobody knew who my parents were.

Then there was my lifelong feeling of bipolarity, of things repressed just beneath the surface. Memories of another life? When I'd been walking around in the White Mansion with Darroc, it had all been so familiar. I'd recognized things. I'd been there before and not just in my dreams.

Speaking of dreams—how could my slumbering mind conjure up a fourth prince that I'd never seen? How could I have known Cruce had wings?

I could sense the *Sinsar Dubh*. It kept finding me,

liked to play with me. Why? Because in an earlier incarnation—when it had been the Unseelie King, not a book of the banished knowledge—it had loved me? Did I sense it because I'd loved the earlier incarnation of *it*?

I buried my hands in my hair and tugged, as if the pain might clarify my thoughts or perhaps fortify my will.

See me, Barrons kept saying.

And, more recently, *If you can't face the truth of your reality, you can't control it.*

Ryodan had been right: I was a loose cannon, but not for the reason he thought.

I didn't know the truth of my reality. And until I did, I was a wild card, something that could flip. The question keeping me awake at night wasn't whether or not *sidhe*-seers were an Unseelie caste. That was small compared to my problem. The question that kept me from sleeping was much more alarming.

Impossible as it seemed, was I somehow the Unseelie King's concubine? Reincarnated and brought back to life in a new body? Fated for her inhuman lover, destined to a tragic cycle of rebirth?

And just what were Barrons and his eight? My ill-fated lover split into nine human vessels? That was a doozy of a thought. No wonder the concubine had found the king insatiable. How could one woman handle nine men?

"What are you doing, Ms. Lane?" As if my thoughts had conjured him, Barrons' voice slid out of the darkness behind me.

I looked at him. I'd flipped on the exterior lights outside BB&B, powered by the store's immense generators, but the light was at his back and he was heavily shadowed. Still, I would have known it was him even if I were blind. I could feel him on the air; I could smell him.

He was furious with me. I didn't care. He was back.

He was alive. My heart did a flip-flop. I thrilled to his presence. I would anywhere, anytime, under any circumstances. No matter what he was, what he'd done. Even if he was one-ninth of the Unseelie King who'd begun it all.

"Something's seriously wrong with me," I said, half under my breath.

"Just now figuring that out, are you?"

I gave him a look. "Good to see you alive again."

"Good to be alive."

"Do you really mean that?" He'd made comments about death in the past, which now made sense to me. Apparently he would never experience it, and at times he'd seemed almost . . . envious.

"Nice tan. You just can't stay away from the Fae when I'm gone, can you? Did V'lane take you to the beach again? Did you get a sand burn when he fucked you?"

"Are you the Unseelie King, Barrons? Is that what you and your eight are? Different facets of you, crammed into human form, while you search Dublin for your missing Book?"

"Are you the concubine? The Book certainly seems enamored of you. Can't stay away. Kills everyone else. Plays with you."

I blinked. He was always way ahead of me, and he didn't even know about my dream of the winged prince or my déjà vu experience in the mansion. We'd been thinking the same things about each other. I'd had no idea he'd been wondering if I was the allegedly dead concubine.

"There's one way to find out. You keep telling me to see you, to face the truth. I'm ready." I held out my hand.

"If you think I'm letting you into my head again, you're wrong."

"If you think you could stop me if I wanted to, you're wrong."

"Aren't you full of yourself?" he mocked.

"I want you to come somewhere with me," I said. Did Barrons know full well what he was and would just never admit to it? Was it possible the king could subdivide himself into human parts and forget who he was? Or had he been tricked into human form, his individual facets forced to drink from the cauldron, and now the most feared of the Unseelie walked the earth with no greater clue to what he was than his oblivious concubine?

One way or another, I wanted answers. I was sure enough of the truth about myself to run the gauntlet. If I was wrong about him, he didn't have much to lose, just the equivalent of a few days' "nap." And somehow I knew that wouldn't be the case. I was right about this one. I had to be.

He stared at me in silence.

"C'mon, Barrons. What's the worst that can happen? I lead you into some trap and you die for however long it is you go away? Not that I'm going to," I added hastily.

"It's hardly pleasant, Ms. Lane. It's also highly inconvenient."

Inconvenient. That's what dying for me back on the cliff had been. An inconvenience. And I'd been ready to wipe out a world for him. "Fine. Do what you want. I'm going."

I turned and pushed into the wall.

"What the fuck do you think you're—get your ass out of—Ms. Lane! Fuck! Mac!"

As I vanished into the wall, I felt his hand close on my coat, and I laughed. He'd called me Mac, and I wasn't even dying.

* * *

"Which mirror now, Ms. Lane?" He glanced around the white room, scanning the ten mirrors.

"Fourth from the left. *Jericho*." I was sick of him calling me Ms. Lane. I picked myself up off the white floor. Once again the Silver had spit me out with entirely too much enthusiasm, and I didn't even have the stones on me. I didn't have anything but the spear in my holster, a protein bar, two flashlights, and a bottle of Unseelie in my pockets.

"You don't have the right to call me Jericho."

"Why? Because we haven't been intimate enough? I've had sex with you in every possible position, killed you, fed you my blood in the hopes that it would bring you back to life, crammed Unseelie into your stomach, and tried to rearrange your guts. I'd say that's pretty personal. How much more intimate do we have to get for you to feel comfortable with me calling you Jericho? *Jericho*."

I expected him to pounce on the sex-in-every-possible-position comment, but he only said, "You fed me your—"

I pushed into the mirror, cutting him off. Like the first one, it resisted me, then grabbed me and squirted me out on the other side.

His voice preceded his arrival. "You bloody fool, do you never stop to consider the consequences of your actions?" He barreled out of the mirror behind me.

"Of course I do," I said coolly. "There's always plenty of time to consider the consequences. After I've screwed up."

"Funny girl, aren't you, Ms. Lane?"

"Sure am. Jericho. It's Mac. I'm Mac. No more fake formality between us. Get with the program or get the hell out of here."

His dark eyes flared. "Big talk. *Ms. Lane.* Try to enforce it." Challenge burned in his gaze.

I sauntered toward him. He watched me coldly and I was reminded of the other night, when I'd pretended to be coming on to him, because I was angry. He thought I was doing it again. I wasn't. Being in the White Mansion with him was doing something strange to me. Unraveling all my inhibitions, as if these walls had no tolerance for lies, or within them there was no need.

Then he was staring past me. "I don't believe it. We're in the White Mansion. You just casually lead me in here like you're running errands to the drugstore. I've been looking for this bloody place forever."

"I thought you'd been everywhere." He'd never been here? Or did he not remember being here, long ago, in another incarnation?

He turned in a slow circle, absorbing the white marble floors, the high arched ceilings, the columns, the sparkling windows opening on a brilliant, frosted winter's day. "I knew where it was supposed to be, but the White Mansion shows itself only when and to whom it chooses. This is incredible." He walked to the window and stared out. Then he turned on me. "Have you found the libraries?"

"What libraries?" I was having a hard time looking at him, mesmerized by the glittering winter day beyond his shoulder. How many times had I sat in that snowy garden, surrounded by dazzling ice sculptures and frozen fountains, waiting for him?

Fire to his chill. Ice to her flame.

I loved this wing. As I stared out the window, the concubine was suddenly there, but she was faint around the edges, a little misty, a partially realized memory.

She sat on a stone bench, in a dress of blood-red and diamonds, through which I could see snow and iced branches. The light was strange, as if everything but her was painted in halftones.

I jerked. The fourth Unseelie Prince, the winged War/Cruce, had just appeared. He was also semitransparent, a residue from a time long past. At his wrist glinted a wide silver cuff, and around his neck was an amulet, very different from the one Darroc had worn.

I watched with astonishment as the concubine rose and greeted him with a kiss on both marble-white cheeks. There was affection between them. Once, long ago, the beautiful woman in my dream hadn't been afraid of him. What had changed? The raven-winged prince carried a silver tray, upon which sat a single teacup and an exquisite black rose. She laughed up at him, but her eyes were sad.

Another of his potions to change me?

War/Cruce murmured something I couldn't catch.

She accepted the cup. *Perhaps I do not want his salvation.* But she drank deeply, until the cup was empty.

"The king kept all his notes and journals on his experiments in the White Mansion, to prevent those in his Dark Court from stealing his knowledge." Barrons' voice jarred me.

I blinked, and the memory was gone.

"You sure do know a lot about the king." I was going to say more, but I suddenly felt as if a rubber band attached to my belly button had contracted, yanking me toward the other end. I'd been too far away, gone too long.

Without another word, I turned and ran down the corridor, away from him. Gone was all desire to fight with him. I was being summoned. Every fiber in my being was drawn, the same way it was the last time I was here.

"Where are you going? Slow down!" he called behind me.

I couldn't have slowed if I'd wanted to, and I didn't. I'd come here for a reason, and that reason was where I was being pulled. The black floors of the Unseelie King were calling me. I wanted to be in that boudoir again. I wanted to see him this time, to see the king's face. Assuming he had one.

I passed over rose marble, skidded onto bronze floors, dashed through turquoise corridors, and flew through halls of yellow, until I felt the sultry warmth of the crimson wings. I could feel Barrons behind me. He could have caught me if he'd wanted to. He was fast like Dani, like all his men. But he let me run, and he followed.

Why? Because he suspected the same things I did? Because he wanted it out in the open? My heart was pounding with fear and anticipation to have it finally over, to know what I was, what he was.

Barrons was suddenly beside me. I glanced over at him, and he gave me a look that was equal parts fury and lust. He was really going to have to get over that fury part. It was beginning to piss me off. I had just as much to be mad at him about.

"I *didn't* have sex with Darroc." I was mad all over again, itching for physical contact. "Not that I should have to explain myself to you. It's not like you ever explain yourself to me. But even if I did, even if I was the traitor you're determined to believe I am, he's dead, so according to the philosophy of Barrons, who cares? Here I am, with you again. Actions speak, right? You got the action you wanted. OOP detector back under control, tightly leashed. Lead me around by the collar, why don't you? Isn't that when you're happiest? *Ruff-ruff*," I mock-barked, seething.

"You haven't fucked me since you were *Pri-ya*. There's an action for you. Says pretty much all there is to say."

It burned him. Good. It was burning me, too. "This

is some kind of pissing contest? Darroc got laid but you didn't? That's the only reason you're mad?" What did he think it said? That I would touch him only if I was sex-starved? Or if the alternative was dying a mindless animal?

"You couldn't begin to understand."

"Try me." If he'd ever just admit to one little feeling about me, I might admit to one about him.

"Don't push me, Ms. Lane. This place is getting to me. You want the beast on your hands?"

I glanced at him. His eyes were sparking crimson and he was breathing hard, but not from exertion. I knew him. He could run for hours. "You want me, Jericho. Admit it. A lot more than once or twice. I'm under your skin. You think about me all the time. I keep you awake at night. Go ahead, say it."

"Fuck you, Ms. Lane."

"Is that your way of saying it?"

"That's my way of saying grow up, little girl."

I skidded to a halt, slipping and sliding on the black marble floor. The instant I stopped running, he did, too, as if we were bound by the same tether.

"If I'm a little girl, then that makes you a serious pervert." *The things we did together* . . . I shot him a graphic reminder with my eyes.

Oh, so you're finally ready to talk about them, his dark gaze mocked. *Maybe I don't want to now.*

Too bad. You were always slapping me in the face with reminders. Turnabout's fair play. But it sure wasn't a little girl back in that bed, Jericho. It's not a little girl you're messing with now.

I poked him in the chest with my finger. "You died in front of my eyes and let me believe it was real, you bastard!" I felt like I was being torn in half—pulled toward the boudoir by destiny, rooted in place by the need to air my grievances.

He knocked my finger away. "Do you think it was fun for me?"

"I hated watching you die!"

"I hated doing it. It hurts every damned time."

"I grieved!" I shouted. "I felt guilty—"

"Guilt isn't grief," he snapped.

"And lost—"

"Get a fucking road map. Lost isn't grief, either."

"And—and—and—" I broke off. There was no way I was telling him all the things I'd really felt. Like destroying the world for him.

"And *what*? What did you feel?"

"Guilt," I shouted. I punched him, hard.

He shoved me, and I stumbled back against the wall. I shoved him back. "And *lost*."

"Don't tell me you grieved me when you were really just pissed off about the mess you'd gotten yourself into. I died and you felt sorry for yourself. Nothing more." His gaze flickered to my lips. I got that. He was once again furious with me and once again perfectly ready to have sex with me. The conundrum that was Barrons. Apparently it was impossible for him to feel anything as far as I was concerned without getting angry about it. Did anger make him want to have sex with me? Or was it that he always wanted to have sex with me that made him so angry?

"I was grieving more than that. You don't know the first thing about me!"

"And you *should* have felt guilty."

"So should you!"

"Guilt is wasted. Live, Ms. Lane."

"Oh! Ms. Lane! Ms. Frigging Lane! There it is again. You tell me to feel guilty, then you tell me it's wasted. Make up your mind! And don't tell me to live. That's exactly what I was doing that you're so pissed about. I went on!"

"With the enemy!"

"Do you care how I went on, as long as I did? Isn't that the lesson you've been trying to teach me? That adaptability is survivability? Don't you think it would have been easier for me to lay down and quit once I thought you were dead? But I didn't. You know why? Because some overbearing prick taught me that it was how you *go on* that matters."

"The word that was supposed to be emphasized there was *how*. As in honorably."

"What place does honor have in the face of death? And, please, did you *honorably* kill that woman you carried out of the Silver in your study?"

"You couldn't possibly understand that, either."

"That's your answer for everything, isn't it? I couldn't possibly understand, so you're not going to bother telling me. You know what I think, Jericho? You're a coward. You won't use words, because you don't want anyone to hold you accountable," I accused. "You won't tell the truth, because then somebody might judge you, and God—"

"—has nothing to do with this and—"

"—forbid you actually get *personal* with me—"

"—I don't give a damn about being judged—"

"—and I don't mean try to have sex with me—"

"—I wasn't trying to have sex with you—"

"—I didn't mean at this precise moment. I meant—"

"—and it would have been impossible, anyway, because we've been running. I don't have any bloody idea *why* we've been running," he said irritably, "but you're the one who started it and you're the one that stopped."

"—like knock down a few walls between us and see what happens. No, you're such a coward that the only time you can call me by my name is when you're either pretty sure I'm dying or you think I'm so out of my mind that I won't notice. Seems like a hell of a wall to erect between yourself and someone you don't like."

"It's not a wall. I merely endeavor to help you keep our boundaries straight. And I didn't say I didn't *like* you. 'Like' is such a puerile word. Mediocre people *like* things. The only question of any significant emotive content is: Can you live without it?"

I knew the answer to that question where he was concerned, and I didn't like it one bit. "You think *I* need help understanding where our boundaries are? Do *you* understand where our boundaries are? Because they seemed pretty damned mysterious and movable to me!"

"You're the one arguing about the names we call each other."

"What do you call Fiona? Fio! How charming. Oh, and what about that twit at Casa Blanc the night I met that bizarre man McCabe? Marilyn!"

"I can't believe you remember her name," he muttered.

"You called her by her full first name, and you didn't even like her. But not me. Oh, no. I'm Ms. Lane. In bloody frigging perpetuity."

"I had no idea you had such a hang-up about your name, *Mac,*" he snarled.

"Jericho," I snarled back, and pushed him.

He manacled both my wrists with one hand so I couldn't hit him again. It infuriated me. I head-butted him.

"I thought you died for me!"

He shoved me against the wall and braced his forearm across my throat so I couldn't head-butt him again. "For fuck's sake, is that what this is about?"

"You didn't die. You lied to me. You took a little nap and left me on that cliff thinking I'd killed you!"

He searched my face, dark eyes slitted. "Ah, I see. You thought it meant something that I died for you. Did you dress it up in romance? Compose sonnets memorializing my great sacrifice? Did it make you like me better? Did I have to be dead to get you to *see* me? Wake the fuck up, Ms. Lane. Dying is overrated. Human sentimentality has twisted it into the ultimate act of love. Biggest load of bullshit in the world. Dying for someone isn't the hard thing. The man that dies *escapes*. Plain and simple. Game over. End of pain. Alina was the lucky one. Try *living* for someone. Through it all—good, bad, thick, thin, joy, suffering. That's the hard thing."

Alina was the lucky one. I'd thought that, too, and had been ashamed of myself for thinking it. I punched him so hard, he stumbled on the slick black floor, and as he went down, I felt sudden horror at seeing him stumble. I never wanted to see him stumble, so I grabbed him and we both went down to our knees on the black floors. "Damn you, Jericho!"

"Too late, Rainbow Girl." He grabbed a fist of my hair. "Somebody beat you to it." He laughed, and when he opened his mouth over mine, fangs grazed my teeth.

Yes, this was what I needed, what I'd needed since the day I woke up in that basement and left his bed. His tongue in my mouth, his hands on my skin. The burn of his body against mine. I grabbed his head with both hands and ground my mouth against his. I tasted my own blood from a nick on his teeth. I didn't care. I couldn't get close enough. I needed rough, hard, fast sex, followed by hours and hours of slow and intimately thorough fucking. I needed *weeks* in bed with him. Maybe if I had willing, cognizant sex with him long enough, I'd get over him already.

Somehow I doubted that.

He hissed. "Fucking fairy in your mouth. You have me in your mouth, you don't get anybody else. Or you don't get me." He sucked on my tongue, hard, and I could feel V'lane's name unraveling from the center of it.

He spat it out like an unfastened piercing. I didn't care. There hadn't been enough room in my mouth for them both anyway. I pressed into his body, rubbing desperately against him. How long had it been since I'd had him inside me? Too long. I grabbed the sides of his shirt and ripped, sent buttons flying. I needed skin to skin.

"Another of my favorite shirts. What is it with you and my wardrobe?" He pushed his hands up my shirt and unhooked my bra. When his hands rasped over my nipples, I jerked.

Come, you must hurry . . .

Shut up, I snarled silently. I'd left that voice back in Dublin, where it had been torturing me in my bedroom.

All will be lost. . . . It must be you. . . . Come.

I growled. Couldn't she leave me alone? She hadn't spoken in my head for the past forty-five minutes. Why now? I wasn't asleep. I was awake, wide awake, and I needed this. I needed him. *Go away,* I willed. "Please," I groaned.

"Please what, Mac? You'll have to ask for it this time, spell it out in graphic detail. I'm done giving you everything you want without making you ask for it."

"Right. Words mean nothing to you, but now you insist on them," I said against his mouth. "You are *such* a hypocrite."

"And you're bipolar. You want me. You always do. You think I can't smell it?"

"I'm *not* bipolar." Sometimes he struck way too close to home. I popped the button on his pants, unzipped them, and shoved my hands inside. He was rock hard. God, he felt good.

He stiffened, air hissing between clenched teeth.

Make haste . . . He comes. . . .

"Leave me *alone*," I snapped.

"Over my dead body," he said roughly. "You've got

my dick in your hands." He told me where it was going to be next and my bones turned to water, tried to spill my body across the floor and let him do anything he wanted to me.

"Not you. Her."

"Her who?"

A hand tugged at the sleeve of my jacket, and I knew without looking that it wasn't his. "Kiss me and she'll go away." I needed him inside me so badly I hurt from it. I was hot and wet and nothing mattered but this moment, this man.

"Who?"

"Kiss me!"

But he didn't. He pulled back and looked past me, and I knew from the look on his face that I wasn't the only one who could see her.

"I think she's me," I whispered.

He looked at me, back at her, and at me again. "Is that a joke?"

"I know this house. I know this place. I don't know how else to explain it."

"Impossible."

It is nearly too late. Come NOW.

It was no longer a wisp of a plea. It was a command, and the hand was implacable on my arm. I could not disobey, no matter how badly I wanted to stay here and lose myself in sex, no matter how desperately I needed him inside me again, needed to feel we were joined in the most primal way, that I was in Jericho Barrons' arms and mouth and under his skin.

And, God, did I need it! So much that I resented it. I never wanted to want a man this much—so much that *not* having him was physical pain. I never wanted to feel that any man had so much control over me and my life.

I pushed up from my knees and shoved past him.

He grabbed the sleeve of my coat; it ripped as I pulled away. "We need to talk about this! Mac!"

I dashed down the corridor, running after her like a dog chasing its own tail.

The concubine's white half of the boudoir was carpeted in dewy petals and lit by a thousand candles. The winking diamonds that floated on the air were tiny fiery stars. Those few that passed through the enormous mirror to the dark king's side were instantly extinguished, as if there wasn't oxygen enough to support flame, or the darkness there was too dense to permit light.

The concubine sprawled nude on piles of snowy ermine before the white hearth.

In the shadows on the far side of the bedchamber, darkness moved. The king watched her through the mirror. I could feel him there, immense, ancient, sexual. She knew he was watching. She stretched languidly, slid her hands up her body into her hair, and arched her back.

I'd expected to find the other end of the rubber band here, ending with the concubine, but it tugged me still. It stretched invisibly on, through the massive black Silver that divided their bedchamber in half.

I wanted to step through and join that immense ancientness.

I never wanted to step one foot closer to those shadows.

Was the king himself summoning me? Or was part of the king standing behind me, even now? I had to know. I'd called Jericho a coward but could too easily be accused of the same.

I need . . . the voice summoned.

I understood that. I did, too. Sex. Answers. An end to my fears, one way or another.

But the voice hadn't come from the woman on the rug.

It had come from the dark side of the boudoir, which was all bed because he required that much bed. It was a command I couldn't refuse. I would slip through the mirror and Barrons would lay me back on the Unseelie King's bed and cover me with lust and darkness. And we would know who we were. It would be okay. It would all be out in the open finally.

As I stared into the Silver that I knew was a killing mirror for anyone who wasn't the king or his concubine, I was suddenly five again. More details of my Cold Place dream crashed over me and I realized there were many I still didn't remember.

I'd always had to pass through this chamber first: half white, half dark, half warm, half cold. But numbed and frightened out of my childhood wits by the nightmarish things that followed, I'd always forgotten how the dream had begun. It had always been here.

And it had always been so hard to force myself to go through the enormous black Silver, because I'd wanted nothing more than to stay in the warm white half of this chamber forever, to lose myself in endlessly replaying scenes of what had once been but was now lost to me and I could never have again, and grief—oh, God, I'd never really known grief at all! Grief was walking these black halls and knowing they would be haunted for eternity with the residue of lovers too foolish to savor what time they'd had. Memories stalked these corridors, and I stalked those memories like a sad ghost.

Still, wasn't illusion better than nothing?

I could stay here and never have to face that my existence was empty, that emptiness was all my life had ever been about: dreams, seduction, glamour.

Lies. All lies.

But here I could forget.

Come NOW.

"Mac." Jericho was shaking me. "Look at me."

I could see him distantly, through sparkling diamonds and ghosts of times past. And behind him, through the mirror, I could see the monstrous dark shape of the Unseelie King, as if he was casting Jericho as his shadow on the other side, on the white half of the room. I wondered if the concubine's shadow was different, too, through the king's Silver. Did she become like him on his half? Large and complex enough to mate with whatever the king was? Over there, in the blessed, comforting, sacred dark, what was she? What was I?

"Mac, focus on me! Look at me, talk to me!"

But I couldn't look. I couldn't focus, because whatever was beyond that mirror had been calling me all my life.

I knew the Silver wouldn't kill me. I knew it beyond a shadow of a doubt.

"I'm sorry. I have to go."

His hands tightened on my shoulders and tried to turn me away. "Walk away from it, Mac. Let it go. Some things don't need to be known. Isn't your life enough as it is?"

I laughed. The man who always insisted I see things as they were was now urging me to hide? On the rug behind him, the concubine laughed, too. Her head arched, her chin tipped up, as if she was being kissed by an invisible lover.

He had to be the king. I slid my hand down his arm, twined my fingers with his. "Come with me," I said, and ran for the Silver.

26

I was surprised by the ease with which I slid through the black membrane. I was stunned senseless by the cold that knifed into me.

My brain issued an order to gasp. My body failed to obey it. I was crusted from head to toe with a thin sheet of glittering ice. It cracked as I took a step, tinkled to my feet, and I was instantly recoated again.

How was I supposed to breathe here? How had the concubine breathed?

Ice coated the insides of my nose, my mouth and tongue and teeth, all the way down to my lungs, as all the parts of my body I needed to process air were sheathed in an impenetrable layer. I stumbled backward, seeking the other side of the mirror, where there was white and light and oxygen.

I was so cold that I could barely move. For a moment, I wasn't sure I would make it back through the Silver. I was afraid I would die in the Unseelie King's bedchamber, repeating history, only this time I'd have left no note.

When I finally slid through the dark membrane, warmth hit me like a blast oven, and I stumbled, went flying across the room, and slammed into the wall. The concubine stretched on the rug paid me no heed. I sucked in air with a greedy screech.

Where was Jericho? Could he breathe on the other side? Did he *need* to breathe, or was it his natural environment? I glanced back at the mirror, expecting to see him moving darkly on the other side, scowling at me for having forced him to reveal his true identity.

I staggered and nearly went down.

I'd been so certain I was right.

Barrons was collapsed on the floor, at the boundary of light and dark—on the *white* side of the room.

Only two in all existence could ever travel through that Silver: the Unseelie King and his concubine, Darroc had told me. *Any other that touches it is instantly killed. Even Fae.*

"Jericho!" I ran for him, dragged him away from the mirror, and sank to the floor beside him. I rolled him over. He wasn't breathing. He was dead. Again.

I stared down at him.

I stared into the darkness of the mirror.

The Silver hadn't killed me. But it *had* killed him. I didn't like what that meant one bit.

It meant I was indeed the concubine.

It also meant that Jericho *wasn't* my king.

NOW.

The command was enormous, irresistible, Voice to the nth degree. I wanted to stay with Jericho. I couldn't have stayed if my life had depended on it. And I was pretty sure it did.

"I can't breathe over there."

You do not live on this side of the Silver. Alter your expectations. Forgo breath. Fear, not fact, impedes you.

Was that possible? I wasn't buying it. But apparently it didn't matter whether I bought it, because my hands were pushing me up and my feet were moving me straight into the dark Silver.

"Jericho!" I cried as I felt myself being forced away.

I hated this. I hated everything about it. I was the concubine but Jericho wasn't the king, and I couldn't deal with that—not that I was sure how well I would have dealt with it if he *had* been the king. Now I was being summoned to a place where I couldn't breathe, where I didn't really live according to my disembodied tormentor, and I had no choice but to leave him, dead again, by himself.

I suddenly had no desire to learn anything else about myself. This was enough. I was sorry I'd been so hell-bent on knowing to begin with. He'd been right. Wasn't he always? Some things just didn't need to be known.

"I'm not doing this. I'm not playing your stupid games, whatever they are, whoever you are. I'm going back to my life now. That would be *Mac's* life," I clarified. There was no reply. Only an inexorable pull into the darkness.

I was once again puppet to an invisible puppet master. I had no choice. I was being dragged through and there was nothing I could do about it.

Struggling, gritting my teeth, resisting every step of the way, I stepped over Jericho's body and pushed back into the Silver.

27

It was pure instinct to fight for breath.

I was encased in ice again the moment I slid through the Silver.

Passing through the dark mirror peeled back a curtain, exposing more forgotten childhood memories. Abruptly, I recalled being four, five, six, finding myself stuck in this alien dreamscape nightly. No sooner did I say my prayers, close my eyes, and drift off to sleep than a disembodied command would infiltrate my slumber.

I recalled waking from those nightmares, gasping and shivering, running for Daddy, crying that I was freezing, suffocating.

I wondered what young Jack Lane had made of it—his adopted daughter who'd been forbidden to ever return to the country of her birth, who was tormented by terrifyingly cold, airless nightmares. What horrors had he decided I must have suffered to be scarred in such ways?

I loved him with all my heart for the childhood he'd given me. He'd anchored me with the day-to-day routines of a simple life, crammed it full of sunshine and bike rides, music lessons and baking with Mom in our bright, warm kitchen. Perhaps he'd let me be too frivolous, in an effort to counter the pain of those nightmares. But I couldn't say I'd have done any differently as a parent.

The inability to breathe had been only the first of many things my child's mind had found so terrifying. As I'd gotten older, strengthened by the cocoon of parental love, I'd learned to suppress those nocturnal images and the bleak emotions the Cold Place engendered. By my teens, the recurring nightmare had been buried deep in my subconscious, leaving me burdened with an intense dislike of the cold and a vague sense of bipolarity I was finally beginning to understand. If occasionally images that made no sense to me slipped through a crack, I attributed them to some horror movie I'd flipped through on TV.

Do not be frightened. I chose you because you could.

I remembered that now, too. The voice that had demanded I come had tried to comfort me and promised I was capable of the task—whatever it was.

I'd never believed it. If I was capable, I wouldn't have dreaded it so much.

I shook myself hard, cracking the ice. It dropped away, but I immediately re-iced.

I repeated the shaking, the re-icing. I did it four or five more times, terrified all the while that if I didn't keep cracking it, it would build up so thick that I would end up staying right here where I stood forever, a statue of a woman, frozen and forgotten, in the Unseelie King's bedchamber.

When Barrons came back to life, he would stand and stare through the mirror at me and try to roar me back to my senses and into motion, but there I'd be—right in front of his eyes, eternally out of his reach, because nobody but me and the Unseelie race's mysterious creator could enter the king's boudoir. And who knew where the king was?

For that matter, who knew *who* the king was?

And I really wanted to, which meant I had to find a way to move around in his natural habitat. I'd done it before, long ago, in another life, as his lover, so surely I could figure out how to do it again. It seemed I'd left clues for myself.

Fear, not fact, impedes you.

I was supposed to alter my expectations and do without breath.

When I re-iced again, I remained still and let the ice cover me, instead of resisting and struggling to breathe. I tried to imagine it as a comfort, a soothing coolness to a high fever. I made it all of thirty seconds before I panicked. Silvery sheets rained from me and shattered on the obsidian floor as I moved jerkily.

I made it an entire minute the second time.

By my third try, it dawned on me that I hadn't actually drawn a breath since I'd passed through the mirror. I'd been so busy fighting the ice that I hadn't realized I was no longer breathing. I would have snorted but I couldn't. There literally *was* no breath on this side of the Silver. My physicality was a different thing here.

Here I stood, fighting for something I didn't even need, driven by a life of conditioning.

Could I talk on this side? Wasn't voice comprised of breath to drive it?

"Hello." I flinched.

I'd chimed like one of the dark princes, only on a different scale, high and feminine. Although my greeting had been comprised of English syllables, without breath to drive it the notes sounded as if slide-hammered on a hellish xylophone.

"Is anyone here?" I iced again, frozen in place by

sheer astonishment at the bizarre sound. I spoke in shades of tubular bells.

Assured that I wasn't going to suffocate, that I could talk, sort of, and that, as long as I kept moving, the ice would keep cracking, I began to jog in place and took a look around.

The king's bedchamber was the size of a football stadium. Walls of black ice towered overhead to a ceiling too high to see. Spicy black petals from some exquisite, otherworldly rose garden swirled at my feet as I bounced lightly from foot to foot. Clusters of frost that were trying to form on my skin rained down to join them. I was mesmerized a moment by the sparkling crystals against the black floor and flowers.

Falling back, laughing, ice in her hair, a handful of velvety petals fluttering down to land on her bare breasts . . .

Never cold here.

Always together.

Sadness overwhelmed me. I nearly choked on it.

He had so many ambitions.

She had one. To love.

Could have learned from her.

The tiny diamonds from the concubine's—I couldn't bring myself to say *my*, especially not standing so close to the king's bed—side of the bedchamber hadn't been extinguished at all. They'd become something else when they passed through and now shimmered on the dark air, midnight fireflies winking with blue flame.

The bed was draped with black curtains that fluttered around piles of silky black furs and filled up a third of the chamber, the portion visible from the other side. I moved to it, slid my hand over the furs. They were sleek, sensual. I wanted to stretch out naked and never leave.

It wasn't the white warm place I found so comforting and familiar, but there was beauty here, too, on the far side of the mirror. Her world was the bright, glorious summer day that held no secrets, but his was the dark, glittering night where anything was possible. I tipped my head back. Was that a black ceiling painted with stars so high above me or a night sky sliced from another world and brought here for my pleasure?

I was in his bedchamber. I remembered this place. I'd come. Would he? Would I finally see the face of my long-lost lover? If he was my beloved king, why was I so afraid?

Hurry! Almost here . . . Come quickly!

The command came from beyond a giant arched opening far across the bedchamber. The summons was beyond my ability to deny. I broke into a run, following the voice of my childhood Pied Piper.

Once the king had held the Seelie Queen above all others, but somewhere down the eons, things had changed. He had puzzled over it for thousands of years, studying her, challenging her with subtle tests, in an effort to divine if the problem lay within her or within him.

He was comforted on the day he realized it was through no fault of theirs but that the two who were the eternal glue of their race were coming apart because she was Stasis and he was Change. It was their nature. The oddity was how long they had remained together.

He could not have prevented his evolution any more than she could have prevented her stagnation. All that the queen was at that very moment was all she would ever be.

Ironically, the mother of their race—she who wielded the Song of Making, she who could enact the mightiest acts of all creation—was no Creator. She was power without wonder, satisfaction without joy. What was existence without wonder, without joy? Meaningless. Empty.

And she thought *he* was dangerous.

He began to slip off more frequently, exploring worlds without her, hungering for things he could not name. The bright, silly court he once found harmlessly entertaining became to him a place of empty pursuits and jaded palates.

He built a fortress on a world of black ice because it was the antithesis of all the queen had chosen. Here, in his dark, quiet castle, he could think. Here, where there were no garish chaises or brilliantly clad courtiers, he could feel himself expanding. He was not drowned by incessant tinkling laughter, in constant petty disputes. He was free.

Once, the queen sought him in his ice castle, and it amused him to see her horror at being leeched of all her bright plumage by the strange light on the world he had chosen, which cast everything black, white, or blue. It suited his need for Spartan surroundings while he sorted through the complexity of his existence and decided the next thing he would be. It was after he had found his concubine, long after he had realized he was no longer capable of tolerating his own people for more than a few short hours at a time, but before he'd begun his efforts to make his beloved Fae like himself.

The queen had been seductive, she had been full of guile, she had been scornful. She had finally tried to use a small part of the Song against him, but he had been prepared for that because, like her, he looked into the future as far as it would permit and had foreseen this day.

They held each other at bay with weapons for the first time in the history of their race.

As the imperious, unforgiving matriarch of their race stormed from his fortress, he padlocked his doors against her, vowing that until she gave him what he wanted—the secret to immortality for his beloved—no Seelie would ever again walk his icy halls. Only the queen could dispense the elixir of life. She kept it hidden in her private bower. He wanted that, and more: enough to make the concubine his equal in every way.

I shook myself hard and stopped running. I iced instantly, but it didn't terrify me. I waited a few moments before taking a step and cracking it.

The memories on the king's side of the Silver didn't play out before my eyes like the residue of times past on the concubine's side. Here they seemed to slide directly into my brain.

It was as if I'd just been two people: One had been running down enormous halls of black ice, and the other had stood in a kingly reception hall, watching the first Fae queen fight with a mighty darkness, probing for weaknesses, manipulating, always manipulating. I knew every detail of her being, what she looked like in her true form and her preferred guises. I even knew the look on her face as she'd died.

Come to me . . .

I began to run again, down floors of obsidian. The king hadn't been much for decorating. No windows opened onto the world outside his walls, although I knew they once did, in those early days before the queen turned his planet into a prison. I also knew that once there were simple yet regal furnishings, but now the only embellishments were elaborately carved designs in the ice itself, lending the place a certain austere majesty. If the queen's court was a gaily painted whore, the king's was a strange but natural beauty.

I knew every hall, every twist and turn, every chamber. She must have lived here, before he'd made the Silvers for her. Me.

I shivered.

So where was he now?

If I genuinely was his concubine reincarnated, why wasn't he waiting for me? It seemed I'd been programmed to end up here, one way or another. Who was summoning me?

I am dying. . . .

My heart constricted. If I'd thought I couldn't breathe before, it was nothing compared to what those three simple words had just made me feel—that I would give my right arm, my eyeteeth, maybe even twenty years of my life to prevent that from happening.

I skidded to a halt before the gigantic doors to the king's fortress and stared up. Chiseled of ebon ice, they had to be a hundred feet tall. There was no way I could open them. But the voice was coming from beyond them—out there in the dreaded, icy Unseelie hell.

Elaborate symbols decorated the high arch into which the doors were set, and I suddenly understood there was a pass code. Unfortunately, I couldn't reach any of the symbols to press them, and there was no convenient hundred-foot ladder propped nearby.

I felt him then.

Almost as if he rose up behind me.

I heard a command come out of my own mouth, words I was incapable of uttering with a human tongue, and the enormous doors swung silently open.

The icy prison was exactly as I'd dreamed it, with a single significant difference.

It was empty.

In my nightmares, the prison had always been inhabited by countless monstrous Unseelie who had squatted high on cliffs above me, hurling chunks of ice down the ravine as if they were bowlers from hell and I was the pin. Others darted low, taking stabs at me with giant beaks.

The moment I'd stepped through the king's mighty doors, I braced myself for an attack.

It didn't come.

The stark arctic terrain was a great empty hull of a prison with rusted-out bars.

Even devoid of those once incarcerated, despair clung to every ridge, blew down from mountainous cliffs, and seeped up from bottomless chasms.

I tilted my head back. There was no sky. Cliffs of black ice stretched up farther than the eye could follow. A blue glow emanated from the cliffs—the only light in the place. Blue-black fog gusted from crevices in the cliffs.

The moon would never rise here, the sun would never set. Seasons would not pass. Color would never splash this landscape.

Death in this place would be a blessing. There was no hope, no expectation that life would ever change. For hundreds of thousands of years, the Unseelie had abided in these chilling, killing, sunless cliffs. Their need, their emptiness, had stained the very stuff from which their prison was fashioned. Once, long ago, it had been a fine if strange world. Now it was radioactive to the core.

I knew that if I remained long on this barren terrain, I would lose all will to leave. I would come to believe that this arctic wasteland, this frozen oubliette of misery, was all that existed, all that had ever existed and, worse—was exactly what I deserved.

Was I too late? Was I supposed to have answered this summons long before the prison walls fell? Was that why I kept seeing all those hourglasses with black sand running out?

But I kept hearing the voice in my dreams—and now, when I was awake. That had to mean there was still time.

For what?

I scanned the many caves cut into the sheer façade of jagged black cliffs, frigid homes the Unseelie had clawed into the unforgiving landscape. Nothing stirred. I knew without even looking I would find no creature comforts within. Those without hope didn't feather nests. They endured. I was startled by a sudden deep sorrow that they'd been reduced to such straits. What a vindictive act on the queen's part! They might have been brethren to the Light Court, not forced to shiver for eternity in the cold and dark. On sunny beaches, in tropical climes, perhaps they would have become something less monstrous, evolved as the king had. But, no, the vicious queen hadn't been satisfied with imprisoning them. She'd *wanted* them to suffer. And for what crimes? What had they done to deserve it, other than be born without her consent?

I was disturbed by the turn of my thoughts. I was feeling pity for the Unseelie and thinking the king had evolved.

It had to be this place's memory residue.

I crunched over iced drifts, scaled jagged outcroppings, and turned down a narrow pathway between cliffs that were hundreds of feet high. The thin fissure through which I passed was another of my childhood terrors. Barely two and a half feet wide, the narrow passage made me feel crushed, claustrophobic, yet I knew my route went this way.

With each step I took, my feelings of bipolarity grew.

I was Mac, who hated Unseelie and wanted nothing more than to see the prison walls restored, the monstrous killers contained.

I was the concubine, who loved the king and all of his children. I even loved this place. There had been happy moments here before the bitch queen broke everything in those final seconds before she died.

Speaking of dying, I should have. I wasn't breathing.

I had no blood flow. No oxygen. I should have been mortally frostbitten the moment I'd passed through the Silver. There was no plausible way I could be walking through these conditions, yet I was.

I was so cold that dying would have been a welcome relief. It was easy to see why my child's mind had thrilled to the poem "The Cremation of Sam McGee." The notion of being warm again was nearly beyond my comprehension.

Half a dozen times I considered aborting my unwanted mission. I could turn around, go back to the mansion, slip through the Silver, find Jericho, resume our plans, and pretend none of this had ever happened. He'd never tell. He had a few dark secrets of his own to keep.

I could forget I was the concubine. Forget that I'd ever had a past existence. I mean, really, who wanted to be in love with someone they'd never even met—at least not in this lifetime? The thought of the Unseelie King was a big messy knot of emotions inside me that I preferred to leave tangled and unexamined.

Hurry! You must!

Razor-edged snow began to fall. Deep in caves, things chimed horrible, grating sounds. Jericho had told me that there were creatures so twisted and monstrous in the Unseelie prison that they'd stay even if the walls came down, because they liked their home. How was I supposed to have made it through if the place had still been fully populated? For that matter, how was I supposed to have found my way here to begin with? How had things been orchestrated to bring me here, to this moment, in this way—and, more importantly, by whom? Whose puppet was I? I resented being here. I couldn't have turned back for anything.

I have no idea how long I trudged through despair and futility so palpable that every step felt like slogging through wet cement. Temporal divisions did not exist in this place. There were no watches or clocks, no minutes or hours, no night or day, no sun or moon. Just relentless black and white and blue matched by relentless misery.

How many times had I walked this path while I slept? If I'd been having the dream since birth—more than eight *thousand*.

Repetition had made every step instinctual. I skirted dangerously thin ice that I couldn't have known was there. I intuited the location of bottomless drifts. I knew the shape and number of the entrances in the caves in the black walls high above my head. I recognized landmarks too insignificant to be noticed by anyone who hadn't walked this path countless times.

If my heart could have pounded, it would have. I had no idea what awaited me. If I'd ever gotten to the end of my journey in my dreams, I'd blocked it thoroughly.

It had always been a woman's voice commanding me, ordering me to obey. Had my inner concubine been taking over every time I'd fallen asleep and fed me dreams, trying to force me to remember and make me do something?

Darroc had told me that some said the Unseelie King was entombed in black ice, slumbering in his prison eternally. Had he been tricked into a trap and he'd been reaching out to me in the Dreaming to teach me all I needed to know to free him? Was that what my whole life had been about?

Despite the love I knew he and the concubine shared, I resented that my mortal existence had been used up without regard for what it might have been, what *I* might have been. Hadn't she lived long enough once before, waiting for him to wake up, to pull his head out and live?

It was no wonder I'd always felt so psychotic in high school! I'd been walking around since childhood with the suppressed memories of another fantastical lifetime embedded in my subconscious!

I suddenly found everything about myself suspect. Did I really love sunshine so much, or was it a leftover feeling from *her*? Was I really crazy about fashion, or was I obsessing over the concubine's closet of a thousand stunning gowns? Was I truly enthralled by beautifying my surroundings, or was it an outlet for *her* need to change the face of her confinement while she waited for her lover?

Did I even *like* the color pink?

I tried to remember how many of her dresses had been some shade of rose.

"Ugh," I said. It came out as a deep, booming *gong*.

I didn't want to be *her*. I wanted to be me. But, as far as I knew, I hadn't even been born.

A terrible thought occurred to me. Maybe I wasn't the concubine reincarnated; maybe I *was* the concubine and somebody had forced me to drink from the cauldron!

"Right, then sent me to a plastic surgeon and recreated my face?" I muttered. I didn't look anything like the concubine.

My head was spinning with fears, each more disturbing than the last.

I stopped, as if a homing beacon that had been beeping faster and faster inside me had abruptly become a single long sound.

I was there. Wherever "there" was supposed to be. Whatever fate awaited me, whatever, whoever had brought me here, was just over the next ridge of black ice, some twenty feet away.

I stood still so long that I iced again.

Despair filled me. I didn't want to look. I didn't want

to top the ridge. What if I didn't like what I found? Had I blocked this memory because I was going to die here?

What if I was too late?

The prison was empty. There was no point in going on. I should just give in, turn to ice permanently, and forget. I didn't want to be the concubine. I didn't want to find the king. I didn't want to stay in Faery or be his forever love.

I wanted to be human. I wanted to live in Dublin and Ashford and love my mom and dad. I wanted to fight with Jericho Barrons and run a bookstore one day when our world was rebuilt. I wanted to watch Dani grow up and fall in love for the first time. I wanted to replace that old woman at the abbey with Kat and take tropical vacations on human beaches.

I stood, torn by indecision. Go greet my destiny, like a good little automaton? Freeze and forget, as the overwhelming stain of futility in this place was trying to convince me to do? Or turn and walk away? That thought appealed to me a lot. It smacked of personal will, of choosing to set sail on my own course and terms.

If I never crested that ridge and never discovered the end of this dream that had been plaguing me all my life, would I be free of it?

There was no higher power forcing me to go on, no divine being charging me with tracking the Book and getting the walls back up. Just because I *could* track it didn't mean I had to. I didn't have to fight the Fae. I was a free agent. I could leave right now, move far away, shirk responsibility, look out for myself, and leave this mess to somebody else. It was a strange new world. I could stop resisting, adapt, and make the best of it. If I'd proved nothing else to myself over the past few months, I was good at adapting and figuring out how to go on when things weren't remotely what I'd thought they were.

Still . . . could I really walk away now and never know what all this had been about? Live with unresolved bipolarity shaping all my choices? Did I *want* to live that way—a conflicted, screwed-up, half-afraid existence of someone who'd chickened out at the critical moment?

Safety is a fence, and fences are for sheep, I'd told Rowena.

Were it put to the test, she'd replied tartly, *I wonder where you would truly stand.*

This was the test.

I cracked the ice, shook it from my skin, and headed for the top of the ridge.

28

In that moment, just before I could see over the crest, a final memory I'd been suppressing surfaced, a last desperate bid to get me to tuck tail and run.

It nearly worked.

Once I topped the ridge, there would be a coffin chiseled of the same blue-black ice from which the four stones had been carved, standing in the center of a snow-covered dais, surrounded by sheer cliffs.

A chilling, bitter wind would gust down and tangle my hair. I would stand, debating, before moving to the sepulchre.

The lid would be elaborately carved with ancient symbols. I would press my hands to the runes at ten and two, slide the lid away, and look inside.

And I would scream.

My steps faltered.

I closed my eyes, but, try as I might, I couldn't see what was inside the coffin that made me scream. Apparently I was going to have to actually perform the deed to know how my recurring nightmare ended.

I squared my shoulders, marched to the top, and stopped, startled.

There was the icy tomb, elaborately carved and embellished, precisely as I'd just pictured it. It certainly didn't look big enough to hold the king.

But who was *he*?

This was a new twist. In all my nightmares, there'd never been anyone else here but me and whoever was inside that tomb.

Tall, beautifully formed, ice-white, and smooth as marble, with long jet hair, he sat on a bank of crusted snow beside the coffin, face buried in his hands.

I stood at the top of the ridge, staring. Wind gusted down from high cliffs and tangled my hair. Was he a residue? A memory? There was none of that fading at the edges, no transparency.

Was he my king?

As soon as I thought the question, I knew he wasn't.

Then who was he?

What I could see of his ivory skin—a hand on his cheek, one sleek, strong white arm—raced with dark shapes and symbols.

Was it possible there were *five* Unseelie Princes? This wasn't one of the three who'd raped me, and he had no wings, which meant he wasn't War/Cruce, either.

So who was he?

"It's about bloody damned time," he tossed over his shoulder, without turning. "Been waiting weeks."

I jerked. He'd spoken in that awful chiming and, while my mind understood it, my ears would never get used to it. That was only part of what made me jerk, though. Needing to crack my ice was another part of it. But the majority was horror at the realization of who I was looking at.

"Christian MacKeltar," I said, and grimaced. I was speaking the language of my enemies, a language I'd never learned, with a mouth incapable of shaping it. I couldn't get back to my side of the mirror soon enough. "Is that you?"

"In the flesh, lass. Well . . . mostly."

I wasn't sure if he meant it was mostly him or mostly flesh. I didn't ask.

He raised his head and shot me a savage look over his shoulder. He was beautiful. He was wrong. His eyes were full black. He blinked and had whites again.

In another life, I would have gone crazy over Christian MacKeltar. Or at least I would have gone nuts for the Christian I met back in Dublin. He was so different now that, if he hadn't spoken to me, I'm not sure how long it might have taken me to figure out who he was. The good-looking college student with the great body, Druid heart, and killer smile was gone. As I watched shapes and symbols move under his skin, I wondered: If we weren't inside the prison that leached color from everything, would his tattoos still be black or kaleidoscopic?

I stood still too long and was suddenly staring at him through a thin sheeting of ice. He'd been sitting still and was ice-free. Why? Then there was that short-sleeved shirt he was wearing. Wasn't he cold? When I cracked it, he spoke.

"The majority of what happens here is in your mind. Whatever you permit yourself to feel intensifies." The words were dark bells hammered on a bent xylophone. I shuddered. I could hear the hint of Scots brogue in the chiming, and the element of humanity in the inhuman tongue made it all the more disturbing.

"You mean if I don't think about icing, I won't?" I said. My stomach growled and I was suddenly frosted with thick, creamy blue icing.

"Thought about food, did you now, lass?" Amusement leavened the tubular tones, made it slightly more bearable. He stood up but made no move toward me. "You'll find you do that a lot here."

I thought about turning the icing to ice. It was that simple. When I stepped forward, it shattered from my skin. "Does this mean if I think of a warm, tropical beach—"

"No. The fabric of this place is what it is. You can make it worse, but you can never make it better. You can only destroy, not create. That was a bit of added nastiness on the queen's part. I suspect it's not icing on you but flakes of frost creamed with the innards of a thing you'd rather not look at too closely."

I glanced at the sepulchre. I couldn't help it. It hulked, dark and silent, the boogeyman of twenty years of bad dreams. I'd been trying to ignore it but couldn't. It gnawed at my awareness.

I would stand beside it.

I would open it, look inside, and scream.

Right. Not in a hurry to do that.

I looked back at Christian. What was he doing here? Whatever had brought me to this place had consumed all my nightly hours for most of my life. I was entitled to a few minutes of my own before whatever was fated happened.

If they were indeed my own.

It didn't escape me that I'd just found exactly what I needed. How lucky to find the fifth of the five Druids necessary to perform the ritual right here, next to whatever it was I'd been led to!

Too bad I didn't believe in luck anymore.

I felt bitterly manipulated. But by whom and why?

"What happened to you?" I asked.

"Och, what happened to me?" Laughter screeched like metal spikes across chalkboard bells. "That would be you, lass. *You* happened to me. You fed me Unseelie."

I was appalled. This was what feeding him the flesh of dark Fae had done to him? Whatever transformation Christian had begun back on that world where we'd dried our clothes by the loch had continued at breakneck speed.

He looked half human, half Fae, and in this place of shadows and ice, he was leaning toward the Unseelie, not their light brethren. With a few finishing touches, he'd look just like one of the princes. I bit my lip. What could I say? *I'm sorry? Does it hurt? Are you turning into a monster inside, too?* Maybe he'd look better once he was out in the real world, where there were other colors besides black, white, and blue.

He gave me a darker version of that killer smile, white teeth flashing against cobalt lips in a white-marble face. "Och, your heart weeps for me. I see it in your eyes," he mocked. The smile faded, but the hostility in his gaze grew. "It should. I'm beginning to look like one of them, aren't I? No handy mirrors around here. Don't know what my face looks like and doubt I want to."

"Eating Unseelie did this to you? I don't understand. I've eaten Unseelie. So did Mallucé and Darroc, Fiona and O'Bannion. Then there's Jayne and his men. Nothing like this happened to me or any of them."

"I suspect it began happening on Halloween. I wasn't runed well enough." The smile morphed from killer to murderous. "I blame your Barrons for that. We'll be seeing who's the finer Druid now. We'll be having words when we meet again."

From the expression on that white chiseled face, I doubted they would be words. "Was Jericho the one who tattooed you?"

He raised a brow. "So, it's 'Jericho,' is it? No, my uncles Dageus and Cian did the work, but he should have checked me when I was finished, and he didn't. He let me go into the ritual unprotected."

"And just how pissy would your uncles have gotten if he'd tried?" It was instinct to defend him.

"He still should have. He knew more about protection runes than we did. His knowledge is older than ours, which is bloody inconceivable to me."

"What happened that night in the stones, Christian?" Neither he nor Barrons had ever told me.

He rubbed his face with a hand, skin rasping over blue-black stubble. "I suppose it doesn't matter who knows now. I thought to hide my shame, but it looks as if I've ended up wearing it."

He began to walk a slow circle around the black coffin, ice crunching beneath his boots. It was a well-worn path. He'd been here awhile.

I tried to focus on him, but my gaze kept sliding unwillingly to the tomb. The ice was thick, but if I stared, I could see a shape through the frosted sides. The lid was thinner than the rest of the coffin.

Was that the blurred outline of a face through the smoky ice?

I yanked my gaze to Christian's too-white face. "And?"

"We tried to summon the ancient god of the Draghar, a sect of dark sorcerers. They'd worshipped it long before the Fae came to town. It was our only hope to counter Darroc's magic. We succeeded in raising it. I felt it come alive. The great stones that weighted it deep beneath the earth fell away." He paused, letting the echo of his chiming bounce off the walls in ever-diminishing decibels until the icy mountains fell silent. "It came for me. Straight for me. Gunning for my soul. Ever play chicken, Mac?"

I shook my head.

"I lost. It's a wonder it didn't decimate Barrons. I felt it blast past me and into him. Then it was just . . . gone."

"So how was that responsible for what's happening to you?"

"It touched me." He looked repulsed. "It . . . I don't want to talk about it. Then you gave me the blood of dark Fae, and that, coupled with the three years I've been in here—"

"Three *years*?" The words exploded from me in a cacophony of such dissonance that I was surprised the chiming didn't start an avalanche. "You've been in the Unseelie prison for three years?"

"No, I've been in this place for only a few weeks. But I've been in the Silvers for three years by my count."

"But less than a month has passed on the outside since I saw you last!"

"So it's passing faster for me in here," he murmured.

"Which is exactly the opposite of what usually happens. Usually a few hours in here are days out there."

He shrugged. Muscle and tattoos rippled. "Things don't seem to be working right where I'm concerned. I've become a wee bit unpredictable." His smile was tight. His eyes were full black again.

It was on the tip of my tongue to apologize, but I was more pragmatic than I used to be and I was getting tired of being blamed for things. "When I found you in that desert, you were dying. Would you rather I'd buried you in the Silvers?"

The corners of his mouth twisted. "Aye, there's the rub, isn't it? I'm glad I'm alive. And you've no idea what that does to me. I used to be part of a clan that protected against the Fae, upheld the Compact, and kept the truce between us and them. Now I'm turning into one of the bloody buggers. I used to think the Keltar were the good guys. Now I don't believe there *are* good guys."

"There'd better be good guys. I need five of them to perform the ritual." My gaze slid to the coffin again. I shook myself and looked away. Assuming I got out of here with my sanity and life.

"See for yourself and decide. I'll fit in with them now just fine. Uncle Dageus once opened himself up to thirteen of the most evil Druids that ever existed and still can't exorcise parts of them."

So Dageus was the "inhabited or possessed" that the prophecy had mentioned!

"And Uncle Cian was trapped in a Silver for nearly a thousand years, as if he wasn't enough of a barbarian to begin with. He thinks all power is good and would do anything he had to in order to keep himself and his wife alive and happy. Then there's Da, who'll be useless to you. He took one look at the two of them when they showed up and swore off Druid arts forever."

"That's unacceptable," I said flatly. "I need all five of you."

"Good luck with that."

We looked at each other in silence. He smiled thinly after a moment. "I knew someone would come. I just didn't expect it to be you. I thought my uncles would find this place so I'd better stick close. I couldn't find the bloody way out, anyway."

"What have you been eating?"

"Same as we're breathing. It's part of hell. No food, no breath. But hunger, ah, the hunger never goes away. Your stomach gnaws at itself constantly. You just don't die from it. And sex. Och, Christ, the need!" The look he raked over me chilled. It wasn't nearly as bottomless as a prince's, but it wasn't human, either. "You lust in this place, but you can't jack off. Nothing comes of it but greater lust. I lost a few days to a bad spot there, nearly lost my fucking mind. If you and I had sex—"

"Thanks but no," I said swiftly. My life was already too complicated, and if it hadn't been, this wasn't the place I'd choose to complicate it more.

"I suspect it wouldn't work anyway," he finished drily. "Am I that revolting, lass?"

"Just a little . . . scary."

He looked away.

"Still sexy as hell, though," I added.

He looked back, flashed me a smile.

"There's the Christian I know," I tried to tease. "You're still in there."

"Once I get out of the Silvers, I'm hoping it won't be like this. *I* won't be like this."

That would make two of us who hoped things would go back to normal, in a hurry, once we left this place behind.

I glanced at the sepulchre. I was going to have to open it sometime. Face it and get it over with. Was it the king? Did he terrify me? Why? What could possibly be in there that would make me scream?

He followed my gaze. "So now you know why I'm sitting here. Why are you here? How did you find this place?"

"I've been dreaming about it every night since I was a child, as if I was programmed to come here."

His mouth twisted. "Aye, she does that. Fucks with us."

"She? Who?"

He nodded at the coffin. "The queen."

I blinked. "What queen?" This wasn't making any sense.

"Aoibheal, Queen of the Seelie."

"*That's* who's in the coffin?"

"Who were you expecting to find?"

All hesitation gone, I moved to the side of the tomb and stared through the lid.

Beneath smoky ice and runes, I could see the hint of pale skin, golden hair, a slight form.

"We've got to get her out of here, and fast," he said, "if she's even still alive. I can't tell through the ice. I tried to open it but couldn't budge it. A few times, I thought she moved. Once, I could have sworn she made a sound."

I barely heard him. Why would the queen be *here* of all places? V'lane said he was keeping her safe in Faery.

V'lane had lied.

What else had he lied about?

Had he brought her here? If not, who had? Why? And why would opening the lid make me scream? I raked my hair back from my face with both hands and tugged on it, staring down. Something was eluding me.

"Are you absolutely certain it's the queen of the Seelie in this coffin?" Why would the queen have been summoning me—the concubine? How did she even know who I was, once I'd been reincarnated? It wasn't as if I still *looked* like the concubine. It was absurd to think she'd accidentally chosen me. None of this made sense. I couldn't think of any reason seeing the queen of the Seelie would make me scream.

"Aye, I'm certain. My ancestors have been painting her for millennia. I'd know her anywhere, even through the ice."

"But why would she call me? What do *I* have to do with any of this?"

"My uncles say she has meddled with our clan for thousands of years, preparing us for the moment of her greatest need. Uncle Cian saw her four or five years back, standing behind the balustrade of our Great Hall, watching us. He said she came to him later, in sleep, and told him that she'd been killed in the not-so-distant future and needed us to perform certain tasks to prevent it—and the destruction of the world as we knew it—from coming to pass. She foretold that the walls would come down. We did our best to keep them up. He said that even in the Dreaming, she seemed hunted, weak. I suspect now she was projecting herself from her tomb here in this prison somehow. She said she would return to tell him more but never did. It sounds like she must have meddled with your family, as well."

She'd used me. The queen of the Fae had figured out who I was and used me, and I resented it. Though I knew she was a far-distant successor, not the original queen who had refused to make me—the concubine, I amended—Fae and grant the king's wish, and despite that she wasn't actually the bitch who'd sown hatred and revenge when she might have used her vast power for good, how dare *any* queen of the Seelie use me to rescue her? Me, the concubine! I hated her without even seeing her.

Would it never end? Would I eternally be a pawn on their chessboard? Would I just keep getting reborn, or forced to drink from the cauldron, or whatever had happened to me to screw up my memories, and used over and over again?

I turned away, bile rising.

"What's important now is that we get her out of here. I can't go back the way I came. The Silver that dumped me was two stories up, in the side of a cliff. I was stunned by the fall and can't find the bloody thing again. Where'd you come in, lass?"

I dragged my gaze from the coffin to him. How to get him out of here was an entirely new problem I hadn't even thought about. "Well, you certainly can't go out the way I came in," I muttered.

"Why the bloody hell not?"

I wondered how much he'd learned about Fae lore in this place. Maybe my sources were wrong and Barrons had died from some other coincidental cause, not because of the mirror at all. Maybe Christian would hear my answer, laugh at me, and tell me my version was a bunch of baloney, that lots of people and Fae could use that mirror, or that Cruce's curse had messed it up. "Because I came in through the Silver in the king's bedchamber."

He was silent a moment. "Not funny, lass."

I didn't say anything, just looked at him.

"Not possible, either," he said flatly.

I pushed my hands into my pockets and waited for him to deal with it.

"That legend is famous on every world I visited. There are only two who can pass through the king's Silver," he said.

"Maybe Cruce's curse changed it."

"The king's Silver was the first he ever made and of a completely different composition. It was unaffected. It continued to be used as a method of execution long after Cruce's time."

Damn. I'd really been hoping he wouldn't say that. I turned my back on him and moved to the side of the coffin. The queen of the Fae would make me scream. I wondered why. I was sick of wondering. It was time for truth.

Behind me, Christian was still talking. "And, duh—you're neither of those."

"Doona be duh-ing me, laddie," I mocked something he'd said to me once, taking a stab at humor before my life got totally wrecked by whatever I was about to discover.

I pressed my hands to the runes at ten and two. Something clicked. There was a soft hiss of air as the lid raised

beneath my hands. I could feel the spring in it. All I had
to do now was push it aside.

"Only the Unseelie King and his concubine can use
that mirror." Christian was still talking.

I slid the lid away and looked down.

I was silent for a long moment, absorbing it.

Then I screamed.

29

To my credit, I didn't scream for long.

But the short burst in their hellish language was enough to disturb precariously packed snow and ice. My chiming scream echoed off sheer cliffs. Unlike an echo, however, it grew louder with each rebound and I heard a rumble that could presage only one thing: an avalanche.

My head whipped around. "Grab her!"

Christian shook his head, cursing. "Christ, you open your bag of stones. You feed me Unseelie. You scream. You're a walking—"

"Just grab her and run! Now!"

He raced to the coffin, then stood, hesitating.

"What's wrong with you? Pick her up!"

"She's the queen of the Fae." Awe tinged his voice. "It's forbidden to touch the queen."

"Fine, then stay here with her and get buried alive," I snapped.

He scooped her up.

She was so frail, so wasted by . . . whatever wastes fairies, that I could have carried her myself, but I had no desire to touch her. Ever. Which was really kind of funny in a dark and disturbing way, if I thought about it. So I didn't.

Ice cracked and rumbled high above, showering crystals across the dais.

We needed no further encouragement. We slipped and slid down the frozen ridge and fled the way I'd come, heading for the narrow fissure between cliffs. It was going to be a close race and a tight squeeze with Christian's shoulders and with an avalanche chasing us.

"Why'd you scream, anyway?" he shouted at me over the rumbling.

"She startled me, is all," I shouted back.

"Bloody great. Next time put a sock in it, would you?"

Neither of us said anything then, focused on trying to outrun being buried alive. I bounced between the walls of the cliffs like a Ping-Pong ball. Twice I lost my footing and went down. Christian went flying over the top of me but somehow managed to hang on to the frail queen. The avalanche chased us, growling like dark thunder, crashing from ravine to canyon, spraying the deep fissure with snow.

We finally cleared the claustrophobic path through the cliffs, slid on our asses down a steep hill, then raced across the canyon for the towering fortress of black ice.

"The Unseelie King's castle!" Christian marveled as we dashed through the towering doors. He looked up, down, and around. "I grew up on tales of this place, but I never imagined I'd see it. I thought the closest I'd get to one of the legendary Tuatha Dé was standing next to a portrait. And here I am, holding the Seelie Queen, in the Unseelie King's fortress." He gave a bitter laugh. "And turning into one of them."

I murmured the same soft command that had opened

the tall doors and heaved a sigh of relief when they slid silently closed on the thundering rush of snow beyond. Would the avalanche I'd started reach the castle? Pile up outside the doors, sealing us in here more securely than any bolt? I waited for Christian to demand to know how I'd shut them, but he was so engrossed in his surroundings, he'd not even noticed.

"What now?" His fascinated gaze kept sliding between the frail woman in his arms and the interior of the dark fortress.

"Now we head for the Silver in the king's boudoir," I said.

"Why? I can't go through and neither can she."

"I can. And I can get help and bring them back to the mirror to talk to you. We'll make plans to get you out, figure out how and where to meet."

He cocked his head and studied me a moment. "There's a thing you should know, lass. My truth sensor works just fine here in the Unseelie prison."

"So?"

"What you just said wasn't truth."

"I'm going to go through the mirror. Truth?" I said impatiently.

He nodded.

"And I'm going to get help and bring them back for you. Truth?"

He nodded again.

"Then what the hell is the problem?" I had a lot on my mind. Delays were untenable. Standing still, my mind began to think. I needed to keep moving. I couldn't bear to look at the woman in his arms. Couldn't handle thinking what looking at her made me think.

His eyes narrowed. They were full black again. There was a time when it would have made me nervous, but I doubted anything would make me nervous ever again. I was beyond stress, beyond fear, beyond reach.

"Tell me you plan to save me," he ordered.

That was easy. With each passing day, I understood Jericho better. People *didn't* ask the right questions. And if you answered enough of their wrong ones, by the time they ever got around to a right one, you could just snap their head off and shut them up. How many times had he done that to me? I was developing a grudging respect for his tactics. Especially now that I had something to hide.

"I plan to save you," I said, and I didn't need a truth detector to hear the ring of sincerity in my voice. "And I will do it as quickly as possible. It will be my priority to get you out of here." It would. I needed him. More than I'd ever understood.

"Truth."

"Then what's the problem?"

"I don't know. Something." He shifted the queen in his arms.

She wore a sparkling white gown. I knew that dress. Who'd selected it for her? Had she chosen it? How and why? I refused to look at her. I snapped my gaze from her dress to Christian's face.

"Tell me again why you screamed," he fished.

He was getting too close for comfort. But I knew this game. Barrons had taught me well. "I was frightened."

"Truth. Why?"

"Oh, for heaven's sake, Christian, I told you already! Are we going to stand here all day while you interrogate me, or are we going to get out of here?" Beyond the fortress, the avalanche crashed and roared. It was nothing like the roar I felt building in me. "She wasn't what I expected, okay?" *That* was certainly the truth! "Even though you told me it was her in the coffin, I expected it to be the Unseelie King," I tossed, to get him off the scent.

There was just enough sincerity in what I'd said to appease him. But barely. "If you're somehow lying to me . . ." he warned.

He'd do what? By the time he figured out what I was doing, it'd be too late. Besides, I really wasn't someone he wanted to be threatening, no matter who he was turning into or how powerful he was becoming. I'd just found out I was way more terrifying than anything he could possibly be turning into.

"The king's bedchamber is this way," I said coolly. "And don't threaten me. I'm sick of being used and pushed around."

Christian dallied. There was no other word for it. He was fascinated by the Unseelie King's fortress, and his Keltar duties as Fae lorekeeper had been bred into him since birth, despite any misgivings he might have about what was happening to him. He took detailed mental notes on everything he saw, to pass on later to his clan. I was glad he didn't have pen or paper, or I might never have gotten him to the mirror. "Look at this, Mac! What do you think it means?"

I glanced unwillingly where he pointed. It was a door that was much smaller than the others. There was an inscription above the arch. It was a powerful ward. The king had kept things in there he'd never wanted loosed on the world. The ward had been broken long ago. Great. I just hoped they weren't on my world. I resumed walking, staring straight ahead, retracing my earlier steps. Unlike Christian, I didn't want to see a damned thing.

"You'll have time to look around when I'm gone," I said.

"I'll need to stay close to the Silver to know when you return."

"Well, move a little faster, okay? We have no idea how time's passing out in the real world. You slow it down, I speed it up."

"Maybe we'll split the difference."

"Maybe." Would enough time have passed that Barrons would be alive again? Standing at the mirror, waiting for me? Or had so much time passed that he'd have given up? Moved on to other tasks?

I'd know in a few minutes.

"She's not breathing," he said.

"Neither are we," I said drily.

"But I think she's alive. I can . . . feel her."

"Good. We need her. Through here," I said.

Moments later I stepped into the comforting darkness of the Unseelie King's boudoir, where the dark maker of the Court of Shadows had rested—he'd never slept—and fucked, and dreamed.

Jericho wasn't dead on the other side of the mirror, nor was he waiting for me. I assumed that meant we'd been gone a good long time as humans counted it.

Christian made it easy for me.

I couldn't have asked for more.

He laid her on the king's bed, close to the Silver, and tucked furs around her.

"She's so cold. You've got to hurry, Mac. We need to get her warm. In my travels, I heard that during the battle between the king and original queen, some of the Seelie were taken captive before the prison walls went up. The Unseelie planned to torture them for all eternity, but legends say the Seelie prisoners died because this place is the antithesis of all they are and drains their life essence." He gave me a grim look. "I think someone brought the Seelie Queen here, put her in that coffin, and left her to die slowly. Uncle Cian said she wasn't really there when she came to see him but was a projection of herself. As if she was trapped somewhere, focusing all her effort and energy on sending a vision of herself to nudge events around so we would save her when the time was right. Someone wanted revenge. I think she's been here a long time."

And V'lane was looking like the prime suspect, considering that he'd been lying to me about where she'd been since day one. But how could any of this be? Why would V'lane have had this woman to begin with? How had she ended up in the Seelie court?

The truth was, I was standing in the middle of so many lies—some of them hundreds of thousands of years old—that I didn't know where to begin trying to untangle them. If I pulled on one thread, ten others would unravel, and I saw little point in trying to make sense of anything now.

All I could do was what had to be done. Get them both out of here. The sooner the better. Especially her. Not because she was the queen but because Christian's legend resonated with me and I knew it to be true. A Seelie could survive only a finite space of time in here. I doubted a human would survive half that long. And I wasn't entirely sure which she really was.

She was dangerously weak. The slight form on the bed barely made a hump. Masses of silvery hair cloaked a body that had deteriorated to that of a slender, undeveloped child. My dreams had been trying to warn me. I'd waited too long. I'd almost been too late.

"Look over there," I exclaimed, pointing to the far side of the bed. "What's that on the wall? I think I've seen those symbols before."

He was halfway across the bedchamber before that sixth sense of his made him look back over his shoulder. I know, because I was looking over mine.

It was too late.

I'd already scooped her up and pushed into the Silver. She was oddly insubstantial, as if she'd donned physical form to contain the energy of which she was made and, as her life essence evaporated, so did the physicality holding her. Was she beyond saving?

I know what he thought.

I was the traitor.

I was trying to finish the job of killing the queen by forcing her through a mirror only the king and his concubine could pass through. A mirror that killed all other life, including Fae.

But that wasn't it at all.

I wasn't trying to kill the queen. I knew she wouldn't die. I *knew* she could go through the mirror.

Because the woman in my arms wasn't Aoibheal, queen of the Fae.

She was the concubine.

30

That was why I'd screamed. I'd been having a hard enough time dealing with the thought that I was the concubine.

As I'd stared into the coffin and recognized her from the White Mansion, it had taken me only a moment to process that, if the concubine was lying in the coffin and I could pass through the king's Silver, I had a serious problem.

The scream had been instinctive, denial from the very marrow in my bones clawing its way up my throat and past my lips.

If she was the concubine, and I could go through the Silver, too, there was only one other . . . person—and I was using that term *very* loosely—I could be.

"And it's not the concubine, that's for sure," I muttered as I pushed through the Silver and slammed into the wall. I'd expected resistance like in every other Silver, but this one—the first ever created—was untainted by Cruce's curse. I turned at the last moment, cradling her in my arms, taking the brunt of the impact on my shoulder. Not a damned thing about this made sense.

"Mac, what are you doing?" Christian roared, storming toward the mirror.

"Don't touch it!" I cried. "It *will* kill you!" I didn't want him to think for a minute that it wouldn't and try to come through. It had killed Barrons. I had no doubt it would destroy Christian, and he didn't have a get-out-of-death-free card. At least not that I knew of. But as had just become painfully apparent to me, I didn't know much of anything, so maybe he had a whole deck of them. Maybe everyone did but me. Still, I wasn't going to count on it. I needed him. More than ever before, I needed the *Sinsar Dubh* contained, and he was one of the five necessary to do it. I understood why it played with me now.

He stopped inches from the mirror and peered at me through it. "Why didn't it kill her? I'll know the truth," he warned.

I adjusted her in my arms, scooped up a mass of her hair, and draped it over my shoulder so it didn't trail the floor and trip me. I stared back through the mirror at him. "Because she's the concubine. That's why I really screamed. I recognized her."

"But I thought you were the conc—" He gave me a fast once-over. "But you went through the—But that would mean—Mac?"

I shrugged. I couldn't think of anything to say.

"How do you *know* she's the concubine?" he demanded.

"The memory residue of the king and the concubine walks these halls. It's hard not to get lost in them. But I imagine you won't have quite as hard a time as I had, seeing how you aren't quite so . . . personally involved," I said bitterly. "I have no doubt you'll see her while I'm gone." I still wouldn't look at her. It was too disconcerting. She was frighteningly light, delicate, and very, very cold. "I'll be back as soon as I can."

We stared at each other.

"I won't believe it," he said finally.

"It makes too much sense not to be true. There's no record of me being born, Christian. The Book . . . it hunts me. I hear it always has."

"Not buying it."

"Give me another explanation."

"Maybe the legends are wrong. Maybe a lot of people can step through the Silver. Maybe it's all bluff, to keep people from trying."

My heart lurched when he took a step forward. "No, don't! Christian, listen to me. I can't tell you who, but I know you can hear the truth in what I'm saying. I watched the Silver kill someone already."

He cocked his head, then nodded. "Aye, lass. I hear truth in that, but why can't you tell me who?"

"It's not my secret to tell."

"You'll tell me one day."

I didn't reply.

"I'm still not buying it."

"Find me an alternative. Any alternative. I'll happily believe it."

"Maybe you're . . . I don't know . . . Maybe you're their child somehow," he offered.

"Seven-hundred-thousand-plus years later?" I'd already considered and discarded that thought. Not only didn't it resonate with my gut feelings, but "It doesn't begin to explain all the things I know and feel and remember, or why the Book plays with me," I said. I couldn't explain how I knew it, but I wasn't the progeny of the Unseelie King and his concubine. My feelings were far too personal. Far too sexual and possessive. Not a child's feelings at all. But a lover's.

He shrugged. "I'll remain here. But hurry back."

"Promise me you won't try to come through, Christian."

"I promise, Mac. But hurry. The longer I'm in here, the more I feel myself . . . changing."

I nodded. As I turned away with the queen/concubine/woman I'd apparently destroyed worlds for, I couldn't help but wonder where my other parts were.

31

I stared through the front door of Barrons Books and Baubles, uncertain what surprised me more: that the front seating cozy was intact or that Barrons was sitting there, boots propped on a table, surrounded by piles of books, hand-drawn maps tacked to the walls.

I couldn't count how many nights I'd sat in exactly the same place and position, digging through books for answers, occasionally staring out the windows at the Dublin night, and waiting for him to appear. I liked to think he was waiting for me to show.

I leaned closer, staring in through the glass.

He'd refurnished the bookstore. How long had I been gone?

There was my magazine rack, my cashier's counter, a new old-fashioned cash register, a small flat-screen TV/DVD player that was actually from this decade, and a sound dock for my iPod. There was a new sleek black iPod Nano in the dock. He'd done more than refurnish the place. He might as well have put a mat out that said WELCOME HOME, MAC.

A bell tinkled as I stepped inside.

His head whipped around and he half-stood, books sliding to the floor.

The last time I'd seen him, he was dead. I stood in the doorway, forgetting to breathe, watching him unfold from the couch in a ripple of animal grace. He crammed the four-story room full, dwarfed it with his presence. For a moment neither of us spoke.

Leave it to Barrons—the world melts down and he's still dressed like a wealthy business tycoon. His suit was exquisite, his shirt crisp, tie intricately patterned and tastefully muted. Silver glinted at his wrist, that familiar wide cuff decorated with ancient Celtic designs he and Ryodan both wore.

Even with all my problems, my knees still went weak. I was suddenly back in that basement. My hands were tied to the bed. He was between my legs but wouldn't give me what I wanted. He used his mouth, then rubbed himself against my clitoris and barely pushed inside me before pulling out, then his mouth, then him, over and over, watching my eyes the whole time, staring down at me.

What am I, Mac? he'd say.

My world, I'd purr, and mean it. And I was afraid that, even now that I wasn't *Pri-ya,* I'd be just as out of control in bed with him as I was then. I'd melt, I'd purr, I'd hand him my heart. And I would have no excuse, nothing to blame it on. And if he got up and walked away from me and never came back to my bed, I would never recover. I'd keep waiting for a man like him, and there were no other men like him. I'd have to die old and alone, with the greatest sex of my life a painful memory.

So, you're alive, his dark eyes said. *Pisses me off, the wondering. Do something about that.*

Like what? Can't all be like you, Barrons.

His eyes suddenly rushed with shadows and I couldn't make out a single word. Impatience, anger, something ancient and ruthless. Cold eyes regarded me with calculation, as if weighing things against each other, meditating—a word Daddy used to point out was the larger part of premeditation. He'd say, *Baby, once you start thinking about it, you're working your way toward doing it.* Was there something Barrons was working his way toward doing?

I shivered.

"Where the fuck've you been? It's been over a month. Pull a stunt like that again without telling me what you're doing first, and I'm chaining you to my bed when you get back."

Was that supposed to be a deterrent or an incentive? I pictured myself sprawled on my back, his dark head moving between my legs. I imagined Mac 1.0, knowing what I knew now: that in a few months Barrons would be doing everything a man could do to a woman in bed. Would she have run screaming or torn off her clothes right then and there?

As he stepped around the high-back chesterfield, he spotted the slight woman in my arms, her silvery hair trailing the floor. He looked incredulous, which, for Jericho, meant his head took on a slight cant and his eyes narrowed. "Where the hell did you find *her*?"

I shoved the fragile body into his arms. I'd touched her all I ever wanted to. My feelings were too complex to sort out. "In the Unseelie prison. In a tomb of ice."

"V'lane, that fuck—I knew he was a traitor!"

I sighed. That meant Jericho thought she was the queen, too. And he should know. He'd spent time at her court. But I knew she was the concubine. So, who had actually died in the Unseelie King's boudoir eons ago? Had anyone? The concubine hadn't killed herself. How had she gotten from the Silvers into Faery and ended up one day becoming the current queen? Had V'lane lied to me? Or had they all drunk from the cauldron so many times that the Fae didn't have one bit of their own history right? Maybe someone had sabotaged their written records.

"How did you get her out of there? The Silver should have killed her."

"Apparently the queen has the same kind of immunity to the Silver that she has to the *Sinsar Dubh*." I was pleasantly surprised by how smoothly I lied. Barrons has a sharp nose for deceit. "She can touch both. It looks like the king and queen can't cast spells that the other can't break." The best lies are solidly cemented in known exceptions to the rule, and by her very nature as matriarch and ruler of both courts, the queen was the universal exception to every rule that bound the lessers of the Fae court. I wasn't above exploiting it to secure my cover until I knew beyond all shadow of a doubt what to make of myself. In his dark gaze, I saw the moment he accepted the logic of my lie.

How could I be the Unseelie King? I didn't feel like the king. I felt like Mac, with a bunch of memories I couldn't explain. Well, that wasn't the entire truth. There was also that place in my head where I had nifty little things like parasitic runes of ancient origin and—I terminated that line of thought. I didn't feel like taking a tally of all the things I couldn't explain about myself. The list was miserably long.

He took her to the sofa, tucked blankets around her, and shoved the sofa closer to the fire and turned it on. "She's freezing. I've half a mind to take her back and let the place finish her off," he said darkly.

"We need her."

"Maybe." He sounded unconvinced. "Fucking fairies."

I blinked and he was no longer by the couch—he was nose-to-nose with me. My breathing quickened. It was the first time he'd ever put his preternatural speed to full use in front of me.

He tucked a strand of hair behind my ear, trailed his fingers down my cheek. He traced the shape of my lips, then let his hand fall away.

I wet my lips and looked up at him. The lust I felt when standing so close to him was almost unbearable. I wanted to lean into him. I wanted to pull his head down and kiss him. I wanted to strip, and shove him back, and be his reverse cowgirl, ride him hard until he made raw, sexy, rough sounds as he came.

"How long have you known you were the Unseelie King's concubine?" Though his voice was soft, his words were too precise. Tension shaped his mouth. I knew every nuance of that mouth. Fury was gnawing at him and needed an outlet. "You shoved through that Silver with no doubt you'd make it through."

My laughter held a note of hysteria. Oh, if only that was the extent of my problems!

Was I a woman, obsessed with the woman on the couch?

Or was I the male king of the Fae, obsessed with Jericho?

I consider myself open-minded about gender preference—love is love, and who's to say how the body follows the heart?—but both of those scenarios were hard for me to accept for myself. Neither fit me like a glove, and sexuality should. When it's right, it feels good on you, like your own skin, and the only thing that felt like skin to *me* was woman to man. Then there was the whole *Oh, gee,* I'm *the screwup responsible for this whole mess.* No more blaming the Unseelie King for making so many bad decisions and messing up my world. Was I the one who'd messed up theirs? If so, I bore an unbearable amount of guilt.

I raked my hair back from my face with both hands. If I kept thinking about it, I was going to lose it.

I'm not the concubine, Jericho. I'm afraid I must be some part of the Unseelie King in human form. "Not very long," I lied. "I recognized things in the White Mansion, and I kept having dreams that made sense only if I was her. I knew there was a way to test it."

"You bloody fool, if you'd been wrong it would have killed you!"

"But I wasn't wrong."

"Obtuse and illogical!"

I shrugged. Apparently I'd been a lot worse than that.

"You will never do such an idiotic thing again," he said, muscles bunching in his jaw.

Given my track record, I was pretty sure I would. I mean, really, if I *was* the Unseelie King—the most powerful Fae ever—I'd somehow ended up human and clueless. That meant I was not only evil, obsessed, and destructive, I was inexcusably stupid.

He began to circle me, looking me up and down like an exotic in a zoo. "And you thought I was the king. That's why you tried to drag me through it with you. You just can't get enough of killing me, can you? What's the last thing you said to me?" He mocked in falsetto: *"What's the worst that can happen? I lead you into some trap and you die for however long it is you go away?"*

I said nothing. I saw little point in trying to justify myself anymore.

"I imagine it got all your little romantic notions atwitter again, didn't it?"

"Is 'atwitter' even a word?"

"Did you think we were star-crossed lovers, Ms. Lane? Did you need that excuse?"

He gave me that wolf smile and I thought, *Right,*

star-crossed lovers with a double-edged sword. Because that's what this man was. Sharp, edgy, dangerous. With no safe side. And, yes, actually, I had thought we were star-crossed lovers. But I wasn't about to tell him that.

I turned to circle with him, meeting that dark, hostile gaze. "I thought we resolved this in the mansion, *Jericho*. It's Mac."

"It's Mac when I'm fucking you. The rest of the time, it's Ms. Lane. Get used to it."

"Boundaries, Barrons?"

"Precisely. Where's the king, Ms. Lane?"

"You think he calls me to check in? Says, *Honey, I'll be home for dinner tonight at seven?* How the hell should I know?" Which was technically the truth. Even Christian would have had a hard time with that one. I didn't know where all his parts were.

The concubine made a faint sound and we turned to look at her.

His eyes narrowed. "I've got to get her out of here. I won't have the entire Fae race trying to get past my wards. I suppose we'll have to protect her." His distaste couldn't have been more evident. If given a choice between having a razor-blade enema and protecting a Fae—had it been any other Fae than the all-powerful queen—Barrons would have willingly died a few times from internal bleeding.

But she was the one Fae he wasn't willing to sacrifice—yet.

I was definitely up for moving her somewhere else; the farther from me, the better. I'd been worried that he might try to keep her at the bookstore and had been prepared to argue that, no matter how formidable his wards were, with the two of us coming and going constantly, she'd be left alone too much to guarantee her safety. "What do you have in mind?" I said.

* * *

Half a *Dani Daily* flapped on a streetlamp in the chilly night breeze. I plucked it off, scanned it for the date AWC, and did some hasty calculations. If it had been posted today—which it probably hadn't, considering its condition—the date was March 23. Maybe a week later.

I read it and smiled faintly. She'd taken the bull by the horns while I was gone. The kid feared nothing.

The Dani Daily

147 Days AWC

Dudes—Listen Up if You Wanna Survive!

A few simple rules and regs will keep you alive!

1. Skintight clothes or nothing at all! Don't be bashful, don't be shy. Don't leave no place for a book to hide. The fecker's on the rampage, has been for weeks! Need to be seeing with your own eyeballs ain't nothing hiding on your peeps.

2. No splitting up! Do NOT go anywhere alone. That's when it gets you! If you see a book, DON'T PICK IT UP!!!!!

3. Don't leave your hidey-holes at night! Don't know why, but it likes the dark. Yes, I'm talking about the SINSAR DUBH. I said it, you heard me. You dudes who ain't been seeing my rags, it's a book of dark magic created by the Unseelie King almost a million years ago. Past time you know the truth. If you pick it up, it will make you KILL EVERYBODY AROUND YOU, starting with the peeps you love. Start following the rules! No deviations, no stupid fecking

The bottom half had been torn off, but I didn't need to see any more. I'd really just wanted to know the date. I'd missed her birthday. Chocolate on chocolate, she'd said. I'd planned to make her a cake myself. I'd throw a belated party for her, even if it was just the two of us.

Hardly something the Unseelie King would think about: birthday parties for humans.

"You might have all night, but some of us don't," Barrons growled over his shoulder.

I stuffed the paper in my pocket and hurried to catch up. We'd parked the Viper a block away. The queen wore a hooded cloak and was wrapped in blankets.

"You have all night tonight *and* tomorrow night *and* all eternity for that matter. So how long were you dead this time?" I asked, needling him.

The rattle moved in his throat.

I took a perverse pleasure in irritating him. "A day? Three? Five? What does it depend on? How badly you're injured?"

"If I were you, Ms. Lane, I'd never bring that up again. You think you're suddenly a major player because you went through that Silver—"

"I left Christian at the mirror. I found him in the prison," I cut him off.

His mouth snapped shut, then, "Why the fuck does it always take you so long to tell me the important things?"

"Because there are always so *many* important things," I said defensively. "Her hair's dragging again."

"Pick it up. My hands are full."

"I'm not touching her."

He shot me a look. "Issues much, Ms. Concubine?"

"She's not even the real queen," I said irritably. "Not the one that ruined the concubine's life. I just don't like Fae. I'm a *sidhe*-seer, remember?"

"Are you?"

"Why are you so pissed at me? It's not my fault who

I am. The only thing that's my fault is what I choose to do with it."

He gave me a sidelong glance that said, *That might be the only intelligent thing you've said tonight.*

I looked past him to the wrecked façade of Chester's ahead, and for a moment it looked eerily like a ruin of standing stones, black against a blue-black sky, from a faraway time and another place. A full moon hung above it, wearing a halo of crimson, round fat face splattered with craters of blood. More Fae changes in our world.

"When you get inside, go to the stairs and one of them will escort you up. Go *directly* to the stairs," he said pointedly. "Try not to get in trouble or cause a riot on the way."

"I don't think that's a fair statement. Life isn't always chaotic around me."

"Like when isn't it?"

"Like when I'm . . . " I thought a minute. "Alone," I finished pissily. "Or asleep." I didn't ask about my parents. It felt . . . wrong, as if I no longer had any right to ask questions about Jack and Rainey Lane. It made my heart hurt. "Where are you going?"

"I'll meet you inside."

"Because if I knew whatever secret back entrance you're about to use," I said sarcastically, "I might broadcast it to all the Fae, is that it?" He trusted me even less now that he thought I was the king's mortal lover. How would he treat me if he thought I was the Big Bad himself?

"Move it, Ms. Lane," was all he said.

I descended into the belly of the whale to find it crammed to the gills with humans and Unseelie—standing room only at Chester's tonight.

I couldn't be the king. These would be my "children." I didn't feel remotely paternal. I felt homicidal. That sealed it. I was human. I had no idea why the mirror had let me through, but eventually I'd figure it out.

I glanced around, shocked. Things had changed while I'd been gone. The world just kept morphing into something new without me.

There were *Seelie* in Chester's now, too. Not many, and it didn't look like they were getting the warmest welcome from the Unseelie, but I'd already spotted a dozen, and the humans were going crazy over them. Two of those horrid little monsters that made you laugh yourself to death were dive-bombing the crowd, clutching tiny drinks that sloshed over the rims as they flew. Three of those blinding-light trailers were whizzing through the masses. In a cage suspended from the ceiling, naked men danced, writhing in sexual ecstasy, fanned by ethereal, gossamer-winged nymphs.

I continued scanning the club and stiffened. On an elevated platform, in the sub-club that catered to those with a taste for *very* young humans, stood the golden god who'd comforted Dree'lia when V'lane had taken her mouth away.

It was all I could do not to march over there, stab him with my spear, and denounce V'lane as a traitor.

Then I had a better idea.

I pushed through the crowd, pulled myself up next to him, and said, "Hey, remember me?"

He ignored me. I imagined he heard that a lot if he'd been coming here awhile. I stood beside him, looking out over the sea of heads.

"I'm the woman that was with Darroc the night we met in the street. I need you to summon V'lane."

The golden god's head swiveled. Disdain stamped his immortal features. "Summon. V'lane. Those two words do not go together in any language, human."

"I had his name in my tongue until Barrons sucked it out. I need him. Now." This golden god might have disconcerted me once, but I had a spear in my holster and a black secret in my heart, and nothing disconcerted me anymore. I wanted V'lane here, now. He had a few things to answer for.

"V'lane did not give you his name."

"On multiple occasions. And his fury with you will know no bounds if he learns I asked you to get him for me and you refused."

He regarded me in stony silence.

I shrugged. "Fine. Your call. Just remember what he did to Dree'lia." I turned and walked away.

He was in front of me.

"Hey, what the fuck ya think ya doing? No sifting in the club!" someone cried. The golden god jerked and disentangled himself from the arm that he'd materialized around. It seemed to slide from his body, as if the section containing it had abruptly become energy, not matter.

The guy the arm belonged to was young, with a fauxhawk, a petulant expression, and twitchy, restless eyes. He clutched his offended appendage, rubbing it as if it had gone to sleep. Then he seemed to see what had just sifted in next to him and his eyes rounded almost comically.

A drink appeared in the golden god's hand. He offered it to the guy with a murmured regret. "I did not mean to break the rules of the club. Your arm will be fine in a moment."

"S'cool, man," the guy gushed as he accepted the drink. "No worries." He stared up at the Fae worshipfully. "What can I do for ya?" he said breathlessly. "I mean, man, I'd do anything, ya know? Anything at all!"

The golden god bent down, leaning close. "Would you die for me?"

"Anything, man! But will you take me to Faery first?"

I leaned in behind the golden god and pressed my mouth to his ear. "There's a spear in a holster beneath my arm. You broke a rule and sifted. I bet that means I can break a rule, too. You want to try it?"

He made that hissing Fae sound of distaste. But he eased away and stood straight.

"Be a good little fairy," I purred, "and go get V'lane for me." I hesitated, weighing my next words. "Tell him I have some news about the *Sinsar Dubh*."

Laughter and all voices died; the club fell silent.

Movement ceased.

I glanced around, absorbing it. It was as if the entire place had been freeze-framed by the mere mention of the *Sinsar Dubh*.

Though the club was a bubble frozen in time, I swore I felt eyes resting heavily on me. Was there some kind of charm cast over this place so that if someone uttered the name of the king's forbidden Book, everyone but the person who'd spoken the words and the person who'd laid the spell would momentarily freeze?

I scanned the sub-clubs.

Air hissed between my teeth. Two tiered dance floors down, a man in an impeccable white suit was holding frozen court in a kingly white chair, surrounded by dozens of white-clad attendants.

I hadn't seen him since that night long ago, when Barrons and I had searched Casa Blanc. But, like me, he wasn't frozen.

McCabe nodded to me across the sea of statues.

Just as suddenly as everything had frozen, life resumed.

"You have offended me, human," the golden god was saying, "and I will kill you for the slight. Not here. Not tonight. But soon."

"Sure, whatever," I muttered. "Just get him here." I turned away and began shoving my way through the crowd, but by the time I reached the kingly white chair, McCabe was gone.

I had to pass the sub-club where the dreamy-eyed guy tended bar to get to the stairs. "Directly," construed as a geographical command, didn't preclude stopping along the way and, since I was parched and had a few questions about a tarot card, I rapped my knuckles on the counter for a shot.

I could barely remember what it felt like to mix drinks and party with my friends, jam-packed with ignorance and shiny dreams.

Five stools down, a top hat gauzed with cobwebs was a dark, unused chimney badly in need of sweeping. Strawlike hair swept shoulders that were as bony as broomsticks in a pinstriped suit. The *fear dorcha* was hanging with the dreamy-eyed guy again. Creepy.

Nobody was sitting next to it. The top hat rotated my way as I took a seat, four empty stools away. A deck of tarot cards was artfully arranged in its suit pocket, a natty handkerchief, cards fanned. Knobbed ankles crossed, displaying patent-leather shoes with shiny, pointy toes.

"Weight of the world on your shoulders?" it called like a carny selling chances at a booth.

I stared into the swirling dark tornado beneath the brim of the top hat. Fragments of a face—half a green eye and brow, part of a nose—appeared and vanished like scraps of pictures torn from a magazine, momentarily slapped up against a window, then torn off by the next storm gust. I suddenly knew the debonair and eerie prop was as ancient as the Fae themselves. Did the *fear dorcha* make the hat, or did the hat make the *fear dorcha*?

Because my parents raised me to be polite and old habits die hard, it was difficult to hold my tongue. But the mistake of speaking to it was not one I'd make twice.

"Relationships got you down?" it cried, with the inflated exuberance of an OxiClean commercial. I half-expected helpful visual aids to manifest in midair as he hawked his wares—whatever they were.

I rolled my eyes. One could certainly say that.

"Might be just what you need is a night on the town!" it enthused in a too-bright voice.

I snorted.

It unfolded itself from the stool, proffering long bony arms and skeletal hands. "Give us a dance, luv. I'm told I'm quite the Fred Astaire." It tapped out a quick step and bent low at the waist, thin arms flamboyantly wide.

A shot of whiskey slid down the counter. I tossed it back swiftly.

"See you learned your lesson, beautiful girl."

"Been learning a lot lately."

"All ears."

"Tarot deck was my life. How's that?"

"Told you. Prophecies. All shapes."

"Why'd you give me THE WORLD?"

"Didn't. Would you like me to?"

"You flirting with me?"

"If I was?"

"Might run screaming."

"Smart girl."

We laughed.

"Seen Christian lately?"

"Yes."

His hands stilled on the bottles and he waited.

"Think he's turning into something."

"All things change."

"Think he's becoming Unseelie."

"Fae. Like starfish, beautiful girl."

"How's that?"

"Grow back missing parts."

"What are you saying?"

"Balance. World lists toward it."

"Thought it was entropy."

"Implies innate idiocy. People are. Universes aren't."

"So if an Unseelie Prince dies, someone will eventually replace it? If not a Fae, a human?"

"Hear princesses are dead, too."

I gagged. Would human women be changed by eating Unseelie and end up becoming them in time? What else would the Fae steal from my world? Well, er, actually, what would I and my—I changed the subject swiftly. "Who gave me the card?"

He jerked a thumb at the *fear dorcha*.

I didn't believe that for a minute. "What am I supposed to get from it?"

"Ask him."

"You told me not to."

"That's a problem."

"Solution?"

"Maybe it's not about the world."

"What else could it be about?"

"Got eyes, BG, use them."

"Got a mouth, DEG, use it."

He moved away, tossing bottles like a professional juggler. I watched his hands fly, trying to figure out how to get him to talk.

He knew things. I could smell it. He knew a lot of things.

Five shot glasses settled on the counter. He splashed them full and slid them five ways with enviable precision.

I glanced up into the mirror behind the bar that angled down and reflected the sleek black bar top. I saw myself. I saw the *fear dorcha*. I saw dozens of other patrons gathered at the counter. It wasn't a busy bar. This was one of the smaller, less popular sub-clubs. There was no sex or violence to be found here, only cobwebs and tarot cards.

The dreamy-eyed guy was absent in the reflection. I saw glasses and bottles sparkling as they flipped in the air but no one tossing them.

I glanced down at him, pouring high and flashy.

Back up. There was no reflection.

I tapped my empty shot glass on the counter. Another one clinked into it. I sipped this one, watching him, waiting for him to return.

He took his time.

"Look conflicted, beautiful girl."

"I don't see you in the mirror."

"Maybe I don't see you, either."

I froze. Was that possible? Was I missing in the mirror?

He laughed. "Just kidding. You're there."

"Not funny."

"Not my mirror."

"What does that mean?"

"I'm not responsible for what it shows. Or doesn't."

"Who *are* you?"

"Who are *you*?"

I narrowed my eyes. "Somehow I got the idea you were trying to help me. Guess I was wrong."

"Help. Dangerous medicine."

"How?"

"Hard to gauge the right dose. Especially if there's more than one doctor."

I sucked in a breath. The dreamy-eyed guy's eyes were no longer dreamy. They were . . . I stared. They were . . . I caught my lower lip with my teeth and bit down. What was I looking at? What was happening to me?

He was no longer behind the counter but sitting on a bar stool beside me, to my left, no—to my right. No, he was on the stool with me. There he was—behind me, mouth pressed to my ear.

"Too much falsely inflates. Too little underprepares. The finest surgeon has butterfly fingers. Airy. Delicate."

Like his fingers on my hair. The touch was mesmerizing. "Am I the Unseelie King?" I whispered.

Laughter as soft as moth wings filled my ears and muddied my mind, stirring silt from the dregs of my soul. "No more than I." He was back behind the bar. "The cantankerous one comes," he said, with a nod toward the stairs.

I looked to see Barrons descending. When I looked back, the dreamy-eyed guy was no more visible than his reflection.

"I was coming," I said irritably. Fingers handcuffed around my wrist, Barrons dragged me toward the stairs.

"What part of 'directly' didn't you understand?"

"Same part of 'play well with others' you never understand, O cantankerous one," I muttered.

He laughed, surprising me. I never know what's going to make him laugh. At the oddest moments, he seems to find humor in his own bad temper.

"I'd be a lot less cantankerous if you admitted you wanted to fuck me and we got down to it."

Lust ripped through me. Barrons said "fuck" and I was ready. "That's all it would take to put you in a good humor?"

"It'd go a long way."

"Are we having a conversation, Barrons? Where you actually express feelings?"

"If you want to call a hard dick feelings, Ms. Lane."

A sudden commotion at the entrance to the club, two levels above us, caught his attention. He was taller than me and could see over the crowd. "You've got to be kidding me." His face hardened as he stared up at the balconied foyer.

"What? Who?" I said, bouncing on my tiptoes to try to see. "Is it V'lane?"

"Why would it be—" He glared down at me. "I stripped his name from your tongue. There hasn't been an opportunity for you to get it back again."

"I told one of his court to go get him. Don't look at me like that. I want to know what's going on."

"What's going on, Ms. Lane, is that you found the Seelie Queen in the Unseelie prison. What's going on—given the condition she's in—is that V'lane's obviously been lying about her whereabouts for months now, and that can mean only one thing."

"That it was impossible for me to permit the court to know that the queen was missing, and has been missing for many human years," V'lane said tightly behind us, his voice hushed. "They would have fallen apart. Without her reining them in, a dozen different factions would have assaulted your world. There has long been unrest in Faery. But this is hardly the place to discuss such matters."

Barrons and I turned as one.

"Velvet told me you required my presence, Mac-Kayla," V'lane continued, "but he said your news was of the Book, not of our liege." He searched my face with a coolness I hadn't seen since I'd first met him. I supposed my method of summoning him had offended. Fae are so prickly. "Have you truly found her? Is she alive? In every spare moment, I have searched for her. It has prevented me from attending you as I wished."

"Velvet is a Fae name?"

"His true name is unpronounceable in your tongue. Is she here?"

I nodded.

"I must see her. How does she fare?"

Barrons' hand shot out and closed around V'lane's throat. "You lying fuck."

V'lane grabbed Barron's arm with one hand, his throat with the other.

I stared, fascinated. I was so discombobulated by recent developments that I hadn't even realized Barrons and V'lane were standing face-to-face on a crowded dance floor for what was probably the first time in all eternity—close enough to kill each other. Well, close enough for Barrons to kill V'lane. Barrons was staring at the Fae prince as if he'd finally caught a fire ant that had been torturing him for centuries while he'd lay spread-eagled on the desert, coated in honey. V'lane was glaring at Barrons as if he couldn't believe he'd be so stupid.

"We have larger concerns than your personal grievances," V'lane said with icy disdain. "If you cannot remove your head from your ass and see that, you deserve what will happen to your world."

"Maybe I don't care what happens to the world."

V'lane's head swiveled my way, cool appraisal in his gaze. "I have permitted you to retain your spear, Mac-Kayla. You will not let him harm me. Kill him—"

Barrons squeezed. "I said shut up."

"He has the fourth stone," I reminded Barrons. "We need him."

"Keltars!" V'lane said, staring up at the foyer. He hissed through his teeth.

"I know. Big fucking party tonight," said Barrons.

"Where? Is that who just came in?" I said.

Barrons leaned closer to V'lane and sniffed him. His

nostrils flared, as if he found the scent both repulsive and perfect for a fine, bloody filet.

"Where is she?" a man roared. The accent was Scottish, like Christian's but thicker.

V'lane ordered, "Shut him up before his next question is, 'Where is the queen,' and every Unseelie in this place discovers she is here."

Barrons moved too fast for me to see. One second, V'lane was his usual gorgeous self, then his nose was crushed and gushing blood. Barrons said, "Next time, fairy," and was gone.

"I said, where the bloody hell is the—"

I heard a grunt, then the sound of fists and more grunts, and all hell broke loose at Chester's.

"I doona give a bloody damn what you think. She's our responsibility—"

"And a hell of a job you've done with her—"

"She's my queen and she's not going anywhere with—"

"—so far, losing her to the fucking Unseelie."

"—and we'll be taking her back to Scotland with us, where she can be watched o'er properly."

"—a pair of inept humans, she belongs in Faery."

"I'll send you back to Faery, fairy, in a fucking—"

"Remember the missing stone, mongrel."

I looked from the Scotsman, to Barrons, to V'lane, watching the three of them argue. They'd been covering the same ground with no new developments for the past five minutes. V'lane kept demanding she be turned over to him, the Scot kept insisting he was taking her back to Scotland, but I knew Barrons. He wasn't going to let either of them have her. Not only did he trust no one, the queen of the Fae was a powerful trump card.

"How the fuck did you even know she was here?" Barrons demanded.

V'lane, whose nose was once again perfect, said, "MacKayla summoned me. As I walked up behind you, I heard you, as anyone else might have. You jeopardize her life with your carelessness."

"Not *you*," Barrons growled. "The Highlander."

The Scot said, "Nearly five years past, she visited Cian in the Dreaming, telling him she would be here this eve. The queen herself ordered us to collect her, from this address on this night. We have irrefutable claim. We are the Keltar and wear the mantle of protection for the Fae. You will turn her over to us now."

I almost laughed, but something about the two Scots made me think twice about it. They looked like they'd been traveling hard through rough terrain and hadn't showered or shaved in days. Words like "patience" and "diplomacy" were not in their vocabulary. They thought in terms of objectives and results—and the fewer things between the two, the better. They were like Barrons: driven, focused, ruthless.

Both were shirtless and heavily tattooed—Lor and another of Barrons' men I hadn't seen before had made all of us strip down to clothing that couldn't conceal a book, before permitting us access to the upper level of the club. Now the five of us stood, partially dressed, in an unfurnished glass cubicle.

The one arguing, Dageus, was all long, smooth muscle, with the fast, graceful movements of a big cat and cheetah-gold eyes. His black hair was so long it brushed his belt—not that he needed one, in hip-slimming black leather pants. He sported a cut lip and a shiner on his right cheek from the skirmish that had begun at the door and spread like a contagion through several sub-clubs. It had taken five of Barrons' men to get things back under control. Being able to move like the wind gave them a tremendous advantage. They didn't warn the patrons to stop fighting—they simply appeared and killed them. Once humans and Fae figured out what was happening, the outbreak of violence ended as quickly as it had begun.

The other Scot, Cian, had yet to speak a word and had escaped the brawl without a mark, but with all the red and black ink on his torso, I'm not sure I would have noticed blood. He was massive, with bunched short muscles, the kind a man gets from weight training in a gym or working off a long prison sentence. His shoulders were enormous, his stomach flat; he had piercings, one of his tattoos said JESSI. I wondered what kind of woman could make a man like him want to tattoo her name on his chest.

These were the uncles Christian had talked about, the men who'd broken into the Welshman's castle the night Barrons and I had tried to steal the amulet, the ones who'd performed the ritual with Barrons on Halloween. They were nothing like any uncles I'd ever seen. I'd expected time-softened relatives in their late thirties or forties, but these were time-hardened men of barely thirty, with a dangerous, sexy edge. Both had an unfocused distance in their eyes, as if they'd seen things so disturbing that only by refocusing with everything slightly *out* of focus could they gaze on the world and bear it.

I wondered if my own eyes were beginning to look like that.

"One thing's for certain: She doesna belong with you," Dageus said to Barrons.

"How do you figure, Highlander?"

"We protect the Fae and he *is* Fae, which gives both of us greater claim than you."

I felt someone staring at me, hard, and looked around. V'lane was watching me, eyes narrowed. So far everyone had been so busy arguing about what to do with the queen that no one had bothered asking how I'd found her or how I'd gotten her out of the prison. I suspected that was what V'lane was wondering now.

He knew the legend of the king's Silver. He knew only two could pass through it—unless I'd serendipitously stumbled on a truth with my lie and whoever was the current queen *was* immune to the king's magic, which I doubted. The one person the king would have wanted to protect the concubine from the most would have been the Seelie Queen. He'd barred his castle against the original, vindictive queen the day she'd come to his fortress and they'd argued. He'd forbidden any Seelie from ever entering it. I had no doubt he'd used the same spells or worse on the Silver that connected his boudoir to the concubine's. V'lane had to be wondering if he had any idea who their queen really was, who *I* really was, or if maybe their entire history was as suspect and inaccurate as ours. Regardless, V'lane knew *something* about me wasn't what it seemed.

Besides myself, only Christian knew the queen was really the concubine. And only I knew of this duality inside me that could be neatly explained away if I was the other half of their royal equation.

After a long, measuring moment, he gave me a tight nod.

What the hell did that mean? That for now he would keep his silence and not raise any questions that might further muddy already-muddied waters? I nodded back as if I had some clue what we were nodding about.

"You couldn't even perform the bloody ritual to keep the walls up and you want me to trust you with the queen? And you," Barrons turned on V'lane, who was maintaining a careful distance, "will never get her from me. As far as I'm concerned, you put her in the coffin she was found in."

"Why don't you ask the queen yourself?" V'lane suggested coolly. "It was not I, as she will tell you."

"Conveniently for you, she's not talking."

"Is she injured?"

"How would I know? I don't even know what you fucks are made of."

"Why would anyone put her in the Unseelie prison?" I said.

" 'Tis a slow but certain way to kill her, lass," Dageus said. "The Unseelie prison is the opposite of all she is and, as such, leaches her very life essence."

"If someone wanted her dead, there are quicker ways," I protested.

"Maybe whoever took her couldn't get the spear or sword."

That ruled out V'lane. He took it from me regularly, like now. Darroc did, too. Whoever had taken the queen captive had to have been powerful enough to take her but not powerful enough to get the spear or sword, two conditions that seemed mutually exclusive. Was it possible her kidnapper had a reason to want to kill her slowly?

"V'lane told me all the Seelie Princesses are dead," I said. "There's a Fae legend that says if all successors to the queen's power are dead, the True Magic of their race would be forced to pass to their most powerful male. What if someone was trying to time taking possession of the *Sinsar Dubh* with killing all the female royalty, ending with Aoibheal herself, so when the queen died, he would end up with not only the power of the Unseelie King but the True Magic of the queen, making him the first patriarchal ruler of their race? Who is the most powerful male?"

All heads swiveled toward V'lane.

"What do you humans say? I have it: Oh, please," he

said drily. The look he gave me was equal parts anger and reproach. As if to say, *I'm sitting on your secrets, don't turn on me.* "It is a legend, nothing more. I have served Aoibheal for my entire existence and I serve her now."

"Why did you lie about her location?" Dageus demanded.

"I have been masking her absence for many human years to prevent a Fae civil war. With the princesses dead, there is no clear successor."

Many human years? It was the second time he'd said as much, but the ramifications only now penetrated. I stared at him. He'd told me far more than just one lie. On Halloween, he'd told me he had been otherwise occupied, carrying his queen to safety. Where had he really been that night when I'd so desperately needed him? I wanted to know right now, demand answers, but there was already too much going on here, and when I interrogated him, it would be on my terms, my turf.

"And just how did they die?" Barrons said.

V'lane sighed. "They vanished when she did." He looked at me again.

I blinked. His gaze held sorrow—and a promise that we would talk soon.

"Convenient for you, fairy."

V'lane cut Barrons a look of disdain. "Look beyond the tip of your mortal nose. The Unseelie Princes are easily as powerful—if not more so—than I. And the Unseelie King himself is far stronger than us all. The magic would most certainly go to him, wherever he is. I have nothing to gain by harming my queen and everything to lose. You must let me have her. If she was in the Unseelie prison the entire time that she has been missing, she may be very close to death. You must permit me to take her to Faery, to regain her strength!"

"Never going to happen."

"Then *you* will be responsible for killing our queen," V'lane said bitterly.

"And how do I know that's not what you've been after all along?"

"You despise us all. You would allow the queen to die to satisfy your own petty vengeances."

I wanted to know what Barrons' petty vengeances were. But I was feeling that damned duality again. What was unfolding here wasn't remotely what anyone thought. Only I knew the truth.

This was not the queen they were fighting over. It was the concubine from hundreds of thousands of years ago, who'd somehow ended up becoming the Seelie Queen. Had the king finally gotten what he'd hoped for? Had protracted time in Faery made his beloved Fae? Had the balance that the world "listed" toward, as the dreamy-eyed guy proposed, turned a mortal into a replacement queen, as it would ultimately turn Christian into a re-placement prince?

If I was the king, why didn't that elate me? The con-cubine was finally Fae! I shook my head. I couldn't think that way. It just didn't work for me. "Mac," I muttered. "Just be Mac."

Barrons cut me a hard look that said, *Shelve it for later, Ms. Concubine.*

"Look, boys," I said. Four ancient sets of eyes skew-ered me, and I blinked at the two Scotsmen. "Oh, you two aren't at all what you seem to be, are you?"

"Is anyone in this room?" Barrons said irritably. "What's your point?"

"She's safest here," I said succinctly.

"That's what I've been saying all along," Barrons growled. "This level is warded the same way the book-store is. Nothing can sift in—"

V'lane hissed.

"—or out. Nothing Seelie or Unseelie can get to her. We don't let anyone enter the room clothed. Rainey is nursing—"

"You put her in with my parents?" I said incredulously. "People are visiting naked?"

"Where else would I put her?"

"The queen of the Faery is in that glass room with my mom and dad?" My voice was rising. I didn't care.

He shrugged. His eyes said, *Not really, and we both know that. You aren't even from this world.*

Mine said, *I don't give a shit who I might have been in another lifetime. I know who I am now.*

"It takes time and resources to ward a place as well as the room where Jack and Rainey are. We're not duplicating our efforts," he said.

"Castle Keltar was warded by the queen herself," Dageus said. "Far from Dublin, where the *Sinsar Dubh* seems inclined to prowl, 'tis the better choice."

"She stays. Not open to discussion. You don't like that, try to take her," Barrons said flatly, and in his dark eyes I saw anticipation. He hoped they would. He was in the mood for a fight. Everyone in the room was. Even me, I was startled to realize. I had a sudden, unwanted appreciation of men. I had a problem I couldn't fix. But if I could create a manageable problem, like a fistfight, and kick the shit out of it, it sure would make me feel better for a while.

"If she stays, we stay," Dageus said flatly. "We guard her here or we guard her there. But we guard her."

"And if they stay, I stay, too." V'lane's voice dripped ice. "No human will protect my queen so long as I exist."

"Simple solution to that, fairy. I make you stop existing."

"The Seelie are not our enemy. You touch him, you take us all on."

"You think I couldn't, Highlander?"

For a moment the tension in the room was unbearable, and in my mind's eye I saw us all going for one another's throats.

Barrons was the only one of us that couldn't be killed. I needed the Scotsmen to perform the re-interment ritual and V'lane and his stone to help corner the Book. A fight right now was a very bad idea.

"And that's settled," I chirped brightly. "Everyone's staying. Welcome to the Chester's Hilton! Let's get some beds made up."

Barrons looked at me as if I'd gone mad.

"Then let's go out and find some things to kill," I added.

Dageus and Cian growled assent, and even V'lane looked relieved.

32

I stepped out of the shower and looked at myself in the mirror. Since dragging my aching body up the back stairs of BB&B to my bedroom twenty minutes ago, my bruises had faded by forty percent. I traced my fingers across a particularly bad one on my collarbone. I'd thought I heard a *crack* and was worried something had broken, but it was only a hot, swollen contusion and was healing remarkably fast.

What was with me? I might have suspected it was something to do with my being . . . well, Not the Concubine, but I'd never healed like this when I was a kid. I'd run around with skinned knees constantly.

Was McCabe one of my parts? Was that why he hadn't frozen, too? Could the dreamy-eyed guy be a part? Who else? How many parts did Not the Concubine have?

"I am *not* the king," I said out loud. "There's some other explanation." There had to be. I simply wouldn't accept it.

Tonight had been a rush. We'd run into Jayne, his guardians, and Dani near Fourteenth and cut a wide swath through the city. Dageus, Cian, and V'lane had pummeled; Dani and I had sliced and diced. Barrons had done whatever it was he did, but he'd done it too fast for me to see. After a time I'd stopped trying, too lost in my own bloodlust.

When I'd finally quit counting, the death toll had been in the hundreds.

How could it feel so good to kill Unseelie if I was their creator?

"See? More proof I'm not," I told myself in the mirror with a nod. My reflection nodded sagely back. I selected the medium heat setting on my dryer and began to blow-dry my hair.

The Unseelie had retreated. Word of us had spread through the streets and they'd withdrawn from combat, flapped, sifted, and slithered away. I guess after being locked up for their entire existence, they were in no hurry to die now that they were free. I'd left Barrons, the two Keltar, and V'lane looking remarkably unsatisfied and about to fall at one another's throats. I'd been tired, sore, and beyond caring. If they were stupid enough to kill each other, they deserved the resultant problems it would create.

As I slipped into pajamas, a pebble rattled against my bedroom window.

I was so not in the mood for V'lane right now. Yes, I had questions, but tonight was not the night to ask them. I needed rest and a clear head. I kicked away the backpack, crawled in bed and pulled the covers over my head to block out the blazing light from five lamps. The Shades were supposedly gone. "Supposedly" isn't a word I live with well.

Another pebble.

I squeezed my eyes shut and waited for it to stop.

Five minutes of incessant pebbles later, a stone crashed through my window, spraying glass and scaring the hell out of me.

I shot up in bed and glared at the mess on the floor. I couldn't even march over and snap his head off. I had to dig around for shoes first.

A chilly breeze flapped the curtains.

I tugged on boots and crunched to the window. "I'm not talking to you until you fix the damned glass, V'lane," I snapped. Then, "Oh!"

A cloaked, hooded figure stood in the alley below, and for a moment it reminded me of Mallucé. Dark robes swirled in a gossamer cloud as the figure moved jerkily forward, as if every step was agony. The exterior spotlights gleamed across the cloak, and I saw it was fashioned of frothy light chiffon.

My first thought was of the *Sinsar Dubh,* hiding somewhere beneath those many secretive folds.

"Drop the cloak. I want to see hands, everything."

I heard a sharp inhalation, a wheeze of agony. Arms moved with arthritic carefulness, loosening a brooch at the throat. The hood fell and the cloak rustled to the ground.

I nearly vomited. I bit back a scream. I wouldn't wish it on my worst enemy. It was Fiona, in the badly mutilated flesh.

"Merssseee." Skinned lips parted on a sibilant hiss.

I turned away from the window and leaned back against the sill, hand over my mouth. My eyes were closed, but there was no escape. I could see her on the backs of my lids.

She'd tried to kill me, in what seemed another lifetime. She'd taken up with Derek O'Bannion, then Darroc.

All because she loved Jericho Barrons.

The night the Book had brought her to my balcony, skinned alive, I'd wondered if all the Unseelie she'd eaten would keep her from dying. Eating Unseelie has remarkable healing properties. But apparently growing a new human skin—or maybe healing from any magical injury the *Sinsar Dubh* had inflicted—was beyond its ability.

"I thought the Book killed everyone it possessed," I said finally. My words rang out in the hushed night.

"It has . . . different appetites for . . . us . . . who eat Unseelie." Her pained voice floated up.

"It killed Darroc. He ate Unseelie."

"Silencing , . . him. For what . . . he knew."

"Which was?"

"If only . . . I knew. I would . . ." She made a garbled sound, and I assumed from the wheezes and moans that she was stooping to retrieve her cloak. I tried to imagine what would hurt worse on flayed flesh—the cold night breeze or clothes. Both would be a walking hell. I couldn't imagine how she stood the pain.

I didn't say anything. There was nothing to say.

"Try it . . . myself," she finally continued, "pray it . . . killed me . . . too."

"Why are you here?" I turned and stared down at her. Although she'd put her cloak back on, she'd left the hood down.

"Can't heal." Gray eyes shimmered with constant pain in bloody sockets. Even her lids were gone. "Can't die. Tried . . . everything."

"Still eating Unseelie?"

"Dulls . . . pain."

"It's probably what's keeping you alive."

"Too . . . late."

"You mean you think you've been eating it so long that even if you stopped now you might not die?"

"Yesss."

I considered that. Depending on how much she'd eaten, it was possible. Mallucé had been marbled with Fae like a steak with fat. Maybe even if she stopped entirely, she would never be fully human again. I'd eaten it only twice in my life and hoped it had passed from my body forever.

"Can't find . . . " Her gaze drifted to the abandoned Dark Zone, and I understood that she'd hunted for a Shade to kill her. But they'd moved on long ago to greener pastures, literally, and she didn't look capable of walking very far. I couldn't imagine her driving a car, sitting on that flayed flesh. I shuddered. "Only spear . . . sword . . . will—"

"—make the Fae parts quit keeping you alive," I finished. I looked away, stared out over the roof of Barrons' garage at the hundreds of dark roofs beyond. "You want me to kill you." There was a terrible irony here.

"Yesss."

"Why not try Dani? Don't you think you might have better luck there?"

"Said no."

I blinked. She'd actually known about Dani, found her, and Dani had refused?

"Said . . . you had to . . ."

"And you think I have mercy?"

"Can't . . . look . . . at me."

I jerked my gaze back to her skinned face. "I can ignore you for the rest of my life." But it wasn't true. And she knew it.

"Merssseee," she hissed again.

I punched the ledge of the window.

There were no easy choices anymore. I didn't want to go down there and look at her. I didn't want to stab her. I couldn't possibly let her go on suffering if I could do something about it, and I could.

I gazed longingly at my bed. I wanted nothing more than to crawl back in.

My window was broken. The room would be freezing in no time.

I reached for my holster, strapped it on over my pajama top, slid the spear beneath my arm, grabbed a coat from the chair, and headed for the stairs.

I had a small epiphany on the way down.

My spear would kill the Fae parts of Fiona, granting her the ultimate demise she wished, but very slowly. It had taken months for Mallucé to die. When I stabbed a Fae, it was entirely Fae and died swiftly. But when a human eats Unseelie, it laces the human's body with pockets and threads of immortal flesh, and there's no way to stab each and every thread or pocket, so the wound works instead like a slow poison. I wonder if whoever created the immortal-slaying weapons deliberately designed them that way, to carry out a horrific punishment for a horrific crime.

However, there was another potential method of execution that would either kill her instantly—or answer a question I badly wanted answered.

The entire time I'd been fighting tonight, I'd been thinking about it.

I wanted to test the Silver in the White Mansion.

Maybe lots of people and Fae could go through it.

I'd been considering taking an Unseelie captive and forcing it into the Silver.

Now I didn't have to. I had a volunteer.

And, even better, she was mostly human.

If Fiona could pass through the king's Silver without dying, that would mean the legend was a bluff.

It killed Barrons.

I shrugged. That might have been an anomaly. Barrons defied the laws of physics. Maybe humans could pass through it just fine. Maybe the Unseelie King hadn't warded it as well as he thought he had. Maybe humans from our planet were different from his mortal concubine, and how could you ward against something you didn't even know existed? All I knew was I wasn't the king, and here was my chance to prove it. I hated losing more time, but my peace of mind was worth losing time for.

I stepped into the alley and moved slowly toward her. "Hood up."

She made a sound that was almost laughter but made no move to lift it.

"Do you want to die? If so, hood up."

Eyes hot with hate, moving stiffly and with painstaking care, she adjusted the fabric to shadow her face.

As she put her arms back down, a gust of wind blew the stench of her straight into my nostrils. I gagged. She smelled of blood and decaying flesh with a strong medicinal odor, as if she was eating painkillers by the handful.

"Follow me."

"Where?"

"The spear will kill you, but it will do so slowly. I might have a way to kill you instantly."

The hood turned toward me as if she was searching my face to divine my motives.

Daddy told me once that we believe others are capable of the worst we ourselves are capable of. Fiona was wondering if I might be as cruel to her as she'd have been to me in the same position.

"It will be hell for you to have to walk there. But I think you'd rather spend twenty minutes getting there to die than the weeks or even months it could take to die from the spear wound. Because of the Unseelie you've been eating, you'll die slowly."

"Spear . . . not instant?" There was shock in her voice.

"No."

I knew the moment she accepted it. When I turned

and headed for the Silver in the brick wall, she followed. I heard the soft *swish* of her cloak behind me.

"There's a price, though. If you really want to die, you're going to have to tell me everything you know about—"

"I can't leave you alone for a minute, can I?" Barrons said. "Where the hell do you think you're going this time, Ms. Lane? And who is that with you?"

The three of us went in together.

It was one of the most awkward, uncomfortable walks I've taken.

I had one of those outside-my-skin-watching-from-above moments. Eight months ago, when I'd first ducked into BB&B, seeking sanctuary from my first encounter with a Dark Zone, I'd never have imagined this moment: pushing into a brick wall behind the bookstore—I mean, really, a brick wall!—with the badly skinned and heavily narcotized woman who'd run BB&B with Barrons, who was waiting for me to put him in a good mood again with sex and who turned into a nine-foot-tall beast on occasion, all so I could find out if I was the king and creator of the monsters that had overtaken my world. If I'd thought my life would come to this, I'd have marched straight for the airport that day and flown back home.

Fiona hadn't uttered a syllable since Barrons had appeared in the alley. She'd drawn her hood tightly around her face. I couldn't imagine what she had to be feeling as she marched to her suicide between the man she'd loved to her own destruction and the woman she believed had taken him from her.

At first, Barrons had disagreed with my plan vehemently.

He'd wanted to use the spear and kill her without

going back into the Silvers and wasting weeks, possibly months, doing it. But after I pulled him aside and explained that she was the perfect test, he'd reluctantly agreed, and I realized that he, too, hoped the legend was an erroneous myth.

Why? He thought I was the concubine. Considering what *I* was afraid I was, the concubine didn't seem like such a bad thing to be.

Unless he'd concluded that, if I was the concubine, the king himself was destined to come for me at some point, and that was one foe he might not be able to take on, even in beast form. Perhaps he worried that the king would take his OOP detector, and then where would he be?

But if you ask her one thing about me, Ms. Lane, he'd murmured against my ear, *I'll kill her where we stand, and you won't get your little test.*

I glanced at him from the corner of my eye. Could he? In the same way he killed Fae, whatever it was? Yet he didn't offer it as mercy. I wondered what he was feeling as we moved down a rosy corridor. Did he mourn her, this woman who'd run his store for years, this woman he'd trusted with more of his secrets than he'd ever entrusted to me? He hadn't offered to kill her swiftly, to end her suffering. He'd used it only as a threat to keep me from prying into his business.

His face was set in hard, cold lines. He looked down at the top of Fiona's head and his face changed; then he saw me looking at him and it was again a mask of stone.

He did mourn her—not her suffering or death but that she'd chosen the path that had led her here. I suspected that he would never have stopped caring for her, and taking care of her, if she hadn't turned on me. But that action had sealed her fate.

Barrons was one of the most complicated men I'd ever met and at the same time one of the simplest: You were with him, or you were against him. Period. End of story. You got only one chance with him. And if you betrayed him, you ceased to exist in his world until he got around to killing you.

Fiona had ceased to exist when she'd let Shades into the bookstore to devour me while I was sleeping—thereby stealing his only chance at something he wanted very badly, whatever it was—and the only thing he felt now was a twinge of wishing it hadn't turned out this way, a whisper of a regret. Not so long ago he'd put a knife through her heart, and if she hadn't been eating Unseelie, it would have killed her. He'd been ready to kill her in the alley, and not mercifully.

I stole another look at him, realizing the full extent of what I'd just been mulling over.

He thought I'd betrayed him by taking up with Darroc when I'd believed he was dead. But he hadn't excised *me* from his life. Whatever he wanted from the *Sinsar Dubh,* he wanted very badly.

And according to my own assessment of him, once he had it, he would kill me.

He must have felt my gaze, because he looked at me. *Something wrong, Ms. Lane?*

My gaze mocked, *Is there anything* right *about this situation?*

He smiled without humor. *Besides the obvious.*

I shook my head.

You're looking at me as if you expect me to kill you.

I jerked. Was I that easy to read?

You're wondering what kind of man I am and how I feel about all this.

I stared.

You think you betrayed me and one day I will kill you for it.

I'm not sure why I even bother talking. My eyes flashed with temper. I hated being so transparent.

That you allied with Darroc to attain your goals did not betray me. I'd have done the same.

Then why are you so pissy?

That you fucked him will be forgiven once you fuck me. Another woman might run headlong toward absolution.

I put an end to our discussion by staring straight ahead.

It was slow going. Fiona couldn't move very quickly. We proceeded at a snail's pace through rose halls, to sunshine, to bronze.

"The libraries," Barrons said as we passed. "We'll stop on the way back, since we're in here anyway. I want another look around."

I felt a sudden tension in the cloaked figure next to me as the dark hood turned my way.

I didn't need to be able to see her face to sense the bitterness of her gaze or divine the morbid turn of her thoughts.

His comment had driven home that he and I would be walking out of here together and she would be dead. And I knew she thought we would be having a fabulous time, dancing and fighting, having sex and living, while her existence would be over, extinguished as if she'd never been born, unmourned, unmissed.

I felt hatred emanating from beneath that cloak, malevolent and dark, and was glad to see black floors ahead.

I felt like we were prison guards, taking the long, slow, hellish walk to the electric chair. The convict between us would have done anything to escape her sentence, but fate had left her no choice but to crave oblivion.

"How?" she whispered, as we entered the black tunnel.

I looked at Barrons and he looked at me. Once we'd stepped onto the black floors, I'd begun to feel the sexual tension this part of the castle inevitably stirred. One glance at his face confirmed he was feeling it, too.

I was horrified to realize that Fiona must be feeling it, too.

Barrons replied tightly, "There is a Silver that divides the chamber of the Unseelie King and the concubine's. Only those two can step through it. All others die instantly."

"Even . . . you?"

So she knew he could die. And come back.

"Yes."

There was that awful wet sound, laughter but not. "She . . . knows now."

Barrons gave me a look that clearly said, *Shut her up or I'll end it now.*

"Yes. I know all of it, Fiona," I lied.

She moved forward, silent once again.

Christian was asleep in the Unseelie King's big bed, long black hair a silken fan across a pillow.

If Fiona hadn't been skinned and in so much pain, I would have pushed her across the white half of the boudoir into the mirror to get it over with, but I couldn't bring myself to touch her.

"Who the—What the fuck?" Barrons stalked across snowy furs, through diamond-studded air, to the enormous Silver, staring at the male in the bed.

I glanced at the fireplace, expecting to see the concubine, trying to figure out how I would explain things to Barrons if the queen's memory residue was stretched out there, but the furs were empty, the fire banked to low white embers.

His voice startled Christian awake; the young Scot rolled over and sprang to his feet.

Silk sheets dripped from his body, leaving him nude and visibly aroused. For a moment I thought he'd gotten rid of the tattoos, but they appeared, moving up his legs, his groin, and his abdomen, then around the side of his chest, before vanishing again.

I joined Barrons at the edge of the mirror, trying not to stare, but gorgeous naked men are gorgeous naked men.

I wondered if memories of the king and queen's lovemaking had been affecting him the way they'd got to me. His eyes glittered with lazy sensuality, and I could too well imagine the bent of his dreams. He might be difficult to pry out of the chamber when the time came.

He stood on the dark side of the boudoir and looked at me. "I must be dreaming. Bring that sweet ass over here and I'll show you what God made women and well-hung Scotsmen for."

"Who the bloody hell is that?" Barrons demanded.

"Christian MacKeltar."

"That's not Christian MacKeltar!" Barrons exploded. "That's Unseelie royalty!"

"Ah, fuck me." Christian ran his hands through his long, dark hair, muscles rippling in his shoulders. "Is that really what I look like, Mac?"

I almost said, *I don't know, I can't stop looking at your—*

Fiona pushed me.

The bitch actually shoved me from behind.

I was so flabbergasted, I didn't even gasp. I was speechless. I'd come here on a mission of mercy and she'd tried to kill me *again*!

She'd concluded from what Barrons had told her that I would die if I touched the Silver, too, and her final act had been to try to take me with her.

She pushed me hard enough that I shot straight through the unresisting Silver and crashed squarely into

Christian, knocking him backward onto the bed. We got tangled up in each other, trying to get out.

Behind me, Barrons roared.

On top of me, Christian made a raw, horny sound and ground himself against me.

I sucked air between my teeth. Every instinct in my body wanted to have sex, here, now, with anyone. This place was dangerous. "Christian, it's the chamber. It makes sex—"

"I know, lass. Been here awhile." He raised one of his arms that was pinning me to the bed. "Get out from under me. Move your ass!" he gritted.

When I didn't react instantly, he snarled, "Now! I won't be able to say it again!"

I looked at him. His eyes were out of focus, fixed on some point inside me, like a Fae prince. I shot out from beneath him and scrambled from the bed.

He crouched there a moment on his hands and knees, balls heavy, erection huge and flat to his stomach, then he lunged to his feet, trying to cover himself, his hand a hopelessly inadequate shield. He tried to yank a sheet from the bed, but the black silk was king-sized, for acres of bed. Cursing, he began digging among pillows and furs, looking for his clothes, while I tried not to watch and failed miserably.

"Mac!" Barrons thundered.

My heart was pounding. I wanted Barrons, not Christian, but the man I wanted was on the other side of the mirror, and this damned half-white, half-black boudoir was Ecstasy on steroids with a shot of adrenaline, and it made things so dreamy and confused . . .

It was the awful sound of Fiona's laughter that broke the spell.

I turned to see her standing right next to the mirror, looking up at Barrons, her hood down.

She spoke the longest sentence she'd said tonight.

"How does it feel to want someone more than they want you, Jericho?" Her voice dripped venom. "If she went through that mirror, she belongs to the king. I hope wanting her eats you alive. I hope he takes her from you. I hope you suffer for all eternity!"

Barrons said nothing.

"You should have left me to die where you found me, you bastard," she said bitterly. "All you did was give me a life that made me want things I couldn't have."

I would have told her it wasn't like that at all. Barrons didn't feel that way about me, or about anyone, but before I could say a word, Fiona threw herself at the mirror.

I braced myself for her to slam into me.

I was *that* sure I wasn't the Unseelie King.

I was ready for the stench of her to assault my nostrils, her mutilated body to slam into mine. I would deflect her toward the bed, where I would stab her and put us all out of her misery, once and for all.

Fiona fell over dead the instant she touched the mirror.

"Hello, Ms. Concubine," Barrons mocked.

Oh, if he only knew.

But Christian didn't tell him before we left, and neither did I.

33

CONS: Why I'm not the king

1. I was a baby twenty-three years ago. I saw pictures of me, and I remember growing up. (Unless someone planted false memories.)

2. I don't even *like* the concubine. (Unless I fell out of love with her a long time ago.)

3. I don't feel like I'm split into multiple human parts, and I've never been attracted to women. (Unless I'm repressing.)

4. I hate Fae, and especially Unseelie. (Am I overcompensating?)

5. If I were the king, wouldn't the Unseelie Princes have known me and not raped me? Wouldn't somebody . . . recognize me or something?

6. Where have I been for six or seven hundred thousand years? And how could I not know about it? (Okay, so maybe somebody forced me to drink from the cauldron.)

PROS: things that make it look like I could be

1. I knew what the White Mansion looked like inside. I also knew every step I walked in the Unseelie prison. Same with knowing that Cruce had wings. I have a ton of knowledge I can't

explain having. (Maybe somebody planted memories. If they can plant false ones, why not real ones?)

2. I've been dreaming of the concubine all my life and, even though she was unconscious, she managed to summon me. (Maybe she was manipulating me in the Dreaming like she did the Keltars.)

3. I can conjure runes that are supposedly part of what was used to reinforce the Unseelie prison walls. (Not sure which column this goes in. Why would the king have helped?) (Maybe it's part of my *sidhe*-seer gifts.)

4. The Book hunts me and plays with me like a cat worrying a mouse. (Can't think of a way out of this one. There's obviously *something* different about me.)

5. K'Vruck poked at me mentally, then said, "Ah, there you are." (WTF????)

6. I can go through the mirror that only the king and concubine can go through, and the queen is the concubine. Barrons can't. Fiona couldn't.

7. When I was in the White Mansion, I could see the concubine but not the king, which makes perfect sense if it was the king's memories I was living, because when you're remembering something, you don't see yourself in the memory, you see who else was there and what happened around you.

I dropped my pen and snapped my journal shut. Daddy could have used those last two PROs to get me life without parole.

I needed to perform more experiments with the Silver. That was all there was to it. Once I proved someone else could go through, I could quit driving myself nuts.

"Right," I muttered. "More experiments. Sound like someone else we know?" Like maybe an obsessed king that had experimented an entire race of monsters into being. There was no getting around a brutal fact: If my tests failed, my test subjects would die. Was I so desperate to exonerate myself that I was willing to become a murderer? Sure, I'd killed a lot in the past few months, but in the heat of the fight, not premeditated, and Fiona had *wanted* to die.

A pure human would be the best test.

I could probably find someone hanging out at Chester's who was in love with dying. Or too drunk to—

Was I losing my humanity? Or had I always been a little short to begin with?

I clutched my head and groaned.

Suddenly every muscle in my body tensed as if standing up in greeting, even though I didn't move. "Barrons." I dropped my hands and raised my head.

"Ms. Lane." He took a chair across from me with such eerie grace that I wondered how I'd ever believed he was human. He poured himself into the brocade wing chair, like water over stone, before settling into sleek muscle. He moved as if he knew where everything in the room was, in precise measurements. He didn't walk, stalk, or prowl; he glided with flawless awareness of all other atoms in relation to his. It made it easy for him to conceal himself behind inanimate objects and to assume a similar . . . structure or something.

"Have you always moved like that in front of me and I just never noticed? Was I oblivious?"

"No and yes. You were oblivious. Head up that tight pink ass. But I never moved this way in front of you." His look dripped sexual innuendo. "I might have moved this way a time or two *behind* you."

"Not hiding anything from me anymore?"

"I wouldn't go that far."

"What does someone like you conceal?"

"Wouldn't you like to know?" His glittering eyes raked me with a hard once-over.

It had been nearly a week since we'd killed Fiona in the Silvers, and my wardrobe was giving me more fits than ever. I was wearing distressed black leather pants with a tattooed gray grunge element and my favorite baby-doll pink tee that said *I'm a JUICY girl* across the front and had chiffon cap sleeves. I'd tied a Goth scarf around my blond curls and had on a pair of Alina's dangling heart earrings. My fingernails had grown out and I'd done a French manicure on my hands, but I'd painted my toenails black. The dichotomy didn't end there. I had on a black lace thong and a pink-and-white-striped cotton bra. I was having issues.

"Identity crisis, Ms. Lane?"

There was a time when I'd have fired back a pithy retort. But I was drunk on the moment: sitting in my bookstore, sipping hot cocoa, staring across a coffee table at Barrons by candle and firelight, with my journal and iPod handy and the assurance that my parents were well and my world was mostly fine except for my own little personality crisis. Friends and loved ones were safe. I breathed. So did the people that mattered to me. Life was good.

Not long ago, I'd thought I would never step foot in this place again. Never see the faint, sexy lift of his lips that told me he was amused but still waiting to be *really* wowed. Never bicker and banter and argue and plan. Never bask in the knowledge that, so long as the previous owner of this establishment was alive, this place would stand bastion in far more than mere latitude and longitude, keeping Dark Zones, fairies, and monsters at bay. It was the place of last defense in my heart.

Although I hated him for letting me grieve, I couldn't be more grateful that he was unkillable, because it meant I would never have to grieve him again.

I could never be broken about Barrons. Nothing could hurt me where he was concerned, because he was as certain as the nightfall, he would recur as eternally as the dawn. I still had questions about what he was and concerns about his motives, but they could wait. Time might sort things out in ways pushing and prying never could. "I don't have any idea what to wear anymore, so I tried to cover all bases."

"Try skin."

"Little chilly for that."

We looked at each other across the coffee table.

His eyes didn't say, *I'd heat you up,* and mine didn't say *What are you waiting for?* His didn't reply, *Fuck if I'm making the first move,* so I was careful not to say, *I wish you would, because I can't, because I'm . . .* and he didn't snap . . . *choking on your pride?!*

"As if you aren't."

"Excuse me?"

"Really, Barrons," I said drily. "I'm not the only one who didn't just not have that conversation, and you know it."

There was the faint, sexy lift of his lip. "You're a piece of work, Ms. Lane."

"Right back at you."

He changed the subject. "The Keltar moved their wives and children into Chester's."

"When?"

Our sojourn in the White Mansion had cost us nearly five weeks, Dublin time. We'd stopped in the libraries on the way out and taken as many of the Unseelie King's books as we'd been able to wrap up and carry out along with Fiona's body. I'd not only missed Dani's birthday, I'd missed my own, on May 1. Time sure did fly.

"About three weeks ago. Long enough that they've settled in. They refuse to leave until we give them the queen."

"Which will be never," I said.

"Precisely."

"How many kids?" I tried to picture Chester's with families living on the cool chrome-and-glass top floor. Towheaded tots carrying blankets and sucking their thumbs, walking along the balustrade. It seemed terribly wrong—and laughably right. Maybe it could eradicate some of the fundamental badassness of the place.

"The four Keltar Druids brought their wives and children. They breed like it's their personal mission to populate their country in case somebody attacks again, as if anybody wants the bloody place. There were dozens of them. Everywhere. It was total chaos."

"Ryodan must be losing his mind." I had to bite my lip not to laugh. Barrons sounded downright consternated.

"A child followed us on our way to see the queen. Wanted Ryodan to fix a toy or something."

"Did he?"

"He got upset because it wouldn't shut up and tore its head off."

"The child?" I gasped.

He looked at me like I was crazy. "The bear. The battery was dying and the audio file was looping. It was the only way to make it stop."

"Or put a new battery in."

"Child screamed bloody murder. Army of Keltars came running. I couldn't get out of there fast enough."

"I want to see my parents. I mean, visit with them."

"V'lane agreed to help the Keltar get Christian out of the Unseelie prison. He has them rebuilding the dolmen at LaRuhe he crushed for you." He shot me a look that said, *Too bad you didn't think before you did that one; would have saved time.* "He believes that once it's complete he can reestablish the connection and bring him out."

So V'lane was playing nice, batting hard for the team. We had serious unfinished business, but I no longer had his name in my tongue and I suspected he was avoiding me. I'd been in no mood for confrontations in the past week. Confronting myself was hard enough. "If you don't arrange it, I'll go by myself." We'd have Christian

soon! The moment I'd returned from Fiona's mercy killing, I'd begun lobbying to get Christian out of the Unseelie prison. I would have begun my campaign sooner,
but finding out I was Not the Concubine had thrown me
for a wicked, mind-numbing loop. "When will he be
back?"

"Your pretty college boy isn't so pretty anymore."

"He isn't *my* pretty college boy."

Our gazes locked.

"But I still think he's pretty pretty," I said, just to
antagonize him.

*See you in bed with him like I saw in the Silvers, I'll kill
him.*

I blinked. I did *not* just see that in Barrons' eyes.

He evaporated from the chair and reappeared five
feet away, standing in front of the fire, his back to me.

"They expect to have him back any day now."

I wanted to be there when they got Christian out, but
the Keltar had made it clear they didn't want me around.
I should never have told them I'd fed their nephew Fae
flesh. I wasn't sure if they found it cannibalistic, sacrile-
gious, or both, but it had certainly offended them. I'd
gone light on details about what it had done to him.
They'd find out soon enough.

I shivered. The time was approaching. We would be
doing the ritual soon. "We need to have a meeting with
everyone. Keltar, *sidhe*-seers, V'lane. Iron out the details." What would happen when we finally had the
Book under lock and key? How did Barrons think he
was going to use it once it was contained? Did he know
the First Language? Was he that old? Had he learned it
over time, or been taught? Did he plan to let us re-inter
it at the abbey again, then sit down and read it?

And do *what* with the knowledge?

"Why don't you just tell me what you want the *Sinsar
Dubh* for?"

No longer staring into the fire, he faced me.

"Why do you keep moving like that? You never used to do it before." It was unnerving.

"Does it unnerve you?"

"Not at all. It's just . . . hard to follow."

A haze of red slithered through his eyes. "Doesn't faze you at all?"

"Not a bit. I only want to know what changed."

He shrugged. "Concealing my nature requires effort." But his eyes said, *Think you accepted the beast? Stare at it, day in, day out.*

Not a problem.

"The queen came to—"

"She's conscious?" I exclaimed.

"—briefly before she went under again."

"Why does it always take you so long to tell me the important things?"

"While the queen was lucid, Jack had the presence of mind to ask her who sealed her in the coffin."

Expectancy straightened my spine. "And?"

"She said it was a Fae prince she'd never seen before. He called himself Cruce."

I stared, stunned. "How is that possible? Is anyone who's supposed to be dead actually dead?"

"Doesn't seem like it."

"Did he have wings?"

He gave me a look. "Why?"

"Cruce does."

"How do you—ah. Memories."

"Does it bother you? That I'm . . ." *Not the Concubine.* I couldn't finish the sentence.

"No more human than I? On the contrary. You've either lived a very long time or you prove reincarnation. I'd like to know which it is, so we'd know whether you can die. Eventually the Unseelie King will come looking for you. He and I are overdue for a talk."

"What do you want the Book for, Barrons?"

He smiled. Well, he showed me his teeth, anyway. "One spell, Ms. Lane. That's all. Don't worry your pretty little head."

"Don't talk down to me. It used to shut me up. Doesn't work anymore. A spell for what? To change you back to whatever you were before? To let you die?"

His eyes narrowed and the rattlesnake stirred in his chest. He looked at my face closely, as if reading the tiniest nuances of the way my nostrils flared on each breath, the shape of my mouth, the movement of my eyes.

I raised a brow, waiting.

"Is that what you need to think of me? That I want to die? Must you dress me up in chivalry to find me palatable? Chivalry demands a suicidal bent. I don't have one. I can't get enough of life. I get off on waking up every day for infinity. I *like* being what I am. I got the best end of the deal. I'll be here while it's happening. I'll be here when it ends. And I'll stand up from the ashes and do it all over when it begins again."

"You said somebody beat me to damning you."

"Melodrama. Did it curry favor? You kissed me."

"You don't feel damned?"

"God said, Let there be light. I said, Say please."

He was gone. No longer standing in front of me. The bookstore seemed empty and I looked around, wondering where he'd gone so quickly and why. Had he melted up against a bookcase, faded into a drape, wrapped himself around a pillar?

Suddenly there was a fist in my hair, behind me, pulling my head back, arching my spine up from the sofa.

He closed his mouth over mine and pushed his tongue in, forcing my teeth wide.

I grabbed his arm, but as sharply as he had my head pulled back, all I could do was steady myself.

He wrapped his other hand around my neck, forcing

my chin higher, kissing me more deeply, harder, keeping me from resisting.

Not that I wanted to.

Heart slamming in my chest, my legs moved apart. There are different kinds of kisses. I'd thought I'd experienced them all, if not prior to coming to Dublin, certainly after months of being *Pri-ya,* in bed with this man.

This was a new one.

All I could do was hold on to his arm and survive.

"Kiss" wasn't the right word at all.

He fused us together—my jaws so wide, I couldn't even kiss him back. I could only take what he was doing to me. I felt the sharp slide of fangs over my tongue as he sucked it into his mouth.

I knew then—as he'd never let me see in our bed in that basement—that he was far more animal than man. Maybe he hadn't always been, but he was now. Maybe, long ago, in the beginning, he'd missed being a man—if, in fact, he'd been one to begin with. But he didn't anymore. He'd gone native.

I was kind of astonished by it: What a man he'd chosen to be! He could easily have gone feral. He was the strongest, fastest, smartest, most powerful creature I'd ever seen. He could kill everything and everyone, including Fae. He could never *be* killed. Yet he walked upright and lived in Dublin and he had a bookstore and great cars and collected rare things of beauty. He bitched when his rugs got burned and got pissy when somebody messed with his clothes. He took care of some people, whether he seemed to like doing it or not. And he had a sense of honor that wasn't animal.

"Honor *is* animal. Animals are pure. People are fucked up. Quit fucking thinking." He let go of my mouth long enough to speak, then I couldn't breathe again.

I didn't play nice. I wasn't feeling nice. I was plastered

at an awkward angle against the couch, completely in his control unless I wanted to try to break my own neck to get free. I wanted to know what spell he wanted, though, so I drew in on myself and volleyed into his head.

Crimson silk sheets.

I'm in her and she's looking at me like I'm her world. The woman undoes me.

I flinch. I'm having sex with me, seeing myself from his eyes. I look incredible naked—is that how he sees me? He doesn't see any of my flaws. I've never looked half as good to myself. I want to pull out. It feels perverse. I'm fascinated. But this was not what I was hunting for at all . . .

Where are the handcuffs? Ah, grab her fucking head, she's going down on me again. She'll make me come. Tie her up. Is she back? How much longer do I have?

He senses me there.

Get out of my HEAD!

I deepen the kiss, bite his tongue, and he is violent with lust. I take advantage, diving deep. There's a thought he's shielding. I want it.

Nobody home but She for Whom I Am the World. Can't go on like this, can't keep doing it.

Why couldn't he go on? What couldn't he keep doing? I'm having sex with him, any way he wants me, while I stare up at him with utter worship. Where was the problem there?

Weariness suddenly crashes over me. I'm in his body, and I'm coming beneath him, and I'm checking my eyes warily.

What the fuck am I doing here?

He knew what he was, what I was.

He knew we came from different worlds, didn't belong together.

Yet for a few months there'd been no lines of demarcation between us. We'd existed in a place beyond definitions, where no rules had mattered, and I wasn't the only one who'd reveled in it. But the entire time I'd been lost in sexual bliss, he'd been aware of time passing, of everything that was happening—that I was mindless, I wasn't willing, and when I snapped out of it I'd blame him.

Keep hoping to see the light in her eyes. Even knowing it'll mean she's saying good-bye.

I had. Irrational or not, I'd held it against him. He'd seen me naked, body and soul, and I hadn't seen him at all. I'd been blinded by helpless lust that hadn't been for *him*. I had been lust, and he'd been there.

Just one time, he's thinking as we watch my glazed eyes go even emptier.

One time, what? Instead of pushing, I try a stealth attack. I pretend to retreat, let him think he's won, and at the last minute turn around. Instead of lunging for his thoughts, I stay very, very still and listen.

He pushes my hair out of my face. I look like an animal. There's no sentience in my gaze. I'm a cavewoman, with a minuscule, prehistoric brain.

When you know who I am. Let me be your man.

He blasts me from his skull with such force that I nearly pass out. My ears ring and my head hurts.

I'm sucking air. He's gone.

34

I walked through Temple Bar with a spring in my step. I'd woken early, taken one look at the sunshine shafting in through my bedroom window, dressed, and headed out to run errands.

The fridge was empty, I had two birthdays I was determined to celebrate before they got any more belated, and I was going to have to do some serious improvising with ingredients to bake a cake. Since Halloween, butter, eggs, and milk were a scarce commodity, but a Southern woman could do a lot with shortening, condensed milk, and powdered eggs. I was going to bake a chocolate cake with thick, creamy double-chocolate fudge icing if it was the last thing I did. Dani and I would watch movies and paint our fingernails. It would be like old times with Alina.

I turned my face up to the sun as I hurried down the street. After what seemed an interminable hiatus, spring had returned to Dublin.

The season of sunshine and rebirth was overdue for me. Though I'd managed to avoid miserable months of cold weather, busy in Faery or the Silvers, it had still been the longest winter of my life.

Spring didn't *look* any different than winter, but you could feel it in the air—the kiss of warmth on the breeze, the scent blowing off the ocean that carried the promise of buds and blossoms, if not here, somewhere else in the world. I'd never thought I'd miss flies and insects, but I did. There wasn't a single thing growing in Dublin—and that meant no moths, butterflies, birds, or bees. Not a single flower bloomed, no shoots pushed out from young limbs, not a blade of grass grew. The Shades had decimated the city on their way out, before slamming the door shut with a bang last Halloween. The soil was barren.

I was no horticulturalist, but I'd been doing some research. I was pretty sure if we reintroduced the right nutrients into the soil, in time, we'd be able to grow things again.

We had a lot to reclaim. Trees to remove and replace. Planters and flower boxes to fill. Parks to redesign. I planned to start small, haul dirt back from the abbey, grow a few daisies, buttercups, maybe some petunias and impatiens. Fill my bookstore with ferns and spider plants and begin taking back the night in my own space before spilling over onto the rooftop garden and beyond.

One day Dublin would live and breathe again. One day all these husks of what had once been people would be swept up and buried in a memorial ceremony. One day, tourists would come to see ground zero and reminisce about the Halloween when the walls fell—maybe even mention in passing a girl who cowered in a belfry before helping save the day—then head off to one of six hundred newly restored pubs to celebrate that the human race had taken back what was theirs.

Because we would. No matter who or what I was, I was determined to capture and re-inter the Book, then get to work figuring out a way to put the walls back up.

Along the way, I'd find proof that I wasn't the king, just a human woman with a lot of memories someone else had planted for reasons that would make sense when I finally knew them. I wasn't the fulcrum of a prophecy that would either save or doom the human race. I was merely the person who'd been pre-programmed by the queen—or who knew? Maybe the king—to track the Book in case it escaped, just like the Keltar had been manipulated: one small part of the equation for sealing it away again, forever this time.

As I sauntered through the morning, I tried to slip back into the mind of the young woman who'd stepped off the plane, taken a cab through Temple Bar, and checked in to the Clarin House late last summer, bemused by the thick accent of the leprechaun-like old man behind the reservations desk. Starving. Scared and grieving. Dublin had been so huge, and I'd been so small and clueless.

I looked around, absorbing the silent shell of a city, remembering the hustle and bustle. The streets had been crammed with *craic*—vibrant life that took itself entirely for granted.

"Morning, Ms. Lane." Inspector Jayne moved into step with me.

I assessed him quickly. He wore tight khaki-colored jeans with a plain white T-shirt stretched over his barrel chest and military boots laced up outside his pants. He was draped in ammo, pistols in his waistband and arm holster, Uzi over his shoulder. No place for an evil Book to hide. Months ago he'd had the start of a paunch. It was no longer there. He was rangy with muscle, long limbed, and walking like a man who had his feet planted firmly on the ground for the first time in years.

I smiled, genuinely pleased to see him, but it was all I could do not to reach for my spear. I hoped he wasn't still after it or holding grudges.

"Fine morning, isn't it?"

I laughed. "I was thinking the same thing. Is there something wrong with us? Dublin's a shell, and we look ready to burst into a cheery whistle." The Unseelie-spiked-tea-drinking inspector and I had certainly come a long way.

"No paperwork. I used to hate paperwork. Didn't know how much of my life it was eating up."

"New world."

"Bloody strange one."

"But good."

"Aye. The streets are quiet. Book's laying low. Haven't seen a Hunter in days. We Irish know to make the most of the times of plenty, for sure enough they'll be famine again. Made love to my wife last night. Children are healthy and strong. It's a good day to be alive," he said matter-of-factly.

I nodded in complete understanding. "Speaking of Hunters, you'll be seeing at least one in the skies soon." I filled him in on the outline of our plan—that I would be scouring the streets by Hunter, looking for the *Sinsar Dubh*. "So don't shoot me down, okay?"

His eyes narrowed shrewdly. "How do you control it? Can you force it to take you to its lair? We could wipe out the lot of them if we could only find the den."

"Let's get the Book off the streets first. Then we'll help you hunt, I promise."

"A promise I'll be holding you to. I don't like using the girl, but she insists. That one's had a hard enough life. She should be home, somebody watching out for her. Kills like she was born to it. Makes me wonder how long she's been—"

"MacKayla," V'lane said.

Jayne was frozen, mouth ajar, mid-step. Not iced. Just immobilized.

I stiffened and reached for my spear.

"We need to talk."

"Understatement. *You* need to explain." I spun in a circle, spear up. For whatever reason, I still had it.

"Sheathe the spear."

"Why haven't you taken it?"

"I offer you a show of good faith."

"Where are you?" I demanded. I could hear his voice, but he wasn't visible and the source of his voice kept moving.

"I will appear when you have given me *your* show of good faith."

"Which is?"

"I choose to let you keep it. You choose to sheathe it. We will honor each other with trust and confidence."

"Not a chance in hell."

"I am not the only one that has some explaining to do. How did you bring the queen out through the king's mirror?"

"Let me tell you what I don't understand. Last Halloween I got raped by Unseelie Princes. You told me you were busy carrying your queen to safety on human feet. But now I know the queen had been in the Unseelie prison for—how did you word it?—many human years. Where were you *really* that night, V'lane?"

He materialized in front of me, a dozen feet away.

"I did not lie to you. Not entirely. I told you I could not be in two places at once, and that much was true. However, I misspoke when I said I was carrying my queen to safety. Instead, I was taking advantage of those hours, searching for her in Darroc's Silvers. I was certain he was behind her disappearance. I believed he had imprisoned her in one of the stolen mirrors at LaRuhe, but I could not search those Silvers until the magic of the realms was neutralized. When I crushed his dolmen for you—which we rebuilt, and I succeeded in retrieving Christian only last night, or I would have come to explain myself sooner—I endeavored to search them then. But Darroc had learned much from journals stolen from the White Mansion, and I was unable to break his wards."

"You spent the night I was getting raped searching his house and finding nothing?"

"A regrettable decision only because it did not yield fruit. I was certain she was there. If she had been, it would have been worth it. As it was, when I discovered what had transpired, I felt . . . " He lowered his lids over his eyes, leaving only a thin band of silver glittering beneath his lashes. "I *felt*." His mouth shaped a bitter smile. "It was untenable. Fae do not feel. Certainly not the queen's first prince. I tasted envy of my dark brethren for knowing you in a way I never would. I choked on rage that they harmed you. I grieved the loss of something of incomparable measure I could never have again. Is that not human regret? I felt . . . " He inhaled slow and deep, then blew it out. "Shame."

"So you say."

The smile twisted. "For the first time in my existence, I wanted to experience a temporary oblivion. I was unable to make my thoughts obey me. They wandered of their own accord to matters that were hellish to suffer. I was unable to make them stop. It made *me* want to stop. Is that love, MacKayla? Is that what it does to you? Why, then, do humans long for it?"

I jerked, remembering a moment when I'd considered stretching on the ground next to Barrons and bleeding out next to him.

"I am tired of being in impossible positions. For an eternity, my first allegiance has been to my queen. Without her, my race is doomed. There is no successor to her throne. There is none worthy or capable of leading my people. I could not choose to help you over attempting to recover her. My emotions, to which I had no right, could not be permitted to interfere. For too long I have been all that stands between peace and war." He locked gazes with me. "Unless . . ."

"Unless what?"

"Still you point that spear at me."

I stalked toward him, drawing my spear arm back.

He vanished.

He spoke behind me. "Could it be you are becoming like us?"

I whirled, eyes narrowed. "What do you mean?"

"Are you becoming Fae, in the way some long ago were born? I suspect the young Druid also suffers birth pains. It is a most unexpected development."

"And unwelcome."

"That remains to be seen."

Was that his breath at my ear, his lips against my hair?

"It's unwelcome to me! I'm not going to become one of you. Get it out. I don't want it."

I felt his hands on my waist, sliding lower, over my ass. "Immortality is a gift. Princess."

"I'm not a princess and I'm not turning Fae."

"Not yet perhaps. But you are something, are you not? I wonder what. I weary of watching Barrons piss circles around you. I tire of waiting for the day you will finally look at me and see that I am so much more than a Fae and a prince. I am a male. With hunger for you that knows no bottom. You and I, more than anyone else in the universe, are perfect for each other."

He was half a dozen feet away, facing me, looking down into my eyes.

"I do not wish to continue like this. I am divided and know no peace. Pride has prevented me from speaking plainly. No more."

He vanished and reappeared right in front of me, so close I could see a shimmer of rainbows in his iridescent eyes.

The spear was between us.

I tightened my hand on the hilt. He closed his over mine, pointed the spear at his chest, and leaned into me. I could feel him, rock hard and ready, against me. He was breathing fast and shallow, eyes glittering.

"Accept me or kill me, MacKayla. But choose. Just fucking choose."

35

The last time I talked with my mom in person was on August 2, the day I said good-bye and caught a plane for Dublin. We'd fought bitterly about my going to Ireland. She hadn't wanted to lose a second daughter to what she'd called "that cursed place." At the time, I thought she was being melodramatic. Now I know she had reason to believe she should never have let Alina go and was terrified to see me follow. I've hated that our last words spoken face-to-face were harsh. Although I've spoken to her on the phone since then, it's not the same.

I saw Daddy three weeks later, when he came to BB&B looking for me. Barrons Voiced him to make him go home and planted subliminal commands to prevent him from returning to Ireland. They worked. Daddy went to the airport several times to come back for me but couldn't make himself get on a plane.

I saw them both again two weeks after Christmas, when I'd surfaced from being *Pri-ya* and V'lane had taken me to Ashford to show me that he'd helped re-store my hometown and was keeping my folks safe.

I hadn't talked to them then. I'd crouched in the

bushes behind my house and watched them on the lanai, talking about me and how I was supposedly going to doom the world.

I'd seen them both when Darroc was holding them captive. They'd been gagged and bound.

Then I'd seen them here, at Chester's, on the night the *Sinsar Dubh* took control of Fade and killed Barrons and Ryodan, but that was only through a glass pane.

Chronologically, it had been nine months since they'd seen me. With the time I'd lost in Faery, being *Pri-ya*, and in the Silvers, it felt more like three months to me, albeit the longest, most crammed-full three months of my life.

I wanted to see them. Now. Although I hadn't accepted V'lane the way he'd wanted me to, I hadn't stabbed him, either, which turned out to be fortuitous, because he'd finally gotten around to telling me that we were all supposed to meet at Chester's today at noon to iron out our plans to capture the Book. He'd been dispatched as a sifting messenger to round everyone up.

I decided my errands could wait. Knowing that we were so close to making a serious attempt at capturing the Book had filled me with urgency to see Mom and Dad before the big meeting. Before the ritual. Before anything else in my life could go wrong. Personal identity crisis aside, they were my parents and always would be. If I'd lived before as someone or something else, that life had paled in comparison to this one.

I blasted into Chester's, sailed coolly through the bars, which were depressingly packed so early in the day, and headed for the stairs. I had no desire to talk to any of the cryptic denizens of the club.

At the foot of the stairs, Lor and a massively muscled man with long white hair, pale skin, and burning eyes moved together, blocking my way.

I was debating what I might have in my deep glassy

lake to use—Barrons had slurped down my crimson runes like truffles—when Ryodan called down, "Let her up."

I tipped my head back. The urbane owner of the largest den of sex, drugs, and exotic thrills in the city stood behind the chrome balustrade, big hands closed on the chrome railing, thick wrists cuffed by silver, features darkened by a convenient shadow. He looked like a scarred Gucci model. Whatever kind of life these men had lived before they'd become whatever they were, it had been violent and hard. Like them.

"Why?" Lor demanded.

"I said so."

"Not time for the meeting yet."

"She wants to see her parents. She's going to insist."

"So?"

"She thinks she has something to prove. She's feeling pushy."

"Gee, this is nice. I don't even have to talk," I purred. I *was* feeling pushy. Ryodan brought out the worst in me. Like Rowena, he'd prejudged me.

"You ooze emotion today. Emotional humans are unpredictable, and you're more unpredictable than most to begin with. Besides," Ryodan sounded amused, "Jack's building up immunity to Barrons' Voice. He's been demanding to see you. Said he'll take the queen hostage if we don't bring you to him. I don't worry about the queen's safety. Rainey likes her, and Jack likes anything Rainey likes. But I have concerns he might debate us to death."

I smiled faintly. If anyone could win, it was my daddy. I pushed past Lor, clipping him with my shoulder. His arm shot out like a bar across my neck and stopped me.

"Look at me, woman," Lor growled.

I turned my head and met his gaze coolly.

"If he tells you anything about us, we'll kill you. Do

you understand that? One word, you die. So if you're walking around feeling cocky and protected because Barrons likes to fuck you, think again. The more he likes to do you, the more likely it is that one of us will kill you."

I looked up at Ryodan.

The owner of Chester's nodded.

"Nobody killed Fiona."

"She was a doormat."

I pushed the arm away from my neck. "Get out of my way."

"I would suggest you cure him of his little problem if you want to survive," Lor said.

"Oh, I'll survive."

"The farther away from him you get, the safer you are."

"Do you want me to find the Book or not?"

Ryodan answered. "We don't give a fuck if the Book is out there. Or that the walls are down. Times change, we go on."

"Then why are you helping with the ritual? V'lane said Barrons asked you and Lor to handle the other stones."

"For Barrons. But if he breathes one word about himself, you're dead."

"I thought he was the boss of you guys."

"He is. He made the rules we live by. We'll still take you from him."

Take you from him. Sometimes I was so dense. "And he knows that."

"We've had to do it before," Lor said. "Kasteo hasn't said a word to us since. I say get over it already. It's been a thousand fucking years. What's a woman worth?"

I inhaled slow and deep as the full ramifications of what they'd just told me sunk in. This was why Barrons never answered any of my questions and never would.

He knew what they would do to me if he told me—whatever they'd done to Kasteo's woman a thousand years ago. "You don't need to worry about it. He hasn't told me anything."

"Yet," Lor said.

"But more importantly," I said, looking up at Ryodan, "I won't ask. I don't need to know." I realized it was true. I was no longer obsessed with having a name and an explanation for Jericho Barrons. He was what he was. No name, no reasons, would alter anything about him. Or how I felt.

"So every woman has said at some point. Are you familiar with the tale of *Bluebeard*?"

Sure. He'd asked only one thing of his wives: that they never look in the forbidden room upstairs—where he kept the bodies of all the wives before them, whom he'd killed for looking in the forbidden room upstairs. "Bluebeard's wives didn't have a life." I studied him. They were all so controlled, so hard and ruthless. "How many have you taken from one another? So many that you hate the sight of one another? Has the merry band of brothers become a walking, talking, immortal Cold War?"

His face hardened. "Strip if you're coming up."

I gave him a look. "I have on skintight clothes."

"Non-negotiable. All of it. Nothing but skin."

Lor folded his arms, leaned back against the staircase, and laughed. "She's got a great ass. If we're lucky, she's wearing a thong."

The white-haired man rumbled with laughter.

"You've never made anyone strip before," I said.

"New rules." Ryodan smiled.

"I'm not—"

"Seeing your parents if you don't," he cut me off.

"I don't want to see them if I have to be naked. My mother would never recover."

He held up a short robe.

"You planned this." The prick.

"Told you. New rules. Can't be too careful with the queen here."

He didn't think I'd do it. He was wrong.

Bristling, I kicked off my shoes, tugged my shirt over my head, skinned off my jeans, popped my bra, and stripped off my thong. Then I put my shoulder holster back on, tucked my spear into it, and walked up the stairs naked. I put a little jiggle in my walk and held his gaze the whole time.

At the top, Ryodan practically accosted me with the short robe. I looked back at Lor and the other guard. They were both staring at me. Neither of them was laughing anymore.

The second floor of Chester's smelled good. I cocked my head, sniffing. Perfume and . . . cooking? Was there a kitchen up here?

Three women popped out of a wall, talking and laughing, carrying covered dishes, then vanished behind another hissing panel. I was piqued. They knew how to open and close the doors and I didn't.

Ryodan thrust my clothes at me. "The Keltar women are out of control. They cook. They chatter. They laugh. Idiots."

I looked at him. He was already stalking away. It was all I could do not to laugh. I stepped to the side of the hall and dressed as I watched him disappear into one of the glass-paneled rooms.

When I began walking again, Lor moved into step beside me. I didn't like the way he was looking at me—with the hot, fixed gaze of an intensely sexual man who'd seen me naked and jiggling and wasn't about to forget it soon.

"Jack and Rainey are down here." He turned left in the honeycomb of glass and chrome, down a hallway I hadn't even realized was there. The reflective glass walls created a hall-of-mirrors illusion. Chester's was even larger on the second floor than I'd thought.

"You moved them."

"Needed a place we could ward better, with the queen here."

Ahead, Drustan and Dageus were standing in the hallway, talking to a—I stared. Fae? I wasn't getting a Fae read off him. What was he? Long black hair, gold-dust skin, loads of charisma. Fae but not Fae.

As we approached, I heard Dageus say impatiently, "All we're asking is that you confirm she's truly Aoibheal. You were her favorite for five thousand years, Adam. You know her better than any of us. She's wasted and weak and, though we're fair certain it's her, we'd be resting easier if we heard it from one who was once her right hand."

"I'm mortal, Gab's pregnant, and I'm not dying in a bloody Fae war. This isn't my battle. This isn't my life anymore."

"We're only asking you confirm it's her. We'll have V'lane sift you out of here—"

"You tell that fuck I'm here, you won't get a thing from me. No one is to know I'm in Ireland. Not a single Fae. Got it?"

"You believe they'd still hunt you?"

"They have long memories, the queen is weak, and I was never their favorite. Some of them don't drink from the cauldron as often as I'd like. One look. I'll confirm it for you, but then I'm out of here. Don't come looking for me again."

Dageus said coolly, "You had the chance to kill Darroc. You made him mortal instead."

Adam's dark eyes glittered. "I knew one of you bastards would try to blame me for what happened. I let him live. Humans let Hitler live. I'm not responsible for the destruction of a third of the world's population."

"Be damned glad none of the casualties were Keltar, or we'd be hunting you ourselves."

"Don't threaten me, Highlander. I wasn't called the *sin siriche du* for nothing, and I didn't go native without taking precautions. I still have a few tricks up my sleeve. I've got my own clan to protect."

I stared at him as we passed. Suddenly his head whipped around and he stared straight back at me, eyes narrowed. His gaze followed me until I'd passed.

"Who's she?" I heard him ask.

"One of the queen's chosen, it seems. She can track the Book."

"I bet she can," Adam murmured.

I looked sharply over my shoulder and began to turn around. I wanted to know why he'd said that.

Lor's hand clamped around my arm. "Keep walking. Visiting hours at Chester's . . . well, for you, there aren't any."

He stopped at the far end of the hall in front of a smooth wall of glass that was heavily painted with smoky runes and pressed his palm to the panel. As the door slid aside, I looked down and saw that the floor was covered with more runes.

"If you tire of Barrons." His cold eyes fixed on my face. "Assuming you survive."

I shot him a look of mock astonishment. "Will wonders never cease? Lor's idea of a proposition. Somebody catch me while I swoon."

"Charm takes energy better spent fucking. I prefer a club over the head." He turned and began to walk away.

I rolled my eyes and, squaring my shoulders, stepped over the runes.

Or rather I *tried* to step over the runes.

They repelled me violently, and every alarm in the building went off.

"I'm not carrying the Book! You saw me naked. Get off me!"

Lor's arm was around my throat, crushing my windpipe. A bit more pressure and I'd pass out from lack of oxygen.

"What happened?" Ryodan demanded, storming up.

"She tripped the wards."

"Why is that, I wonder, Mac?"

"Get this prick off me," I said.

"Let her go." Barrons had joined Ryodan in the hall. "Now."

Ryodan looked at Barrons and something passed between them, and I realized they'd been expecting this. They'd known at some point I would demand to see my parents. The only reason Ryodan had let me up was to subject me to this test. But what had it proved?

"Doesn't change anything," Barrons said finally.

"No," Ryodan agreed.

"What?" I demanded.

"The wards recognize you as Fae," Barrons said.

"Impossible. We all know I'm not. It must be picking up that I've eaten Fae."

"You've eaten Fae?" Adam sounded disgusted.

"Do you recognize her? You looked at her oddly when she passed," Lor said.

"Only that she's Fae-touched," Adam replied. "Somewhere in her bloodline. Royal. Don't know the house. Not mine."

They were all staring at me. "You guys should talk. None of you is human. Well, maybe Cian and Drustan, but there's that whole chosen-by-the-queen, trained-as-her-Druids thing. So don't be staring at me like I'm the freak du jour. Maybe any *sidhe*-seer would set it off. Supposedly the UK had a hand in making us. I never set off the alarms at the abbey that were designed to keep Fae out."

Or had I? Each time I'd gone there, I'd been found remarkably quickly. Then there was the blond woman who'd barred the corridor with her implacable *You are not permitted here. You are not one of us.* What wasn't I? A *sidhe*-seer? A Haven member? A human?

"I want to see my parents," I said coolly.

Barrons and Ryodan exchanged a look again, then Ryodan shrugged. "Let her. Set them up in the room next door."

"Mac!" Jack exclaimed, rushing me the moment I stepped in the door. "Oh, God, we've missed you, baby!"

I disappeared into a bear hug that smelled of peppermint and aftershave. They say scent is the strongest memory association we possess. The smell of my daddy's hug peeled away the months like calendar pages tossed into a trash can.

I wasn't Fae, I wasn't possibly the Unseelie King, I wasn't going to doom the world. I was safe, protected, right, loved. I was his little girl. Always would be.

"Daddy!" I pressed my nose to his shirt. "And, Mom," I choked out, burying my face in her shoulder. The three of us clung to one another, hugging like there was no tomorrow.

I pulled back and looked at them. Jack Lane was tall, handsome, and composed as ever. Rainey was smiling radiantly.

"You guys look fantastic. And, Mom, look at you!"

There was no trace of grief or fear in her gently lined face. Her eyes were clear, her fine features glowing.

"Doesn't she look great?" Jack said, giving her hand a squeeze. "Your mom's a changed woman."

"What happened?"

Rainey laughed. "Living in a glass room with the queen of fairies might have something to do with it. Then there's the music coming up through the floors at all hours. And let's not forget all the naked people dropping by."

Dad growled.

I smiled. I'd wondered how my parents were handling that. Mom was getting a crash course in bizarreness. "Welcome to Dublin," I told her.

"Not that we've gotten to see much of it." She shot a pointed look at the glass, as if she knew exactly where Ryodan was standing. "Anytime now would be nice." She glanced back at me. "Don't get me wrong. I had a difficult time when we first got here. Your father had his hands full. But one morning I woke up and it was as if all my fears had melted away while I slept. They never came back."

"Because so much was weird that fear didn't have any place anymore?" I asked.

"Exactly! None of the rules that I'd lived by for so long applied. Things were so far outside my box, I had to either go crazy or throw the box away. I'm excited to be alive in a way I haven't felt since you girls were little, since before I began to worry about you and your sister all the time. Now the only thing I've been worried about was when I might get to see you again, and here you are and you look amazing, and, Mac, I love your hair! The shorter look is perfect on you. But you've lost weight, honey. Too much. Are you eating? I don't think you're eating. You can't be eating enough and be so thin. What did you have for breakfast?" she demanded.

I looked at Daddy and shook my head. "Is she still making cheese grits and pork chops for breakfast? Are they letting her in the kitchen here?"

"Lor sneaks her in every now and then."

"Lor?"

"He likes her hoecakes."

I blinked. Lor snuck my mother into the kitchen to make hoecakes?

"Your Barrons prefers my apple pie," Rainey said, beaming.

"He's not my Barrons, and there's no way that man eats apple pie." Barrons and apple pie were as wrong together as . . . well, vampires and puppies. It was hard to even hold them in the same thought.

"But no ice cream. He hates ice cream."

My mother knew more about Barrons' eating habits than I did. Unless one counted all the animal scraps he'd left when he was in beast form. I knew he didn't like the paws, and the only bones he chewed on were marrow-filled. The hearts were always gone, even if he ate nothing else.

"I hear they plan to try the ritual soon," Jack said.

"Do they tell you guys everything?" I said, exasperated. They trusted my parents but not me? That was just wrong.

"The Keltar men talk," Rainey said. "Their wives visit."

"And we might pry a little." Daddy winked. I wondered how long it would take the Keltar wives to realize all that flattering, focused attention Jack Lane could turn on at the drop of a hat that made you feel like the most special and interesting person in the world was a cover for his interrogations. That he was methodically turning them inside out, looking for admissible—and nonadmissible—evidence. He'd pulled more confessions out of his charmed, disarmed prey than any attorney in Ashford and the surrounding nine counties.

"Speaking of talk," I said, "I have a confession to make."

"You came to see us in January but you didn't stay," Rainey said. "We know. You left us a picture of Alina. We were surprised you put it in the mailbox. We might never have looked there. We found it only because your father went after a nest of wasps that had taken up residence in the milk can that holds the post."

The simplest things elude me. "Duh. There's no mail running."

"They kept it up for a while, but too many postal workers were getting killed in those dimensional shifts or attacked by Unseelie. Nobody's willing to run the routes," Jack said.

"We found it the day that man came and abducted us," Rainey said.

"That's not when I left it, though." I looked at Daddy. "I was there one night when you and Mom were out back on the lanai, talking. About me."

Jack searched my eyes, left to right, rapidly. "I think I remember that night."

"You and Mom were talking about how there were things you guys had never told me." That was nice and innocuous. I knew Ryodan and Barrons were outside, listening to every word we said. I wanted to know about the prophecy but not enough to ask up front. Considering I'd just set off the wards, I was worried that if we said anything about me dooming the world, I'd get shut out of the ritual. And I needed to be there. I wasn't going to be excluded from the big showdown. I had a part to play. A good, wholesome part. All I had to do was fly the Hunter and point at the evil Book.

"Yes," Jack said, watching me, "we were. You always think of things you'd wish you'd said when you're afraid you might never get another chance. We weren't sure we'd ever see you again."

"Well, here I am," I said brightly.

"And we missed you so much, baby," Jack said.

I knew he'd gotten the message.

We all got a little teary-eyed then, hugged some more, and made small talk. They told me about Ashford, who'd lived and who'd died. They told me the Shades had tried to take over (they'd known only because of the husks), then the Rhino-boys had come, but "that handsome fairy prince who is utterly infatuated with you, and you could certainly do worse than a prince, honey, and you know it, he could protect you and keep you in style and safety," according to my mom, had arrived and saved my hometown single-handedly.

I encouraged her to gush unabashedly about V'lane, hoping it would drive Barrons and Ryodan away. Or at least nuts.

The time went much too quickly. Before I knew it, nearly half an hour had passed and someone was rapping on the glass, barking that it was quarter to twelve and my time was up.

I hugged them both on the way out and got teary-eyed again. "I'll be back to see you again as soon as I can. I love you, Mom."

"Love you, too, honey. Hurry back." I clung to her for a moment, then turned to Daddy, who wrapped me in a bear hug.

"Love you, too, Mac." Against my ear he whispered, "The crazy woman was Augusta O'Clare from Devonshire. Had a granddaughter named Tellie she said helped your mother get the two of you out of the country. You're sunshine and light, baby. There's not a damned thing wrong with you, and don't you ever forget that." He pulled away and smiled down at me. Love and pride blazed in his eyes.

Tellie. It was the same name Barrons had mentioned in his phone conversation with Ryodan the morning after I'd discovered he was alive. He'd wanted to know if Ryodan had located Tellie yet and instructed him to get more people involved in the search.

"Get on with saving the world, baby."

I nodded, lower lip trembling. I could hunt monsters. I could have sex with men who turned into beasts. I could kill in cold blood.

And Daddy could still make me cry just by believing in me.

"I won't have her on the ground with us," Rowena was saying fifteen minutes later. "There's no reason for it. We'll have our radios. She need only fly overhead, spot the Book, talk us into position with the stones, then fly off on her demon steed." She shot me a look full of venom that said no *sidhe*-seer alive would ride a Hunter, and there was all the proof she needed of my treason. "The Keltar will chant and carry it to the abbey, where they will teach my girls to re-inter it. There is no purpose for her presence."

I snorted. The air was so thick with tension, I was getting light-headed from lack of oxygen. I'd never stood in a room packed with so much distrust and aggression as I was standing in today. That Ryodan had made everyone strip and have their clothes searched before returning them at the top of the stairs had only added to their bad tempers. I knew why he'd done it. It wasn't about new rules. It was about throwing everyone off balance, establishing from the get-go that they weren't in control of anything, not even their person. Being naked in front of clothed guards makes anyone feel intensely vulnerable.

I surveyed the room. On the east wall of the glass room, five heavily tattooed Keltar hulked in tight pants and shirts.

On the south wall, Rowena, Kat, Jo, and three other *sidhe*-seers—all dressed in drab, snug pantsuits—stood at attention, minus Dani. I was surprised Rowena hadn't brought her, but I guessed she'd decided her risks outweighed her benefits—the most risky of her flaws being that she liked *me*.

On the north wall, V'lane, Velvet, Dree'lia—who once again had a mouth but was wisely keeping it closed—and three other Seelie of the same caste posed arrogantly, draped in see-through short shifts, their flawless faces matched by flawless genitalia.

Barrons, Lor, Ryodan, and myself occupied the west wall, closest to the door.

Rowena glared at the five Scots lined shoulder-to-shoulder like the Falcons' defense. "You *do* know how to seal it away, do you not?" she demanded.

Oozing varying degrees of hostility, they glared back at her.

The Keltar were not the kind of men a woman ordered around, especially not an old woman like Rowena, who hadn't been bothering to exercise an ounce of diplomacy or charm since she'd been escorted, blindfolded, into one of the glass rooms on the top floor of Chester's.

Perversion and decadence, she'd snapped the moment they'd removed her blindfold. *You condone this . . . this . . . consorting? The flesh of human and Fae mix in this place. Och, and you'll be the damnation of the human race!* she'd hissed at Ryodan.

Fuck the human race. You're not my problem.

I'd almost laughed at the expression on her face, but I wasn't laughing now. She'd been trying to shut me out of the ritual. Acting like I was a pariah that shouldn't even be allowed in the room where this meeting was taking place.

"Och, and of course we ken it." The speaker was Drustan, the Keltar who would be picking up the *Sinsar Dubh* and carrying it to the abbey. According to his brother, he'd been burned on a pyre of sorts and had an incorruptible heart. I didn't believe it for a minute. Nobody has an incorruptible heart. We all have our weaknesses. But I had to admit that the man who looked out from those silvery eyes exuded some kind of . . . serenity, at utter odds with his appearance. He looked like a man who would have been more comfortable centuries in the past, stomping around the Highlands with a club in one hand and a sword in the other. They all did, except for Christopher, who strongly resembled Drustan, without the throwback gene. But Drustan had presence. He had a way with words and a voice that was deep, full of command, yet gentle. He spoke more softly than any of the other Keltar, but he was the one I found myself trying hardest to hear when they were all talking at once, which was pretty much all the time.

I looked at Christian and gave him a faint smile, but his expression didn't defrost one bit.

It was only last night that V'lane and the Keltars had succeeded in reconnecting the dolmen at 1247 LaRuhe to the Unseelie prison, then stormed the king's fortress to retrieve him. He'd been out roughly sixteen hours and didn't look much better than he had inside the Silvers. He was no longer a study in marble, cobalt, and jet but he was . . . well, it made no sense, but he gave the fleeting impression of those colors. If I looked directly at his hair, I could pick out strands of copper and even a hint or two of sun-burnished gold in the dark ponytail, but if I caught it from the corner of my eye, it looked ebony and longer than it was. His lips were pink and utterly kissable, unless I turned my head suddenly. Then for a moment I'd swear they were blue with cold and lightly frosted. His skin was golden, smooth, and touchable, but if I glanced sharply his way he would glow like backlit ice.

His eyes were changed, too. Lie detector extraordinaire, he now seemed to be looking right through everything around him, as if he was seeing the world completely different than the rest of us.

His father, Christopher, studied him when he thought Christian wasn't paying attention. Somebody needed to tell him there was never a time his son wasn't paying attention. Christian might seem to check out for a few moments, but if you were looking straight into his eyes, you could see that he was even more intensely focused on his surroundings—so focused that he'd gone still and seemingly absent, as if opening an inner ear that demanded absolute concentration.

"Lie," he said now.

Drustan scowled at Christopher. "I told you to make sure he'd haud his bloody whist."

"He's not hauding his whist for anyone anymore," Christian said flatly.

"What do you mean—lie?" Rowena demanded.

"They don't know for certain that their chant will work. The old texts stored in Silvan's tower had deteriorated, leaving them no choice but to improvise."

"And we're bloody good at it. We got you out, didn't we?" Cian growled.

"It's *his* fucking fault I ended up in there to begin with." Christian jerked his head toward Barrons. "I don't even know why he's here."

"He's here," Barrons said coolly, "because he has three of the stones necessary to corner the Book."

"Hand 'em over and get the fuck out."

"It's not my fault you're turning into a fairy."

V'lane said stiffly, "Fae. Not fairy."

"You knew my tats weren't protection enough—"

"I'm not your babysitter—"

Christopher hissed, "You should have checked him—"

"For the love of Mary," Rowena snapped. "I've a plague of barbarians and fools!"

"—and it wasn't my job to tattoo you. Pack your own fucking parachute. It wasn't even my job to try to keep the—"

Drustan said softly, "We *should* have checked him—"

Dageus snarled, "Doona be acting like 'twas some bloody favor you did—"

"You didn't try to get me out of the Silvers. Did you even tell anyone I was there?"

"—but the hour grew late," Drustan said, "and time can no longer be undone."

"—for the human race, when you're part of it," Dageus finished.

"—walls up. And it *was* a bloody favor, though you wouldn't know by the bloody thanks I've gotten, and don't be lumping me in the same gene pool as you, Highlander."

"Oh, shut up, all of you," I said, exasperated. "You can fight later. Right now we have work to do." To the Keltar, I said, "How certain are you of the parts you improvised?"

No one spoke for a moment as they finished the battle in silence, with glares and wordless threats.

"As certain as we can be," Dageus finally said. "We're not new to this. We've been the queen's Druids since before the Compact was negotiated. We sat with them in the Old Days, when the great hill of Tara had yet to be built, and learned their ways. Plus we've a few other . . . bits of arcane lore at our disposal."

"And we all know how well that turned out for you last time," Barrons said silkily.

"Mayhap you weren't helping but hindering, Old One," Dageus growled. "We ken you've your own agenda. What is it?"

"Stop it, all of you!" Rowena snapped.

The tension swelled.

"Barrons and his men will place three of the stones." I tried to get things back on track.

"He will give them to my *sidhe*-seers," Rowena said sternly. "We will place the stones."

Barrons gave her an incredulous look with the subtle arch of a brow. "In whose fucking reality do you think that's going to happen?"

"You have no business being involved."

"Old woman, I don't like you," Barrons said coldly. "Be careful around me. Be very, very careful."

Rowena closed her mouth, perched her glasses on her nose, and pursed her lips.

I looked at V'lane. "Did you bring the fourth stone?"

He looked at Barrons. "Did he bring his three?"

Barrons bared his teeth at V'lane.

V'lane hissed.

The Keltar growled.

And so it went.

Forty-five minutes later, when we all stalked from the room, two of the walls were shattered and the floor was cracked.

But we'd nailed down the nuances of our plan.

I would fly a Hunter over the city and locate the *Sinsar Dubh*, radioing back the location.

Barrons, Lor, Ryodan, and V'lane would close in with the four stones, while the Keltar began the binding spell to seal its covers so it could be moved.

Drustan would pick it up.

Barrons, Rowena, Drustan, V'lane, and I would ride together in Barrons' Hummer to the abbey (because no one trusted V'lane or any other Fae to sift him with the Book there and wait for everyone else to arrive).

Rowena would drop the wards, and all of us who were in the room today would enter the underground tomb that had been created eons ago to contain the *Sinsar Dubh*.

Dageus would complete the binding spell that would seal its pages closed and—according to their lore—turn the keys in the locks, which would silence it in a vacuum of eternal awareness, alone forever. *A hellish thing, to be sure,* he'd said grimly.

And something he'd seemed to know a thing or two about.

There's no reason for her *to be there,* Rowena had continued to protest, giving me the gimlet eye, even as they were blindfolding her and the *sidhe*-seers. Ryodan didn't want them seeing his club or knowing the back way in.

There's no reason for you to be there, either, old woman, Barrons had said. *Once you drop the wards, we don't need you.*

You're not necessary, either.

You think only Dageus should go in, with Drustan and the Book? I'd said acerbically.

She'd fumed the entire way out.

As I stepped into the overcast afternoon, I shivered. All trace of spring had vanished. The day was dark as dusk again, heavy with rain. Tomorrow night we would meet at O'Connell and Beacon.

And, with luck, by dawn the next day the world would be a safer place.

In the meantime, I was desperate for some downtime away from all the men in my life. I needed a girl's night and the comforts of normalcy.

I turned to V'lane and touched his arm. "Can you

find Dani for me and ask her to come to the bookstore tonight at eight?"

"Your wish, my command, MacKayla." He smiled. "Shall we spend tomorrow at the beach together?"

Barrons moved beside me. "She's busy tomorrow."

"Are you busy tomorrow, MacKayla?"

"She's working on old texts with me."

V'lane gave me a pitying look. "Ah. Old texts. A banner day at the bookstore."

"We're translating the *Kama Sutra*," Barrons said, "with interactive aids."

I almost choked. "You're never around during the day."

"Why is that?" V'lane was the picture of innocence.

"I'll be around tomorrow," Barrons said.

"All day?" I asked.

"The entire day."

"She will be naked on a beach with me."

"She's never been naked in a bed with you. When she comes, she roars."

"I know what she sounds like when she comes. I have given her multiple orgasms merely by kissing her."

"I've given her multiple orgasms by fucking her. For months, fairy."

"Are you still fucking her?" V'lane purred. "Because she does not smell like you. If you are, you are not marking her enough. She is beginning to smell like me. Like Fae."

"Unbelievable," I heard Christian mutter behind me.

"She toops them both?" I heard Drustan ask.

"And they permit it?" Dageus sounded baffled.

I looked between V'lane and Barrons. "This isn't even about me."

"You're wrong about that." Barrons reached into his pocket and pulled out a cell phone. "You know how to find me if you want me." He was walking away.

"More nifty acronyms?"

He was gone.

"And you know how to find me, as well, Princess." V'lane turned me toward him and closed his mouth over mine.

"Mac, what the bloody hell do you think you're doing?" Christian demanded.

I staggered a little when V'lane released me. His name was once again coiled in my tongue.

"You know what?" I said irritably. "You can all just butt out of my business. I don't have to answer to any of you."

There was definitely too much testosterone in my life.

A girl's night in was just what I needed.

PART

III

Between the desire
And the spasm
Between the potency
And the existence
Between the essence
And the descent
Falls the Shadow
      —T. S. ELIOT

Que sera, sera
Whatever will be will be
The future's not ours to see
      —DORIS DAY
(LIVINGSTON AND EVANS)

I AM NOT EVIL.

Then why do you destroy?

CLARIFY.

You do heinous things.

EXPOUND.

You kill.

THOSE THAT ARE KILLED BECOME ANOTHER THING.

Yes, dead! Destroyed.

DEFINE DESTROY.

To demolish, damage, ruin, kill.

DEFINE CREATE.

To give rise to, fashion something from nothing, take raw material and invent something new.

THERE IS NO SUCH THING AS NOTHING. ALL IS SOMETHING. WHERE DOES YOUR "RAW MATERIAL" COME FROM? WAS IT NOT SOMETHING BEFORE YOU FORCED IT TO BECOME SOMETHING ELSE?

Clay is just a lump of clay before an artist molds it into a beautiful vase.

LUMP. BEAUTIFUL. OPINION. SUBJECTIVE. THE CLAY WAS SOMETHING. PERHAPS YOU WERE AS UNIMPRESSED WITH IT AS I AM BY HUMANS, YET YOU CANNOT DENY IT WAS ITS ESSENTIAL SELF. YOU SMASHED IT, STRETCHED IT, PULLED IT, SMELTED IT, DYED IT, AND FORCED IT TO BECOME SOMETHING ELSE. YOU IMPOSED YOUR WILL UPON IT. AND YOU CALL THIS CREATION?

I TAKE A BEING AND MAKE ITS MOLECULES REST. HOW IS THAT NOT CREATION? IT WAS ONE THING AND IS ANOTHER. ONCE IT ATE, NOW IT IS EATEN. DID I NOT CREATE SUSTENANCE FOR ANOTHER WITH ITS NEW STATE? CAN THERE BE ANY ACT OF CREATION THAT DOES NOT FIRST DESTROY? VILLAGES

FALL. CITIES RISE. HUMANS DIE. LIFE SPRINGS FROM THE SOIL WHEREIN THEY LIE. IS NOT ANY ACT OF DESTRUCTION, SHOULD TIME ENOUGH PASS, AN ACT OF CREATION?

— CONVERSATIONS WITH THE *SINSAR DUBH*

36

"Happy birthday!" I cried, as I opened the front door of BB&B. When Dani stepped inside, I stuck a pointy party hat on her head, snapped the elastic string beneath her chin, and handed her a party horn.

"Gotta be kidding me, Mac. It was months ago." She looked embarrassed, but I saw the sparkle in her eyes. "V'lane said you wanted me. Gotta love that, dude—a Fae prince comes looking for the Mega! What's up? Ain't seen you for a while."

I led her to Party Central in the back of the bookstore, where a fire leapt, music played, and I'd piled wrapped packages on a table.

Her eyes widened. "This all for me? Ain't never had a party."

"We've got potato chips, pizza, cake, cookies, and candy, and all the sweets are triple chocolate fudge, chocolate mousse, or chocolate chip. We're going to be total couch potatoes, open presents, gorge, and watch movies."

"Like you and Alina used to?"

"Just like." I put my arm around her shoulder. "But first things first. Sit down and stay right there."

I hurried back to the front of the store, removed the cake from the fridge, stuck fourteen candles on it, and lit them.

I was proud of my cake. I'd taken my time icing it, with swoops and swirls, then decorated it with shavings of bittersweet chocolate.

"You've got to make a wish and blow out the candles." I placed it on the coffee table in front of her.

She stared down at the cake with a dubious expression, and for a moment all I could think was, *Please don't smash it into the ceiling.* It had taken me all afternoon and three tries to bake one that had finally turned out well.

She looked at me, squeezed her eyes shut, and screwed her face into a pucker of fierce determination.

"Don't hurt yourself, honey. It's just a wish," I teased.

But she wished like she did everything else: one hundred fifty percent. She stood there so long I was beginning to suspect she had a little bit of an attorney in her and was adding codicils and caveats.

Then her eyes popped open and she flashed me that cocky grin. She nearly blew the icing off the cake. "Means it'll hafta come true, right? Cause I blew 'em out?"

"Haven't you had a birthday cake before, Dani?"

She jerked her head.

"From this day forward, there will be at least one birthday cake for Dani Mega O'Malley each year," I proclaimed solemnly.

She beamed, cut the cake, and plunked two huge wedges on plates. I added cookies and a handful of candy.

"Dude," she said happily, licking the knife, "what are we gonna watch first?"

* * * *

Since I came to Dublin, there haven't been many moments in my life when I've been able to sit back, relax, and forget.

Tonight was one of them. It was bliss. For a stolen evening, I was Mac again. Eating good food, enjoying good company, pretending I didn't have a care in the world. One thing I've learned is that the harder your life gets, the gentler you have to be with yourself when you finally get some downtime, or you can't be strong when you need to be.

We watched a dark comedy and laughed our petunias off, while I painted her stubby fingernails black.

"What's this?" I said, noticing her bracelet.

Her cheeks pinked. "Ain't nothing. Dancer gave it to me."

"Who's Dancer? You have a boyfriend?"

She wrinkled her nose. "Ain't like that."

"What's it like?"

"Dancer's cool, but he ain't . . . he's got . . . just a friend."

Yeah, right. The Mega had blushed. Dancer was more than a friend. "How'd you meet him?"

She wriggled uncomfortably. "We watching this movie or being sissies?"

I picked up the remote and hit the pause button. "Sisters, not sissies. Spill, Dani. Who's Dancer?"

"You never tell me nothing about *your* sex life," she said crossly. "Bet you and Alina talked about sex all the time."

I sat up straight, alarmed. "Are you *having* a sex life?"

"Nah, man. Ain't ready yet. Just saying. Wanna talk like sisters, gotta do more than read me the riot act."

I breathed again. She'd been forced to grow up so fast. I wanted some part of her life to unfold slowly, perfectly, with roses and romance. Not in the heat of the moment, with the console of a Camaro digging into the small of her back and some guy she barely knew on top of her, but in a way that she'd remember forever. "Remember when I said we were overdue for a talk?"

"And here comes the lecture," she muttered. "Dude, ears up, they didn't tell us all the important stuff about the prophecy. Left out a lot."

She sprang it on me out of the blue, derailing me completely, as she'd known she would.

"And you're just *now* telling me this?"

She poked out her bottom lip. "Was getting around to it. You're the one that wanted to talk stupid stuff while I was trying to be professional-like. Just heard it myself. Ain't been hanging around the abbey much. Moved out long time ago."

I'd assumed she'd moved back in! One day I'd learn to quit making assumptions. "Where have you been staying? With Jayne at Dublin Castle?"

She crossed her arms over her chest, preening. "Pop by to kill the Fae fecks they catch, but got my own digs. Call it Casa Mega."

Dani was living on her own? And she had a boyfriend? "You just turned *fourteen*." I was horrified. The boyfriend part was fine—well, maybe, depending on what he was like, how old he was, and if he was good enough for her—but the living on her own part of things was going to have to change, fast.

"I know. Long overdue, huh?" She flashed me that gamine grin. "Got a couple o' places for different moods. 'S all there for the picking. Even got a crotch rocket!" She waggled her fingers. "Five-finger discount. I was *made* for this world."

Who would take care of her if she got the flu? Who would talk to her about birth control and STDs? Who would bandage her cuts and scrapes and make sure she ate right?

" 'Bout the prophecy, Mac. There's a whole 'nuther part they didn't tell us."

I shelved parental concerns for the moment. "Where did you hear that?"

"Jo told me."

"I thought Jo was loyal to Rowena."

"Think Jo's got stuff going on the side. She's part of Ro's Haven, but don't think she likes her none. Said Ro wouldn't let 'em tell you the whole truth and they kept it from me 'cause they don't trust me neither. Think I tell you everything."

"So, spill," I urged.

"Prophecy has a whole buncha other parts, more deets about peeps and the ways things'll happen. Says the one who dies young is gonna betray the human race and hook up with those that made the Beast."

I shifted uneasily. A thousand years before Alina had even been born, it had been foretold that she would join Team Darroc?

"Says the one who longs for death, the one that's gonna hunt the Book—that's you, Mac—ain't human, and the two from the ancient bloodlines ain't got a snowball chance in hell o' fixing our mess, 'cause they ain't gonna want to."

I shaped my mouth around words but nothing came out.

"Says the whole gig's got 'bout twenty percent chance o' working, and, if it don't, the second prophecy has about two percent odds."

"Who writes prophecies with such sucky odds?" I said irritably.

She cracked up. "Dude—I said the same thing!"

"Why didn't they tell me? They made it sound like I was virtually insignificant." I'd liked it that way. I had enough problems to deal with.

Dani shrugged. "Whole thing about Ro never telling

us we might be an Unseelie caste—said if you knew, it might be like a self-fulfilling prophecy. I say you gotta know what'cha are, know? Look in the mirror, eyes gotta meet eyes or quit looking."

"What else?" I demanded. "Was there more?"

"There's like this whole other . . . sub-prophecy. Says if the two from the ancient bloodlines are killed, things'll play out different and the odds of success'll be higher. Younger they're killed, the better."

A chill slid up my spine. That was brutal and to the point. Who would go how far to skew the odds more strongly in favor of the human race? I was surprised we hadn't been killed at birth. Assuming I'd had one.

"So I was thinking that's prolly why you and Alina got gave up. Somebody didn't wanna kill you guys as little kids, so they sent you away."

Of course. And we'd been forbidden to return. But Alina had wanted to go to Dublin to study abroad, and Daddy had never been able to deny us anything.

One decision, one tiny decision, and the world as we knew it began to fall apart.

"What else?" I pressed.

"Jo said they been talking to Nana O' behind Ro's back. Said the old woman was at the abbey the night the Book got out. Saw things. *Sidhe*-seers ripped to pieces, hacked apart. Said they only found little pieces of some. Others, they never found."

"Nana was there when the Book got out?" She hadn't mentioned a word of it the night Kat and I had talked to her at her cottage by the sea. Short of calling me Alina, telling us that her granddaughter, Kayleigh, had been Isla's best friend and fellow Haven member, and that she'd felt dark stirrings in the soil, she'd told us little else.

Dani shook her head. "Showed up after. Said her bones told her her daughter's immortal soul was in peril."

"You mean her granddaughter, Kayleigh."

"I mean her daughter." Dani's eyes sparkled. "Ro."

My mouth shaped a silent O. "Rowena is Nana's daughter?" I finally managed. Rowena was Kayleigh's mother? How much more had Nana O'Reilly neglected to tell me?

"Old woman despises her. Won't claim her. Kat and Jo searched Nana's cottage while she slept and found things—pictures and baby books and stuff. Nana thinks Ro's part of how the Book got out. Said Kayleigh told her they'd created a backup mini-Haven that Ro knew nothing about, with a leader that didn't even live at the abbey. Name was Tessie or Tellie or something funny like that. Case something happened to the Haven members that lived at the abbey."

My head was spinning. They'd been keeping me completely out of the loop. If I'd postponed celebrating Dani's birthday, I never would have learned any of this. Here was the mysterious Tellie that Barrons and my father had both mentioned! She'd been leader of a secret Haven. She'd helped my mother escape. I needed to find her. *Have you located Tellie yet?* I'd overheard Barrons saying. *No? Get more people on it.* It seemed Barrons had once again beat me to the punch and had his men out hunting for her already. Why? How did he know about the woman? What had he learned that he hadn't told me? "And?"

"Said your m—well, supposedly you ain't human, so I guess she ain't your mom—Isla got out alive. Nana O' saw her leaving that night. Ain't never gonna guess with who!"

I didn't even trust myself to speak. Rowena. And the old bitch had probably killed her. Whether she was my mom or not, I still felt tied to her, protective of her.

"Aw, c'mon, you gotta guess!" She was getting blurry around the edges with excitement.

"Rowena," I said flatly.

"Guess again," she said. "This one's gonna fry your mind. Nana never woulda known, 'cept you stopped by with him. Well, she don't call him a him, she calls him an it."

I stared at her. "Who?" I demanded.

"Saw Isla getting in a car with something she calls the Damned. Dude that drove off twenty-some years ago with the only survivor of the abbey's Haven was Barrons."

I was so wound up after everything Dani told me that there was no way I was going to be able to do something as lethargic as curl on a sofa and watch a movie. Plus, I had so much sugar running through my system I was nearly vibrating like Dani.

After she dropped the Barrons' bomb, she hit play and began cracking up again. The kid is resilient.

I sat and stared at the screen, not seeing a thing.

Why would Barrons keep from me that he'd been at the abbey when the Book escaped twenty-odd years ago? Why hide from me that he'd known Isla O'Connor, my sister's mother? I could relinquish a mother I'd never had, but I couldn't give up my sister. Whether she was mine or not, that was how I was thinking of her, period. The end.

I remembered coming down the back stairs, catching him talking to Ryodan on the phone, hearing him say, *After what I learned about her the other night.* Had he been referring to the night we'd gone to the cottage? Had he been as surprised as I was to hear Nana tell me the woman he'd left the abbey with two decades ago had supposedly been my mother?

Had he taken her to this Tellie woman, who'd then helped Alina and me find an adoptive home in America?

If Isla had left the abbey alive, why, how, when had she died? Had she even made it to Tellie, or had the woman agreed in advance to get her children out if anything happened to her? What part had Barrons been playing in all this? Had he killed Isla?

I shifted restlessly. He'd seen the cake. He knew I had a birthday party planned. He hated birthdays. There was no way he'd show his face tonight.

I picked at a piece of chocolate mousse icing. I stared around the bookstore. I contemplated the mural on the ceiling and fiddled with the cashmere throw. I plucked crumbs from the corner of the sofa and lined them up on my plate.

Rowena was Nana's daughter. Isla and Kayleigh had practically grown up together. Isla had been the Haven Mistress. They'd felt it necessary to form a Haven behind Ro's back. One that didn't even live at the abbey. Isla had run the formal one, and the mysterious Tellie had run the secret one. All these years my mom—Isla—had been taking the blame for the Book escaping, and now it looked like it had been Rowena behind things.

She'd let us all take the blame: first Isla, then Alina, then me.

. . . the two from the ancient bloodlines ain't got a snowball's chance in hell o' fixing our mess, 'cause they ain't gonna want to.

I sighed. When I'd overheard my mom and dad in Ashford that night, talking about how I might doom the world, I'd felt condemned. Then Kat and Jo had showed me the prophecy—what I now knew was an abbreviated version—and I'd felt absolved.

Now I was back to feeling condemned. It was more than a little disturbing to hear that the sooner my sister and I got killed, the better off the human race would be.

If she'd lived, would Alina have chosen Darroc? In a fit of grief, I'd wanted to unmake this world for a new one with Barrons in it. Were we both fatally flawed? Instead of having been smuggled from the country for our own good, had we been exiled for the sake of the world? Was that why the DEG had given me THE WORLD card? To warn me that I was going to destroy it if I wasn't careful? That I needed to look at it, see it, choose it? Who was he, anyway?

When I'd first arrived in Dublin and begun finding things out about myself, I'd felt like a reluctant hero, questing on an epic journey.

Now I just hoped I wouldn't end up screwing things up too much. Big problems demanded big decisions. How could I trust my own judgment when I wasn't even sure who I was?

I crossed my legs. Uncrossed them and raked a hand through my hair.

"Dude—you watching or doing couch calisthenics?" Dani complained.

I gave her a stark look. "You want to go kill something?"

She beamed. She had a chocolate ice-cream mustache. "Man, I thought you'd *never* ask!"

Each time Dani and I have fought back-to-back is a golden memory I've tucked away in the scrapbook of my mind.

I can't help but think it's what things would have been like if Alina had trusted me and we'd gotten to fight together. Knowing that you've got somebody watching your back, you're a team, you'd never leave each other behind, you'd break each other out of enemy camps, is one of the greatest feelings in the world. Knowing that no matter how bad the trouble is you've gotten yourself into, that person will come for you and go on with you—that's love. I wonder if Alina and I were weak because we let ourselves get divided, separated by an ocean. I wonder whether she'd still be alive if we'd stayed together.

I may never know where I came from, but I can choose my family from here on out, and Dani's a non-negotiable part of it. Jack and Rainey are going to love her when they finally meet her.

We blasted through the rain-slicked streets, killing Unseelie with a vengeance. With each one I stabbed, I grew more convinced I wasn't the king. I would have felt something if I had been: remorse, guilt, *something*. The king had been unwilling to give up his shadow children. I felt no pride of creation, no misguided love. I felt nothing but satisfaction at ending their immortal, parasitic existences and saving human lives.

We ran into Jayne and the Guardians and helped them out of a tight spot with a couple of sifters. We saw Lor and Fade on the prowl. I thought I glimpsed a Keltar on a rooftop, but he vanished so quickly I was left only with the impression of sleek tattooed muscle in the darkness.

Near dawn, we ended up a little too close to Chester's and I decided we should probably call it quits for the day. I was finally tired enough to sleep and I wanted to be at my best to track the *Sinsar Dubh*.

Tonight, it would finally end. Tonight we would seal the Book away forever. Then I would pick up the pieces of my life and begin rebuilding it, starting with my mom and dad. I would continue with my missions to find out who'd killed Alina and who I was, but once the Book was locked down again, I'd finally be able to breathe a little easier. Take more time like tonight for myself, time to live . . . and love.

"Let's head back to the bookstore, Dani."

A strangled sound was the only reply.

I spun and sucked in a screech of breath. I didn't

think. I just lunged and slammed my palms into her to Null the bitch.

The Gray Woman froze, but I was too late.

I stared in horror. While I'd been lost in my own thoughts, the lesion-covered, beauty-sucking Gray Woman had sifted in, grabbed Dani unaware, and begun devouring her. Right behind me, and I hadn't even noticed!

All I could think was, *But this isn't her MO—the Gray Woman devours men!*

Dani tried to shake her off but couldn't. "Dude, how bad'm I?"

I looked directly at her and nearly lost it. Bad. I gaped. This was not happening. This was unacceptable. I couldn't do this. I couldn't lose Dani. I felt something wild and dark stir inside me.

"Aw, man, get her *off* me!" she cried.

I tried. I couldn't. Dani tried, too, but the Gray Woman's hands created an unbreakable suction, fusing her victim to her until she chose to release it. I kept hitting her with my palms to keep her frozen, running a constant Null effect on her, trying to clear my head and figure out what to do. I kept stealing sideways glances at Dani. What was left of her hair was no longer auburn. Big bald patches showed, and lesions had formed on her scalp. Her eyes were sunken holes in a bloodless face. She was covered with sores and looked like she'd lost fifty pounds, and she couldn't have weighed more than twice that soaking wet.

"Shoulda known," Dani said miserably. "She hangs here. Likes Chester's. I been hunting her. Guess she knew it. Ow!" She touched her mouth.

Her lips were cracked, oozing. It looked as if her teeth were about to start falling out.

Tears stung my eyes. I slammed my palms into the

frozen Gray Woman. "Get off her, get off her!" I
shouted.

"Too late, Mac. Ain't it? That's what I'm seeing in
your eyes."

"*Never* too late." I pulled my spear out and pressed it
to the Gray Woman's throat. "Do what I say, Dani.
Don't move. Just let me handle this. I'm going to let her
unfreeze."

"She'll finish me!"

"No, she won't. Trust me. Hang on." I closed my
eyes and opened my mind. I stood on the black beach
and stared at the dark waters. Deep down, something
stirred, whispered welcome, greeted me with affection.
Missed you, it said. *Take these, they are all you need.
But come back soon, there is so much more.* I knew
that. I could feel it. The lake was like the padlocked box
in which I kept thoughts I couldn't face. There were
chains to break, a lid to lift. The runes I gathered seeped
out cracks. But one day I was going to have to open that
dark place of power and look deep. I scooped crimson
runes from the black waters. I opened my eyes and
pressed one into the Gray Woman's oozing cheek, another into her leprous chest.

I waited.

The instant she unfroze, she tried to sift, but as my
dark lake had promised, the runes prevented her. The
more she resisted, the brighter they pulsed. I realized
this was the Song of Making ingredient Barrons had
told me about, the one that had added the punch to the
prison walls. The more powerful the Fae that tried to
push through, the more resistant the walls became.

She exploded away from Dani and began trying to
tear the runes from her skin, shrieking. They seemed to
burn. Good.

Dani whooshed to the ground like a sheet of paper,
thin, white, and badly crumpled.

I kicked the Gray Woman. Hard. Again and again. "Fix her."

She rolled over and hissed up at me.

I raised a fist, dripping blood and runes, flung a third one at her.

She screamed and curled in on herself.

"I said fix her!"

"It is impossible."

"I don't believe you. You sucked it out. You can give it back. And if you can't, I will trap you in your own leprous skin and torture you for eternity. You think you're hungry now? You have no idea what hunger is. I'll show you pain. I'll keep you in a box and make it my personal mission in life to—"

With a snarl of rage and pain, she rolled over and clamped her oozing hands to Dani's face. "Free passage!" Bloody spittle flew from her lips.

"What?"

"You will not kill me if I do this. You and I will have—how do they say?—détente. We will be comrades. You will owe me."

"I will give you your life. That's all you get."

"I can take hers before you can take mine."

"Feck that noise," Dani cried. "Kill the bitch. You ain't owing her nothing, Mac."

There was something bothering me. This had the feel of a personal attack. "You don't kill females. Why did you come after Dani?"

"You killed my mate!" she snarled.

"The Gray Man?"

"He was the only other. Now I hurt you. Get them out of me!"

"Give her back what you took. Make her like she was before and I'll remove them. Otherwise, I'll skin you in them."

She writhed on the pavement.

"By the count of three, bitch. One, two . . ."

She held up a thin, sucker-covered, oozing hand. "Make oath with me. Free passage or she dies." She laughed bitterly. "We were separated when we escaped. We were going to hunt together, feed together. Who knows? In this world, perhaps we might have had young. I never saw him alive again." Her lips peeled back. "Choose. I weary of you."

"Feck her," Dani seethed.

"I want more than her life. You will never harm any of mine. I won't waste my breath explaining to you who is mine. If you think there's even a minuscule possibility that I might know the person you're thinking about feeding on, don't, or our truce ends. Understand?"

"Neither you nor any you consider yours will ever hunt me. Understand?"

"You will leave no trace of your foul touch on her."

"You will grant me a favor one day."

"Agreed."

"No, Mac!" Dani cried.

I pressed my palm to the Gray Woman's. I felt the sting of a single sucker mouth as it bled me and we made the oath.

"Fix her," I said. "Now."

"Can't fecking believe you did that," Dani muttered for the tenth time.

Her cheeks were flushed, her eyes sparkling, her curly auburn hair more lustrous than ever. She even looked a little plumper, as if she had an extra layer or two of collagen beneath her skin.

"Think she gave you a little extra back, Dani," I teased. But I wasn't entirely certain the Gray Woman hadn't. Dani glowed, her skin shimmered translucent, her eyes were so green they were mesmerizing. Ruby lips pursed in a pretty moue.

"Think my boobs are bigger," she said with a smirk. Then she sobered. "Shoulda let her kill me, and you know it."

"Never gonna happen," I said.

"'Stead you went and made some kinda devil deal with the creepy feck."

"And I'd do it again in a heartbeat. We'll figure it out when it becomes a problem. You're alive. That's all that matters."

Dani keeps it cool, all the time. On the rare occasions she lets you see a feeling, it's one she's chosen to paste on her face and let you see. She has a vast arsenal of scowls and disgruntled sneers, she's nailed every nuance of saucy grins and cocky swaggers known to man, and I suspect she perfected the Look of Death by five.

Her face is naked now, wide open. Unadulterated adoration blazes in her eyes. "This is the best birthday ever! Ain't never had nobody do something like that for me," she said wonderingly. "Not even Mom—" She broke off, clamping her lips in a thin line.

"Peas in the Mega pod," I said, tousling her curls, as we headed down the alley behind the bookstore. "Love you, kid."

She jerked but quickly slapped an insouciant grin over her shock. "Dude, I'm even gonna let you get away with calling me kid. Really think I'm prettier? Not that I care or nothing, just wanna know what kinda pain in the ass it's gonna be when I'm even hotter than I was before, and Dancer gets a good—"

"Brought ussh tasshty to drink, fassht one? Lassht one wassh sshweeeeet."

I whirled, spear up. They'd either sifted in or been hiding in the shadows, motionless, and we'd been so caught up in relief at our near escape that we'd been oblivious.

A pair of Unseelie I'd never seen before stood by the trash dumpster by the rear door of BB&B. They were identical, each with four arms and four slender, tubular legs, three heads apiece, and dozens of mouths on their flat, horrific faces, with tiny, needle-sharp teeth. At the corners of the many mouths were pairs of much longer thin teeth, and I knew, without knowing how I knew, that they used them as straws.

My sister had been missing the marrow in her bones, her endocrine glands had been drained, her eyeballs were collapsed, and she'd had no spinal fluid. The coroner had been at a complete loss.

I wasn't. Not anymore.

I knew what caste had killed Alina. What had gnawed and ripped and torn at her flesh to slowly and carefully remove all her inner fluids as if they were gourmet delights.

What they'd said penetrated, belatedly.

Brought us tasty to drink, fast one? Last one was sweet.

I froze, horrified. Surely that didn't mean what it sounded like it meant. Dani was the fast one. What—Why—My brain turned to sludge.

They were staring behind me with hopeful expressions. "She issh ourssh, assh well?" Six mouths spoke as one. "You mussht take her sshpear for ussh. You mussht make her helplessh, like you did other blondie. Leave in alley with ussh again."

Dani. I open my mouth. I can't seem to make a sound.

I hear a choking noise behind me, a strangled sob.

"Do not go, fassht one!" Six mouths cry, gazes fixed behind me. "Come back, feed ussh again! We are ssho hungry!"

I turn and stare at Dani.

Her eyes are enormous, her face pale. She's backing away from me.

If she draws her sword, it'll make everything easy.

She doesn't.

"Draw your sword."

She shakes her head and takes another step backward.

"Draw your fucking sword!"

She bites her lower lip and shakes her head again. "Ain't doing it. I'm faster. Ain't killing you."

"You killed my sister. Why not me?" The dark lake in my head begins to boil.

"Ain't like that."

"You brought her to them."

Her face screws up with anger. "You don't know a fecking thing 'bout me, you stupid fecking fecker! You don't know *nothing*!"

I hear rustles behind me, leathery wet sounds, and I whirl. The freaks that killed my sister are taking advantage of the distraction and trying to leave.

Not a chance in hell. This is what I've been living for. This moment. My revenge. First them, then her.

I lunge for them, screaming my sister's name.

I slice and rip and tear.

I begin with my spear and end with my bare hands.

I fall on the pair like the beast form of Barrons. My sister died in an alley with these monsters working on her, and now I know it wasn't fast. I can see her, white-lipped with pain, knowing she's going to die, scratching a clue into the pavement. Hoping I'll come, afraid I'll come. Believing I could succeed where she failed. God, I miss her! Hatred consumes me. I devolve into vengeance, I embrace it, I become it.

When I finish, there are no pieces larger than my fist.

I'm shaking, gasping, covered with bits of flesh and gray matter from smashing their skulls.

Feed ussh again! they'd demanded.

I double over and hit the pavement, puking. I puke until I dry-heave, then I dry-heave until my ears ring and my eyes are stinging.

I don't have to look behind me to know she's long gone.

I finally got what I came to Dublin for.

I know who killed my sister.

The girl I'd begun to think of as my sister.

I curl in a tight ball on the cold pavement and cry.

37

As I stepped out of the shower, I caught a glimpse of myself in the mirror. It wasn't pretty.

In all the time I'd been in Dublin, with all the horrors I've encountered, I've never seen quite this expression on my face.

I look haunted. Haunted is all about the eyes.

I *feel* haunted.

I came here for revenge. I brace my palms on either side of the bathroom sink and lean close into the mirror, studying myself.

Who's in there, behind my face? A king that wouldn't think twice about killing a fourteen-year-old girl I love? Loved. Hate her now. She took my sister to an alley, gave her to monsters that slaughtered her.

I can't even think things like *why*? It doesn't seem to matter. She did it. *Res ipsa loquitur* as Daddy would say. The thing speaks for itself.

I don't have the emotional energy to dry my hair or put on makeup. I dress and drift downstairs where I slump on the sofa in the rear seating area, as thunder rolls in the leaden sky. The day is so thick with rain that it looks like dusk at noon. Lightning crashes.

I've lost so much. And gained precious little.

I'd had Dani in the gains column.

Finding out who killed Alina made the pain of her death fresh again. It made it all too visual for me. I'd told myself she died instantly and whatever had been done to her had happened postmortem. I knew better now. While they'd slowly drained her, she lay there scratching a clue into the pavement for me. I sat, torturing myself with thoughts of her torture, as if that might accomplish something useful, besides torturing myself.

Leftover cake mocked me on the coffee table. Unopened presents teetered nearby. I'd baked a cake for my sister's murderer. I'd wrapped presents. I'd painted her nails. I'd sat and watched movies with her. What kind of monster was I? How could I have been so blind? Were there clues I'd never noticed? Had she ever slipped? Revealed knowledge of Alina she shouldn't have had but I hadn't been paying enough attention?

I dropped my head in my hands and squeezed, rubbing my temples, tugging my hair.

The journal pages!

"She has Alina's journal," I said, incredulous. The journal pages that had shown up for a brief time had made no sense to me. They'd never really told me anything and they'd appeared at the strangest times. Like the day Dani had brought my mail in and there'd been one in the stack. In a thick, fine envelope, just the kind a corporation like Rowena's might use.

But why would she have given me those entries? They'd pretty much just been about . . .

"How much Alina loved me." Tears stung my eyes.

The bell over the door tinkled.

I rose in a half crouch and waited. Who was here in the middle of the day?

My muscles stayed tense, and my gut tightened with anticipation. I eased back down to the sofa.

I responded that way to only one man. Jericho Barrons.

I was lost in grief and fury and hated being alive. And still I wanted to stand up, stripping as I went, and have sex with him right here on the bookstore floor. Was that the sum total of my existence? I didn't get the erudition of *I think therefore I am*. Instead, I got *I am, therefore I want to fuck Jericho Barrons*.

"Got a little messy in my back alley, Ms. Lane." His voice floated around bookcases, preceding him.

Not nearly as messy as I'd've liked. I wished I had those Unseelie bastards alive right now to kill all over again. How was I going to do what I was supposed to do?

Maybe I could just take *her* to an alley and give *her* to some monsters to die. She would be hard to catch, but my dark, glassy lake was stirring, whispering, offering all kinds of assistance, and I knew that I had more than enough juice to catch the kid. To do anything I wanted. There was something very cold inside me. Always had been. I wanted to welcome it now. Let it chill my blood and frost all my emotions until there was nothing left in me that was haunted because there was nothing left in me.

"The rain'll clean it up."

"I don't like messes on my—"

"Jericho." It was plea, lament, and benediction.

He stopped speaking instantly. He appeared around the last bookcase and stared at me. "You can say it that way anytime, Mac. Especially if you're naked and I'm on top of you." I could feel his gaze on me, searching, trying to understand.

I didn't understand myself. The plea had been to not pick on me right now. Sarcasm would undo me. The lament had been a sharing of my pain, because I knew he understood pain himself. The benediction was the part I couldn't explain. As if he was sacred to me. I looked up at him. He'd been with my alleged mother the night she'd left the abbey, the night the Book had escaped, and never told me. How could I revere him? I didn't have the energy to confront him. Learning that Dani had killed Alina had left me feeling like a popped balloon.

"Why are you sitting in the dark?' he said finally.

"I know who killed Alina."

"Ah." The single word said more than most people can say in entire paragraphs. "Beyond a shadow?"

"Black and white."

He waited. He didn't ask. And I suddenly understood that he wouldn't. This was part of who he was. Barrons *did* feel, and when he felt most strongly, he spoke the least, asked the fewest questions. Even from here I could feel the tension in his body as he waited to see if I would tell him more. If I didn't, he would continue walking through the store and vanish as silently as he'd glided into view.

But if I spoke? What if I asked him to make love to me? Not fuck me hard, but make love.

"It was Dani."

He said nothing for so long that I began to think he hadn't heard me. Then he released a long, weary-sounding breath. "Mac, I'm sorry."

I looked up at him. "What do I do?" I was appalled to hear my voice crack.

"You've done nothing yet?"

I shook my head.

"What do you want to do?"

I laughed bitterly and nearly began sobbing. "Pretend I never found out and go on like it never happened."

"Then that's what you do."

I tipped my head back and looked up at him in disbelief. "What? Barrons, the great hand of vengeance, is telling me to forgive and forget? You never forgive. You *never* walk away from a fight."

"I like to fight. You do, too, sometimes. But in this case, it doesn't sound like it."

"It's not that I—I mean . . . it's . . . God, it's so complicated!"

"Life is. Imperfect. Royally fucked up. How do you feel about her?"

"I—" felt like a traitor answering him.

"Let me rephrase that: How did you feel about her before you found out she'd killed Alina?"

"—loved her," I whispered.

"Do you think love just goes away? Pops out of existence when it becomes too painful or inconvenient, as if you never felt it?"

I looked at him. What did Jericho Barrons know of love?

"If only it did. If only it could be turned off. It's not a faucet. Love's a bloody river with level-five rapids. Only a catastrophic act of nature or a dam has any chance of stopping it—and then usually only succeeds in diverting it. Both measures are extreme and change the terrain so much you end up wondering why you bothered. No landmarks to gauge your position when it's done. Only way to survive is to devise new ways to map out life. You loved her yesterday, you love her today. And she did something that devastates you. You'll love her tomorrow."

"She killed my sister!"

"With malice? Spite? Out of cruelty? Hunger for power?"

"How would I know?"

"You love her," he said roughly. "That means you know her. When you love somebody you see inside them. Use your heart. Is Dani that kind of person?"

Jericho Barrons was telling me to use my heart. Could life get any stranger?

"Think maybe somebody told her to do it?"

"She should have known better!"

"Humans, in their infancy, tend to be infants."

"Are you making excuses for her?" I snarled.

"There is no excuse. I'm merely pointing out what you want me to point out. How has Dani treated you since the day you met?"

It hurt to even say the words. "Like a big sister she looked up to."

"Has she been loyal to you? Taken your side against others?"

I nodded. Even when she'd thought I'd hooked up with Darroc, she'd have remained at my side. Followed me into hell.

"She must have known you were Alina's sister."

"Yes."

"Coming to see you would have felt like facing the firing squad, every time."

I'd told her we were like sisters. And *sisters,* I'd told her, *forgive each other everything.* I'd caught a glimpse of her face in the mirror after I'd said it, when she hadn't known I was looking. Her expression had been bleak, and now I understood why. Because she'd been thinking, *Yeah, right. Mac's gonna kill me if she ever finds out.* Yet she'd still kept coming. When I thought about it, I was astonished she hadn't hunted down and killed those Unseelie, removing the damning evidence from the face of the earth.

He was silent a long moment, then, "Did she actually kill Alina? With her hands? A weapon?"

"Why do you ask?"

"Everything has degrees."

"You think some ways of killing are better?"

"I know they are."

"Death is death!"

"Agreed. But killing is not always murder."

"I think she took her somewhere she knew she'd be killed."

"Now you don't sound certain she killed her."

I told him what had happened last night, what the Unseelie had said, how Alina's body had looked, how Dani had vanished.

He nodded in silent agreement when I was finished.

"So, what do I do?"

"Are you asking me for advice?"

I braced myself for a sarcastic comment. "Don't snap my head off, okay? I had a bad night."

"Wasn't going to." He sat down on his heels in front of me and looked into my eyes. "This one got you. Worse than all the other things that happened to you. Worse than being turned *Pri-ya*."

I shrugged. "I got to have sex nonstop, no blame, no shame. You kidding me? Compared to the rest of my life, that was a joy."

He didn't say anything for a long time. Then, "But not something you'd care to repeat in full possession of your senses."

"It was . . ." I searched for words to explain.

He was motionless, waiting.

"Like Halloween. When people rioted. They loot. Do crazy things."

"You're saying *Pri-ya* was a blackout."

I nodded. "So what do I do?"

"You pull your fucking—" He bared his teeth on a silent snarl and looked away. When he looked back again, his face was a cool mask of urbanity. "You choose what you can live with. And what you can't live without. That's what."

"You mean can I live with killing her? Can I stand myself if I don't kill her?"

"I mean can you live without her. You kill her, you snuff her life forever. Dani will never be again. At fourteen, she'll be done. She had her chances, she fucked up, she lost. Are you ready to be her judge, jury, and executioner?"

I swallowed and dropped my head, shielding myself with hair as if I could hide behind it and not have to come out. "You're saying I won't like myself."

"I think you'd deal with it fine. You find places to put things. I know how you work. I've seen you kill. I think O'Bannion and his men were the hardest for you because they were your first humans, but after that, you took to it with a bit of stone cold. But this would be a chosen killing. Premeditated. It makes you breathe different. To swim in that sea, you have to grow gills."

"I don't understand what you're saying. Are you telling me to kill her?"

"Some actions change you for the better. Some for the worse. Be sure which one it is and accept it before you do anything. Death, for Dani, is irrevocable."

"Would *you* kill her?"

I could tell he was uncomfortable with the question, but I didn't know why.

After a strained silence, he said, "If that's what you want, yes. I'll kill her for you."

"That's not what I—no, I wasn't asking you to kill her for me. I was asking if you would in my shoes."

"The shoes you wear are beyond my ability to fathom. It's been too long."

"You're not going to tell me what to do, are you?" I wanted him to. I didn't want any of the responsibility for this. I wanted someone to blame if I didn't like how it turned out.

"I respect you more than that."

I almost fell off the couch. I parted my hair and looked up at him, but he was no longer squatting in front of me. He'd stood and moved away.

"Are we, like, having a conversation?"

"Did you just, like, ask me for advice and listen with an open mind? If so, then yes, I would call this a conversation. I can see how you might not recognize it, considering all I usually get from you is attitude and hostility—"

"Oh! All I ever get from you is hostility and—"

"And here we go. She's bristling and my hackles go up. Bloody hell, I feel fangs coming on. Tell you what, Ms. Lane," he said softly, "anytime you want to have a conversation with me, leave the myriad issues you have with wanting to fuck me every time you look at me outside my cave, come on in, and see what you find. You might like it."

He turned and began moving toward the entrance to the rear part of the store.

"Wait! I still don't know what to do about Dani."

"Then that's your answer for now." He stopped at the door and glanced back at me. "How much longer will you dissemble?"

"Who *uses* words like dissemble?"

He leaned back against the door and folded his arms. "I won't wait much longer. You're on your last chance with me."

"I don't know what you're talking about." What was he saying? Would Barrons walk away from me? Me? He never walked away from me. He was the one who would always keep me alive. And always want me. I'd come to count on those things like I counted on air and food.

"During a blackout, people do what they've wanted to do all along but have repressed, afraid of the consequences. Worried what others might think of them. Afraid of what they'll see in themselves. Or simply unwilling to get punished by the society that governs them. You don't care what other people think anymore. Nobody's going to punish you. Which raises the question: Why are you still afraid of me? What haven't you wrapped your head around yet?"

I stared at him.

"I want the woman I think you are. But the longer you dissemble, the more I think I made a mistake. Saw things in you that weren't there."

I fisted my hands and bit down a protest. He made me feel so conflicted. I wanted to shout, *You didn't make a mistake. I am her!* I wanted to cut my losses and run before the devil owned more of my soul.

"There was purity in that basement. That's the way I live. There was a time I thought you did, too."

I did, I wanted to say. *I do.*

"Some things are sacred. Until you act like they're not. Then you lose them."

The door swung silently shut.

38

"You okay, Mac?" Kat sounded worried. "You don't look so good."

I forced myself to smile. "I'm fine. Little nervous, I guess. I just want everything to go right and get this over with. You?"

She smiled but it didn't reach her eyes, and too late I remembered her touch of emotional telepathy. She could feel how badly off balance I was.

I felt doubly betrayed, first by Dani, then by Barrons for telling me he wouldn't wait forever. And ashamed for things I didn't understand. But it went all the way back to believing he was dead, then finding out he was alive, and it had something to do with my sister. No, it went back farther than that, to the end of my being *Pri-ya*. I sighed. I couldn't pin it down.

"Last night I found the Unseelie that killed Alina," I told Kat, figuring that would get her off my back.

The sharp focus of her gaze softened. "Did you have your revenge, then?"

I nodded, not trusting myself to speak.

"But it failed to ease your pain as you expected it

would." She was silent a moment. "When the walls came down, Rowena didn't tell us about eating Unseelie. I lost both my brothers to Shades. I've killed dozens of them since. It never makes me feel better. If only revenge would bring them back, but it doesn't. It adds to the body count."

"Wise as ever, Kat." I smiled. But inwardly I seethed.

I didn't want wise. I wanted blood. Crushed bones. Destruction. My dark lake had rippled into crashing waves last night, with a dark wind blowing hard across it.

I am here, it was saying. *Use me. What are you waiting for?*

I had no answer for it.

I continued to march toward O'Connell and Beacon, checking my watch. It was ten to nine. Kat had fallen into step with me a few blocks back.

"Where's Jo?"

"Food poisoning. Bad can of beans. Thought about bringing Dani but couldn't find her. Brought Sophie instead."

Hearing Dani's name impacted me hard. Kat looked at me sharply. I squared my shoulders and marched on. At the intersection, V'lane and his Seelie waited, on the opposite side of the street from Rowena and her *sidhe-seers.*

My dark lake boiled at the sight of her, hissed and steamed: *Think she doesn't know Dani did it? She knows everything. Did she order it?* I locked my jaw down and fisted my hands.

I would take care of my personal vendettas later. First things first. If I *was* the Unseelie King, I needed the Book locked away, the sooner the better. If I wasn't the Unseelie King, I still needed it locked away, because, for whatever reason, it kept coming for me and those I loved. My parents and I would never be safe, as long as it was loose.

All I had to do was play my small part. I would fly the Hunter over the city—supplied courtesy of Barrons, dampened and controlled—and help them corner it. Once it was contained, I would join them on the ground.

Just to be on the safe side, I planned to keep my distance. I didn't want any more surprises in my life.

My body tensed with sexual awareness.

"Mac," Ryodan said coolly as he pushed past me.

The sexual tension heightened to a painful state, and I knew Barrons was behind me. I waited for him to pass.

Kat walked by, Lor passed, and then they were all at the intersection. Still I stood, waiting for Barrons to get out from behind me.

Then his hand was on the nape of my neck and I felt the hardness of him against my ass. I inhaled sharply and leaned back against him, pushing for him with my hips.

He was gone.

I swallowed. I hadn't seen him all afternoon, since he'd told me I could lose him.

"Ms. Lane," he said coolly.

"Barrons."

"The Hunter is landing in . . ." He looked up. "Three . . . two . . . now."

It flapped down into the center of the intersection, wings churning black ice crystals in the air. It settled with a soft whuff of breath, swung its head low, and glared at me with fiery eyes. It was subdued—and pissed as hell about it. I felt for it with my mind. It was seething, rattling the bars of whatever cage Barrons was capable of creating with his mysterious runes and spells.

"Good hunting," he said.

"Barrons, I—"

"You've got rotten timing."

"You two gonna stand there fucking each other with your eyes all night, or can we get on with it?" Christian demanded.

The Keltar had arrived. Christopher, Drustan, Dageus, and Cian stalked from a nearby alley.

"Get on your demon horse, girl, and fly. But remember," Rowena shook a warning finger at me, "we're watching you."

And although I knew now why she was so convinced I was a threat—since Dani had told me about the *real* prophecy—I still consoled myself with the thought of deposing and killing her.

This Hunter was larger than the last one Barrons had "charmed." It took Barrons, Lor, and Ryodan to help me get up on its back. I was glad I'd remembered to bring gloves and to dress warmly. It was like sitting on an iceberg with sulfur breath.

Once I was settled between its icy wings, I looked around.

This was it.

The night we were going to take down the *Sinsar Dubh*.

At the meeting yesterday, no one had even raised the question: *What then?*

Rowena hadn't said: *The Seelie won't be permitted anywhere near it! It will be ours to guard, and we will keep it under lock and key forever!*

As if anybody'd believe that. It had gotten out once.

And V'lane hadn't said: *Then I will take my queen to Faery, with the Book, where she will recover and search it for fragments of the Song of Making, so she can reimprison the Unseelie and re-create the walls between our worlds.*

I wouldn't have believed that, either. What made them so certain fragments of the Song were in the Book?

Or that the queen could even read it? The concubine might have once known the First Language, but she'd obviously drunk from the cauldron too many times to remember it now.

And Barrons hadn't said: *Then I will sit down and read it, because somehow I know the First Language, and once I get the spell I'm after, you all can do whatever the fuck you want. Fix the world or destroy it, I don't care.*

And Ryodan hadn't said: *Then we're killing you, Mac, because we don't trust you and you'll no longer be necessary.*

Unfortunately, I believed the last two.

The tension I felt was unbearable. I hadn't realized how much I took Barrons for granted until he'd made it plain earlier today that his time with me had an expiration date.

I could lose him.

Maybe I didn't know what I wanted from him, but at least I knew I wanted him around. That had always seemed to be enough for him.

Unfair as hell and you know it, a small voice inside me said.

At my hip, my radio squawked. "Check, Mac."

I pressed a button. "Check, Ryodan."

We tested the radios all around.

"What are you waiting for, girl?" Rowena barked. "Get up there and find it!"

I nudged the Hunter with muscles and mind and watched her dwindle beneath me, as great black wings powerfully churned the night air. I wanted to squash her with my thumb like the infuriating speck she was.

Then I forgot her in the pleasure of the moment.

This was a rush.

This felt . . . good.

Familiar.

Free.

We rose higher and higher into the sky. Rooftops receded beneath us.

In front of me was the silvery coastline. Behind me, open country.

The air was crisp with a tang of salt. Lights beneath us were few and far between. I laughed out loud. This was amazing. I was *flying*.

I'd done it before, with Barrons, but this was different. It was just me and my Hunter and the night. I felt wide open with possibilities. The world was my oyster. No, the *worlds* were my oysters.

Damn, it was good to be me!

I suddenly knew something about Hunters—maybe it fed it to me with its mind. Not only were the massive icy dragons sifters, they made the Silvers obsolete. They weren't Fae. They never had been. They were amused by us. Aloofly entertained. They hung out with the Unseelie because they found it . . . interesting to pass time in such a fashion. They'd never been imprisoned.

No one owned them.

No one ever could.

In fact, we didn't even begin to understand what they really were. (Not alive the way we thought. Was I flying on a huge breathing meteor through the sky? Carved from that of which the universe had begun?)

I reached out for the Hunter's mind. *You can sift worlds!*

It turned its head and fixed me with a fiery orange eye, as if to say, *How stupid are you? You knew that.*

No, I didn't.

It snorted a tendril of smoky fire back at me, scorching my jeans.

"Ow!" I clapped a hand over my knee.

Don't need blinders. Wipe off his marks. Interfere with my vision. That one should be terminated. He plays with the instruments of gods.

"Barrons? What marks?"

On my wings, the back of my head. Wipe them off.

"No."

It was disappointed but fell silent, accepting my decision.

I opened my *sidhe*-seer senses. Or was it that part of me that was the Unseelie King? I gasped.

I knew where the *Sinsar Dubh* was. It was outside Barrons Books and Baubles. Looking for me.

"East," I said into my radio. "It's at the bookstore."

They crept around it, draping a net of stones chiseled from the cliffs of its home, closing in slowly but surely, with my guidance.

It could sense me near. It wasn't sure where. But it didn't seem to be able to sense them.

I listened to chatter on my radio.

Rowena had begun with her demands that the Seelie not be allowed to see the Book once it was sealed away, although Kat tried desperately and diplomatically to curb her imperious attitude.

The Seelie were growing more incensed by the moment. And getting more imperious by the moment.

Drustan was trying to run interference, but the other Keltar began bickering among themselves about the role of the Seelie and the role of the *sidhe*-seers, insisting their part to play was more important.

Barrons was getting angrier with each passing minute, and Lor had just threatened to drop the stone and leave if everyone didn't shut the fuck up.

"Two blocks west of you, V'lane," I said. He was

walking, not sifting. Said the Book would sense his presence if he did.

"It's moving again, fast," I cried. It had just shot three blocks in a matter of seconds. "It has to be in a car. Whoever it's got is driving it. I'm going to try to get closer for a better look."

"Don't you dare!" Rowena said. "You stay up there, far away from it, girl!"

I scowled. A Hunter-sized bowel movement on her head would go a long way toward making me feel better. For now. I was afraid killing her might be all that would satisfy me long term.

"Get off my back, old woman," I muttered, and turned the voice function of my radio off so I could hear them but they couldn't hear me.

I didn't want anyone to pick up on the *whoosh-whoosh* of the wings that had abruptly appeared beside me—which were much too massive to belong to the Hunter I was on.

I stared down the leathery wing of my Hunter at the one that was flying tandem with us.

K'Vruck.

Nightwindflyhighfreeeeeee.

I hastily checked my internal radar. It was hardly a typical *Sinsar Dubh* thought, but I couldn't be too safe. Only when I was certain the Book was still on the ground did I breathe easily again.

What was K'Vruck doing here if the Book hadn't brought him? Its thought had been less words and more an observation of the moment.

Was K'Vruck . . . happy?

It turned its head sideways and gave me a toothy, leathery-lipped grin. The tips of its wings worried my Hunter's span, making it rear in alarm.

"What are you doing?"

What are you?

"Huh?"

I *fly.*

I looked at it blankly. It had emphasized the word "I."

Used to ride me, it chuffed with reproach. *Old friend.*

I stared at it, nonplussed.

My eyes narrowed. It was clearly part of some conspiracy to make me think I was the Unseelie King. That was one load of crap I wasn't buying. "Go away." I swatted at it like a fly. "Shoo. Get out of here." I was shooing finality more final than death.

I was dimly aware of Barrons shouting on my radio.

It turned its leathery smile forward and sailed serenely along, barely moving its enormous wings, surfing a breeze. It was five times the size of my Hunter, several houses of leathery wings and hooves and enormous oven eyes and whatever held all that icy blackness together. As it passed through the dark sky, the breeze that sloughed off its titanic body steamed like dry ice.

"Go!" I snarled.

"Mac, where the hell is the Book?" Ryodan's voice sounded tinny on the radio. We were higher than I'd meant to be. "Where are you? I can't see you up there. I see a couple of Hunters flying together, but I don't see you. Fuck, is that one enormous or what?"

Great, just what I needed. Somebody to look up and catch me flying side by side with the Unseelie King's favorite Lamborghini. I thumbed my volume back on. "I'm here. In a cloud. Hang on. You'll see me in a few minutes," I lied.

"There aren't any clouds up there, Mac," Lor said.

Christian snapped, "Lie, MacKayla. Try again. Who are you flying with?"

"Where's the Book?" V'lane demanded.

"It's—Oh, there it is! Damn! Now it's four blocks to

the west, down by the docks. I'm going down for a closer look."

When I nudged my Hunter into a dive, K'Vruck dove with us.

"Ms. Lane," Barrons demanded, "what are you doing flying with the Hunter that killed Darroc?"

39

They refused to let me land.

I couldn't exactly blame them.

It wasn't so much that I had my own Satanic wing man—there wasn't anybody on the ground that night who hadn't dipped a toe into something dark at one point or another—as that they worried the Book would grab K'Vruck somehow and then we'd all be, well . . . K'Vrucked.

I couldn't shake him. The Hunter who called himself something more final than death simply would not leave my side. And a secret part of me was a little thrilled by it.

I flew over Dublin with Death.

Heady stuff for a bartender from small-town Georgia.

I had to watch from the air as the debacle unfolded. And it was a debacle.

They cornered it, hemmed it in with stones, whittled in and down until they finally had it penned on the steps of the church where I'd been raped. I had to wonder if it somehow knew that and was trying to mess with my head.

I kept waiting for it to speak in my mind, but it didn't. Not once. Not a word. It was the first time I'd ever been in its vicinity that it hadn't tried to mess with me somehow. I figured the stones and the Druids had a dampening effect.

As I watched, they moved the four stones—east, west, north, and south—in closer and closer until they formed the corners of a box, ten feet by ten feet around it.

A soft blue light began to emanate between the stones, as if forming a cage.

Everyone backed away.

"What now?" I whispered, circling over the steeple.

"Now it's mine," Drustan said calmly. The Keltar Druids begin to chant, and the silver-eyed Highlander moved forward.

I had a sudden vision of him, broken and dead on the church steps. The Book morphing into the Beast, towering over them all, laughing. Taking out one after the next.

"No," I cried.

"No, what?" Barrons said instantly.

"Stop, Drustan!"

The Highlander looked up at me and stopped.

I studied the tableau below. Something wasn't right. The *Sinsar Dubh* was lying on the steps, an innocuous hardcover. No towering Beast, no chain-saw-toothed O'Bannion, no skinned Fiona.

"When did it get out of the car?" I demanded.

Nobody answered me.

"Who was driving it? Did anyone see the Book get out of the car?"

"Ryodan, Lor, speak up!" Barrons snapped.

"Don't know, Barrons. Didn't see it. Thought you did."

"How did it end up on the steps?"

V'lane hissed. "It is an illusion!"

I groaned. "It's not really there. I must have lost track of it. I wondered why it wasn't messing with me. It *was*. Just not the way it usually does. I screwed up. Oh, shit—V'lane—look out!"

40

"Do you hear that?" It was driving me nuts.

"What?"

"You don't hear someone playing a xylophone?"

Barrons gave me a look.

"I swear I hear the faint strains of 'Qué Sera Sera.'"

"Doris Day?"

"Pink Martini."

"Ah. No. Don't hear it."

We walked in silence. Or, rather, he did. In my world, trumpets were blaring and a harpsichord was tinkling and it was all I could do not to go spinning in wide-armed circles down the street, singing: *When I was just a little girl, I asked my mother, "What will I be? Will I be pretty, will I be rich?" Here's what she said to me . . .*

The night had been an abysmal failure on all fronts.

The *Sinsar Dubh* had tricked us, but I was the one to blame. I was the one who could track it. I'd had a tiny part to play and hadn't been able to get it right. If I hadn't clued in at the last minute, it would have gotten V'lane and probably killed us all—or at least everyone that could be killed. As it was, I'd given V'lane just enough warning that he'd been able to sift out before it could turn the full brunt of its evil thrall on him and get him to take it from the hand of the *sidhe*-seer who'd been standing there offering it to him.

It had conned Sophie into picking it up right under our noses, while we'd all been focused on where it was making me *think* it was.

It had been walking along with us for God only knew how long, working its illusions on me, and I had misled them. Very nearly to a mass slaughter.

We'd run like rats from a sinking ship, scrambling over one another to get away.

It had been something to see. The most powerful and dangerous people I've ever known—Christian, with his Unseelie tattoos; Ryodan and Barrons and Lor, who were secretly nine-foot-tall monsters that couldn't die; V'lane and his cohorts, who were virtually unkillable and had mind-boggling powers—all running from one small *sidhe*-seer holding a book.

A Book. A magical tome that some idiot had made because he'd wanted to dump all his evil from himself so he could start life over again as patriarchal leader of his race. I could have told him that trying to shirk personal responsibility never works out well in the end.

And somewhere out there tonight or tomorrow, though nobody would go looking for her or try to save her, Sophie would die.

Along with who knew how many others? V'lane had sifted to the abbey to warn them she was no longer one of them.

"What was going on with the Hunter up there, Ms. Lane?"

"No clue."

"Looked like you had a friend. I thought maybe it was the concubine's Hunter."

"I hadn't thought of that!" I forced myself to exclaim, as if stunned.

He gave me a dry look. "I don't need a Keltar Druid to know when you're lying."

I scowled. "Why is that?"

"I've been around a long time. You learn to read people."

"Exactly how long?"

"What did it say to you?"

I blew out a breath, exasperated. "It said I used to ride it. It called me 'old friend.' " One nice thing about talking to Barrons was that I didn't have to mince words.

He burst out laughing.

I've heard him laugh openly so few times that it kind of hurt my feelings that he was laughing now. "What's funny about that?"

"The look on your face. Life hasn't turned out like you thought it would, has it, Rainbow Girl?"

The name slid through my heart like a dull blade. *You're leaving me, Rainbow Girl.* Then it had been laced with tenderness. Now it was merely a mocking appellation.

"Clearly I was misled," I said stiffly. That damned harpsichord was back, the trumpets swelled.

When I grew up and fell in love, I asked my sweetheart, "What lies ahead? Will there be rainbows, day after day?" Here's what my sweetheart said . . .

"You don't really believe you're the Unseelie King, do you?"

The trumpets warbled, the harpsichord fell silent, and the needle screeched as it was abruptly yanked from the record. Why did I even bother talking? "Where did you get that idea?"

"I saw the queen in the White Mansion. I couldn't think of any reason for her memory residue to be there. Occam's razor. She's not the queen. Or she wasn't then."

"So who am I?"

"Not the Unseelie King."

"Give me another explanation."

"It hasn't presented itself yet."

"I need to find a woman named Augusta O'Clare."

"She's dead."

I stopped walking. "You knew her?"

"She was Tellie Sullivan's grandmother. It was to their home Isla O'Connor asked me to take her the night the Book escaped from the abbey."

"And?"

"You're not surprised. Interesting. You knew I was at the abbey."

"How well did you know my moth—Isla?"

"I met her that night. I visited her grave five days later."

"Did she have two children?"

He shook his head. "I checked later. She had only one daughter. Tellie was babysitting her that night. I saw the child at her house when I took Isla there."

My sister. He'd seen Alina at Tellie's. "And you think I'm *not* the Unseelie King?"

"I think we don't have all the facts."

I felt like crying. The day I'd set foot on the Emerald Isle, the slow erosion of me had begun. I'd arrived, the beloved daughter of Jack and Rainey Lane, sister of Alina. I'd accepted being adopted. I'd been elated to discover I had Irish roots. But now Barrons had just confirmed that I wasn't an O'Connor. He'd been there when Isla died and she'd had one child. No wonder Ryodan had been so sure. There was nothing to identify me at all but a lifetime of impossible dreams, an oubliette of impossible knowledge, and an evil Book and a ghastly Hunter with a disturbing fondness for me.

"What happened that night at the abbey? Why were you there?"

"We'd gotten wind of something. Talk in the country-side. Old women gossiping. I've learned to listen to old women, read them over a newspaper anytime."

"Yet you made fun of Nana O'Reilly."

"I didn't want you to go back and dig deeper."

"Why?"

"She would have told you things I didn't want you to know."

"Like what you are?"

"She would have given you a name for me." He stopped, then chewed out the next words. "Inaccurate. But a name. You needed names then."

"You think I don't now?" The Damned, she'd called him. I wondered why.

"You're learning. The abbey was the focus of the talk. I'd been watching it for weeks, trying to devise a way in without setting off their wards. Clever work. They sensed even me, and nothing senses me."

"You said 'we'd' gotten wind. I thought you worked alone. Who is we?"

"I do. But dozens have hunted it over time. It's been the Grail for a certain type of collector. A sorcerer in London that ended up with copies of pages that night. Mobsters. Would-be kings. Following the same leads, we glimpsed one another now and then, gave each other a wide berth as long as we thought the other might one day provide a valuable lead, although I never saw the Keltar. I suspect the queen cleaned up after them, kept her 'hidden mantle' well hidden."

"So, you were outside the abbey?"

"I had no idea anything was going on inside. It was a quiet night, like any other I'd watched it. There was no commotion. No shouting, no disturbance. The Book slipped out into the night unnoticed, or bided its time and left later. I was distracted by a woman climbing out a window in the rear of the abbey, holding her side.

She'd been stabbed and was badly injured. She headed straight for me, as if she knew I was there. *You must get me out of here,* she said. She told me to take her to Tellie Sullivan in Devonshire. That the fate of the world depended on it."

"I didn't think you gave a rat's petunia about the fate of the world."

"I don't. She'd *seen* the *Sinsar Dubh.* I asked if it was still at the abbey and she said it had been but was no longer. I learned that night that the damned thing had been practically beneath my nose for the past thousand years."

"I thought it was always there, since the dawn of time, long before it was an abbey." I wasn't above prying into his age.

"*I've* been in Ireland only for the past millennia. Before that, I was . . . other places. Satisfied, Ms. Lane?"

"Hardly." I wondered why he'd chosen Ireland. Why would a man like him stay in one place? Why not travel? Did he like having a "home?" I supposed even bears and lions had dens.

"She said it killed everyone in the Haven. I had no idea what the Haven was at the time. I tried to Voice her, but she was slipping in and out of consciousness. I had nothing with which to stem her injuries. I thought she was my best bet to track it, so I put her in my car and took her to her friend. But by the time we got there, she was in a coma."

"And that's all she ever told you?"

"Once I realized she wasn't coming out of it, I moved on, unwilling to let the trail cool. I had competition to eliminate. For the first time since man learned to keep written archives, the *Sinsar Dubh* had been sighted. Others were after it. I needed to kill them while I still knew where they were. By the time I returned to Devonshire, she was dead and buried."

"Did you dig—"

"Cremated."

"Oh, isn't that just convenient. Did you question Tellie? Voice her and her grandmother?"

"Look who's all ruthless now. They were gone. I've had investigators hunting for them off and on ever since. The grandmother died eight years ago. The granddaughter was never seen again."

I rolled my eyes.

"Yes, it stinks. That's one of many reasons I don't believe you're the king. Too many humans went to too much effort to conceal things. I don't see humans doing that for any Fae, especially not *sidhe*-seers. No, there was something else going on."

"You said one of many reasons."

"The list is endless. Do you remember what you were like when you first came here? Do you really think he'd wear pink? Or a shirt that said *I'm a JUICY Girl*?"

I looked at him. The corners of his lips were twitching.

"I just don't see the most dreaded of the Fae wearing a matching thong and bra with little pink and purple appliqué flowers."

"You're trying to make me laugh." My heart hurt. Thoughts of what to do about Dani, fury at Rowena, anger at myself for having misled everyone tonight—there was a knot of emotions inside me.

"And it's not working," he said, as we stepped into the alcove of Barrons Books and Baubles. "How's this?" He drew me back out into the street and cupped my head with his hands. I thought he was going to kiss me, but he tipped my head back so I was looking up.

"What?"

"The sign."

The placard swaying on a polished brass pole read: MACKAYLA'S MANUSCRIPTS AND MISCELLANY.

"Are you kidding me?" I exploded. "It's mine? But you just said I was on my last chance with you!"

"You are." He released my head and moved away. "It can be removed as easily as it was hung."

My sign. My bookstore. "My Lamborghini?" I said hopefully.

He opened the door and stepped inside. "Don't push it."

"What about the Viper?"

"Not a chance."

I moved in behind him. Fine, I could deal without the cars. For the moment. The bookstore was mine. I was feeling choked up. MINE with all capital letters, just like the sign. "Barrons, I—"

"Don't be trite. It's not you."

"I was just going to thank you," I said crossly.

"For what? Leaving? I changed the sign because I don't plan to be here much longer. It has nothing to do with you. What I want is nearly within reach. Good night, Ms. Lane."

He vanished out the back. I don't know what I expected.

Actually, I do. I expected him to try to get me into bed again.

Barrons has been predictable in his treatment of me since the day I met him. Initially he used references to sex to shut me up. Then he used sex to wake me up. After I was no longer *Pri-ya,* he'd returned to using references to sex to keep me on edge. Forcing me to remember how intimate we once were.

Like everything else about him, I'd begun to count on it.

Innuendo and invitation. Eternal as the rain in Dublin. I was the one the dangerous lion licked. And I liked it.

Tonight, when we'd walked back to the bookstore, talking, sharing information freely, I felt something warm and new blossom between us. When he'd shown me the sign, I melted.

Then he'd splashed ice water on me.

For what? Leaving? I changed the sign because I don't plan to be here much longer.

He'd walked off without making innuendo or extending an invitation.

He'd just *left*.

Giving me a tiny taste of what it felt like. Barrons walking off, leaving me alone.

Would he really go away for good when this was done? Vanish without saying good-bye the moment he had his spell?

I trudged into my fifth-floor bedroom and threw myself across my bed. I usually pretend there's nothing strange about sometimes finding my room on the fourth floor and sometimes on the fifth. I've become so inured to "weird" that the only thing that worries me much anymore is the possibility that my bedroom might one day disappear entirely. What if I'm in it when it goes? Will I go, too? Or be stuck in a wall or floor as it makes its grand exit, yelling my head off? As long as it's still somewhere in the store, I feel reasonably secure with my parameters. After the way my life has turned out, if it does disappear, I'll probably just sigh, gear up, and go hunting for it.

It's hard to lose the things you've come to think of as yours.

Was all this going to be over soon? Sure, we'd screwed up tonight, but I wouldn't screw up next time. We were meeting at Chester's tomorrow to make a new plan. We had our team; we'd keep trying. Conceivably, we could have the *Sinsar Dubh* stowed securely away in a matter of days.

And what would happen then?

Would V'lane and the queen and all the Seelie leave our world and go back to their court? Would they manage to get the walls back up somehow and scrape the Unseelie blight from my world?

Would Barrons and his eight close up Chester's and disappear?

What would I do, with no V'lane, no Unseelie to fight, no Barrons?

Ryodan had made it clear that no one was allowed to know about them and live. They'd been hiding their immortal existence among us for thousands of years. Would they try to kill me? Or just leave and remove all trace of evidence that they'd ever been here?

Could I search the world over and never find any of them again? Would I age and begin to wonder if I'd imagined those crazy, passionate, dark days in Dublin?

How could I age? Who would I marry? Who would ever understand me? Would I live out the rest of my life alone? Become as cantankerous and cryptic and strange as the man who'd made me this way?

I began to pace.

I'd been so worried about my problems—who he was, who I was, who Alina's killer was—that I'd never looked into the future and tried to project the likely outcome of events. When you're fighting every day simply for the chance to have a future, it's kind of hard to get around to imagining what that future might be like. Thinking about *how* to live is a luxury enjoyed by people who know they're *going* to live.

I didn't want to be alone in Dublin when this was all over!

What would I do? Run the bookstore, surrounded by memories for the rest of my life as those of us who remained painstakingly rebuilt the city? I couldn't stay here if he didn't. Even if he left, he'd still be here, everywhere I looked. It would almost be worse than him dying. Barrons' residue would stalk this place as vividly as the concubine and the king lived in the White Mansion's inky corridors. I'd know he was out there, forever beyond my reach. Glory days: achieved and gone by twenty-three, like a has-been high school football player sitting in his double-wide, chugging beer with his friends at thirty, two kids, a nagging wife, a family van, and a grudge against life.

I slumped down on my bed.

Everywhere I turned, I'd see ghosts.

Would Dani's ghost haunt me in the streets? Would I make that happen? Would I go that far? Premeditated murder of a girl who was little more than a child?

You choose what you can live with, he'd said. *And what you can't live without.*

It had never occurred to me that the outcome of my time in Dublin might be a future of living in a bookstore without Barrons ever again, walking the streets filled with my—

"Oh, feck it, she was my sister," I growled, punching my pillow. I didn't give a damn if we weren't born to each other: Alina had been my best friend, my heart-sister, and that made us sisters any way I looked at it.

"Where was I?" I muttered. Ah, yes, streets filled with my sister's ghost, compounded by the ghost of the teenager I'd come to think of as my little sister, who'd been involved with killing my sister. Would I walk the streets with those phantoms every day?

What an awful, empty life that would be!

"Alina, what should I do?" God, I missed her. I missed her like it was yesterday. I heaved myself up from bed, grabbed my backpack, dropped cross-legged on the floor, pulled out one of her photo albums, and opened the sunny yellow cover.

There she was with Mom and Dad at her college graduation.

There we were, at the lake with a group of friends, drinking beer and playing volleyball like we were going to live forever. Young, so damned young. Had I ever really been that young?

Tears slipped down my cheeks as I turned the pages.

There she was on the green at Trinity College, with new friends.

Out in the pubs, dancing and waving to the camera.

There was Darroc, watching her, his gaze possessive, hot.

There she was looking up at him, completely unguarded. I caught my breath. Goose bumps rose on my arms and neck.

She *had* loved him.

I could see it. I knew my sister. She'd been crazy about him. He'd made her feel what Barrons made me feel. Bigger than I could possibly be, larger than life, on fire with possibilities, ecstatic to be breathing, impatient for the next moment together. She'd been happy in those last months, so alive and happy.

And if she'd lived?

I closed my eyes.

I knew my sister.

Darroc had been right. She would have gone to him. She would have found a way to accept it. To love him anyway. We were so fatally flawed.

But what if . . . what if her love might have changed him? Who could say it wouldn't have? What if she'd gotten pregnant and there was suddenly a baby Alina, helpless and pink and cooing? Might love have softened his edges, his need for revenge? It had worked greater miracles. Maybe I shouldn't think of her as flawed but as a wrench in the works in a good way, who might have changed the outcome for the better. Who could say?

I turned the page and my cheeks flamed.

I shouldn't look. I couldn't help it. They were in bed. I couldn't see Alina. She had the camera. Darroc was naked. From the angle, I knew Alina was on top of him. From the look on his face, I knew he was coming when she took it. And I could see it in his eyes.

He'd loved her, too.

I dropped the album and sat staring into space.

Life was so complicated. Was she bad because she'd loved him? Was he evil because he'd wanted to reclaim what had been taken from him? Hadn't the same motives driven the Unseelie King and his concubine? Didn't the same motives drive humans every day?

Why hadn't the queen just let the king have the woman he loved? Why couldn't the king be happy with one lifetime? What might have happened to the Unseelie if they'd never been imprisoned? Might they have turned out like the Seelie court?

And what about my sister and me? Would we really doom the world? Nurture or nature: What were we?

Everywhere I looked, I could see only shades of gray. Black and white were nothing more than lofty ideals in our minds, the standards by which we tried to judge things and map out our place in the world in relevance to them. Good and evil, in their purest form, were as intangible and forever beyond our ability to hold in our hand as any Fae illusion. We could only aim at them, aspire to them, and hope not to get so lost in the shadows that we could no longer see the light.

Alina had been aiming for the right thing to do. So was I. She hadn't made it. Would I fail? Sometimes it was hard to know what the right thing to do was.

Feeling like the worst kind of voyeur, I reached for the photo album, pulled it back on my lap, and began to turn the page.

That's when I felt it. The pocket was too thick. There

was something behind the photo of Darroc staring up at Alina like she was his world, coming inside her.

I slid the photo out with trembling hands. What would I find secreted away here? A note from my sister? Something that would give me more insight into her life before she'd died?

A love letter from him? From her?

I withdrew a piece of old parchment, unfolded it, and gently smoothed it open. There was writing on both sides. I turned it over. One side was covered from upper margin to lower. The other side had only a few lines on it.

I recognized the paper and script on the full side instantly. I'd seen Mad Morry's writings before, although I didn't read Old Irish Gaelic.

I turned it over, holding my breath. Yes, he'd translated it!

IF THE BEAST OF THREE FACES IS NOT CONTAINED BY THE TIME THE FIRST DARK PRINCE DIES THE FIRST PROPHECY SHALL FAIL FOR THE BEAST SHALL HAVE GORGED ON POWER AND CHANGED. ONLY BY ITS OWN DESIGN WILL IT FALL. HE WHO IS NOT WHAT HE WAS SHALL TAKE UP THE TALISMAN AND WHEN THE MONSTER WITHIN IS DEFEATED SO SHALL BE THE MONSTER WITHOUT.

I read it again. "What talisman?" How accurate was his translation? He'd written, He *who is not what* he *was*. Had Darroc really been the only one who could merge with the Book? Dageus wasn't what he was. I was willing to bet Barrons wasn't, either. Really, who of us was? What a nebulous statement. I'd hardly call that definitive criteria. Daddy would have a heyday in court with such a vague phrase.

By the time the first dark prince dies . . . It was already too late, if that was true. The first dark prince was Cruce, who couldn't possibly be alive. At least once in the past seven hundred thousand years, he would have shown his face. Someone would have seen him. But even if he was alive, the moment Dani had killed the dark prince who came to my cell at the abbey, it had been too late for the first prophecy to work.

The shortcut was a talisman. And Darroc had had it.

Something nagged at my subconscious. I grabbed my backpack and began to rummage through it, hunting for the tarot card. I dumped out the contents, picked up the card, and studied it. A woman stared off into the distance while the world spun in front of her.

What was the point? Why had the DEG—or the *fear dorcha,* as he'd claimed—given me this particular card?

I took painstaking note of the details of her clothing and hair, the continents on the planet. It was definitely Earth.

I examined the border of the card, looking for concealed runes or symbols. Nothing. But wait! What was around her wrist? It looked like a fold in her skin until I looked closer.

I couldn't believe I'd missed it.

It had been worked into the border, cleverly concealed as a sort of pentacle, but I knew the shape of the cage that housed the stone. Around the woman's wrist was the chain of the amulet Darroc had stolen from Mallucé.

The dreamy-eyed guy *had* been trying to help me.

The talisman from the prophecy was the amulet. The amulet was Darroc's shortcut!

It had been within my reach the night the *Sinsar Dubh* popped Darroc's head like a grape. I'd touched it. It had been so close. Then the next thing I knew I was over a shoulder and it was gone.

I smiled. I knew where to find it.

As a man, Barrons collected antiquities, rugs, manuscripts, and ancient weapons. As a beast, he'd collected everything I touched. The pouch of stones, my sweater.

No matter his form, Barrons was a ferret after shiny baubles that smelled good to him.

There was no way he'd walked away from it that night. I'd touched it.

I slipped the parchment, translation, and tarot card in my pocket and stood up.

It was long past time to find out where Jericho Barrons went when he left the bookstore.

He didn't go far.

In all the time I'd known him, I was willing to bet he never had.

When I reached the bottom step, I smelled him. The faint hint of spice hung in the air outside his study. The study where he kept his Silver.

The entire time I was *Pri-ya,* I'd never seen him sleep. I would drift off, but each time I'd wake, he'd be there, lids heavy on glittering dark eyes, watching me as if he'd been laying there just waiting for me to roll over and ask him to fuck me again. Always ready. As if he lived for it. I remembered the look on his face when he'd stretch himself over me.

I remembered how my body had responded.

I'd never done Ecstasy or any of the drugs some of my friends had tried. But if it was like being *Pri-ya,* I couldn't imagine wanting to do it willingly.

A part of my brain had still been aware, in a dim sort of way, while my body was out of my control.

If he'd brush a hand over my skin, I'd nearly scream from needing him inside me. I would have done anything to get him there.

Being *Pri-ya* was worse than being raped by the princes.

It had been hundreds of rapes over and over again. My body had wanted. My mind had been vacant. Yet some part of the essential me had still been there, fully aware that my body was completely out of my control. That I wasn't choosing. All my choices had been made for me. Sex should be a choice.

Only one had been left to me: more.

When he'd push inside me and I'd feel him begin to penetrate, it had turned me into a wild thing—hot, wet, and desperate for more of him. With every kiss, every caress, every thrust, I'd just needed more. He'd touched me, I went nuts. The world dwindled down to one thing: him. He really *had* been my world in that basement. It was too much power for one person to have over another. It could put you on your knees, begging.

I had a secret.

A terrible secret that had been eating me alive.

What did you wear to your senior prom, Mac?

That had been the last thing I'd heard, *Pri-ya*.

Everything from that moment on had really happened.

I'd faked.

I'd lied to him and myself.

I stayed.

And it hadn't felt any different.

I'd been just as insatiable, just as greedy, just as vulnerable. I'd known exactly who I was, what had happened at the church, and what I'd been doing for the past few months.

And every time he'd touched me, my world had dwindled down to one thing: him.

He was never vulnerable.

I'd hated him for that.

I shook my head, scattered the broody thoughts.

Where would Barrons go to be alone, relax, maybe sleep? Beyond the reach of anyone. Inside a heavily warded Silver.

With the scent of him still hanging in the air, I ransacked his study.

I was feeling ruthless and tired of playing by rules. I didn't know why there should be any rules between us, anyway. It seemed absurd. He'd been in my space since the moment I'd met him, larger than life, electrifyingly present, shaking me up and waking me up and making me just this side of insane.

I grabbed one of his many antique weapons and pried open the locked drawers of his desk.

Yes, he'd see that I broke into it. No, I didn't care. He could just try to take his anger out on me. I had a fair share of my own.

He had files on me, on my parents, on McCabe, on O'Bannion, people I'd never heard of, even his own men.

There were bills for dozens of different addresses in many different countries.

In the bottom drawer, I found pictures of me. Stacks and stacks of them.

At the Clarin House, stepping out into the dewy Dublin morning, tan legs gleaming beneath the short hem of my favorite white skirt, long blond hair swinging in a high ponytail.

Walking across the green at Trinity College, meeting Dani for the first time, by the fountain.

Coming down the back steps of Alina's apartment, exiting into the alley.

Slinking down the back alley, looking at O'Bannion's abandoned cars, the morning I'd realized that Barrons had turned out all the lights and let the Shades take the perimeter, devouring sixteen men to kill a single one who was a threat to me. There was shock, horror, and something unmistakably relieved in my eyes.

Fighting back-to-back with Dani, sword and spear blazing alabaster in the darkness. There was a whole series of those shots, taken from a rooftop angle. I was on fire, face shining, eyes narrowed, body made for what I was doing.

Through the front window of the bookstore, hugging Daddy.

Curled on the sofa in the rear conversation area of BB&B, sleeping, hands tucked against my chest. No makeup. I looked seventeen, a little lost, completely un-guarded.

Marching into the Garda station with Jayne. Heading back to the bookstore, without flashlights. I'd never been in danger that night. He'd been there, making sure I survived whatever came my way.

No one had ever taken so many pictures of me before. Not even Alina. He'd caught my subtlest emo-tions in each shot. He'd been watching me, always watching me.

Through the window of a crofter's cottage, I was touching Nana's face, trying to push into her thoughts and see my mother. My eyes were half closed, my fea-tures drawn with concentration.

Another rooftop shot. I had my palm on the Gray Woman's chest, demanding she restore Dani.

Was there anything he didn't know?

I let the photos fall back into the drawer. I was feeling light-headed. He'd seen it all: the good, the bad, and the ugly. He never asked me any questions, unless he thought *I* needed to figure out the answers. He never decked me out in convenient labels and tried to stuff me in a box. Even when there were plenty of labels to stick to me. I was what I was at that moment and he liked it, and that was all that mattered to him.

I turned and stared into the mirror.

The reflection of a stranger stared back.

I touched my face in the reflection. No, she wasn't a stranger. She was a woman who'd stepped out of her comfort zone in order to survive, who'd become a fighter. I liked the woman I saw in the looking glass.

The surface of the mirror was icy beneath my fingers.

I knew this Silver. I knew all the Silvers. They had something of . . . K'Vruck in them. Had the king selected an ingredient of their creation from the Hunter's home world?

As I gazed into it, I sought that dark, glassy lake and told it I wanted in.

Missed you, it steamed. *Come swim.*

Soon, I promised.

Alabaster runes popped up from the black depths, shimmering on the surface.

It was that easy. I asked, it gave. Always there, always ready.

I scooped them up and pressed them, one after another, to the surface of the Silver.

When the final one was in place, the surface began to ripple like silvery water. I trailed my fingers through it and the waters peeled back, receded to the black edges of the mirror, leaving me staring down a fog-filled path through a cemetery. Behind tombstones and crypts, dark creatures slithered and crept.

The Silver belched a gust of icy air.

I stepped up, into the mirror.

As I suspected, he'd stacked Silvers to form a gauntlet no intruder would make it through alive, protecting his underground abode.

Nine months ago, if I'd been able to figure out how to get in, I'd have gotten killed within the first few feet. I was attacked the instant I stepped inside. I didn't have time to draw my spear. When the first volley of teeth and claws came at me, my lake instantly offered and I accepted without hesitation.

A single purple rune glowed in my palm.

My attackers fell back. They hated it, whatever it was.

I swirled through fog to my waist, absorbing the barren landscape. Skeletal trees glowed like yellow bones in the sickly moonlight. Crumbling headstones listed at acute angles. Mausoleums hulked behind wrought iron gates. It was brutally cold here, almost as frigid as the Unseelie prison. My hair iced, my brows and nose hairs frosted. My fingers began to numb.

The transition from this Silver to the next was seamless. All of them were. Barrons was far more adept at stacking Silvers than Darroc had been and even more skilled, it seemed, than the Unseelie King.

I didn't even see the change in my environment coming. I suddenly had one foot in an icy cemetery and the other in a stifling desert of black sand, sun beating down on me. I glided forward into the searing heat and was instantly parched. Nothing attacked me on this scorched terrain. I wondered if the sun alone would keep certain trespassers out. The next mirror gave me fits. Abruptly, I was underwater. I couldn't breathe. I panicked and tried to back out.

But I hadn't been able to breathe in the Unseelie prison, either.

I stopped fighting it and half-swam, half-walked on the ocean floor of some planet—not ours, because we didn't have fish that looked like small underwater steamboats with whirling wheels of teeth.

My glassy lake offered a bubble of sorts, scaled it around me, and everything that came at me bounced off.

I was beginning to feel downright indestructible. Cocky. I put a little swagger in my rolling steps.

By the time I passed through half a dozen more "zones," I was beyond cocky. Every threat that came at me, my dark lake had an answer for. I was getting drunk on my own power.

From a landscape that would have been called "Midnight on a Far Star" if it had been a painting, I burst into a dimly lit room and blinked.

It was Spartan, Old World, and smelled *good*. Deep, drugging spices. Barrons. My knees felt soft. I smell him, I think of sex. I'm a hopeless case.

I knew instantly where I was.

Beneath the garage behind Barrons Books and Baubles.

41

I wanted to explore. I would have explored, except for the child crying.

Of all the things I expected Barrons to have secreted away from the world and protected so well, a child wasn't on my list.

Clues to his identity? Surely.

A luxurious home? Definitely.

A kid? Never.

Bemused, I followed the sound. It was faint, coming from below. The child was sobbing as if its world was ending. I couldn't tell if it was a girl or a boy, but the pain and sorrow it felt was soul-shredding. I wanted to make it stop. I *had* to make it stop. It was breaking my heart.

I moved through room after room, barely noticing my surroundings, opening and closing doors, looking for a way down. I was distantly aware that the true jewels of Barrons' collection were here, in his underground lair. I passed things that I'd seen in museums and now knew had been copies. Barrons didn't mess with copies. He loved his antiquities. The place hummed with OOPs somewhere. I would find them eventually.

But, first, the child.

The sound of it crying was killing me.

Did Jericho Barrons have children? Maybe he'd had one with Fiona?

I hissed, then realized how Fae I'd sounded and pretended I hadn't just done that. I stopped and cocked my head. As if he'd heard my tight-lipped exhalation, the crying got louder. Saying, *I'm here, I'm near, please find me, I'm so scared and alone.*

There had to be stairs.

I stalked through the place, yanking open door after door. The crying was getting on my last maternal-instinct nerve. I finally found the right door and stepped inside.

He'd taken serious precautions.

I was in a fun-house room of mirrors. I could see stairs in a dozen different places, but I had no way of distinguishing between reflection and reality.

And knowing Barrons as well as I did, if I went for the reflection, something very nasty would happen to me. He obviously cared a great deal about the protection of the child.

My dark lake offered, but I didn't need it.

"Show me what is true," I murmured, and the mirrors fell dark, one after the next, until a chrome staircase gleamed in the low light.

I moved silently down it, drawn by the siren lure of the child's sobs.

Once again, my expectations were shot.

The crying was coming from behind tall doors that were chained, padlocked, and engraved with runes. I shouldn't have been able to hear it at all. I was astonished I'd ever been able to hear Barrons roaring this far underground.

It took me twenty minutes to break the chains, wards, and runes. He obviously wanted this child protected to the hilt. Why? What was so important? What was going on?

When I pushed open the doors, the crying stopped abruptly.

I stepped into the room and looked around. Whatever I'd expected, it wasn't this. There was no opulence here, no treasure or collectibles. This was little better than Mallucé's grotto beneath the Burren.

The room was hewn from stone, a cave cleared out in the bedrock of the earth. A small stream ran through, appearing in the east wall, disappearing beyond the west. There were cameras mounted everywhere. He would know I'd been here, even if I walked back out right now.

In the center of the room was a cage that was twenty by twenty, made of massive iron bars, closely spaced. Like the doors, it was heavily runed. It was also empty.

I moved toward it.

And stopped, stunned.

It wasn't empty as I'd thought. A child lay in the cage, curled on its side, naked. He looked about ten or eleven.

I hurried to him. "Honey, are you all right? What's wrong? Why are you in there?"

The child looked up. I staggered and went to my knees on the stone floor, stupefied.

I was looking at the child from the vision I'd shared with Barrons.

Every detail of it was crystal clear in my head, as if I'd lived it yesterday—a rare glimpse into Barrons' heart. I could close my eyes and be back there again with him, that easily. We were in a desert.

It's dusk. We hold a child in our arms.

I stare into the night.

I won't look down.

Can't face what's in his eyes.

Can't not look.

My gaze goes unwillingly, hungrily down.

The child stares up at me with utter trust.

"But you died!" I protested, staring at him.

The boy moved toward me, came to stand at the edge of the cage and wrapped his small hands around the bars. Beautiful boy. Dark hair, gold skin, dark eyes. His father's son. His eyes are soft, warm.

And I'm Barrons, staring down at him . . .

His eyes say, I know you won't let me die.

His eyes say, I know you will make the pain stop.

His eyes said, Trust/love/adore/youareperfect/youwill alwayskeepmesafe/youaremyworld.

But I didn't keep him safe.

And I can't make his pain stop.

We'd been in the desert holding this child, this very boy in our arms, losing him, loving him, grieving him, feeling his life slip away . . .

I see him there. His yesterdays. His today. The tomorrows that will never be.

I see his pain and it shreds me.

I see his absolute love and it shames me.

He smiles at me. He gives me all his love in his eyes. It begins to fade.

No! I roar. You will not die! You will not leave me!

I stare into his eyes for what seems a thousand days.

I see him. I hold him. He is there.

He is gone.

But he's not gone. He's right here with me. The boy presses his face to the bars. He smiles at me. He gives me all his love in his eyes. I melt. If I could be someone's mother, I would take this child and keep him safe forever.

I push to my feet, moving as if I'm in a trance. I've held this child, inside Barrons' head. As Barrons, I loved him and I lost him. In sharing that vision, it became my wound, too.

"I don't understand. How are you alive? Why are you here?" Why had Barrons experienced his death? There was no question that he had. I'd been there. I'd tasted it, too. It was reminiscent of the regrets I'd felt about Alina . . .

Come back, come back, you want to scream . . . just one more minute. Just one more smile . . . one more chance to do things right. But he's gone. He's gone. Where did he go? What happens to life when it leaves? Does it go somewhere or is it just fucking gone?

"*How* are you here?" I say wonderingly.

He speaks to me, and I don't understand a word of it. It's a language dead and forgotten. But I hear the plaintive tones. I hear a word that sounds like Ma-*ma*.

Choking back a sob, I reach for him.

As I slip my arms through the bars and gather his small, naked body into my arms, as his dark head floats into the hollow where my shoulder meets my neck, fangs puncture my skin, and the beautiful little boy rips out my throat.

42

I die for a long time.

Much longer than I think it should take.

Figures I'd die slow and in pain. I pass out several times and am surprised that I regain consciousness. I feel fevered. The skin of my neck is numb, but the wound burns like I've been injected with venom.

I think I left half of my neck in the child's impossibly expandable jaws.

He began to change the moment I took him in my arms.

I managed to tear myself from his preternaturally strong grasp and stumble from the cage before he completed the transformation.

But it was too late. I'd been a fool. My heart had wed Barrons to a sobbing child and embraced sentimentality. I'd seen the chains, padlocks, and wards as Barrons' way of keeping a child safe.

What they'd really been was his way of keeping the world safe from the child.

I lie on the floor of the stone chamber, dying. I lose awareness again for a time, then am back.

I watch the child become the night version of Barrons' beast. Black skin, black horns and fangs, red eyes. Talk about homicidally insane. He makes the beast Barrons was in the Silvers seem downright genial and calm.

He bays continuously while he changes, head whipping from side to side, spraying me with his spittle and my blood, staring at me with feral crimson eyes. He wants to sink his teeth into me, shake me, and crush every last drop of blood from my body. The mark Barrons placed on my skull doesn't do a thing to defuse his bloodlust.

I am food and he can't reach me.

He rattles the bars of the cage and he howls.

He morphs from four to ten feet tall.

This is what I heard beneath the garage. This is what I listened to while looking at Barrons across the roof of a car.

This child, caged down here, forever imprisoned.

And I understand, as my lifeblood seeps out, that this is why he was bringing the dead woman out of the Silver.

The child had to be fed.

He held this child, watched him die. I try to think about it, wrap my brain around it. The child has to be his son. If Barrons didn't feed him, the child suffered. If he did feed him, he had to look at this monster. How long? How long had he been caretaker for this child? A thousand years? Ten? More?

I try to touch my neck, feel the extent of my wounds, but I can't raise my arms. I'm weak, dreamy, and I don't really care. I just want to close my eyes and sleep for a few minutes. Just a short nap, then I'll wake up and get busy finding something in my lake to help me survive this. I wonder if there are runes that can heal torn-out throats. Maybe there's some Unseelie in here somewhere.

I wonder if that's my jugular gushing. If so, it's too late, way too late for me now.

I can't believe I'm going to die like this.

Barrons will come in and find me here.

Bled out on the floor of his bat cave.

I try to summon the will to search my lake, but I think I lost too much blood too fast. I can't care, no matter how I try. The lake is curiously silent. Like it's watching, waiting to see what happens next.

The roaring in the cage is so loud, I don't hear Barrons roaring, too, until he's scooping me up into his arms and carrying me from the room, slamming doors behind him.

"What the fuck, Mac? What the fuck?" He keeps saying, over and over. His eyes are wild, his face white, his lips thin. "What were you thinking coming down here without me? I'd've brought you if I thought you'd be so stupid. Don't do this to me! You can't fucking do this to me!"

I look up at him. Shades of Bluebeard, I muse dreamily. I opened the door on his slaughtered wives. My mouth won't shape words. I want to know how the child is still alive. I feel numb. *He's your son, isn't he?*

He doesn't answer me. He stares at me as if memorizing my face. I see something move deep in his eyes.

I should have made love to this man. I was always afraid to be tender. I'm bemused by my own idiocy.

He flinches.

"Don't you think for a fucking minute you can put all that in your eyes, then die. That's bullshit. I'm not doing this again."

Got any Unseelie? I half-expect him to race above-ground to hunt one and bring it back. But I don't have that much time and I know it.

"I'm not good, Mac. Never have been."

What—true-confession time? my eyes tease. *Don't need it.*

"I want what I want and I take it."

Is he warning me? What could he possibly threaten me with now?

"There's nothing I can't live with. Only things I won't live without."

He stares at my neck, and I know it's a mess from the look in his eyes. Savaged and shredded. I don't know how I'm still breathing, why I'm not dead. I think I can't talk because I no longer have intact vocal cords.

He touches my neck. Well, at least I think he does. I see his hand beneath my chin. I can't feel anything. Is he trying to rearrange my internal parts like I once did to his, in the early-morning sun on the edge of a cliff, as if I could put him back together by sheer force of will?

His eyes narrow and his brows draw together. He closes his eyes, opens them again, and frowns. He shifts me in his arms and studies me from a different angle, glancing between my face and neck. Comprehension smooths his brow, and his lips twist in the ghastly smile people give you right before they tell you they have good news and bad news—and the bad news is really bad. "When you were in Faery, did you ever eat or drink anything, Mac?"

V'lane, I say silently. *Drinks on beach.*

"Did they make you sick?"

No.

"Did you drink anything at any time that made you feel like your guts were being ripped out? You'd want to die. From what I hear, it would have lasted about a day."

I think a moment. *The rape,* I finally say. *He gave me something. The one I couldn't see. I felt pain for a long time. Thought it was from the princes being inside me.*

His nostrils flare, and when he tries to speak, only a deep rattle comes out. He tries twice more before he gets it right. "They would have left you like that forever. I'm going to slice them into tiny pieces and feed them to one another. Slowly. Over centuries." His voice is as calm as a sociopath's.

What are you saying?

"I wondered. You smelled different afterward. I knew they'd done something. But you didn't smell like the Rhymer. You were like him but different. I had to wait and see."

Staring up at him, I take a fresh mental assessment of myself. I am beginning to feel my neck again. It burns like hell. But I can swallow.

Not dying?

"They must have been afraid they'd kill you with their—" He looks away, muscles working in his jaw. "An eternity of hell. You would have been *Pri-ya* forever." His face is tight with fury.

What did they do to me? I demand.

He resumes walking, carries me through room after room, finally stopping in a chamber nearly identical to the rear seating cozy in BB&B: rugs, lamps, chesterfield, fluffy throws. Only the fireplace is different: enormous, with a stone hearth a man can stand in. Gas logs. No wood smoke seeping out somewhere to give him away.

He props pillows against the arm and places me gently on the sofa. He moves to the fireplace and turns it on.

"The Fae have an elixir that prolongs life."

They gave it to me.

He nods.

Is that what happened to you?

"I said prolongs. Not turns you into a nine-foot-tall horned insane monster." He watches my neck. "You're healing. Your wounds are closing. I know a man that was given this elixir. Four thousand years ago. He smells different, too. As long as the Rhymer is never stabbed by the spear or sword, he lives, un-aging. He can only be killed in the ways a Fae can be killed."

I stare up at him. *I'm immortal?* I can move my arms again. I touch my neck. I feel thick ridges as the skin fuses back together. It's like when I ate Unseelie. I'm healing beneath my hands. I feel things crunching, moving in my neck, growing new and strong.

"Think of it as long-lived and hard to kill."

Four thousand years long-lived? I stare at him blankly. I don't want to live four thousand years. I think about that Unseelie, badly mutilated, left in my back alley. Immortality is terrifying. I just want my small lifetime. I can't even conceive of four thousand years. I don't want to live forever. Life is hard. Eighty or a hundred years would be just perfect. That's all I ever wanted.

"You might want to seriously reconsider carrying that spear. In fact, I may decide to destroy it. And the sword." He unbuckles the holster from my shoulder and throws it to the floor, near the fireplace.

I watch it clatter to a stop against the façade of the hearth, relieved. I can die. Not that I want to right now. I just like options. As long as I have the spear, I have options. I'm never getting rid of that thing. It's my date with a gravestone, and I'm human. I want to die one day.

"But he can't." It's the first complete sentence I speak since I was attacked. "Your son can't die, can he? No matter what. Ever."

43

If I'd never eaten Unseelie, healing miraculously would have messed with my head.

As it was, I pretended I *had* eaten Unseelie. I couldn't deal with the whole elixir-that-prolongs-life scenario. It made me want to kill Darroc all over again. Violently. Sadistically. With lots of torture.

He'd not only turned me *Pri-ya,* he'd planned for me to live that way eternally. I'd softened when I saw those pictures of him with Alina, imagining a different outcome for them, but now all softness vanished. If Barrons hadn't saved me—I couldn't even begin to imagine the horrors. I didn't want to. I would have been pathologically insane in a very short time. What if he'd locked me away, refused to give me what I needed? Kept me somewhere small and dark and—

I shuddered.

"Stop thinking about it," Barrons said.

I shivered. I couldn't help it. There really *were* worse things than dying.

"It didn't happen. I got you out and brought you back. It all worked out in the end. You're tough to kill. I'm glad."

I'd bled out, according to Barrons, several times. Too much of my throat had been torn away for my body to repair me quickly enough. While I'd been dead—or at least no longer breathing—my body had continued repairing itself. I'd regain consciousness, only to bleed out again. Eventually enough of me had been restored that I'd remained conscious for the rest of the process. I was covered with blood, crusted with it.

Barrons picks me up and is carrying me again. We pass through luxurious rooms, down stairs and more stairs, and I realize there are more than three levels beneath his garage. He has a whole world down here. I usually hate being underground. But this is different. There's a sensation of expansiveness, of space not being quite what it seems. I suspect he has more Silvers in here, many ways in and out. It's the ultimate survivalist fantasy. The world could be nuked, and life would go on down here, or we could pass through to some other world. With Barrons, I suspect, no catastrophe is ever final. He always goes on.

Now, so will I.

I don't like that. I've been reprogrammed, changed in so many ways. This one is going to be the hardest to deal with. It makes me feel less human, and I was already feeling detached. Am I part of the Unseelie King, now nearly immortal? I wonder if this is a loop. Are we reborn over and over again, to repeat the same cycles?

"Would it be so bad?"

"Are you reading my mind?"

"You're thinking with your eyes." He smiles.

I touch his face, and the smile vanishes. "Do it again."

"Don't be a jackass."

I laugh. But there's no amusement left in his face. It was swiftly erased.

He looks at me with cold, hard eyes. I see what's in

thcm now. To the rest of the world, they might seem empty. I remember thinking a few times myself that they were void of all humanity, but that's simply not true.

He feels. Rage. Pain. Lust. So much emotion, electric beneath his skin. So much volatility. Man and beast, always at war. I know now it's never easy for him. The battle he fights is nonstop. How does this man go on every day?

He stops and lowers me to my feet. He moves through the shadows, turns on a gas fire, and begins to light candles.

We are in his bedroom. It's like the Unseelie King's lair: opulent, luxurious, with an enormous bed, draped in black silk, black furs. I can't see past it. All I can see is myself there, naked with him.

I'm trembling.

I'm awed that I'm here. That he wants me.

He lights more candles near the bed. He picks up pillows and pushes them into a pile I remember from being *Pri-ya.*

In that long-ago basement, he mounded them beneath my hips. I sprawled over them with my head on the bed and my ass in the air. He would rub himself back and forth between my legs until I was begging, then push slowly into me from behind.

He places the last pillow on the pile, and looks at me. He jerks his head toward the pile of pillows.

"I watched you die. I need to fuck you, Mac."

The words slam into me like bullets, taking my knees out. I lean back against a piece of furniture—an armoire, I think. I really don't care. It holds me up. It wasn't a request. It was acknowledgment of a requirement to make it from this moment to the next, like *I need a transfusion, my blood has been poisoned.*

"Do you want me to?" There is no purr, or coyness,

or seduction in his voice. There is a question that needs an answer. Bare bones. That's what he's after. That's what he offers.

"Yes."

He strips his shirt over his head and I catch my breath, watching those long, hard muscles ripple. I know how his shoulders look, bunched, when he's on top of me, how his face gets tight with lust, as he eases inside me. "Who am I?"

"Jericho."

"Who are you?" He kicks off his boots, steps out of his pants. He's commando tonight.

My breath whooshes out of me in a run-on word: "Whogivesafuck?"

"Finally." The word is soft. The man is not.

"I need a shower."

His eyes glitter, his teeth flash in the darkness. "A little blood never bothers me." He glides toward me, in that way that barely displaces air. A velvet shadow in the darkness. He is the night. He always has been. I used to be a sunshine girl.

He circles me, looking me up and down.

I watch him, holding my breath. Jericho Barrons is walking naked circles around me, looking at me like he's going to eat me alive—in a good way, not like his son. As I watch him, emotion staggers me and I realize that I never completely thawed from what I'd done to myself back there on the cliff, when I'd believed he was dead. I'd stripped away so much of me in order to survive. When I'd realized he was alive, there were so many other things going on and I was angry because he hadn't told me, and I'd shoved the messy tangle away, refused to look at it. I'd walked through the past few months refusing to let any of what was happening really touch me. Refusing to accept the woman I'd become, denying that I'd even become it.

Now I thaw. Now I stand and look at him and realize why I never turned it all back on.

I *would* have destroyed the world for him.

And I couldn't face that. Couldn't stand what it said about me.

I want to slow this moment down. Once before, I ended up in bed with him inside me, but I was *Pri-ya*—it happened so quickly and without conscious choice that it was over before it began. I want this to happen in slow motion. I want to live every second like it's my last. I've chosen this. It feels incredible. "Wait."

His demeanor changes instantly, his eyes haze with crimson. "I haven't waited long enough?" His chest rattles. His hands are at his sides, curling, flexing. He breathes hard and fast.

In the flickering light, his skin begins to darken.

I stare at him. Just like that, lust to fury. I think he might launch himself on me, take me down, shredding my clothes as we go, and shove inside me before we even hit the floor.

"I'd never take it." His eyes narrow. Crimson stains the white, bleeds into them with tiny rivers. Suddenly his eyes are black on red, no whites at all. "But I won't tell you I haven't thought about it."

I inhale deeply.

"You're here. In my bedroom. You have no fucking idea what that does to me. If a woman comes to this place, she dies. If I don't kill her, my men do."

"Has a woman ever come to this place?"

"Once."

"Did she find her own way in? Or did you bring her?"

"I brought her."

"And?"

"I made love to her."

I jerk, turning with him, staring into his eyes. That he says those words about another woman makes me feel like launching myself at him, tearing off my clothes, and slamming him home inside me before we reach the floor. Erasing her. He wants to fuck me. He made love to her.

He's watching me closely. He seems to like what he sees.

"And?"

"When I was done I killed her."

He says it without emotion, but I see more in his eyes. He hated himself for killing her. He believed he had no choice. He succumbed to a moment of wanting someone in his bed, in his home, in his world. He wanted to feel . . . normal for a night. And she paid for it with her life.

"I'm not the hero, Mac. Never have been. Never will be. Let us be perfectly clear: I'm not the antihero, either, so quit waiting to discover my hidden potential. There's nothing to redeem me."

I want him anyway.

It's what he wanted to know.

I exhale impatiently and shove hair from my face. "Are you going to talk me to death or fuck me, Jericho Barrons?"

"Say it again. The last part."

I do.

"They'll try to kill you."

"Good thing I'm hard to kill." Only one thing concerned me. "Will you?"

"Never. I'm the one who will always watch over you. Always be there to fuck you back to your senses when you need it, the one who will never let you die."

I pull my shirt over my head and kick off my shoes. "What more could a woman ask?" I skinny out of my jeans but get a foot tangled up trying to get out of my underwear. I stumble.

He's on me before I hit the floor.

Since the moment I laid eyes on Jericho Barrons, I wanted him. I wanted him to do things to me that pink and clueless MacKayla Lane was shocked and appalled and . . . okay, yeah, well, utterly fascinated to find herself thinking about.

I admitted none of it to myself. How could a peacock lust for a lion?

I'd been as fancy as one of the proud males, in my useless plumage. I'd strutted around, stealing glances at the king of the jungle, denying what I felt. I'd assessed my tail and his killing claws and understood that if the lion were ever to lay down with the peacock—it would only be on a nest of bloody feathers.

It hadn't stopped me from wanting him.

It made me grow claws.

As I fall to the floor beneath him, I think, here I am now: a featherless peacock with claws. My lovely tail lost, in one ordeal or the other. I look in the mirror and have no idea what I am. Don't care. Perhaps I'll grow a mane.

Relief floods me when his body slams into mine. Barrons moves like a sudden dark wind. He's not only on me but pushing *in* me before we hit the floor.

Oh, God, yes, *finally*! My head slams back into wood but I barely feel it. My neck and back arch, my legs spread. My ankles are on his shoulders and I suffer no conflicts. There is only need and the answer to it all shoving inside me—sleek, hard, animal dressed up in the skin of a man.

I look up at him and he's part beast. His face is mahogany, his fangs are out. His eyes are Barrons. The look in them isn't. It makes me wild. I can be whatever I want to be with him. No inhibitions. I feel him growing harder, longer inside me.

"You can do *that*?" I gasp. The beast was bigger than the man.

He laughs, and it is definitely *not* a human sound.

I moan, I whimper, I writhe. It's incredible. He's filling me up, gliding deep and deliciously inside me where I've never felt a man before. Oh, God! I come. I explode. I hear someone roaring.

It's me. I laugh and keep coming. I think I scream. I use my claws and he bucks in me, sudden and rapid. He makes that sound in the back of his throat I'm so crazy about. I love that sound.

I'd walk through hell and back, smiling, as long as he was beside me. As long as I could glance over at him and our eyes would meet and we'd share one of those wordless looks.

"You haven't lost your feathers." His words are strange, guttural, forced out around fangs.

I'd snort, but then his tongue is in my mouth, my jaws are wide, and I can't breathe, and he's right. One day you *do* meet a man who kisses you and you can't breathe around it and you realize you don't need air. Oxygen is trivial. Desire makes life happen. Makes it matter. Makes everything worth it. Desire *is* life. Hunger to see the next sunrise or sunset, to touch the one you love, to try again.

"Hell would be waking up and wanting nothing," he agrees. He knows what I'm thinking. Always. We're connected. The atoms between us ferry messages back and forth.

"Harder. Deeper. Come on, Barrons. More." I feel violent. I am unbreakable. I am elastic around him. Insatiable. His hand is on the side of my neck, around my throat, half cupping my face. His eyes bore into mine. He watches every nuance, every detail of every expression, as if his existence depends on it. He fucks with the single-minded devotion of a dying man hunting God.

As he fills me, I wonder if—in the same way that sex makes its own unique perfume—we don't really "make" love. As in create, manufacture, evoke an independent element in the air around us, and if enough of us did it really well, for real, not just for the hell of it, we could change the world. Because when he's in me, I feel the space around us changing, charging, and it seems to set off some kind of feedback loop, where the more he touches me, the more I need him to. Having sex with Barrons sates my need. Then feeds it. Sates, then feeds. It's a never-ending cycle. I get out of bed with him, frantic to be back in it again. And I—

"—hated you for it," he says gently.

That was my line.

"I never get enough, Mac. Drives me bug-fuck. I should kill you for what you make me feel."

I understand perfectly. He is my vulnerability. I would become Shiva, the world-eater, for him.

He withdraws and I nearly scream from the emptiness.

Then he's lifting me into his arms and I'm on the bed, and he's spreading me over the mound of pillows, nudging my legs wide, and when he pushes into me from behind, I sob with relief. I'm whole, I'm alive, I'm—

I close my eyes and ride the mindless bliss. It's all I can do. Be. Feel. Live.

I'm *Pri-ya* again.

I always will be with this man.

* * *

Much later, I look up at him. He's on top of me, barely inside me. I'm swollen, hot, and fiercely alive. My hands are over my head. He likes to tease, an inch, maybe two, until I'm crazy with need, then drive it home hard. It undoes me every time.

I know part of what turns me on so hard, makes me so violent with lust, is that he's dangerous. I fell for the bad guy. I'm crazy about the one who's trouble. The alpha that doesn't play well with others and doesn't take orders from anyone.

What else would I expect? It's possible I'm part of the ancient creator of the Unseelie race.

He's kissing me. V'lane's name is long gone from my tongue. There's only him, and he's right: No other man would fit.

"Maybe there's nothing wrong with you at all, Mac," he says. "Maybe you're exactly what you're supposed to be, and the only reason you feel so conflicted about it is that you keep trying to bat for the wrong team." He thrusts deep, rocks his hips forward with a muscle I'd be willing to bet no human man had.

I arch my back. "Are you saying you think I'm evil?"

"Evil isn't a state of being. It's a choice."

"I don't think—"

My mouth is suddenly busy. By the time I get around to finishing my sentence, I have no idea what I was going to say.

We end up in the shower, an enormous affair of Italian marble and showerheads on all walls. A dozen feet long, six feet wide, it has a bench that's just the right height. I think we stay in there for days. He brings in food and I eat in the shower. I wash him, slide my hands over his beautiful body.

"When you die, do your tattoos disappear?" Wet, his hair is darker, glossy, his skin a deep bronze. Water runs over muscle, sprays off his erection. He's always hard.

"Yes."

"That's why they were different." I frown. "Do you come back exactly how you were when you died the first time?"

"Were you *Pri-ya* the entire time?"

I gasp and try to duck my head so he can't see my eyes. My eyes betray me sometimes, no matter how hard I try, especially when my feelings are intense.

He grabs my head and holds it with two fistfuls of my hair, forcing me to look at him.

"I knew it—you weren't!" His mouth is on mine, he has me against the wall. I can't breathe and I don't care. He is exultant. "How long?" he demands.

"What happens when you die?" I counter.

"I come back."

"Duh, obviously. How? Where? Do you eventually just stand up from your ashes again or something?"

I hear a rattle and suddenly he's on the floor, head back, muscles rippling, fighting to remain a man. He's losing the battle. He has talons. Black fangs slide from his mouth, gouging into his skin. I can tell he doesn't want to turn, but something I asked him has made him frenzied.

I can't stand watching him struggle. I wonder if anyone has ever tried to help Barrons. I answer, talk to him to keep him grounded in the here and now. "I knew what was happening from the moment you asked me what I wore to the prom." I drop to my knees beside him, take his head in my arms and cradle him at my breast. His face is half beast, half man. "I began to surface. It was like I was there but trying not to be there. I'm here, Jericho. Stay with me."

Later we sleep. Or I do. I don't know what he does. I'm exhausted and warm and feel safe for the first time in a long time, drifting off in Barrons' underground world, next to the king of beasts.

I wake to him pushing into me from behind. We've had sex so many times, so many ways, I can barely move. I've come so many times I think it's impossible for me to even *want* to come again, but then he's inside me and my body tells a different story. I need so badly I ache. I slip my hand down and, as soon as I touch myself, I come. He shoves into me deep, rocking into my climax. I'm on my side. He's tucked me into his body, spooned close. His arms are around me, his lips on my neck. Teeth graze my skin. When I stop shuddering, he pulls out and immediately I want him again. I push back with my rump and he's back. He goes slow, so slow it's torture. He thrusts, I clench. He withdraws, I lay tense, waiting. Neither of us says a word. I barely breathe. He stops and stays perfectly still for a while but not to tease. He likes being hard inside me. Connected, we lie there in silence. I don't want the moment to end.

But it does, and when we're separate, we don't speak for a long time. I watch the shadows flickering on a famous painting on the wall. He's not asleep. I can feel him back there, aware.

"Do you ever sleep?"

"No."

"That must be *hell*." I love sleeping. Curling up, napping, dreaming. I need to dream.

"I dream," he says coolly.

"I didn't mean—"

"Never pity me, Ms. Lane. I like what I am."

I roll over in his arms, touch his face. I let myself be tender. Trace his features, slide my fingers into his hair. He seems both put off and entranced by the way I'm touching him. I rearrange my head to accommodate the advantages of never sleeping. There are a lot. "How do you dream if you don't sleep?"

"I drift. Humans need to shut down to let go. Meditation accomplishes the same thing, lets the subconscious play. That's all you need."

"What happened to your son?"

"Aren't you question girl?" he mocks.

"He's why you want the *Sinsar Dubh*."

I feel the sudden violence in his body. It gusts like a sirocco, and just like that I'm inside his head and we're in a desert and I wonder with a strange sense of duality in which I am him and I am me why it always seems to come back to this place for him. Then . . .

I'm Barrons, and I'm on my knees in the sand.

The wind is kicking up; the storm comes.

I was stupid, so stupid.

Death for hire. I laughed. I drank. I fucked. Nothing mattered. I swaggered through life, a god. Grown men screamed when they saw me coming.

I was born today. I opened my eyes for the first time.

It all looks so different now that it's too late. What a grand fucking joke on me. I should never have come here. This is one battle-for-hire I should never have taken.

I hold my son and I weep.

The sky opens, letting the storm free. Sand comes, so thick it turns day into night.

One by one, my men fall around me.

I curse the heavens as I die. They curse me back.

There is black. Only black. I wait for the light. The Old Ones say there is light when you die. They say to run for it. If it goes away, you drift the earth forever.

No light comes to me.

I wait all night in the dark.

I'm dead yet I can feel the desert beneath my corpse, the abrasion of sand on my skin, up my nostrils. Scorpions sting my hands, my feet. Open, dead eyes crusted with sand watch the night sky as the stars pop and vanish, one by one. The darkness is absolute. I wait and wonder. The light will come. I wait, I wait.

The only light that comes for me is dawn.

I stand up, and my men stand up and we stare uneasily at one another.

Then my son stands up and I don't care. I spare no thought for the strange night that shouldn't have been. The universe is a mystery. The gods are fickle. I am and he is and that is enough. I toss him on my horse and leave my men behind.

"My son was killed two days later."

I open my eyes, blinking. I can still taste sand, feel the grit in my eyes. Scorpions crawl at my feet.

"It was an accident. His body disappeared before we could bury it."

"I don't understand. Did you die in the desert or not? Did he?"

"We died. It was only later that I pieced it together. Things rarely make sense while they're unfolding. After my son died the second time, he died many more times, simply trying to get back to me and come home. He was deep in the desert without conveyance or water."

I stare. "What are you saying? That every time he died, he came back in the same place he'd died that first time with you?"

"At dawn the next day."

"Over and over? He would try to make it out, die of heatstroke or something, then have to start all over again?"

"Far from home. We didn't know. None of us died for a long time. We knew we were different, but we didn't know about the dying. That came later."

I watch him and wait for him to speak again. This is the crux of Barrons. I want to know. I won't push.

"That wasn't the end of his hell. I had rivals who rode the desert, too. Death for hire. Many were the times we'd thinned each other's pack. One day, they found him walking the sands. They played with him." He looks away. "They tortured and killed him."

"How do you know this?"

"Because when I finally put things together, I tortured and killed a few of them and they talked while they died." His lips smile; his eyes are cold, merciless. "They set up camp not too far from where he was reborn every dawn and found him the next day. Once they realized what was happening, they believed he was demon spawn. They tortured and killed him over and over. The more he came back, the more determined they were to destroy him. I don't know how many times they killed him. Too many. They never let him live long enough to change. They didn't know what he was, nor did he. Just that he kept coming back. One day another band attacked, and they didn't have time to kill him. He was left alone, tied up in a tent for days. He got hungry enough that he turned. He never turned back. It was a year before we were hired to hunt the beast that was scouring the country, ripping out the throats and hearts of men."

I was horrified. "They killed him every day for a year? And you were hired to kill him?"

"We knew it was one of us. We'd all changed. We knew what we'd become. It had to be him. I hoped." His mouth twisted in a bitter smile. "I actually hoped it was my son." There was naked hunger in his eyes. "How long was he a child tonight? How long did you see him before he attacked you?"

"A few minutes."

"I haven't seen him like that in centuries." I could see him remembering the last time. "They broke him. He can't control his change. I've seen him as my son only five times, as if for a few moments he knew peace."

"You can't reach him? Teach him?" Barrons could teach anyone.

"Part of his mind is gone. He was too young. Too frightened. They destroyed him. A man might have withstood it. A child had no chance. I used to sit by his cage and talk to him. When technology afforded, I recorded every moment, to catch a glimpse of him as my son. The cameras are off now. I couldn't watch the recordings, looking for him. I have to keep him caged. If the world ever found him, they would kill him, too. Over and over. He's feral. He kills. That's all he does."

"You feed him."

"He suffers if I don't. Fed, sometimes he rests. I've killed him. I've tried drugs. I learned sorcery. Druidry. I thought Voice might make him sleep, even die. It seemed to hypnotize him for a time. He's highly adaptable. The ultimate killing machine. I studied. I collected relics of power. I drove your spear through his heart two thousand years ago, when I first heard of it. I forced a Fae princess to do her best. Nothing works. He's not in there. Or if he is somewhere, he is in constant, eternal agony. It never ends for him. His faith in me was misplaced. I can never—"

Save him, he doesn't say, and I don't, either, because if I'm not careful I'm going to start crying, and I know it would only make things worse for him. He's thousands of years past tears. He just wants release. Wants to lay his son to rest. Tuck him in and say good night forever, one last time.

"You want to unmake him."

"Yes."

"How long has this been going on?"

He says nothing.

He will never tell me. And I realize a number doesn't really matter. The grief he felt in the desert has never abated. I understand now why they would kill me. It's not just his secret. It's theirs, too. "All of you return to the place you first died every time you die."

He is instantly violent. I understand.

They kill to keep anyone from doing to them what was done to his son. It is their only vulnerability: wherever they come back at dawn the next day. An enemy could sit there, waiting for them, and kill them over and over again.

"I don't want to know where that is. Ever," I assure him, and mean it. "Jericho, we'll get the Book. We'll find a spell of unmaking. I promise. We'll put your son to rest." I feel suddenly vicious. Who had done this to them? Why? "I swear it," I vow. "One way or another, we'll make it happen."

He nods, folds his arms behind his head, stretches back on a pillow, and closes his eyes.

As the moments pass, I watch the tension leave his face. I know he's in that place where he meditates, where he controls things. What extraordinary discipline.

How many thousands of years has he been taking care of his son, feeding him, trying to kill him and ease his agony, if only for a few moments?

I'm back in the desert again, not because he takes me there but because I can't get the look on his son's face out of my head.

His eyes say, *I know you will make the pain stop.*

Barrons has never been able to. It never ended. For either of them.

The child, whose death destroyed him, has destroyed him every single day since. By living.

Dying, Barrons said, *is easy. The man who dies escapes, plain and simple.*

I'm suddenly glad Alina is dead. If the light comes for anyone, it came for her. She rests somewhere.

But not his son. And not this man.

I press my cheek to his chest, to listen to his heart beating.

And for the first time since I met him, I realize it isn't. Have I never heard his blood rush before? His heart pound? How could I not have noticed?

I look up at him to find him staring down his chest at me, an unfathomable expression in his eyes. "I haven't eaten lately."

"And your heart stops beating?"

"It becomes painful. Eventually I would change."

"What do you eat?" I say carefully.

"None of your fucking business," he says gently.

I nod. I can live with that.

He moves differently down here. He doesn't try to conceal anything. Here, he is himself and moves in that way that seems one with the universe, smooth as silk, flowing noiselessly from room to room. If I forget to pay attention to where he is, I misplace him. I discover he's leaning against a column—when I'd thought he *was* the column—arms folded, watching me.

I explore his underground lair. I don't how long he's lived, but it's clear he has always lived well. He was a mercenary once, in another time, another place, who knows how long ago. He liked fine things then, and his taste hasn't changed.

I find his kitchen. It's a gourmet chef's dream—stainless-steel top-of-the-line everything. Lots of marble and beautiful cabinets. Sub-Zero fridge and freezer well stocked. Wine cellar to die for. As I devour a plate of bread and cheese, I imagine him here all those nights when I trudged up to my fourth- or fifth-floor bedroom and slept alone. Did he pace these floors, cook himself dinner, or maybe eat it raw, practice dark arts, tattoo himself, go for a drive in one of his many cars? He was so close all that time. Down here, naked on silk sheets. It would have driven me crazy if I'd known then what I know now.

He peels a mango while I wonder how he managed to get his hands on fruit in post-wall Dublin. It's so ripe it drips down his fingers, his arms. I lick the juice from his hands. I push him back and eat the pulp off his stomach, lower, then end up with my bare ass on the cool marble of the island and him inside me again, my legs locked around his hips. He stares down at me, as if he's memorizing my face, watches me like he can't quite believe I'm here.

I sit on the island while he makes me an omelet. I'm ravenous, body and soul. Burning off more calories than I can eat.

He cooks naked. I admire his back and shoulders, his legs. "I found the second prophecy," I tell him.

He laughs. "Why does it always take you so long to tell me the important things?"

"You should talk," I say drily.

He slides the plate in front of me and hands me a fork. "Eat."

When I finish, I say, "You have the amulet, don't you?"

He catches his tongue in his teeth briefly and gives me a full-on smile. It says: *I'm the biggest baddest fuck and I have all the toys.*

We go back to his bedroom and I get the page from Mad Morry's notebook and the tarot card from my pocket.

He looks at the card. "Where did you say you got this?"

"Chester's. The dreamy-eyed guy gave it to me."

"Who?"

"The good-looking college-age guy that bartends."

His head moves funny, like a snake drawing back to strike. "How good-looking?"

I look at him. His gaze is cool. *If you want that kind of life, get the fuck out of my house now,* his eyes say.

"Nothing like you, Barrons."

He relaxes. "So, who is he? Have I ever seen him?"

I tell him when and where and describe him, and he looks puzzled. "I've never seen the kid. I saw an elderly man with a heavy Irish accent pouring drinks a few times when I came to get you, but no one like you're describing."

I shrug. "Point is, it's too late for the first prophecy to work." I hand him the page. "Darroc was convinced he was the one who could use the amulet. But I read his translation and it sounds like it could be you or Dageus. Or any number of men."

Barrons takes the parchment from me and scans it. "Why would he think it was him?"

"Because it says *he who is not what he was.* And he used to be Fae."

He turns it over, looks at Darroc's translation, then flips back to Mad Morry's prophecy.

"Darroc didn't speak Old Irish when I trained him and, if he picked it up since then, he didn't learn it very well. His translation is wrong. It's a rare dialect and gender neutral. It says *the one that is possessed . . . or inhabited.*"

"That's what the first prophecy said."

He looks at me and raises a brow. It takes me a moment to interpret his expression.

"You think it's me." Somehow that doesn't surprise me. As if some part of me always knew it was going to come down to this in the end: Me against the *Sinsar Dubh,* winner take all. It smacks of fate. I hate fate. I don't believe in her. Unfortunately, I think the bitch believes in me.

He moves to a vault behind the painting I'd been watching candlelight flicker over earlier and removes the amulet. It's dark in his hands. The moment he approaches me, it pulses faintly.

I reach for it. It blazes when I touch it. It feels right in my hands. I've wanted it since the moment I first saw it.

"You're the wild card, Mac. I've thought that since the beginning. This thing thinks you're epic. So do I."

Quite a compliment. I cup the amulet in my hands. I know this piece. I turn inward, hunting, searching. I've learned so much tonight, about him, about myself. In this place, I feel fearless. Nothing can touch me, nothing can do too much damage to me. I feel calmer than I've felt in a long time. If I can use this, I can find the spell to unmake his son. I can end their suffering.

Show me what is true, I say, and shake off my blinders. I quit trying to force myself on the truth to reshape it, and I let the truth force itself on me. What have I been hiding from? What monsters have been stalking me, waiting patiently for me to look at them?

I close my eyes and open my mind. Fragments of times forgotten flash past me so fast I see only blurs of color. I trust my heart to take me where I need to go and tell me when to stop.

The images slow, become static, and I am in another place, another time. It's so real, I can smell the scent of spiced roses nearby. I love the smell because it makes me think of her. I keep the roses everywhere. I look around.

I am in a laboratory.

Cruce is gone.

I watched him leave.

He loves me, but he loves himself more.

I finish the fourth amulet without him. The first three were imperfect. This one does what I want it to do.

Balances the scales between us.

She will shine as brilliantly in the night sky as do I. Giants mate with giants or not at all.

I will take it to my beloved myself.

I cannot make her Fae, but I will give her all our powers in other ways.

Perhaps I am a fool to give her an amulet capable of weaving illusion that could seduce even me, but my faith in my love knows no bounds.

My wings trail the floor as I turn. I am enormous. I am singular. I am eternal.

I am the Unseelie King.

44

Dusk comes hard-edged and violet.

Dancer'd like that thought. He's a poet, brilliant cool with words. Wrote a piece the other day 'bout murdering clocks 'cause they feck us up, keep us stuck in the past and keep us from living the day. Used to have this thing in my past riding me all the fecking time, but now she knows, and I say, fine, get the monkey off my back.

I shift, restless, staring down at BB&B. There's a limo out front. Pulled up hours ago, ain't moved since. Couldn't see who got out. Somebody changed the sign. I think it musta been Mac, and it cracks me up but I don't laugh from the belly like I used to. Swallow it instead.

Ain't like she ain't gonna try to kill me.

And I ain't gonna die, so.

There we are.

Guess somebody's gonna bite it.

Been watching the place off and on for days. Watching the watchers. Everybody's nervous. Chewing each other's heads off.

Book went nuts the other day. Turned some guy into a suicide bomb, walked him right into Chester's. Lots o' peeps died getting him outta there, blown up when it blew. They're paranoid out at the abbey. Think it's gonna be next. Ain't nobody can track the thing, 'cause Mac's gone missing.

So's Barrons.

Without 'em, we're stuck. Ain't nobody can sense the Book 'til it's on top of us. Dancer thinks it'll make a nuke one day. End us all. He says we gotta put it down fast.

I watch, knees up, arms around, perched on a water tower. Nobody looking this high.

I been shut out. Ro won't let me near none o' the action. Kat and Jo keep me in the loop. They don't know I killed Alina. Mac don't know, 'cause I just found out, but there's a *third* prophecy. Something 'bout mirror images and sons and daughters and monsters within being monsters without. Jo wasn't done translating yet but she was worried big-time. Seems the longer the Book's loose, the worse the odds get.

I heard Ry-O telling that white-haired dude with the freaky eyes that Mac's gotta die. But not before the Book gets shut down. Pissed him off real bad that it came into his club and tried to blow it. You don't mess with Ry-O.

He's got dudes on top of the bookstore. They move funny.

Jo's hanging on a roof a few buildings over, with Kat and her trusty little group of *sidhe*-sheep. *"Baaaaa,"* I say under my breath. They're staring through binocs. Never look my way. Only see what they 'spect to see. What she tells 'em to see. Dickheads. Pull your heads out, I think. Smell the sheep shit.

The things I know.

The Scots are on top of a five-story in the Dark Zone. They got binocs, too.

These eyeballs of mine don't need no help seeing. I'm supercharged, superwired, super-D! All-seeing, all-hearing, all-jamming, all the time.

I smell V'lane. Spice on the wind. Dunno where he is. Somewhere near.

Five days Mac and Barrons been gone. Since the night they tried to trap the Book.

Ro's blaming it all on Mac. First, she was glad Mac was gone. Said we didn't need her, didn't want her. But she came to her senses when it strolled into Chester's. See, she was there when the Book paid its little visit wearing a corset of dynamite, and ain't nothing Ro likes better than her own wrinkly ass. Gah. That's a visual I coulda done without.

Ry-O's blaming the Druids. Saying they must've got the chant wrong.

The Scots are blaming Ry-O. Saying evil can't trap evil.

Ry-O laughs and asks what the feck they are.

V'lane's pissed at everybody. Says we're all inept, puny mortals.

I snicker. Dude, got that right. I sigh, dreamy-like. Think V'lane's got the hots for me. Wanna ask Mac what she—

I rip open a protein bar and munch it, scowling. What was I thinking? As if I'm ever gonna ask Mac anything again. I shoulda hunted those feckers that killed Alina. Shoulda got rid of 'em. She never woulda known. I smile, thinking about killing 'em. I scowl, thinking about how I didn't.

"Dither much, kid?"

Voice like knives. I stiffen and try to freeze-frame out, but the feck's got my arm and he ain't letting go.

"G'off me," I spit around a mouthful of chocolate and peanut, thinking, *Who* uses *words like that?* But I know who it is, and he worries me 'bout as much as the Book does. "Ry-O," I say, real cool.

He smiles like I think Death must smile, all fangs and hard eyes that ain't never held an ounce of—

I breathe in sharp-like without meaning to, 'stead of swallowing, and choke on peanuts. Throat squinches up, can't breathe, start thumping my chest.

He dressing for Halloween? Ain't here yet.

Pounding my sternum ain't gonna work and I know it. I need the Heimlich but can't do it on myself 'less he lets go of me so I can slam myself into the ledge. I use superstrength to yank my arm free, practically pull it outta the socket.

He's still got me. Ain't goin' nowhere.

He manacles my wrist with long fingers and studies me. Watching me choke. Cold fecker. Watching me foam, my eyes get wild. I'm drooling! Dude—this is *so* not cool.

Gonna die up here on a water tower, choking on a fecking protein bar. Topple off, splat to the pavement. Everybody's gonna see.

Mega O'Malley croaks like a Joe!

No fecking way.

Just when I'm getting light-headed, he slams a fist into my back and I spit out a mangled mouthful. Can't breathe for a minute. Then screech it in. Air ain't never been sweeter.

He smiles. His teeth are normal. I stare at him. Mind playing tricks? I been watching too many movies.

"Got a job for you."

"No way," I say instantly. Ain't falling in with his crowd. Got the feeling you don't get to fall back out. You just fall. 'Til you hit bottom. Ain't going that low. Got trubs of my own.

"Didn't ask, kid."

"Don't work for nobody calls me kid."

"Let her go."

I screw my face up in a scowl. "Who sent the party invites for *my* water tower?" I'm pissed. Whatever happened to a little privacy?

One of the Keltars oozes from the shadows. Only seen him from a distance. Don't know how either of 'em got so close to me without me knowing. Freaks me. I got supersenses and they snuck up on me.

Scot laughs. But he don't look like a Scot no more. He looks sorta like . . . I whistle and shake my head sympathetically. He's going Unseelie Prince.

They forget me. Busy looking at each other. Ry-O folds his arms. The Scot does the same.

I take advantage of the moment. Ain't sticking around to find out what job Ry-O has in mind for me. Never wanna know. And if some dude turned dark side thinks he's gonna score redemption playing avenging angel for me, I got news for him. I don't want it.

My ticket to hell's already been punched, bags on board, steam whistle blowing.

I'm fine with it. Like knowing 'zactly where I stand.

I freeze-frame out.

No night. No day. No time.

We get lost in each other.

Something happens to me down there in the underground. I'm reborn. I feel peaceful for the first time in my life. I'm no longer bipolar. There's nothing I'm hiding from myself.

Being afraid is debilitating. I'll take truth over fear of it any day.

I am the Unseelie King. I am the Unseelie King.

I say it over and over in my mind.

I accept it.

I don't know how or why and may never, but at least now I've looked hard at the darkest part of me.

It really was the only explanation all along.

It's almost funny in a way. The whole time I was so worried about what everyone around me might be, *I* was the biggest bad of all.

That dark, glassy lake I've got is him. Me. Us. That's why it always terrified me. Somehow I managed to partition my psyche and store him away. Me. The parts of me that weren't born twenty-three years ago, if I actually was born.

I can't think of any scenario that explains how I came to be what I am. But the truth of my memory is indisputable.

I *did* stand in that laboratory, nearly a million years ago. I *did* create the Hallows and I *did* love the concubine and I *did* give birth to the Unseelie. That was all me.

Maybe that's why Barrons and I can't resist each other. We both have our monsters. "You really think evil is a choice?" I ask.

"Everything is. Each moment. Each day."

"I didn't sleep with Darroc. But I would have."

"Irrelevant." He moves inside me. "I'm here now."

"I was going to seduce the shortcut out of him so I could get the Book. Then I was going to unmake this world and replace it with another, so I could have you back."

He freezes. I can't see his face. He's behind me. It's part of why I can say it. I don't think I could say it to his face and see myself reflected in his eyes.

I wasn't going to unmake the world for my sister. I'd loved her all my life. I'd known him for only a few short months.

"Might have been a bit strenuous for your first attempt at creation," he says finally. He's trying not to laugh. I tell him I would have doomed mankind for him, and he tries not to laugh.

"It wouldn't have been my first attempt. I'm a pro. You were wrong. I *am* the Unseelie King," I tell him.

He begins moving again. After a while, he pulls me around and kisses me. "You're Mac," he says. "And I'm Jericho. And nothing else matters. Never will. You exist in a place that is beyond all rules for me. Do you understand that?"

I do.

Jericho Barrons just told me he loves me.

"What was your plan?" I ask much later. "When we got the Book locked down, how were you going to get the spell you wanted?"

"The Unseelie have never drunk from the cauldron. All of them know the First Language. I made a few deals, set things in motion."

I shake my head, frowning at myself. Sometimes I miss the most obvious things.

"But now I have you."

"I'll be able to read it." That was creepy. Now at least I knew why I had such a strong negative reaction to the *Sinsar Dubh*. All my sins were trapped between its covers. And the damn thing just wouldn't go away. I'd tried to escape culpability, and my culpability had had the nerve to take on a life of its own and hunt me.

I understood why it stalked me. Once it had become sentient—a mind with no feet, no wings, no method of locomotion and nothing else in all of existence quite like it, except me, and I'd obviously despised it—it must have hated me. And since it *was* me, it loved me, too.

The Book I'd written had become obsessed with me. It wanted to hurt me, not kill me.

Because it wanted my attention.

So many things made sense now that I'd accepted I was the king.

I'd wondered why the Silvers had always been so hard for me to get in and out of. "Cruce's" curse, which had really been cast by the other Unseelie Princes, had sensed me and tried to keep me out. Of course I knew my way around the black fortress and the Unseelie hell. It had been my home. Every step had been instinctive because I'd walked those icy paths millions of times, called greetings to the cliffs, wept for the cruel confinement of my sons and daughters. I understood why the concubine's memories had played out before my eyes but the king's had sort of slid into my brain. I knew now why I'd known the command to open the doors to the king's fortress.

I might be the king, but at least I was the "good" king. I preferred to think of myself as the Seelie King, because I'd eradicated all my evil. The obsessed maniac who'd done experiments on anything and everything to achieve his ends was out there in Book form, not inside me, and that was no small comfort. I'd chosen to get rid of my evil—I'd made a choice, like Barrons had said— and I'd been trying to destroy those blackest parts of me ever since.

Barrons was speaking. I'd forgotten we were talking.

"I'm counting on you being able to read it. Makes everything simpler. We just have to figure out how to capture it with three stones and no Druids. I'm damned if I'm letting those fucks near it again."

I looked down at the silver and gold chain, the stone housed in the ornate gilt cage. Did I even need the stones or the Druids to trap my Book, or was the amulet what

I'd been hunting for all along? I certainly fit into the "inhabited" or "possessed" category. I was the king of the Fae inside a female human's body.

I wondered how the concubine had lost the amulet. Who had taken it from her, betrayed me? Had someone abducted her, faked her death, then whisked her off to the Seelie court while I'd been insane with grief, busy divesting myself of my sins?

She never would have taken it off willingly, yet here it was, in the world of man. If someone had come for her, might she have cast it off rather than let it fall into the wrong hands, patiently sowing clues, taking her chances that one day events would align, I would remember, and we would escape whatever had been done to us and be together again? Too bad I didn't want to be with her.

She'd always hated illusion. When she'd planted gardens and added on to the White Mansion, she'd done it in the old ways. The Faery court reverted to nothingness if the Fae attending it failed to maintain it. The White Mansion had been fashioned differently and would stand the test of time with or without her, apart from anyone.

How had she become the Seelie Queen? Who had kidnapped her, interred her in a tomb of ice, and left her to a slow death in the Unseelie hell? What games were being played, what agenda was being pursued? I knew the patience of immortality. Who among the Fae had been biding their time, waiting for the perfect moment, the ultimate payday?

The timing would have to be flawless.

All the Seelie and Unseelie Princesses would have to be dead and the queen killed at the precise moment—there could be no contenders to the throne of matriarchal power—once whoever it was had merged with or acquired all the knowledge from the Book.

All the power of the Seelie Queen and the Unseelie King would be deposited in a single vessel.

I shuddered. That could never be permitted to happen. Anyone with that much power would be unstoppable by anyone, by any means. He or she would be undefeatable, uncontrollable, unkillable. In a word: God. Or Satan, with the home-court advantage. We would all be doomed.

Did they believe me dead? Gone? Apathetic? Think I would just stand by and let this happen? Was this unknown enemy responsible for the condition I was currently in—human and confused?

My power and the queen's magic. Who was behind this? One of the dark princes?

Perhaps it had been Darroc all along, and the Book had popped that plan like the grape his head had been. Perhaps Darroc had only been taking advantage of someone else's cunning, riding on the coattails, so to speak, of a more clever and dangerous foe.

I shook my head. The magic wouldn't have gone to him, and he'd known it. Eating Fae wasn't enough. The successor to Fae magic had to *be* Fae.

The concubine had awakened and said a Fae prince she'd never seen before, who had called himself Cruce, had entombed her.

According to V'lane, he'd brought Cruce to the original Queen of the Seelie (the bitch) and she'd killed him in front of my eyes.

Did I possess that memory?

I turned inward, searching.

I clutched my head as images slammed into me. Cruce had not died easily or well. He raged and ranted, was ugly at the end. Denied being the one, denied having betrayed me to the queen. I was ashamed of his death.

But who'd faked my concubine's death?

How had I been deceived?

Deceived.

Was that the key?

ONLY BY ITS OWN DESIGN WILL IT FALL, the prophecy said.

Limited in form, what was the Book's design? How did it get around and accomplish its ends?

Its currency was illusion. It deceived people into seeing what it wanted them to see.

Was that why the *fear dorcha*—who was probably one of my good friends if I had time to pick through all my memories—had given me the tarot card, pointing me toward the amulet?

The amulet could deceive even *me*.

I'd worried about giving it to the concubine for that very reason. What enormous love, what dangerous trust.

The Book was only a shadow of me.

I was the real thing, the king who'd made the Book.

And I had the amulet capable of creating illusions that could deceive us.

It was simple. In a contest of wills, I was the guaranteed victor.

I felt almost giddy with excitement. My deductions had the ring of truth to them. All arrows pointed north. I knew what had to be done. Today, I could put the Book down once and for all. Not inter it to *slumber with one eye open*, like the first prophecy had said, but defeat the monster. Destroy it.

After I'd gotten a spell of unmaking for Barrons. Ironic: I'd given all my spells over to a Book to get rid of them, and now I needed one back from it.

Once I had it, I would roust the traitor, kill him or her, restore the concubine to being the Seelie Queen (because I sure didn't want her, and she didn't remember anything, anyway), where she would grow strong enough to lead again. I would walk away, leaving the Fae to their own petty devices.

I would return to Dublin and become just-Mac.

That couldn't happen soon enough for me.

"I think I know what to do, Jericho."

"What would you want if you were the Book and it was the king?" Barrons asked later.

"I thought you didn't believe I *was* the king."

"It doesn't matter what I believe. The Book seems to."

"K'Vruck does, too," I reminded him. Then there was the dreamy-eyed guy. When I'd asked him if I was the Unseelie King, he'd said, *No more than I*. Was he one of my parts?

"Have an identity crisis later. Focus."

"I think it wants to be accepted, absolved—prodigal son and all. It wants me to welcome it back into me, say I was wrong, and become one again."

"That's what I think, too."

"I'm a little worried about the part where it says *once the monster within is defeated, so shall be the monster without*. What monster within?"

"I don't know."

"You always know."

"Not this time. It's your monster. Nobody can know another person's monster, not well enough to cage it. Only you can do that yourself."

"Speculate," I demanded.

He smiled faintly. He finds it amusing when I throw his own words back at him. "If you are the Unseelie King—and note the word 'if' there, I remain unconvinced—one might speculate that you have a weakness for evil. Once you acquire the *Sinsar Dubh*, it's conceivable that you would feel tempted to do what it wants. Instead of trying to lock it away, you might choose to relinquish human form and restore yourself to your former glory—take all the spells you dumped into it back and become the Unseelie King again."

Never. But I've learned never to say never. "What if I am?"

"I'll be there, talking you out of it. But I don't think you're the king."

What other possible explanation was there? Occam's razor, my daddy's criteria for conviction, and my own logic concurred. But with Barrons there to shout me back and my determination to live a normal human life, I could do it. I knew I could. What I wanted was here, in the human world. Not in an icy prison with a pale silvery woman, caught up in eternal court politics.

"I'm more concerned about what your inner monster might be if you're not the king. Any ideas?"

I shook my head. Irrelevant. He might be having a hard time accepting what I was, but he didn't know everything I knew, and there wasn't time to explain. Every day, every hour, that the *Sinsar Dubh* was free, roaming the streets of Dublin, more people would die. I had no illusions about why it kept going to Chester's. It wanted to take my parents from me. Wanted to strip away everything I cared about, leaving only it and me. As if it could force me to care about it. Force me to welcome its darkness back into my body and be one again. I now believed Ryodan had been right all along: It had been trying to get me to "flip." The Book thought if it took enough from me, made me angry and hurt enough, I wouldn't care about the world, only about power. Then it would conveniently appear and say, *Here I am, take me, use my power, do whatever you want.*

I inhaled sharply. That was exactly the frame of mind I'd been in when I'd thought Barrons was dead. Hunting the Book, ready to pick it up and merge with it and unmake the world. Believing I would be able to control it.

But I was on guard now. I'd experienced that grief once. Besides, I had Darroc's shortcut in my hand. I had the key to controlling it. I wasn't going to flip. Barrons was alive. My parents were well. I wouldn't even be tempted.

I was suddenly impatient to get it over with. Before anything could go wrong.

"I need to be certain you can use the amulet."

"How?"

"Deceive me," he said flatly. "And convince me of it."

I fisted my hand around the amulet and closed my eyes. Long ago, in Mallucé's grotto, it had not been willing to work for me. It had wanted something, had waited for what I'd thought was a tithe, as if I needed to spill blood for it or something.

I knew now it was much simpler than that. It had flared with blue-black brilliance for the same reason the stones did, because it recognized me.

The problem was I hadn't recognized myself.

I did now.

I am your king. You belong to me. You will obey me in all things.

I gasped with pleasure as it blazed in my fist, brighter than it had ever burned for Darroc.

I looked around the bedroom. I remembered the basement where I had been *Pri-ya*. I would never forget any of the details.

I re-created it now for us, down to the last detail: pictures of Alina and me, crimson silk sheets, a shower in the corner, a Christmas tree twinkling, fur-lined handcuffs on the bed. For a time, it had been the happiest, simplest place I'd ever known.

"Not exactly incentive to get me out of here."

"We have to save the world," I reminded.

He reached for me. "The world can wait. I can't."

PART

IV

This is the way the world ends
This is the way the world ends
This is the way the world ends
Not with a bang but a whimper.
—T. S. Eliot

Don't talk to it, beautiful girl.
Never talk to it.
—The dreamy-eyed guy

45

I knew the moment he began to reconsider.

I could feel the tension in his body, see the tightening around his eyes, which meant he was thinking hard and not liking the topic. "It's not enough of a plan," he said finally, and got out of bed.

It was nearly impossible to make myself move. I wanted to stay in bed forever. But until this was over, no one I cared about was safe and I wasn't going to be able to relax and get on with life. I pushed up, tugged on my jeans, buttoned the fly, and yanked my shirt over my head.

"What do you suggest? That we get everyone together and make them all hold the amulet? See if it responds to anyone else? What if it lights up for someone like, say, Rowena?"

He glared at me as I slipped the amulet around my neck and tucked it beneath my shirt, where it lay cool against my skin. I could see the strange dark light of it through my shirt. I tugged my leather jacket on over it and belted it.

It didn't flare with blue-black light for him. I knew if

it had, and he'd known what the second prophecy said, he'd have gone after the Book long ago.

"I don't like this one bit."

Neither did I, but I didn't see any alternative. "You helped make this plan."

"That was hours ago. Now we're about to walk out into the streets and you're going to pick the bloody thing up, believing in some prophecy scribbled by a mad washerwoman who used to work at the abbey, with no concrete idea what to do, trusting that the amulet will help you deceive it into submission. It's the ultimate in seductive evil, and you expect to wing it. The plan stinks. That's all there is to it. I don't trust Rowena. I don't trust—"

"Anyone," I finished. "You don't trust anyone. Except yourself, and that's not trust, that's ego."

"Not ego. Awareness of my abilities. And the limitless nature of them."

"You got killed on a cliff by Ryodan and me. Classic case of a time when a little trust might have gone a long way."

His eyes were black and bottomless. I was just about to look away when something moved in them. *I trust you.*

I felt like he'd handed me the keys to the kingdom. That sealed it: I could do anything. "Prove it. You've been training me since the moment I got here to make me strong enough, smart enough, tough enough to do whatever has to be done. I've been through hell and back and survived. Look at me. What is it you say? See me. You made me a fighter. Now let me fight."

"*I* fight the battles."

"You *are* fighting this battle. We're going after it together."

"Watching. Who's driving this motorcycle and who's in the bloody sidecar? I don't ride in the sidecar. I wouldn't even *own* a pussy bike with a sidecar." He looked aggrieved to the bottom of his soul.

"More than watching. Keeping me tethered, like you did when I was *Pri-ya* and couldn't find my way back. I never would have made it without you, Jericho. I was lost, but I could feel you there, grounding me, holding my kite string." He'd stalked into hell for me, sat down on my sprung sofa in my insane place, and kept me from being stuck there forever. He'd dragged me out by sheer force of will. He always would. "I need you," I said simply.

A haze of crimson stained his eyes. He pulled a sweater over his head, muscles flexing, tattoos rippling. "It's not too late," he said roughly. "We can let the world go to hell. There are other worlds. Plenty of them. We can even take your parents. Whoever you want."

I searched his eyes. He meant it. He'd leave with me, go through the Silvers, and live somewhere else. "I like this world."

"Some prices are too high. You aren't invincible. Merely long-lived and hard to kill."

"You can't protect me forever."

He gave me a look that said, *Are you crazy? Of course I could.*

You would ask me to live that way?

Key word there being: live.

Don't put me in a cage. I expect better from you.

He smiled faintly. *Touché.*

"We could see if it works for Dageus. He's inhabited, too, or so they say."

"Funny girl, aren't you? Over my dead body."

"Then stop tilting at windmills. You can't use the amulet. That leaves me, with you at my side. It's the only choice. You can't die—I mean, you can, but you'll always come back. And we know it won't kill me. We're perfect for this."

"Nobody's perfect for battling evil. It's seductive. When we find it, it's going to come at you with everything it's got."

I was braced for it. I knew it would. I took a deep, slow breath, filling my lungs, squaring my shoulders. "Jericho, I feel like my whole life has been pushing me toward this moment."

"That's it. Fate's a fickle whore. We're not going. Take your clothes off and get back in my bed."

I laughed. "Come on, Barrons. When have you ever run from a fight?"

"Never. And others paid for it. I won't have the same happen to you."

"I don't believe this," I said with mock horror. "Jericho Barrons is vacillating. Will wonders never cease?"

The rattle moved in his chest. "I'm not vacillating. I'm . . . ah, fuck."

Barrons doesn't lie to himself. He was vacillating and he knew it.

"The moment I laid eyes on you, I knew you were trouble."

"Ditto."

"I wanted to drag you between the shelves, fuck you senseless, and send you home."

"If you'd done that, I never would have left."

"You're still here anyway."

"You don't have to sound so sour about it."

"You're upsetting my entire existence."

"Fine, I'll leave."

"Try and I'll chain you up." He glowered at me. "*That's* vacillating." He sighed.

After a moment, he held out his hand.

I slipped mine into his.

* * *

The Silver in Barrons' study belched me out. I went flying across the room and slammed into the wall.

I was tired of the mirrors not liking me. When this was over, I wanted Cruce's curse lifted. In my free time, I might like exploring the White Mansion.

I frowned. But then again, I might not. Maybe I needed to cut all my ties with my past.

Barrons glided out behind me, looking urbane and unruffled as usual, dark hair and brows frosted, skin icy. "Stop," he ordered instantly.

My feet rooted to the floor. "What?"

"People on the roof. Talking." He stood still so long that the frost began to slide in droplets down his cheeks and neck. "Ryodan and others. The Keltar are near. They're waiting for—what the hell was that noise?" He strode past me and stalked from the study.

He pushed through the door that joined the rear, private residence part of the bookstore to the public portion.

I followed, hot on his heels. It was dark outside, drizzly with a light fog beyond the tall windows, and the interior was lit only by the soft amber glow of the recessed lights I left on all the time so the store would never be fully dark.

"Jericho Barrons," an elegantly cultured voice said.

"Who the fuck are you?" Barrons demanded.

I caught up with Barrons just in time to see a man step from the shadows in the rear conversation area.

He walked toward us, offering his hand. "I am Pieter Van de Meer."

Long and lean, with the impeccable posture of a man trained in martial arts, he was in his mid to late forties. Blond hair framed a Nordic face with deep-set pale-green eyes. He had the quietly watchful air of a snake, coiled but not about to strike unless he had to.

"Take one more step and I'll kill you," Barrons said.

The man paused, looking surprised and impatient. "Mr. Barrons, we don't have time for this."

"I'll decide what we have time for. What are you doing here?"

"I'm with the Triton Group."

"So?"

"Let us not play games. You know who we are," the man chided.

"You own the abbey, among other things. I don't like your kind."

"Our kind?" Pieter Van de Meer afforded a small smile. "We have watched you for centuries, Mr. Barrons. We are not a 'kind.' You are."

"And why am I not killing you now?" Barrons purred.

"Because 'my kind' is often useful, and you've long sought a way to infiltrate our ranks. You never succeeded. You are curious about us. I've brought something for the girl. It's time for the truth."

"What would anyone in the Triton Group know of truth?"

"If you will not hear me out with any degree of objectivity, perhaps you will listen to someone else."

"Get out of my store right now and I'll let you live. This time. There won't be another."

"We can't do that. You're on the cusp of making a grave mistake, and we have been forced to show our hand. It's her choice. Not yours."

"Who is us?" I'd been alternately eyeing Pieter and peering into the dimly lit conversation area, keeping a careful watch on the other figure seated there. There wasn't enough light to make out her features, but there was enough that I knew it was a woman. I had butterflies in my stomach and a strong sense of foreboding.

Pieter's pale-green eyes drifted from Barrons to me. His features softened.

I was instantly uneasy. He was looking at me like he knew me. I didn't know this man. I'd never seen him before in my life.

"MacKayla," he said gently. "How lovely you are. But I knew you would be. Letting you go was the hardest thing we ever did."

"Who the hell are you?" I didn't like him. Not one bit.

He extended a hand toward the person on the sofa.

She rose and stepped into the light.

I gaped.

Although time had worked delicate changes on her face, softening the jaw, brushing creases at the corners of the eyes and mouth, and her hair was much shorter now, barely brushing her shoulders, there was no doubt who she was.

Blond hair, blue eyes, beautiful. I'd seen her, twenty years younger, standing guard in a warded corridor at the abbey. She'd said: *You do not belong here. You are not one of us.*

I was looking at the last known leader of the Haven, Alina's mother.

Isla O'Connor.

"How—what—" I stammered.

"Please forgive me." The plea was soft in her words, anguished in her eyes. "You must know it was necessary. I had no choice."

Barrons said, "You died. I saw you. You were in a coma. I went to your funeral."

I jerked. He'd just confirmed it. She was Isla O'Connor. I didn't know why I cared. She wasn't my mother. Alina had been her only child. I was the Unseelie King.

"It's a long story," she said.

Barrons shook his head. "And one we're not listening to."

"But you must. Or you'll make a terrible mistake," Pieter said grimly. "And MacKayla will pay for it."

"He's right. We need to talk now, before it's too late." Isla didn't seem to be able to take her eyes off me. "*You* want to hear it, don't you?"

I shook my head. I didn't trust myself to speak. How did I keep getting so brutally blindsided by life? When we'd walked into the Silver, I'd fully expected to walk out the other side, get in a car, and go driving around, hunting for the *Sinsar Dubh*.

Not for one moment had I entertained the possibility that Isla O'Connor might be waiting for us in the bookstore, long black limousine parked out front, a wide-shouldered chauffeur by the passenger doors, scanning the street up and down. I was willing to bet that beneath that dark uniform I'd find a gun or two. What was the Triton Group, besides the company that owned the abbey? Why did Barrons dislike them so much? What was Isla—one more person who was supposed to be dead but wasn't—doing here?

Her fine-boned features crumpled and tears spilled down her cheeks. "Oh, darling, giving you up was the hardest thing I ever did. If you will hear nothing else from me, hear that. You were my baby. My sweet, help-less baby, and they said you were going to doom the world. They would have killed you if they'd known about you! Both my daughters were in danger. We all knew about the prophecy. Knew it had been foretold that sisters would be born to one of the most potent bloodlines. Rowena was watching me. She'd hated me since the day my talents began to manifest. She wanted her daughter, Kayleigh, to become Haven Mistress, wanted the O'Reillys to run the abbey forever. She never forgave Nana for turning her back on the order. She would have done anything to get rid of me. If she'd known I was pregnant again . . . I had no choice. I had to give you up and go away, pretend to be dead."

"You weren't pregnant when I helped you leave the abbey," Barrons said coolly.

"Nearly five months. I carried well and dressed to hide it. It was a miracle my baby wasn't injured when I escaped. I was so afraid I would lose her." More tears spilled.

I was still shaking my head. I didn't seem to be able to stop.

"Oh, MacKayla! It was torture every day, knowing you were out there, being raised by someone else, knowing that I could never see you or Alina again without putting you in danger. But you're here now, and you're about to do something that would have terrible consequences. It's time for the lies to stop. You need to know the truth."

I shoved my fists in my pockets and turned away.

"Don't turn your back on me," she cried. "I'm your mother!"

"Rainey Lane is my mother."

"Unkind and unfair," Pieter said. "You aren't even giving her a chance."

"Why do you care?" I said irritably.

"Because I'm her husband, MacKayla. And your father."

46

I had brothers: Pieter, Jr., who was nineteen, and Michael—everyone called him Mick—who was sixteen. They showed me pictures. We looked alike. Even Barrons seemed rattled.

"We staged your mother's death, cremated a Jane Doe, and smuggled the two of you from the country. Took you to the States and did our best to find you a good home far from danger." Pieter took Isla's hand and clasped it between his own. "Your mother nearly didn't survive it. She didn't speak for months afterward."

"Oh, Pieter, I knew it had to be done. It was just—"

"Hell," he said flatly. "It was absolute hell giving them up."

I jerked. They were saying all the things I wanted to hear. It was breaking my heart. I had parents. Brothers. I'd been born. I belonged. I only wished Alina had lived to see this day. It would have been perfect.

"You said you had something important to tell her. Say it and get out," Barrons ordered.

I looked at Barrons, torn. Part of me wanted to tell him to be quiet so I could hear more, and part of me wanted them to go away and never come back. I'd just gotten my head wrapped around one reality. Now they wanted me to abandon that reality and embrace a new one. How many times was I supposed to decide who I knew and what I was, only to learn I was wrong? I was no longer feeling bipolar, I was feeling schizophrenic, with multiple personalities.

"If I'm your daughter, then why do I have memories that belong to the Unseelie King?"

Isla gasped. "You do?"

I nodded.

"I told you she might do it," Pieter reminded.

"Who?" I demanded. "Do what?"

"The Seelie Queen came to see us shortly after the Book escaped, before we left Dublin. She said she would do everything in her power to help recover it," Pieter said.

"She was very interested in you," Isla said grimly. "You were barely three months old. I remember like it was yesterday. You had on a pink dress with tiny flowers and a rainbow hair ribbon. You couldn't stop looking at her. You kept cooing and reaching for her. The two of you seemed fascinated by each other."

"We were afraid then that the queen had meddled with you. She's notorious for that. She looks to the future and tries to adjust minuscule events, nudging here and there to achieve her ends," Pieter said. "A few times I was almost certain someone had been in your nursery moments before I walked in."

"And you think she planted memories of the Unseelie King? How would she have any to plant? I thought she drank from the cauldron. It would have erased everything she knew."

"Who could say with her?" Isla shrugged. "Perhaps they were false memories, cleverly crafted, or lifted from another. Perhaps she never truly drank from the cauldron. Some say she pretends."

"Who gives a fuck? What did you come here for?" Barrons said impatiently.

Isla looked at him as if he must be crazy. "You've been taking care of her, and for that we can't thank you enough, but we've come to take her home."

"She *is* home. And she's got a world to save."

"We'll take care of that," Pieter said. "It's what we do."

"Bang-up job you've been doing so far."

Pieter gave him a look of rebuke. "Not as if you've been doing any better. We've been directing the majority of our efforts to hunting the amulet. The true one."

I narrowed my eyes. "Why?"

"The Triton Group has been searching for it for centuries for various reasons. But recently it became critical that we find it, because we've discovered it's the only way to re-inter the Book," Pieter said. "A representative from our company heard—too late—about the auction where it was sold. We arrived at the Welshman's castle shortly after Johnstone's massacre. But the Goth punk seemed to vanish into thin air."

"Thick rock," I muttered. I would never forget my hellish incarceration beneath the Burren.

"We had no idea where it was for months. We suspected Darroc had it but couldn't get any of our people close enough. He had no tolerance for humans. Then we received reports that MacKayla had infiltrated his camp and was at his right hand." His gaze glowed with pride. "Well done, darling! You are as brilliant and resourceful as your mother."

"You said 'the true one,' " I said.

"According to legend, the king made many amulets," Isla replied. "All capable of sustaining varying degrees of illusion. Used together, they are formidable. But only the last one he made can deceive the king himself. The Book has grown too powerful to be stopped by any other means. Illusion is the only weapon that will work against it."

"We were right!" I exclaimed, looking at Barrons.

"The prophecy is clear. The one who was inhabited must use the amulet to seal it away."

"Already on it," Barrons said coolly.

"It's not your fight," Pieter said gently. "We started this. We will end it."

I sat forward on the edge of the sofa, elbows on my knees. "What are you saying?"

"Your mother is the one who has to do it. Although if you're anything like her, darling, you think it's your problem. That's what we were worried about, why we rushed here tonight. Isla is 'the inhabited.' Twenty-three years ago, when the Book escaped, it possessed her, inhabited her. She knows it. She has been it. She understands it. And she's the only one who can lay it to rest."

"It never leaves a human alive," Barrons said flatly.

"It left Fiona alive," I reminded.

"She'd been eating Unseelie. She was different."

"Isla was able to wrest it from her body," Pieter said. "She is the only one we know of that has ever been able to resist to the point where it jumped from her while she was still alive and took another, more complacent host."

Barrons didn't look remotely convinced. "But not before it made her kill most of the Haven."

"I never said it was easy," Isla said softly, eyes dark with remembered grief. "I despise what it made me do. I live with it every day."

"But it's been tracking *me*," I protested.

"Sensing your bloodline, looking for me," Isla said.

"But I'm epic," I said numbly. Wasn't I? I was so tired of not knowing my place in things.

Was I going to doom the world? Was I the concubine? Was I the Unseelie King? Was I even human? Was I the person who was supposed to re-inter the Book?

The answer was no to all of the above. I was just Mac Lane, bumbling around, getting in the way a lot, and making stupid decisions.

"You are, darling," Isla said. "But this isn't your battle."

"Your destiny is another day," Pieter said. "This is only the first of many battles we'll be called upon to fight. There are dark times ahead. Even with the Book contained, there's still the matter of the walls between realms. They can't be rebuilt without the Song of Making. We have our work cut out for us." He smiled. "Your brothers have their talents, too. They can't wait to meet you."

"Oh, MacKayla, we'll be a family again!" Isla said, and began to cry. "It's all I ever wanted."

I looked at Barrons. He wore a grim expression. I looked back at Pieter and Isla. It was all I'd ever wanted, too. I wasn't the king. I'd been born. I was a person with a family. I couldn't wrap my head around it. But my heart was already trying.

Family reconciliations aside, Barrons didn't like the change in the game plan, and neither did I.

We'd spent months building to this moment, and now, on the eve of battle, in walked my biological parents, telling us we were no longer necessary. They would fight the war and finish it.

It chafed.

"Can you track it?" Barrons demanded.

Pieter answered. "Isla can. But it can sense her, as well, which made it too dangerous for her to be in Dublin until we were certain MacKayla had the amulet."

"How did you know I had it?" I said.

"Your mother said she felt you connect with it tonight. We came at once."

"I thought I felt you connect with it once before, at the beginning of October last year," Isla said, "but the feeling was gone almost as suddenly as it came."

I blinked. "I *did* touch it last October. How did you know that?"

"I have no idea," she said simply. "I felt the joining of two great powers. Both times I felt *you*, MacKayla. I felt my daughter!" Her face crumpled. "I felt Alina once, too." She looked away, stared into the cold fireplace for a long moment, then shivered. "She was dying. Could we please have a fire?"

"Of course," Pieter said immediately. He rose and moved to the fireplace, but Barrons beat him there.

He glared at Pieter. *You may be trying to claim the woman,* his eyes said, *but make no mistake, she and the fucking fireplace are mine.*

After a long moment, Pieter shrugged and moved back to the sofa.

"We'll sleep on it," Barrons said. "Leave now. We'll be in touch tomorrow."

Pieter snorted. "We can't leave, Barrons. This has to end here, tonight, one way or another. There's no time to waste."

I couldn't stop looking at Isla. There was something about her face. Looking at her made me think of Rowena. I guess because the old woman had persecuted us for so long. "Why does it have to end tonight?"

Isla gave me an odd look. "MacKayla, don't you feel it?"

"Feel wh—" I broke off. I hadn't been trying to feel it. I'd been keeping my *sidhe*-seer volume all the way down for so long it had become instinct. "Oh, God, the *Sinsar Dubh* is heading straight for us." I opened my senses as far as I could. "It's . . . different." I looked at Isla, who nodded. "It's more intense. Like it's all pumped up and ready. It's been waiting for this." My eyes widened. "It's got a suicide bomber again, and it's going to blow us all to hell if we don't stop it!"

"It knows I'm here," Isla said. Her face was pale, but her eyes were narrowed with determination that I recognized. I'd seen it in my own face. "It's all right," she said with a tight smile. "I'm ready, too. It may have stolen my children and torn my family apart twenty-three years ago, but tonight we're putting it back together."

Pieter and Isla excused themselves for a moment and stepped away, talking in hushed, urgent tones.

I sat on the chesterfield with Barrons, watching them. This was all so surreal. I felt as if I'd stepped through the Silver into an alternate reality, one with a happily-ever-after. This was exactly what I'd wanted: a family, a safe haven, no responsibility to save the day.

Then why did I feel so deflated and off kilter?

Out there in the night, I could feel the Book coming. It had slowed for some reason, nearly stopped. I wondered if it was swapping "rides." Maybe it had found a better one.

In spite of myself, despite my love for Jack and Rainey, looking at my biological parents was doing something funny to me. Knowing that they hadn't wanted to give me up had released a knot of tension I hadn't even known I'd been carrying. I guess some part of me had felt like the devil-child that everyone was afraid of, who'd been banished only because no one had wanted to kill a baby. But all these years my real parents had been out there, missing Alina and me, longing for us. They'd hated giving us up and had done so only for our own safety. We were connected by a mother–daughter bond. We were going to be a family again. I had so many questions!

"I don't trust a bloody thing about them," Barrons said. "This is bullshit."

Barrons was perfectly paranoid. *Perfect awareness,* he called it. It was exactly what I expected him to say. "It *is* hard to believe," I murmured.

"Then don't."

"Look at her, Barrons. She's the woman that warded me out at the abbey, the last leader of the Haven. The woman you picked up that night. For heaven's sake, we look alike!" When I'd first arrived in Dublin, we hadn't. I'd been soft and curvy and still holding on to a smidge of baby fat in my face. Now I was like her, older, leaner, my face less round, my features more distinct.

He glanced between us. "She could be a cousin."

"She could also be my mother," I said drily. "And if she is, I'm not the Unseelie King." There went the weight of countless sins from my shoulders. Believing I was the ultimate villain, responsible for so many twisted births and billions of deaths, had been a crushing load to carry. "Maybe they're right, Barrons. Maybe this never was my battle. Maybe Alina and I just got caught in the crossfire. The Book sensed us as part of her bloodline and harassed us, screwed up our lives."

"Dani killed Alina," he reminded sharply.

Why did he have to remind me of that now? I turned to scowl at him.

Face contorted, he was staring at me, dark eyes wild, roaring Rowena's name so loud I was surprised the windows didn't shatter.

I blinked. He was just Barrons again. Looking at me strangely.

"Are you okay?"

"What did you just say?"

"I said, are you okay?"

"No, what did you say before that?"

"I said Dani killed Alina because of Rowena, never doubt it. What's wrong? You're white as a sheet."

I shook my head, embarrassed. Then I jerked and my head whipped toward the window. "Oh, no!" The *Sinsar Dubh* had begun moving again, rapidly.

"It's coming!" Isla cried at the same moment.

"How long?" Pieter demanded.

"Three minutes, maybe less. It's in a car," Isla said.

I needed to know we were both sensing it in the same general vicinity. With two of us, we would be harder to deceive. I'd be damned if what had happened the last time we'd tried to corner it was happening again. "Where do you sense it?"

"Northwest of the city. Three miles at the most."

I was relieved. That was exactly where I felt it, too.

"What part of this place is most securely warded?" Isla asked Barrons.

He gave her a look. "All of it."

"What's the plan?" I said.

"You must give your mother the amulet," Pieter said.

I touched the chain around my neck and looked at Barrons. He took a slow breath and opened his mouth. It stretched wide on a soundless roar.

I blinked and looked again. He was composed and urbane as ever.

"It's your call," he said. "You have to decide this one."

I felt so strange. Mac 1.0, bartender, daydreamer, and professional sun worshipper, would have wanted nothing more than to pass off any and all responsibility to someone else. To be taken care of. Not to be the one taking care. I no longer knew that woman. I liked making the hard decisions and fighting the good fight. Getting to lay down responsibility no longer felt like relinquishing a burden—it felt like being shut out of the most important parts of my life.

"MacKayla, time is of the essence," Pieter said softly. "You don't have to fight anymore. We're here now."

I looked at Isla. Her blue eyes shimmered with unshed tears. "Listen to your father," she said. "You'll never be alone again, darling. Give me the amulet. Release your burden and let me carry it for you. It was never meant to be yours."

I looked back at Barrons. He was watching me. I knew him. He wouldn't force my hand.

I did a double take. Who was I kidding? Of course Barrons would try to force my hand on this. He wanted the spell of unmaking to end his son's life. He'd been hunting it for nearly his entire existence. He would stomp and argue and roar. He'd never get this close only to back off and give me space to make my own decisions.

"Don't do it," he snarled. "You promised."

"The *Sinsar Dubh* has entered the city," Isla said simply. "You must decide."

I could feel it, too, rushing toward us, as if it knew that if it hurried, it could catch us with our pants down, me undecided, all of us exposed by my inability to commit.

I moved toward Isla, playing the chain through my fingers. How could I accept that I didn't have to fight this battle? I'd been preparing for it. I was ready. Yet here she stood, telling me I didn't need to worry. I wouldn't doom the world, and I didn't need to save it. Others had been preparing for the same moment and were more qualified.

That surreal feeling was back. And what was that buzzing at my ear? I kept thinking I was hearing Barrons roaring, but every time I looked at him, he wasn't saying a word. "I need a spell from the Book," I said.

"Once it's locked up, we can get anything you need.

Pieter knows the First Language. It's how your father and I met, working on ancient scrolls."

I stared into the face so like my own but older, wiser, more mature. I wanted to say it, needed to do this, at least once. I might never get the chance again. "Mother," I tried the word on my tongue.

A tremulous, radiant smile curved her lips. "My dear, sweet MacKayla!" she exclaimed.

I wanted to touch her, be in her arms, breathe in the scent of my mother, and know I belonged. I focused on my only memory of her, deeply buried until this moment. I focused on it hard, thinking about how treasured it was. How I couldn't believe I'd forgotten it all these years. How my child's mind had taken a single snapshot: Isla O'Connor and Pieter staring at me with tears in their eyes. They'd been standing by a blue station wagon, waving good-bye to us. It was pouring rain, and someone had held a bright pink umbrella with green cartoon flowers above my baby carriage, but the wind had whisked a chill mist beneath it. I'd flailed my tiny fists, cold and crying, and Isla suddenly broke away from Pieter to tuck the blanket more securely around me.

"Oh, darling, it was the hardest thing I ever did that day in the rain, letting you go! When I tucked you in, I wanted so desperately to snatch you up and keep you with us forever!"

"I remember the umbrella," I said. "I think it must be where I got my love of pink."

She nodded, eyes shining. "It was bright pink with green flowers."

Tears stung my eyes. I stared at her a long moment, memorizing her face.

Isla opened her arms. "My daughter, my beautiful little girl!"

Bittersweet emotion flooded me as I moved into my mother's arms. When they closed warm and comforting around me, I began to cry.

She stroked my hair and whispered, "Hush, darling, it's all right. Your father and I are here now. You don't need to worry about a thing. It's all right. We're together again."

I cried harder. Because I could see the truth. Sometimes it's there in the flaws.

And other times it's there in too much perfection.

My mother's arms were around my neck. She smelled good, like Alina, of peaches-and-cream candles and Beautiful perfume.

And I didn't have a single memory of this woman.

There'd been no blue station wagon. No pink umbrella. No day in the rain.

I slid the spear from my holster and drove it up between our bodies.

Straight into Isla O'Connor's heart.

47

Isla inhaled, sharp with pain, and went stiff in my arms, clutching at my neck.

"Darling?" Blue eyes stared into mine, blank and confused. She was Isla.

"You stupid little bitch!" Blue eyes stared into mine, fiercely intelligent, furious, hard with rage. She was Rowena.

"How could you do this to me?" Isla cried.

"If only I'd killed you that night in the pub!" Blood-tinged spittle sprayed from Rowena's lips.

"MacKayla, my darling, darling daughter, what have you done?"

"Och, and 'tis because of you all this happened!" Rowena spat. "You bloody damned O'Connors, bringing naught but trouble and misfortune to us all!"

I felt her legs buckle, but she caught herself on my shoulders and didn't go down. She was one tough old woman.

I shuddered. I'd never been talking to Isla. It was Rowena all along, carrying the *Sinsar Dubh*, possessed by it. But now she was dying, and the Book's ability to maintain a convincing illusion was dying with her. She was flashing back and forth between the illusion of Isla and the reality of Rowena.

"Did you kill my sister?" I shook the old woman so hard her hair spilled loose from its tight bun.

"Dani killed your sister. And the two of you were always cozying up. Och, and I imagine you feel differently about her now!" She cackled.

I used Voice. *"Did you order her to do it?"*

She writhed, mouth contorting. She didn't want to answer me. She wanted me to suffer. "Yesss!" the word exploded in an unwilling hiss. I hoped it hurt.

"Did you use your mental coercion to make her do it?"

Her jaw locked and her eyes narrowed to slits. I repeated the question, rattling the windows in the study with the multilayered thunder of compulsion.

"Yesss! 'Twas my right. 'Tis why I was given such gifts! *And* the cleverness to use them. It requires the layering of many subtle commands, knowing precisely where to nudge. No other could have done it." She gave me a smug stare, proud of herself.

I grimaced and looked away, stilled by the horror of it.

Here it was at last—the truth of my sister's murder. I finally knew what had happened to Alina.

The day she'd discovered Darroc was the Lord Master, the same day she'd called me, crying, and left a message, was the day she'd been killed—but not at all for the reasons I'd thought. If it hadn't been for Rowena, Alina would have lived through that day.

I'd have gotten a new phone, called her in a few days, and she'd have answered. Life would have gone on for the two of us. She and Darroc would probably have gotten back together, and who knew how things might have turned out? Her message had been misleading from the beginning, but she'd had no idea this old woman was her enemy.

This bitch, this meddling tyrant who believed it was her right to use her "gifts" to force a child to kill, had ordered Dani to take Alina to a dark alley to be murdered.

My hands trembled. I wanted to kill her the same way.

Had Rowena specified the monsters Dani should find and leave Alina with? Had she insisted Dani stay and watch the deed be done? Had Alina begged? Had they both wept, knowing the wrongness of it? I'd been forced to want sex. Dani had been forced to murder. My sister. At thirteen. I couldn't imagine what it would feel like to watch yourself kill someone you didn't want to kill. Had Dani known Alina? Liked her? And been compelled to kill her anyway?

"And I tried to kill you in your cell when you were a mindless whore, but you wouldn't die! I slit your throat. I suffocated you. I gutted you, I poisoned you! Still you came back. Finally I painted over the wards to let them take you and destroy you!"

"*You* painted over the—you were going to give me back to the princes?" I was flabbergasted. She *had* tried to kill me. I hadn't just dreamed it. I shoved both thoughts from my mind. I wanted answers and, from the look of her, she wasn't going to last long. Voice echoed out of me, reverberating off the walls. "*Why did you kill Alina?*"

"Are you daft? She consorted with the enemy! My spies followed her to his house and saw him with Unseelie! 'Twas reason enough! Then there was the prophecy! I'd've killed her at birth if I could've. If I'd known she was still alive, I'd've hunted her!"

"Did you know who she was when you killed her? Did you know she was Isla's daughter?"

"Och, of course," she sneered. "I had Dani lure her to us when my girls told me they'd spotted an untrained *sidhe*-seer, same as I sent her to you! Alina Lane, she called herself, but I knew the instant I saw her who she was. Isla, all over again, plain as day! And my Kayleigh dead because of her mother!"

I wanted to strangle her with my bare hands, choke the breath out of her. Over and over.

"Did you know who I was when you saw me that first night?"

A troubled look creased her brow. "'Tis impossible. *You* can't be. You weren't born. I'd have known were Isla pregnant! Women talk. They never spoke of it!"

"How did the Book get out?" I demanded.

A crafty light entered her eyes. "You think I let it out. I did no such thing. I do the work of angels! An angel came to me and warned me that the spells holding it had weakened. It bid me enter the forbidden chamber and strengthen the runes. Only I could do it. I had to be brave! I had to be strong! I was both. I see, serve, and protect! I have always been there for my children!"

I caught my breath. The Book seduced. I was willing to bet there had been no angel. The old woman charged with protecting the world from the *Sinsar Dubh* hadn't strengthened the runes. She'd erased them.

"I did as the angel instructed. 'Twas your mother who let it out!"

"What happened the night the Book escaped? Tell me everything!"

"You are an abomination. The doom of us all." The light in her eyes was matched by a craftier smile. "I'll die here, well I ken it, but I'll not be giving the likes of you any peace. Isla was a traitor and a whore, and you're more of the same." She grabbed my hand and thrust her small frame forward on the spear, twisting it as she went. "Ahhhh!" she cried. Blood gushed from her mouth.

She died sudden, mouth open, eyes wide.

Disgusted, I dropped her and stepped back, watched her fall to the floor. The *Sinsar Dubh whumped* to the floor. I stepped back hastily.

Behind me, Barrons was roaring. I glanced over my shoulder. He was hammering at an invisible barrier, his eyes wild, shouting.

"It's okay," I told him. "I have it under control. I saw through it." I was trembling, cold and hot and nauseated. It had all been so real. It felt as if I'd killed my mother, even though my brain knew I hadn't. For a short time, I'd believed the lies. And my heart hurt as if I'd lost a family I'd never had.

I looked back at Rowena. She stared up at the ceiling, eyes empty, mouth slack.

The *Sinsar Dubh* lay between us, closed, seemingly inert, a massive black tome with many locks.

I had no doubt it had chosen Rowena for her knowledge of wards so she could carry it past Barrons' protective spells, straight into the heart of our heavily warded world.

I thought back, isolating the moment the illusion had begun. From the instant I'd stepped out of the Silver tonight, nothing had been real.

Rowena and the *Sinsar Dubh* had been waiting to ambush me in the bookstore the moment I'd appeared. It had skimmed my mind, picking out the details I would find most convincing.

I'd never left the study, never followed Barrons into the rear conversation area, or sat on the couch, or met my mother. It had "tasted me" on many occasions. It knew me. And it had played me like a virtuoso, sawing away at one heartstring after the next.

Creating a "father" for me had been a masterstroke. It had married memories to longings and given me what I wanted most: family, safety, freedom from crushing choices.

All to get me to hand over the amulet, to con me into placing the one thing capable of deceiving both of us into Rowena's hands.

And if I had—oh, God, if I had! I would never have known from that moment forward what was real and what wasn't.

I'd been so close to doing it, but the Book had made two mistakes. I'd fed it a thought about Barrons and it had immediately altered him to bring him in line with my expectations. Then I'd fed it a false memory, amplified it with the amulet, and it had played it right back at me.

I had no doubt the real Barrons had been walled off from me the entire time. The Barrons who had stood beside me in the bookstore had been an illusion the Book had constantly tweaked, according to the feedback it had been getting from me.

Almost had you . . . it purred.

"Almost only counts in hand grenades and horseshoes." I stared down at the *Sinsar Dubh,* with its black cover and many complicated locks. But something wasn't right. It had never looked right to me.

I consulted my memories. I remembered the day the Unseelie King had created it. This was not what he'd made. "Show me what is true," I murmured.

When the *Sinsar Dubh*'s true form was revealed, I gasped. Sung into existence from slabs of purest gold and shards of obsidian, it was exquisite. I'd summoned crimson stones from one of the galaxies the Hunters liked to fly that housed tiny dancing flames. And although I'd put locks on my Book, top and bottom, they were decorative, never meant to secure it. My encryption was protection enough.

Or so I'd thought.

I'd made it lovely. I'd hoped the beauty of its binding might temper the horror of its contents.

I smiled sadly. For a brief time I'd believed I was Isla's daughter. No such luck. I was the Unseelie King. And it was long past time for my battle with my darker half to end. According to the prophecy as I understood it, I'd triumphed over my "monster within." It had been my hunger for illusion, to lose myself in a life I'd never had.

I fisted my hand around the amulet. It blazed with blue-black light. I was epic. I was strong. I had created this horror and I would destroy it. I would not be defeated.

Not defeat, MacKayla. I want you to come home.

"I am home. My bookstore."

Is nothing. I will show you wonders beyond your imagining. Your body is strong. You will hold me and we will live. Dance. Fuck. Feast. It will be grand. We will K'Vruck the world.

"I'm not holding you. Ever."

You were made for me. I for you. Two for tea and t-t-t-tea for two.

"I'll kill myself first." If I thought it might come to that, I would.

And let me win? You would die and let me rule? Allow me to encourage you.

"That's not what you want, and you know it."

What do you think I want, sweet MacKayla?

"You want me to forgive you."

I have no need of absolution.

"You want me to take you back."

In, sweet thing, take me in. Warm and wet like sex is warm and wet.

"You want to be the king. You want to turn us evil again."

Evil, good, create, destroy. Puny minds. Puny caves. Time, MacKayla. Time absolves.

"Time does not define the act. Time is impartial; it neither condemns nor absolves. The action contains intent, and intent is where the definition lies."

Bore me with human law.

"Enlighten you with universal law."

You convict me of evil intent?

"Unequivocally."

In your eyes I am a monster?

"Absolutely."

I should be—how do you say—put down?

"That's what I'm here for."

What, then, does that make you, MacKayla?

"A repentant king. I eviscerated my evil, imprisoned you once before, and I will again."

How you amuse.

"Laugh all you want."

You believe you are my maker.

"I know I am."

My sweet MacKayla, you are such a fool. You did not make me. I made you.

A chill slid down my spine. Its voice oozed satisfaction and mockery, as if it were watching me head straight toward a train wreck and enjoying every minute of it. My eyes narrowed. "Not falling for the chicken/egg discussion. Your evil didn't make me the king. I was the king, and I turned evil. I wised up and dumped my evil into a book. You were never supposed to live. And I plan to rectify that."

Not chickens and eggs. A human woman. And you—a tiny little embryo.

My mouth opened on a retort, but I hesitated.

Of all the lies it had woven so far, this one held a startling ring of truth. Why?

What I told you before was true. I took Isla to escape the abbey. And she was *pregnant. I did not expect to find you in her. I did not know how humans replicated. As I used her to kill the other humans who had dared to restrain me—ME, locked in a cold stone vacuum for an eternity of nothingness, have you any idea the HELL?— there you were. The wonder. Unformed life in her body. Mine for the taking. I marveled at the beauty of you. Unshaped, unfettered by scruple, unhampered by human weaknesses. Your race and its obsession with sin! You chain yourselves to the whipping post because you fear the sky. It is those chains, those limits, that make the bodies I take so fragile, tear them apart so soon after I possess them.*

But you were different. You hungered, you slept, you dreamed, but you were pure. You knew no right or wrong; you were empty. You did not resist me. You were open. I filled you. I nestled down inside you, replicated myself and left it there. You are my child. You suckled at my breast, MacKayla. I was your mother's milk; I gave you your defenses against the world. On that day, before your body could sustain itself separately, before you ever had the chance to do something so stupid and small as become human, I claimed you. I gave birth to you. Not Isla.

"You're lying. I'm the king," I said flatly.

You seek truth? Can you face it?

I said nothing.

The truth is within you. It always has been. It is there in the one place you refuse to go.

I narrowed my eyes. Perhaps I'd been congratulating myself on subduing my inner monster too soon. *Don't talk to it, beautiful girl,* the dreamy-eyed guy had said, long ago in Chester's, long before I'd met the *fear dor-*

cha. Never talk to it. I wondered if he'd meant the *Sinsar Dubh* then. Too late. I was waist-deep in quicksand. Struggling would only hasten my descent.

You have only ever taken what I offered, what I floated to the surface. Dive in, MacKayla. Graze the bottom of your lake. You will find me down there, shining in all my glory. Lift my lid. Know the truth of your existence. If I am evil, we are evil. If I should be "put down," so must you. There is no sentence you can cry upon me that you must not carry out upon yourself. There is no point in fighting me. You are me. Not a king. Me. Always have been. Always will be. You can't eviscerate me. I am your soul.

"Those runes I found are my *sidhe*-seer gifts."

From the walls of the Unseelie prison? The universe abhors a boring liar. Flamboyance, MacKayla. Get some if you wish to spend an eternity with me.

"It's because I'm the king. The good part of him. I have his memories to prove it."

We possess memories from a portion of his existence. It was impossible for him to dump his knowledge without imbuing my pages with the essence of the being that created them. I was sentient from the moment he finished scribing my pages. Do you recall anything that happened before the day the queen denied the king his concubine's immortality?

I turned inward, searching.

There was nothing. A white expanse of emptiness. It was as if life began that day.

It did. It was the day he wrote his first spell of creation, performed the first of his experiments. We know his life from that day on. We know nothing of his existence before then. And we know little of his life since— only when I tracked and glimpsed him. You are not the king. You are my child, MacKayla. I am mother, father, lover, all. It is time to come home.

Was it possible that it was telling me the truth? I wasn't the concubine, wasn't the king? I was just a human who'd been touched by evil before birth?

More than touched. As the king poured himself into me, I am in you. Your body grew around me like a tree absorbs a nail and now waits to be reunited. You miss me. You are hollow without me. Haven't you always known it? Felt empty, hungry for more? If I am evil, so are you. That, my sweet MacKayla, is your monster within. Or not.

"If you made me, where have you been for the past twenty-three years?"

Waiting for the mewling infant to grow strong before we reunited.

"You needed me to flip. That's why you tried to kill the people I loved."

Pain distills. The clarifying emotion.

"You screwed up. You came too soon. I can deal with pain, and I haven't flipped."

Lift my cover and embrace your dreams. You want Alina back? Snap of a finger. Isla and your father? They are yours. Dani as a young, innocent child with a bright future? One word can make it so. The walls back up? We will do it immediately. Walls are no hindrance to us. We pass through them.

"It would all be a lie."

Not a lie, a different path, equally real. Embrace me and you will understand. Do you want the spell to un-make his child? Is that what you want? The key to releasing Jericho Barrons from the eternal hell of watching his son suffer? He has been tortured for so long. Has it not been long enough?

I caught my breath. Of all the things it might say, this was the one thing that tempted me.

I am not without mercy, MacKayla, the *Sinsar Dubh* said gently. *Compassion is not beyond me. I see it in*

*you. I learn. I evolve. Perhaps you do have the good
parts of the king in you after all. Perhaps your humanity
will temper me. You will make me kinder, more forgiving. I will make you stronger, less breakable.*

Memories swarmed through my mind. I knew the
Book was sifting through them, manipulating me. It had
found the images Barrons showed me in the desert of the
child dying in our arms. It embellished upon what Barrons had told me about his enemies, nearly drowned me
in images of barbaric men torturing and killing the child
again and again.

Behind those images, a father stalked through eternity, hunting for a way to release his son and grant him
peace.

And gain it himself.

*He gave you everything and has never asked you for
a thing in return. Until this. He will die for you over and
over. And all he wants you to do is free his son.*

There was nothing it had just said that I could argue
with.

*Open me, MacKayla. Embrace me. Use me for good,
out of love. How could a thing given from love be bad?
You said it yourself—it is the intention that defines the
action.*

And there it was in a nutshell, the ultimate temptation: to pick up the Book, crack it open, and read it,
looking for the spell so Barrons could unmake his child,
because I would be doing it for all the right reasons.
Even Barrons had said evil wasn't a state of being, it was
a choice.

The Unseelie King had not trusted himself to retain
the power contained within the pages of the *Sinsar
Dubh*. How could I?

I stared at it, debating.

Irony, perfect definition: Barrons had said, *that for*

which I want to possess it, I ⸏ould no longer want once I possessed it.

If I picked it up—even with the most merciful of reasons in my heart—would I still care about releasing the child once I raised the cover? Would I care about Jack and Rainey, about the world, about Barrons himself?

Foolish fears, my sweet MacKayla. You have free will. I am only a chisel. You are the sculptor. Use me. Shape your world. Be a saint if you wish. Plant flowers, save children, champion small animals.

Was it that easy? Could it be true?

I could make the world perfect.

It's an imperfect world, Mac, I could almost hear Barrons roaring.

It was. Royally screwed up. Packed with injustices that needed to be righted, bad people and hard times. I could make everyone happy.

You have the amulet. With it you will always have control over me. You will always be stronger than I. I am merely a book. You are alive.

It *was* just a book.

Take me, use me. It is as Barrons has always told you—it is how you go on that defines you. You make the choices. His child suffers. There is so much suffering in this world. You can make it all go away.

I stared at it, hands flexing. That was the hard thing. The pain. He and his son suffered endlessly and would continue to do so every day, eternally. Unless I could get the spell of unmaking I'd promised him.

I have such a spell. We will lay the child to rest together. You will be his savior. We will free him now, this very night. Open me, MacKayla. Open yourself. I have been unguided. You will teach me.

I bit my lip, frowning. Could I guide the *Sinsar Dubh*? Would my humanity give me the edge I needed? I turned inward, searching my heart, my soul. What I found there straightened my spine and squared my shoulders.

"I can," I said. "I can change you. I *can* make you better."

Yes, yes, do it now. Take me, hold me, open me, it whispered. *Love you, MacKayla. Love me.*

I couldn't wait another moment. I reached for the *Sinsar Dubh*.

48

The Book was icy beneath my hands, but the flames in the rubies warmed my soul.

I was touching the *Sinsar Dubh*.

The contact took my breath away. We were twins separated at birth, rejoined. I'd been waiting for it all my life. With it in my hands, I was complete. I hugged it to my chest, shivering, trembling with emotion. A dark song began to build inside me. The Book was a finger and I was the wine-damp rim of a fine crystal goblet. It slid round and round, playing a melody that came from deep within my compromised soul.

I ran my hands lovingly over the jeweled cover.

I felt the immense power it contained. It inflated me, swelled inside me, made me drunk on it, giddy. The baby I'd once been, who'd known no right or wrong, was still in there. Unborn, we have yet to develop morality. I suspect there's some part of us that remains that way until death.

We choose. That's what it's all about.

When I stopped embracing it, held it away to admire it, the crimson rune that had been hidden in one of my palms pulsed wetly, expanded, and latched tiny suckers onto it, binding the covers closed.

WHAT ARE YOU DOING! the *Sinsar Dubh* screamed.

"Making you better." I began to cry as I scooped another bloody rune from the glassy black surface of my lake. I wanted the Book like I wanted to breathe. Now I knew why it had hunted me. I *was* its perfect host. We were made for each other. With it, I would never fear anything. Rejecting it was the hardest thing I'd ever done in my life. More bitter still was the knowledge that with each rune I pressed into the boards and binding, I was condemning Jericho and his son to continue living in an eternal hell.

HOW DARE YOU DECEIVE ME?

"The nerve of me." I wanted to tear the runes off, crack open the Book, take my spell of unmaking. I didn't dare. If I opened the gold, black, and crimson cover the tiniest sliver, its dark song would rush out and consume me.

She would doom the world, they'd said.

I'd been tempted, so tempted. I wanted Alina back. I wanted the walls up. I wanted Dani to be innocent and young and not my sister's killer. I wanted to be Jericho Barrons' hero. I wanted to release him from endless pain. See him walk into the future with hope and maybe even smile every now and then.

YOU SAID THE WORLD WAS IMPERFECT!

"It is." I pressed another dripping rune into the cover.

But it was my world, filled with good people, like my father and mother, patient Kat, and Inspector Jayne, who were always doing their parts to make it a better place. Unseelie might be overrunning our planet, but we'd been long overdue for a threat to unify us as a race and turn our petty angers away from one another.

There was pain, but there was also joy. It was in the

tension between the two that life happened. Imperfect as it was, this world was real. Illusion was no substitute. I'd rather live a hard life of fact than a sweet life of lies.

I flipped the Book over and pressed a rune into its back.

Its voice was muffled, growing weaker.

He will hate you!

That was the crushing blow. I'd been a breath away from what Barrons had devoted his entire existence to getting, and I'd turned my back on it. I'd promised him. I'd told him we would find a way, and I'd failed him. There was no way to lift a single spell of such power from the *Sinsar Dubh*. It would never have floated it to the surface and given it to me willingly. Even now it was regretting that it had ever floated anything to the surface for me, but it had taken calculated risks, tempting me to look deeper. It had given me what I'd needed to stay alive, to keep me heading toward merging with it, taking it in, letting it have my body and have control. It knew what I wanted now and would never give it up unless I merged with it completely. If I'd raised that lid—even a scant inch, just for a quick peek—looking for the spell, it would have been all over. It would have taken up squatter's rights and obliterated me. Perhaps some tiny part of me would have remained cognizant, screaming in eternal horror, but not enough to matter.

Ryodan had been right. The *Sinsar Dubh* was after a body, and it had wanted mine. If I believed its story, it had prepped me to be possessed since before I was born. Waited until I'd become the perfect host. But it hadn't waited quite long enough. Or maybe it had waited too long. *Evil is a completely different creature, Mac,* Ryodan had said. *Evil is bad that believes it's good.*

I hadn't understood what he was saying at the time. I did now.

I pressed another rune onto the binding.

I would never lay Barrons' child to rest now. Never free the man.

Destroy you, bitch! Not the end. Never the end!

Four more runes and the *Sinsar Dubh* was silent.

I sat back on my heels. My hands were shaking, I was exhausted, and my cheeks were wet.

I was about to lay my hand against the cover to confirm what I sensed, that it was contained—at least as well as it could be until we got it to the abbey—when the invisible barrier restraining Jericho evaporated.

Then I was in his arms and he was kissing me, and all I could think was that I'd done it, I'd survived, but at what cost?

From the day I'd met him, he'd been after one thing and one thing only. He'd been hunting it for thousands of years with single-minded focus.

I was a woman he'd known for a few months. What could I possibly mean to him compared to that?

49

Shocked by the news that Rowena was dead, the surviving members of the Haven took one look at Drustan MacKeltar carrying the Book, identified themselves—and, yes, Jo was one of them—then removed the wards and opened the corridor to allow access to the chamber in which the *Sinsar Dubh* had originally been interred.

I was thrilled Drustan was carrying it. I wanted nothing more to do with it. I never wanted to touch it again. If I did, I'd have to think about the spell Barrons wanted, how close it was, and how all I'd have to do was lift that cover and . . .

I shook my head, forcing the thought away.

I'd done my part. It was here, and now it was their responsibility. I'd ridden in the Hummer with the Keltar clan to the abbey as a precaution. It was hard to believe it was almost over. I couldn't shake the feeling that the other shoe hadn't dropped yet. In movies, the villain always twitched one last time, and my nerves were a wreck, waiting for it.

Jo and the other Haven members led our procession into the bowels of the stone fortress, followed by Ryodan and the others. The Keltar Druids were next. Barrons and I followed, with Kat and half a dozen more *sidhe*-seers bringing up the rear. V'lane and his Seelie were due to sift in at any moment.

I kept a careful eye on the Book as Drustan carried it down the corridor, past a now silent image of Isla O'Connor that I could barely look at, into an underground chamber, down more stairs, into another chamber, and down still more stairs.

I quit counting after a dozen flights. It was deep. I was once again underground.

I kept waiting for the Book to somehow sense it was approaching the place where it had been caged for so long and make a final, deadly gambit for my soul. Or body.

I looked at Barrons. "Do you feel like—"

"The fat lady hasn't sung?"

I love that about him. He gets me. I don't even have to finish my sentences.

"Ideas?" I said.

"Not a one."

"Are we being paranoid?"

"Possibly. Hard to say." He looked at me. Although his eyes were empty of conversation, I knew he wanted to know everything that had happened while I'd been battling the Book but wouldn't ask until we were alone. The entire time the *Sinsar Dubh* had been playing its head games with me, all he'd been able to see was me standing in silence with Rowena, me killing Rowena, then me standing in silence near the Book. The illusions it had woven for me had taken place only in my head. The battle had been invisible to the naked eye, but the hardest ones are.

He'd been a silent mountain of barely contained hostility the entire way out here. Since the moment the barrier restraining him had evaporated, he hadn't stopped touching me. I was sucking it up. Who knew how he'd feel soon.

I couldn't get to you, he'd exploded when he'd finally stopped kissing me long enough to speak.

But you did, I'd told him. *I heard you roaring. It was what tipped me off. You got through.*

I couldn't save you. His expression had been stark, furious.

I couldn't save him, either. And I was in no hurry to tell him that.

Did you get it? The spell of unmaking?

Ancient eyes had stared at me, filled with ancient grief. And something more. Something so alien and unexpected that I'd almost burst into tears. I'd seen many things in his eyes in the time that I'd known him: lust, amusement, sympathy, mockery, caution, fury. But I had never seen this.

Hope. Jericho Barrons had hope, and I was the reason for it.

Yes, I lied. *I got it.*

I would never forget his smile. It had illuminated him from the inside out.

I blew out a breath and focused on my surroundings. There was a small underground city beneath the abbey. Even Barrons was beginning to look impressed. Wide streetlike tunnels intersected neatly; narrower alleys ran off them in dizzying slopes. We passed an enormous hive of catacombs that Jo told us held the remains of every Grand Mistress that had ever lived. Somewhere among those labyrinthine tunnels, hidden in row after row of mausoleums, was the crypt of the first leader of the first Haven. I wanted to find it, run my fingers over the inscription, know the date our order had been founded. There were secrets down here entrusted to only the initiate, and I wanted to know them all.

Kat, too, was a member of the Haven, a secret she'd not betrayed.

"Rowena would have shut me out if I'd told you, and I'd have had no control over the inner doings of our order. It wasn't a risk I could take. You did well tonight, Mac. She was wrong about you. With both prophecies against you, still you came through for us." Serene gray eyes searched mine. "I can't begin to imagine what you went through." The look on her face told me she'd like to know and that she wouldn't be waiting long to ask me in detail. "We can't thank you enough."

"Sure you can." I gave her a tired smile. "Never let it get out again."

There was a sudden commotion ahead of us.

The Seelie had just sifted in, minus V'lane, in close proximity to Ryodan, Lor, and Fade.

I wasn't sure who was more disgusted. Or more homicidal.

Velvet hissed. "You have no right to be here!"

"Kill it," Ryodan said flatly.

"Don't you dare!" I heard Jo snap.

"Fucking fairies," Lor muttered.

"Touch one of them and I'll—"

"What, human?" Ryodan barked at Jo. "Just what will you do to stop me?"

"Don't push me."

"Stop it," Drustan said quietly. "'Tis a Fae Book and they've come to see it contained, as is their right."

"*They're* the reason it got out in the first place," Fade said.

"We are Seelie, not *sidhe*-seers. The *sidhe*-seers let it out."

"*You* made it."

"We did not. The Unseelie made it."

"Seelie, Unseelie—you're all fairies to me," Lor grumbled.

"I thought there was no sifting in this part of the abbey," I said.

"We had to drop all the wards to let everyone in. There's too much diversity in . . . "

"Everyone's DNA?" I said drily.

Kat smiled. "For lack of a better word. The Keltar are one thing, Barrons and his men another, the Fae yet another."

And me? I wanted to ask, but didn't. Was I human? Had the Book told me any of the truth? Did I really have the *Sinsar Dubh* inside me? Had it stamped its imprint, word for word, into my defenseless infant psyche? Over the years, had I always sensed it—something fundamentally wrong with me—and done my best to wall it off or submerge it in a dark glassy lake to protect myself?

If I *did* have the entire Book of dark magic inside me, and Kat found out about it, would they try to lock me up down here, too?

I shivered. Would they hunt me like we'd hunted the *Sinsar Dubh*?

Barrons looked down at me. *What is it?*

Just cold, I lied. If I did have the *Sinsar Dubh* inside me, did that mean the spell I'd walked away from was in my glassy lake? There at the bottom, like the Book had said? What was the difference, then? Had I really subdued the monster, or was it still inside me? Was the monster temptation, and I'd defeated it?

"Where's V'lane?" I asked, desperate for concretes.

"He is collecting the queen," Velvet said.

That started another fight.

"If you think we're going to let her come here and open the *Sinsar Dubh,* you're wrong."

"How do you expect her to rebuild the walls without it?" Dree'lia demanded.

"We don't need walls. You die as easy as any humans," Fade said.

"Is she even conscious?" I asked.

"*We* need the walls," Kat said quietly.

"She surfaces but is still mostly out of it," Ryodan said. "Point is, if anybody's reading that damned Book, it's not going to be a fairy. They started this fucking mess."

Everyone was still arguing ten minutes later when we reached the cavern that had been designed to contain the *Sinsar Dubh*.

As we approached the doors, Christian glanced back at me and I nodded. I knew what he was thinking. We'd seen doors like this before, at the entrance to the Unseelie King's fortress of black ice, however these were much smaller. Kat pressed a hand to a pattern of runes on the door and they swung open silently.

The blackness beyond was so enormous and complete that the thin beams of our flashlights were swallowed a few feet in.

I heard a match being struck, then Jo lit an oil torch mounted in a silver sconce on the wall. It flared into life, fed into the next and the next, until the cavern was brilliantly illuminated.

A hush fell over us.

Chiseled of milky stone, the cavern soared to an impossibly high ceiling with no visible means of support. Every inch of it—floors, walls, ceiling—was covered with silver runes that glittered as if they'd been branded into stone with diamond dust. The torchlight danced off the runes, making the chamber almost too bright to see. I squinted. Figured the only place in Dublin I'd ever need my sunglasses was underground.

The cavern was easily as large as the Unseelie King's bedchamber. Between the doors and the size of the place, I wondered how much credence there was to the theory that the king was the one who'd founded our order, who'd originally brought his cursed Book here to be entombed.

In the center was a slab laid across two stones. It was also covered with glittering symbols, but these moved constantly, sliding up and across the slab like the tattoos that moved beneath the Unseelie Princes' skin. They disappeared over the edge and began again at the floor.

"Seen runes like these before, Barrons?" Ryodan said.

"No. You?" Barrons said.

"New to me. Could be useful."

I heard the sound of a phone taking pictures.

Then I heard the sound of a phone being crushed against rock.

"Are you out of your mind?" Ryodan said disbelievingly. "That was my phone."

"Possibly," Jo said. "But no one records anything here."

"Crush something of mine again, I'll crush your skull."

"I weary of you," Jo said.

"I weary of your ass, too, *sidhe*-seer," Ryodan growled.

"Leave her alone," I said. "It's their abbey."

Ryodan shot me a look. Barrons intercepted it and Ryodan looked away—but only after a long, tense moment.

"You must place the Book on the slab," Kat instructed. "Then the four stones must be positioned around it."

"Then, MacKayla, you must remove the runes from the binding," V'lane said.

"What?" I exclaimed, whirling to face him as he sifted in. "I'm not taking those runes off!"

Barrons said, "I thought you were bringing the queen."

"I am making certain it is safe for her first."

V'lane scanned the chamber, studying each person, Fae and Druid. I could tell he wasn't comfortable with the risk. His gaze rested on Velvet for a moment, who nodded. Then he looked at me. "I apologize, but it is the only way to protect her. I cannot be two of me at once without halving my abilities."

"What are you talking about?"

He didn't answer.

My parents were suddenly there. My mom and dad—here with the *Sinsar Dubh*—in the last place I would ever have brought them. And supposedly I was going to have to remove the runes, but we'd see about that.

My dad had the Seelie queen in his arms, heavily wrapped in blankets. She was so well swaddled that all I could see of her were a few strands of silvery hair and the tip of her nose. My mom was pressed close to my dad's side, and I understood why V'lane had apologized. He should have.

He had my parents protecting the queen with their bodies.

"You're using my parents as her shield?"

"It's all right, baby. We wanted to help," Jack said.

Rainey agreed. "You're so much like your sister, facing everything alone, but you don't have to. We're family. We face things together. Besides, if I have to stay one more moment in that glass cage, I'll lose my mind. We've been stuck in there for months."

Barrons jerked his head, and Ryodan, Lor, and Fade closed in around my parents, shielding them.

"Thank you," I said softly. He was always protecting me and mine. God, I sucked.

V'lane was still eyeing all the occupants of the room. "I had no choice, MacKayla. Someone kidnapped her. At first I believed it must be one of my race. Now I wonder if it was not one of yours."

"Let's just get this over with," I said tightly. "Why do I have to remove the runes?"

"They are unpredictable parasites and you have placed them directly on a sentient being. On walls, on a cage, they are useful. On a living, thinking entity, they are unbelievably dangerous. In time, it and they will transmogrify. Who knows what kind of monster we will be dealing with then?"

I blew out a breath. It made perfect Fae sense. I'd applied something Unseelie and alive to something else Unseelie and alive. Who could say whether it would ultimately make the Book stronger, maybe even give it whatever it needed to free itself?

"It must be re-interred precisely as it was before. Without the runes."

"She's not removing them," said Barrons. "It's too dangerous."

"It is too dangerous if she does not."

"If it becomes something else, we'll deal with it then," said Barrons.

"You may no longer be around," V'lane replied coolly. "We cannot always count on Jericho Barrons to save the day."

"I'll always be around."

"The runes on the walls, ceiling, and floor make them obsolete. They will contain it."

"It escaped before."

"It was carried out," Kat said. "Isla O'Connor carried it out. She was the leader of the Haven and the only one with the power to carry it past the wards."

I was quiet, thinking. The truth of what V'lane had said resonated deep inside me. I feared the crimson runes myself. They were potent; they'd been given to me by the *Sinsar Dubh,* which in itself was enough to make them suspect. Was this another of its patient gambits?

Had I sealed it with precisely what it needed to one day break free again?

Everyone was looking at me. I was tired of making all the decisions. "I see both sides. I don't know the answer."

"We'll vote," Jo said.

"We're not voting on something this important," Barrons said. "This isn't a fucking democracy."

"Would you prefer a tyranny? Who would you place in charge?" V'lane demanded.

"Why isn't it a democracy?" Kat said. "Everyone here is present because they are useful and important. Everyone should have a say."

Barrons cut her a hard look. "Some of us are more useful and important than others."

"My ass, you are," Christian growled.

Barrons folded his arms. "Who let the Unseelie in here?"

Christian lunged for him. Dageus and Cian were on him in an instant, restraining him.

The muscles in the young Highlander's arms bulged as he shook his uncles off. "I have an idea. Let's subject Barrons to a little lie-detector test."

I sighed. "Why don't we subject everyone to one, Christian? But who's going to test you? Will you be judge and jury of us all?"

"I could," he said coldly. "Got a few secrets you don't want to get out, Mac?"

"Gee, look who's talking, Prince Christian."

"Enough," Drustan said. "No one of us is any better qualified to make the choice alone. Let's take the bloody vote and be done with it."

The Fae voted to remove the crimson runes and trust V'lane, naturally. As longtime Druids to the Fae, the Keltar did, too. Ryodan, Lor, Barrons, Fade, and myself voted against it. The *sidhe*-seers were split down the middle, with Jo for removing them and Kat against. I could barely see the tip of my father's head between Lor, Fade, and Ryodan, but my parents weighed in on my side. Smart parents.

"They shouldn't count," Christian said. "They're not even part of this."

"They're protecting the queen with their lives," Barrons said flatly. "They count."

We still lost.

Drustan placed the Book on the slab. Barrons took the stones from Lor and Fade and placed the first three around it. V'lane laid the final stone in place. As soon as the four were positioned, they began to glow an eerie blue-black and emit a soft, constant chime.

The entire top of the slab was bathed in blue-black light.

"Now, MacKayla," V'lane said.

I bit my lower lip, hesitating, wondering what would happen if I refused.

"We voted," Kat reminded.

I sighed. I knew what would happen. We'd still be down here tomorrow and the next day and the next, arguing about what to do.

I had a really bad feeling about this. But I'd had really bad feelings before that had amounted to nothing more than a case of nerves and, after everything I'd been through, I could understand how I might feel dread merely being in the Book's presence.

I looked at V'lane. He nodded encouragingly.

I looked at Barrons. He was so inhumanly still that I almost missed him. For a moment, he looked like someone else's shadow in the bright cavern. It was a neat trick. I knew what that kind of stillness meant. He didn't like it, either, but had come to the same conclusions as me. Ours was a volatile group. It had voted. If I went against that vote, all hell would break loose. We'd turn on one another, and who knew how ugly things might get?

My parents were here. Did I remove the runes and potentially expose them to risk? Or refuse and potentially expose them to risk?

There were no good choices.

I reached into the blue-black light and began to peel the first rune from the spine. As I pried it away, it pulsed like a small angry heartbeat and left a lesion that pooled with black blood before vanishing.

"What am I supposed to do with them?" I held it in the air.

"Velvet will sift them away as you remove them," V'lane said.

One by one, I tugged them away and they popped out of existence.

When there was only one left, I stopped and pressed both my hands to the cover. It felt inert. Were the runes on the inside of these walls really enough to hold it? I was about to find out.

I tugged the final one from the binding of the book. It came away reluctantly, squirming like a hungry leech, and tried to attach to me once I'd broken the bond.

Velvet sifted it out.

I held my breath as the crimson rune vanished. After about twenty seconds, I heard a small explosion of gusty exhales. I think we all expected it to morph into the Beast and rain down the end of days on us.

"Well?" V'lane said.

I opened my *sidhe*-seer senses, trying to feel it.

"Is it contained?" Barrons demanded.

I reached with everything I had, stretching, pushing that part of me that could sense OOPs as far as it could go, and for a brief moment I felt the entire interior of the cavern and understood the purposes of the runes.

Each had been meticulously chiseled into the stone interior so that if lines were drawn connecting them, from floor to ceiling and wall to wall, they would reveal an intricate tight grid. Once the Book had been positioned on the slab and the stones arranged around it, the runes had begun to activate. They now crisscrossed the room with a gigantic invisible spiderweb. I could almost see the tensile silvery strands shooting past my head, feel them slicing through me.

Even if the Book somehow got off the slab, it would be instantly stuck in the first of countless sticky compartments. The harder it fought, the more the web would twist around it, eventually cocooning it.

It was over. It was really over. There was no other shoe that was going to drop.

There was a time I'd thought this day would never come. The mission had seemed too difficult, the odds too strongly stacked against us.

But we'd done it.

The *Sinsar Dubh* was shut down. Locked up. Caged. Imprisoned. Put to rest. Neutralized. Inert.

So long as nobody ever came down here and set it free again.

We were going to need better locks on the door. And I was going to make a motion that no one in the Haven got to have a key this time around. I wasn't sure why they'd been able to get in to begin with. There was no reason anyone should enter this cavern. Ever.

Relief flooded me. I was having a hard time processing that it was really, truly over and comprehending all that meant.

Life could begin again. It would never be as normal as it used to be, but it would be a lot more normal than it had been for a long time. With the biggest, most immediate threat out of the way, we could focus our efforts on reclaiming and rebuilding our world. I could get some pots and dirt and start a rooftop garden at the bookstore.

I'd never have to walk down a dark street and be afraid the Book might be waiting for me, ready to crush me with a bone-deep migraine, set my spine on fire, or tempt me with illusion. It would never again possess one of us, never slaughter its way through our midst or threaten the people I loved.

I didn't have to strip when I went to Chester's anymore! Skintight clothing was a fad whose time had passed.

I turned around. Everyone was looking at me expectantly. They looked so wired and anxious, I suspected they'd jump out of their skins if I said, *Boo*. And for a moment I was tempted.

But I didn't want anything to detract from the joy of the moment. I spread my hands and shrugged, smiling. "It's over. It worked. The *Sinsar Dubh* is just a book. Nothing more."

The cheers were deafening.

50

Well, okay, so maybe the cheers weren't deafening, but they felt deafening to me, because I was cheering, too, and louder than most. The reality of the situation was that the *sidhe*-seers cheered, Mom and Dad hooted, Drustan whooped, Dageus and Cian grunted, Christopher looked worried, Christian turned and began to walk away in silence, Barrons scowled as did the rest of his men, and the Seelie glared.

Then the fighting broke out. Again.

I sighed gustily. They really needed to get with the program and learn to celebrate the good times a little longer before dwelling on the problems. I'd been walking around under the sentence of a prophecy that I would doom or save the world and I'd . . . well, technically, I hadn't done either. I hadn't doomed it. But I couldn't see any way I'd saved it. Unless I'd saved it simply by not dooming it. But, still, I knew the importance of celebrating every now and then to alleviate the stress.

"We cannot restore the walls without the Song," V'lane was saying.

"Who says we *need* the walls back up?" Barrons demanded. "You're roaches, we're Raid. We'll get rid of you eventually."

"We. Are. Not. Insects," Velvet said tightly.

"I was talking about the Unseelie. I figured you prancing fairy bastards would get off our world voluntarily after helping eradicate your skulking half."

"*I* do not prance." Dree'lia was insulted. "You would do well to recall the delights found in our arms."

I glanced at Barrons disbelievingly. "You had sex with her?"

He rolled his eyes. "It was a long time ago and only because she pretended to know something about the Book."

"Lies, ancient one. You panted around behind me—"

"Barrons has never panted around behind anyone," I said.

His dark gaze shimmered with amusement. *Unexpected, but thanks for the defense.*

Well, you haven't. Not even me.

Debatable. Ryodan would disagree with you.

Sleep with another fairy and I'll turn into V'lane's personal Pri-ya.

His eyes were murderous, but he kept his tone light. *Jealous much?*

What's mine is mine.

He went very still. *Is that how you think of me?*

Time seemed to stand still while we looked at each other. The arguing receded. The cavern emptied and it was just him and me. The moment stretched between us, pregnant with possibility. I hate moments like this. They always demand you lay something on the line.

He wanted an answer. And he wasn't moving until he got one. I could see it in his eyes.

I was terrified. What if I said yes and he came back with a mocking retort? What if I got dewy and emotional and he left me hanging all exposed? Worse yet, what was going to happen when he found out I hadn't gotten the spell to free his son? Would he take down my sign, batten up my beloved store, steal off with his child in the dark of night, burning off like mist in the morning sun, and I would never see him again?

I'd learned a thing or two.

Hope strengthens. Fear kills.

Bet your ass you're mine, bud, I shot at him. I was staking my claim and I'd fight for it—lie, cheat, and steal. So I hadn't gotten the spell: Yet. Tomorrow was another day. And if that was all he'd wanted me for, he didn't deserve me.

Barrons tossed his head back and laughed, teeth flashing in his dark face.

Only once before had I ever heard him laugh like that: the night he caught me dancing to "Bad Moon Rising," wearing the MacHalo, leaping small couches in a single bound, slaying pillows and slashing air. I caught my breath. Like Alina's laugh, which used to make my world brighter than the hot afternoon sun, it held joy.

The rest of the occupants faded back in. They'd all gone silent and were staring at Barrons and me.

He stopped laughing instantly and cleared his throat. Then his eyes narrowed. "What the fuck is *he* doing? We haven't made a decision."

"I was trying to tell you," Jack said. "But you didn't hear a thing I said. You were looking at my daughter like—"

"Get away from the Book, V'lane," Barrons growled. "If anyone's going to be looking at it, it'll be Mac."

"Mac's not touching it," Rainey said instantly. "That terrible thing should be destroyed."

"Can't be, Mom. It doesn't work that way."

While everyone was fighting and Barrons and I were absorbed in a wordless conversation, V'lane had taken the bundled queen/concubine from my daddy and was now standing near the slab, looking down at the *Sinsar Dubh*.

"Don't open it," Kat warned him. "We need to talk. Make plans."

"She's right," Dageus said. "'Tis no' a thing to be undertaken lightly, V'lane."

"There are precautions that must be observed," Drustan added.

"There has been enough talk," V'lane said. "My duties to my race are clear. They always have been."

Barrons didn't waste any breath. He moved like the beast, too fast to see. One moment he was a few feet from me, the next he was—

—slamming up against a wall and bouncing off it, snarling.

Clear crystal walls erupted around V'lane. Lined with blue-black bars, they extended all the way up to the ceiling.

He didn't even turn. It was as if he'd tuned us out. He placed the unconscious body of the queen on the ground next to the slab and reached for the *Sinsar Dubh*.

"V'lane, don't open it!" I cried. "I think it's inert, but we don't have any idea what will happen if you—"

It was too late. He'd opened the Book.

Arms spread, hands splayed on either side of it, head down, V'lane began to read, his lips moving.

Barrons flung himself at the wall. He bounced off.

V'lane had shut us out.

Ryodan, Lor, and Fade joined him, and moments later all five Keltar and my dad were at it, too, pounding on the walls, blasting into it with their shoulders and fists.

Me, I just stood, staring, trying to make sense of it, thinking back to the day I'd met V'lane. He'd told me he served his queen, that she needed the Book in order to have any chance at re-creating the lost Song. At the time, the only thing I'd been worried about was finding Alina's murderer and keeping the walls up. I'd very much wanted the queen to find that Song and reinforce them.

However, he'd also told me it was legend that if there were no contenders for the queen's magic at the time of her death, all the matriarchal magic of the True Race would go to the most powerful male.

Surely he wouldn't have told me that if he'd planned all along to be the one. Would he? Was he that stupid?

Or so arrogant that he'd given me all the clues, laughing the entire time, as the "puny human" failed to put them together?

If he read the entire *Sinsar Dubh*, would that make him—unquestionably—the most powerful male, stronger even than the Unseelie King?

I hadn't seen a single Unseelie Princess. Not one. All the Seelie Princesses were—according to V'lane—missing or dead.

What if he finished reading the Book and killed the queen?

He would have all the dark knowledge of the Unseelie King *and* all the magic of the queen. He would be unstoppable.

Was he the player who'd been manipulating events, biding time, waiting for the perfect moment?

I felt for my spear in the holster. It wasn't there. I inhaled, nostrils flaring. How long ago had it disappeared? Had he taken it to kill the queen? Would he even need it? Once he'd absorbed the Book, could he simply unmake her?

Was I being totally paranoid?

This was V'lane, after all. He was probably just looking for the fragments of the Song for his queen and once he'd found them he would close the deadly tome.

I sidled in for a better view.

The men were blasting the walls with everything they

had. Christopher and Christian were doing some sort of chant, while the others hammered at it. Nothing they did was having the slightest effect.

Peering between them, I suddenly got a clear look at V'lane. Unruffled by the assault on the walls he'd erected, he stood, head thrown back, eyes closed. His hands weren't spread on each side of the Book as I'd thought.

They were *on* it, a palm pressed to each page.

How was he touching an Unseelie Hallow? The pages were entrancingly beautiful, each made of hammered gold, embellished with gems, covered with a strikingly bold, dynamic script that rushed across the pages like ceaseless waves. The First Language was as fluid as the original queen had been static.

V'lane wasn't *reading* the *Sinsar Dubh*.

The spells scribed upon the gold pages were vanishing from the Book, passing up his arms, into his body, leaving the pages empty. He was draining it. Absorbing it. Becoming it.

"Barrons," I shouted to be heard over the roars and grunts as bodies imploded with an unyielding barrier, "we've got a serious problem!"

"Same page, Mac. Same bloody word."

51

When I was fifteen, Dad taught me how to drive. Mom was terrified to let me behind the wheel. I hadn't been that bad.

I remember swerving wide around a bend, narrowly missing a mailbox, and asking Daddy, *But how do you stay on the road? What keeps people from just running off it? It's not like we're on rails.*

He'd laughed. *Ruts in the road, baby. They aren't really there, but if you keep doing it over and over, eventually you begin to feel them, and a sort of autopilot kicks in.*

Life is like that. Ruts in the road. My rut was that V'lane was one of the good guys.

But be careful, Jack had added, *because autopilot can be dangerous. Drunk driver might come at you head on. The most important thing to know about ruts is how and when to get out of them.*

I was immobilized by indecision. Was V'lane *really* one of the bad guys? Was he really trying to usurp all Fae power and rule? Was I supposed to intervene? What could I do?

As my mom and I watched, Kat, Jo, and the other

sidhe-seers joined the assault on the walls. I was about to step in myself when my mom said, "Who's that handsome young man? He wasn't here be—" She froze, midword.

So did everyone in the cavern.

The Keltar stopped chanting. Barrons and my daddy were frozen mid-lunge. Even V'lane was affected, but not completely. The spells moving up his arms slowed from a fast-moving river to a stream.

I looked where my mother had been pointing and lost my breath.

He was by the door. No, he was behind me. No, he was right in front of me! When he smiled at me, I got lost in his eyes. They expanded until they were enormous and I was swallowed up in darkness, drifting between supernovas in space.

"Hey, beautiful girl," the dreamy-eyed guy said.

"Butterfly fingers," I managed finally. "You."

"Finest surgeon," he agreed.

"You helped."

"Told you not to talk to it. You did."

"I survived."

"So far."

"There's more?"

"Always."

I couldn't stop staring. I knew who he was. And now that I knew, I couldn't believe I hadn't seen it before.

"Never let you, small thing."

"Let me now."

"Why?"

"Curiosity."

"Dead cats."

"Nine lives," I countered.

He smiled and his head swiveled in a distinctly Unseelie manner. I was also seeing, superimposed on a space of air that couldn't exist—at least not in this realm—an enormous darkness regarding me. Its head didn't swivel: It grated like stone on stone. It was as if the king was so vast that no single realm could contain him, around him dimensions splintered, overlapped, shifted. His eyes locked with mine, opening wider and wider until they swallowed the entire abbey, and I went spinning, head over heels, into them, with the abbey tumbling beside me.

I was wrapped in enormous black velvet wings, taken into the heart of darkness that was the Unseelie King.

He was so far beyond my comprehension that I couldn't begin to absorb it. "Ancient" didn't come close, because he was newborn in each moment, as well. Time didn't define him. *He* defined time. He wasn't death or life, or creation or destruction. He was all possibles and none, everything and nothing, a bottomless abyss that would look back at you if you gazed into it. He was a truth of existence: Once you'd been exposed to him, you'd never be the same. Like a contagion that infected the blood and brain, he forced new neural pathways to develop merely to handle the brief contact. That or you went nuts.

For a split second, drifting in his vast, ancient embrace, I understood everything. It all made sense. The universes, the galaxies—existence was unfolding precisely as it should, and there was a symmetry, a pattern, a stunning beauty to the structure of it.

I was tiny and naked, lost in black velvet wings so lush, rich, and sensual that I never wanted to leave. His darkness wasn't frightening. It was verdant, teeming with life on the verge of becoming. There were shiny pearls of worlds tucked into his feathers. I rolled between them, laughing with delight. I think he rolled with me, watching my reaction to him, learning me, tasting. I tumbled among planets, constellations, stars. They hung from his quills, suspended, trembling with growing pains. Waiting for the day he would unfasten them, bat them off into the ballpark, and see what they might do. *A home run—hey, batter, batter! Fly ball, watch out! That ball sucks, didn't stitch it tight enough . . . coming apart at the seams . . .*

I saw us through his eyes: dust motes floating in a shaft of sunlight that stabbed through the rusted-out roof of a barn. He was as likely to swipe his hand through us and watch us scatter as he was to turn and walk away from this particular hole-in-the-roof byproduct. Or maybe sneeze us all into the great outdoors, where we would go whirling off in a dozen different directions, lost in lonely oblivion, never to come together again.

By our standards, he was mad. Utterly and completely mad. But every now and then, he surfaced and walked a fine line of sanity. It never lasted long.

By his standards, we were paper dolls, flat and one-dimensional. Barking mad as far as he was concerned. But every now and then, one of us walked a fine line of sanity. It never lasted long.

Still, all was well. Life was, and change happened.

Me. He thought *I* was relatively sane. I laughed until I cried, rolling around in his feathers. Because of his imprint inside me? If I was a shining example of my race, we should all be shot.

He showed me things. Took my hand and escorted me into an enormous theater, where I watched an endless play of light and shadows from a prime seat in the front row. He watched me, chin on a fist, from a red crushed-velvet chair in a box near the stage.

"Never did get it all out." His voice came from every speaker: huge, melodic.

"The Book?"

"Can't eviscerate essential self."

"Playing doctor again?"

"Trying. You listening this time?"

"He's stealing your Book. You listening?"

The dreamy-eyed guy's head swiveled away from the stage, and suddenly the theater was gone and we were back in the cavern.

Wings no longer cradled me.

I was cold and alone. I missed his wings. I yearned for him. It hurt.

"It will pass," he said absently. "You will forget the pain of separation. They always do." His eyes narrowed on V'lane. "Yes. He is."

"Aren't you going to stop him?"

"*Que sera, sera.*"

I was being stalked by a song, haunted by the calliope from hell. "It's your responsibility. You should take care of it."

"Should is a false god. No fun there."

"Some changes are better than others."

"Expound."

"If you stop him, the changes will be much more interesting."

"Opinion. Subjective."

"So is yours," I said indignantly.

His starry eyes glinted with amusement. "If he replaces me, I will become something else."

I could almost hear the *Sinsar Dubh* saying, *Is not any act of destruction, should time enough pass, an act of creation?* The apple didn't fall far from the tree.

"I don't want you replaced. I like you as you are."

"Flirting with me, beautiful girl?"

I tried to breathe and couldn't. The Unseelie King was touching me, kissing me. I could feel his lips on my skin, and I—I—I—

"Breathe, BG."

I could breathe again.

"Please, stop him." I wasn't above begging. I'd get on my knees. If V'lane succeeded in gaining ultimate power, I didn't want to live in this world. Not with him in charge. With a spell of unmaking he could kill Barrons, and he'd made it clear, every chance he got, that he wanted to. He had to be stopped. I wasn't losing any of my people. My parents were going to live to a ripe old age. Barrons was going to live forever. Me? Well. I wasn't sure exactly what I was going to do. But I planned on having a long, full lifetime. "It would mean a lot to me."

"You would owe me. Like you owe my Gray Woman."

Was there anything he didn't know? *Deals with devils* . . . Barrons would have said, if he hadn't been frozen. "Deal."

He winked. "I'd planned to, anyway."

"Ooh! Then why did you—"

"Pretty girl and all. Asking. Gotta love that. Stuff of heroes. Don't get the role often."

He was gone. He reappeared near the slab, staring at V'lane through crystal walls.

I was horrified to realize V'lane was more than halfway through the *Sinsar Dubh*.

But it was going to be okay. The king was going to stop him, crush him like a bug. V'lane would take one look at who'd come after him and sift out with his tail tucked, whimpering with fear. The king would reseal the cavern, and all would be well. No one would have any spells of unmaking. Barrons would continue to be unkillable. That was a constant, eternal rock beneath my feet that I needed.

"—fore. Where on earth do you think he came from?" My mother finished her sentence. She frowned. "And where did he go?"

Time resumed and everyone in the cavern began moving again.

V'lane's head dropped down and his eyes slid open.

His reaction wasn't at all what I expected.

His mouth ticked up in a cool smile. "About fucking time you showed your face, old man."

"Ah," said the Unseelie King. "Cruce."

52

Cruce? V'lane was Cruce?

I glanced around the cavern. Everyone looked as stupefied as I felt, staring between V'lane and the dreamy-eyed guy.

When I'd stood at Darroc's side, watching the Seelie and Unseelie armies face off in a snowy Dublin street, I'd been awed by the mythic proportions of the event.

Now, according to the dreamy-eyed guy who was really the Unseelie King, the Seelie who'd been masquerading as V'lane for hundreds of thousands of years was really the legendary Cruce, aka War—the final and most perfect Unseelie ever sung into existence.

And he was facing off with his maker.

Cruce was staring down the Unseelie King.

It was the stuff of million-year-old legends.

I looked from one to the other. You could have heard a pin drop in the cavern.

I glanced at Barrons, who had both brows raised in an expression of complete shock. For a change, there was something he hadn't known, either. Then his eyes narrowed on the dreamy-eyed guy.

"*He's* the king? That frail old geezer?"

"Geezer? You mean the pretty French woman," Jo said. "She's a waitress at Chester's."

"French woman? It's the Morgan Freeman lookalike from the bar on the seventh level at Chester's," Christian said.

"No," Dageus said, " 'tis the ex-groundskeeper from Edinburgh Castle who took on a bussing job at Ryodan's pub when the walls fell."

And I saw a young, dreamy-eyed college guy. He winked at me again. We all saw something different when we looked at him.

I stared back at V'lane . . . er, Cruce.

How had I not known? How had I been so completely duped? It had never been a Seelie Prince facing an Unseelie Prince that night in the snowy Dublin street but *two* Unseelie Princes. If War's brother had recognized him, he'd never given it away.

V'lane was Cruce.

V'lane was War.

I'd walked hand in hand with him on a beach. I'd kissed him. More times than I could count. I'd had his name in my tongue. I'd trembled with orgasm after orgasm in his arms. He'd given me Ashford back. Had he taken it to begin with?

War. Of course. He'd turned my world on itself. He'd set armies against each other and sat back watching the chaos he'd created. He'd even gotten out in it and fought with us. No doubt laughing inside, enjoying the added chaos, being in the thick of the fight, watching his handiwork up close and personal.

Was he behind it all? Had he been nudging Darroc for millennia, priming him to defy the queen? And when Darroc was made mortal, had Cruce whispered in a few Unseelie ears, maybe planted key information, and helped him bring down the walls from far behind the scenes? Had he been watching, waiting for the day he might get close enough to the *Sinsar Dubh* to steal the king's knowledge and kill the current queen and take her magic?

Did Fae really possess such patience?

He'd killed all the princesses and secreted the queen away to kill at the right time.

He'd turned the Seelie and Unseelie courts against each other, using our world as their battlefield.

We were all pawns on his chessboard.

I had no doubt he was after the ultimate power. The nerve of him, the arrogance—*he* was the one who'd told me it could be done and how! He was the one who'd recounted the legend to begin with. Unable to resist bragging? When I'd asked him about Cruce, he'd gotten irritated, saying: *One day you will wish to talk of* me. He'd been jealous of himself, angry that he couldn't reveal his true majesty. He'd said, *Cruce was the most beautiful of all, although the world will never know it—a waste of perfection to never have laid eyes upon one such as he.* How it must have chafed him to have to hide his true face for so long.

I'd tanned in a silk chaise, lying next to him. I'd dipped my toes in the surf, holding hands with War. I'd admired an Unseelie Prince's naked body. Wondered what it would be like to have sex with him. I'd conspired with the enemy and never even guessed it. All the while he'd been touching and adjusting things, nudging us this way and that.

And it had worked.

He'd gotten exactly what he'd wanted. Here he was: standing over the king's Book, absorbing the deadly knowledge, with the unconscious queen lying at his feet so he could kill her and take the True Magic of their race, too. He'd put her on ice in the Unseelie prison to keep her under control and alive until he was certain he was the most powerful male among them all. The king had given up his dark knowledge. Once Cruce had it, would he really be stronger than the king?

I watched the spells scribed in the *Sinsar Dubh* slide off the page, move up his fingers into his hands, arms, shoulders, and vanish beneath his skin. He was almost done. Why wasn't the king stopping him?

"Begun. Can't be stopped. Think I'd leave part of the Book in two places when they couldn't even guard one?" the king said.

Barrons and the rest of the men were back to slamming the walls, trying to tear them down to get to Cruce.

But it was too late. He had only a few pages left to go.

I stood, shivering, looking between the king and Cruce, hoping the king knew what he was doing.

Cruce turned the last page.

As the final spell vanished, the Book collapsed into a thin pile of gold dust and a handful of winking red gemstones on the slab.

The *Sinsar Dubh* had finally been destroyed.

Too bad it now lived and breathed inside the most powerful Unseelie Prince ever created.

The transition was seamless.

One moment I was in the cavern with everyone else. The next I was standing on a giant grassy swell of a hill with Cruce and the king.

An enormous moon obliterated the horizon. Welling up from behind the planet, it blocked out the night sky entirely but for a smattering of stars against a cobalt palette above it.

The rounded pasture climbed gently for miles, vanishing into the moon and making it seem like, if I walked to the top of the ridge, I might hop the pine-board fence and bridge planet to moon with a single leap. The air hummed with a low-level charge, and in the distance, thunder rolled. Black megaliths jutted like the fingers of a fallen giant poking into the cool, unblinking eye of the moon.

We stood between towering stones—Cruce facing the king, me at midpoint between them.

The queen was slumped at Cruce's feet.

I backed out and away for a wider view. I wondered who'd brought us here and left all the others behind. Cruce or the king? Why?

Wind whipped my hair into a tangle. The breeze was rich with spice and the fragrance of night-blooming jasmine. Hunters glided past the moon, gonging deep in their chests, and the moon answered.

I had no idea what world I was on, what galaxy I was in, but some part of me—my inner king—knew this place. We'd chosen the hill of Tara for the resemblance, but Tara was a pale imitation. On Earth, the moon was never so near as it was here, and there was only one, not three, in the night sky. Power pulsed in this planet's rocky core and mineral veins, earth's magic had been bored to death by humans long ago.

"Why the three of us?" I said.

"Children," the king replied.

I didn't like what his answer seemed to imply. War was *so* not my brother.

"MacKayla," Cruce said softly.

I gave him a cool look. "Did you think it was funny? You lied to me over and over. You used me."

"I wanted you to accept me as I was, but—how is it you say?—my reputation preceded me. Others filled your head with lies about Cruce. I endeavored to correct them, open your eyes."

"By telling me more lies? V'lane didn't kill Cruce the day the king and queen fought. You switched places with V'lane."

"With the three amulets the king never believed good enough, I deceived them all. Together they are strong." He touched his neck, a smug glint in his eyes, and although I couldn't see them, I knew he wore them still. He'd used them to maintain his flawless glamour of Seelie Prince. I'd seen it flicker only a few times, when he'd been near the abbey's wards.

"That day I called you to help me defeat the guardian in the abbey, the day you hissed and vanished—"

"It was a truth ward made of blood and bone. It sensed me as Unseelie. Had I stayed, I would have been unable to maintain the glamour. But you could not pass it, either. Why is that?"

I didn't answer. "The queen killed V'lane with her sword, and never even knew it. You've been impersonating him ever since."

"He was a fool. After I had my audience with the queen, it was V'lane she dispatched to confine me in her bower. I took his face and gave him mine. He was not half the Fae I am. He knew nothing of true illusion, could not have created an amulet capable of such if he'd lived a million years. Then I took him to her to kill. He was pathetic. Pleaded his innocence. Whimpered at the end and made a mockery of my name. The other Unseelie Princes tried their hand at a curse and blamed that on me, as well."

"You hid among the Seelie all this time."

"Never drinking from the cauldron. Watching. Waiting for the perfect convergence of events. The Book was missing for an eternity. The old fool hid it. Twenty-three years ago I felt it and knew the time was right. But enough about me. What are you, MacKayla?"

"You set Darroc up."

"I encouraged where encouragement was useful."

"You want to be king," I said.

Cruce's iridescent eyes flashed. "Why would I not? Someone needs to take over. He turned his back on his children. We were an accident of creation he sought to contain and hide. He fears power? I do not. He refuses to lead our people? I will champion them as he never did."

"And when they weary of your rule?" the king said. "When you realize you can never please them?"

"I will make them happy. They will love me."

"So all gods think. At first."

"Shut up, old man."

"Still you wear V'lane's face. What do you fear?" the king said.

"I fear nothing." But his gaze lingered on me a long moment. "I fight for my race, MacKayla. I have since I was born. He would conceal us in shame and condemn us to a half life. Remember that. There are reasons for all I have done."

Abruptly his golden mane was raven, his gold-velvet skin bronzed.

Iridescent eyes emptied. A torque threaded with silver slithered around his neck. Beneath his skin, kaleidoscopic tattoos crashed like waves in a turbulent sea. He was beautiful. He was horrifying. He was soul-destroying. A nimbus of gold surrounded his body.

And his face, oh, God, his face, I knew that face. I'd seen that face. Bending over me. Holding my head in his arms. Cradling me.

While he moved inside me.

"*You* were the fourth at the church!" I cried. He'd raped me. With his other dark brethren, he'd turned me into a mindless shell of a person, left me shattered and naked in the street. And I would have remained broken forever, except that Barrons had come charging in after me with men and guns, taken me away, and put me back together again.

The Unseelie Prince cocked his head, looking every bit as unnatural as his brothers. Sharp teeth gleamed white against the dark skin of his face. "They would have killed you. They had never had a human woman. Darroc underestimated their ardor."

"You raped me!"

"I saved you, MacKayla."

"Saving me would have been getting me out of there!"

"You were already *Pri-ya* when I found you. Your life was ending. I gave you my elixir—"

"*Your* elixir?" the king said mildly.

"—to stem your wounds."

"You didn't have to have sex with me to do it!"

"I desired you. You refused me. I wearied of your protests. You wanted me. You thought about it. You were not even there. What difference?"

"You think that makes it okay?"

"I do not understand your objections. I did nothing that had not already been done by others. Nothing you had not considered. And I did it better."

"What *exactly* did you give me?"

"I do not *exactly*"—he imitated my tone perfectly—"know. I have never given it to a human before."

"Was it the queen's elixir?"

"It was mine," the king said.

"I improved it. You are the past," Cruce said. "I am the future. It is time for you to be unmade."

He was going to unmake the king? Was it possible?

"Kids. Pain in the ass. Don't know why I ever made them. Hell on relationships."

"You have no idea," Cruce said. "Getting the queen to kill V'lane was not the first illusion I wove and left for you, old fool, although it was the first you saw. *This* was." He bent and grabbed a fistful of the queen's hair, raising her by it. As he did, her blankets fell away.

The king went perfectly still.

In his eyes I saw the black-and-white boudoir, void of all but empty memories, the endless barren years, the eternal grieving. I saw loneliness as vast and all-encompassing as his wings. I knew the joy of their union and the despair of their separation.

I no longer trusted anyone's face. I sought my *sidhe-* seer center, reinforced it with the amulet, and demanded to be shown what was true.

She was still the concubine. The king's mortal beloved, the one he'd gone insane over, created the *Sinsar Dubh* because of, walked away from his entire race for.

"As the current queen, her death will grant me the True Magic of our race. I saved her to kill in front of you before I unmake you. But this time when you see her dead, it will be no illusion."

When the king said nothing, Cruce said impatiently, "Do you not wish to know how I did it, you stubborn old fuck? No? You never would speak up when it mattered. The day you went to battle the queen, I took the concubine another of your famous elixirs, but this time it was no potion: It was a cup stolen from the cauldron of forgetting. She stood in your boudoir while I erased all memory of you. When she was a blank slate, I bent her over your bed and fucked her. I hid her from you where I knew you would never look. The Seelie court. I took V'lane's place and pretended she was a human I'd become enamored of. Over time, as the courtiers drank from the cauldron and forgot, as Seelie Princesses rose to power and were deposed, she became one of us. I achieved what your potions never did. Time in Faery, our potions, and our way of life made her Fae. Is it not ironic? The day came when she was so powerful she became our queen. She was always there—alive—but you never even looked. I kept her in the one place I knew the arrogant Unseelie King would not go. Bedding down with your grudges while I bedded your bitch. Your concubine became my lover, my queen. And now her death will make me *you*."

The king's eyes were sad. "In more ways than you know, if it were true. But another stands in your way." He glanced at me.

My eyes widened and I shook my head instantly. "What are you trying to do? Get him to kill me? I'm not in his way."

"Our magic prefers a woman. I believe it would choose you."

"I have the *Sinsar Dubh*," Cruce said. "She does not."

The king laughed. "You think to become me. She becomes her. Not the only possible."

I was horrified. I thought I understood what he was saying and didn't like it one bit.

"Perhaps Barrons becomes Cruce. Who, then, would cry judgment?" the king said.

"Barrons wouldn't become War," I said instantly.

"Or me. Depends on the nuances." The king looked at the concubine in Cruce's grasp. "Irrelevant, all of it. I'm not done yet."

She was gone.

"What the—?" Cruce's hands were suddenly empty. He lunged forward and slammed into an invisible barrier. His eyes narrowed and he began to chant in a voice that made my blood ice, chiming like the full-blooded Unseelie Prince he was.

The king waved a hand and Cruce stopped chiming.

Cruce sketched a complicated symbol in the air, eyes narrowed on the king. Nothing happened. He began to chime again. The king silenced him.

Cruce conjured a rune and flung it at the king. It hit the invisible barrier and dropped. He flung a dozen more. They all did the same. It was like watching a man and a woman fight, where the man was simply trying to keep the woman from hurting herself too much.

Cruce rocked back on his heels and his wings began to open, black velvet and enormous, framing a nude, muscled body of such perfection that my cheeks were suddenly wet. Long black hair streamed down his shoulders; brilliant colors rushed beneath his bronze skin.

I touched my face and my fingers came away bloody.

I was awed by the dark majesty of him. I knew why War was as often revered as feared. I knew what it felt like to be cradled in those wings while he moved inside me.

The Unseelie King watched him, paternal pride glittering in his eyes.

Cruce was trying to destroy him, and he was *proud* of him.

Like a parent watching his child kick off the training wheels and take off down the drive for the first time without help.

And I knew that Cruce had never stood a chance, so long as the king cared to exist.

The danger would never be whether the king was powerful enough—he was and always would be the strongest of them all.

The true danger would always only be whether he *cared* enough.

He saw existence differently from everyone else. What *we* might view as defeat and destruction, *he* saw—like the Book he'd created—far down the arrows of time, as an act of creation.

Who knew? Maybe it was.

But I liked existing here and now, and I'd fight for it.

I didn't have a bird's-eye view and didn't want it. I liked padding around on dog paws, kicking up fall leaves and digging in spring dew, sniffing up scents on the ground, and living a life. I was only too happy to leave the flying for those with wings.

I reached for my spear. It was in my holster. And I realized it always had been whenever "V'lane" was around. It was part of the complex illusion he'd maintained. As an Unseelie, he'd never been able to touch it yet could have been killed by it, so whenever we were together, he'd fed me the glamour that it was no longer in my holster. Just as the Unseelie Princes had fed me an illusion that I'd been turning it on myself there in the church.

I never had. I'd chosen to throw it away because I'd believed the glamour. I could have killed them that night, if I'd been able to see through it. The power had always been right here, inside me, if I'd just known it.

I would kill him now.

"Don't even think about it," the Unseelie King said.

"He took your concubine. He faked her death. He *raped* me!"

"No harm, no foul."

"Are you kidding me?"

He looked at his concubine. "Today amuses."

Abruptly, the moon and megaliths were gone. We were back in the cavern.

Cruce chimed, his wings open to their full majestic glory, eyes blazing with righteous fury, lips peeled back in a snarl.

The king iced him like that.

A nude, avenging angel, encased in clear crystal. Blue-black bars shot up from the floor, framing his prison.

I should have told the king to put clothes on him.

Make the ice cloudy so no one could see him. Hide those stunning velvety wings. Tone down the golden halo around him.

Make him look less . . . angelic, sexual, erotic. But you know what they say about hindsight.

The king said to Kat, "He is your *Sinsar Dubh* now."

"No!" Kat exclaimed. "We don't want him!"

"Your fault it got out. Contain it better this time."

I heard Barrons say, "McCabe? What the fuck are you doing here?"

People began to appear in the cavern, sifting in. The white-suited McCabe from Casa Blanc was joined by the leprechaun-like reservations clerk from my first night at the Clarin House and by the news vendor from the street who'd given me directions to the Garda, the one who'd called me a hairy jackass.

"Liz?" Jo said. "Where did you come from?"

Liz said nothing, simply moved, as they all did, to join the Unseelie King.

"He's too big for one body," I said numbly.

"I *knew* there was something wrong with her!" Jo exclaimed.

The king had been watching the *sidhe*-seers and Barrons. He'd posed as one of the players hunting his own Book. He'd been watching me all this time. Since the day I'd come to Dublin. He'd checked me into the Clarin House.

"Before that, beautiful girl." The king slanted me a look that horrified me. Pride glittered in his starry eyes.

My high school gym coach joined him. When my grade school principal appeared, I locked my jaw and gave the king a mutinous glare. *Since the beginning.* "Little help might have been nice."

The king cradled the concubine tenderly to his chest. "What would you change?"

"You must give her to us," Dree'lia demanded. "We need her. Without V'lane, who will lead us?"

"Find a new queen. She is mine."

Velvet bristled. "But there is no one—"

"Grow a pair, Velvet," the king snapped.

"We don't *want* Cruce. *You* take him," Kat was insisting.

"What the bloody hell is going on? You can't take the queen. We work for her," Drustan was saying.

"What about the Compact?" Cian said. "We need to renegotiate it!"

"Change me back!" Christian demanded. "I ate only one bite. That's not enough to do this to me. Why am I being punished?"

The king only had eyes for the woman in his arms.

"You can't leave until you put the bloody walls back up," Dageus was growling. "We've no idea how to go about—"

"You'll figure it out."

Skins began to drop to the floor, empty shells of the king's parts. For a moment, I was worried my own might fall off, but it didn't.

Barrons had pulled me back from being *Pri-ya*. I had no doubt the king would find his concubine, too. Wherever she was, in whatever cave of amnesia she was trapped, he would join her. Tell her stories. Make love to her. Until one day they both got up and walked out of it.

The dreamy-eyed guy began to change, absorbing the shadows that passed from the skins.

He stretched and expanded until he towered over us like the *Sinsar Dubh*'s beast, but without the malevolence, and when his wings spread wide, eclipsing the chamber in night, stars and worlds dangling from his quills, I felt his joy.

The thought that she'd left him by choice had driven him mad.

But she hadn't. She'd been taken.
He'd loved her for all time.
Before she was made.
After he'd believed she was gone.
Sunshine to his ice. Frost to her fever.
I wished them forever.
You, too, beautiful girl.
The Unseelie King was gone.

PART

V

When my faith is getting weak
And I feel like giving in
You breathe into me again . . .
—SKILLET, "AWAKE AND ALIVE"

53

The sign was heavy, but I was determined.

Although Barrons' strength would have made things a lot easier, I managed without him. I wasn't in the mood for an argument.

As I unscrewed the last bracket suspending the gaily painted sign from the brass pole bolted into the brick above the door of the bookstore, it slipped from my hands, fell to the sidewalk, and cracked down the middle.

MACKAYLA'S MANUSCRIPTS AND MISCELLANY bit the dust before a single customer ever looked up and saw the sign.

I was okay with that. It didn't have the right ring to it. Although I'd loved seeing my name up there, I'd never have gotten comfortable with it. This place was . . . well, MM&M just didn't roll off the tongue.

I had no intention of giving him back the bookstore.

I was keeping it forever. And I planned to keep the name, too. I'd never be able to think of it as anything else.

Twenty minutes later, the original sign was restored.

I dusted off my hands, propped the ladder against a column, and stepped back to view my work.

The four-story—I looked up. It was five stories tonight. The five-story building was officially BARRONS BOOKS AND BAUBLES again. Owned by one MacKayla Lane. He'd given me the deed last night.

I walked out into the middle of the street and assessed my bookstore with a critical eye. It was mine to take care of, and I wasn't yielding one inch of it to vandals or the elements. It had weathered the storm of Unseelie better than most places in the city, protected by wards and a man who could never die.

I remembered the first time I'd seen it. I'd come barreling out of the Dark Zone, terrified, alone, desperate for answers. It had blazed with the holy light of salvation for me that night.

My sanctuary. My home.

The updated façade of dark cherry and brass gleamed. The alcoved entrance, between stately pillars, sported a new light fixture that cast a warm amber glow on the handsome cherry door and stained-glass sidelights.

The tall windows on the sides of the building, framed by matching columns and delicate wrought-iron latticework, didn't have a single crack, and there were no chips on the pillars. The foundation was solid, strong. Powerful spotlights mounted on the rooftop, controlled by timers, would be coming on any minute now. The lighted sign in the old-fashioned green-tinted windows winked OPEN.

The Dark Zone might be empty, but this place would always stand as a bastion of light, as long as it was mine. I'd needed it. It had saved me. I loved this place.

And the man.

And there was the rub.

It had been days since the showdown beneath the abbey, and we still hadn't talked about it.

After the king left, we'd all just kind of looked at each

other and headed for the door, as if we couldn't get back to where we felt safe and comfortable fast enough.

Mom and Dad took one look at Barrons and me and decided to go back to Chester's. I've got the smartest, coolest parents. Barrons and I went back to the bookstore, straight to bed. We'd gotten out only when near starvation had forced us.

The finale hadn't been perfect and certainly not what I'd expected last fall, when we were making our desperate plans to keep the walls up between the realms of Fae and man.

The *Sinsar Dubh* had been destroyed.

But in the way of Fae things, another had come into being.

The *sidhe*-seers were furious that they'd been left in charge of the new one, but it's hard to argue with an absentee king.

Kat had stepped up to the plate, taking over for Rowena, agreeing to lead until the abbey was cleared of Shades and their numbers were partially restored, at which time they would revert to a democratic vote and rebuild the Haven.

I intended to snag a spot in that inner sanctum, where I would lobby for significant changes—first and foremost that we permanently and irrevocably seal the cavern where the *Sinsar Dubh* was currently frozen in its much-too-exquisite temptation. Line it with iron. Pump it full of concrete.

The Keltar had returned to Scotland, taking Christian with them, but none of us believed we'd seen the last of them.

Before Halloween, we'd all thought life might one day get back to normal. Those days were gone forever.

We'd lost nearly half the world's population—more than three billion people dead.

The walls were down and I was pretty sure they'd

stay that way, with no queen and no one to lead the Seelie. I had no doubt the king was on extended sabbatical.

Jayne and his men were out in force, kicking ass, hell-bent on emptying the streets of Unseelie and the skies of Hunters. I planned to talk to him about that. I wondered if we might be able to negotiate a treaty with the Hunters. I didn't like the thought of K'Vruck being shot at.

Kat had connected with Post Haste, Inc.'s international branches. She told me that Dark Zones abounded around the world, but Dani's Shade-Buster recipe had been translated into virtually every language and manufacturing MacHalos was a booming business. In certain parts of the world, you could trade one for a cow. There were millions of surplus houses, cars, electronics, all the things I used to dream about one day owning, lying around out there for the taking. And all I could think was that I might cheerfully give up Barrons' 911 Porsche turbo for a glass of fresh-squeezed orange juice.

IFPs were drifting around like small tornados, but Ryodan and his men knew a way to tether them and had begun weeding the worst out of the city. Not because he cared, Ryodan had informed me coolly, but because they weren't good for business.

Chester's was rocking like never before. Today when I was out running errands, some chick had actually chirped, "See you in Faery!" As if she was saying, "Dude, have a good day."

It was a strange new world.

The war was on, but it was a subdued war. Seelie and Unseelie were fighting each other but keeping it quiet for now, as if they weren't sure what we might do if they messed up any more of our world and they weren't ready to find out.

Yet.

The only good Fae is a dead Fae, in my book. PS: Hunters aren't Fae.

The power was still down in most places. Generators were hot commodities. The cell towers didn't work—Barrons' and his men's phones the mysterious exceptions. The Internet had crashed months ago. Some people were talking about maybe not restoring things to the way they were, going in a new direction that was a little less plugged in. I imagined there'd be a lot of different schools of thought, with enclaves springing up here and there, each espousing their own philosophy and social order.

I had no idea where the future was headed.

But I was glad to be alive and couldn't think of anywhere I'd rather be than here and now, watching it all unfold.

I felt like Barrons: I'd never get enough of living.

Only yesterday, Ryodan's men had finally located Tellie, and I'd gotten to speak with her briefly on Barrons' cell phone. She told me Isla O'Connor really was pregnant with me the night the Book escaped. I *had* been born. I did have a biological mother. Tellie was on her way here to give me the whole story, would be arriving in a few days.

My parents were healthy and happy. The bad guys bit it and the good guys won the day. This time around.

It was a wonderful life.

With a single painful exception.

There was a child behind my bookstore, beneath the garage, and he was in agony every second he lived.

And there was a father who hadn't said a word to me about him or the spell since we'd left the cavern beneath the abbey.

I didn't have the faintest idea why. I'd expected him to demand the spell of unmaking the moment we got back to the bookstore. It was what he'd existed for, been hunting for an eternity.

But he hadn't, and with each passing day I grew to dread my inevitable confession more. The lie loomed larger, seemed increasingly impossible to retract.

I would never forget the hope in his eyes. The joy in his smile.

I'd put it there. With a lie.

He was never going to forgive me when he found me out.

You can still do it . . .

I squeezed my eyes shut.

That insidious voice had been torturing me ever since we'd left the abbey: the *Sinsar Dubh*. I couldn't decide if it was a memory of what it had said to me when it tempted me to embrace it—or a reality that was actually inside me.

Had the Book really "downloaded" a copy of itself into me while I was still an unformed fetus inside my mother?

Had it really created the perfect host for itself twenty-three years ago, making me a human facsimile of it, waiting for me to mature?

Most important of all: Was the spell to lay his son to rest *really* inside me?

Could I give it to him? Hear the joy in his laughter again? Free them both? At what cost?

I dug my nails into my palms.

Last night, right before I drifted off to sleep, I'd heard the child/beast howl. Hunger, anguish, eternal misery.

We'd both heard it. He kissed me, pretending he hadn't. Then later, when he left to go do whatever it was he did for the child, I'd choked back tears of shame and failure.

He'd asked me for *one* thing. And I hadn't been strong enough to get it for him and survive the getting.

I opened my eyes and stared at the bookstore, at the sign swaying gently in the breeze. Dusk brushed the store in shades of violet. A tinge of a metallic silver gauzed the windowpanes, one of the many new Fae hues.

Barrons would be back soon. I had no idea where he went when he left. But I'd learned the pattern. When he returned, I would be able to feel his heartbeat.

I didn't let myself think about doing it. I knew if I thought about it, I never would. I'd chicken out. I let my eyes drift out of focus and took the plunge.

The water was frigid, unwelcoming, black as pitch, black as original sin. I couldn't see a thing. I kicked deep.

I felt small, young, and afraid.

I kicked deeper.

The lake was enormous. I had miles and miles of dark, icy water inside me. I was surprised my blood didn't run black and cold.

Melodrama. See you finally got some, a familiar voice purred. *How is that flamboyance coming? Universe hates a dull girl.*

"Where are you?"

Keep swimming, MacKayla.

"Are you really in here?"

Always have been.

I kicked harder, pushing deeper into the blackness. I couldn't see a thing. I might as well have been blind.

Suddenly there was light.

Because I said let there be, it said silkily.

"You're not God," I muttered.

I am not the devil either. I'm you. Are you finally ready to see yourself? What lies at the bottom, the great taproot?

"I'm ready." I'd no sooner said it than there it was. Shining, resplendent, at the bottom of my lake. Golden rays shot out from it, rubies shimmered, locks gleamed.

The *Sinsar Dubh*.

I have been here all this time. Since before you were born.

"I beat you. In the study, I saw through your games twice. I walked away from the temptation."

Can't eviscerate essential self.

I was no longer swimming but dripping wet and floating to the floor of a black cavern. I drifted to my feet, boots lightly touching down. I looked around, wondering where I was. In the dark night of my soul? The *Sinsar Dubh* was open on a regal black pedestal in front of me. Gold pages shimmering, it waited.

It was beautiful, so beautiful . . .

Inside me all this time. All those nights I'd been hunting it, it had been right under my nose. Or, actually, behind it. Just like Cruce, I *was* the *Sinsar Dubh,* but unlike Cruce, I'd never opened it. Never welcomed or read it. That was why I'd never understood any of the runes it had given me. I'd never looked inside. Only taken what it offered to use it as recommended.

If I'd ever dived to the bottom of my glassy lake and opened the Book, I'd have had all the king's dark knowledge at my disposal, in detail. Every spell and rune, the recipe for every experiment, including how to create the Shades, the Gray Man, even Cruce! It was no wonder the Unseelie King had regarded me with paternal pride. I possessed so many of his memories, so much of his magic. I supposed that was as close to having a daughter as the king would ever get. He'd spat out a part of himself, and it was in me now. Sperm, essential self: what difference to a Fae? He could see himself in me, and the Fae liked that.

It was also no wonder K'Vruck had pushed at me mentally and recognized me. He'd found some part of the king inside me, and to him, king was king. He'd missed his traveling companion. Ditto with the Silvers. They'd recognized the essence of the king in me, and while most had resisted me pushing into them and spat me out enthusiastically—thanks to Cruce's botched curse that hadn't been Cruce's at all—the oldest and first Silver that joined the king and concubine's boudoir was unaffected by the curse and had permitted me passage for the same reason. I was wearing Eau d'King. Even Adam had sensed something about me, and I knew Cruce must have, too. They just hadn't known exactly what. Then there was the time the dreamy-eyed guy had told the *fear dorcha* to look deeper and the pin-striped terror had backed off.

I am open to the spell you want. You need only come close enough to read me, MacKayla. It is that easy. We will be rejoined. And you can lay the child to rest.

"I suppose you have a perfectly good reason for destroying my sign?" Jericho appeared beside me. "I had to paint the bloody thing myself," he said pissily. "There's not a sign-maker left in the city. I have better things to do than paint."

I gaped. Jericho Barrons was standing beside me.

Inside my head.

I shook it, half expecting him to be knocked off his feet and go rattling around.

He remained standing, urbane and implacable as ever.

"This isn't possible," I told him. "You can't be here. This is *my* head."

"You push into mine. I merely projected an image with the push this time, to give you something to look at." He gave me a faint smile. "Wasn't easy getting in. You give a whole new meaning to 'rock-head.' "

I laughed. I couldn't help it. He invaded my thoughts and gave me guff even here.

"I found you standing in the street, staring at the sign over the bookstore. Tried talking to you but you didn't respond. Thought I'd better take a look around. What are you doing, Mac?" he said softly—Barrons at his most alert and dangerous.

My laughter died and tears sprang to my eyes. He was in my head. I saw little point in hiding anything. He could take a good look around and see the truth for himself.

"I didn't get the spell." My voice broke. I'd failed him. I hated myself for that. He'd never failed me.

"I know."

My gaze flicked to his face, bewildered. "You . . . know?"

"I knew it was a lie the moment you said it."

I searched his eyes. "But you looked happy! You smiled. I saw things in your eyes!"

"I *was* happy. I knew why you'd lied." His dark gaze was ancient, inhuman, and uncharacteristically gentle. *Because you love me.*

I drew in a ragged breath.

"Let's get out of here, Mac. There's nothing for you down here."

"The spell! It's here. I can get it. Use it. Lay him to rest!"

"But you wouldn't be you anymore. You can't take a single spell from that thing. It's all or nothing. We'll find another way."

The *Sinsar Dubh* poisoned the moment. *He lies. He hates you for failing him.*

"Shut it down, Mac. Ice the lake over."

I stared at the Book, shining in all its glory. Power, pure and simple. I could create worlds.

Ice his ass over. He's just worried you'll be more powerful than he is.

Barrons held out his hand. "Don't leave me, Rainbow Girl."

Rainbow Girl. Was that who I was?

It seemed so long ago. I smiled faintly. "Remember the skirt I wore to Mallucé's the night you told me to dress Goth?"

"It's upstairs in your closet. Never throw it away. It looked like a wet dream on you."

I took his hand.

And just like that, we were standing in the street outside Barrons Books and Baubles.

Deep inside me, the Book *whumped* closed.

As we headed for the entrance, I heard gunshots, and we looked up. Two winged dragons sailed past the moon.

Jayne was shooting at Hunters again.

Hunters.

My eyes widened.

K'Vruck!

Could it be that simple?

"Oh, God, that's it," I whispered.

Barrons was holding the door open for me. "What?"

Excitement and urgency flooded me. I clutched his arm. "Can you get me a Hunter to fly?"

"Of course."

"Hurry, then. I think I know what to do about your son!"

54

Jericho Barrons buried his son in a cemetery on the outskirts of Dublin, after five days of keeping vigil beside his lifeless body, waiting for it to disappear and be reborn wherever it was they were reborn.

His son never disappeared and was never reborn.

He was dead. Truly dead.

I kept a vigil of my own at the door to his study, watching him stare at the beautiful boy through the long days and nights.

The answer was so simple once I'd thought of it.

It had taken a while to find him flying over the city, but he'd finally soared in beside me, blacker than blackness, with his *Nightwindflyhighfreeeeeee* comments and his *old friend* remarks—serene and smooth, chuffing the night air in small frosted puffs. The wind had steamed like dry ice in his wake.

I'd asked a favor. It had been the best kind for a Hunter. It had amused.

It took Barrons and five of his men to get the beast from beneath the garage up onto the roof of a nearby building, safely restrained.

Once they'd been far enough away, they radioed me and I had my new "old friend" fly in and do what he does best.

Death isn't nearly as final as a good K'Vrucking.

When he closed his great black leathery wings around the beast and inhaled long and deep, the beast turned into the boy.

And the boy died.

As if K'Vruck had simply inhaled his life essence.

After he'd suffered who-knew-how-many thousands of years, the child was finally at peace. So was Barrons.

Ryodan and his men had sat with Barrons through the days and nights, waiting, wondering if it was possible one of them could actually be killed. They'd seemed as offended as they'd been relieved. Kasteo had sat in the room and stared unblinking at me for hours. Ryodan and the others had to drag him away. I wondered what they'd done to him a thousand years ago. I knew what grief looked like when I saw it.

And when they'd left, although hostility had poured off them in my direction, I knew I'd won a stay of execution.

They wouldn't kill me. Not now. I didn't know how long they might feel benevolent toward me, but I'd take what I could get.

And if one day they decided it was war between us, it was war they'd get.

Somebody'd made me a fighter. With him by my side, there was nothing I couldn't do.

"Hey baby, you up there?" Daddy's baritone soared up from the street.

I peeked over the edge of the rooftop and smiled. Mom, Dad, and Inspector Jayne were standing down below, in front of the bookstore. Daddy was carrying a bottle of wine. Jayne had a notebook and a pen, and I knew he was planning to grill me about methods of Fae execution and try, once again, to get his hands on my spear.

I was thrilled my parents had decided to stay in Dublin. They'd taken a house in the city, so we could visit. One of these days, I would give Mom most of Alina's stuff back. We would sit and talk, go visit her apartment. I'd take Mom to the college where Alina had been happy for a time. We'd remember her and celebrate what we'd had with her while we had it. Mom was a different woman now, stronger, more alive than ever before.

Dad was going to be some kind of *brehon,* or lawmaker, and work with Jayne and his crew to maintain order in New Dublin. He wanted to fight, but Mom wasn't real keen on that idea.

She was spearheading a group called NDGU. New Dublin Green-Up was devoted to making the city green again—fertilizing the soil, filling the planters, putting down sod, and eventually bringing the parks and commons back to life. It was the perfect job for her. She was the ultimate nester, and Dublin's nest was sorely in need of some feathering.

"It's open, come on up," I called. Mom was carrying two pretty ceramic pots, and I could see the green tips of bulbs sprouting. All my window boxes and planters were still empty. I hadn't had time to get out to the abbey yet and dig a few things up. I hoped they were a housewarming gift.

I turned and checked the table. The drinks were chilled, the plates out, the napkins folded. It was my first garden party.

Barrons was looming over a gas grill, searing thick steaks and trying, unsuccessfully, to hide his disgust. I wasn't sure if he found the act of cooking meat revolting— as opposed to eating it raw—or if he just wasn't much for dead cow because he preferred *live* . . . cow. Or live something.

I didn't ask. Some things are better left unsaid.

He looked at me and I shivered. I never get enough of him. Never will.

He lives.

I breathe.

I want. Him. Always.

Fire to my ice. Ice to my fever.

Later we would go to bed, and when he rose over me, dark and vast and eternal, I'd know joy. Who knew? Much later we might fly a couple of Hunters to the moon.

While I waited for our dinner company to come up the stairs, I stared at the city. It was mostly dark, with only a few lights flickering. It wasn't remotely the same city I'd met last August; still, I loved her. One day she would be filled with life, teeming with *craic* again.

Dani was out there in the streets somewhere. Soon I would go looking for her.

But not to kill her.

We'd fight back to back.

Sisters and all.

I think Alina would understand.

The good guys and bad guys aren't as easy to tell apart as I used to think they were. You can't look at someone with your eyes and take their measure.

You have to look with the heart.

The end . . .

. . . for now.

ACKNOWLEDGMENTS

This novel would never have reached readers' hands if not for my brilliant dynamo of an agent, Amy Berkower, nor would it have been remotely what it is without all the wonderful people at Random House. Special thanks to Gina Centrello, for listening and for being there. Words can't express my gratitude! And to Shauna Summers, my fabulous editor and biggest fan, and to the rest of the team at Random House: Libby McGuire, Scott Shannon, Matthew Schwartz, Sanyu Dillon, Gina Wachtel, Anne Watters, Kristin Fassler, the art department for the sensational cover, the sales team for getting my books out there, and the booksellers for hand-selling the series with so much enthusiasm. Thanks to my first readers who see the manuscript before anyone else and give me their unflinching critique: the talented and amazing Genevieve Gagne-Hawes, and my husband, Neil Dover (chef, musician, editor, and my inspiration in so many ways!)—I couldn't do it without you two. Thanks to Leiha Mann, for making all things cyber-Fever and event-related run smoothly and feel magical. Last but by no means least, thanks to YOU, dear readers, for your feverish commitment that has made the Fever series such a success, and allowing me to do what I love most every day.

Sometimes characters just won't cooperate. Mac and Barrons kept trying to have sex before it was time and screwing up the way the story was supposed to go. I finally wrote a sex scene to keep them occupied so I could write the book the right way in peace. Funny thing was, once I wrote them a sex scene, the novel got back on track and never derailed again. This was the scene I deleted for the current Chapter Thirty-three. It took place right after Mac had killed Fiona (in the wrong version, she did it without Barrons). Mac had been gone for weeks and had just walked back into the bookstore.

Finding out that I was adopted had triggered a slow but relentless erosion of my identity. I tried to roll with the punches, be a good trooper, go with the flow.

When I'd learned that maybe I wasn't even Alina's real sister, I'd kept my chin up. When Darroc had proposed that I might be a stone, I'd laughed in his face. When Ryodan had suggested that perhaps I'd never actually been born, I hadn't let it get me down. When Barrons had accused me of being the Unseelie King's creation, one of his final castes, I'd doggedly persevered. I'd even been levelheaded and optimistic in the face of discovering I was the ill-fated, star-crossed love of the Unseelie King's life.

But there was no escaping what Fiona's death had just proved.

I was the Unseelie King.

I stared around the bookstore.

I loved this place. The bookstore was where I wanted

to be. And the woman that I felt like here was *who* I wanted to be. From my magazine rack to my gas fireplaces, from my cash register to the joy of ordering books and introducing people to new worlds, from earning my keep at the end of the day to knowing my constant jackass was always going to be out back, breathing down my neck, I wanted to be who I was here. And wasn't that the defining quality of "home"? You liked the person you were inside those walls.

I felt as if most of the living I'd done in my twenty-two years had taken place in BB&B. Definitely the most intense and formative parts. Ashford seemed a million miles away, a lifetime ago. None of my memories of home were as vivid and real as my memories here. I'd accumulated so many defining experiences in such a short time.

I'd learned about OOP-detecting. I'd touched copies of pages of the *Sinsar Dubh* and felt my latent power. I'd discovered monsters were real. I'd sat on the rooftop, my arm splinted, watching the world's most improbable nail technician paint my fingernails. He'd taught me to look inside myself without flinching. He'd taught me to kill. I'd fought Shades, invented a MacHalo, danced, and been caught making a complete fool of myself. And although he'd tried not to laugh, it had been one of the few moments I'd ever seen him unguarded—except in bed. In a basement, with me Pri-ya, he'd been raw, open, animal without apology. I'd learned about hard decisions and consequences. I'd let go of the pink and embraced the black.

That day, so long ago, when I'd gotten lost in the Dark Zone, I'd burst through the front doors seeking sanctuary, and the fact of the matter was, I'd found it.

Unconditional sanctuary.

I reached into my pocket for my new iPod and thumbed it on. He'd loaded it with music. The playlists were titled with nifty little acronyms. Jericho Barrons had picked out a pink iPod for me, hooked it up to a computer and downloaded music. I could more easily envision a lion donning a frilly apron and cooking a scrumptious vegetarian dish.

I scanned the playlists. There was HOHW, OTB, WYB, WIFYS&E, WIFYF&H.

I thumbed up HOHW and laughed. Even though he'd had dozens of hits, Louis Armstrong's "What a Wonderful World" topped the list of Happy One Hit Wonders. It would always be a painful song to me.

OTB had to be On The Beach, and was full of songs that were perfect for tanning, including my favorite Beach Boys songs. The man had definitely snooped in my old iPod.

WYB was a puzzle at first, until I saw "My Violent Heart" by Nine Inch Nails. "When You Brood," I said, getting it.

I scrolled down. Lust softened my knees and muscled my spine. These were the songs I remembered from my time in the basement. "I Came For You," "Awake and Alive," "Because the Night" and dozens of others. "So what is WIFYS&E?" I liked the game of trying to think like him.

"When I fuck you slow and easy," Barrons said, tight and hard, at the back of the store.

All the moisture in my body went south, leaving my mouth painfully dry. The next playlist began with "Pussy Liquor." I pressed the play button. "And WIFYH&F?" I'd already figured it out. I just wanted to hear him say it out loud.

"When I fuck you fast and hard," he said slow and precise and each word was plucked on tight strings in my groin as if he was purring them with his mouth to my clitoris.

Wanting him is visceral. Undeniable. Doesn't matter

if I was born, who I might have been in any other life-time, or what I'm headed for.

Barrons lives.

I breathe.

I want. Him. Always.

Fire to my ice. Ice to my fever.

"What do you want, Ms. Lane?"

I opened my mouth with a complete sentence formed and ready to come out but all I managed was an incoherent sound of pain and lust.

"Finally speaking a language I understand."

I'd never felt so exposed, so vulnerable. I hated everything about it.

Here I am, his dark gaze said. *Don't expect me to make the first move. I've been making it since the day you sashayed your manicured, deluded little self in here.*

You did not. You treated me like—

A woman I wanted to fuck. You aren't my type. It pissed me off.

Get over yourself—you aren't my type, either!

I'm your only *type. Admit it.*

You admit it.

I wanted to send Fiona home, drag you behind a bookcase and grow your fancy pink ass up in a hurry. Mark you. Fuck you till you figured out you belonged to me.

How shocked pink Mac would have been! How horrified. How turned upside down. How . . . turned on. All that wasted time. We could have been fighting and having sex and getting inside each other's skin. *Women don't belong to men.*

Bullshit.

Fine. Then you belong to me, Barrons.

There was an unholy light in his eyes. He caught the tip of his tongue between his teeth, fangs gleaming into view, and smiled. *You think you could keep something like me happy? I have large appetites.*

I don't think you know the meaning of the word "happy," Broody, pissy bastard.

You want me, stake your claim.

I'll stake your fanged ass.

I'd come back from that, too, so don't get your hopes up.

I lunged for him but he was already halfway there. We would have slammed into each other but at the last minute, I leapt and he caught me by the waist. I wrapped my legs around him, then his tongue was in my mouth, and we were falling back to the floor. I straddled him, riding him to the flawlessly raunchy beat of Rob Zombie, reveling in the raw energy, lust, and life flowing between us.

He wanted a spell of unmaking.

I would *never* give it to him. I didn't give a damn if he'd lived so long that now he wanted to die. Barrons was not dying. Not in my lifetime. And it looked like mine was going to be every bit as long as his.

I tore my mouth from his, sat back on my heels and, when he reached for me, shoved him back on the floor. "Hands off. This one is for me. You had your turn when I was Pri-ya."

You're not Pri-ya now.

"Point?" I asked dryly. But I knew what it was. It burned him that I'd only had sex with him when I was out of my mind and had no idea who he was. It would have burned me, too, if the tables were turned.

You know who I am. Say my name.

"Jericho."

You chose this. Tell me.

"I'm choosing this. Right here. Right now. I know who you are, I know who I am. And I want this."

What am I? His eyes glittered with expectation.

I remembered him saying this, back in a basement when I was Pri-ya. He wanted me to tell him he was my world. "How would I know?" I asked glibly. "You never cooperate."

I was so aroused, it was painful. I felt violent with emotion. If I couldn't control my lust, at least I could control him.

We'll see about that. Mockery glinted in his dark eyes, and something else I was having a hard time defining. A shimmer of disappointment? Had he just muttered something beneath his ocular breath? *A pity. Not as ready as I thought you were . . .*

Stay out of my head. I stripped off my shirt and bra and gasped at the coolness of the air on my fevered skin.

When he reached for me, I pushed him back with a boot square in his chest. "I said 'my turn.'"

He laughed and lay back on the floor and folded arms his behind his head. I wasn't fooled. I could feel the violence in him, too. We were like two great boulders, crashing into each other, chipping away, seeing if the other might crack.

I kicked off my boots, stripped off my jeans and thong, and stood over him, looking down my naked body at his face. His eyes narrowed, his lips tightened. Lust in those ancient eyes makes me feel elated to be alive. He unzipped his pants, made an adjustment, and his dick sprang free.

I finally had Jericho Barrons exactly where I wanted him. Rock hard, ready, and between my thighs.

Inexhaustible didn't begin to cover it. Insatiable couldn't describe it.

Bottomless need is what I feel for him. I love it and hate it. Feeling so intensely is a blessing and a curse.

I've never known a man as beautiful as Barrons. I've

never been with anyone as sexual and uninhibited. Sex is Jericho Barrons' religion. He worships, he defiles. He fucks with the single-minded devotion of a dying man in search of God. He leaves no part of a woman untouched. When he's inside me, the world ceases to exist. On the floor, on the counter, on the Chesterfield, across a chair, in his study over the desk, it was as if we were the only two people alive. Nothing mattered. The world could have ended and neither of us would have given a damn as long as the bookstore remained standing around us and we could continue fucking.

It was about the obsession we'd both been afflicted with the moment we'd laid eyes on each other. For whatever reason—I no longer even cared—my body demanded I have him—and he'd been poisoned by the same sickness. I took, he fought. He took, I fought. Neither of us gave easy. It's not our nature. Sex for us was a battlefield, and when we finally exhausted ourselves—at least for a time—the store was worse for the wear. Books spilled across the floor, two of the recently reinstalled bookcases listed at dangerous angles, the new coffee table was shattered, lamps were broken, and my TV had gotten knocked off the counter and cracked.

Wedged into a tight space between the broken coffee table, the sofa, and his body, I felt magnificent.

*Don't miss any of the books
in Karen Marie Moning's
"addictively dark, erotic
and even shocking"* series.*

Feel the heat, catch the fever . . .

*Publishers Weekly

KAREN MARIE MONING

DARKFEVER

A MacKayla Lane Novel

DARKFEVER

My name is MacKayla, Mac for short. I'm a sidhe-seer, a person who can see the Fae, a fact I accepted only recently and very reluctantly.

My philosophy is pretty simple—any day nobody's trying to kill me is a good day in my book. I haven't had many good days lately. Not since the walls between Man and Fae came down. But then, there's not a sidhe-seer alive who's had a good day since then.

When MacKayla's sister is murdered, she leaves a single clue to her death—a cryptic message on Mac's cell-phone. Journeying to Ireland in search of answers, Mac is soon faced with an even greater challenge: staying alive long enough to master a power she had no idea she possessed—a gift that allows her to see beyond the world of Man, into the dangerous realm of the Fae.

As Mac delves deeper into the mystery of her sister's death, her every move is shadowed by the dark, mysterious Jericho, while at the same time, the ruthless V'lane—an immortal Fae who makes sex an addiction for human women—closes in on her. As the boundary between worlds begins to crumble, Mac's true mission becomes clear: find the elusive *Sinsar Dubh* before someone else claims the all-powerful Dark Book—because whoever gets to it first holds nothing less than complete control of both worlds in their hands.

KAREN MARIE
MONING

BLOODFEVER

A MACKAYLA LANE NOVEL

BLOODFEVER

I used to be your average, everyday girl but all that changed one night in Dublin when I saw my first Fae, and got dragged into a world of deadly immortals and ancient secrets. . . .

In her fight to stay alive, MacKayla must find the *Sinsar Dubh*—a million-year-old book of the blackest magic imaginable, which holds the key to power over the worlds of both the Fae and Man. Pursued by assassins, surrounded by mysterious figures she knows she can't trust, Mac finds herself torn between two deadly and powerful men: V'lane, the immortal Fae Prince, and Jericho Barrons, a man as irresistible as he is dangerous.

For centuries the shadowy realm of the Fae has coexisted with that of humans. Now the walls between the two are coming down, and Mac is the only thing that stands between them.

KAREN MARIE MONING

FAEFEVER

A MACKAYLA LANE NOVEL

FAEFEVER

He calls me his Queen of the Night. I'd die for him. I'd kill for him, too.

When MacKayla Lane receives a page torn from her dead sister's journal, she is stunned by Alina's desperate words. And now MacKayla knows that her sister's killer is close. But evil is closer. And suddenly the *sidhe*-seer is on the hunt: For answers. For revenge. And for an ancient book of dark magic so evil that it corrupts anyone who touches it.

Mac's quest for the *Sinsar Dubh* takes her into the mean, shapeshifting streets of Dublin, with a suspicious cop on her tail. Forced into a dangerous triangle of alliance with V'lane, a lethal Fae prince, and Jericho Barrons, a man of deadly secrets, Mac is soon locked in a battle for her body, mind, and soul.

NEW YORK TIMES BESTSELLER

KAREN MARIE MONING

DREAMFEVER

A MacKayla Lane Novel

DREAMFEVER

They may have stolen my past, but I'll never let them take my future.

When the walls between Man and Fae come crashing down, freeing the insatiable, immortal Unseelie from their icy prison, MacKayla Lane is caught in a deadly trap. Captured by the Fae Lord Master, she is left with no memory of who or what she is: the only *sidhe*-seer alive who can track the *Sinsar Dubh*, a book of arcane black magic that holds the key to controlling both worlds.

Clawing her way back from oblivion is only the first step Mac must take down a perilous path, from the battle-filled streets of Dublin to the treacherous politics of an ancient, secret sect, through the tangled lies of men who claim to be her allies into the illusory world of the Fae themselves, where nothing is as it seems—and Mac is forced to face a soul-shattering truth.

Who do you trust when you can't even trust yourself?